WHITE NIGHTS

THE COMPLETE DUET

ANNA ZAIRES

CHARMAINE PAULS

GREY EAGLE
PUBLICATIONS

Published by Grey Eagle Publications
www.greyeaglepublications.com

Cover by The Book Brander
thebookbrander.com

ISBN: 978-1-64366-472-9
Print ISBN: 978-1-64366-476-7

WHITE NIGHTS

PROLOGUE

$\mathcal{T}$he assassin takes aim.

This is his favorite moment, right before he pulls the trigger. He's calm and focused, his senses heightened. In that split second before he takes a life, it's as though everything happens in slow motion. He's aware of his own breathing, deep and even, and of the steady beating of his heart.

One living being about to destroy another. There's power in that, and beauty. He's grown to appreciate it over the years, to derive enjoyment from something that had initially eaten at his soul.

He's not a psychopath. Maybe others of his kind are. If so, he envies them. No, he has emotions, deep, strong emotions that fill him to the brim. He loves and hates with equal passion.

Yet he rarely feels anything during a hit. Not anymore. When he's on the job, he simply thinks of himself as a hunter— a hunter with a very specific prey.

This particular hunt has been longer and more difficult than most. His target is as dangerous as the assassin himself. The man he's about to kill displays many of his own traits, and he has no doubt his prey was once a predator himself.

Then again, none of the men he's commissioned to kill are angels. He doesn't kill the innocent. He dispatches the guilty.

The man in the scope of his rifle is fully deserving of what's about to befall him.

Taking a deep breath, the assassin gently squeezes the trigger.

"*K*ate, I'm sorry, but we need you right now."

June Wallers, the nursing supervisor, bursts into the tiny room where I'm wolfing down my dinner.

Sighing, I put down my half-eaten sandwich, take a sip of water, and follow June down the hall. It's not the first time this week that my allocated dinner hour has turned into a ten-minute snack break.

The economic climate has taken its toll on New York hospitals, with budget cuts leading to hiring freezes and staff layoffs. Even now, the Emergency Room at Coney Island Hospital is three nurses short of what it needs to function properly. Other departments are also short-staffed, but their patient flow is more predictable. At the ER, however, it's always a madhouse.

This week is particularly trying. With the beginning of winter, it's flu season, and one of the nurses got sick. It's the worst time for her to be off, given the extra influx of patients. This is my fifth twelve-hour shift this week, and it's a night shift, something I hate to do but can't always avoid. June begged and I gave in, knowing there was no one else available.

So here I am, skipping dinner again. At this pace, I'll be skin and bones before the flu season is over. *The flu season diet,* my mom likes to call it.

"What's the emergency?" I ask, walking faster to keep up with June. At fifty-five years of age, my supervisor is as spry as a twenty-year-old.

"We've got a gunshot wound."

"How bad?"

"We're not sure yet. Lettie's shift just ended, and Nancy is with the patient."

Shit. I almost break into a run. Nancy is a first-year nurse. She's trying hard, but she needs a lot of guidance. She should never be on her own without a more experienced nurse present.

"Now you see why we need you," June says.

I nod, my pulse speeding up. This is why I went into nursing. I like the idea of being needed and helping people. A good nurse can mean the difference between life and death for a patient, particularly in the ER. It's a heavy responsibility, but I don't mind. I like the fast pace of work here, the way twelve hours fly by. By the end of each day, I'm so exhausted I can barely walk, but I'm also satisfied.

The ER teems with activity when I enter. Approaching one of the curtained-off sections, I pull back the drapes and take everything in with a quick glance. The gunshot victim lies on the stretcher. He's a large man, tall and broad. I guess him to be somewhere in his late twenties or early thirties.

Nancy, the first-year nurse, is applying pressure to the chest wound to stop the bleeding. Two men stand nearby, but I pay them little attention, all my focus on the patient.

After making quick work of washing my hands and pulling on a pair of gloves, I take charge. The patient's pulse is weak, and he's having difficulty breathing. The bullet must've hit a lung.

"He's going into hypotensive shock," I call out.

Dr. Stevenson rushes over. He swiftly confirms that the patient is experiencing a tension pneumothorax. A few minutes later, we've got a tube inserted into his chest.

The patient's pneumothorax decompresses, and he drags in a breath. Good. Now we need to stop the bleeding. There's both an entrance and an exit wound. The bullet went straight through. Judging by the location of the injuries, it must've just missed his heart. Another inch and the man would be occupying a body bag instead of this stretcher.

I don't wonder who shot this man or why. That's not my job. My job is to help the doctor save his life.

Finally, the victim is stable and can be wheeled to Radiology for a CT scan. Barring any unforeseen complications, the man will live.

Stripping off my gloves, I walk over to the sink to wash my hands again. The habit is so deeply ingrained I never have to think about it. Whenever I'm in the hospital, I wash my hands compulsively every chance I get, both for my own health and that of my patients.

Letting the warm water run over my hands, I roll my head from side to side to relieve the tension in my neck. As much as I love my job, it's both physically and mentally exhausting, particularly when someone's life is on the line. Full-body massages should be part of the benefit package for nurses. If anyone needs a rubdown at the end of a twelve-hour shift, it's a nurse.

Turning away from the sink, I glance back at where the wounded man was—and catch a pair of steely blue eyes looking at me.

It's one of the men who'd been standing near the victim, likely one of his relatives. Visitors are generally not allowed in the hospital at night, but the ER is an exception.

Instead of looking away, as most people will when caught staring, the man continues to study me.

Both intrigued and slightly annoyed, I study him back.

He's tall, well over six feet in height, and broad-shouldered. He's not handsome in the traditional sense. That's too weak of a word to describe him. Instead, he's magnetic.

Power. That's what comes to mind when I look at him. It's there in the arrogant tilt of his head, in the way he looks at me so calmly, utterly sure of himself and his ability to control all around him. I don't know who he is or what he does, but I doubt he's a pencil pusher in some office. This is a man used to issuing orders and having them obeyed.

His clothes fit him well and look expensive. Maybe even custom made. He's wearing a gray trench coat, dark gray pants with a subtle pinstripe, and a pair of black Italian leather shoes. His dark brown hair is cut short, almost military style. The simple haircut suits his face, revealing hard, symmetric features. He has high cheekbones and a blade of a nose with a slight bump, as though it had been broken once.

I have no idea how old he is. His face is unlined, but there's no boyishness to it. No softness whatsoever, not even in the curve of his mouth. I guess his age to be early thirties, but he could just as easily be twenty-five or forty.

He doesn't fidget or look uncomfortable as our staring contest continues. He simply stands there quietly, completely still, his blue gaze trained on me.

To my shock, my heart rate picks up as a tingle of heat runs down my spine. It's as though the temperature in the room has jumped ten degrees. All of a sudden, the atmosphere becomes intensely sexual, making me aware of myself as a woman in a way I've never experienced. I can feel the silky material of my matching underwear set brushing between my legs and against my breasts. My entire body seems flushed and sensitized, my nipples pebbling underneath my layers of clothing.

Holy shit. So this is what it feels like to be attracted to someone. It's not rational, not logical. There's no meeting of minds and hearts involved. No, the urge is basic and primitive. My body has sensed his on some animal level, and it wants to mate.

He feels it too. It shows in the way his blue eyes darken, lids partially lowering, and in the way his nostrils flare as if trying to catch my scent. His fingers twitch, then curl into fists, and I somehow know he's trying to control himself, to avoid reaching for me right here and now.

If we were alone, I have no doubt he'd be on me already.

Still staring at the stranger, I back away. The strength of my response to him is frightening, unsettling. We're in the middle of the ER, surrounded by people, and all I can think about is hot, sheet-twisting sex. I have no idea who he is, whether he's married or single. For all I know, he's a criminal or an asshole. *Or a cheating scumbag like Tony.* If anyone has taught me to think twice before trusting a man, it's my ex-boyfriend. I don't want to get involved with anyone so soon after my last, disastrous relationship. I don't want that kind of complication in my life again.

The tall stranger clearly has other ideas.

At my cautious retreat, he narrows his eyes, his gaze becoming sharper, more focused. Then he comes toward me, his stride graceful for such a large man. There's something panther-like in his leisurely movements, and for a second, I feel like a mouse being stalked by a big cat. Instinctively, I take another step back, and his hard mouth tightens with displeasure.

Dammit, I'm acting like a coward.

I stop backing away and stand my ground instead, straightening to my full five-foot-seven height. I'm always the calm and capable one, handling high-stress situations with ease, yet I'm behaving like a schoolgirl confronted with her first crush. Yes, the man makes me uncomfortable, but there's nothing to be afraid of. What's the worst he can do? Ask me out on a date?

Nevertheless, my hands shake slightly as he approaches, stopping less than two feet away. This close, he's even taller than I thought, a few inches over six feet. I'm not a short woman, but I feel tiny standing in front of him. It's not a feeling I enjoy.

"You're very good at your job." His voice is deep and a little rough, tinged with some Eastern European accent. Just hearing it makes my insides shiver in a strangely pleasurable way.

"Thank you," I say, a bit uncertainly. I *am* good at my job, but I didn't expect a compliment from this stranger.

"You took care of Igor well. Thank you for that."

Igor must be the gunshot patient. It's a foreign-sounding name. Russian, perhaps? That would explain the stranger's accent. Although he speaks English fluently, he's not a native speaker.

"Of course." I'm proud of the steadiness of my tone. Hopefully, the man won't realize how he affects me. "I hope he recovers quickly. Is he a relative?"

"My bodyguard."

Wow. I was right. This man is a big fish. Does that mean—

"Was he shot in the course of duty?" I ask, holding my breath.

"He took a bullet meant for me, yes." His tone is matter-of-fact, but I get a sense of suppressed rage underneath those words.

I swallow hard. "Have you already spoken to the police?"

"I gave them a brief statement. I will talk to them in more detail once Igor is stabilized and regains consciousness."

I nod, not knowing what to say to that. The man standing in front of me was nearly assassinated today. Who is he? Some mafia boss? A political figure?

If I had any doubts about the wisdom of exploring this strange attraction between us, they're gone. This stranger is bad news, and I need to stay as far away from him as possible.

"I wish your bodyguard a speedy recovery," I say in a falsely cheerful tone. "Barring any complications, he should be fine."

"Thanks to you."

I give him a half-smile and take a step to the side, hoping to walk around the man and go to my next patient.

He shifts his stance, blocking my way. "I'm Alex Volkov," he says quietly. "And you are?"

My pulse quickens. The male intent in his question makes me nervous. Hoping he'll get the hint, I say, "Just a nurse working here."

He doesn't catch on, or he pretends not to. "What's your name?"

He's certainly persistent. I take a deep breath. "I'm Katherine Morrell. If you'll excuse me—"

"Katherine," he repeats, his accent lending the familiar syllables an exotic edge. His hard mouth softens a bit. "Katerina. It's a beautiful name."

"Thank you. I really have to go."

I'm increasingly anxious to get away. He's too large, too potently male. I need space and some room to breathe. His nearness is overpowering, making me edgy and restless, leaving me craving something that I know will be bad for me.

"You have your job to do. I understand," he says, looking vaguely amused.

Still, he doesn't move out of my way. Instead, as I watch in shock, he raises one large hand and brushes his knuckles over my cheek.

I freeze as a wave of heat zaps through my body. His touch is light, but I feel branded by it, shaken to the core.

"I would like to see you again, Katerina," he says softly, dropping his hand. "When does your shift end tonight?"

I stare at him, feeling like I'm losing control of the situation. "I don't think that's a good idea."

"Why not?" His blue eyes narrow. "Are you married?"

I'm tempted to lie, but honesty wins out. "No, but I'm not interested in dating right now."

"Who said anything about dating?"

I blink. I assumed—

He lifts his hand again, stopping me mid-thought. This time, he picks up a strand of my hair, rubbing it between his fingers.

"I don't date, Katerina," he murmurs, his accented voice oddly mesmerizing. "But I would like to take you to bed. And I think you'd like that too."

12

2

_____

"*A*re you serious? He said that to you? What did you do next?"

Joanne, my best friend since high school and a newly promoted investment banking associate at Goldman Sachs, stares at me in fascination.

I settle deeper into the soft velvet of the booth, happy to exchange the chilly November weather outside for the warm interior of the restaurant. "I said no, I wouldn't like that, and that I needed to go."

I cringe a little when I remember how I stuttered those words yesterday while stepping out of the man's reach. Within a two-minute conversation, Alex Volkov stripped away my hard-earned composure, reducing me to a trembling, uncertain girl instead of the confident woman I've worked hard to become.

"And he just accepted that?" Joanne's green eyes are wide and curious.

He didn't, exactly. Instead, he looked at me with that hard blue gaze and smiled for the first time—a sharp, predatory smile that made my knees weak. Only then did he step away, letting me escape.

I don't feel like explaining this to my friend, though. "What else was he going to do?"

"I don't know. I've never met anyone like that, so I have no idea."

"I have no idea either. What, you think I'm used to being propositioned in the ER?"

"I don't know," Joanne says with a straight face. "You certainly get into more interesting situations than me."

"Oh, please. You're hardly the poster child for normal relationships. Do I need to remind you about Larry?"

"Hey, that was in tenth grade! You can't hold that against me."

I grin at my friend. "I can and I will."

We'd been thick as thieves in high school, gossiping about boys and clothes, and we're still close. If not for Joanne's crazy work hours, we'd probably hang out every weekend. As is, days like today, when we meet up for lunch in Chinatown, are only an occasional indulgence.

Why my friend chose a career in finance, I'll never understand. Yes, the money is great, but the work-life balance is horrendous. For the past three years, Joanne has been working like a slave, putting in between eighty and a hundred hours a week. More often than not, my friend's pretty face looks pale and strained, with bluish shadows underneath her eyes.

I also work hard, but I have a life. Granted, it's not much of a life these days, but at least I have time off. Joanne has no such assurance. With her job, she's on call twenty-four-seven. Even now, she keeps checking her phone every couple of minutes, just in case she has to rush back to the office for some emergency.

"Seriously, they can't get along without you for an hour?" I ask in exasperation after Joanne covertly looks at her phone for the fifth time.

As a nurse dealing with real emergencies, I find it ridiculous that Joanne's colleagues consider a PowerPoint presentation important enough to make someone work on the weekend.

She sighs. "Sorry about that. I'm so used to checking my phone that it's like a compulsion."

I level a serious look at her. "Is it going to get better now that you're an associate and not a lowly analyst?"

"Hopefully. Now I can get some poor first-year analyst to stay there until midnight, and I can maybe go home at nine."

"You're insane."

"Yes, yes, I know. But let's not talk about my work. That's too depressing. Tell me more about Mr. Tall and Sexy. You said he had an accent?"

"Mm-hmm. My best guess is he's Russian or something along those lines. He said his name was Alex Volkov."

She gasps. "What? Did you just say *Alex Volkov*? As in Alexander Volkov?"

I frown. "Yeah. Why? You know that name?"

"Duh. Of course I know that name. Anybody who reads the newspapers knows that name, Katie girl. Don't tell me you've never heard of him?"

I shake my head, still frowning. "No. Why? Is he some big kahuna?"

"The biggest there is. Fuck, Kate, I can't believe you met one of the wealthiest men in the world and didn't have a clue who he was!"

"What?" I stare at my friend in shock. "What do you mean?"

"I mean... wow. Alexander Volkov. He's one of those Russian oligarchs who made a fortune in oil. Now he runs what amounts to an empire. And you're telling me he propositioned you?"

"He didn't *proposition* me. He just said he wanted to take me to bed."

"Uh-huh. If that's not a proposition, I don't know what is. Fucking-A. The man is a freaking gazillionaire! And you found him hot! I can't believe you told him you're not interested."

"I'm not interested, Jo. You know I just broke up with Tony."

"Oh, please, that asshole doesn't deserve even a mention from you. I always hated his guts. I told you he was wrong for you from the beginning."

It's true. She'd taken an immediate dislike to Tony, calling him bland and boring. She didn't understand why I was dating the skinny surgery resident when I never had trouble attracting men—her words. The thing is, Tony seemed like a safe, easy choice. We shared the same interests, and I enjoyed spending time with him. Our sex might've been mediocre at best, but it was nice to have a steady boyfriend, someone I thought I could trust.

Little did I know. It had been almost comical finding Tony fucking some blond bimbo in my apartment, a studio to which I'd given him the keys only two weeks earlier. I'd caught a stomach bug, so I came home early that day, hoping to crawl into bed with a mug of ginger tea. Instead, I found my boyfriend of eight months there—and he wasn't alone.

At the sight of his bony ass buried between the blonde's pale thighs, I literally threw up. Just barfed right there in the door-way. Tony and his blond squeeze were forced to step through the vomit to leave the apartment.

It was actually quite funny, especially after the fact.

Forcing my attention back to the present, I give my friend a sarcastic smile. "Yes, you are all-seeing and all-knowing, Miss Grand Psychic. How could I have ever doubted your wisdom?"

"That's right. How could you have?" Joanne grins at me. "But back to your Russian billionaire. Are you going to do it?"

"Do what?"

"Sleep with him."

I shoot her an incredulous look. "Um, no. The guy basically told me all he wants is sex. Besides, don't you think it's sketchy that someone wants to kill him?"

"That part is a bit problematic." She looks thoughtful for a moment, twirling a strand of reddish-gold hair around her finger. "Don't all wealthy people attract crazies, though? Isn't that why they have bodyguards in the first place?"

"I don't know. I just don't need those complications in my life right now."

"Honestly, Katie girl, there's nothing that complicated about having sex with a guy you're attracted to. When was the last time you had awesome, mind-blowing sex?"

I can't recall. "Not for a while," I admit.

Actually, maybe never. My best sex was with my college boyfriend after we'd gotten drunk and smoked weed, and even that had been just pretty good.

"In that case, you're way past due. Did that douchebag even give you orgasms?" She's obviously referring to Tony.

"Sometimes," I say reluctantly.

"Oh my God, I'm so glad he's out of your life. It should've been every single freaking time."

I scoff. "Look who's talking. When was the last time you went on a date, much less got laid?"

"Hey, at least I have an excuse. I work too much and don't have time for boyfriends. You, on the other hand, actually had a boyfriend."

"Whatever." I sigh. "I don't know if I can simply sleep with a guy like that. I'm more of a relationship person."

"Relationships with boring-as-hell guys? How well has that worked out for you?"

Not that well, I have to admit, since I'm twenty-five and single.

"You see!" Her eyes glitter with triumph. "Something clearly needs to change in your approach. Let loose for a change and stop going for your usual, overly logical choice. A hot Russian billionaire wants to take you to bed? Why not freaking let him?"

WHY NOT, INDEED?

Joanne's words linger in my mind as I walk down Broadway, heading toward the Staten Island Ferry. Once every couple of weeks, I meet my Manhattan-dwelling friends somewhere downtown and then take the ferry to visit my mom. Today is one of those times, and I'm glad I made the plans earlier in the week. I don't want to sit home and brood about my strange reaction to a man I've known for all of five minutes.

Why had he affected me so strongly? The way all my senses focused on him had been both frightening and exhilarating.

Even now, just thinking about him, my heart beats faster and my belly tightens with excitement.

This is ridiculous. I haven't even kissed the guy. How can he turn me on so much? I have no idea what he's like in bed. For all I know, he's a wham-bam-thank-you-ma'am type who just wants to have a quickie with a pretty nurse. Yet I can't stop thinking about him, imagining all the delicious things he might do to me if I took him up on his offer.

Why am I so drawn to him? Is it the aura of power he projects? I can't deny I find strong men attractive, even if Alex intimidates me on some level. Something feminine deep within me likes the idea of a bigger, more powerful man, someone who can protect me from dangers both real and imaginary. With his air of calm confidence and male arrogance, Alex definitely gives off that vibe in spades.

Now that I know who he is, I'm not surprised he came across the way he did. Although I've never heard of him specifically, I know a bit about Russian oligarchs and the sway they have in Russia. The man is a ruler in his corner of the world. My friend Nadia, a Ukrainian nurse who works in the Pediatric ER Department, told me about the so-called New Russians and their ruthless rise to the top in post-Communist Russia. Their history sounded brutal and mafia-like, and I bet things haven't changed that much since. No wonder the man had bodyguards. Who knows what he did to piss someone off?

Yes, Alex Volkov is definitely bad news. It would be smart to avoid any involvement with him.

Still, I can't get him out of my head. I've never dated any Russian men, although I've been asked out by plenty. Coney Island Hospital is located in an Eastern European area of Brooklyn, and many of my coworkers and patients come from the local Russian or Ukrainian community. For an American, I'm fairly well versed with Alex's culture and can even speak a few words of his language. Not that I'd need to use my minuscule linguistic skills. Alex is obviously fluent in English.

Ugh, stop it, Kate. You won't need to use your Russian knowledge because you won't see the guy again.

That's what I need to keep in mind. He expressed interest, I refused, and that's the end of it. A man like him, wealthy and attractive, doesn't need to chase women. He won't bother pursuing a nurse he met only once. I have nothing to fear. Even if I were inclined to agree to his rather crude offer, which I'm not, it's too late.

I'll never see him again.

It's for the best... even if, for some odd reason, I find that thought depressing.

MY MOM, LAURA MORRELL, LIVES IN A QUIET AREA OF STATEN Island near the Ferry, less than two blocks away from the ocean. The neighborhood is a bit rundown, but it makes for a cheap, convenient commute into Manhattan. That feature is less relevant now that my mom can no longer work, but it served her well back when she waitressed at the fancy steak-houses in the Financial District.

Although not glamorous, the job brought in good money, enabling my mom to raise me on her own without help from anyone else. She even managed to save enough money to buy a two-bedroom apartment when I was seven years old. It wasn't until two years ago that my mom's rheumatoid arthritis got bad enough that she was forced to file for disability. Now, at only forty-three years of age, my mom lives off disability payments and the money I regularly deposit into her bank account, ignoring her protests.

My own tiny studio is in Brooklyn, in the Park Slope area where I moved three years ago after college graduation. It's a short commute to the hospital and is, in general, a great neighborhood for a twenty-five-year-old single woman. Although I miss my mom, I don't regret moving to Brooklyn. I can't imagine spending two hours a day traveling to and from work, or having to take a ferry or an express bus to go anywhere outside of Staten Island. However, visiting my mom at my childhood home is something I very much enjoy.

"Hi, Mom," I say with a smile as she opens the door.

Her youthful face lights up. "Katie! Oh, I was just thinking about you. Come in, honey. I made your favorite split-pea soup."

With her blond hair, blue eyes, and smooth skin, my mom is a remarkably pretty woman. As her disease has progressed, she's gradually become less active and has slowly gained weight over the years. Now curvy rather than slim, she's still beautiful and still goes through men like Kleenex, just like she did in her twenties and thirties.

"Thanks, Mom," I say, grinning.

My mom's cooking is second to none, and she loves spoiling her only daughter. I've always found her mature-and-motherly manner endearing and somewhat surprising. After all, she's only eighteen years older than I am. Growing up, I often had to explain that the young woman with me was indeed my mother and not my babysitter, and the differences in our appearances didn't make it easier. While I've inherited some features from my mom, my darker coloring is from my father, whoever he may be. My mom has no clue herself, having fallen pregnant by accident after attending one of the frat parties at a nearby college—a development that didn't exactly please her conservative New England family.

Upon learning of her intent to keep the baby, they disowned their wild, rebellious daughter, forcing her to scrap her college plans and find a job immediately upon high school graduation. It had been a harsh dose of reality, and my mom still hasn't forgiven them for it. As a result, I've never met my grandparents—a situation I'm fine with, given the way they'd treated their only daughter. I hardly ever think about them at all, in fact.

I do, however, wonder about my father. My mom is blond and pale, so my olive-hued skin, wavy brown hair, and hazel eyes must've come from his side of the family. I could easily be part Latino, Middle Eastern, Italian, or Greek. One of these days, I'll do a DNA test and figure it out once and for all.

My mom bustles around the kitchen, moving with unusual ease. "So, tell me, honey, how's work?"

This is one of her better days. On bad days, her joints ache so much even simple household tasks are painful to perform. I contemplated moving back in, but my mom wouldn't hear of it. The last thing she needs is an adult daughter underfoot, she said. Mom loves the freedom of having the apartment to herself. My moving out has given her love life a boost.

"Oh, the usual," I reply. "Lots of flu patients."

I'm tempted to tell her about the man I met, but for some reason, I decide against it. Although my mom is as much a friend as she's a parent, something about that encounter makes me hesitant to talk about it.

She pauses for a second to frown at me. "Are you eating

properly? You look thinner than the last time I saw you."

"It's an illusion, I promise," I say with a smile. "The flu season has just begun, so I haven't had a chance to lose any weight yet."

"I don't like it that you skip meals during work." She looks fretful as she places a bowl of soup on the table in front of me. "You've been working way too much."

I pick up my spoon. "I don't have any shifts for the next two days. Besides, I don't work nearly as much as Joanne does."

"That girl is insane," Mom says, sitting down across from me. "Does she date at all?"

"Not really. She just got a promotion at work, though. Hopefully, that means she'll be able to work a little less and have a life."

My mom sighs and shakes her head, apparently as worried about my friend as she is about me.

Dipping my spoon into the soup, I bring it to my lips and take a sip. As usual, the hearty flavor brings me back to my childhood, when Mom made the healthy dish almost every week. Despite her youth, she's been a great parent, always putting my needs before her own and ensuring I had the best childhood possible. Even with the constant parade of her ever-changing boyfriends, I grew up feeling secure and loved.

"How's Martin doing?" I ask between spoonfuls of soup.

Mom's full lips curve into a happy smile. Martin, a forty-six-year-old lawyer, is her current boyfriend. They've been dating for the past four months, a remarkably long stretch for my mom. As a teenager, I often wondered why she couldn't find someone to settle down with. Finally, I concluded that my mom simply enjoys variety when it comes to relationships. She likes men far too much to choose just one.

"He's good," she says. "He invited me to go to Cancun next week."

"Wow. Are you guys getting serious?"

Her smile grows wider. "Perhaps. I do like him a lot, and he's been very good to me. He doesn't even mind this ridiculous disease I've got. Plus, he's really good in the sack."

I burst out laughing. I can't imagine other mothers telling their daughters these sorts of tidbits. As I've gotten older, I've become my mom's closest friend and confidante, and I frequently hear far too many details about her love life. Although it can be weird at times, I appreciate that I know my mother as a real person and not just as the woman who gave birth to me.

For the next couple of hours, we chat about work and her upcoming trip to Mexico. Martin bought a beachfront condo there and can't wait to show it off to his girlfriend. He's so eager, in fact, he bought her a plane ticket before she'd even agreed to go there. As I listen to her relay the story, my chest warms with happiness. Good for my mom. She deserves to be spoiled.

The afternoon comes to an end much too soon, and before I know it, it's time to kiss my mom goodbye and head back home, where no exciting love life or enticing adventures await.

It makes me think as I walk the two blocks to the ferry. Maybe it's time to throw some of my caution to the wind.

THE NEXT MORNING, I WAKE FEELING REFRESHED AFTER GOING TO bed at a reasonable time. Night shifts always mess me up. My body dislikes abrupt changes in sleeping patterns.

Stretching, I yawn and enjoy the luxury of not being rushed. For the first time in weeks, I have no plans or commitments. I can lounge in my pajamas all day, and no one will say boo.

I briefly consider calling some friends and going out for lunch, but I decide against it. Chill days are far too rare. Instead, I get up and make my usual breakfast—a bowl of oatmeal with cranberries and walnuts—and I eat it on the couch while watching an episode of *Downton Abbey*.

Just as I'm starting on the next episode, my phone rings.

June, my supervisor, sounds harried. "Kate, I'm so sorry. I know you have the day off, but is there any way you could swap shifts with Rose? She's had a death in the family, and she won't be able to come in today. She was supposed to start at ten."

So much for that chill day. "Sure. I'll be there."

THE SHIFT IS GRUELING WITH A NEVER-ENDING STREAM OF patients. One man is brought in with chest pains, but most of the other cases aren't true emergencies. Many people go to the ER instead of seeing a regular doctor simply because they lack health insurance.

Feeling unusually tired, I take a quick break to visit the restroom and splash cold water on my face. I have three hours left on my shift, and I'm looking forward to going home and falling straight into bed.

I'm walking back from the restroom when I see him again.

My heart leaps, needles of adrenaline biting into my skin.

Walking toward me is none other than the man who's been on my mind for the past two days.

Alex Volkov, the Russian oligarch himself.

3

*a*lex is strolling leisurely down the hallway, dressed in a pair of jeans and a gray sweater. The clothes hug his large frame, revealing wide shoulders and a muscular build. A pair of hard-looking men are walking a few yards behind him, their eyes sharp and vigilant. His bodyguards.

He's looking at the phone in his hand, and I speed up, hoping I'll be able to walk past him unnoticed.

No such luck.

As though sensing my gaze on him, he looks up, and his blue eyes narrow with recognition. Then a small smile curves his lips, softening them a bit.

A warm shiver snakes down my spine, heating my skin, even as some instinct tells me to run. The urge is so strong my leg muscles tighten with it, the needles of adrenaline sinking deeper into my skin and spiking my heart rate.

Don't be a coward, Kate.

Steeling my spine, I continue walking toward him, trying

not to react to the way his eyes rake over my body and finally linger on my mouth. When he meets my gaze again, there's so much heat in the look he gives me I may burn on the spot. My core clenches, and liquid warmth dampens my underwear.

Dammit. This is insane.

He stops in front of me. I'm cognizant of his bodyguards a few yards away, but all my attention is focused on him. I'd forgotten how tall he is, how big his body is compared to mine. I have to crane my neck to meet his eyes, and I can't help but be conscious of his size, his strength, his sheer maleness.

His accented voice is soft and slightly mocking, as if he knows the effect he has on me. "Hello, Katerina."

I stare up at him, Joanne's words ringing in my ears. I've always approached my relationships the same way as every-thing else, with a calm, steady rationality. I've never been one to leap before I looked. That's my mom's way, not mine. I like to think, to apply the same logical reasoning to dating as I do to my career. Casual hookups weren't my thing in college, and I've never had a one-night stand. The risks have never been worth the benefits. Instead, I've dated men I've liked and respected, with whom I've connected on a mental and emotional level. A man's personality has always been far more important to me than his looks.

I have no idea what Alex's personality is like. I don't know him at all. There's nothing logical in the way he makes me feel, nothing rational in the way my body reacts to his. Something within me responds to him on a subconscious, instinctive level, and there's nothing I can do about it.

Worst yet, what little I do know about him is frightening. He's a wealthy man from a place where wealth and corruption go hand in hand, and he's pissed off someone enough that they want to kill him. How crazy would it be to get involved with someone like that?

Insane. Completely, totally, and utterly irresponsible.

Yet yesterday's thought about throwing caution to the wind keeps wiggling into my mind. What if Joanne is right? It's not as if I'm going to marry or even date the guy. All he wants is a brief sexual fling. I can sleep with him, get this strange craving out of my system, and go back to my normal life. I'm not ready for another relationship—the incident with Tony has left a sour taste in my mouth—and Alex isn't looking for one. Would it really be so terrible to do something impulsive for once and give in to this attraction? To hook up with an attractive man?

Before I can think better of it, I give Alex an answering smile. "Hi. How's Igor doing?"

Something dark flashes across his face before his expression smooths out and turns inscrutable. "He's much better, thanks."

His eyes travel down my body again, making me feel flushed all over. I've never felt so blatantly desired in my life, and it's incredibly seductive.

When he looks back at me, there's a cynical tilt to his lips. "What time does your shift end?" His voice is low and deep, his tone self-assured. Somehow, he's sensed my weakening resolve.

I swallow. "At ten."

I can't believe myself. Am I really going to do this? Agree to a purely sexual arrangement with a man I barely know?

He flashes me a darkly sensual smile that makes my core tighten with desire. "I'd like to see you tonight. How about we grab a bite to eat after your shift ends?"

I hesitate. Despite his animal magnetism, there's something unsettling about him, some hardness in the line of his mouth that makes me think he can be ruthless. How can I even think about getting involved with a man like that? Someone who's a total stranger? What if he's as corrupt and dangerous as Nadia portrayed the wealthy Russians to be?

As though sensing my reservations, he says quietly, "It will be just dinner, I promise. I won't force you to do anything you don't want."

I blink, surprised. "A dinner at ten?" I thought *grabbing a bite to eat* was a euphemism for sex, at least the way he said it.

"Won't you be hungry after your work is done?"

"Probably," I say slowly.

I was planning on grabbing a quick sandwich at home before plopping into bed, but dinner with Alex sounds much more appealing. True, he unnerves me, but he also fascinates me. Surely a dinner won't be a big deal.

"Then it's decided," he says, his tone brooking no argument. "I'll send a car to pick you up here after work. The restaurant is nearby, but I don't want you to walk alone. I'll meet you there."

Before I can reply, he heads down the hallway, his body-guards trailing in his wake.

THE REST OF THE SHIFT DRAGS. I KEEP WATCHING THE CLOCK, MY heart racing with a mixture of nervous excitement and feverish anticipation. I feel like a teenager again, waiting to be picked up for my very first date.

It's not a date. Alex doesn't date. This dinner is his attempt to convince me to sleep with him, nothing more.

Of course, one can argue that all dates are ultimately just that. All social niceties disguise a mating dance as old as time. Still, I prefer to think the men I usually go out with want more than just my body, that they enjoy my company and like me as a person. With Alex, I can't pretend that's the case. He's been honest about his intentions.

In some ways, it's liberating to know exactly where I stand with him. He doesn't want a relationship, and at the moment, neither do I. We're both adults and attracted to each other. Why shouldn't I act on that attraction?

A memory of the way he touched me the first time we met flashes through my mind, the way he brushed his fingers over my cheek and how my skin burned afterward. If a simple touch can turn me on so much, how will it feel to kiss him? To feel his hands on my body? To have him inside me?

Stop it, Kate. You probably won't sleep with him tonight. It's just dinner.

Yeah, right. Just dinner with a man I find so hot I fantasized about him while changing bloody bandages. With a man who made me feel more aroused with a single look than my last boyfriend did with foreplay. A man who outright told me he wanted to take me to bed.

Yeah, just dinner.

Finally, it's ten.

Rushing to the locker room, I change out of my scrubs, wash my face, and apply the mascara and lip gloss I always carry in my purse. Thankfully, I don't need more than a light application of cosmetics, having been blessed with clear, even-toned skin and dark, well-defined eyebrows and eyelashes, the latter courtesy of my father's mysterious genes. When I was a child, I disliked my coloring, wishing I had blond hair and blue eyes like my mother. As I got older, however, I grew to appreciate the olive hue of my skin and the thickness of my long, wavy brown hair.

I give myself a quick once-over in the mirror. My face glows with excitement, and my eyes sparkle with anticipation. Thank goodness I didn't wear sweats and old Uggs to work. That's my usual go-to outfit for days when I'm called in unexpectedly. Instead, I'm dressed in a form-fitting sweater, my favorite jeans, and a pair of Frye boots I got on sale last week. It's not a fancy outfit, but it flatters my figure. Unless Alex is taking me to a fancy restaurant, I'm reasonably presentable.

I also shaved my legs this morning and got a Brazilian wax a couple of weeks ago, so I'm ready in that department if things progress that far.

With a last look in the mirror, I exit the restroom and head outside, hoping the car is already waiting.

As soon as I step outside, I hear my name being called.

I turn toward the voice. A sleek black car is parked at the curb. A tall, sandy-haired man stands in front of it, watching me with a sharp gaze.

Seeing me looking his way, the man comes over, his posture reminding me of someone in the military.

"I'm Yuri, Alexander's driver," he says in a heavily accented voice. "He'd like you to come with me."

I nod, my heart pounding in my chest. I can't believe I'm about to get into a car with a strange man to go on a date—*no, not a date*—with one of the wealthiest men in the world. It's the kind of stuff I can tell my grandkids about when I'm old and gray.

Trying to act like I'm not freaking out inside, I say calmly, "It's nice to meet you, Yuri. Where are we going?"

"To a Russian restaurant nearby." He leads me toward the car and opens the door. "Romanoff's. Perhaps you've heard of it?"

I stop in my tracks. I *have* heard of it. Nadia went to a wedding there once and showed me pictures of the place. Apparently, it's one of the most popular places for major celebrations in the Russian community, famous for fine dining and over-the-top dinner shows. If I remember correctly, all the guests in Nadia's pictures wore extravagant attire.

"Wait, Yuri, I think there's been a mistake. I'm not dressed for that. Alex said we're just grabbing a bite to eat, but this sounds much fancier."

"Alexander said you're not to worry. Everything is taken care of."

I lift a brow in surprise but climb into the car. Is Alex planning to give me a change of clothes when I get there?

Yuri closes the door and gets into the driver's seat, leaving me alone in the back of the car. A partition separates us, like in a limo, although the car is more of a full-sized, luxuriously appointed sedan.

Before I've even settled into the plush leather seat, he smoothly pulls away from the curb and onto Ocean Parkway.

Three minutes later, we're in front of the restaurant.

Tightly clutching my purse, I exit the car and follow Yuri inside.

4

$\mathcal{I}$ step through the doors and stop, staring at my surroundings in awe.

The restaurant is opulent. There's no other way to describe it. The interior is huge, easily fitting in five hundred guests or more. Soft music plays in the background. Everything is decorated in shades of red and gold with richly textured fabrics and gleaming surfaces. I can easily imagine some nineteenth-century czar dining here, surrounded by his loyal nobles.

Of course, instead of a czar, I'm meeting Alex Volkov, who's as close to a czar as one can get in modern-day Russia.

I walk deeper into the empty restaurant. Where are the diners? The tables are pushed to the walls, leaving a large empty space in the middle. Only one round table remains, and a familiar figure is waiting for me there.

At my approach, Alex rises to his feet. Like me, he's dressed casually, in the same jeans and sweater I saw him wear earlier. Maybe the restaurant isn't as dressy as I imagined, or—more likely—Alex doesn't have to follow any rules and dresses however he pleases.

I bet he can wear rags, or nothing at all, and still look like the most powerful man in the room. It's not the clothes that make him so impressive. It's something within him, some inner steel that's as much a part of him as his muscular body and chiseled jaw.

He watches me walk toward him with a hooded gaze, his face giving away nothing of his emotions. Doubt creeps in again, making me question the wisdom of coming here. But then his mouth softens, one corner curving upward, and I forget about my reservations, again feeling that inexplicable pull of attraction.

Reaching the table, I pause for a second to look up at him. "Are we the only two people here?" His height is both arousing and intimidating, making me feel helpless and feminine in a way I've never experienced.

"We are," he says, pulling out a chair for me. "I hope you don't mind."

Uttering a shaky laugh, I sit down. "No, but why this huge place?"

"I like their food and music," he says as he walks around to take his seat across from me.

I give him a disbelieving look. "So you rented out the whole enormous restaurant?"

"Why not? I like my privacy."

Why not, indeed? When one is richer than Croesus, what does a measly few grand matter? Trying to match his casual attitude, I nod as though it makes sense.

"Tell me about yourself, Katerina."

His softly worded command catches me by surprise. Does

he truly want to get to know me, or is he making polite conversation? Either way, there's one thing I definitely want to tell him. "Please call me Kate." I give him a smile. "That's what I usually go by."

"Kate," he repeats, his blue eyes gleaming. Somehow, he manages to make even that simple word sound deliciously foreign. "Kate. Hmm, I'm not sure if it suits you. Too simple. Not like you at all."

"Oh? How would you know what I'm like?"

His lips curve into something resembling a smile. "I don't know what you're like, Katyusha, but I'd like to find out."

I swallow, my throat suddenly dry. The sexual intent behind his words is unmistakable. And what is that word he used? Katyu-something?

A waiter approaches our table, interrupting my thoughts. He brings a bottle of sparkling water and what looks like high-end vodka.

Alex gestures toward the drinks. "Would you like wine or cognac, or is this okay?"

"This is fine." I'm not a big drinker, so anything he orders is fine with me.

He nods and pours us each a shot of vodka and a glass of Perrier before addressing the waiter in Russian. The man departs and promptly returns with two elaborately decorated menus. I study mine. The dishes are listed in Russian but have English translations.

"Have you ever been to a Russian restaurant?" Alex asks, looking up from his menu.

"Actually, no," I say, slightly embarrassed about the fact. "I work in this neighborhood, but I've never explored it much. By the time I'm done with my shift, I'm usually too tired to go out afterward."

A small smile appears on his lips. "Yet you're out with me tonight."

"So I am."

"Why?" He seems genuinely curious. "I got the impression you weren't that interested at first."

I lift a shoulder in a shrug. "A girl can always change her mind, right?" I could add that I've thought about him constantly for the past two days and realized I'd be an idiot to miss out on this kind of chemistry, but I don't think his ego needs stroking.

He gives me a cynical look. "A girl sure can."

Puzzled, I frown but let it go. "How long have you been in America?" I ask instead. "Your English is excellent for someone who's not a native speaker."

"I came here last year," he says, taking a sip of his water.

"Where did you learn to speak English so well?"

"I studied with a private tutor for a couple of years in my early twenties."

"A couple of years? That's all?" I stare at him in amazement. I studied Spanish in high school for four years, but I'm far from fluent in it.

His tone is casual, as though it's no big deal to gain near-native proficiency in a foreign language in such a short time. "I have a talent for languages. I learn them easily."

I'm beyond impressed. "Do you speak other languages as well?"

"French, Italian, Ukrainian, Polish, Mandarin, and some German."

My jaw drops. The man sitting across the table from me isn't only rich and hot, but also a freaking polyglot.

"Do you know what you'd like to order, or do you need more time?" he asks.

Realizing I've been staring, I close my mouth and turn my attention back to the menu. "Maybe another minute." The majority of the options are unfamiliar, but the potato-mushroom appetizer seems promising.

"Is there anything you don't like or eat?"

"I'm a vegetarian." I look up to measure his reaction. "No meat or fish. I do eat eggs and dairy, though."

"What about caviar?" he asks, seemingly neither surprised nor put off by my dietary preference.

I wrinkle my nose. "I'm afraid not. For its eggs to be harvested, the fish has to be killed."

He nods, again completely unoffended. "How about I order us a few meat-free appetizers then, and you can try different things?"

"That would be great, thanks," I say, offering him a smile. I'm pleasantly surprised by Alex thus far. He's considerate and accommodating, at least when it comes to accepting my diet.

A vegetarian since the age of thirteen, I'm used to having to explain and justify my food choices to my dates. Many omnivores, including the men I've dated, are uncomfortable around vegetarians, as though afraid they'll be lectured on animal cruelty at every meal. That's not my approach. I just quietly practice what I believe. Tony constantly argued with me, trying to convince me to change my stance on the matter, and after a while, it got exhausting. I'm glad Alex is different.

I study his unconventionally handsome face from under my lashes as he summons the waiter and converses in Russian. I listen closely to the foreign sounds, wishing I understood more of their language. Like many nurses at Coney Island Hospital, I know how to ask if a patient is in pain—*bolit?*—and whether they want something to drink—*pit'?*—but that's the extent of my Russian vocabulary.

Once the waiter is gone, Alex returns his attention to me.

"They'll bring us *zakuski*—appetizers—shortly," he says, picking up his shot glass. "In the meantime, how about a toast to girls changing their minds?" He smiles, showing even white teeth.

I hesitate for a second before picking up my glass. Drinking on an empty stomach isn't something I typically do, but nothing about this date is typical.

To hell with caution. For tonight, I just want to enjoy myself.

"Sure," I say, smiling back. "And to your bodyguard's speedy recovery."

"And to Igor's recovery," Alex agrees, clinking his glass against mine.

He knocks back the shot in one smooth swallow. The strong column of his throat moves in a deliciously masculine way, and I fight a sudden urge to walk around the table and lick the side of his neck.

Oh my God, Kate. Control yourself.

Taking a deep breath, I force myself to look away and focus on my own glass of vodka. I can't remember the last time I wanted to touch a man so badly. It's as if my hormones have suddenly decided to come out of lifelong hibernation, and I have no idea how to rein them back in.

Lifting my glass, I drink the shot in two big gulps and pretend the liquor doesn't burn my esophagus on the way down. From the amused look on Alex's face, I don't succeed.

"You're not used to vodka," he says as my eyes water from the strong alcohol.

"Not exactly." I make a face. "Is it obvious?"

"No," he deadpans. "You took that shot like a pro."

I laugh, shaking my head. "I guess my vodka-drinking skills can't compare to yours."

"Well, I *am* Russian." He gives me a self-deprecating smile. "If I couldn't outdrink an American girl, I'd be a very poor representative of my people."

I laugh again, genuinely enjoying myself. The residual warmth from the alcohol has heated my chest and stomach, and the night is taking on a pleasantly surreal glow. "So, is this your usual modus operandi?" I ask with a smile. "Do you bring all the women you're trying to seduce to this fancy restaurant and ply them with vodka?"

He leans forward and covers my hand with his, making me draw in a startled breath. His palm is so large it engulfs mine completely, his skin warm and dry against my own.

"No," he says softly, gently massaging the inside of my palm with his thumb. "I only do it for special ones. Like you."

"Me?" I lift my eyebrows, trying to ignore the way my lower body tightens at his touch. He has what I've always considered a real man's hand, complete with the roughness of calluses on his palm. "What's so special about me?"

"Are you fishing for compliments, Katyusha?" His eyes are warm and amused. "Surely a woman as beautiful as you knows her worth."

I grin. "Surely a man as attractive as you is used to beautiful women."

A cynical note darkens his smile again. "You find me attractive?"

"Why else would I be here?" I ask, puzzled.

"Yes," he drawls. "Why else?" Finding the tender spot near

39

the fleshy part of my palm, he massages until I almost moan out loud from the pleasurable sensation. It's all I can do not to glare at the waiter when he interrupts by serving our appetizers.

As I look at the spread, however, amazement drowns out my disappointment. There must be twenty different dishes, everything from pickled vegetables to delicate Russian blintzes with a filling that looks like cream cheese.

It's enough to feed an army.

When I tell Alex that, he laughs and explains that Russians believe in having plenty of variety on the table, particularly for special occasions. He then describes each dish to me, pointing out his favorites—the beet salad he calls *vinyegret* and the marinated mushrooms with sour cream.

Curious, I try a bite of everything and discover that I especially like the salty flavor of the cream cheese paired with the subtle sweetness of the crepes. I also fall in love with the cheese-and-garlic salad and the homestyle potatoes fried with mushrooms.

"Wow," I say, going for yet another serving of the potato dish. "I can't believe I've been missing out on such delicious food. I'm going to kill Nadia for not taking me to a Russian restaurant sooner."

He lifts an eyebrow. "Nadia?"

"One of my coworkers. She's from Ukraine, and we've become good friends in the past year."

His blue eyes crinkle in the corners. "Yes, she should've definitely introduced you to our cuisine and culture, but I'm happy to remedy her mistake." Filling our shot glasses with more vodka, he lifts his and says softly, "To new experiences."

"To new experiences," I agree, clinking my glass against his and knocking back the shot. It's easier this time, the vodka going down smoothly and leaving a pleasant warmth in its wake. I grin after I've caught my breath. "I think I'm getting the hang of it."

"You might make a good Russian after all," he says, studying me with a look of warm amusement on his face.

My breath catches. With his lips parted in a genuine smile, he looks both strikingly handsome and shockingly approachable. To my surprise, I realize I like him. It's not just a physical attraction. I like the man himself.

"I'm glad I ran into you again," I blurt without thinking. "I was sure I wouldn't see you again after that first time in the hospital. I wasn't even supposed to work today. I was called in because another nurse couldn't make it."

"Oh, you would've seen me again," he says with conviction. "If not today, then soon."

I give him a questioning look.

He reaches across the table again and takes my hand. This time, his touch is more familiar, less shocking, though it turns me on just as much.

"I would've looked for you," he says, caressing the inside of my wrist with this thumb. "I don't accept rejection easily, not when I really want something."

My heart skips a beat. His words are both exciting and unnerving. "Is that right?" I manage to say, trying to keep the breathy note out of my voice.

The simple touch on my wrist alone turns me on more than anything my ex-boyfriend had ever done, and Alex knows it. He knows how to seduce a woman, and he's fully aware of my reaction to him.

"Of course," he murmurs, finding the sensitive spot between my thumb and index finger and pressing on it lightly. "I can't remember the last time I wanted a woman so badly."

I bite my lip to contain a moan of pleasure at what he's doing to me. I can't believe how erotic simple hand-to-hand contact is with him. What will it be like when he gets me into bed?

Because he will. There's no denying it any longer, no doubt in my mind about how the night will end. Whatever my original reservations were, whatever my fears, none of those reasons matter now. Not when he makes me feel like this. Not when my entire body cries out for his touch.

"What would you like for the main course?" he asks softly, still doing something incredibly pleasurable to my palm. "Or do you wish to skip it and go straight to dessert?"

"Dessert, please," I say on an exhale.

I've eaten more than enough, and anything that brings the evening closer to its inevitable conclusion is a good thing. I've never wanted anything in my life as much as I want Alex right now.

Smiling, he releases my hand and signals the waiter, who nods and disappears into the kitchen.

"He'll have dessert for us shortly," Alex says, turning back to me. "In the meantime, could I interest you in a dance?"

"A dance?"

He gestures toward the stage where a band of musicians has appeared seemingly from nowhere.

"Live music?" I can't help but be impressed. "Sure."

He rises from his seat, walks around the table, and courteously offers me his hand.

Heart pounding, I place my hand in his and let him lead me

to the dance floor. The musicians strike up a slow tune I've never heard, and a female voice croons something in Russian.

At the empty area near the stage, he pulls me close, clasping my hand in his and placing a palm on the small of my back. The smell of his cologne is clean and masculine—cardamom and something spicy. As we sway to the music, I look up, struck again by our size difference and the strength of the hard body pressed against mine. Even with the two-inch heels on my boots, I barely reach his chin, and the breadth of his palm covers most of my lower back. His hips are at the level of my middle, his erection pressing against my stomach. My nipples pebble in response, reacting to his nearness and obvious desire for me.

Staring up at him, I moisten my dry lips, and my pulse speeds further as his gaze tracks the path of my tongue. The air between us grows thick and heated, like the blood pumping through my veins. As our eyes meet again, all I can hear is the uneven rhythm of my breath... and then he bends his head and kisses me.

His lips are smooth, warm, and soft. Despite the demanding hardness pressing into my belly, he kisses me gently and patiently, as though we have all the time in the world. As though we're not burning inside, consumed by a lust so intense I'd gladly climb him right here and now, no foreplay necessary.

He traces the seam of my lips with his tongue and slips inside to stroke and caress the interior of my mouth. The taste of vodka on his breath adds to the intoxicating sensations coursing through my body. Moaning, I wrap my arms around his neck and kiss him back, sucking his lower lip into my mouth and biting down on it lightly.

He groans and presses even closer, burying one hand in my hair to hold me in place as he deepens the kiss.

In a foggy corner of my brain, an alarm sounds, briefly penetrating the haze of desire clouding my mind. The musicians, the waiters... Pushing on his shoulders, I tear my lips away.

"Wait, Alex," I whisper, trying to catch my breath. "Not here."

His voice is low and rough with frustration as he releases me. "I know." Heat emanates from his large body. He's just as turned on as I am, if not more. "I didn't mean to get so carried away."

"Why don't we get out of here?"

Did those words just come out of my mouth? I've never been so bold or forward with a man, but I seem to have no shame with Alex.

His eyes darken, his nostrils flaring. "Yes, why don't we?"

Before the touch of his hands on my skin has turned cold, he's already guiding me toward the exit, one arm wrapped possessively around my shoulders.

5

*A*s soon as we're outside, Alex shepherds me toward the black car standing at the curb. The driver, Yuri, is waiting inside.

Wait. We just walked out without asking for a check.

"What about paying for dinner?" I ask.

The chilly November air is quickly clearing my mind, and the full implications of my actions are dawning on me.

By my initiative, I'm about to have sex with a man I hardly know—a man who's now holding open the car door for me, waiting for me to get inside.

One corner of his mouth lifts in a smile. "Don't worry about such matters, Katyusha. It's all taken care of."

There's that Katyu-something word again. "What's that you're calling me?" I pause before the open door, stalling for time. Now that we're away from the seductive atmosphere of the restaurant and he isn't drugging my senses with his touch, my normally cautious nature reasserts itself.

Sex after the first date? How could I have agreed to—no, *insisted on*—doing something so impulsive?

"Katyusha?" He lifts his eyebrows. "It's a Russianized version of your name. An endearment, if you will."

"Oh." How do I respond to that? Truthfully, it doesn't matter what he calls me because this is supposed to be a one-night stand. *If* I go through with it.

"What's the matter?" he asks, frowning when I don't get inside the car.

I swallow. "Alex, I . . ."

He must sense my hesitation because he bends down and kisses me again, his mouth slanting over mine more aggressively, his tongue pushing past my lips in a blatant imitation of the sexual act itself. Burying one hand in my hair, he plants the other on my ass, kneading it softly and pressing me closer to his hard body until I moan helplessly and cling to his shoulders, my doubts melting away in the heated pleasure of his touch.

How we end up inside the car, I don't know. Somehow, we're just there, and he's still kissing me with those deep, penetrating kisses that make a mockery of any attempt at rational thinking. All I can concentrate on is the taste of him, the scent of him... the feel of his large, powerful body as he presses me down onto the plush leather seat.

In the back of my mind, I'm aware we're not alone. The driver is in the car with us, taking us to our destination. But I can't bring myself to care. I'm too caught up in what Alex is doing to me. He slips one hand underneath my sweater and cups the back of my head with the other, holding me still for the continued sensual assault on my mouth. His callused palm is deliciously rough on my bare skin as he strokes my naked back.

Unbearably turned on, I dig my nails into his shoulders, barely cognizant of my actions. His lips brush over my neck, scorching hot and moist on my sensitive skin as he delves deeper inside my sweater, finding the clasp of my bra and undoing it with smooth efficiency.

"Alex, wait," I breathe, the warm pressure of his hand on my naked breast startling me into realizing what's happening.

Is he about to take me right here, in the back of this car, with his driver only a thin partition away?

"Shh," he soothes, kissing me again while kneading my breast, testing its shape and texture.

"No, wait," I moan, arching into his touch despite myself. "We can't. Not here."

He lifts his head, staring down at me with an intent look on his face. "Just let me touch you, *kiska*," he whispers harshly, brushing his palm back and forth against my hard nipple. His accent is heavier than usual, his voice thick with arousal. "I won't do anything else until we get home, but I need this. I need to touch you, to feel you. God, you're driving me crazy. I need to be inside you so fucking bad, but I won't take you, not until we're alone."

I stare at him, my heart pounding like I've just run a marathon. The throbbing between my legs is as strong as if I were on the verge of an orgasm, and he hasn't even unzipped my jeans. With his hand still inside my sweater, he's rolling and massaging my nipple with exactly the right amount of pressure as his heavy weight presses me down, holding me in place.

I want him so badly I can barely think or process the sensations coursing through my body. "Please, Alex," I whisper, not knowing if I'm begging him to stop or continue, but then the car slows down and comes to a stop.

The driver's side door opens and Yuri gets out.

"We're home," Alex says roughly, sitting up and bringing me with him. "Let's go in."

Disoriented, I let him pull me out of the car and lead me toward a large house. His arm is wrapped firmly around my shoulders, as if he's afraid I'll change my mind and run away.

Before I know it, we're in front of the house, and he opens the door and leads me inside. As he turns on the light, I catch a glimpse of modern furniture and gleaming wooden floors. Suddenly, my world tilts as he lifts me, swinging me up into his arms.

Startled, I clutch his neck and shoulders. I'm a grown woman, yet he picks me up as easily as if I weighed five pounds.

"What are you doing?" I manage to say, clinging to him as he carries me up the wide staircase to the first floor.

"Taking you to bed so I can fuck you," he replies, his accent still noticeably pronounced.

He doesn't sound winded in the least, as though it's not a big deal to carry a grown woman up a flight of stairs. And maybe for him, it isn't. The thought gives me a strange inner thrill, as does the steely strength of the arms that hold me so securely. The crudeness of his words both offends and excites me, adding to the pulsing ache between my legs.

Before I can say more, he brings me into a dark room and carefully lowers me to my feet. Releasing me, he steps to the side and flicks on the light switch.

A soft, warm glow floods the room, illuminating a four-poster bed. The sheets are white with dark brown edges, a color scheme prevalent throughout the room. Contemporary paintings decorate the walls, and a red vase with exotic flowers stands on a dresser in the corner.

It's a masculine room, tastefully done, and under different circumstances, I would've loved to explore. Alex doesn't give me time. He takes a step back and brings me toward him with an arm around my waist and a hand in my hair, holding me still for another deep and carnal kiss.

As before, all my worries and inhibitions melt away in the heat of his embrace. Winding my arms around his neck, I kiss him back hungrily, sucking on his tongue and nipping his lower lip. He groans at my passionate response, tightening his hand in my hair almost to the point of pain. Then, with a suddenness that startles me, he pushes me away, leaving a couple of feet between us.

"Take off your clothes," he orders hoarsely, gripping the hem of his sweater and pulling it over his head.

Mouth dry, I watch him undress. Underneath the sweater, he wears a white T-shirt, which he removes next, revealing a powerfully built chest and a flat masculine stomach covered with a layer of hard muscle. His skin is lightly tanned, as though he's been in the sun recently, and a faint dusting of dark hair is visible around his nipples. Without his clothes, he looks even bigger and more intimidating, his muscles sharply defined and his shoulders impossibly wide.

What kind of sport does he do to be in that kind of shape? I doubt it's just going to the gym a couple of times a week. He reminds me of an ancient warrior, a man who wouldn't be out of place swinging a broadsword and riding on top of a giant steed.

Seeing that I'm not undressing, he stops after kicking off his shoes and gives me a narrow-eyed look. "Well?"

For some reason, I feel a strong urge to please him. Not wanting to analyze that too much, I begin to remove my clothing, my hands trembling with a mixture of excitement and trepidation. I take off my boots first and then my sweater. All the while, he watches, his gaze scorching in its intensity.

Finally, I'm clad only in my jeans and a pink bra. It's unfastened in the back from our make-out session in the car and is almost falling off me, exposing far more of my breasts than the manufacturers intended.

Feeling inexplicably shy, I stop. I've always been comfortable with my body, but with Alex, I can't help feeling insecure. Am I pretty enough for someone who probably has the most beautiful women in the world chasing after him?

At my pause, his eyes darken. Stepping toward me, he pulls me against him with a firm grip on my hip. "You're gorgeous," he growls, holding me with one hand and using the other to remove my bra. "I knew you'd be. Even in scrubs, you were so damn sexy I wanted to fuck you right there, right in the middle of the goddamn ER."

I stare up at him, my breath catching. "So why don't you?" I whisper, hardly cognizant of what I'm saying. "Why don't you fuck me right now?"

He gives a harsh laugh. "Oh, I will, kiska. I will."

Pushing me flat onto the bed, he unzips my jeans and pulls them off my legs, leaving me lying in nothing but the pink thong that matches the bra.

He makes quick work of stripping off the rest of his clothes, never moving his eyes from my near-naked body. His face is taut with lust, and as his jeans and briefs come off, I find myself watching him just as intensely.

His thighs and calves are thickly muscled, just like his arms and chest. Whatever he does to stay fit has given him a perfectly proportioned figure. My gaze homes in on his cock, and I swallow hard. He's big, much bigger than any man I've seen outside of a porn video. With a mixture of apprehension and excitement, I realize I won't manage to take him easily.

His eyes still locked on me, he opens a nightstand drawer and takes out a condom. Ripping open the packet, he rolls the condom onto his shaft with a practiced motion before climbing onto the bed. His movements are slow and deliberate. I scoot back, my heart pounding as he leans over me, caging me with his arms.

"Alex..."

Whatever I was going to say gets lost in a gasp as he bends down and takes one nipple into his mouth, sucking the hardened tip deep. I forget my words. All rational thoughts fleeing, I arch off the bed with a strangled cry. His mouth is hot, burning my sensitive skin, and as he slides a hand between my thighs and palms my wet sex through the thong, tension builds inside me, intensifying unbearably as he presses down firmly, stimulating my aching clit.

Beyond aroused, I twist my hips, brushing against his rigid cock. He inhales sharply. With startling roughness, he grips the scrap of fabric that covers me and tears it off, provoking a gasp from me. Before I have time to recover, he pushes his heavy thighs between my legs, spreading them wide, and presses his cock against my opening.

I grip his shoulders, my breath catching from the blunt, firm pressure. Despite my wetness, he doesn't slide inside. His shaft is too thick for me to accept with ease. Instead, he rocks gently, working himself in inch by slow inch. As his inexorable advance continues, my inner muscles stretch uncomfortably, and a whimper of distress escapes my throat.

Pausing, he asks in a low, hoarse voice, "Am I hurting you?"

His body is tense, his jaw tightly clenched, but he holds himself still, giving me time to adjust.

I draw in a breath, forcing myself to relax. "Just give me a second," I whisper, grateful for his restraint. Lying underneath him with his cock halfway inside me makes me feel vulnerable, at his mercy, and I'm grateful he has enough control to pay attention to the cues of my body.

"Of course," he murmurs, holding himself up with one arm and using the other to reach between our bodies. Finding my clit, he rubs around it, spreading my arousal there before gently pinching the sensitive bundle of nerves.

Gasping, I arch against him. The pleasure is so sharp it's almost painful. My action pulls him deeper inside me, stretching me further, filling me in a way I've never experienced. Another pinch, another arch, and he's all the way in, the coarseness of his pubic hair brushing against the smoothness of my sex.

Breathing heavily, he stares at me, holding still to let me get used to the feel of him buried inside my body. He continues petting my folds and toying with my clit until I soften around his hardness. I'm still not completely comfortable with his size, but the extreme fullness is no longer unpleasant. Instead, it adds to the powerful tension growing inside me.

Sensing my increasing desire, he begins to move, rubbing my slick folds and pressing on my clit with a rhythm that makes me spiral higher until I'm teetering on the exquisite edge of release. Letting out a choked cry, I dig my nails into his shoulders, needing him to move faster, harder, to hurl me over the brink. Suddenly, I'm there, my entire body convulsing as a wave of pleasure radiates outward from my core.

At my pulsations, he groans and starts thrusting more

powerfully, pushing me into the mattress with each stroke. To my disbelief, the tension coils inside me again, my sensitized flesh responding as he drives into me with increasing force. He swells inside me, growing impossibly longer and thicker, and another orgasm rips through me, shocking me with its suddenness. At the same time, he reaches his peak, throwing his head back with a hoarse cry and grinding his pelvis against mine.

We stay like this for a moment, our foreheads pressed together as we catch our breath. Then he withdraws from me and discards the condom. Gathering me into his arms, he curves his body around mine from behind. The heat of his flesh penetrates my skin as his heavy breathing slows. My heartbeat, however, is still elevated, as if I've run up ten flights of stairs. I don't know if it'll ever beat normally again.

There's sex, and there's what I've just experienced.

"Are you all right?" he asks softly, draping a heavy arm across my hip. "I hope I didn't hurt you."

I let out a shaky laugh, glad he can't see the dazed expression on my face. "You were very careful, and I enjoyed it very much. Obviously."

"Good," he says quietly, tracing circles on my stomach. "Because I'd like to see you again, Katyusha."

I give an internal start and turn in his arms. "Are you asking me out after we just had sex?"

"Whatever you want to call it." His lips curl into a sensual smile. "I told you, I don't do traditional dating, but I'd like to explore this further."

"You want to have sex with me again?"

He nods, his eyes gleaming. "Absolutely. Unless you have objections?"

Objections? What kind of objections can I have after the best sex of my life? "No objections here."

"Good," he says, a wealth of satisfaction in his tone. "Then it's settled."

I bite my lip. "Should we shake on it?"

"I have a better idea," he murmurs, shifting so his hardening cock brushes against my thigh.

Really? "Again?"

"Unless you have objections?"

"No objections," I repeat dazedly as he reaches across the bed for another condom.

6

ST. PETERSBURG

"What do you fucking mean it failed?"

"His bodyguard took the bullet instead." The assassin's voice is expressionless. "I don't know how he sensed it, but he did. Another second, and I would've had him."

"Fuck." Oleg Pavlov takes a deep breath, gripping the phone so hard the metal edges dig into his palm. "Are you losing your touch, Bes?"

"If you think so, you're welcome to get someone else."

The motherfucking—

Oleg takes another breath, reminding himself why it's not a good idea to piss off Bes. "Look," he says in a more conciliatory tone, "I just need to know if you can get it done or not. You know our agreement—"

"I can get it done."

"Then do it." Putting the phone away, Oleg turns his attention back to the man sitting across the table from him. On the stage in front of them, three blond girls are gyrating to the latest Russian hip-hop imitation, their slim bodies perfectly tanned and surgically enhanced. Under different circumstances, Oleg would've used one—or all three of them—to relieve some of his tension, but now isn't the time to indulge.

Not when he has to explain the situation to one of the most dangerous men in St. Petersburg.

"I take it Volkov is in good health," Vladimir Stefanov says dryly, his fleshy jowls quivering with each movement. With his thick lips and neck rolls, he reminds Oleg of Jabba the Hutt. Inside that bloated frame, however, lurks a razor-sharp intelligence and cunning slyness, something Oleg is careful never to forget.

"For now," Oleg says, nodding. "But Bes will take care of it."

"You place a lot of faith in that cleaner."

"He's never let me down before."

"He's never gone up against Alexander Volkov before either."

Oleg shrugs. "He knows about Volkov's reputation. He'll be careful."

"Oh, really?" Vladimir's lips stretch into something resembling a smile. "You think he knows what Volkov is capable of?"

"He's got the file on him," Oleg says. "The same one you gave me."

Vladimir lets out a harsh laugh, his entire body seeming to oscillate from the movement. "Well, then, let's hope your boy is up to the task. Because if Volkov gets wind of who's behind it all and why, you and I will both wish we'd never been born."

7

I wake up to the unusual aroma of eggs and coffee. Opening my eyes, I stare at the shocking sight of a Russian tycoon standing next to the bed dressed in nothing more than a pair of boxer shorts. He's holding a tray filled with a variety of dishes, apparently the source of the delicious smell.

Blinking, I sit up, holding the blanket up to cover my breasts as I try to orient myself. I must've fallen asleep in Alex's bed, although I don't remember doing so. As I shift to rest my back against the headboard, I become aware of a deep inner soreness, a reminder of last night's sexual marathon.

"Hi," I croak, my voice rough from sleep. Clearing my throat, I manage more normally, "Good morning."

"Good morning," he says, sitting down on the edge of the bed and carefully balancing the tray. He looks amused for some reason, his blue eyes crinkling at the corners. In the bright morning light, he looks strikingly male, every muscle on his incredible body sharply defined and the hard planes of his face darkened by a hint of stubble.

Rubbing my eyes, I realize I went to bed last night without removing my makeup or taking a shower. My hair must look like a rat's nest, and I have no doubt my mascara is smeared all over my face.

This is so not how I want Alex to see me after the amazing night we've just had, especially since he looks so good himself.

Casting a desperate look around, I notice a door leading to a bathroom. "Excuse me," I mumble, scooting to the other end of the bed before letting go of the blanket and executing a quick escape into the bathroom.

Six minutes later, I emerge, looking and feeling much more human. I found a brand-new toothbrush someone had thoughtfully left on the edge of the sink and freshened up, removing all traces of mascara and smoothing my hair. I still need a shower, but that can wait until after breakfast.

"Hi again," I say, trying to ignore the heated look in his eyes as they slide over my naked body. I'm comfortable with nudity, but something about the way Alex stares at me makes me want to blush like a virgin. "Is that what I think it is?"

He raises his eyebrows. "What do you think it is?"

"Breakfast in bed?" I venture, smiling.

"It may be," he concedes, one corner of his mouth tilting up. He's placed the tray in the middle of the bed, and he now lifts the lid from one of the dishes, exposing a fluffy omelet with a side of toasted bread and sliced cucumber.

"Wow, that looks awesome," I say with appreciation, inhaling the appetizing aroma of freshly cooked eggs. Climbing back onto the bed, I rearrange the blankets so that I'm partially covered. My breasts are still mostly exposed, but I don't want to seem like a prude by pulling up the sheets to my chin. It's not as if he didn't see—and explore—every inch of my body last night.

"It tastes even better," he promises, moving the plate toward me. "Go ahead, try it."

I balance the plate on my lap. Grabbing a fork from the tray, I spear a piece of omelet and bring it to my mouth. The rich flavor of eggs, cheese, and grilled tomato explodes on my tongue. "Oh, that's so good. Did you make it?"

He shakes his head, pulling another plate toward himself. "I have a housekeeper who's also a wonderful cook. You can meet her later this morning."

"Please thank her for me in the meantime," I say between bites. "This is the best breakfast I've had in years."

He smiles, looking pleased. "It's all vegetarian. I asked Marusya to make sure there was no meat anywhere near your omelet. Here, try it with the cucumber and the bread. It goes really well like that."

Eggs with a fresh cucumber? Why not? I bite into the crisp vegetable and follow it up with another forkful of omelet and a piece of bread. He didn't lie. The flavors mesh well together, the refreshing taste of the cucumber complementing the richness of the eggs and the hearty taste of the rye bread.

We eat in companionable silence, enjoying the food. I can't remember the last time I've been so content. The sex was out-of-this-world amazing, and now he's feeding me breakfast in bed. If he's representative of Russian men, I've been missing out all these years.

But no. He's unique. For one thing, I've never been so affected by anyone. It would've been surprising if last night had been anything but good, given the strength of our attraction.

"How old are you?" I ask, studying him with curiosity as I

place my empty plate back on the tray. I still can't determine his age. His skin is smooth and taut, yet there's a certain world-weary look in his eyes that makes me think he's older.

"Thirty-six," he replies promptly, seemingly amused at my question. "You?"

"Twenty-five," I answer. Smiling, I add, "I didn't know men over thirty-five could do that."

"Do what?"

"You know"—I wave toward his groin—"have sex so frequently in one night."

He grins and stares pointedly at my breasts. "Men over thirty-five can do all kinds of things with the right incentive."

I laugh. "The right incentive being boobs in the vicinity?"

"No, Katyusha," he says softly, his grin fading. "The right incentive being someone as beautiful and sexy as you."

"Oh, stop it," I say, rolling my eyes. Now he's going over-board. "You'll make me blush."

"Why?" He tilts his head to the side. "Don't you know you're beautiful?"

Beautiful? I've never thought of myself that way. Reasonably attractive, sure. Pretty, maybe. Tony sometimes called me cute. But beautiful? That's a word applied to glamorous supermodels and actresses, and I fit into neither of those categories. Still, I can't help the warm feeling that spreads through me at his words.

"Why, thank you," I say, smiling. "But you don't have to flatter me, you know. You already got me into bed."

He looks at me intently, his eyes startlingly blue in the bright morning light. "And I'd very much like to keep you there."

I grin, trying to ignore the heat washing over my body.

"After last night, you couldn't kick me out if you tried. I came more in a few hours with you than I have in the last few months."

"Oh?" He looks intrigued.

I shrug, already regretting that I've brought up the subject. "My ex and I, our sex life wasn't great."

That should've been a clue from the beginning. Although I enjoyed spending time with Tony, we just didn't have sexual chemistry. At times, he seemed downright disinterested in love-making. I made excuses for him—he was tired from working long hours, he didn't have a strong sex drive, and so on—but the truth was much simpler. We were wrong for each other.

Alex puts his plate on the tray and gets up to leave the tray on the floor before sitting down next to me.

Gently, he runs his knuckles down the side of my face. "Your ex sounds like someone who didn't deserve you," he says quietly, his accented voice sending pleasant shivers down my spine. "I'm glad you're no longer with him."

"I'm glad too," I whisper, mesmerized by the warm glow in his eyes.

"Do you have plans for today?" He plays with my hair, gently massaging my scalp.

I blink, fighting the urge to beg for more as he pulls back his hand. "I have to work," I say regretfully. "My shift starts at three."

He glances at a clock on the nightstand. "It's almost noon. Why don't you stay here until it's time to go?"

He wants to spend time with me? My pulse accelerates with excitement. "You don't have to work or anything?"

He smiles. "I always have work to do. I could be working twenty-four-seven, and it still wouldn't be enough to get everything done. If I can't take a couple of hours to enjoy the company of a beautiful woman, then what good is all this?" He waves a hand to indicate our luxurious surroundings.

"In that case, I'd love to stay. My scrubs are at the hospital, so I can just grab a cab from here."

"You don't need to do that," he says, pushing to his feet. "Yuri will drive you anywhere you need to go."

"Oh, no, I'll be—"

He gives me a look that stops me mid-sentence. "Katyusha, I have a driver for a reason. Let him do his job."

"All right." I can't help but grin. "Thank you." I should protest more, but I like the idea of taking a fancy black car to work. Besides, it seems important to Alex.

He walks into a closet on the other side of the bedroom and emerges a minute later, dressed in a pair of black sweatpants and a white T-shirt.

"Come," he says. "Let me show you around."

I climb out of bed, trying to ignore the heated look in his eyes as I hunt for my clothes. My thong is a goner, but I pull on my jeans, bra, and sweater before turning to face him again.

"Ready," I say, feeling as eager as a kid at an amusement park.

Smiling, he takes my hand and leads me out of the bedroom.

8

To my surprise, Alex's house isn't as over the top as I imagined it might be. While all the furnishings look nice and expensive, the house itself could belong to any wealthy individual. Everything is tastefully decorated, with touches of modern art here and there.

"I like your place," I tell Alex as he leads me downstairs. "It's not exactly what I'd pictured, but I love the airy look and feel. Did you choose all this yourself or hire a decorator to do it?"

He smiles, obviously pleased by my praise. "I have a woman who works for me. She knows my taste, and she makes sure all my properties have what I need."

I try to keep the incredulous tone from my voice. "You have a decorator who works for you full-time? Just how many properties do you have?"

"A lot," he admits, giving me a self-deprecating smile. "I don't really keep track of them all."

I laugh, shaking my head. "Wow. You really do come from a different world, huh?"

"In more ways than you can imagine, Katyusha," he says softly, his smile fading.

Before I can ask him what that means, we enter the kitchen, where a middle-aged woman with dark hair and brown eyes is stirring something in a pot.

"Marusya," Alex says, "I'd like you to meet my guest, Kate. She's the nurse I mentioned to you before, the one who took care of Igor."

"Nice to meet you," the woman says in a heavy Russian accent, a welcoming smile lighting up her broad face.

"It's nice to meet you too," I reply, smiling back. "Thank you for the breakfast. It was delicious."

"Good," she says, nodding. "You too small. Should eat."

I laugh. "Oh, you and my mom both."

She shakes her head. "No, you need"—she draws a rounded shape in the air with her hands—"and should eat."

Alex catches my eye and gives me a wink. To Marusya, he says, "Don't worry. I'll make sure I feed her. Maybe you can pack her something for lunch? She needs to go to work in a couple of hours."

"Oh, no," I say. "You don't have to do that."

"Katyusha," Alex says firmly. "Please let Marusya prepare a few things for you. It'll be good, I promise."

I blink at him, caught off-guard by his unexpected solicitousness. Is he this nice to all the women he sleeps with? If so, how on earth is he still single? "If you're sure. You really don't have to."

"I know I don't have to," he says. "But I want to."

His firm manner says the subject is closed for discussion. I open my mouth to thank him when a large man with a shaved head enters the kitchen and swiftly approaches Alex. Ignoring Marusya and me, he whispers something in Alex's ear, causing Alex to stiffen.

Just like that, the cold, dangerous stranger I met at the hospital is back.

He turns to me. "Katyusha, will you excuse me for a moment? I need to make a phone call. Marusya will show you the rest of the house."

"It's okay," I say, not wanting to be a nuisance when he's obviously distracted by something. "I can go home."

His expression softening slightly, he brushes his knuckles over my cheek. "Please stay. I'll be done in fifteen minutes."

His touch sends warm sensations all the way to my core. "Sure," I whisper. "I'll stay if you want me to."

"I do," he says with finality, leaning down to plant a kiss on my lips. "I'll see you soon."

With a last, strained smile in my direction, he exits with the bald man, leaving me in the kitchen with Marusya.

We stare at each other, at a loss for words. Without Alex acting as an intermediary, I feel a little uncomfortable. From the uncertain look she gives me, so does she.

"If you don't mind," I say, "I'd appreciate the opportunity to have a quick shower."

She nods enthusiastically, her shoulders slumping in obvious relief. "You need things?"

"I'm good, thanks." I don't want to put her out and keep her from her work more than I'm already doing by having her prepare my lunch.

"You call," she says, pointing a thumb at her chest.

"Thanks." I backtrack to the door with an awkward wave and dart through the frame.

~

WITHOUT ALEX, I FEEL LIKE AN IMPOSTER AS I RUSH BACK upstairs and enter the private domain of his bedroom. Sure, he invited me to stay, but I'm certain he didn't intend for me to wander around alone in his house.

I enter the bathroom and shut the door for privacy. The walls, floor, vanities, corner tub, and shower stall are made of the same gray marble. I turn on the tap in the shower and strip while the water runs warm. Using his shampoo and soap, I make quick work of washing myself. I help myself to a clean towel from a rack and leave it in the hamper before putting my clothes back on. Without a brush, the best I can do for my hair is run my fingers through it, but that's fine. The long strands will settle into natural waves when they dry.

When I'm done, I feel almost like my old self. The warm water has relieved the soreness in my muscles, but it'll take more time for the discomfort inside to fade. The thought of the cause of that ache makes my stomach heat.

Giving myself a last look in the mirror, I venture back into the bedroom. The bed has been made with clean linen. Marusya must've done it while I was in the shower. The window is open a crack, letting in the fresh, crisp air.

Alex should be done with his call by now. I exit onto the landing to make my way back to the kitchen, but voices coming from the room next door stop me. One of those voices belongs to Alex. He's in a heated conversation with another man. He sounds upset, enough so to make my stomach tie in an answering knot.

Indecisive, I hover next to the door. Should I make him aware of my presence? I don't want to disturb him when he's involved in a serious discussion. Besides, the conversation is private. Even if they're speaking in Russian, it's not meant for my ears.

I'm about to shoot past the frame when the mention of my name makes me pause. My ears must be playing tricks on me, but no, there it is again. *Katherine Morrell.* My full legal name on Alex's lips catches me off guard. Why are they discussing me?

The relaxing effect of the shower vanishes. I want to both demand an explanation and run. What I don't want is for Alex to think I'm eavesdropping, but it's too late, because when I finally get my feet to move toward the stairs again, Alex's voice stops me in my tracks.

"Katyusha."

The way he says my name now is in stark contrast to what I've just heard. The endearment is spoken tenderly—no, cautiously. Reluctantly, I turn. He stands in the frame, worry lines marring his forehead.

"I…" I swallow to moisten my dry throat. "I had a shower. I hope you don't mind."

He advances toward me, his frown deepening. "Why would I mind?"

The bald man exits behind Alex. He casts a glance in my direction before heading past us down the stairs. Through the open door, I notice a desk and bookshelves. It looks like a study.

Alex draws my attention back to him when he takes both of

my hands, rubbing his thumbs over my knuckles. "I want you to feel at home. You can do whatever you please here."

"Thank you." I study his face for clues of what just happened in his study, but it's an unreadable mask.

"Come," he says, pulling me toward the stairs. "I owe you a tour."

Withdrawing my hands from his, I hang back. He stops and looks at me, his features schooled except for a frown. I don't miss the minute darkening of his eyes that shows his displeasure at my defiance. If he's not going to address the elephant in the room, I will.

"What's wrong?" he asks.

My voice comes out a tad breathless, the tension I'm trying to hide evident in my tone. "Why were you talking about me?"

A pained expression flashes over his face. "I'm sorry you heard that."

"I didn't mean to." I feel compelled to justify myself. "I was just coming out of the room and—"

He clasps my wrist, wrapping his strong fingers lightly around my bones, which feel too fragile in his hold. "You don't have to explain, Katyusha. You didn't do anything wrong."

"Then explain to me what I heard," I say, staring up at his ruggedly handsome face.

He waves a hand. "It's nothing."

Dragging me against his chest, he places a big palm on my lower back and brings his head down. From the way his gaze fixes on my lips, I know he's swooping in for a kiss, but I turn my face away and his lips brush over my cheek in the gentlest of caresses instead.

Craning my neck to look him in the eyes, I say, "It's not nothing. You discussed me with one of your men."

A sigh falls from his lips. "I don't want to worry you with silly details you shouldn't concern yourself about."

"If it's so silly, then tell me."

He purses his lips as he considers me. After a moment, he says, "A man like me is always a target. You understand?"

My neck is starting to feel the strain, bent backward as it is. "What does that have to do with me?"

"Nothing." His expression closes off even as determination settles in his eyes.

When he goes for my mouth again, I push my palms against his shoulders. "Alex, stop."

He gives me a frustrated look. Holy shit. He's trying to distract me with a kiss, knowing the effect he has on my body. I push harder, but he doesn't set me free. One hand is still firmly pressed against my back while the other is curled around my wrist.

I grit my teeth. "What does that have to do with me, Alex?"

A storm brews in his eyes. Whatever that conversation was about, he doesn't want to tell me.

I tense even more, dread creeping into my veins, but it's too late. I can't not know now. "Tell me," I say, my voice hard.

A muscle ticks in his jaw. "It's just a precaution. It means nothing."

A lightbulb goes on, the realization hitting me like a brick between the eyes. *He doesn't trust me. He looked into me.* The knowledge hurts. I don't know why. Maybe because I want him to trust me. Maybe because he should've trusted me before falling into bed with me. The regret in his eyes tells me I'm right. It tells me he knows this is hurting me, even as the hard set of his mouth informs me that if given another chance, he'd do that hurtful thing all over again.

This time, when I shove him, he lets me go.

I stumble back a step, barely regaining my balance in my high-heeled boots. "You did a background check on me." Saying it out loud rubs salt into the wound. My laugh is cynical. "What did you find? My grades? My yearbooks?" If he was looking for a history of drug abuse or something scandalous that could tarnish his billionaire reputation and make it a hazard for him to be seen with me, he would've looked for a long time. When he still says nothing, I add tauntingly, "Bank statements?"

He flinches.

Son of a bitch. I was being sarcastic about the bank statements. "You accessed my bank account?"

"Katyusha." His voice is soft, cajoling.

I stare at him in disbelief. "What were you hoping to find?"

"You have to understand." He spreads his palms. "Some people would pay a lot of money to see me go down, use whatever means they have to."

I take another step back, farther away from him. "You mean bribe me? To do what? Gather information on you?" I wave my arms around. "Plant a bug in your house? Is that what you think of me?"

"No." His tone is harsh. "I told you. It's a precaution."

"Why? What gave you the idea that I'd do something like that?"

"At first, you wanted nothing to do with me. Then I saw you again and you gave me such a pretty, eager smile. You have to admit, it was a rather quick change of mind."

I itch to smack him. If my mother had raised me differently, I might have. To think we toasted to girls changing their minds with his high-end vodka last night. To think I spent the night in his bed with him *inside* me. No, I shouldn't think about that. I'm upset, and anything I say now, I may regret later. Dragging my fingers through my hair, I retreat as far away from him as possible, until my back hits the wall.

"I need to go," I say in a hoarse whisper.

He takes two steps toward me. "Katyusha."

"Stop calling me that. Don't pretend you care."

"That's the problem. I do."

I turn my face away. "Stop it."

He advances more, reaching for me. I see his hands from my peripheral vision, those hands that had been all over my body last night while he secretly ran security checks on me. Before he can touch me, I sidestep him again.

"You're upset," he says.

No kidding. I look back up at him. "You could've told me you planned on running a background check on me."

"I didn't want you to be upset about nothing."

"It's not nothing! What you think of me—" I bite off the words I was about to say, the admission that it's important to me.

Pushing off the wall, I shove my fingers through my hair. "You know what? You're right. It's not important."

"What's that supposed to mean?" His voice is tight as I walk past him.

"Nothing," I say, not looking back at him. Let's see how he feels about that *nothing* he's been giving me as an answer.

"Katerina, come back here."

I all but run down the stairs, looking around for my bag. Where did I leave it?

Marusya comes out of the kitchen with a plastic container in her hand just as I enter the foyer with Alex hot on my heels. Her eyes widen a fraction as she takes us in.

"Um..." I make an effort to calm myself, brushing invisible strands of hair off my face. "Have you seen my bag?"

She points at a wingback chair. My handbag sits neatly on it. I must've dropped it in the car during our heated make-out session last night. Heat floods my cheeks when I think about the driver who probably brought my handbag inside and what he must've been thinking. What the sweet housekeeper is thinking. What *Alex* is thinking: that I had a change of mind because someone paid me to sleep with him.

Hurrying over to the chair, I grab my bag. I need to escape. I need space to calm down and think this through. I spin on my heels, giving Alex a flustered, "Thanks for the dinner and"—I clear my throat—"everything."

He stares at me silently, his blue eyes hard but at the same time soft with something that threatens to steal into my heart. But no. I won't be treated like a spy who can be bought for the right price. Our attraction isn't enough for me to turn a blind eye to the fact that he'd held this opinion of me while we were in bed together, or that he'd invaded my privacy in this awful way. Not even the great sex or tender aftercare this morning is worth it.

Marusya trots across the floor and thrusts the container she's carrying at me, her cheeks flushed. "Your lunch."

"Thank you," I say, taking the container. Since she's gone to the trouble of making the lunch, I'm not going to be rude and throw it back in her face. I'm angry with Alex, not his housekeeper.

For some reason, though, I can't say goodbye to him. The knowledge that I'll never see him again hurts even worse than his reluctant confession. The tears are already burning the backs of my eyes as I escape to the door, cursing my naivety.

I'm no match for a worldly, experienced Russian oligarch with many enemies. The kind of men I'm used to dating don't distrust me. They get to know me over time because we don't fall into bed on the first date. They don't dig up my history while I sleep in their arms, and they certainly don't hack into my bank account.

Kate, you are such an idiot.

I wipe at my eyes and grip the doorknob, but it slides in my sweaty palm. I try twice, and still the damn door doesn't budge. There's no escaping. I'm stuck inside.

A strong, masculine arm circles around me from behind, stilling my hand. I freeze. Alex leans against me, letting me feel his weight as he sandwiches me between his muscular body and the door. Despite everything, he's hard for me. His erection is like a bar of steel pressing on my spine. His heat penetrates my skin, and my body aches for more. It wants his arms around me, soothing me, but my mind is finally back from its sabbatical, functioning despite the haze of the hormones raging through my body.

"Stay," he murmurs, nuzzling my neck.

A heated shiver ripples down my spine. "Why? You got what you wanted."

"I told you, I want more."

"Because whatever you pulled up on me last night confirmed I'm not a threat to you?"

He blows out a long breath, letting it feather along the arch of my neck. "Even if you were a threat, I'd still want more."

Those words should soothe me, but I'm too bruised inside. A part of me wishes I'd heeded the storm in his eyes, but I wanted the truth.

"Let me go." My words are more of a plea than an order.

He heaves a sigh. "You're right. I should've told you. It's standard procedure, so much of a norm for me that I forget how it must feel for an outsider like you."

"I need..." I bite my lip, considering where this leaves us. "I need time."

"Time." He says it like the world rests on his shoulders. "Sure. Of course. I understand."

I wait, but he doesn't let go of my hand. He cups it over the doorknob for another few seconds before he turns the knob and steps away. Cold air rushes down my back as the distance between us lengthens. The door swings open, and a blast of icy air hits me in the face. The wind is strong today, making the chilly fall weather feel even colder.

In the light of day, I notice the manicured front garden and the fountain with a statue of a fallen angel I didn't notice in the dark last night. The angel is draped over the fountain steps, her marble dress dragging in the dirt. One intricate wing is broken, hanging torn at her side. The sight is so sad it jostles my heart, making the tears I'm trying to hold back spill over my cheeks.

The black car from yesterday is parked at the curb. Yuri stands next to it as if he's always waiting to drive Alex on command. Alex follows me out and opens the door for me. I manage to wipe my palms over my cheeks before I slide into the back seat, where he'd almost undressed me.

He leans down, catching my eyes as I shift all the way to the other side. "It was—" He gives a soft smile and a short shake of his head, as if catching himself. "Tell me I'll see you again."

I can't. I can't make a promise if I'm not certain about keeping it. "Alex." My voice holds a plea.

"Fine, Katyusha. You want time? You win." The line of his jaw sharpens as his mouth sets in a determined line. "But rest assured, I'll call you. Very soon." He taps the roof of the car. "For now, my driver will take you wherever you want to go."

When he straightens and closes my door, the driver takes off. I dare a look over my shoulder. Alex stands on the pavement, staring after the car with his hands shoved into his pockets. A lump swells in my throat, and a sharp sense of loss stabs into my heart.

Despite what he said, the look he wears says I won't see him again.

9

My mom bustles around the bedroom, shoving outfits into a suitcase and pulling them out again.

I finish folding a wrap and a matching bathing suit and lay them neatly in her suitcase before flopping down on the bed. "Stop fussing. Whatever you wear, you always look pretty. Besides, it's Mexico. You probably don't need more than this swimsuit and wrap."

"Oh"—she waves a hand—"I'll just go naked when we're at the condo. It's the evenings I'm worried about. Martin said there are a few lovely restaurants to try."

I groan, making a face. "TMI, Mom. Way TMI."

She stops to smooth a hand over my hair like she used to when I was little. "What about you, honey? Are you still going through a dry spell after that horrible Tony? Why don't you let me set you up on a date?"

It's as if a spike pierces my chest every time I think of my disastrous one-night stand. Well, not all of it was disastrous. Just the honesty part, the part where the man who fucked me thought me capable of spying on him. As if I'd even know what to look for.

"Katie?" Mom gives me one of her worried looks. "Did you hear what I said?"

I plaster a smile on my face. "I'm too busy at the moment."

That's not a lie. I've been cramming my shifts to the brink, working around the clock. It's been two days since our date, if I can call it a date, and I haven't heard from Alex. We didn't exchange numbers, but he knows where to get hold of me. Not that I want him to. Or do I? I wanted time to think, and now that I have it, I'm doing my best to avoid thinking by working myself to exhaustion. When I get home, I barely have enough energy to drag myself to bed.

"Maybe when you get back," I say to appease her.

The feeble promise works. Mom's face brightens, as if dating is the solution to all problems in life.

"How do I look?" she asks, fluffing out her hair in the mirror.

"Beautiful," I say honestly, my chest warming as I study her pretty features in the reflection.

"Come on," she says. "Martin will be here any minute. Be a dear and give me a hand with that suitcase."

I zip up the suitcase as she rambles about how much water each plant in the apartment needs and how often.

"Don't worry." I pick up the suitcase and swing an arm around her shoulders. "The apartment will still be standing and the plants will be green when you get back. I grew up here, remember?"

She grabs my face between her palms, pouting my lips. "Oh,

I love you so much. What would I have ever done without you?" She jerks, dropping me like a hot potato when the doorbell rings. "Oh my gosh. That's him." Straightening her dress, she beelines for the door and throws it wide open.

Martin stands on the step, looking handsome in a pair of dark jeans and a white linen shirt. He trails an appreciative look over my mom before pulling her closer for a kiss.

"Oh my," she says when he releases her after a kiss that lasted a few seconds too long to be considered publicly decent. "Would you like to come in? Do we have time for a drink?"

"We'd better get moving. I prefer to get there early. The flights are always overbooked." He glances at me from over my mom's shoulder. "Hi, Kate. How's work?"

"Busy but good, thanks. You?"

"Great. We should all have dinner when we get back. My treat."

"That sounds good," I say, handing him my mom's suitcase.

"Don't forget your copy of the key," Mom says to me. "You know the alarm code. What else? Did I forget anything?"

"Go." I kiss her cheek, grinning at her childlike excitement. "I'll hold down the fort."

"Bye, honey." She waves as Martin takes her arm and escorts her from her ground floor apartment to his car. "I'll send a postcard," she calls back.

"That'll be great." I lean in the frame, watching them load her suitcase into the trunk and get settled.

Like a gentleman, Martin secures my mother's seatbelt before getting his own. She waves again through the passenger window. I lift a hand in return as Martin pulls off and weaves into the quiet, midday traffic. When they turn the corner, I drop my hand. Silence descends on the apartment. A bird chirps somewhere, but without my mom's lively chatter, the apartment feels cold and empty. The weird sense of loss I'd felt when I left Alex's house assaults me anew. I suddenly feel isolated, much like I've felt these past couple of days at work. Even surrounded by my colleagues and patients, I've had a sense of being alone and out of sorts.

Loneliness.

That's what it was. That's what it is right now.

Shaking it off, I go through the apartment and make sure all the windows are closed and the plants aren't thirsty before I lock up and walk to the express bus stop. It's not until I'm on the bus to Brooklyn, seated between a teenager and an elderly man, that I finally allow myself to think.

Despite what he did, I miss Alex. I miss what could've been, and I mourn that I'm missing out on the man who'd booked a whole restaurant just for me. I wish I'd gotten to know better the language of his face, the way his eyes crinkled when he found something amusing and how his gaze heated when he looked at me. The way his body hardened when he leaned against me. No matter how much I try, I can't get those visions out of my head.

We only spent one night together, but it feels like I'm grieving a lifetime of could-have-beens.

I stare at the peeling clear polish on my nails. This has to stop. I have to pull myself together. So Alex isn't who I hoped he was. Neither was Tony. It happens all the time. I'm not the first woman disappointed by a man. There are plenty of fish in the sea. Right?

Picking at the polish, I fish my phone from my pocket and

dial Joanne. I have a few hours off tomorrow, and I can't face staying home alone. Maybe I'm running from my thoughts and feelings, but they're still too raw to analyze them deeply.

Joanne is busy, so we quickly agree on a time and place to meet for lunch tomorrow. When I hang up and lift my gaze, my eyes collide with a pair of brown ones. A man wearing a gray suit is standing in the aisle toward the front of the bus. He has bushy eyebrows and a square jaw. He holds my gaze for a second before looking away.

I frown. Have I seen him somewhere? He looks vaguely familiar. Foreign. Eastern European, maybe. Perhaps we've been on the same bus before. I don't pay him further attention as my stop in Brooklyn approaches.

Pushing past him and a few other passengers standing in the aisle, I get off the bus, rush home, and have a quick lunch. As I'm wolfing down my salad, my gaze falls on Alex's plastic container. I washed it and, not knowing what to do with it, left it sitting on the kitchen counter. Its bright red lid stares at me like a screaming reminder. I could take it to work and leave it in Igor's room. I've been walking circles around the ICU, scared of running into Alex. It's time to stop that. What happened, happened. Pretending it didn't won't make it go away.

I write a quick thank-you note on a Post-it and stick it on the lid. Then I drop the container with a bottle of water and a snack into my tote bag. I have just enough time left to vacuum my apartment before heading back to the hospital, where I change into my scrubs and start my shift.

As always, it's hectic, leaving no time to think about personal problems. A ten-year-old boy with a burst appendix and a young woman with a broken arm are admitted, and my feelings are mercifully squashed under the weight of their much more serious problems. It continues like that for the next twelve hours, and by the end of my shift, I'm so tired I can hardly stand on my feet.

I have one last task to execute. Taking the container from my bag, I walk to the room in the ICU where Igor is recovering. I knock and push open the door, only to freeze in the frame. The man lying in the bed in the private room isn't Igor.

Mumbling an excuse, I shut the door and go to the desk to check the patient list. Apparently, Igor was discharged yesterday. Relief rushes through me, both because Igor is doing well and because there's no longer a chance of accidentally running into Alex in the hospital corridors.

I head back toward the ER with a confusing mixture of relief and disappointment.

"Everything all right, Kate?" June asks, scurrying past me as I exit the elevator.

"Great."

She grabs a stack of medical gloves and turns to me. "You look pale. Maybe you should swap with someone tomorrow and get some rest."

"I'm good. Anyway, we're understaffed as is."

She sighs. "Well, make sure you take care of yourself. I can't afford another sick nurse."

"Yes, ma'am."

She smiles at my playful tone, already heading for the swinging doors.

In the locker room, I dump Alex's dish in my locker, determined to let it gather dust on the shelf until I've forgotten about it.

Pulling on a puffy jacket and my reliable Uggs, I go home to my empty apartment, nuke some frozen soup, and collapse onto my bed. As I'm drifting off, I wonder if it's maybe time to get a cat.

They're a lot less complicated than humans, and they don't cheat on you or think the worst before they even get to know you.

～

"LET ME GET THIS STRAIGHT," JOANNE SAYS, BITING INTO HER pizza before continuing with a full mouth. "You had the best sex of your life, the guy brought you breakfast in bed, and then you ran off because he did a background check on you."

The slice of pizza I've just eaten turns sour in my stomach, which is a shame because the pizza at Oregano is my favorite. "How would you have reacted?"

She chews, seeming thoughtful. When she's swallowed, she says, "I don't know. Don't get me wrong. I get why you're upset, but given who the guy is, I can understand why he's cautious."

"Yeah," I say dryly. "I suppose when you get shot at, you have to be careful about who you take to bed. Your one-night stand may murder you in your sleep."

She stills with the pizza in midair. "You know, it actually doesn't sound *that* far-fetched."

I gape at her. "Are you serious?"

She shrugs. "Things like that happen."

I watch her devour what's left of her slice. "Are you saying I overreacted?"

"No. I'm just saying it can't hurt to give him an opportunity to apologize."

"For what?" I ask, confused. "For looking out for his safety? You just said that's normal."

"For not laying his cards on the table. I know you're one of the kindest people with the most integrity, but he doesn't. Give him a chance to say he's sorry and to get to know you. He said he wanted to see you again, right?"

I push away my plate, not hungry anymore. "I'm not sure he wants to any longer. I haven't heard from him in three days."

"He's busy."

"Indeed."

I drag my hands through my hair. I'm such a mess. On the one hand, I'm still upset with Alex, and on the other, I'm anxious that he hasn't called. Maybe Joanne is right. Maybe I overreacted.

Giving me a pointed look, she says, "You don't have to wait for him to call. You can make the first move. He'll probably appreciate it. Come to think of it, maybe he's not calling you because he feels bad for upsetting you. Maybe it's hard for him to look you in the eyes now."

I scoff. "I doubt that. And there's no way I'm calling him first."

She takes a sip of her water and points a finger at me. "That's your pride talking. Are you going to let your pride keep you from more great sex and breakfasts in bed?"

"If it means saving my dignity."

She studies me from under her lashes. "So you'd rather be alone in bed with your dignity than give Mr. Hot and Handsome another chance?"

When she says it like that, it sounds rather childish, but it's not only about my dignity. It's also about protecting my heart, but I don't feel like laying that vulnerability on the table. It's bad enough that I feel insulted. I don't want to admit that I liked him, *really* liked him, before shit hit the fan. What does that say about my people judgement skills? Besides, I wasn't interested in a relationship when I went out with him, and it only took one date to make me a lot more interested than I should be.

Joanne finishes her last bite and dabs her mouth with a napkin. "You know what I think?" Her smile is compassionate. "You're scared of rejection."

"Of course I am."

She sighs. "What do you have to lose? A bit of dignity? At least you won't have to wonder about the what-ifs."

She's right, but I'm not ready to admit that.

"I don't even have his number," I say. "He never gave it to me."

The screen of her phone, which is sitting on the table next to her, lights up. Shooting a glance at it, she says, "You didn't exactly give him a chance. How difficult can it be to get his number? He runs that huge oil company and a bunch of other businesses, doesn't he? They must have websites with contact information."

"And go through a whole army of underlings to try to reach him? No, thanks. If he doesn't want to speak to me, I'd rather not have some assistant of an assistant relay that message."

She pushes to her feet. "Sorry, Kate. I have to go." She gives me an apologetic smile. "Work."

"Thanks for listening," I say as she scoots out of the booth.

"Anytime, Katie girl." She makes big eyes. "Call him."

When she opens her handbag, I wave her away. "Lunch is on me."

"Thanks. I'll get the next one." She makes her way to the door and exits with a wave.

I sigh, watching her depart. What if I do call first? If he doesn't want to talk to me, he'll tell me so. I won't sleep easy again until I have closure. I left his house in a rush, hurt and angry, but he said he wanted to see me again. If that's still the case, trust is an issue we'll have to address. If not, I need to know for certain, so I can close this chapter of my life. Either way, I have to find out where I stand. I have to know why that farewell on his face when he watched me go seemed so sad.

I'll wait a full week, and then I'll gather the courage to face him. I'm certain his private number won't be listed anywhere, not with how obsessed he is about security, and I'm not going to call his work and fight my way through a million gatekeepers to speak to him. Instead, I'll go to his house to return his plastic container. Yes, that's what I'll do.

My mind made up, I get the bill. I feel a lot lighter when I step outside and head for the subway. As I walk, I send Joanne a text to thank her again.

This is the best I've felt in days.

MY NEXT BREAK ISN'T UNTIL THE FOLLOWING WEEK, AND THE days fly by with no more free time. By the time I catch my breath, it's been six days since I ran out of Alex's house, and my stomach is tight with nerves because tomorrow is my deadline. If I don't hear from him by then—and I doubt I will—I'll face him as I've promised myself.

Every day, I receive a text message and a photo from my mom, showing her face glowing with a healthy tan. Today, she's sent a picture of her snorkeling in turquoise water with colorful fish. Martin took the picture with an underwater camera. She says her mobility is easier in the water, and that all the vitamin D from the sun is doing her good. I send her three emoji kisses from the locker room when my shift ends, assure her the plants are doing well, and tell her to enjoy every minute. She deserves it. My chest swells with happiness for her and gratitude toward Martin.

I'm putting away my phone when Rose, the nurse I stood in for when I ran into Alex the night he took me out to dinner, walks in.

"How are you doing?" I ask, taking in her dejected look and the dark rings under her eyes. She's lost her mom to cancer, and they'd been close.

She rubs her hands over her face. "Some days are better. Others are harder."

Laying a hand on her arm, I give a gentle squeeze. "I know it sounds lame, but if there's anything I can do…"

Her smile is strained. "Thanks. Actually, I owe you a drink for standing in for me."

"Oh, no. You owe me nothing."

"Please?" Her gaze is imploring. "As a matter of fact, it will help. It'll be good for me to get out. There's a bar not far from here, so we can walk."

"Oh." I was planning on going straight home and crashing into bed as I have an early shift tomorrow, but sleep can wait. This is more important. "Of course."

Her expression lifts a little. "Nadia is also getting off now." She takes her phone from her pocket. "I'll check if she wants to join us."

"Great idea," I say as I peel off my scrubs.

To be honest, I can do with a drink. My nerves have been in

tatters all day thinking about going over to Alex's house tomorrow evening with the feeble excuse of returning his container. He's going to see right through me, so I might as well drop the pretense and tell him honestly what the reason for my visit is—that I want to know why he never contacted me, and that I want him to tell me to my face we were never more than a one-night stand. That he lied when he said he wanted to see me again. Or if he hadn't lied, I want him to tell me why he changed his mind. It's the least he owes me.

Pushing the disconcerting thoughts aside, I dress in my jeans, sweater, and boots. Then I wash my face and apply mascara and lip gloss. By the time I've brushed my hair and pulled on my warm jacket, Rose and Nadia are ready.

We walk one block to a bar I've never been to, but Rose says she hangs out there frequently. It's a cozy place with hardwood floors and wooden panels on the walls. A lamp burns on each table. We take one in the corner and order a bottle of wine and a few tapas that will serve as dinner.

Our banter is light and the mood is uplifting. Rose was right. Sometimes, no matter how tired I am, I have to come out and live a little. Often, especially after a strenuous day, I have to force myself to get ready and go someplace, but once I'm there, like now, I end up having fun. In fact, I'm having so much fun it's close to eleven by the time we get the bill.

Rose and Nadia live farther away than I do and decide to share a cab while I choose the cheaper fare of the subway. I earn enough to pay the bills and help out my mom, but I have to budget carefully to afford the luxury of a few nights on the town and lunches with my friends.

I'm a block away from the bar, walking in the direction of the hospital toward the Sheepshead Bay station, when the lettering of Romanoff's shines up ahead. I slow my step as memories of *that* night rush over me.

I'm curious. What does the place look like on a normal evening when it's busy? Yet it's not curiosity but an unfortunate bout of nostalgia that carries my feet in that direction. Instead of turning toward the subway, I walk the remaining distance along a pavement that's still relatively busy at this late hour. This area of Brooklyn isn't Manhattan, but it's lively enough for many people to be out and about in the middle of a weeknight.

I stop at the window, trying to peer inside, but the curtains are closed. Dammit. I want to have a peek at our table, to see if I can spot it in the midst of all the others. I want to experience what I felt that night to make sense of why a single night can hurt so profoundly. How could I have gone from not wanting a relationship to wanting so much more after only one night?

Operating on instinct, I push open the door and enter into the cozy interior. A range of delicious smells greets me—garlic, fried onions, and spices. The place is as opulent as I remember, and the extravagance hits me as though seeing it for the first time. I don't think I'll ever grow used to it, no matter how many times I see it. The warm reds and golds melt together. Music comes from the stage where a band is playing a lively Russian song.

A hostess flutters over. "Good evening." She looks at a clipboard on the counter. "Do you have a reservation?"

The place is packed, every table occupied. The chatter is loud, pierced by occasional laughter. I don't even want to think about how much money Alex forked out to make sure it was empty for us.

"Ma'am?" the hostess says, impatience slipping into her tone.

I open my mouth to tell her I just wanted to have a look when I spot him.

Alex.

He's sitting at one of the big tables close to the stage with three other men and a dark-haired beauty pressed against his side.

10

I nearly choke on my shock. My words fall to the wayside as I take in the scene. Alex's dark hair shines under the lights. He lowers his head to say something to the woman, and she laughs.

I go hot and cold, a sick feeling settling in the pit of my stomach. Betrayal. That's what it feels like, even though it doesn't make any sense. He owes me nothing. I'm the one who ran away.

Well, at least that explains why he didn't contact me.

As though sensing my stare, he turns his head. Our gazes collide over the distance. The smile vanishes from his face. Something else replaces his jovial expression—something calculated, something darker.

Humiliation drenches me. Now he'll think I'm stalking him.

"Ma'am," the hostess says, her pitch persistent now.

I break my stare-off with Alex to look at her.

She's watching me with irritation. "Are you meeting friends?"

"N-no," I stammer, backtracking to the door. "I was just... looking."

She wrinkles her nose and looks me up and down as if I were a beggar who came inside to drool over the food sitting on the tables in front of the people in their fancy clothes.

And the clothes are fancy. The women are dressed in evening dresses and the men in suits. I glance down at my attire, the very same clothes I wore the night Alex brought me here, like I'm so poor I don't own a different outfit.

A movement at the stage draws my attention. Alex has gotten to his feet. Tall and broad, he stands out in the crowd. He's dressed in a tuxedo, the black jacket stretching over his shoulders. The three men at his table turn toward me with frowns. He says something to the woman, who looks in my direction. She's wearing a black dress with diamante detail on the shoulders. Still, I can only stand there, frozen in place under their scrutiny.

"If you don't have a reservation, I have to ask you to leave," the hostess says.

I tear my eyes away from Alex to meet her hostile gaze again. Life flows back into my limbs as the shock turns into nausea. Clutching a hand to my stomach, I say, "I'm going."

I don't look back at the table in front of the stage or the five pairs of eyes fixed with curious animosity on me. I spin around and leave, slamming a palm on the door and stumbling into the frosty night.

My heartbeat is a dull thumping in my chest. I must look like a fool. A total idiot. I glance around me like I'm lost, like I haven't seen or walked this pavement before. Needing to get away, I break into a run. I don't care in which direction I'm going, as long as Alex doesn't come outside and find me here. As long as we don't stand face to face, I can pretend this experience never happened. I can pretend I didn't just come across as a lovesick, mentally unstable person stalking her one-night stand.

The air burns in my lungs. My heels clack loudly on the pavement as I turn the corner just before a deep, low male voice calls my name.

Shit. He followed me outside.

Blindly, I run down the dark side street under scaffolding, pumping my arms in an effort to outrun the steps falling hard on the concrete behind me. They're so close he must've teleported. There's no way he should've caught up with me so fast. I cut the corner, slipping in my haste, and barely regain my balance before I sprint down the block.

All the while, the steps echo closer. He's not even running flat out. It sounds as if he's barely putting effort into it. I duck around the next corner, heading into a narrow street with a service door. Trashcans are lined up against the wall. An odor of fermented food hangs in the air. The passage is dark, and it's a dead end. A brick wall faces me.

I curse and swing around, bumping into a hard chest. For a second, I'm off balance, and before I've found my footing, a large hand curls around my neck and slams my back against the wall. My head hits the bricks with a thud. Pain explodes in my skull, and stars pop behind my eyes. When I open my mouth to scream, a meaty palm slams over it.

Lifting my panicked gaze, I look into a pair of dark eyes set in a square face. It's not Alex. The man is not as tall, but bulkier. His lips tilt into a malicious smile as he tightens his grip on my throat, cutting off my airflow. I fight with everything I've got, clawing at his hands with my nails, but he only grins wider. I swing my fists at him, punching him in the gut, and he doesn't so much as grunt.

Panic sets in as my lungs start burning and spots dot my vision.

He flashes a set of crooked teeth as he lifts me off my feet. Only the toes of my boots are dragging on the ground. I aim for his eyes, but he drops his hand from my mouth and leans back, effectively escaping my efforts to claw at him while keeping me at arm's length and dragging me back to the street. A sliver of light from a window above catches his face, shining over his bald head. An eight-pointed star is tattooed in black ink on his skull. The scream I try to push from my throat comes out as nothing but a croak. I struggle in his grip, kicking at air as he laughs at me quietly while tugging me along like I weigh nothing.

The blood rushes in my ears, amplifying the beat of my heart. From somewhere else, my name comes to me like a sound through water. A figure appears at the top of the alley, his shadow falling tall in the light that comes from the street-lamp on the corner. He doesn't say a word, but he doesn't have to. The menace dripping off him is palpable.

As he comes toward us at full speed, the man hauling me to the street lets me go. The pressure lifts and my lungs expand. I fall to my knees, choking on oxygen while my assailant rips the strap of my bag from my shoulder. I try to scream again, but no sound comes from my raw throat. The man offers me a last grin and sprints to the end of the alley with my bag in his hands.

The man coming to my rescue charges after the bald guy

down the alley, but my attacker is already sailing over the wall at the end. A third man looms over me.

"Katyusha."

Warm hands grip my arms and drag me to my feet.

Blinking, I stare at the face hovering over me. "Alex?"

"Fuck." Alex drags his hands over my body as if he's patting me down for a weapon. "Are you hurt?" The words sound cold and murderous. "Are you bleeding?"

"He's gone," the other man says in a gruff, heavily accented voice as he returns from scaling the wall.

I turn my attention to him, and my mouth goes dry.

It's the man from the express bus with the bushy eyebrows.

I grab Alex's shoulders as fresh fear pounds in my temples. "That man," I say in a thin voice. "He followed me."

Alex puts an arm around me and pulls me to his chest. "It's all right. He's with me."

I point at the man. "I saw him. On the bus. He's following me."

"It's okay, Katyusha," Alex says. "Dimitri's only there for your protection." Glancing toward the man, he says, "Call Yuri. Tell him to bring the car."

Dimitri turns with a "Yes, sir," and promptly leaves, but not before I see him slip a pistol into the back of his waistband under his jacket.

Shivers rack my body despite the warmth of Alex's embrace. "My phone. He took my bag. We have to call the police."

"I'll deal with it. Don't worry." He lowers his head to peer into my eyes. Outwardly, he appears calm, but his tone has an urgent edge. "Are you hurting anywhere?"

I press cold fingers to my neck. "I'm fine. It's just my throat and my head."

His jaw tightens dangerously. "What did he do to you?"

"He knocked my head against the wall and tried to strangle me."

His nostrils flare. "That son of a bitch." Throwing an arm around my shoulders, he turns me toward the street. "I'll kill him when I get my hands on him." He holds me so tightly against him it hurts. "We need to have you checked out at the hospital."

"I said I'm fine. I should know. I'm a nurse, remember?"

Silence.

"Wait," I say when he takes a step, hauling me along. "What are you doing here?"

"I saw you at the restaurant. What are *you* doing here?"

"It's not what it looks like," I say quickly and wince as pain threatens to split my skull in two. "I was only walking by."

He stops. A hint of anger creeps into his voice. "Walking by? Alone? In the middle of the night?"

"It's not even midnight." Wait. Why am I justifying myself to him?

His fingers tighten on my shoulder. "You do not walk around in the city alone. Understand? From now on, I'll send a car for you."

I pull away, anger washing away the shock of the attack. "I don't belong to you. You don't tell me what to do."

A dark look comes over his face. "Think again."

When he grips my arm and continues to drag me behind him, I yank myself free. "Don't manhandle me."

"Don't push me on this, Katerina," he says in a low, rough voice. "Not now." He takes my wrist and turns back toward the street, where a black car pulls up to the curb.

"Where are you taking me?" I ask, stumbling a step.

He steadies me with an arm around my waist. "Home."

"My keys are in my bag. I won't be able to get into my apartment. I need to call a locksmith."

"*My* home." His gaze pierces mine. "Do you think I'd let you sleep alone in your place while that *ublyudok* has your keys and phone?"

"What? No. I'm not going to your place."

His body goes rigid. "He can easily figure out where you live and wait for you there."

"He was after my valuables. He's not coming after me."

"You don't know that," he growls.

To be honest, the thought did cross my mind. "I'll go to my mom's."

"No." He starts walking again, pulling me along.

I have long legs, but I can barely keep up with his strides. Frantically, I consider my options. "Look, thanks for helping me. I owe you. I just—"

He stops dead. Something I can't decipher flashes in his eyes. "You *don't* owe me."

"If you hadn't shown up—"

"Don't." He lifts a finger, briefly pinching his eyes shut. "Don't say it."

"You have guests to get back to. I'd be grateful if you could just call me a cab."

"Like hell," he says, taking his phone from his pocket with one hand while keeping the other locked around my wrist, as if he's scared I'll run again.

He punches in a number and presses the phone to his ear while walking us closer to the car. When whoever it is answers, he barks out something in Russian. The conversation is short.

He ends the call before we get to the car and holds the back door open for me, helping me inside.

I'm without money, bank cards, keys, or phone, and I do need a ride, so I shift all the way to the other side and make myself small against the door. Yuri turns in his seat, handing me a bottle of water and a box of pills.

"Painkillers," he says. "Mr. Volkov said you may need some."

So he's the person Alex spoke to in Russian on the phone. I'm so grateful I don't bother to ask where he got painkillers from so quickly. As I push two pills from the foil casing and swallow them with the water, Alex gets inside and tells Yuri to go.

When the car pulls away from the curb, Alex puts an arm around me and pulls me against him. He makes another call and fires off something in rapid Russian. His presence is warm and comforting. His smell wraps around me, making me want to burrow my nose in his neck and soak up the safety he offers, but then a vision of the dark beauty pressed up against him in the restaurant flashes through my mind, and I stiffen.

"Don't you have guests to get back to?" I ask.

"They can wait," he replies with that exotic foreign accent. "You're more important."

"Really?" I ask with sarcasm.

He looks down at me. "Yes. Really."

"Is that why you never contacted me?"

He rubs a thumb over the padded shoulder of my jacket. "I had to take care of business in Moscow."

I add a heavy note of sarcasm to my voice. "And I suppose you didn't have roaming."

His features soften. "Did you want me to call you?"

"No," I say, crossing my arms.

A faint smile caresses his lips. "Right." His tone matches the soft look in his eyes. "It's not that I didn't want to. I was busy."

Right. I wriggle out from under his arm. "When did you get back?"

"Yesterday."

"Ah."

I turn my face to look through the window, but he grips my chin and forces me to face him. "It's not what you think."

"What am I supposedly thinking?"

He traces my bottom lip with his thumb. "It was business."

I feign ignorance. "What was business?"

"Tonight."

"You don't owe me explanations."

His steely blue eyes tighten. "I disagree."

The car comes to a halt, preventing me from arguing more. Alex says something to Yuri in Russian before getting out and opening the door for me. When we've stepped onto the pavement, Yuri pulls away.

"Come," Alex says, guiding me to the door with his hand on my back.

The broad expanse of his palm burns through my jacket, but I ignore the effect as I climb the steps to his front door.

The house is quiet. A dim light shines in the entrance. The temperature inside is comfortable. I shiver a little as my cold body adjusts to the warmth.

Gripping my shoulders, Alex turns me to face him and reaches for my jacket zipper. My eyes are drawn to his with the same pull I experienced the first time I felt his gaze on me. He's staring at me like he may eat me alive, but there's also something dark underneath the desire, something almost violent.

Mesmerized, I stand quietly as he pulls down the zipper and

brushes the edges of my jacket open. Sliding his hands under the fabric over my shoulders, he frees my arms from the sleeves. Heat gathers in my core from the simple act. Even if I have unanswered questions, such as the real reason he didn't call and who the woman at his side tonight truly was, I'm helpless against the reaction he elicits.

He watches me with that sharp blue gaze as he takes off his own jacket and hangs it with mine on the coat stand. I feel like the mouse who's about to become the cat's dinner as he advances on me until our bodies are flush together.

Gripping my chin between a forefinger and thumb, he says, "You're never to wander the streets alone again."

The unreasonable command reignites my anger. We're nothing to each other. Since he made that clear by ignoring me, he has no right to make demands of me. "I'm not never going out again because of a mugging."

He drags his gaze over me, pausing on my breasts before meeting my eyes again. "Why did you come to the restaurant tonight?"

"Don't worry," I say with a sardonic smile. "I wasn't spying on you."

Annoyance flashes across his face. "I apologized for that. I explained why the background check had to be done. Do you want to hear it again? I'm sorry I made you feel bad. It wasn't my intention. In my world, security precautions mean the difference between life and death. I don't know you well enough to exempt you from how I treat everyone who comes into my house for the first time, but I do intend to rectify that."

If that speech is supposed to make me feel better, it doesn't work. Backing away, I escape his touch. "Do you say that to all the women you bring home?"

He advances a step, the set of his jaw hard. "Only to the ones I intend to sleep with more than once."

I'm not sure I can do this. I thought I could handle a one-night stand with him and look where that has left me. In the span of a short week, I've turned into a mass of nerves just because he thinks little of me and hasn't called. How will I react after a second no-strings night with him? I have to face the truth. I'm not the one-night stand type. Sex has never been meaningless for me the way it has been for him. That's the problem. That's why this can never work. The sooner I get out of here, the better. First, though, I have an urgent matter to attend to.

I take in a tremulous breath. "May I please use your phone? I need to cancel my bank cards."

His voice is clipped. "It's done."

I gape at him. "The call you made in the car?"

"Yes."

"I see," I say slowly, not seeing at all. Does he have a private banker on standby that he can call in the middle of the night? Probably. And since he's already accessed my bank account, what's getting his unorthodox banker to cancel my cards? The thought is disconcerting, but I try to focus on what still has to be done. "In that case, may I please call a locksmith?"

"Yuri is taking care of it," he says in the same matter-of-fact tone.

"Oh. Thank you." I guess.

Instead of pleasing him, my expression of gratitude seems to upset him. He's not breaking our eye contact, but a shutter drops in front of his eyes as he says, "There's no need to thank me."

Rubbing my arms, I say, "I'll reimburse you."

His voice turns hard. "I don't need your money."

"I don't like to feel like I'm taking advantage."

"Advantage?" He scoffs, lifting a strand of my hair between his fingers. "It's the least I can do."

"Why?" I sidestep the touch. "What happened isn't your fault."

For a moment, he only looks at me, seeming to wage an internal battle. Finally, he says, "Why did you come to the restaurant tonight? Tell me the truth."

"I was out at a bar that isn't far from the restaurant. I happened to walk past and just wanted to see what it looks like when a tycoon hasn't booked out the whole place."

He gives me a measuring look. "Out with who?"

I shrug. "Friends."

"Male friends?"

"Female, not that it's any of your business."

His smile is calculated. "Oh, but I intend to make it my business." He crosses the distance I've put between us, the gleam in his eyes predatory. "I'm going to take you to bed again, Katyusha. And again. And while you're in my bed, you won't let another man into your body. You won't even smile at another man. I don't like to share. Think you can handle that?"

My back hits the wall. I stare up at the hard lines of his face. My heart says no, but my lips don't form the word. I don't want him to know how weak he makes me, how vulnerable.

"Good," he murmurs, leaning in for a kiss.

I splay my palms on his chest. "This isn't what I want."

"No?" He raises a brow. "Let me kiss you and tell me again you don't want me."

"That's not fair," I say on a whisper. He knows the power he wields over me.

Victory shines in his eyes. "Just one little kiss. If you still tell me no, I'll book you into a hotel."

"You will?" I hate how breathless I sound.

"Yes," he says, planting his hands next to my face on the wall. "I promise."

I steel myself when he brings his mouth lower, but when he brushes his lips over mine, yearning spreads through my body. I couldn't summon enough willpower to push him away even if I wanted to. His touch is too potent. Sparks ignite under my skin as he traces the curve of my lips with his tongue and sucks gently to mold my mouth to his rhythm.

However hard I try, I can't be unaffected. He knows this, and he's using it to his advantage, but I can't bring myself to care, not when he slides his tongue into my mouth and sweeps it over my own. Just like that, my resolve goes up in flames, especially when he slips a hand between our bodies and cups my sex over my jeans.

Shamelessly, I arch my hips into his palm, craving more friction. He doesn't hesitate. He delivers, rubbing the heel of his palm in a circular motion. My toes curl from the pleasure. Heat coils through my insides, hard and fast. He groans into my mouth as I grab the lapels of his fancy waistcoat, holding him to me as if my life depends on it. The cold of earlier is gone, the pain much less. My head is still throbbing a little, but the discomfort takes a back seat to the endorphins drenching me in a deliriously happy glow.

It's temporary, Kate, my mind whispers, but I shut it down. I'm too lost in the moment, too needy for release to let logic derail me. My body dictates my moves. When he pushes a thigh between my legs, I rub against him. He triples the intensity of his assault on my mouth, not by violent and frantic kissing, but by pleasuring my mouth with slow, meticulous precision, turning me into putty in his hands. He abandons my sex to frame my face between his large hands, letting me relieve my ache on the hard muscle of his leg. His hard-on presses against my stomach. I slide a palm over his chest to the hardness under his waistline. His cock is the only remedy that can cure my need.

"What you do to me," he growls into our kiss.

I don't resist when he sweeps me off my feet and carries me upstairs, even though I know our destination before he pushes open the bedroom door with a shoulder.

He lays me down gently on the mattress before removing my clothes and quickly undressing himself. I shiver with anticipation when he takes a condom from the nightstand drawer, makes quick work of rolling it on, and crawls over me, igniting every inch of my skin with the naked feel of his.

"How's your head?" he asks when he reaches my neck, planting soft kisses along the arch.

"Better." The knock was hard, but not so hard that I'll have a concussion.

He drags a finger over my throat, fury etched in his features. "He left marks on you."

"They'll fade," I say, cupping his cheek. I don't want to think about the attack. Not now, and maybe not ever.

"I'll be careful, but I can't go slow," he says with a hint of warning. "Not after what almost happened in that alley."

I swallow and nod. "Skip the foreplay. I need you *now*."

He drags a palm down my body and between my legs. He teases the inside of my folds with a fingertip before tracing my slit. My arousal is slick on his finger. He uses it to lubricate my clit and rub it in lazy circles as he aligns his cock with my opening. Then he pushes forward, carefully stretching me.

The way he fills me is delicious. The slight discomfort from his largeness only makes me burn hotter. I arch my hips, trying to make him move, but he sinks deeper slowly, inch by inch. When he's buried to the hilt, he pauses, giving me time to adapt. He's not only inside but also around me, overwhelming each of my senses. His arms are wrapped around my body, his muscular thighs wedged between mine. His weight anchors me, his warmth seeping through my skin to dispel the chill as the spicy, masculine scent of his cologne teases my nostrils. He makes a sound of pleasure in the back of his throat, sending goosebumps over my arms.

When he finally moves, my world falls apart. I sink deep into languid pleasure, so deep I'm scared I may never be able to resurface. I may never be able to come back from this. Chasing away the thought, I cling to him as if he's a buoy in stormy waters. I hold on like he's my salvation and the answer to everything. And as long as he's gently rocking inside me, he is.

The pleasure that's been building since the foyer starts to unravel in that way that promises closure. Just a little more. Angling my hips, I find the right friction, and when he slides backward and forward over my clit, I come with a cry.

"Yes, Katyusha," he growls. "Just like that."

My orgasm pleases him. The possessive look in his eyes tells me that. Holding my gaze, he comes a second later, his cock swelling even thicker and every muscle in his body locking tight.

When he's spent, he catches his weight on his arms and kisses me like he hasn't just explored the depths of my mouth. He kisses me like it's our first time, and I fall a little more for him. Kissing has always been my weakness, and I appreciate a man who knows how to use his lips.

Rolling off me, he gathers me in his arms. I shouldn't spend another night in his bed, but the episode in the alley has left me drained. I don't have enough energy to deal with locksmiths and replacing my stolen cards right now. Just for a short while, I want to bask in his strength.

It's cozy and safe in his arms, and it doesn't take long before I doze off.

11

A knock on the door startles me. The sun is barely up, the light in the room still gloomy. It takes me a moment to realize where I am and what happened last night.

Alex gets up from the bed and pulls on the boxer briefs he retrieves from the floor. I draw the blankets up to my chin even though he opens the door only a crack, carefully blocking me from view with his body.

"What is it, Leonid?" Alex asks.

A man replies in Russian. I recognize his voice. It's the man who spoke to Alex in his study the first time I slept over.

They exchange a few words, and then Alex shuts the door.

He turns to me with an apologetic look. "I have to go." Walking back to the bed, he brushes his knuckles over my cheek. "It's early. Go back to sleep. You need the rest."

I glance at the clock on his nightstand. It's seven in the morning. "Is everything all right?"

"Problems at work," he says tightly, dropping his hand. "What time is your shift?"

"I'm starting at ten."

"Marusya will make you breakfast. When you're ready, Yuri will drive you home if you'd like to change before your shift." He gives me a thoughtful look, his blue eyes piercing. "Maybe you should leave some clothes here. That way, you don't have to make the detour to your place before going to work."

My mouth almost drops at the statement. "I thought…"

"I said I wanted to sleep with you again," he says in a blasé way, walking to the bathroom.

It's the blasé that gets stuck in my throat, the easy way in which he brushes off the sex as if it holds no value. Again, my mind screams I'm no match for him. A man like Alex will chew me up and spit me out. The sex is great, but I realized something last night. It's not enough. Not in the long term. Besides, his iffy answers about his trip to Moscow and that woman in the restaurant bug me. I'm less experienced than him, but I'm not naïve.

Slipping out from under the covers, I pad over the wooden floor to the bathroom. Steam billows from over the glass wall of the shower cubicle. Alex's strong body is a murky picture in the mist. Even hazy and frayed around the edges, the image sends a bolt of heat to my abdomen. My stomach flutters like I'm a schoolgirl experiencing her first crush.

Despite everything, I still like Alex. I like the man I caught a glimpse of in Romanoff's. After last night's ordeal, he's been angry and more reserved than on our first date, but who can blame him? I gatecrashed his party and then he had to run after me only to save me from the clutches of a mugger.

Still, I can't ignore the question in the back of my mind.

Would I even be here if I hadn't walked into that restaurant and gotten attacked? The seesaw of emotions I'm riding is exhausting, first fretting about Alex forgetting about me and now worrying that sleeping with him was nothing but a result of unfortunate circumstances.

The toothbrush I used the last time I was here stands in a glass next to the basin. Alex's toothbrush is neatly arranged in a similar glass next to the twin basin, which I presume to be his side. The setup screams of the exclusivity he asked of me last night. Like him, I don't like to share, but I know myself well enough to know I need more. I need emotions, deep and lasting ones. I need trust. Especially after Tony, trust is non-negotiable, and trust is the one thing Alex and I don't share. He obviously doesn't trust me, and after last night, I don't trust him either. Not fully. He's evasive. He's not completely honest with me. I thought I knew exactly where I stood with him, but now I'm not so sure. This road I'm heading down with him is a dangerous one. There's only one way it can end—with my broken heart.

I know what I have to do. I should've done it right from the start. It's called self-preservation, and it means walking away. The mere thought makes my chest tighten painfully. Dammit. How did Alex get under my skin so fast? It must be the emotional bonding that comes with sex. I can't help it. It's just how I'm programmed.

I hover in front of the fancy shower, considering walking away without a goodbye, but I'm not strong enough. Opening the door, I step inside the spacious cubicle. Alex turns, brushing back his wet hair with both hands. Surprise flares in his eyes, but his lips curve in a pleased way. He wraps an arm around my waist and drags me closer, his head already coming down for a kiss. I'm only making this harder on myself, but I let him kiss me while the water cascades over us.

He tears his mouth from mine as he crushes my body against his. He's hard, and the molten look in his eyes says he wants me. He drags his hand up the inside of my thigh, holding my gaze as he slips a finger inside. My wetness tells him I want him too. The knowledge shines with a light of fever and victory in his crystal-blue eyes.

When he gives a shallow pump, I rise on tiptoes from the fire that immediately ignites in my lower body. My moan is lost in the sound of the water, but his gaze fixes on my parted lips as he curls his finger and rubs a sensitive spot. Clutching his shoulders, I gasp. He holds me up with his arm around my waist as he makes my knees weak with a single finger.

"More," I push from a throat still raw after last night's attack.

As always, he obliges. He doesn't make me beg or wait. He gives me two fingers, his pace turning faster. He quickly brings me to the edge but pulls out before I go over. Carefully, he turns me around and pushes me down with a hand between my shoulder blades.

"Hands on the wall," he says.

I splay my palms over the coolness of the tiles as warm water runs over my back. He wedges a thigh between my legs, spreading me with his arm secured around my waist so I don't slip. Bent over in a wide stance, I'm vulnerable and on display, but my body is the one thing I do trust him with.

He plants a kiss on every vertebra of my back, then goes down on his knees behind me and drags his tongue through my folds. I shiver at the promise of that touch, hoping that, like last night, he'll skip the foreplay. He doesn't disappoint. He sucks my clit into his mouth and grazes it with his teeth. My back arches from the pleasure. I drag my nails over the wall as he licks me like candy. I can't find purchase on the smooth surface of the tiles, but he keeps me steady with his broad palms on my hips as he fucks me with his tongue and tortures me with sucks and licks until my thighs quiver and my legs threaten to cave.

Before I find release, he straightens behind me. I'm panting, dragging in air and swallowing drops of water. The smooth, hot crest of his cock nudges my entrance. The breath leaves my lungs as he slides inside, splitting me open. He's excruciatingly gentle, taking his time to stretch me and circling my clit with a finger until my inner muscles relax enough to let him in all the way. He doesn't start moving until I soften around him, but when he does, the pleasure is unbearable. Reaching behind me, I grip his wrist for a point of contact. I need to hold on to him when he makes me come undone. I'm almost there when he picks up his pace, but then he stills.

"Katyusha." His voice is hoarse. "I'm not using a condom."

I've never had unprotected sex, even though I'm on the pill. That it doesn't faze me now should scare me, but somehow it feels right. Perfect.

"I'm clean," he says raggedly, rubbing a hand over my back. "You have nothing to worry about. I won't come inside you."

I glance at him from over my shoulder, taking in his harshly handsome features and the need etched on his face. "No. I want you to."

His eyes flare and darken, a possessive look coming over his face. "Are you sure?"

"I'm on birth control."

That's all the convincing he needs. Punching his hips, he pulls mine toward him. Our groins slap together, the sound of our wet skin reverberating in the steam-filled space. Every thrust he slams into me is a beat that keeps time with the harsh rhythm of my heart. In no time, my inner muscles clench around him. His cock swells inside me. He slips a hand around my waist and between my legs to help me get there with him— and I do. It's not his animalistic groan or the heel of his palm on my clit that triggers my climax but the knowledge that he's inside me without the barrier of a condom.

I come so hard I see stars. If not for his hand on my hip and the other cupped between my legs, I'd be sliding to the floor.

"Katyusha."

The way he says my name sounds primal. It's naked and stripped from pretenses, vulnerable and exposed, telling me what my body does to him.

He lowers his chest over my back and kisses my neck. From the way he sucks on my skin, I know he's going to leave a mark, but even this seems right.

He nips at my skin and licks away the bite of pain with his tongue. Kissing the shell of my ear, he says, "I've never done that before."

The confession makes warmth spread through my stomach. With a man as experienced as Alex, I would've thought there could be no more firsts for him. I'm glad it's me. I'm happy I could give him this.

Straightening, he brings me with him and turns me in his arms. He kisses me again, taking his time to enjoy my mouth. I all but melt. I'll never get enough of his skillful kisses. When he finally pulls away, I'm breathless again.

He cups my breast, lazily flicking his thumb over my nipple. "My beautiful Katyusha. You're perfect in every way."

I'm far from perfect, but I bask in the compliment anyway,

nestling against his chest when he brings his arms around me and holds me tightly. For a moment, we just stand like this, exchanging breaths and warmth.

I mourn the loss of his heat when he puts distance between us to grab the shampoo. Squirting some into his palm, he washes my hair and softly massages my scalp. He does the same with my body, cleaning me from head to toe. He only washes between my legs at the end, leaving his residual release on my thighs for as long as possible.

When I'm clean, he turns off the water and hands me a towel. We dry and dress in silence. He shows me where he keeps a hairdryer, saying he doesn't want me to catch a cold, and then he gives me a heated kiss and one last scorching look before walking out of the room.

Once more, I'm alone in his domain, colder since he's gone. Unanswered questions churn in my head now that it's no longer spinning from my orgasm. When the front door clicks shut, I move to the mirror to dry my hair. My neck sports a few blue marks, obviously left by fingers, and on top of one of those is a darker bruise—Alex's hickey. It's as if he wanted to erase the nasty bruises with a mark of his own.

I finish quickly, then go onto the landing and peer downstairs. The house is quiet and dark, except for the light burning in the entrance. Alex said Marusya will feed me breakfast, but without him, I once more feel like an intruder, one who's ripped him away from his dinner guests by playing the damsel in distress. I can't bear to linger any longer, not when I know what I have to do.

With a last look around, I go downstairs and pull on my jacket. When I step outside, Yuri is waiting next to the car.

I shiver in the early morning cold as I make my way toward him. "Morning, Yuri."

"Morning, Miss."

"Please, call me Kate."

"Kate," he says with a nod.

"Thank you for last night, for taking care of the locksmith."

"You're welcome." He takes a set of keys from his pocket and hands them to me. "Your new keys."

I drop them in my pocket. "I really appreciate that."

He opens the back door. "Why don't you get in? It's cold."

"What about Alex?" I don't want to inconvenience him by using his car. "How is he getting around?"

"He took the Bugatti."

"Oh." Alex has a Bugatti? Of course he does. I climb into the back and settle into the pleasant heat of the car.

"Where to?" Yuri asks when he's taken the wheel.

"My place, please."

I said I was going to reach out to Alex to get my closure. This is not the closure I envisioned, but it's something. This chapter of my life is now finished.

Even though it's for the best, tears burn at the backs of my eyes at the thought.

12

$\mathcal{I}$t's another hectic day at the ER. The influx of patients never diminishes. When it's time for my lunch break, I hurry to the breakroom to quickly eat the sandwich I prepared at home, but Rose rushes toward me with a cooler bag in her hand. I haven't told her or Nadia about last night's mugging because I don't want to explain why I was visiting the restaurant where my one-night stand took me on our sex date. To hide the marks, I've tied a scarf around my neck and claimed it's to prevent myself from catching a cold.

"Hey, Kate," she says, out of breath. "This was just delivered for you."

I look at the blue bag in her hand. "For me?"

"Yep." She hands it over. "I grabbed it since I was on my way up. I hope you don't mind."

I scrutinize the bag. "That was kind of you. Thanks."

"Lunch break?" She scoots past me to the breakroom, in just as much of a hurry as myself.

"I hope," I say with a sigh. "If it's not interrupted."

"I know." She opens the door and holds it for me. "I haven't finished a single lunch this week."

"Mm." I enter and deposit the bag on the table. "My mom calls it the flu season diet."

Her face falls as she lets the door shut with a click.

"Oh, Rose." I lay a hand on her arm. "I'm sorry. That was insensitive."

"Not at all." Tears shimmer in her eyes. "Your mom's great. Enjoy every moment you have together."

Taking a seat, I study her face as she sits down opposite me. Dark rings still mar her eyes, but they're less puffy and less red from crying. "How are you holding up?"

"I'm dealing with it." She shrugs, arranging the strap of her tote bag over the back of the chair. "You know."

"Yeah." I pat her hand. "You miss her."

She sniffs and puts on a bright smile. "Don't keep me in suspense. What's in the bag? The guy who delivered it was rather mean-looking."

My stomach tightens with suspicion and a tinge of appreciation I shouldn't feel. "Did he drive a fancy black car?"

"Yes. Who *is* that?"

"I'm not sure." But I have an idea. "I think it may be the driver of my one-night stand." Make that my two-night stand.

Her eyes grow big. "You had a one-night stand?"

"I know, right?" I make a face. "What was I thinking?"

"Actually, I think that's exciting. I just didn't peg you for the casual sex type. When you spoke about your ex, your decisions sounded logical and very much long-term oriented."

"Exactly." I blow out a long breath. "That's why the one-night thing was a huge mistake."

"Yet..." Her expression brightens. "He sent his driver to deliver stuff." She waves at the bag. "Open it before June charges in here and tells us we're needed at another emergency."

Smiling at her enthusiasm, I unzip the bag. I have to admit, I'm just as curious as Rose about the contents of the mystery bag. A delicious waft of melted cheese and mushrooms reaches my nostrils. Inside sits a plastic container with a red lid—the twin of the one I shoved into the back of my locker. Steam escapes from a lifted corner of the lid. Whatever is inside is piping hot. Someone prepared it a short while ago. A silver fork and knife wrapped in a linen napkin are neatly arranged on top of the dish. In a side compartment of the bag is a bottle of water complete with a slice of lemon and a mint leaf drifting inside.

"Wow." Rose makes a puppy face and bats her eyelashes. "That's so considerate. He sent you lunch."

"Um, yes." It is indeed a very considerate act, which doesn't help the closure I'm after.

"It smells delicious," she says. "What is it?"

I take out the dish and remove the lid. It looks like lasagna. Unable to resist the scrumptious aroma, I dip the fork inside and cut off a small corner. Portobello mushrooms and sweet peppers are layered between the pasta, topped with a bechamel sauce and melted cheese.

"Wow," Rose says again.

"Wow," I agree.

Giving my lunch an envious look, Rose takes a sandwich from her tote bag and unwraps it. "Are you sure it was a one-night stand?"

"Yes," I say a little too quickly and motion at the dish. "This is a huge portion. Do you want to share?"

"Oh, no." She waves a hand. "He wanted you to eat it. You go on. Tell me what it tastes like."

I bring the bite to my mouth and inhale the mouth-watering aroma once more before slipping the fork between my lips. Oh, yum. This is so tasty. Marusya is an excellent cook. My own peanut butter sandwich is forgotten as I dig into the treat of the warm meal. I only had a banana and a cup of herbal tea for breakfast, and I am truly starving.

Rose finishes her sandwich in a few big bites and dusts her hands as she gets to her feet. "I've got to run. I promised June I'd check on a patient before two." She lifts her gaze to the clock. "Damn. Forget about running. I'll have to sprint." Gathering her napkin and empty wrapper, she adds with a wink, "Enjoy your lunch."

I do. I savor every bite, washing it down with the lemon-and-mint-infused water. When I'm done, I rinse the plastic dish and cutlery in the sink and put everything back into the bag.

It's not until the end of my shift that I think about the kind gesture again. A few other nurses are changing out of their scrubs. After dressing and pulling on my warm jacket, I drop the plastic dish in my locker into the cooler bag and take it with me, undecided as to how to return it. If I go to Alex's house, my willpower may evaporate. The man has way too strong of an effect on me. Maybe I'll just send the bag back with a courier.

Outside the building, my step slows. The black car is parked at the curb, with Yuri leaning on it. He straightens when he sees me.

At least this solves how I'll return Alex's dishes.

I resume walking, albeit with hesitation. "What are you doing here?" I ask when I'm within earshot.

He opens the back door. "Mr. Volkov sent me. I'm your ride."

"That's very kind, but I can make my own way." I hold out the cooler bag. "If you don't mind, I'd appreciate it if you could return this to Marusya and thank her for me for the lunch."

He takes the bag, offering me a tight smile. "Sure, but I can't *not* take you home. Mr. Volkov was very clear on the matter."

A car honks behind us. The driver hangs from his open window. "Hey, this is a drop-off zone. Are you leaving or staying?"

"Come on," Yuri says, attempting a broader smile, and I get the impression the gesture doesn't come easily for him. "Just get in. Mr. Volkov will be upset if I don't do my job."

After another bout of honking, I get in with a mumbled, "Thank you."

The interior is warm. Yuri must've left the heater running. I wrap my jacket tighter around myself and settle back into the seat. I might as well enjoy the comfort of the ride, seeing that this will be the last ride Alex offers me.

Yuri gets behind the wheel and takes an envelope and a box from the glove compartment. He hands both to me. "Your bank cards and a new phone."

"My cards? Wait, what? A new phone?"

"Mr. Volkov had them replaced. The new security pins for your cards are in the envelope too."

I stare at the box of the latest iPhone in my hands. "I can't—"

"Mr. Volkov said I'm not allowed to take no for an answer." With that, he faces back to the front and starts the engine, indicating the subject is closed for discussion.

Letting Alex replace my phone and cards isn't ideal, but it does save me a lot of hassle, not to mention time. I suppose it's part of the perks of being a billionaire. Not that I expected him to do this for me.

"I was going to go past the bank and police station during my break tomorrow afternoon, but thanks," I say.

Yuri glances at me in the rearview mirror as he steers us into traffic. "The police station is taken care of. You don't need to go there."

"What about my statement? Don't they need it?"

"Mr. Volkov took care of everything."

Right. Another perk of being an oligarch.

We don't speak for the remainder of the ride to my apartment. Yuri parks in front of the main entrance of my building and comes around to get the door.

"Thank you," I offer again. "Please tell Alex I appreciate the ride."

He gives a slight nod and goes ahead to open the main entrance door of my building for me.

When he enters behind me, I say lightly, "You don't have to play doorman. I'll manage from here."

His face remains serious. "Mr. Volkov wants me to see you inside safely."

That's a bit over the top, but since it's clear that Yuri isn't going to budge, I let him walk up the stairs ahead of me and check out the landing before he lets me unlock my door.

"Goodnight, Kate. Lock the door behind you."

"Goodnight," I say as I go inside. "Thanks again for the ride."

He stands at attention until I close the door. His footsteps only fade on the landing after I've turned the key.

Already, my front door sports a brand-new double-bolt lock with a peephole and a camera allowing me to see who's outside. The added measures of safety are enough. Alex doesn't have to send Yuri to escort me like a bodyguard. This morning, Yuri waited outside my apartment until I'd changed to drive me to work. I told him then I didn't need another lift, but he's following Alex's orders and will keep on doing so until I've dealt with Alex.

At least I haven't seen Dimitri since last night.

Sighing, I kick off my shoes and sit down on the sofa to rub my aching feet. It's been a grueling day. I yearn for a warm, relaxing bath, but I first want to charge the new phone.

I'm surprised to find it fully charged and set up when I take it out of the box. Alex saved his number in the contact list. Great. Now I have to call Alex and tell him our sex dates are over, so he stops it with the gifts and kind gestures.

You can do it, Kate.

Taking a deep breath, I dial his number.

He picks up on the first ring. His tone is warm and pleasant, as if he's genuinely happy to hear from me. "Katyusha. How was your day?"

"Tiring."

Voices sound in the background. "Hold on. I'm in a meeting. Give me a moment to step outside."

"Oh, no. I—" I was going to say I don't want to bother him and can call back later, but he's already put me on hold.

His voice comes back a moment later. "How about dinner at my place? If you're tired, we can have it in bed."

My insides tighten in a disconcertingly delicious way. But no. However tempting, I've made my decision. I can't go down this road.

Self-preservation, Kate, remember?

"Actually, I'm calling to tell you that seeing each other again isn't a good idea."

He's silent for a while. If not for a door that slams in the background, I would wonder if he's still there.

"I'm sorry," I say when another second passes. "I appreciate the lunch and the rides, and that you've taken care of the police statement for me. Not to mention my new bank cards and phone. I just don't think I can do this."

"Do what?" he asks gently. "You enjoyed it, didn't you?"

I bite my lip. "You know I did."

"Then what's holding you back?" He adds with an attempt at humor, "Are you into kink? Something you're not telling me? If you need me to brush up on my skills in bed, I'm happy to oblige. I'm not against experimenting. You want handcuffs? Ropes? You just have to name it."

It's hard to resist him when he's both kind and trying hard to be funny. I like the kind and playful Alex too much.

"This isn't about the sex."

"Then what is this about? Why are you having doubts, Katerina? Is it because of what happened last night?"

I'm not sure if he's referring to the mugging or catching him with a woman at his side. The mugging wasn't his fault. As to the woman, he claimed the dinner was business, not that it's any of my business. It's not as if we're in a relationship.

"Tell me what's bothering you," he coaxes. "I'll fix it."

I pinch the bridge of my nose. Should I even attempt this when I've already decided this is a bad idea? Ugh. I can't resist. "You're not being honest with me. Tell me the real reason why I hadn't heard from you in a week."

"You said you needed time."

I can't argue that, but there's something else. I can feel it. "The woman from last night, have you slept with her?"

His hesitation gives me my answer. I swallow hard. Casual

dating isn't supposed to hurt like this. The knowledge shouldn't be a branding iron burning into my heart.

"It was a while ago," he says softly. "Before I met you."

"How long?"

He blows out an impatient sigh. "What does it matter? She means nothing to me."

"How long?"

"A couple of weeks," he admits with strained reluctance.

The week before he took me to bed. Why does that even shock me? Why did I expect anything different? I have no right to be upset over this, but I can't help the painful way my chest constricts. He doesn't date. He's free to have dinner with whomever he wants whenever he wants, but I don't want to be one of his fucks squeezed into his busy schedule between his Monday and Thursday lays. I want to be more than that, more special, and when we were together, he'd made me believe I was. It wouldn't hurt so much now if he'd been honest with me, but the words he spoke last night come back to lash me like a whip.

Only the special ones.

"Katyusha, talk to me."

"Did you book out Romanoff's for her?"

His Russian accent is thick with frustration. "Katerina."

"Did you?"

Another hesitation.

Oh my God.

"She's the daughter of a business associate," he says carefully. "It was her birthday."

"You don't have to explain. I only wanted a simple yes or no answer."

"It's not as simple as that," he all but growls.

No, it seems not. With him, nothing is simple. I've always had my head screwed on straight, but I'm not experienced in his kind of life. I don't know how to deal with his nuances and shades of truth.

"What do you want?" he asks, irritability slipping into his tone. "Flowers? Chocolates? Hearts and cupids? You think that will make what we share more special, more meaningful? I don't say things I don't mean. You *are* special, more than Dania."

Ugh. Great. Now I know her name. "Stop it, Alex."

"What do you want me to say? Tell me, and I'll say it."

"How kind of you," I say, hiding my hurt with sarcasm.

"That's not what I meant and you know it. I want to see you again, and I know you want to see me too. Don't fight it. Don't fight us. Just let me make it good for you. Come over. Yuri can be at your place in ten minutes. Stay over. I'll forever regret not exploring this chemistry with you if you say no."

But his exploration may happen at the cost of breaking my heart. "I can't."

"Why not?"

"You're not into dating, and I'm not into casual sex. I'd rather end this now before..." *One of us really gets hurt, that someone being me.*

"Katyusha, listen."

I don't. I'm not the kind of person who hangs up on others, but we're talking in circles. "I'm sorry," I whisper, ending the call.

13

*A*fter crying myself to sleep, I wake up groggy and with a blotchy, puffy face. No matter how many times I tell myself it's for the best, I don't feel better. Whenever I think about Alex, I want to cry all over again. It's ridiculous. I didn't cry this much about Tony, and we'd been together for months.

I rush through my morning routine since I have an early shift starting at six, and when I fling open my door to leave, I stop in my tracks. A huge bouquet of pink roses wrapped in cellophane and tied with a white ribbon sits on my doorstep. There must be at least two dozen. The blooms are gorgeous, their petals wide open.

Unable to resist, I pick up the heavy arrangement and inhale the sweet fragrance of the flowers. There's no card, but I know who sent them. It's the man who asked me if I wanted flowers and chocolates. I do love flowers, it's true. I've always thought them romantic. Still, I'd rather have honesty and a steady relationship.

Instead of taking the flowers inside, I bring them with me. To my surprise, Yuri is waiting downstairs.

"Oh no," I say as I approach him. "I told Alex I don't want anything from him any longer." Well, not exactly in those words, but that's what I implied when I said our fling was over.

He shrugs and opens the back door. "Just following orders, ma'am."

"Kate."

"Kate." He even attempts another smile.

"We can't keep on doing this, Yuri."

The smile drops from his face. "You'll have to take it up with Mr. Volkov."

"How did you even know when my shift starts?"

He gives me a blank look. "I'm afraid you'll have to take that up with Mr. Volkov as well."

With a sigh, I get inside. Yuri is here now anyway. I'm not going to send him away and waste his time, but I'll have to be firmer with Alex.

Placing the flowers on the back seat next to me, I send Alex a text message, asking him to please stop sending Yuri to drive me around. It's rude not to thank him for the flowers, but I don't want to encourage him, so I say nothing about the pretty roses lying next to me.

When we arrive, I thank Yuri for dropping me off and stress the fact that I won't need a ride home. On my way to the ER, I make a detour to the recovery wing, where I leave the flowers in a vase in an elderly lady's room.

"My," she says as I remove the cellophane wrapping. "Whatever are those for?"

I give her a smile. "They're just too pretty to waste."

"Well, I'll certainly enjoy them."

"Good," I say, patting her hand.

My phone buzzes in my pocket, but I don't take it out to check the message. I'm certain it's from Alex, and I don't want to deal with our short-lived sex dating right now. I need to focus. People's lives depend on my presence of mind.

As patients with life-threatening and serious injuries fill my day, I temporarily forget about my insignificant problems. However, by lunchtime, I get a call from reception, informing me of a delivery. It's a blue cooler bag.

This time, I resist the curiosity to peek inside. Grabbing the bag, I walk outside to look for Yuri, but neither the scary-looking Russian nor the black car is anywhere in sight. I'm about to turn when I spot a man across the road, leaning on a lamppost.

Dimitri.

He doesn't even pretend not to look at me. Since I now know who he is, he stares openly. He continues to stare as I cross the road and stop in front of him.

Shoving the bag into his hands, I say, "Enjoy your lunch break."

He barely catches the bag before it falls.

I don't look back to check what he does. I walk back briskly, wolf down my sandwich, and have just enough time left for a hot cup of tea. While the infusion brews, I check my phone.

The text message from this morning wasn't from Alex. It was from my mom. My stomach tightens as I read the message. She's on her way back earlier than planned due to a bad spell of arthritis. She must be at the airport right now.

With only a couple of minutes left before I'm due back at my station, I dial my mom's number. Thankfully, she picks up.

"Hey." I blow out a sigh of relief. "I just read your message. Are you at the airport?"

"Hi, honey. I'm about to board the plane."

I'm about to board? Not *we're* about to board? "Where's Martin?"

"Oh, he decided to stay."

"What? He's letting you fly back alone when you're unwell?"

"There's no point in spoiling both of our holidays. He still has a few days of vacation left. It would've been a shame to waste them."

There's more behind her nonchalant words. Her high-pitched voice tells me she's close to tears.

"Are you kidding me? What kind of a boyfriend does that?"

"Well…" There's a small pause. "Actually, we're not together anymore."

"What?" I exclaim. "I thought you really liked him."

She sighs. "It seems my illness is too much for him to handle. Martin is a virile and active man. He doesn't want to be bogged down with someone who can hardly move on some days when he can be out dancing and scuba diving."

"Oh, Mom." My heart breaks for her. "I'm so sorry." I can't believe Martin did this to her. "You know what? Good riddance. It's his loss."

"You know what they say. There's plenty of fish in the sea."

Her pep talk doesn't fool me. She's devastated. For once, my butterfly mom believed she was going into something long-term with a man, and he couldn't handle her off days.

"Are you all right, though?" I ask, my chest tight with worry.

"I'll be fine. I took my pills. I'm looking forward to a long nap on the plane."

"Send me your flight number. I'll meet you at the airport."

"Oh, no, Katie. There's no need to put yourself out. I'm a big girl. Listen, I have to go. The boarding gate is about to close. I'll see you soon."

"Love you, Mom. Be safe."

"Love you too, honey."

I end the call, fuming. How could Martin do this to her? Being sick isn't her fault. She has better days. Why couldn't he just be happy with those and be there for her on her worse days? Clearly, he wasn't as much in love with her as he appeared to be.

Concern for my mom hovers in the back of my mind for the rest of the workday. At least I get off at three this afternoon.

When my shift ends, I change quickly and offer my colleagues a hurried goodbye before making my way outside— only to stop in the open doors. The black car is parked in its usual spot, with Yuri sitting in the driver's seat. Dimitri is no longer at his post across the street.

Turning on my heel, I go back inside and take a side exit. From there, I walk toward the bus stop and catch an express bus to my mom's. I can't accept Alex's charity any longer. It's over. He has to get the message.

For the rest of the afternoon, I forget about Alex as I clean my mom's apartment, do the laundry, air all the rooms, and cook spaghetti. Throughout the afternoon, my phone lights up with text messages from Alex demanding to know where I am, but I delete them without replying. My whereabouts are none of his business.

I'm cleaning the mess I've made in the kitchen with my homemade tomato sauce when a new message comes in from him.

Katerina, just let me know you're safe. Please.

I frown at the sinister note of the text. Overprotective much? Maybe he's overreacting because of the mugging. Picking up my phone, I type a quick reply. I don't want to go down the non-dating road with him again, but letting him worry is cruel.

I'm fine.

I hesitate with my finger on the screen, contemplating my words.

Please don't contact me again.

I stare at my phone for a whole ten seconds after hitting send, but nothing appears. No reply. He finally got the message. Good. Right? Then why does my chest ache so much it's hard to breathe?

Shaking it off, I set the table and fold the laundry as I wait.

The taxi pulls up to the apartment at almost eight. The sight of my mom when she emerges shocks me. She's bent over, looking ninety instead of forty-three. I hurry outside to meet her. Fishing out a bill from my pocket, I pay the driver and take her arm to steady her while he gets her bag from the trunk.

"Thank you," I say to the driver, taking her suitcase in one hand and offering my arm to help her to the door.

Renewed anger toward Martin bubbles up inside me. How could he let her leave alone like this?

"Mom," I say, close to tears when we're inside. "You should've told me it was this bad."

She waves a hand, the gesture stiff. "It's been worse. Gosh, am I glad to be home."

"Come on." I lead her to the kitchen and help her sit down at the table. "Are you hungry?"

"Starving."

"Good." I force a tremulous smile onto my face. "I made spaghetti."

"Mm." She flinches as she shifts into a comfortable position. "After all that fancy seafood, pasta is exactly what I crave."

I dish up the food for both of us, keeping a close eye on her. When I'm seated opposite her, I say, "We should call your doctor. I think he needs to up the dose of your medication."

"There isn't much he can do. It's just the way this illness goes. We simply have to accept and adjust."

The speech is supposed to make me feel better when she's the one who needs the comforting. The words of solace I want to offer get stuck with the tears in my throat. I don't utter them because they won't make a difference. They're just empty, meaningless words. Helplessness engulfs me as I watch her try to wind the spaghetti around her fork. After two failed attempts, I can't just sit and look any longer.

"Here." I take the chair next to her. "Let me."

Our roles are reversed as I feed my mom just like she used to feed me at this very table when I was little. The scene breaks my heart, but I keep the conversation upbeat for her benefit. It's hard enough for her as is. She doesn't need the burden of my sorrow on top of everything else.

"So," she says when we're sipping herbal tea in the living room after dinner, "it looks like we're both back in the dating game." She adds with a wink, "We should try double-dating."

That makes me break out in a laugh. "Ugh, Mom. Please. I don't want to be on a date with you."

She makes a shocked face. "You hurt my feelings. No, but seriously, now that I'm back, I should set you up on a date."

"Later, okay? I have too much on my plate at work."

"You work too hard. You're young and pretty. You should go out and have some fun. You *deserve* some fun. Let me arrange a blind date with Phillip for you. He's a really nice guy, and the two of you have a lot in common."

"Your physiotherapist? That Phillip?"

"Yes. He's handsome and single, and he's very interested in meeting you."

"Please tell me you haven't discussed me with him."

"Just your positive attributes, like how beautiful you are, that you're a kind and generous person, that you work in the medical profession like him, and that you have a very sexy body."

"Mom!"

"What?" She shrugs. "It's the truth."

"You sound like a walking billboard advertisement. You've overpromised, and now I'll underdeliver."

She gives me a shrewd look. "Is that a yes?"

"No!"

"Oh, come on. What can it hurt? Just have drinks with him."

"We'll see." I check my watch. "I have to get to bed soon. I have an early shift tomorrow." There's no way I'm leaving her alone tonight, not when she's in this state. "Is it okay if I sleep over? It'll allow me to catch an extra hour of sleep."

"Of course. You don't have to ask. This is always your home."

"Come on." I push to my feet. "I'll run you a bath. I'm sure you'll feel better after relaxing in warm water."

While my mom shuffles around the bedroom, unpacking her cosmetics, I fill the bathtub. When she was first diagnosed, we had her bathroom adapted with a spa bath sporting a built-in bench, special bars on the sides, and a shower nozzle attached to the wall. It's close to the design of a Jacuzzi, which allows my mom to get in and out easily with a few steps on either side of the tub, and to be submerged in the water in a sitting position. The last thing I want is for her to be stuck in the bath and unable to get out, or to slip when she's weak.

I add Epsom salts to the water to help relieve the pain in her joints and switch on the jets to massage her back and legs. Hanging a towel on the bench next to the bath, I leave her to unwind while I finish unpacking her suitcase and put her dirty clothes in the washing machine.

It's close to ten when we finally go to bed, and the moment my head hits the pillow in my childhood bedroom, I'm fast asleep.

THE RING OF THE ALARM ON MY PHONE WAKES ME AT FIVE. I switch if off quickly so I don't wake my mom. After dressing, I go to the kitchen to make coffee and toast. I always keep a few items of clothing in my old bedroom in case I have to sleep over when my mom is having a bad spell. I dress in a clean pair of jeans, a warm sweater, and my puffy jacket. Then I set the alarm and lock up before making my way to the bus.

I half expect to see a black car in the street, but Alex doesn't know where I am. Even if he wanted to be stubborn and send Yuri again, he couldn't. Which is for the best. Maybe sleeping over at my mom's last night was a blessing in disguise.

My phone rings as I get off the bus. I check the screen. It's Alex. Without giving it another thought, I reject the call. A moment later, my phone pings with a voicemail notification. I make it one whole block before I cave and listen.

"Katyusha, where are you? You didn't sleep at home last night. Please tell me you're safe. That's all I want to know, I promise. Just call me."

Biting my lip, I consider his persistent need to know that I'm safe. I want to keep him at arm's length, but I can't bring myself to let him worry.

I type a text message while I'm walking.

I'm fine. I had to take care of my mom yesterday. You have to stop worrying about me. I'm not your responsibility. We're over.

I watch the blue line run from zero to one hundred percent as my message is delivered. I give it a couple of seconds, but there's no reply.

There. It's done. I couldn't have made it any clearer.

As I near the ER, I keep vigilant, but I don't spot Dimitri or Yuri. The pavement in front of the main entrance is void of big Russian men, and no fancy cars are parked at the curb.

A cold wind rips around the corner of the building, making my eyes water. I rush through the sliding doors, grateful for the warmth inside.

June catches up with me on the stairs. "Kate, you have to come see this."

My senses go on high alert. "Is something wrong?"

"No, quite the opposite."

She leads the way to the recovery wing. Pushing open the door of the first room, she stands aside for me to enter. A huge bouquet of white roses stands on the trolley at the foot-end of the bed, hiding the patient who lies under the covers.

I frown. "What did you want to show me?" I don't see anything out of order.

"The flowers," she says with meaning.

"They're pretty, but why show *me*?"

"Because..." She gives me a piercing look. "There's a bouquet in each and every room of the hospital, and the guy who delivered them says they're from your boyfriend."

14

$\mathscr{I}$ stare at June in shock. "I don't have a boyfriend."

"Well," June says, "you'd better explain that to the guy waiting in reception for you."

My heart hammers in my chest, mimicking my steps as I make my way back to reception. I brace myself before I turn the corner, expecting to see a strong body, a sinfully yet unconventionally handsome face, and piercing blue eyes, but there's no tall Russian emanating danger among the throng of people in the reception area.

A guy wearing overalls and a baseball cap stands at the desk. Next to him is a huge pink box with a white ribbon, along with a smaller one.

He straightens when I near. "Miss Morrell?"

I look between him and the boxes. "Yes?"

He shoves a clipboard and a pen toward me. "Please sign here."

"Wait." I shake my head, frowning as I look at the name

printed at the top of the form. It's not a courier company I'm familiar with. "What for?"

"I don't know, Miss. I'm just making the delivery."

"From whom?" I ask, even if I already know.

He taps a finger on a white envelope that lies on top of the clipboard. "From him. Can you please sign? I have another delivery to make."

I hold up a finger. "Just hold on a minute. Did you deliver the flowers?"

"Yes." He motions at a delivery van parked outside. "Took me three trips to the store to get everything here." He checks his wristwatch. "Are you signing or not?"

I shouldn't. I should let him take the boxes back with him, but I'm too baffled by the flowers that June claims decorate every room. What is Alex up to? Why send flowers to every patient in the hospital?

"Did you tell everyone the flowers are from my boyfriend?"

He gives me an exasperated look. "They asked. What did you want me to say?"

"Is that what the man who ordered the delivery told you?"

Sighing, he rolls his eyes. "A guy orders a few grand's worth of flowers? Yeah. If that's not a boyfriend, then I don't know what is."

Not Alex. He's the one man in this city—in the world—who isn't boyfriend material.

"Look, are you signing?" he asks. "If not, I'm supposed to leave this anyway." He waves at the boxes. "If you don't sign, my boss won't know I made the delivery. I'm just covering my own ass here."

A glance at the clock on the wall confirms I only have a few minutes before I'm on duty, and I still have to change into my scrubs. Like the delivery man, I'm running against the clock. However, it's not the clock but his next words that finally make the decision for me.

"If I don't have proof of the delivery, Miss, I'll be in trouble with my boss."

Taking the pen, I sign my name on the form. The man grabs his clipboard and makes his way to the exit without another word, leaving me standing there with the two boxes and the envelope.

As always, it's busy in the reception area with patients filling out admission forms and making payments. I'm obstructing the flow of the queue. Stacking the small box on top of the big one, I go to the locker room.

Nancy, the first-year nurse, passes me in the hallway. "Hey, Kate." She turns, skipping backward as she says, "Is it true that your boyfriend sent flowers to everyone in Recovery?"

I barely hide my irritation as I say from over my shoulder, "He's not my boyfriend."

She grins. "In that case, can I have him?"

At my eyeroll, she gives a merry laugh before continuing on her way.

I nudge the door open with a shoulder and drop the boxes on the bench next to my locker. I've signed for the goods. I may as well check what's inside.

Starting with the big box, I lift the lid. An arrangement of arum lilies tied with a white ribbon rests on a bed of tissue paper. The flowers are stately and elegant, something that would fit in Alex's house. The smaller box contains a gourmet panini, a tub of natural yogurt, fresh berries, and a small pot of honey. Lunch, I assume.

I leave the card for last on purpose, wanting to delay what-

ever message it contains for as long as possible. Not being able
to put it off any longer, I tear open the envelope and take out a
red card with a pink heart in the middle. My hands shake a little
as I open it. The inside is blank except for the strong hand-
writing scribbled in black ink on the white stock of the card.

Maybe roses aren't your style. I'm learning by trial and error.

The message is signed with a simple A.

Blowing out a breath, I close the card and shove it into my
locker with the boxes. I make quick work of changing, winning
me another couple of minutes before I have to go on duty. A
few nurses come in as I swipe across the screen of my phone,
accessing my recent calls list. I hit dial and press the phone to
my ear with a shoulder while I wash my hands at the basin.

Alex's smooth voice comes on the line, the deep timbre
sending a shiver down my spine. "Katyusha, what a pleasant
surprise."

A pleasant surprise? His feigned ignorance angers me. He
knew very well what he was doing when he sent all those gifts.
He knew I'd have no choice but to call him.

"Hello?" he says. "Are you there?"

Hold on. He sounds out of breath, like he does after sex. The
image of us together, our limbs entangled and him rocking into
me at a leisurely but intense pace sends a flash of heat through
my body. Just as quickly, the mental picture of him fucking
someone else in his bed right now dispels the heat, leaving me
frozen.

"Are you busy?" My tone is more hostile than I intended. "I
can call back later."

"Never too busy for you. I was just working out."

Relief washes over me. It's so intense that I feel weak, much
like an energy crash after a bout of adrenaline. What this man

does to me should be illegal. All the more reason to stick to my guns.

"What were you thinking?" I grit out, glancing around to make sure I'm not overheard.

"About what?" he drawls. "You have to be a little more specific."

I clench my teeth. He knows exactly what I'm talking about. "Sending the whole hospital flowers."

"Not the whole hospital. I was told flowers aren't allowed in the ER."

"Cut it out, Alex." I take a paper towel from the dispenser and dry my hands. "I don't have time for games."

"Since you seem to have a tendency of donating your flowers to the patients who don't have any, I'm just making sure you keep yours this time."

"What do you mean?" I say, making my way out the door.

"If every patient has their own flowers, you don't need to give yours to them."

The soles of my shoes squeak on the floor as I walk down the hall with fast, angry steps. "You can't keep doing this."

"Doing what?"

"Don't play ignorant with me."

"You have to say it, Katyusha." The gruffness of his tone strokes over my senses. "I've done a lot of things that are out of character for me since I've met you. Be specific."

"Sending me gifts and lunches."

"Isn't that how the game works?"

A doctor walks past, nodding in greeting. I return the nod and lower my voice. "This isn't a game, Alex."

"No." Seriousness creeps into his tone. "It's not a game."

"Then stop it," I hiss.

"I thought this is what you wanted—the hearts and the flowers."

I pause in front of the doors giving access to the emergency room. "I never said that was what I wanted. That's what you assumed."

"Come on," he says with a hint of humor, "you have to help me out here. I'm new to this. I've never done dating. Except for the flowers and hearts, Google isn't much help."

Despite myself, I can't help the smile that tugs at my lips. "You're into dating now?"

"If that's what it takes to get to see you."

That's not dating. That's manipulation, a way of getting me back into his bed until he tires of me. "I have to go. My shift is about to start."

"Can I see you tonight?"

"No," I say firmly. "It's better like this."

"Better for whom?"

"For me."

"I'm not so sure about that. I know I can make you feel good, better than any other man you've been with. You've admitted as much yourself."

Dammit. I should never have told him I had more orgasms with him in one night than in all my time with Tony. That's only fueled his ego and given him ammunition against me.

"I'm not giving up, Katyusha."

I take a deep breath. "You should."

I end the call just as I catch June's gaze through the window in the door. She waves me in, her manner saying it's urgent.

Putting everything else out of my mind, I slip my phone into my pocket and go inside.

"We have a victim with multiple stab wounds," she says in a strained voice. "I need you with Dr. Miller."

"Got it," I reply, already running.

AFTER DODGING YURI, WHO'S WAITING OUTSIDE THE HOSPITAL IN the car again, I come home with the big box of flowers under my arm, only to find another one waiting on my doorstep. I'm about to pick it up when Yuri speaks behind me.

"Refusing my service isn't helping either of us."

I jump, almost dropping the box. "Shit. You scared me."

"Sorry," he says, not looking one bit sorry. "If I don't drive you, I don't get paid."

"What?" I gape at him. "Alex can't do that."

"He's my boss," he says in a dry tone. "He can do whatever he wants. So either you pay me, or you let me drive you. I have mouths to feed, you know."

"You have a family?" Now I just feel awful.

"What?" he says, lifting his shoulders up to his ears. "A man like me can't have a family?"

"What? No!" Balancing the flowers in one arm, I bend to pick up the box on my doorstep. "That's not what I meant. I'm just shocked that Alex would stoop that low."

"He's not a bad man. He just wants to save you the trouble of commuting in the cold." He raises a brow. "What can it hurt?"

He has no idea. What do I have to do to get Alex out of my life? Maybe I should just sleep with him until he gets me out of his system. But no. That voice of self-preservation holds me back. He may fuck me out of his system, but he'll only get deeper under my skin.

"You're serious?" I scrutinize Yuri's face. "He won't pay you if I don't let you drive me?"

He doesn't so much as blink. "No work, no pay."

"Fine," I say with annoyance. "Until I've sorted this out with Alex, I'll take a ride to work and home, but that's it. When I'm free, I'm on my own."

"You'll have to take that up with—"

"Yes, I know," I say, seething. "With Mr. Volkov."

"Exactly." Yuri's flat smile says he's happy that I finally got it through my thick skull.

I exhale through my nose. Inhale the good, exhale the bad. "I'll see you tomorrow morning then."

"Good," he says, as if talking to a child. "Now go inside. I'm supposed to wait until you've locked the door behind you."

I all but slam the door in his face—not that it's his fault I'm angry. The reason for my irritability is the man who won't take no for an answer. What will it take? A restraining order?

Even as I think it, I can't imagine doing that to Alex. It's not as if he's stalking me. He's just not used to being told no. I bet panties drop at the flick of his fingers.

Dumping everything on the kitchen table, I call my mom to see how she's doing while I put the lilies in water. The flowers are too stunning to let them shrivel and die.

My mom sounds only a little better, but when I propose to come over and cook for us, she profusely declines.

"Why?" I ask, carrying the vase to the living area and placing it on the bookshelf under the window where the flowers will get the best natural light. "Don't you want to see me?"

"Of course I do, honey." She clears her throat. "It's just that I'm expecting company."

I still. "Mom."

"Hmm?"

"You've just broken up with Martin."

"So? Ludwick is a bodybuilder. Apparently, he's very good at massage."

"Okay, that's more information than I wanted to know."

"Do you think I should wear the black negligee or the red one? The black is more flattering for my figure, but it makes me look paler. The red goes better with my skin tone."

"I doubt Ludwick is going to notice the color when he sees you in a negligee," I say with a smile.

"Got to go. Have to make my face pretty."

"Do you want me to come over and wash your hair? I can be there in an hour."

"I had Patricia come out today. She gave me a haircut and a blow-dry. I needed it after all that sun and sea water. My hair felt like grass."

"Fine," I concede with a sigh. "Just promise you'll call if you need me."

"Oh, honey. I'm the one who's supposed to be the parent, not you. I'm so sorry for doing this to you."

I look away from the beautiful flowers. "You *are* the parent, Mom. You've always been. I couldn't have asked for a better one."

"You're the best, you know that?"

"Go on. Have fun. But tell Ludwick to be gentle."

"Gentle sex isn't what I had in mind."

"Mom! I was talking about the massage."

"Oh, yes. Well, whatever."

I can only shake my head as I hang up, both happy for and concerned about my mom.

The box on the kitchen table catches my attention. Going

over, I wiggle the lid loose, expecting dinner or more flowers, but the most delicate white-and-pink chocolates, each in a mini paper cup, sit in the box.

Flowers, hearts, and chocolates. Alex wasn't joking. He really did look up *romance* on Google. The tokens are clichés at best, and since their intention is manipulating me back into his bed, I'm more determined than ever not to let him win.

I won't give in. Not again. Once—make that twice—was a big enough mistake. I'm not willing to repeat the error.

Which is why, when I receive a text message much later from my mom, saying that Phillip wants to meet me for drinks on Friday, I say yes.

15

It would be too weird to let Yuri drive me to my Friday night date, so when he drops me off at home after work, I tell him to have a good weekend. He mumbles something in return, waits until I've locked myself in, and leaves.

I've been sending Alex text messages all week, asking him to stop sending Yuri to drive me to work and home, but I haven't heard a single word back. He hasn't called or tried to make contact again, but the gifts—chocolates, fluffy bears, and healthy meals—arrive like clockwork at my doorstep. I have no idea how to make him quit. The worst is that I can't stop thinking about him. As long as he keeps peppering me with reminders, I can't get him out of my head.

The best thing for me is to move on, which is why I get dressed up for my date with Phillip even though I lack enthusiasm. I make an effort with my appearance, wearing a red dress and my boots and applying light makeup. I leave my hair down in natural waves. Giving myself a critical look in the mirror, I notice the dullness of my eyes and the paleness of my cheeks. The image forms a sharp contrast to the memory of my reflection in the mirror before my date with Alex, when my eyes were shining and my cheeks glowing. Discarding the mental picture, I dab red lipstick onto my lips and brush a bronzer over my cheeks. There. That looks better.

My phone pings with an incoming message just as I grab my coat. It's from my mom.

Enjoy tonight with Phillip.

She adds three tongue-dragging emojis.

I reply with a kissing emoji and check the time. We're meeting at a bar in Manhattan on 9th Avenue. I still have plenty of time to make it there, so I water the flowers before I go. My studio looks like a fairground with candy, bears, cards, and boxes of chocolates everywhere. I've handed out the gifts to my neighbors and the other nurses at the ER, but I'm running out of people.

An hour before the agreed meeting time, I lock up and take a brisk walk to the subway. The cold wind cuts through my coat. I shove my hands deep into my pockets to keep my fingers warm and keep an eye out for Dimitri, but he hasn't been lurking in front of the ER or my apartment building for the past week. I take that as a good sign.

I arrive early at the bar and take a table in the corner. It gives me time to gather myself and mentally prepare for a date I'm not in the mood for. A waitress comes over to ask what I'd like to drink as I pull off my coat. I order a glass of red wine, which she delivers promptly.

My glass is already half-empty and my spirits fortified with liquid courage when Phillip arrives exactly on the hour. I recognize him from the photo on Facebook that my mom sent me. I study him while he searches the bar, which has quickly filled up and is now packed with people. He's tall and willowy, sporting a tuft of blond curls. There's something boyish about his face, and his brown eyes seem lively and curious.

He grins when he finally spots me, making his way over with a wave. There's no immediate attraction or sparks like with Alex, but his smile is warm when he shakes my hand.

"Kate." He sounds out of breath. "I hope I didn't make you wait long."

"I was early." I wave at what's left of the wine in my glass. "As you can see."

The waitress comes up while he's wrestling out of his coat. "What can I get you?"

Phillip motions at my glass. "I'll have the same. On second thought…" He looks at me. "Shall we just get the bottle?"

"I'm not a big drinker."

"The bottle," he says, looking back at the waitress. Then his gaze returns to me. "We have all night to polish it off. Unless you'd prefer to go out for dinner later?"

This is progressing too fast for me. "We can just have a snack here."

He doesn't seem offended or put off. "Good." He hangs his coat on the wall hook and takes a seat next to me. "Your mother has told me so much about you."

"Oh, no." I groan. "She must've been boring you."

"Not at all." He rubs his hands together. "I loved the stories about how you chased the boys around the neighborhood with your toy gun."

I laugh. "I was a bit of a tomboy. I can't believe she told you that."

"You're all she ever talks about." His eyes warm a few degrees. "She obviously loves you very much."

"Yes." A fuzzy, happy feeling spreads through my chest. "She's great. How about you? Did you grow up around here?"

"Vermont, actually. I moved here after I finished my studies."

"Are your parents still there?"

"Yep. They still live in the same house I was born in. I doubt they'll ever move."

"Same here. It's nice to have roots."

The waitress arrives with a bottle of red, already corked, and pours him a glass.

"Do you like to travel?" he asks.

"I think I do, but I haven't had the opportunity yet. I'm working long hours, and it'll probably take me a few years to save up enough money."

He holds my gaze with that curious light shining in his. "Where would you like to go?"

Russia jumps into my head. "I haven't thought about it," I say, frowning at the foreign thought threatening to ruin my date with images of another man.

"India is my dream," he says. "I'd like to visit the Taj Mahal."

Genuinely interested, I ask, "What's the attraction?"

"I love curry," he says with a shrug.

I laugh at that.

"Seriously." He brushes back his hair. "I've been fascinated by the Bollywood culture since I was a kid."

"Really?" I have a hard time pegging him as a Bollywood fan.

He grins. "That's probably not the kind of information I should be sharing on a first date."

"No," I agree, laughing more. "But since the cat is out of the bag, tell me more about your fascination."

As he chats about his love of Indian food, movies, and fashion, I discover two things. One, Phillip is easy to talk to, and two, he's uncomplicated and sincere. He's everything the left side of my brain approves of in terms of relationship material. I can see why my mom wanted me to meet him. He's the kind of guy who will make a good father and faithful husband—reliable, loving, and trustworthy.

I focus on those pros, and by the time we've shared a plate of baked nachos and I've finished my second glass of wine, I can't come up with any cons. I'm buzzing a little from the alcohol, my cheeks hot from the stuffy, artificial heat inside, so when he grows quiet and leans over to my side, I don't pull away. I close my eyes when he presses his lips to mine and focus on analyzing the feeling.

His lips are soft for a man. He doesn't try to part my lips or sneak his tongue inside my mouth, but I can taste the wine and guacamole on his lips. I wait for the sparks or a flicker of arousal, but there's nothing. No zap of lightning or heat igniting under my skin. I'm relieved when he pulls away, but the slight shaking of his hand as he brushes my hair over my shoulder tells me his reaction to the kiss isn't the same.

It would be wrong to give him hope when there's no attraction from my side. That lesson is the one good thing I've taken from my fling with Alex. If being with him has taught me anything, it's that without the attraction, all the pros in the world aren't enough. The signs were there with Tony, and I didn't heed them.

"Phillip." I gather my words, trying to think of a tactful way to break it to him.

He gives me a half-smile. "That didn't rock your world, did it?"

My answering smile is apologetic. "I'm sorry."

"It was a bold move, a bit too soon as well, so maybe I should try again. What do you say? Shall we start over?"

I open my mouth to give him another apology when he's jerked from his chair so suddenly that the glass of wine in front of him topples over. The wine splashes over the table, drops landing on my chest as the bulk of it runs into my lap. I jump up, soaked in wine and confusion.

Alex is pinning Phillip to the wall between our coats, his forearm pressed on Phillip's neck. "Don't ever lay your hands on her."

"Alex!" My chair falls over in my rush to get to them. I grab Alex's bicep, trying to pull him off Phillip. "Let him go."

Phillip raises his hands, his voice steady. "I'm not touching her."

Alex's calm returns as the words register. Slowly, the scowl on his face evens out. The bar has gone quiet, all heads turned our way.

"Let him go," I say again, tugging on Alex's arm. I may as well be trying to move a tree trunk.

"Don't touch her *ever* again," Alex says with a clenched jaw.

"She's all yours," Phillip says, not breaking eye contact with Alex. He's treating him like a feral predator, I realize. Which is what Alex might as well be at the moment.

Alex lets him go with a shove. "Get out of my sight before I break your fingers."

"Alex!" I can't believe my ears. "Phillip, I'm so sorry."

"It's not your fault," Phillip says, barely glancing at me as he takes his coat from the hook on the wall. His gaze is still fixed on Alex as he takes his phone from his pocket and asks, "Do you want me to call the police, Kate?"

Alex watches me with a dark smile, waiting for my verdict as if he's intrigued about what my answer will be. I *should* call the cops on his ass, but it's hardly the way to repay him after he's saved me from an attack in a dark alley and replaced my bank cards, phone, and keys.

"No," I say. "I'll handle this."

Phillip gives me doubtful look. "Are you sure?"

"Yes." I bite my lip, guilt eating at me for how Alex is behaving when Phillip has been nothing but nice. "I'm really sorry about this."

Alex narrows his eyes. Standing there with his bulging muscles and intimidating stare, he looks more like the devil than a man.

"You're not welcome," he says harshly to Phillip. "I suggest you leave while you still can."

Ignoring Alex, Phillip says, "Fine, Kate, but whatever is going on between the two of you, you'd better deal with it before you decide to go on another date."

At the word *date*, Alex balls his hands at his sides.

"I'm really sorry." I'm repeating the same words over and over, but what else can I say?

Phillip takes a few bills from his pocket and leaves them on the table. "So am I."

"No, please." I push the bills back to him. "It's on me. It's the least I can do."

Phillip gives me a lopsided smile and pushes the bills back. "That wouldn't be very gentlemanly of me, would it?"

Directing his attention to me, Alex asks with a growl, "Are you done?"

"Wait." I catch Phillip's sleeve when he makes for the exit, earning another dark look and flaring nostrils from

Alex. "Please don't mention this to my mom. I don't want to worry her about anything. She's got enough on her plate."

"Don't sweat it," Phillip says. "I'm not the spiteful kind."

With a last look in Alex's direction, he leaves the bar. It's only then that I allow my anger to erupt.

"What were you thinking?" I whisper-scream, aware of the eyes of everyone in the bar on us.

Taking my coat from the hook, Alex holds it open for me. I yank the coat from his hands and pull it on myself before stomping out of the bar without looking to see if he's following. I smell like wine, my dress and underwear are soaked with it, and my blood is boiling with anger. He catches up with me by the exit, grabbing my arm and holding the door for me like a gentleman, which he isn't.

I pull on his hold, but he tightens his fingers and pushes me toward the black car waiting at the curb.

"No," I say, yanking on his hold again. "I'm not going anywhere with you."

"We're going to talk about this," he says through clenched teeth. "There are things I need to say to you."

I hang back. "Good, because there are things I need to say as well, but we'll say them right here."

He makes a frustrated sound in the back of his throat. "It's cold. Get in the car."

I've had enough. "You don't tell me what to do."

"*Radi boga*, Katerina. Why are you being so hardheaded?"

"Me?" I exclaim. "You're the one who won't give up."

"Because we're not done." His voice is low, laced with intent. "Not by a long shot."

"That's your opinion."

"Yes," he says, pulling me toward the car again. "That's exactly my opinion."

People stop and stare. Someone even takes out a phone to record our fight, but no one does a thing when Alex lifts me effortlessly into his arms and carries me kicking and protesting to his car. He lowers me to my feet, holding me prisoner against his chest with one arm while opening the back door. Cell phones flash as he deposits me like a parcel onto the back seat before shifting in next to me.

Shutting the door so hard the whole car shakes, he says something in Russian to Yuri, who shoots me a cutting look from over his shoulder before he steers the car into the traffic.

"Fuck," Alex says, dragging a hand through his short hair. "We did not need the scene you made out there."

My jaw drops. "If you hadn't kidnapped me, I wouldn't have needed to make a scene." I cross my arms. "Where are you taking me?"

"Home," he says evenly.

"I'm *not* going to your place."

"To your place then."

I don't argue. I need to get home anyway. "You're not coming inside."

He gives me a flat smile. "We'll see."

Ugh. He's insufferable. "If I'd known you were like this, I never would've agreed to go out with you."

"You prefer your men to be soft, like *Phillip*?" His lips curl around the name as if it's something distasteful.

"You had no right to treat Phillip like that. He's a nice guy who's done nothing to you."

His eyes gleam as he pins me with a stare. "He *touched* you. I've cut off men's fingers for less than that." The corner of his mouth lifts in something that resembles a smile, but it's far from friendly. His accent is more pronounced when he continues. "I treated him rather kindly, all things considered."

The part about cutting off fingers should shock me, but it doesn't. Deep inside, I know what this dangerous Russian is capable of. Igor didn't take a bullet for him for nothing. Alex's life involves violence. I bet his business is shady.

"What?" he taunts. "Aren't you going to thank me for sparing your soft boy's pampered fingers?"

I glare at him. "What were you doing at the bar tonight? How did you know I was there?" A disconcerting thought rattles me. "Are you still having me followed?"

"For your safety."

Holy shit. He doesn't even bother to deny it.

"Dimitri?" I ask as my anger bubbles up and threatens to spill over into something uglier, something like the violence I condemn in his life.

"Yes," he says with a straight face.

"I haven't seen him in a week."

"His presence upsets you, so I told him to keep out of sight."

I'm at a loss for words. "You're a bastard."

"That's not what you said when I had you pinned underneath me in my bed."

Heat creeps over my cheeks. I glance in Yuri's direction, at which he presses a button to lift the partition that gives us privacy. Too little too late.

Humiliation burns in my gut. "For that, you're a double bastard."

Something flashes in Alex's eyes, but he turns his face away, preventing me from seeing his expression.

I fall quiet. Getting into a war with Alex won't gain me

anything. He's a master at warfare. There's no way I can win. Not for the first time, I think that maybe I should just give in and let him have his way until the novelty wears off and he goes looking for another challenge.

The strained atmosphere prevails until we park outside my building. Alex is out of the car before I can reach for my door. He offers me a hand to help me out, and when I ignore it, he takes my arm and pulls me to my feet on the sidewalk.

Like a considerate lover, he snakes an arm around my waist and shelters me from the cold as he guides me to the entrance of my apartment block. It's warm in the crook of his arm, and I resent the welcome heat that seeps through the layers of his clothes and envelops my body.

He ushers me inside and up the stairs. When he takes a pair of keys from his pocket and unlocks my door, I lose it.

My voice echoes shrilly in the hallway. "You can't do that." I hold out my palm. "Give them to me."

"Keep your voice down," he says through gritted teeth. "You'll wake every goddamn person in the building."

"Then so be it. You can't change my lock and keep a set of keys for yourself."

Holding my gaze, he makes a statement by dropping the keys back into his pocket.

Son of a bitch. "Give them to me!"

He's on top of me in a flash, slamming a hand over my mouth and lifting me off my feet. I swallow the gasp that's trapped behind his palm as he opens my door, punches in the code to deactivate the alarm, and shuts the door with a click before lowering me to the floor.

The minute he removes his hand from my mouth, I back up into the small living space.

He frowns. "You don't have to be frightened of me, Katyusha. I'd never hurt you."

I hate that I'm shaking and that it reflects in my tremulous words. "I want you to leave. I told you, it's over."

"Is it?" He advances, making me scoot around the table. "I don't think it is."

"That's not for just you to decide." I lift my chin as my back hits the wall. I've run out of space to flee.

"No, it takes two to tango." He watches me with the intensity of a snake about to strike. "And I bet if I touch you, your body will sing another tune."

He stops flush in front of me, so close that when he leans in, the lengths of our bodies are pressed together. He must've put a spell on me, because on cue, my skin catches fire. The flames creep over my cheeks and down to my core. Every molecule in my body comes alive. The hair on my arms rises, drawn to him as if by static electricity. I flatten myself against the wall in an attempt to put space between us, but it's futile. His hard-on grows against my stomach, and in answer, my nipples tighten and my center clenches.

"You want me," he says, victory riding on the words.

The way he searches my eyes to confirm the truth is just an afterthought. My body has already told him everything.

"It's not that simple," I whisper.

He leans a hand on the wall next to my face and drags a finger over my leg, catching the hem of my dress. "What if it is?"

"With you?" I utter a soft laugh. "Nothing is simple."

He lowers his head and brushes soft words over the shell of my ear. "For you, I can try."

"Try what?" I tilt my head away. "Try to make it simple, or try to make it more complicated?"

"I've already tried more." He slides his palm under my dress and up the inside of my thigh. "You don't seem to like it."

"You mean this?" I wave a shaky hand at the gifts littering my studio.

He brushes his mouth over my jaw, the roughness of his stubble igniting sparks on my skin. "I've been patient, Katyusha. I've given you the time you asked for, but my patience is running out."

My breath catches when his hand reaches the juncture of my legs. "We've long since passed the phase of me asking for time."

"Is that so?" He nuzzles my neck. "Then what are you asking for now?"

It takes all the self-control I can muster to utter the words. "I'm asking you to leave."

He cups a hand between my legs. "You're soaking wet." His voice is low and gruff, his lips ghosting over the arch of my neck. "Are you sure you want me to leave?"

"It's the wine," I say, almost swallowing the last word when he pushes the elastic of my underwear aside.

Brushing a thumb over my slit, he hums his approval as he finds me slick. "You can lie to yourself if it makes you feel better, but you can't lie to me."

Unexpectedly, he curls the digit and presses the pad of his thumb inside my heat. My whole body jerks as if he's zapped me with a thousand volts. The need isn't a lie, but it's a weakness. I fight for strength, gripping his wrist to move his hand away, but when he sinks the length of his middle finger inside me, I all but melt into a puddle. If not for the wall at my back, my legs would cave.

"I want you," he says in a deep, dark whisper that feathers over my ear.

I'm still clinging to his wrist as he starts moving his finger, pumping in and out at a leisurely pace. It only takes a few strokes to make me come undone. My resolve vanishes like mist, replaced with a hazy fog of desire that clouds my mind.

The final nail in my coffin is when he presses his lips against mine. It's not a kind or static kiss. His lips are both gentle and rough, confusing me with promises of tenderness and dominant possession. He takes softly but wholly, invading the depths of my mouth and staking claim to my tongue as if he wants to consume every part of me.

My body reacts to the multiple stimulations, tightening in pleasure as he fucks my mouth with his tongue and drives me closer to release with his finger. I'm helpless against the onslaught—I've always been—and when he reaches between our bodies for the buckle of his belt, I don't stop him. I return his kiss with fervor as he breaks down my defenses and steals his way back inside my body. There's nothing left of my resistance as I thread my fingers through his hair and claw at him to get closer.

He groans deep in his chest, uttering his approval into my mouth with a muffled, "Fuck, yes," and then he catches fire.

We devour each other, fumbling through layers of clothes. Somehow, he manages to free his cock and roll on a condom while kissing me. That kiss is the magic spell that keeps us in this dark place of need, and he doesn't want to break it.

When he yanks my wine-stained dress up to my waist and hoists me up, I wrap a leg around his ass. He doesn't even bother with removing my thong. He barely pauses to pull the elastic aside before tearing into me. He takes too much too fast, but I encourage him, lifting onto my toes.

He growls into our kiss, fastening his hands on my breasts as he bends his knees and drives home. The pleasure makes my insides clench, the burn making me moan. He swallows that sound and gives me more, taking me harder than ever, yet I'm still craving more.

We're making out against the wall, fully dressed, soaked in wine and anger, and it's the hottest sex of my life. If this is what angry sex feels like, I can handle the fights. Except the fights with Tony never felt this good. I wipe the thought away as soon as it forms. There's no space for another man between us. That was the point Alex was making tonight, and I feel it as he drives it home over and over, pushing me ever closer to the breaking point.

My lower body tightens as his pace turns more grueling. The breath leaves my lungs with every thrust that shoves me up the wall. He rolls my nipple between a forefinger and thumb, and slides a palm over my stomach to the place that aches between my legs. When he presses two fingers on my clit, it's over. I come without warning, spasming so hard around him that he falters in his rhythm.

He follows suit, dropping a curse into the kiss as he goes rigid and grows thicker inside me. The aftershocks keep my body in a vise of spasms, and he doesn't stop kissing me until I go limp. Catching me in his arms, he holds me to him as he nips my bottom lip and kisses away the sting before finally lifting his head.

The startling blue of his eyes is doused in passion, the black of his pupils big and inky with lust. He seems virile and ready to go for round two while I'm certain my legs won't carry me to the bathroom.

"How are you doing?" he asks in a tender voice, all the fight from earlier gone.

"I don't know," I admit, and I don't mean on a physical level.

He kisses my forehead. "I'll take care of you."

I flinch at the burn when he pulls out. He tests my balance before he lets go, and as I watch him with caution slipping back into my heart, he gets rid of the condom. He uses the tissues on the island counter to clean himself and dumps everything in the trashcan before adjusting his clothes. Then he looks over at me. My dress is still scrunched up around my waist, baring the underwear that sits askew, exposing my well-used lady bits.

Self-conscious now, I work my dress down over my defiled nakedness.

He makes it back to me in two long strides and takes my face between his hands. "Don't hide from me, Katyusha. You're mine to look at."

"Am I?"

His jaw sets in a hard line. "You're mine to strip naked whenever I want to look at your beautiful body. I don't care if it's in the middle of the day or while you're talking on the phone."

"That sounds one-sided," I say with lethargic contentedness, my brain still floating in the after-sex space.

"Not while my hard-on is tenting my pants." He drops his hands from my face. "I can assure you, the proof of my attraction will be very visible to you."

The sour smell of wine reaches my nostrils. Lifting the hem of my dress, I press it to my nose. "Eww. I need a shower."

He brushes his thumbs over the sensitive skin under my eyes. "You need to eat."

"I did."

"Nachos aren't food."

I blink. The words sift into my consciousness and grow ugly thorns that hook into my heart. Just like that, the lust clears and reality crashes down on me.

Pushing away his hands, I ask, "How do you know what I ate?"

He regards me through hooded eyes. "I know everything that matters."

I escape his nearness, sidestepping toward the kitchen. "You can't spy on me."

"It's not spying. It's taking an interest in your well-being," he says in a reasonable tone that only infuriates me more.

"You can't do this, Alex." My hands are shaking both from the aftermath of our wild sex and from renewed anger.

"Do what?" He follows my movement with his gaze. "Take care of you?"

"Take over my life." I ball my hands to still the trembling of my fingers.

"I've given you time. I've given you romance. What else do you want, Katerina?"

"Honesty."

He stills, a war seeming to rage in his eyes. After a moment, he says, "Honesty is *not* what you want. Believe me."

I lift my chin. "Try me."

He exhales through his nose. "Let it go, Katyusha."

"No." This time, I'm standing my ground.

He studies me for another few seconds, his body rigid, and then his shoulders slump. When he walks to the island counter,

I take three steps back. I need to keep some distance between us. His closeness makes me forget my own name. If I'm to get the truth out of him, I can't allow him to corrupt my body with his touch again. The power he has over me—be that a spell or a curse—is too potent.

Placing his hands on the counter, he looks at me from under his dark lashes. "I own an oil company and several other businesses, and in Russia, business and corruption go hand in hand. I have no choice but to deal with some very dangerous people on occasion. People who wouldn't hesitate to exploit any weakness of mine... such as you."

"What do you mean by 'dangerous people?' Are you talking about *mafia*?" I ask, feeling slightly hysterical, but somehow doing a good job of not showing it—or reacting to the knowledge that he considers me a weakness.

His grin is humorless. "Call them what you will. But that's why I went to Moscow. Some things can't be discussed over the phone, not even on a secure line."

"Go on."

"Dania's father, Mikhail Turgenev, owns a rival oil company. He's hoping to consolidate our businesses by marrying his daughter to me." He fixes me with a stare. "That marriage isn't going to happen. Nothing romantic is going to develop between Dania and me. The sex was purely physical."

"All right," I say as a fountain of relief rushes through me. I have no right to feel as light as I do, but I can't help it. "Thank you for being honest with me." For once. "Are you stalking me?"

He doesn't so much as wince at the accusation. "Just keeping you safe."

"By attacking my dates?"

His gaze darkens. "He touched what's mine. Next time, I won't be so lenient."

"You're making one-sided declarations again."

Anger washes over his features. "Are you still going to deny it after tonight? Let's face it, kiska. We can't keep our hands off each other. You're mine, end of story."

I scoff. "We've only been together for a couple of nights. That doesn't make me yours."

"It's gone beyond a couple of nights." His voice is calm, but tension is steaming off of him. "I want to see more of you. Much more. I've given you everything you asked of me, including honesty. Haven't I lived up to all of your expectations?"

I give a small shake of my head. "You can't change who you are."

"You want me to change?" he asks incredulously.

"You don't date. I do. I thought I could play it your way, but I'm afraid that's not who *I* am." Not to mention, his business dealings are dangerous. He's just told me as much.

He considers my words for a while before saying, "What are you asking of me?"

My lips feel numb as I force the words from them. "I'm asking you to go."

He blows out a sigh and fixes his gaze on the ceiling. When he finally looks back at me, his expression is unreadable. "Eat something healthy and go to bed, Katyusha. You look tired."

He raps his knuckles on the counter, and without another word, he turns and leaves my apartment.

16

MOSCOW

"*H*ave you seen this?" Vladimir pushes his phone toward Oleg and leans back in the visitor's chair facing Oleg's desk, lighting a cigarette as he watches him with shrewd attention.

Oleg takes the phone with caution. He can't fucking wait for Bes to finish the job. The sooner Vladimir gets out of his hair, the better. The man not only postponed his flight back to St. Petersburg, but he apparently also thinks he can walk uninvited into Oleg's Moscow residence, checking up on him like he's a kid who can't be trusted to do his homework.

Reminding himself with whom he's dealing, Oleg bites his tongue and keeps his face blank. All he dares is a glance at Vladimir before he takes the phone and checks the screen.

It's a video of Alexander Volkov with a young, pretty woman in his arms on the pavement in front of a bar. He fleetingly meets Vladimir's eyes before pressing *play*. The woman makes a scene as Volkov picks her up and drops her like a parcel in a

waiting car. Arching a brow, Oleg replays the whole embar-
rassing scene, which is very uncharacteristic for the calculated
and controlled billionaire.

"Interesting," he says, rubbing his jaw. "Looks like Volkov
has a romantic interest."

Vladimir blows out a thin ribbon of smoke, his eyes
narrowing with intent. "Very out of character for him."

"So?" Oleg lifts a shoulder. "He's getting some pussy."

"Volkov is always getting pussy, but never the same pussy
more than once."

Irritation eats at Oleg's gut, but he keeps his voice respectful. "What are you getting at?"

"Emotion, my dear friend, is a powerful bargaining chip."

Oleg puts the phone back on the desk. "Who's to say he feels
anything for the woman?"

Vladimir's expression is smug. "Because of how he's acted
recently. He booked out Romanoff's to take her to dinner there.
A man doesn't go to such lengths and costs if he's not seriously
invested in a woman. He's only done that once before for
Turgenev's daughter, and that was a birthday gift to a family
member of an important business associate. The dinner with
the American woman was different. She's not related to anyone
he's doing business with. She's the nurse who treated Volkov's
guard, the one who took the bullet for him. That dinner was
romantic. They left the restaurant kissing like horny teenagers.
The man I've got on Volkov's tail showed me the photos. I
know for sure that this woman, Katherine Morrell, means
something to him."

That expression alone is enough to make Oleg's back go
rigid. Vladimir has no right to meddle in the job. Oleg said he
would take care of it. Meddling in another man's business is

like overstepping boundaries in his territory—a blatant show of disrespect. "Is that so? How did you figure that out?"

"I sent a man to snatch her. Unfortunately, she got away, but not without a good scare."

Oleg stills. He doesn't give a shit about the girl. For all he cares, Vladimir can give her scares for the rest of her life. What bothers him is the fragile agreement he's got with the NYPD. They have a deal, for fuck's sake. If Vladimir starts stirring up the waters in New York City, the commissioner Oleg has in his pocket may just decide the deal's off.

"What did you do?" Oleg asks in a voice a tad bit scratchy.

"Don't worry." Vladimir takes a drag on the cigarette and blows the smoke straight into Oleg's face. "He made it look like a mugging."

Oleg swallows but doesn't blink, not even when the smoke burns his eyes. He doesn't dare show weakness or disagreement. Inwardly, he calms himself by imagining putting that cigarette out in Vladimir's eye.

"What happened?" he asks like a good lapdog. He knows what's expected of him and how to play the part.

Vladimir grins, his fleshy jowls shaking. "Volkov came to her rescue. He left Mikhail Turgenev in Romanoff's to go running after her like a dog saving his favorite bone."

"Fine, so he feels something for her." Maybe. "What do we care?"

"Bes is having difficulty getting his target. Alex is too well guarded, too careful, especially after the failed shooting attempt. But now he has a weakness."

"You want me to get the girl to get to him?"

"Took you long enough to figure that out. Is the old brain less sharp these days?"

The rebuke gets Oleg's hackles up. "Just checking if you want a specific course of action."

"Be creative." Vladimir's jovial gaze hardens as he stumps out his cigarette on the polished surface of Oleg's ten-thousand-dollar antique cherry-wood desk and drops the butt on his priceless Persian rug. "Use her to get Volkov alone. Kidnap her, kill her... I don't fucking care." He pushes to his feet, the action heavy. His measured words are thick with a threat, this one aimed at Oleg. "Just do the job. Alexander is much too powerful to fuck this up."

Oleg swallows again, getting up so as not to disrespect Vladimir by remaining seated, even as his hands shake with the urge to strangle the man facing him. "I'll get the results you want, but you have to let me do this in my own time. I have an agreement with the NYPD that—"

"Your time has run out." Vladimir turns for the door, paying Oleg the ultimate insult by giving him his back as he says, "Do it, or I'll find someone else."

17

*A*nother crazy work week flies by while the first early snow covers the streets with a layer of white powder that quickly turns muddy in the late morning. Alex calls every day, but I reject his calls.

We're in a strange kind of ceasefire where Yuri doesn't show up to drive me around and Dimitri isn't standing on the street corner of my apartment building or sitting in the same subway carriage as me, at least not within my sight. No more gifts and meals are delivered. Alex must've realized I'm immune to them. Well, kind of immune, because I'd be lying if I said the gestures didn't touch me in some way. Who doesn't like to receive flowers and beautiful messages hand-scribbled in cards?

What I minded weren't the gestures, but the motivation behind them. Alex sent me flowers not because he wanted to, but because he thought that's what I wanted him to do, which shows how little he understands me. It's not about the dinners or the flowers for me. It's about bonding, building a meaningful relationship. And since a meaningful relationship isn't Alex's objective, we keep on turning in this infinite circle of exhausting unfinished business, with him chasing and me running.

Joanne says I'm over-analyzing and over-thinking the whole situation. According to her, guys all have the same agenda when they send flowers. She says it's just a different kind of foreplay or seduction. When I look at it like that, I have to conclude that Alex is really pursuing me hard. For someone who can have any woman in the world, he seems to truly want me. There's hope in that, a small possibility that there's something more in our attraction than just the sex. If it were only the sex, he would've already replaced me with someone else.

And maybe he has. The mere possibility makes my chest ache. I don't want him for only sex, but I also don't want him to have anyone else. It's a selfish notion that borders on jealousy. Oh, who am I kidding? I'm swamp-monster green when I imagine him with another woman. Just look what seeing him with Dania did to me.

Round and round in circles my mind goes. While I'm debating seeing him or not, I'm avoiding him as I try to come to some kind of decision that involves a truce between my mind and my heart. As much as the latter is begging me to give in, the rational side of me is screaming for me to run in the opposite direction and protect my feelings. And more than my feelings. The man has dealings with the Russian mafia, for crying out loud.

To distract myself, I go out for lunch with a couple of the nurses I work with, and I have dinner at my mom's place twice during the week. I cram every free minute I have full of activities and people to avoid coming to the decision I can't bear to make.

Joanne cheers me on from the sidelines, encouraging me to take the biggest risk of my life, but I don't tell her how scared I am that Alex will crush me when he finally leaves. I simply can't admit the strength of my feelings, not even to myself. Neither do I tell her about the criminals he deals with. Doing so will only put her in a compromising position.

I prepare myself for another pep talk as I get ready to meet Joanne for a Sunday lunch in Chinatown. For a change, I have the whole day to myself. I've spent the morning cleaning and doing grocery shopping, and I'm looking forward to a few hours of relaxing time with my friend.

The restaurant is a cozy place with only six tables and no menu. The meal consists of five courses and can last the whole afternoon.

I rub my gloved hands together and shake the dusting of snow from my coat in the foyer before entering the restaurant. It's only twelve, but all the tables are already occupied. The nameless restaurant is popular, so Joanne booked our table weeks in advance. A whiff of coriander and lemongrass reaches me as I shrug out of my coat and look around the noisy, packed space for my friend. Every round table can seat six people, and Joanne and I are used to having four strangers dining with us. The place is small and the owner fills every seat, resulting in one often sharing meals with strangers. It's part of the unexpected, exotic charm of the place.

Joanne's copper curls catch the light. As I suspected, every chair at the table where she's seated is already filled, except for the one on her left. She hasn't spotted me because she's deep in conversation with the guy on her right. So deep, in fact, that her nose is almost buried in his neck.

Going over, I call out, "Hi," before I reach them to warn her of my presence. I don't want to make her feel like I've walked in on something private.

She jerks her head up at the sound of my voice, her cheeks flushing bright red. "Oh, hi. You're early."

"I'm always early," I say with a smile that I follow up with a raised brow aimed in silent question at my friend.

I cast a glance in the direction of the man, who looks between Joanne and me as if he's waiting for an introduction. He wears his brown hair in a manbun and has a tan, like he spends a lot of time outdoors. His green eyes are warm and friendly as he assesses me.

"Um, Kate." Joanne pushes a bouncy curl behind her ear. "This is Ricky."

He leans over Joanne and extends a hand. "Hi, Kate. Joanne has told me a lot about you."

Stunned, I accept his handshake. Joanne didn't mention anything about bringing a date. "It's nice to meet you," I say, draping my coat over the back of the chair before taking my seat.

"I owe you an apology for crashing your lunch," he says to me. "I slept over at Joanne's last night, so I made her drag me along." He flashes her a heated smile. "It's your own fault for not feeding me breakfast, baby girl."

At the endearment, the blush spreads from Joanne's cheeks to her neck. "I hope you don't mind, Kate. I didn't have time to warn you."

"We literally woke up thirty minutes ago," Ricky says. "It was a race to get here. That was my fault too. You can pin all the blame on me."

This is going so fast my head is spinning. I drop my gaze and notice Joanne's hand is clasped in his, resting on his thigh.

Wow. I'm so happy for her. It's about time she got her mind on something other than spreadsheets and figures. "Of course I don't mind. How did you guys meet?"

"He almost ran me over yesterday," Joanne says, making puppy eyes at her date.

"She had her nose in her phone." Ricky gives her a peck on the cheek. "Wasn't watching where she was going."

"Yep. And he stopped to see if I was all right," she says, "not caring that he was holding up the whole street. Then he somehow convinced me I needed something warm and sweet to drink to ease the shock."

"Which turned into a dinner," he says, kissing her again. "And the dinner—"

Joanne raises a palm, blushing to her roots this time. "I think she gets the idea."

This is so not like the friend I know. Joanne has never been the blushing type. Ricky has really swept her off her feet.

By the time the first course of vegetable broth with noodles arrives, I know Ricky is an artist who's making a name for himself with metal sculpturing. His work caught the eye of a big gallery owner, who offered to exhibit his sculptures, and from there, his work took the media by storm. He's originally from Brazil—Ricky is short for Ricardo—but grew up in Canada, hence the absence of a Portuguese accent.

He's agreeable and fun, and clearly mad about Joanne. He never misses an opportunity to touch her, and seeing them so into each other warms my heart.

"Would you like to join us for some Latin dancing tonight?" he asks when we've finished our bow ties for dessert. "I promised Jo I'd show her a club that's open on Sunday evenings. The owners are friends of my parents. We have to work off all this food we've just eaten."

Latin dancing? I don't know the first thing about samba or merengue, and I don't want to be the third wheel. They deserve a romantic evening alone.

"I promised my mom I'd go over for dinner," I say, "but thanks for the invite."

"Maybe next time," he says as our waitress brings the bill.

After paying, Joanne and I excuse ourselves to visit the ladies' room while Ricky gathers our coats and makes his way to the foyer.

"Holy shit," I say, grabbing her arm when we're out of earshot. "Why didn't you tell me?"

Joanne glows. "He's great, isn't he?"

"I really like him. You seem to have hit it off straight away."

"I never thought I'd believe in love at first sight, but this feels like fate."

Holding her back, I slow my step. "He's great, Jo, and I'm so happy for you. Just don't fall for him too fast. You barely know him."

She gives me a wistful look. "I know what matters."

"I'm not trying to be pessimistic. I'm just trying to protect you from getting hurt."

Stopping, she turns to face me. "He's not Alex, Kate."

"That's not what I said."

"If anything, you should be worried about Ricky. He's the one who wants six kids and a dog. I'll be happy with a few nights of his sexy body in my bed."

"Wow. Sounds pretty serious. Just don't let him rush you if you're not sure."

She takes my hand and gives it a squeeze. "That's your analytical brain speaking. You know that you have to let your heart win in some life decisions, right?"

I make a face. "I do. I let it."

"Oh, yeah? Like when?"

"Every time I order something from a menu."

"Liar." She slaps my arm playfully. "You analyze every ingredient and have an internal debate about whether it's cruelty-free before you order so much as a coffee from Starbucks."

"I'm not that bad," I say with disdain, but she's already walking toward the ladies' room, laughing at me over her shoulder.

"You make me sound like a stick in the mud," I complain, hurrying after her.

"Sometimes, Kate, I'm afraid you are."

"What?" I stop at the door, gaping at her.

"I love you, but you really need to learn how to let your hair down."

"I do!"

"Really?" She lifts a brow. "When was the last time you did something impulsive?"

"I went on a date with Phillip."

"That wasn't *your* impulse. You went because your mother wanted you to."

"I still went. That counts."

"Okay," she says, pushing open the door. "But it didn't work out, did it?"

"I told you." I follow her inside. "We didn't connect."

She goes into the first stall and closes the door. "Because?"

"Because there was no spark, no attraction."

"Why?"

I shrug, even though she can't see me. "Not everyone has chemistry."

"Or maybe it's because you're still stuck on another man."

"I'm over him," I say defensively, but the words sound weak, even to myself.

"Right," she says in a knowing tone.

When the door opens and two women enter, she falls silent and I'm stuck in front of the mirror, unwilling to face myself. How ironic is it that her new guy's idea of six kids and a dog appeals to me, while the man I'm attracted to wants nothing but a few nights with my body in his bed? If I mentioned six kids or a dog, he'd probably run for the hills.

There's a line by the time Joanne is done, so we thankfully don't discuss my inhibitions any longer as we wash our hands and make our way to the front to meet Ricky.

He holds Joanne's coat open for her and buttons it up, reminding me of the way Alex took care of me. I miss the attentive care of a man. Seeing Joanne and Ricky together both gladdens me and makes me miss what I don't have.

Chewing my lip, I contemplate this in-between place in which Alex and I exist. We're not in any kind of relationship—neither sexual nor emotional—but contrary to what I've been telling myself and everyone else, we're not completely over either. We feel like unfinished business. Not wanting the memory of his strong hands and skillful kisses to eat away at my resolve, I push the subject of my tormented thoughts away.

I decline Joanne's offer to share their taxi to Brooklyn. Instead, I walk down to the Staten Island ferry. I'm so full after the long, five-course lunch that I can't eat another morsel, but my mom promised to cook something light, and inviting me over for dinner is just an excuse to see me. Being as close as we are, I'm always happy to oblige.

Eager to share Joanne's exciting news with my mom, I let myself in with my key without knocking and hurry to the kitchen, where the only light in the apartment is burning. My mom's voice reaches me with the aroma of my favorite split-pea soup. She's chatting amiably, probably to her neighbor, Mrs. Davis, who drops in from time to time.

I round the corner with a grin on my face, only to stop dead in the doorway.

The picture in front of me burns into my brain, but my mind has difficulty processing it. My mom is stirring something in a pot on the stove, her cheeks flushed and her eyes shining, and in a chair by the table sits none other than Alex Volkov.

18

"*H*ello, Katyusha," Alex says in a deep, level voice. The bulk of his frame looks ridiculous in the small chair. He reminds me of the big, bad wolf in one of the three pigs' little houses. His size makes the room look smaller, and the walls close in around me as he pins me with a stare that dissects like a blade. His dark hair is perfectly trimmed, and the black rollneck jersey he wears with faded blue jeans shows off the width of his shoulders and the impressive size of his biceps. Despite the casual attire and relaxed pose, he looks no less dangerous or intimidating than he did in a power suit, rescuing me from an attacker in a dark alley.

"What are you doing here?" I ask when I finally manage to find my voice.

He waves a big hand toward my mom. "Laura invited me to stay for dinner. Your mother is very nice."

They're on a first-name basis? Already?

"How long have you been here?" I ask, suspicion coiling in my gut.

He holds my gaze without faltering. "I just came over for a cup of coffee and a slice of Laura's delicious chocolate cake, but she invited me to stay for dinner." He narrows his strikingly blue eyes so fractionally I doubt my mom notices, but I do. "You don't mind, do you?"

"Of course she doesn't," Mom says, waving away the comment as she finishes stirring the soup before coming over to kiss my cheek. "Why would she?" She points the wooden spoon at me. "Shame on you for not telling me about your handsome date."

"Hopefully," Alex says, his voice laden with nuance, "soon to be boyfriend."

"Oh, how wonderful." My mom beams. "It's about time you had a man in your life again, Katie."

I stare daggers at him. How dare he use my mom against me?

"Dinner is ready." She flits around to collect bowls and cutlery, flustered like she usually is when she's trying to impress someone. Pushing a tray with the crockery and soup spoons into my hands, she says, "Why don't you set the table, Katie?"

Alex gets up. "I'll help."

When he takes the tray from my hands, our fingers brush. Tingles ignite under my skin, traveling up my arm. The corner of his mouth lifts as he looks down at me, knowing very well the reaction he elicits.

Turning my back on him, I set the table in the kitchen. I'm bristling inside, but I can't bring myself to say something in front of my mom and shatter her obvious delight at having my *date* over for dinner.

From the way she fusses over him, dishing up a double portion and asking if he'd like more salt, pepper, bread, or anything at all, she approves of my choice of a so-called date. She'd be horrified if she found out I don't have a choice in the matter right now.

She turns to Alex when we're seated at the table. "We chatted the whole afternoon away, but you never told me what you do for a living."

Like me at first, my mom doesn't know he's one of the wealthiest—and most persistent—men in the world. She doesn't read the financial news, so the Russian oligarch's name has never blipped on her radar.

Her ignorance doesn't faze him. He smiles warmly at her. "I'm in the oil industry, but I dabble in real estate, clean energy, information technology, pharmaceuticals, and many other investments."

Mom blinks. I think it's starting to dawn on her that he's wealthier than she suspected. Undaunted, she dips her spoon into the soup and continues her interrogation. "What brought you here from Russia?"

"Business opportunities," he says evasively.

My mom's face brightens as she asks hopefully, "Then you live here permanently?"

Could she be any more transparent? She may as well tell him straight to his face that she hopes he's not going to whisk me away to a foreign country. I wish I could disappear inside my bowl of soup.

"I split my time between my various business holdings," he says. "But I plan to be in New York for the foreseeable future."

"Great," my mom says, patting his hand. "If you've settled

here, you won't take my daughter away to a faraway place like Russia."

"Mom!" My cheeks burn with embarrassment. "Alex and I—"

"You don't have to worry about that," Alex says in his hypnotic Russian accent. "I have a house in Brooklyn."

I turn a glaring gaze on him, but he's immune to my scolding, putting on a charming show for my mom as he compliments her on the food and asks questions about her medical condition, obviously a subject they discussed before my arrival.

Mom falls head over heels for Alex's charm, not that I can blame her. He's good at making conversation and showing a genuine interest in her life and her daughter—me. Over the course of the dinner, they chat like old friends, with Alex doing his best to draw me into the conversation, and then they talk about their favorite local dishes and share a few laughs about anecdotes from my childhood over after-dinner tea.

It's close to ten o'clock when we finally clear the table.

"My goodness," Mom says, gathering our dirty bowls, "I haven't laughed this much in ages." She pauses to pat Alex's arm. "I'm so glad you came over." Giving me a chiding look, she adds, "I can't fathom why Katie hasn't invited you sooner."

"Yes," he drawls, pinning me with one of his meaningful stares. "Me neither."

When my mom makes her way to the sink, Alex intercepts her. "Let me take that." He takes the bowls from her hands. "This is heavy."

"Oh"—Mom gives him another approving look—"that's so gallant of you. Thank you very much."

While I rinse the dishes, Alex packs the dishwasher, brushing our hips together on purpose every time he reaches for a bowl. Mom gives us space, wiping down the counters and the table as she hums contentedly to herself.

The kitchen is spotless before Alex and I say our goodbyes. Mom must assume that we'll leave together in his car, because she kisses Alex on the cheek like an old acquaintance when she sees us off at the door and says, "Please make sure Katie locks her door." She adds in a conspiratorial tone, "Unless you're staying over at her place, of course. Then you can lock the door yourself."

She did *not* just say that. I wish the earth would open up and swallow me.

"Bye, Mom." I grab Alex's arm and all but drag him to the street before he can make a promise I don't intend to keep.

A midnight-blue sports car is parked across the street. I noticed the fancy car absentmindedly when I arrived, but I thought it belonged to someone visiting the neighbors. It doesn't surprise me when Alex heads in that direction. Neither does the presence of the black car parked a short distance away. Alex brought protection.

The minute my mom closes the door after a last wave, I let go of Alex's arm as if it's on fire and put distance between us.

"How could you do that?" I grit out, keeping my voice low so as not to attract any unwanted attention from the neighbors.

His mouth curves as he looks down at me. "Do what?"

"Don't play games with me. How could you drag my mom into this?"

He shrugs. "I wanted to meet her. Isn't that how it works? We go on a few dates, I send you flowers and all the things women like, and then you introduce me to your parents."

"You had no right to come here." I take a breath and moderate my tone. "My mom is unwell, Alex. She's suffering enough as is. I don't need to add disappointment to her burden."

He watches me quietly for a few moments. Just when I think he's not going to grace me with an answer, he wraps his arms around me and pulls me close. "You're shivering. It's cold."

His warmth seeps through my clothes and penetrates my skin. It feels good to be in the circle of his arms, but I'm not going to admit it.

"I didn't mean to upset you or your mother," he says in a soft tone. "I just wanted to take this to the next level since you seem too stubborn to admit we deserve a chance."

"I don't know what you're talking about," I mumble against his chest, not fighting his tight hold.

"I'd hate to disappoint your mother. I really like her. I meant it when I said she's nice. So why don't you come home with me, and everyone will be happy."

"Everyone?"

I pull away to look into his eyes. Snowflakes are falling around us, clinging to his dark lashes. The blue of his eyes is gray in the dim glow of the yellow lamplight. That gray bleeds into the black of his pupils, but the lack of color doesn't make the look in them any less intense.

"Come home with me," he urges, tightening his arms around me. "Give us another shot, Katyusha. We deserve it, don't you think?" He brushes a thumb over my numb, frozen lips. "A connection like ours doesn't happen every day."

No, it doesn't. I'm not sure if it's our chemistry, the longing that stirred in me when I saw Joanne and Ricky together, or how well my mom got on with Alex that makes me consider his suggestion. It was a low blow from Alex to play that dirty, inviting himself to my mom's house, but my mom never behaved like this with Tony. She never made a secret of disliking my ex. She merely tolerated him for my sake, which meant acting politely on the rare occasions when we'd have dinner together. With Alex, these occasions wouldn't be rare. It's easy to picture the three of us sharing many more of these congenial moments.

It's that idyllic, wishful part of me that wavers, and Alex is enough in tune with me to notice. The moment he senses my weakness, he swoops in with a kiss, taking away the last of my restraint and all my reason. His lips are warm, his kiss tender yet deliberate. There's nothing tentative about the caress or the hand he slides down my back to cup my buttocks. He knows how to make me melt, and I love how he takes control.

"Katyusha," he groans into my mouth, making my arousal spike instantaneously.

Like all the other times, I cling to him as he presses our bodies together, letting me feel his hardness. My moan is fuel on his fire. He kneads my ass, impatiently sucking my tongue into his mouth.

"I want you," he says in a voice thick with need.

I want him too, enough to slip my hands under his coat and drag them over the hard edges of his abs to my prize under the waistline of his pants.

"Katerina…" He catches my wrist. "If you don't want to be fucked on the pavement in front of your mother's house, I suggest you let me take you home."

My breath catches. Giving voice to my decision will be my final surrender. He won't let me take it back. Once I've given him my consent, he'll consume me. But I'm losing the battle against logic, against that voice in my head that warns me not to get involved with a man so dangerous. The feelings he elicits are much too strong.

He waits, tense but patient. Yet when I finally give a small nod, the tight set of his shoulders doesn't ease. He holds on to my wrist, keeping me close to him as he demands, "Say it. Give me your answer in words."

My answer isn't meek. If I'm taking this leap, I'm not doing it in a half-assed manner. The step is too significant, too huge. It's all or nothing. My voice is strong when I give him my all. "Yes."

He looks simultaneously relieved and victorious. Crushing me to his body, he takes my mouth in a brutal kiss. It's so overwhelming my knees buckle. He steadies me with an arm around my waist, tearing himself away to stare down at my face.

His voice is laced with lust. "Come."

Not giving me any more lenience, he pulls me to the fancy sports car. The black car starts up, its headlights coming on even before Alex has opened the door for me and helped me inside. My face heats when I think about how we were grabbing at each other right there on the pavement, under the streetlight for anyone to see—including Yuri, who I'm assuming will be following us in the black car.

Alex seems unbothered about who bears witness as he palms my breast while securing my seatbelt. He's rushed, his need running as high as mine.

I lean back into the butter-soft leather as he starts the engine and heat fills the interior. His hand is already between my legs before he's steered us onto the road. I stifle a moan as he brushes a finger over my clit and then moves lower to find the wetness that's gathered there for him.

To my dismay, I see the curtains in the window of my mom's

bedroom move as he passes her house. I bet she's been watching through the window. Just as well I decided to let him take me home. Otherwise, she would've known something wasn't right.

Not that I can think about right and wrong when he's tracing my slit ever so lightly with the pad of his finger.

He lets go when he needs to change gears, leaving me cold. I want his hand back there. I want him on my skin and inside me.

Taking my hand, he places it on his thigh. I tighten my fingers on the hard male leg, feeling those powerful muscles tighten as he steps on the clutch. He handles the car with ease. We're sliding effortlessly through the traffic while I'm burning up inside.

For some reason, I feel at home even before he pulls up in front of his house. I feel like I belong inside the warm safety of this car with this dominant, possessive man. The front garden with the broken angel weeping on the fountain steps is already one of my favorite places, and when he leads me inside his house, it feels as if I've seen the contemporary paintings and decorations a thousand times instead of twice.

His bedroom is like an old family resort that welcomes its visitors every year—a second home away from home. It's like booking the same room in the same hotel for every Easter holiday. Everything is familiar, except him. I can never get used to him, or to the perfection of his body as he peels away his layers of clothes. By the time he's stripped down to his underwear, I've barely shrugged out of my coat.

Coming to me naked, he pushes me backward with a hand on my shoulder. My coat and bag fall on the floor, forgotten at my feet as he steers me deeper into the room. My knees bend when they hit the mattress, and I'm on my back before a gasp leaves my lips.

He crawls over me like a predator about to devour its prey, but then he takes his time to arrange me how he wants me with my hands above my head and my legs pressed together. I'm fully dressed, wearing my wool dress, thick tights, and long boots. He doesn't undress me. He simply drags the dress up over my hips and wiggles the tights with my underwear down my thighs. Trapped by the tights, I can't open my legs, but that doesn't seem to be his aim. He's too impatient.

"Don't move," he says, dragging a gaze over how I'm presented.

The hard length of his cock brushes against my naked thigh as he leans over me to get a condom from the nightstand drawer. The crest is slick with precum. His muscles ripple in the glow of the lamp, mesmerizing me. I lift a hand to trail my fingers over the dark dusting of hair on his chest, but he catches my wrist and places it above my head again.

"Like this," he says, burning a path over me with his eyes.

I lie back, relaxing deeper into the mattress and giving over to the passive position he wants me to take. I watch as he sheaths the condom and strokes himself. I'm already impossibly wet when he reaches for the buttons of my dress, slowly popping each one through the hole. He stops at my waist, baring only the lacy cups of my bra. It's a pushup that gives me the cleavage my breasts don't manage unassisted, and when he unclasps the clip in the front, the cups fall open, letting my breasts spill out.

My nipples tighten instantaneously. The temperature in the room is warm, but I'm so sensitive that the contact with the air distends the tips into hard points that ache for his touch. He doesn't disappoint me. Filling his hands with my curves, he plumps them up and lowers his head for a kiss. When the wet heat of his tongue makes contact with my left breast, my whole body jerks.

He hums his approval as he licks and gives a soft nip. "Very sensitive. You're going to come so hard for me tonight."

My body prepares itself at the promise, more liquid heat gathering in my core.

He takes his time kissing my breasts, starting on the outer curve and working his way to the center. I'm a squirming mess when he finally takes the tip into his mouth again, sucking deeply. I arch off the bed with a moan, lost in the sensation that coils around my abdomen and ends with a pulsing ache in my clit.

He sucks and licks, grazing me with his stubble until my skin is oversensitive and the scruff on his cheeks feels too abrasive. The side of my breast is red and raw, sporting two hickeys when he finally gives it a rest only to attack the other breast.

The slow torture starts all over again. He's gentle, but he bites and sucks my curves and nipple for so long that I can't stand the touching any longer when he finally moves to my mouth. In contrast, the kiss he plants on my lips is chaste. It's a small warning, a tender consolation, before he flips me over and drags me to my knees. Again, he arranges my dress around my waist, exposing my lower body. My breasts are swaying lightly, free for the exploration of his wandering hands. He tests his reach, cupping one in each palm and uttering his approval with a satisfied hum that comes from deep in his chest.

"You look so dirty with your underwear around your knees," he says in a low, lazy voice, stroking a hand over my back. "So willing like this, on your knees."

The dirty talk makes my insides clench. I'm so needy it won't take much to make me come.

He bends over me and presses hot, soft, decadent words to my ear. "Are you going to take me like a good girl?"

I whimper in response, long lost to the need he makes me feel.

"Is that a yes?" he demands, kissing the soft spot behind my ear.

"Yes," I say in a breathy voice.

"All of me?"

I turn my head to look at him. His face is wicked, diabolic in his lust. He looks like both a devil and an angel, as if he may sprout horns and wings at once.

"Take me, Alex. Don't make me wait."

He grabs my face in a big hand, splaying his fingers over my cheeks, and steals a wet, sloppy kiss. "I like it when you tell me what you want."

"You," I say without hesitation.

"Yes," he agrees, something dark flashing in his eyes, something that looks a lot like possessive satisfaction. "Only me."

He releases my face to grab my hip. Taking his cock in one hand, he positions the crest at my entrance. Vividly remembering how big he is, I brace myself, locking my elbows and lifting my hips to offer more.

He moves forward carefully, slowly stretching me, but with my legs pressed together, the friction feels more intense. Despite how wet I am, I battle to take him. He inches forward and then slides back, using my arousal to lubricate himself as he slips deeper inch by inch.

When he's fully inside me, we're both breathing hard. I need him to move to find the release that remains out of reach, but he's taking his time, rolling his hips instead of pumping. The circular movement stirs something inside.

Somehow, it feels deeper and more unbearable than when he takes me hard.

I reach behind me and catch his wrist where he's gripping my hip, urging him to move, but he lowers his chest over my back and palms a breast.

"Alex, please."

"Shh." He kisses the top of my spine. "I'll get you there. Just let me enjoy you first."

Enjoying me first means being buried deep inside me while he plays with my nipples and strokes my clit. It means pushing me to the edge and leaving me hanging until I'm certain I'll go out of my mind. He appeases me with a few shallow strokes, giving me a teasing preview of what's to come, all the while driving my need higher. It's only when my arms give out and I catch myself on my elbows that he starts to pump his hips.

My vision blurs from the force of his thrusts. Sweet relief winds closer, coiling tighter. The rougher he gets, the softer my body goes around him. I scrunch the sheets in my fists as the pleasure climbs, winding me even tighter. A hot current of ecstasy runs all the way from the base of my spine to my toes.

I open my mouth on a moan and swallow a gasp when he rolls my clit between his fingers and increases his pace. "I'm going to—"

The rest of what I was going to say is lost as I orgasm. I go over the edge, not caring how far or fast I'm falling, because even as I go down, my body collapsing onto the mattress, his promise in my ears is a sweet compensation.

"I've got you."

He covers me with his body, letting his heat wrap around me while keeping his weight on his arms. We stay like this, me in the safe cocoon of his arms with him buried inside me, until I drift off. I'm vaguely aware of the mattress dipping and a warm blanket replacing his heat. A short while later, the blanket lifts, and a warm, wet towel is pressed between my legs. The warmth is soothing, absorbing some of the ache.

It's dark in the room. He must've switched off the bedside lamp to let me sleep. I can't see his expression, but I can feel his meticulous attention as he undresses me like a doll. When I'm free from the restraining clothes and underwear, he pulls me against his body under the covers. His skin is damp and smells clean, like he's had a shower.

"Rest," he says, kissing the top of my head as he tugs me to his chest. "I'm not letting you go."

I stiffen, all drowsiness fading at his words. Literally, they mean he'll hold me for now, and maybe all through the night, but there's an underlying darkness to his words, a nuance that hints at forever.

"Relax," he coaxes, kissing my neck.

This is too important to let go. I utter an uncomfortable laugh. "If you put it like that, it sounds rather sinister."

His hot breath fans over my nape. "Does it?"

"It sounds as if you mean forever, like locking the princess in the tower kind of forever."

I hold my breath, waiting for him to deny the silly deduction, but he says, "I would've preferred you didn't run away in the first place."

Tensing more, I whisper, "You know why I didn't want to see you."

"And I explained why running the background check on you was necessary."

I turn in his arms to face him, the recollection assaulting me anew. I don't know how I could've forgotten about that. Maybe

I suppressed it because I don't want to acknowledge the truth: that the man in front of me is not someone I should trust.

He must see something on my face because he says, "I apologized for running that background check on you more than once, but I'll apologize again if it makes you feel better." He adds in a softer tone, "I thought we moved past this."

He's right. I can't continue to harp on something he's repeatedly apologized for. Yet I still feel a little bitter over the invasion of privacy and the perceived betrayal, no matter how much sense it logically makes. "I suppose then it's a good thing you didn't find anything dubious in the information you dug up about me."

His expression darkens as determination laces his tone. "Either way, it wouldn't have made a difference."

"No?" I arch an eyebrow.

"Like I told you before, I would've made you mine no matter what I found."

With that heavy declaration, he plants a tender kiss on my forehead. "Go to sleep. I've worn you out."

19

*S*oft shaking pulls me from a deep sleep. I open my eyes, feeling groggy and sore, and then I smile as I remember why I'm hurting inside and out. Alex woke me up twice in the night, but the climaxes he brought me to make my tiredness and aching body worth every second.

The man responsible for my worn-out state is standing next to the bed with a glass in one hand, gently stroking my bare shoulder. He's dressed in tailored gray pants and a black open-neck shirt, looking unfairly fresh, handsome, and alert.

"Wake up, Katyusha," he says in a sexy, deep grumble that makes my insides clench despite how bruised they feel. His tone turns regretful. "It's time to get ready for work."

Groaning, I sit up and rub my eyes. The curtains are already pulled open. The room is basked in the soft light of early morning, the weak sunbeams filtering through the window.

"Here." He holds out the glass, which contains a fizzy orange liquid.

Automatically reaching for it, I ask, "What is this?"

"Vitamin C." He sits down on the edge of the bed. "You need the boost this morning. I don't want you to get sick because I didn't let you rest enough and made you go out in the cold to work when you're overtired. We'll catch a full night's sleep tonight, I promise."

I raise a brow. "We will?"

He takes my hand and brushes a thumb over my knuckles. "I thought you'd welcome a break from my advances. I'm sure you must be tender, no?"

I blush like a teenager, heat crawling over my cheeks at the accurate yet somewhat clinical observation. "I wasn't referring to having more sex. I was asking if we're spending another night together." At the darkening of his expression, I add, "So soon. I'm sure you're a busy man with a hectic schedule."

"Of course we are," he says a tad too forcefully. "Would you prefer we sleep over at your place?"

I want to argue that we don't have to sleep over at each other's every night, but the challenge in his gaze tells me he's up for a fight and determined to get his way. It's not that I don't want to sleep in his arms and benefit from his incredible skills and super-hot body every night. I just don't want to put him under any kind of pressure. For a man who's never been into dating, our newfound relationship is moving pretty fast—if it can even be called a relationship. Is that the label for a prolonged one-night stand?

I might be back together with Alex, but I still don't know where I stand.

Instead of making a big deal out of it, I say, "No, we don't have to sleep over at my place. Here is fine." It's certainly more comfortable than my tiny studio and twin bed.

"Good," he says, approval lighting up his eyes. "I'll let you get ready. Breakfast will be waiting downstairs when you're done. I got Yuri to fetch your clothes from your apartment." Getting to his feet, he adds with a smile, "I hope you don't mind."

He hopes I don't mind? He mentioned it like an afterthought, as if the statement carries no weight. The fact that he has a key to my apartment and sent his driver to go through my closet and personal belongings doesn't strike him as another invasion of my privacy.

When he bends down and kisses the crown of my head, I swallow the retort that's on the tip of my tongue. Alex has strange notions of right and wrong, and the borders of personal space seem to be fuzzy for him, but making sure I have clean clothes to wear to work is a considerate act. He probably did it to let me sleep an extra hour, as I now don't have to travel back to my place to change before going to work.

He's already at the door before I gather my thoughts. "You got up early to arrange this for me, didn't you?"

His smile turns ten degrees warmer. "I needed a workout and a shower. I was up anyway."

I feel the effect of that smile in the heat that spreads through my chest. "Thank you," I say softly.

Whenever he's angry, the blue of his eyes looks like the Arctic glaciers. Now the color is the hue of the sky on a summer day. His Russian accent is a soft, melodic sound in my ears as he says, "You're welcome."

He holds my gaze for another moment, and then he turns and leaves.

Shaking off my reverie, I check the clock on his nightstand. I have thirty minutes to get ready and have breakfast.

I down the fizzy drink, thankful for his thoughtfulness, and hurry through a shower. With towels wrapped around my wet hair and my body, I search for the clean clothes he mentioned, but there's nothing in the bathroom or bedroom. Not wanting to step out of his room dressed only in a towel in case I run into any of his staff, I dart into his walk-in closet to borrow one of his T-shirts and a pair of shorts, only to halt in the doorway.

When Alex mentioned that Yuri had gone to my apartment for my clothes, I imagined a change of clothes—a pair of jeans and a sweater maybe—not a solid portion of Alex's massive closet filled with my dresses, jeans, and blouses. Padding inside as if I'm walking on glass, I gape at the shelves filled with my favorite T-shirts and turtlenecks. My shoes are lined up neatly on the bottom shelf. I open a drawer to find my underwear arranged inside. The second drawer holds my socks and scarves. This isn't a change of clothes. This is my whole closet, winter as well as summer garments.

Summer is two seasons away. Summer clothes scream long-term.

I don't get it. Why would Alex move everything into his house? He mentioned keeping a few items of clothing here, but *all of them*? Baffled, I grab the first sweater my hand falls on and pull it on with a pair of jeans and my Uggs. I take a few minutes to dry my hair, leaving it naturally wavy, and apply mascara and lip gloss before looking for my coat and handbag. My bag sits on the dresser next to a vase of fresh flowers, but my coat is nowhere to be seen. Alex must've taken it downstairs.

As I exit into the hallway, I almost bump into a hulk of a man who's making his way to the staircase with brisk strides.

"Pardon me, ma'am," he says, stepping aside to let me go ahead of him.

"Igor." I recognize him from the hospital. At six-foot-ten, he looks a lot bigger on his feet than on a hospital gurney. His blond hair is cropped close to his skull and his sharp jaw is clean-shaven. The ashen pallor of his face from the last time I saw him has been replaced with a healthy color. "Please, call me Kate." I motion at his chest. "How's the wound?"

"Pretty much healed." He offers me a semblance of a smile. "Almost as good as new."

"I'm glad to hear that. You look well."

"Much better than when we met. I haven't yet had the chance to thank you for saving my life."

"That's very kind of you, but I can't take the credit. The doctor did all the work. I only stabilized you."

"Thank you all the same." He gives a stiff, military kind of nod. "I'm grateful for your capable hands."

"You're welcome. I'm happy that you're fully recovered." I wasn't going to bring this up, but since the opportunity has presented itself... "Um, Igor?"

He watches me with a level stare, giving me his full attention. "Kate?"

"I was wondering... Who was it that shot you?"

His expression betrays nothing. He doesn't move a muscle. There's not even a twitch of his eyelashes. "We're not sure yet, but Mr. Volkov is working on finding out."

"Does he have any suspicions? What did the police say?"

He regards me with the same blank look. "You'll have to ask Mr. Volkov about that."

"Right." It seems that's the only reply I'll ever get from Alex's staff. Well, it was worth a try. "Take care of yourself."

I'm on the first step when he speaks again.

"Kate? I wouldn't ask too many questions if I were you."

Freezing, I turn to face him. "Why's that?"

"Alex's business shouldn't concern you. The less you know, the better. It's for your own safety."

I swallow back a denial. I want to say that if Alex's life is in danger, no matter the reason, it's very much my business too, but I can only stake claim to that statement if I'm something more to Alex than a casual bed partner. As a fuck buddy, I have no right to act like a concerned girlfriend. Even with all of my clothes in Alex's closet, I don't have a say in his life. That's what Igor is really telling me, that I shouldn't stick my nose in where it doesn't belong. That privilege is saved for family and wives.

"Does it happen often? Alex getting shot at?" I ask, my voice suddenly thick with the concern I apparently don't have the right to express.

"No," Igor says curtly before waving a hand at the staircase. "I'm sure Mr. Volkov is waiting for you."

Without sparing him another glance, I make my way downstairs. Yuri is waiting in the foyer, standing on duty by the front door.

"Through here," he says, opening a door leading off the foyer.

"Thanks," I mumble, entering into a large dining room with a table big enough to seat twenty people. The table has a wooden top and metal legs, and the plastic chairs boast a sleek, contemporary design. The elements mix nicely together, creating a welcoming yet modern look.

Alex sits at the head of the table, a spread of cutlery and an empty plate in front of him.

He puts away the tablet he was reading and gets to his feet. In a wordless command, he pulls out the chair on his left.

I walk over and take my place, letting him seat me.

"Did you find everything you needed?" he asks, ringing a small brass bell that stands next to his place setting.

"My clothes…"

I'm about to ask him why he had everything moved over when Marusya enters with a plate that she puts down in front of me.

"Good morning, Kate." Her round face is bright with a smile. "It's good to be back."

"She means it's good to have you back," Alex says.

"You eat up." She arranges the salt and pepper next to my plate. "You need it."

"Thank you," I say as she bustles through the door.

"Yes," Alex says. "You need your strength." He pulls back his sleeve and checks his watch. "You have ten minutes, or else you'll be late."

Without further prompting, I delve into the fluffy scrambled eggs on rye toast. After last night's marathon in bed, I'm hungry enough to clean off my plate in a few minutes.

Alex rises to his feet as I'm dabbing my lips with the napkin. "There's no time for coffee, so I asked Marusya to prepare you one to go."

On cue, the housekeeper appears with a travel mug and the infamous blue cooler bag.

"Thank you," I say, accepting both items from her. "That's very kind."

Alex takes my arm and leads me to the entrance, where he hands my bag, coffee, and lunch to Yuri before helping me into my coat. The three of us make our way outside, but to my surprise, Yuri doesn't drive. Instead, he gets the passenger door of Alex's sports car for me and lets me settle and secure my seatbelt before he hands me the coffee. My coat and bag he leaves on the back seat. Alex takes the wheel.

"You're driving me?" I ask.

Alex casts a glance in my direction as he starts the engine. "Why wouldn't I?"

"Don't you have a business to run?"

He smiles. "The business won't run away. This is more important."

"Driving me?"

"Yes," he says in a non-negotiable manner.

I watch him as he steers us onto the road. His strong features are relaxed, but his gaze is sharp, his comportment vigilant. He's a careful driver, paying attention to everything happening around him while still driving like a true local, maneuvering the car into the fastest-moving lanes.

"Alex," I say, biting my lip.

He gives me another quick glance. "What is it, Katyusha?"

"Why did you have all my clothes moved to your place?"

His smile returns, but I don't miss the strain in the way his eyes tighten minutely. "Drink your coffee, my love. It's getting cold."

My love.

My love.

My mind gets stuck on the phrase, and a giddy happiness bleeds out from my heart and infiltrates my chest. The term of endearment makes me deliriously content. Maybe I'm making too much of it, but I can't help the way his words give wings to my romantic soul. Only I can't let him sidetrack me. The declaration of affection may be completely meaningless.

To appease him, I take a sip of the coffee, then try again. "I thought you'd let Yuri bring a sweater and a pair of jeans. Instead, he emptied out my closet."

He keeps his eyes on the road as he navigates the rush-hour traffic. "There's a good reason for that."

"There is?"

He stops at a red light and turns to face me. "Yes."

"What may that be?" I ask, keeping my tone light.

"I want you to move in with me."

20

What? I can't believe my ears. Did I just hear him ask me to *move in* with him?

Alex frowns. "You don't look happy."

He did say it then. I swallow hard, trying to wrangle my wildly spinning thoughts. "It's not that I'm not enjoying spending time with you, but moving in together is a huge step."

He arches an eyebrow. "Your point is?"

"I thought you weren't the dating type."

The light changes. He focuses back on the road and steps on the gas. "I told you that you're different. I thought we were giving us a shot."

"Yes, but isn't moving in a bit hasty? We barely know each other."

He changes gears smoothly, moving into the fast lane when we reach Ocean Parkway. "I know we're right for each other. Why wait when I know what I want?" He gives me a sidelong glance. "Unless it's not what you want."

It meaning him. "It's not that." I chew my bottom lip, searching for the right words. "You've just sprung this on me a bit suddenly."

His lips tilt in that sexy way that makes me want to kiss the corner of his mouth. "Unexpectedly?"

"Yes."

He cups my hand where it lies on my thigh. "Take some time to think about it today. You can give me your answer later."

"How much later?"

He flashes me a warm, reassuring smile. "Whenever you're ready. I don't want to rush you into anything you don't want."

The declaration eases my tension, and I relax back into the seat, even as my mind continues spinning. It's a lot to process. We only met a few weeks ago, and he told me he doesn't date. What was supposed to be a one-night stand has quickly turned into so much more. And I've been wanting more, but we're moving forward in giant leaps.

"Just to be clear," I say. "Does that mean we're dating?"

"Yes," he says as if the answer is obvious. "We're exclusive and spending our free time together, so by general understanding, that makes me your boyfriend."

Another rush of giddiness saturates my chest. "Then that makes me your girlfriend."

He lifts my hand to his lips and kisses my fingers. "Correct. You, Katherine Morrell, are officially my girlfriend. A first and only for me, may I add."

His first and only girlfriend. I like that statement a little too much.

"Here we go," he says, pulling up at the ER. "I'll fetch you after your shift. We'll have an early dinner so I can put you to bed. You need to catch up on your rest."

"Thank you." I'm already leaning over to kiss him when a thought hits me. "Wait." I pull back. "How did you know when my shift starts?"

"I checked with the ER. As your boyfriend, your schedule is something I should know, don't you think?"

I open my mouth to argue that working hours are confidential, but before I can get a word out, he cups my nape, drags me closer, and presses our mouths together. His lips are warm and soft, but the kiss is firm and demanding. Sparks ignite in my stomach, and in an instant, heat gathers in my core. A moan escapes my lips, betraying my arousal. He tightens his fingers on the back of my neck and deepens the kiss, making me forget where we are or why we're here. I want to climb over the console and into his lap to relieve the ache building between my legs. I want to crawl inside him, and even then, it won't be enough.

It's Alex who keeps enough of a level head to bring the kiss to a halt and tear away from me. Brushing a thumb over my bottom lip, he says roughly, "I'll miss you all fucking day long."

If I smile any harder, my face is going to split. "I'll miss you too."

He stares at me for another moment before retracting his hand. "If I don't let you go now, a lot of sick people are going to be short of a very capable nurse."

The compliment makes me glow. I love my job and I enjoy working hard.

He plants a kiss on my forehead before coming around and getting my door. "See you tonight, Katyusha."

"Later," I say, all but floating on a cloud to the door.

When I glance back from the elevator, he's still leaning on his car with his arms and ankles crossed, watching me through the glass doors. I wave, earning another one of his sexy, crooked smiles. The elevator arrives with a ping. People push outside. I get in with a large group, holding his gaze until the doors shut out his image.

I'm a different person from the one who came to work yesterday overtired, overstressed, and uncertain about her love life, and it must show because my colleagues and patients comment on the change.

"You look like you've won the lottery," June says as she walks into the staffroom where I'm having my lunch break a few hours later.

Rose, whose shift has ended and who's on her way out, says, "A gorgeous man dropped her off in a gorgeous car this morning."

June nudges me. "Good for you, Kate. Way to go."

"Anyone we know?" Rose asks, wagging her eyebrows.

"I don't think so," I say evasively, burying my face behind the berry smoothie Marusya packed for dessert.

"What's his name?" Rose asks. "You can't keep us in suspense."

"Alex Volkov."

"Wait." June makes big eyes. "Isn't that the Russian guy who brought in the gunshot patient?"

"Um, yes." I clear my throat. "That's how we met."

"The same one who delivered flowers to all the patients?" June asks.

"Mm-mm." My cheeks heat as I realize they both know about all the flowers and chocolates I rejected and handed out at the hospital.

"He's really been chasing you hard," June says. "I thought you didn't want to see him. What changed your mind?"

"He convinced me to give it a shot." I don't want to go into detail about how it happened.

"I've read about him somewhere," June says with a frown. "I can't remember if it was on social media or in the news. The guy is loaded."

"Not to mention hot," Rose pipes up.

"What a catch." June grins. "You deserve it, kiddo. Especially after Tony."

"Got to run," Rose says. "I promised my sister I'd pick my nephew up from school." Rushing through the door, she calls back, "You're filling me in tomorrow, Kate. I'm not letting you off the hook."

"I'd better get on with my lunch before another crisis hits," June says. "We're bursting at the seams with emergencies today. I don't know why it always escalates at this time of the year."

"June?" I say before she has a chance to walk away. "Our working schedules are confidential, right?"

"Yes. Why do you ask?"

"No reason." I shake my head. "I was just wondering." She's about to move on, but I stop her again. "If someone needed that information, who would be able to disclose it?"

"Me and HR. Or anyone in admin with access to the records, I guess." She frowns. "Is there a problem with your schedule?"

"Oh, no. I'm just curious."

"Okay. I'm going to buy a sandwich downstairs. Enjoy that gorgeous boyfriend of yours." She winks. "And give him my thanks for all the flowers."

I slip outside to where the smokers usually gather to call my mom before my break is over. Since her bad days are getting more frequent, I like to check on her daily.

"Katie," she says in an amiable tone. "How nice to hear from you. Did you go back to Alex's place?"

"Mom!"

"What? I'm your mother. I have a right to ask."

"Exactly. You're my mom. That kind of sharing is crossing a line."

"Ah. Good. Was the sex great?"

I laugh. "You sound better."

"I'm a whole lot better today. You really don't have to worry so much, you know."

"I'm your daughter. That's my job."

She sighs. "The worrying is supposed to be *my* job."

I don't want her to feel guilty about an illness she has no control over. "Are you busy tonight?"

"Ludwick is coming over." I can hear the smile in her voice. "He's cooking."

"That sounds like fun. At least you'll have a break from kitchen duty. I can come over on Wednesday evening if you like. We can watch a movie and eat a TV dinner on the sofa like we used to do on the weekends."

"Don't put yourself out on my behalf. I'll manage just fine. I'm seeing you on Sunday anyway."

"You are?"

"Didn't Alex tell you?" she says, sounding surprised. "He invited me for lunch."

"Oh. No, he hasn't told me yet, but that's great."

"He said it was to make up for the dinner he invited himself to. Not that he needs to make up for anything, but it's sweet of him anyway."

"Yes." Absolutely. My mom is important to me. I don't want to miss out on seeing her just because I have a new *boyfriend*.

206

A thrill runs through me at the thought. The notion is still novel.

We say our goodbyes, and then I quickly call Joanne to check how her evening with Ricky went.

"It was amazing," she says, whispering since she's on her lunch break at the office—meaning scarfing down a sandwich at her desk—and probably doesn't want her colleagues to over-hear. "We danced until late, and then I went home to his loft. Oh, my. The man's skills in bed are out of this world."

"You sound happy. I'm so glad for you. You deserve it. It's about time you did something other than work."

She chuckles. "Enough of me. What's the latest on Mr. Stalker?"

"Well…" I kick at a lump of iced slush on the concrete. "As it turns out, he's now my boyfriend."

"What?" She squeals so loudly it hurts my eardrum. "Good for you," she says, lowering her voice again. "I know you have reservations, but at least you're giving it a shot. It would be so much worse to never know what could've been. What swayed you?"

I tell her about discovering Alex at my mom's place and how well they got on, as well as going home with Alex, but I decide to omit the part about his asking to move in together until I've made up my mind.

"The four of us have to get together," she says. "How about this weekend? Are you free for lunch?"

"I'm free on Saturday, but I'll have to ask Alex about his plans."

"Great. Check with Alex, and then we can arrange some-thing. I have to go. I'll catch up with you later."

I hang up, pocket my phone, and pull my coat tighter

around my body. When I look up, I notice Dimitri standing a short distance away, huddled in his coat with his hands shoved into his pockets.

Checking the time to make sure I have another minute, I jog over. "Hey."

He gives me a tight-lipped smile.

"Why don't you wait inside? If you're going to be hanging around, you may as well stay warm."

He grunts, but when I turn back for the entrance, he follows.

"You can make yourself comfortable in the cafeteria," I say. "You'll be able to see me come and go through the glass walls."

He scoffs at my attempted humor, but when I make my way back upstairs, he slips through the sliding doors of the cafeteria and heads toward the coffee corner.

I'm still not sure how to feel about having a bodyguard, but instead of fighting it, I decide to accept Alex's good intentions. He's only trying to keep me safe. Given what happened to Igor, I understand why he'd be overprotective.

As promised, Alex is there to pick me up after my shift. To my embarrassment, a small crowd of colleagues has gathered in the entrance to gawk as he whisks me off.

"Sorry about that," I say when I've settled into the comfortable warmth of his car. "You seem to be attracting a lot of attention."

He flashes me a smile before directing his attention to the road again. "The only attention I want is yours."

I put my hand over his where it rests on the gearstick. "You've got it."

Closing his fingers around mine, he brings my hand to his mouth and gently bites down on my index finger. In an instant, I go up in flames. The gentle nip is delivered playfully, but the implication is so suggestive and loaded that it's one of the most erotic moments of my life.

"All of your attention?" he asks in a deep, dark voice.

The single word I manage comes out breathless. "Yes."

"Good." He kisses my fingers and places my hand on his thigh.

"You didn't mention that you invited my mom for lunch on Sunday."

He glances at me. "I was going to bring that up tonight. I hope you don't mind."

"Of course not. On the contrary."

"I gather you spoke to her today."

"Yes."

He squeezes my hand before letting go to change gears. "How is she doing?"

I can't help the worry that slips into my tone. "Better."

"It must be tough," he says with compassion. "For both of you."

"I wish I could make it easier for her, but other than the chronic medication she's on, there's not much I can do."

"She's lucky to have you," he says with a soft smile.

"I'm lucky too."

"Doesn't it bother you not to know who your father is?"

I look at him quickly. "How do you know that?" As soon as the question is out, the answer hits me. "Oh, of course. You did that background check."

"With good intentions."

"Fine," I admit with a sigh. "With good intentions."

"The *best* intentions," he reassures me, sweetening the bitterness that still lingers. "Tell me something. How does a mother who leads a promiscuous life raise a daughter who's so prim and proper?"

"Prim and proper?"

He pulls up in front of his house and cuts the engine. "It's a compliment."

"That's debatable," I say, reluctantly removing my hand from his strong thigh. "Besides, 'promiscuous' is a negative term, and I don't see my mom as such."

"Again, no insult intended. I'm just curious."

"It skips a generation, remember?" I say with a wink. "At least, that's what they say."

"Right." He leans over, catching my chin. "Promiscuous or conservative, I don't care either way. You could've been a nun or a prostitute, I would've wanted you all the same. You can be whatever you like, but you'll still be mine."

The speech takes my breath away. At a loss for words, I can only stare at him as he plants a chaste kiss on my lips before setting me free.

"Would you like to find your father?" he asks.

"I've never felt the need. My mom has always given me attention and love in abundance—maybe to make up for the absence of a father in my life. She might be a butterfly when it comes to men, but she's made sure I've never lacked anything— neither material things nor love."

"You're lucky," he says again, reaching for his door handle.

"What about your parents?"

He hesitates for a moment, as if he's considering whether to answer. Finally, he says, "Both of my parents passed away when I was fifteen."

My heart clenches. "At the same time?"

He nods grimly. "It was an accident."

Oh, Alex. I can't begin to imagine what he went through. "Did you go live with your family?"

"No," he says harshly.

He must've gone into foster care then. Placing a hand on his arm, I say, "I'm so sorry."

He shrugs. "Doesn't matter. In a warped way, I should be thankful. My loss has made me stronger and taught me how to fight. If my life hadn't taken that course, I'm not sure I'd be where I am today."

"Where would you be?"

His blue eyes glitter like hard gemstones in the light that falls through the window. "Somewhere in St. Petersburg, living paycheck to paycheck in a one-bedroom apartment with a tired wife and two kids." He softens his voice. "Instead, I'm here with you."

I'm internalizing the information, still processing what he's shared with me, when he gets out and comes around to open my door.

The snow covers the angel like a thin, white sheet, the powder forming a layer on top of the fountain. He ushers me inside where it's warm and takes my coat.

Leaving it on the coat stand, he asks, "Would you like to freshen up before dinner? I thought we'd have an early one tonight."

"That would be nice," I say, grateful for the consideration. I'm really tired after a long night and exhausting day at work.

"Go ahead." He kisses my forehead. "I'll meet you in the dining room when you're ready."

I venture upstairs, already feeling more at home and less like an intruder, and rush into the closet to grab a clean sweater—only to stop in my tracks for the second time today.

The other half of *my* side that was still empty this morning has been filled to the brink with clothes—clothes that aren't mine. There's everything I could ever need, including pants, blouses, dresses, evening gowns, exercise gear, sleepwear, underwear, and shoes. My mouth drops open as I scan the array of colors and fabrics neatly folded and arranged on the shelves.

I go over to the rail and check the label of one of the expensive-looking dresses. It's a designer brand. I check out several other dresses. Everything has an exclusive designer tag and is in my size. There are no prices, but I can only imagine the small fortune the wardrobe must be worth.

Selecting an old sweater, I change quickly, freshen up in the bathroom, and go downstairs.

Like this morning, Alex is already seated at the head of the table, reading something on his phone.

"Alex," I exclaim, going over. "What's the meaning of the clothes?"

He arches a brow. "Don't you like them?"

"No." I stop next to his chair. "I mean, yes. Obviously, I like them, but I can't afford even one of those dresses, let alone the store you must've cleared out to fill all the shelves in your huge closet."

"*I* can afford them," he says nonchalantly.

"I can't accept it. It's too much."

"Nothing is too much for you." Getting up, he pulls out the chair on his left. "Sit."

I flop down into the chair, staring at his stoic expression. "I'm serious, Alex."

He unbuttons his jacket before taking his seat again.

"Ordering you a few things to wear gave me great pleasure. Besides, you'll feel more comfortable in the right clothes when we have to attend certain events."

"Certain events?" I ask just as Marusya enters with a tray.

"Good evening, Kate." She places a bowl of soup in front of me. "Good day?"

A delicious aroma of porcini mushrooms rises with vapor from the bowl. "Yes, thank you so much."

"Eat up," she says in a sing-song voice as she serves Alex before disappearing through the doorframe.

"Certain events as in work-related networking," Alex says, holding my gaze with a level stare.

"Are you saying my clothes aren't good enough? They may not cost a fortune, but I worked hard for the money that paid for them, and I like them."

His tone is patient. "That's not what I implied. The people who move in my circles can be cruel and the media even crueler. They'll pull you apart and dissect everything about your appearance, from the color of your lipstick to the brand of your shoes. I'm not going to dump you into my world at an unfair disadvantage. When we're not attending one of these pain-in-the-ass, high-class affairs, you can wear whatever you like. I'd never be so audacious as to dictate how you should dress. I'm doing my duty as your boyfriend, which means protecting you more than just physically. I also have to shield you against the media vultures."

I consider his words. "Do you mean that?" Because when he puts it like that, it sounds rather sweet.

"Yes," he replies with determination. "Believe me when I say I had no ill intentions, Katyusha. I love what you wear." His gaze darkens. "In fact, I prefer it when you wear nothing at all."

A wave of heat works its way up my neck at the lust in his eyes and the heat in his tone. "I guess then there's only one thing to say."

He waits.

"Thank you."

His smile is so warm it feels as if the sun is shining from the ceiling of his dining room. "You're welcome. Now, with that settled, eat."

Feeling a few tons lighter, I dip my spoon into the soup and take a sip. "Mm. This is delicious."

"I'm glad you approve." He lifts a bottle of wine from an ice bucket. "Pinot Noir? Chilled to the right temperature, it complements the soup nicely, but if you'd prefer, I can get a bottle of white from the cellar."

"The red will do, thank you." After he's poured us each a glass, I wave at his bowl of soup, which is identical to mine. "You don't have to avoid meat on my behalf. I know you're not a vegetarian."

He smiles. "I asked Marusya to cater to your diet from now on."

I pause with my spoon midway in the air. "Now I feel bad."

"I don't mind."

"Really?"

"Don't worry. If I want a steak, I'll ask her to cook me one. For now, I'm good with this."

"All right." I'm getting whiplash at how fast we're laying down the rules of our new living arrangement. Not only do I have a new wardrobe of fancy clothes, but Alex's household is turning vegetarian to accommodate me.

"Speaking of events," he says, "I have a business dinner on Saturday night. I was hoping you'd join me."

"Oh." I wipe my mouth with my napkin when Marusya enters with a soufflé and a salad that she places in the center of the table.

"Cheese soufflé," she announces proudly, clearing away our bowls. "French menu tonight."

"Wow, that looks gorgeous." She's already at the door as I add, "Thank you so much."

Alex takes my plate to serve me. "Well? I know you're not working on Saturday night."

"My best friend, Joanne, suggested we go out with her and her friend Ricky. She'd like to meet you, but we can move that to another day."

"And I'd like to meet them, just at any other time." He puts the plate in front of me and dishes up a helping of salad on the side. "Let me know when so I can add it to my calendar."

"Great." I iron out my napkin. "How did you know I'm off on Saturday?"

He stills in the middle of dishing up for himself. "I have contacts everywhere in this city. It's imperative in my business."

"Does that mean you have access to any information you want?"

"Just about," he admits without flinching.

I pick up my knife and fork. "Right. Does money buy you everything?"

"Not everything." He reaches across the table and clasps my hand in his big, warm palm. "Money can't buy you love. Isn't that how the saying goes here in America?"

My throat is suddenly dry. "That's right," I manage to say. "How does it go in Russia?"

He brings his glass to his lips. "We say that love doesn't fill an empty stomach."

"That sounds a bit cynical," I say with a small laugh.

Behind the brilliant blue of his eyes, something hard flashes. "Only to those who don't know what it feels like to go hungry." Then the look is gone, replaced by his soft smile. "Now, thanks to Igor getting shot, I have everything."

I'm unable to look away from the magnetic pull of his gaze. "Do you?"

"I have money, power, and the only woman I can't seem to get out of my mind."

I dampen my lips. "Money and power can be dangerous. Getting shot at seems like a steep price to pay."

"But the woman at my side is a nurse. What more can a man who's being shot at ask for?"

"Not to be shot at?"

He squeezes my fingers and releases my hand. "It's unavoidable in my business."

"The oil business? I don't see other oil barons getting shot at."

Leaning closer, he says in a low voice, "But I'm so much more than that, my love. You already know that."

21

As far as sayings go, there's another one about love. They say love makes you blind. I'm not worldly or sophisticated like my oligarch boyfriend, but I'm not naïve enough to believe that when it comes to business, he doesn't play dirty. He's already admitted to dealing with the mafia, but is that where it ends?

I consider his confession as I get dressed for the party on Saturday night. Since the evening he confessed in not so many words to be a dangerous man, I've done my own background check on him. I've pulled up every article and piece of information about Alex Volkov I could get my hands on.

What I've learned baffles me. There's no information about his childhood or teenage years. From what I could gather, he entered a business school in Russia at nineteen. After graduating, he got a job at a major Russian oil company and quickly worked his way from the ground up, winning the favor of senior management and making powerful alliances both in the business world and in the Russian government—alliances that he parlayed into starting an oil company of his own after discovering a new oil field in Siberia.

He fast became as wealthy and powerful as the oligarchs of old who gained their wealth with the fall of the Soviet Union. His hostile takeover of a Ukrainian oil company that was owned by a descendant of Russian royalty made international news. The deal is said to have catapulted him from billionaire to zillionaire status. By his early thirties, he'd already diversified his holdings, acquiring real estate and stakes in various international companies. His influence has continued to rise since, and his advice is said to be valued by politicians and tradesmen alike, his name connected to several high-profile Russian trade deals.

It's both awe-inspiring and intimidating to know what kind of man I'm dating. When I was still in high school, he was already on the cover of *Forbes*, and by the time I started college, he was voted one of the most eligible bachelors in Russia. There's never been a shortage of women in his life. To my dismay, I've also learned that he has a reputation as a playboy, having been linked with famous models and actresses from around the world. However, he's never been seen with the same woman on his arm more than once.

I suppose tonight makes me a debutante of sorts. If I make it to a second night out with my Russian playboy, it will make the news. To say I'm nervous about the upcoming event is an understatement. I now understand why he insisted on giving me a wardrobe full of suitable clothes.

Taking a step back from the vanity, I study my reflection in the mirror. The long red dress drapes softly around my frame. The color goes well with my complexion, and the fabric is kind to my curves. With a high neckline and low back, it's a flattering cut. The bodice fits snuggly while the skirt flares out from my hips. Since I'm relatively tall, the hem ends just above my ankles, exposing my exquisite strappy silver heels. The shoes aren't practical for the weather, but practical isn't what I'm aiming for.

Instead of letting my hair dry naturally, I visited a salon for a change. It took an hour for the stylist to blow-dry my hair straight before taking it up in a simple but stylish French roll. I spent another hour applying my makeup, going for a darker eyeshadow that makes the green flecks in my hazel eyes pop and a paler lipstick that gives my lips extra volume.

To finish off my look, I splurged and got a manicure and pedicure while having my hair done. I'm not wearing much jewelry, though, because nothing I own fits the dress. My only accessory is the silver ring with the rose design my mom gave me for my twenty-first birthday.

With five minutes to spare, I give myself a last critical once-over, then grab the clutch that came with the dress and make my way to the door. I'm about to exit the bedroom when Alex enters, looking mouthwateringly handsome in a tux and bowtie.

"Hey," he says in a low voice, dragging his gaze over me.

My throat goes dry, my reply scraping over my vocal cords. "Hey."

He takes my hand and makes me twirl. "Look at you."

"You like?" I ask when I come to a breathless halt facing him again.

"More than like." His tone turns husky. "Although there's nothing sexier than you in nursing scrubs."

I swat his arm. "What is it with men and nurse costumes?"

Tony always wanted me to get dressed up in a slutty nurse uniform when he'd had a drink too many.

"Oh, there are quite a few male fantasies I could enlighten you about, but since I'm the only one allowed to fantasize about you, only my fantasies matter."

"And what are your fantasies?" I ask, smiling up at his harshly handsome face.

"You in my bed is enough. I've fantasized about that since the moment I set eyes on you."

The deep timbre of his voice strokes over my senses, lighting sparks in my belly.

"I have something for you," he says, taking a small velvet box from his pocket.

My heart skips a beat when he hands it to me. It's a box every woman recognizes on sight, a box that can only house one thing—jewelry. I flip back the lid to reveal two red stones surrounded by sparkling white ones.

"Rubies," he says, "to go with your dress. The rest are diamonds."

I open my mouth to say I can't accept such a gift, but he speaks before I have a chance to utter the words.

"Please don't say you can't accept them. It's a gift from the heart, one I can well afford, and the stones are conflict-free."

The white and red gemstones catch the light and reflect it back in small rainbows. "I... It's very pretty, but—"

"Good."

He takes the box from my hand, removes one of the earrings, and leans closer to fit it in my ear. My stomach tightens from the mere brush of his fingers over the shell of my ear. I'm already impossibly turned on by the time he's fitted the other earring.

He takes a step back to study his work. "Perfect." Taking my shoulders, he turns me toward the mirror hanging above the dresser. "Take a look. They suit you."

The earrings are indeed intricate pieces of art. They look priceless.

Lowering his head, he brushes his lips over my neck in a tender caress. "We'd better go or we'll be late."

Goosebumps run over my arm and tingle down my spine. "Thank you."

"You're most welcome, Katyusha."

He places a soft kiss on my temple and takes my hand. "Yuri will drive us. I may have to down a few shots of vodka with some business partners tonight."

In the foyer, he produces a faux-fur coat that he drapes over my shoulders. "This should keep you warm enough between the house and the car. I'm afraid there's nothing I can do for the shoes, except this."

I utter a squeal as he lifts me into his arms. Folding my hands around his neck, I cuddle closer to the warmth of his strong body. Yuri appears with a matching faux-fur blanket that he wraps around my legs, covering me all the way to my feet.

"You're very considerate, Mr. Volkov," I say with my nose pressed against his neck.

"Just taking care of what's mine."

He's careful to deposit me on the back seat without creasing my dress. After spreading out my skirt and adjusting the fur blanket around me, he comes around and takes the seat next to me.

The minute Yuri pulls onto the street, Alex takes out his phone. He's busy typing messages as we drive, but I don't mind, because he places his free hand on my knee, drawing lazy patterns with this thumb. It's a subtle way of keeping me connected to him and telling me he's aware of my presence even if his mind is occupied elsewhere.

I've been working back-to-back shifts all week and haven't had a chance to ask him much about the party. In the little free time I've had, we've been mostly occupied in other ways that ended up with no talking and a lot of action in his bed. Since he's busy, I refrain from asking where we're headed. I'll just have to wait and see.

I'm surprised when Yuri pulls up in front of the city hall.

"Wow," I say, turning to Alex when he finally puts away his phone. "What kind of a dinner is this?"

"Senator Keaton's wife organized a fundraiser for the Autism Society."

"That's a worthy cause," I say when he helps me from the car.

I discard the blanket but pull the coat tightly around me as we make our way up the steps and inside the hall.

The minute we clear the doors, cameras flash in our faces. The lights are blinding and the mob that descends on us is more than a little frightening, but Alex folds his strong hand around mine in a reassuring way, grounding me as he shelters me against his large frame.

Thankfully, someone more famous enters behind us, and we're relieved from the unwelcome attention. After checking in my coat, we make our way through the lobby to the main hall.

I regard Alex's broad frame. He didn't even put on a coat. "Aren't you cold?"

He smiles down at me. "This isn't cold. I'm from Russia, remember?"

The interior has been decorated like a winter wonderland,

complete with an igloo on an icy landscape in the center. Artificial snowflakes fall from the ceiling, clinging to the elegant dresses and tuxedos of the high society in attendance. A brass band set up on the stage is playing a waltz.

Cocktail tables are scattered around. They're all occupied, so Alex steers me to a quieter corner in the back, grabbing two glasses of champagne from a passing waiter on his way. People glance at us as we walk by, and I catch more than a few envious —and in some cases, contemptuous—looks in my direction from the female attendees.

"The house parties are normally better," Alex says, bending low to brush the words against my ear. "The big ones like these are always overdone with the decoration and lacking in the quality of the food."

As if to prove his point, a waiter offers us a tray set with a variety of sad-looking tarts, sliders, and corndogs.

As I haven't eaten since lunch, I pop one of the bite-sized ricotta-and-tomato tarts into my mouth. The flavors are bland, just like Alex predicted.

Our peace and quiet doesn't last long. A tall man with a thin frame and hawk-like nose swoops in to steal Alex's attention.

"There you are," he says to Alex, fleetingly blinking in my direction. "I was wondering when you'd show. There are some investors who'd like to meet you."

Alex looks like he's about to tug me along, but I smile and wave him off. "You go ahead. I have to visit the ladies' room."

"Okay. Come find me after," he says as the man pulls him away.

I make my way through the throng of people to the restroom and freshen up. When I return, I spot Alex across the room, deep in conversation with a group of men who must be the aforementioned investors. I'm not sure I should interrupt, so I look around for something or someone to occupy me in the meantime. The problem is, I feel out of my depth. I don't know with whom to strike up a conversation or what about. I doubt anyone is interested in the latest flu statistics.

"Well, well," a suave, accented female voice says. "If it isn't Alex's little nurse."

I turn around and come face to face with none other than Dania, the Russian beauty I'd seen at Alex's side in Romanoff's. She's wearing a sleek silver dress that hugs her perfect figure, and her dark curls are hanging down to her waist. With flawless creamy skin and matte red lipstick, she looks like Snow White, only the adult, more seductive version.

"Do we know each other?" I ask as she looks me up and down.

She puts her empty glass on the table next to us and flicks her fingers at the nearest waiter. The man all but falls over his feet to get to us.

"A vodka for me and my friend," she says to the man as soon as he's within earshot.

He turns and runs to execute the order like his coat tails are on fire. I suppose that's because her father is someone important in these circles.

"Dania," she says, offering a gloved hand. "Alex told Papa and me all about Igor getting shot and how you saved his life."

"I didn't save his life."

"Well." She waves a hand. "That's how Alex made it sound." She gives me another once-over. "Like you're a perfect heroine."

Not sure how to reply to that, I keep quiet.

"I remember you from Romanoff's," she continues. "You're

the woman who came in looking for Alex and then ran away like a jealous girlfriend."

Heat rises from my neck, scorching my cheeks. "I didn't go looking for him there. It was pure coincidence."

"Was it now?" she drawls.

I narrow my eyes. "Yes."

The waiter arrives with the vodka, serving us each a glass.

"A toast," Dania says when he's gone, raising her glass. "Let's drink to Alex."

"To Alex," I agree, holding her gaze as she knocks back the alcohol.

I take a small sip of mine.

"That's not the way to do it," she says, motioning at the liquor in my hand. "Not if you want to fit in."

"Who says I want to fit in?"

She sets her glass on the table with a loud clink. "You'd better enjoy your time with him. It's limited."

I raise a brow. "Says who? You?"

Her smile is humorless. "You don't know how things work in our world. Alex and I, we will marry and strengthen the business. I will give him an heir, a son to carry forward his name, and then some more children to inherit his riches and build his empire. You will always be the piece on the side, the distraction he needs before taking his vows. Powerful men like Alex like to feel great. They need to have women at their feet." Her tone turns bitter. "Me? I'll look the other way." She leans closer. "You want to know why? Because he'll always come back to me, and you'll end up like all the others. Forgotten."

Straightening her dress, she gives me a pretty smile. "Enjoy the rest of your evening. I suggest you try the blinis. They're the least offensive of the dishes on the menu." Then she turns and walks off with a regal posture.

Too flabbergasted to find words, I can only stare at her back while she moves through the crowd. I follow her with my gaze as she goes up to an elderly gentleman with silver hair. It's the same one from the restaurant, presumably her father, Mikhail Turgenev. She goes on tiptoes and says something in his ear. His smile fades as he listens, and when he turns his gaze on me, his gray eyes are cold.

Ignoring them, I look over to where I last saw Alex. Despite the packed room, he's easy to spot. He's a head taller than everyone else, his hair shining like onyx in the lights of the chandelier. He's surrounded by an even bigger group of men now, all of whom appear to be vying for his attention. As if feeling my eyes on him, he lifts his head. Our gazes lock over the distance, and he offers me a soft smile. Ignoring his companions, he runs a heated gaze over me, leaving me with no doubt about what's going through his mind.

I look away. Dania's speech has unsettled me. Not because of whatever untruths she spewed about Alex marrying her, but because of the one truth she did mention. Alex and I aren't from the same realities. I don't belong here, among all these rich and famous people with potentially shady connections. I don't know how to navigate this complicated world he's created for himself. But I've never been a quitter, so I shoot back the rest of my drink, leave my glass next to the one with Dania's lipstick imprint, and walk around until I spot a group of relatively friendly-looking women.

"Hi," I say when I reach them. "I'm Kate. Am I the only one here not knowing anyone?"

A woman with wavy auburn hair gives a tight smile. "It

would appear so." She turns her back on me, and they carry on with their conversation.

Fine. Definitely not a group I want to get to know better. Keeping an eye on Alex, who is now doing vodka shots with another man, I try to make my way over to him, but it's difficult to get through the sea of people.

Giving up, I veer toward the terrace on the left, exhaling a sigh of relief when I step through the double doors into an empty space. The terrace is covered for the winter and warmed by gas heaters. Ashtrays are scattered on the tables. This must be the smokers' corner. For the moment, it's thankfully void of smokers, or at least that's what I think before I spot the quiet figure in the far dark corner.

"Oh." I give a start. "I didn't notice you."

"You sound guilty," a male voice replies. "Did you come out here for a forbidden cigarette?"

There's a foreign accent to his English, slight enough that I wouldn't have noticed if it weren't for the way he rolls his Rs.

The man steps from the shadows, his tall, broad form making the big terrace feel crowded in the same way Alex makes a room feel too small.

He walks over to me in long, unhurried steps. His blond hair is cut short, similar to how Alex wears his, and his square chin is dimpled. His eyes are the most unique green color, a mix between turquoise and emerald, and his gaze is arresting as he watches me.

Taking a packet of cigarettes from his pocket, he shakes one out and holds it to me. "Need a partner in crime? Someone to seduce you into doing something you shouldn't?"

I shake my head. "I don't smoke, but thanks."

He pushes the cigarette back into its packet and puts it away.

"Escaping the crowd of good, amiable people?" he asks with a cynical smile.

"Something like that."

Leaning closer, he says, "You don't look like a good and amiable person."

I frown. Is he insulting or complimenting me? "I'm not sure how to take that."

When he lifts his hand, I freeze, but he just tucks a strand of hair that's escaped my French roll behind my ear. Leaning in even closer, he opens his mouth to answer, but a loud voice booming from the door makes both of us jump.

"Get your fucking hands off her."

Alex.

Ignoring the threat in Alex's furious tone, the man puts his lips next to my ear and whispers, "You can take that as a warning."

22

*a*lex closes the distance in three long strides and pushes me behind his back. Fisting his hand in the lapel of the man's jacket, he growls, "I'll fucking crack your skull in two."

The man raises his hands. "We were just getting acquainted."

"You don't get acquainted with her." Alex gives the guy a shake. "You don't talk to her. If you value your life, you don't put a finger on her. The only reason I'm not offing you is because of the favor I owe you." Letting him go with a shove, Alex adds grimly, "Consider us even."

Grinning, the man straightens his jacket. "To be fair, I was here before her."

"Get out of my sight before I change my mind about crushing your thick skull like a nut."

"I'm out," the stranger says with a smirk, not glancing in my direction as he walks back into the hall.

I stare at Alex with my heart thumping in my chest as he turns back to face me. His features are set in harsh lines, the look in his eyes scary. He threatened the guy's life, but that was only overprotective testosterone talking. Right?

"Who's that man?" I ask in a shaky voice.

"Adrian Kuznetsov," he says, his lips curling with disdain.

I peer at his face. "What was that all about?"

"Adrian is a corporate spy. He makes a business of selling information to the highest bidder. You're not to speak to him under any circumstances." He cups my cheek. "Understand?"

The warmth of his palm seeps into my skin, making me aware of how cold I suddenly feel. "What favor did he do for you?"

He drops his hand. "He got me some information I needed."

"What kind of information?"

"Nothing you need to concern yourself over."

"What information, Alex?"

"Just business stuff," he says in a clipped tone as he takes my hand. "Come. Let's go back inside."

"Wait." I hang back. "If Adrian helped you, why do you hate him so much?"

"He can't be trusted. He's a man with no integrity who only answers to money."

I think back to the odd warning Adrian gave me. "He did seem a bit strange."

"That's one way of putting it," Alex says darkly. He takes a breath, his face smoothing out. "Enough of that. We've been here for over an hour, and you haven't had any fun. Am I right?"

"Yes," I admit.

He pulls me toward the door. "Then let's get out of here."

I can't wait. "That sounds like a great idea."

When we go back inside, there are many eyes on us. Alex

acts oblivious to the attention, tugging me along to the main exit. We don't greet anyone on our way out.

Yuri waits in the foyer with a few other men dressed like chauffeurs. When he sees us, he gets to his feet and disappears outside while Alex gets my coat and helps me into it.

A few minutes later, Yuri's car pulls up to the curb. Another car, a similar black one, follows and stops behind. Igor is in the driver's seat, and Leonid sits next to him. Alex's bodyguards.

Alex leads me to Yuri's car and settles me inside. Once he's seated next to me, he flicks his fingers, at which Yuri pushes the button that raises the partition. The minute the barrier is in place, Alex grabs me. He's like a mad man, crushing our mouths together while dragging his hands over my body as if he needs to brand me.

My body is already primed from my arousal earlier this evening, when he'd fitted my new earrings. The urgency of his touch as he lifts me to straddle him makes my need spike alongside my pulse, the way he's groping and devouring me igniting flames under my skin. Heat gathers in my core as he pushes the dress up to my waist and rips off my underwear. He's bruising my lips with the intensity of his kiss, but I welcome his out-of-control hunger, kissing him back with the same fervor.

I gasp into the kiss as he sinks a finger inside me without warning. The intrusion is sudden, the brutal pace of his hand almost too much, but it hurls me into a building orgasm.

"So tight," he groans, nipping my bottom lip. "Think you can take my cock like this—here, now?"

I moan my agreement.

My coat falls on the floor as he pushes it off my arms. Taking a foil packet from his pocket, he rips it open with his teeth, his gaze locked on mine. Since that one time in the shower, we haven't gone bareback again, even though I told him I'm on the pill. Double precaution, I guess. Breathing hard, I fumble with his belt and zipper, unable to believe I'm going to have sex in his car with his driver less than a yard away. We're both out of control, but our need for each other is too fierce to contain.

The windows are tinted, yet the streetlights filtering in from outside make me feel exposed. My sense of vulnerability grows as Alex lowers the zipper at the back of my dress and pushes the sleeves over my shoulders. With the low back of the dress, I'm not wearing a bra, and my nipples contract when the fabric pools around my waist, exposing my breasts to the air.

I finally manage to pull down Alex's zipper and push down the elastic of his briefs to free his cock. He's thick in my hands, my fingers barely overlapping as they circle his girth. When he brings the condom to the crest, I still him with a hand on his wrist. Sliding to the floor, I kneel in front of him, the faux-fur coat forming a soft cushion underneath me. His eyes darken in the light from the lampposts when he realizes my intention.

Holding his gaze, I lower my mouth over the large head of his cock and trace the circumference with my tongue before licking up the drop of precum that leaks through the slit. He tastes like man and power, a heady cocktail that makes me crave more.

I barely get a few licks in before he catches my face in one big hand, his fingers splayed over my cheeks.

His voice is thick with lust. "Enough. You'll make me come like this."

Tightening his hold, he pulls me closer and kisses me fervently before letting me go to roll on the condom.

With his hands under my armpits, he drags me back onto

his lap and guides me onto my knees. I barely have time to take a breath before he lowers me over his erection, sheathing himself inside my body to the hilt.

The stretch makes my back arch with pleasure. As always, it's a tight fit, a little uncomfortable, but I'm aroused enough not to mind the burn.

The car speeds along, taking the exit to his neighborhood as he starts pumping. The light in his eyes is as feverish as his earlier kisses. He seems to want to stamp his ownership on me with his powerful thrusts.

Gripping my nape, he brings my mouth to his, whispering over my lips, "Come with me."

Always knowing how to get me there, he steals a wet, greedy kiss before pushing me back with a hand on my shoulder and sliding his free hand between our bodies. I have to catch my weight with my hands on his knees to keep my balance as he presses his thumb to my clit. It only takes a few strokes to send me over the edge. I come even before we're halfway home, my inner muscles clenching hard around him. He follows with a grunt, lifting his hips to penetrate me even deeper as he fills the condom with his release.

When it's all over, I feel depleted. My limbs are useless, shaking like jelly. He presses me close, cradling me against his chest, and plants a kiss on the top of my head. We sit like that for a while, semi-naked without breaking our physical connection. I'm already dozing off when Alex nudges me gently.

"We're almost home," he says, my cue for getting dressed.

He adjusts my clothes and gets rid of the condom, wrapping it up in a tissue before dropping it in a trash bag he must keep handy for quickies in his car. He then fixes his own clothes and stuffs my torn underwear into his pocket. By the time Yuri gets my door, the only evidence of what has happened in the back of the car is my disheveled hair and what I can only imagine to be my smeared makeup.

Ushering me out of the car, Alex rushes me inside and up the stairs. It's as if the sex in the car never happened. We barely make it to the landing before he drags me down to the floor. It's a good thing it's late because I'd hate for Marusya or one of his bodyguards to walk in on us in our compromising position.

I'm out of my dress and naked on the carpet in seconds, with Alex buried so deep inside me I no longer care where we are. I revel in his brutal claiming, knowing how much he wants me as I give him my all. This time, he comes inside me, somehow making what we started in the car feel complete.

It's only later when I'm drifting off in his arms in bed, exhausted and thoroughly used but happy, that I recall the strange words Adrian had spoken. There's only one way to interpret those words.

He'd told me the same thing Dania had, that I don't belong here.

23

My mom beams as Alex takes her on a tour of his house. She sent me a text message first thing this morning after seeing a tabloid photo of us that was taken at the party. Joanne sent me a few links from online gossip rags, joking that I'm famous. I can't say I'm pleased. I've never liked being in the spotlight, but this is what dating Alex is going to be like, so I guess I'd better get used to it.

I tag along with my mom and Alex, not mentioning that it's my first official tour too. Alex wanted to show me around the morning after our first date, but I ran out on him before he had a chance. Since moving in, I've discovered the rooms by myself.

"This is so cozy," my mom says as Alex shows her his indoor pool.

She ooohs and aaahs as we visit the sauna, gym, kitchen, and upstairs level. When we enter the walk-in closet, she gives a squeal.

"You've moved in together." She grabs my hand. "Why didn't you tell me?"

"It was a bit sudden and soon," I say, glancing at Alex.

"Not soon enough," he says with meaning.

A private look passes between us.

"I'm so happy for both of you." Mom lets me go to give Alex a hug.

To his credit, he doesn't try to escape the maternal gesture. I'm only thankful she doesn't try to ruffle his hair or pinch his cheeks.

"Shall we go down for lunch?" he asks when she finally sets him free. "My housekeeper is off on the weekends, but she left a casserole in the oven we can heat up. I'm afraid I'm not much of a cook."

"Well," my mom says, "you're already perfect. Being a good cook as well would've been simply too good to be true. Did I mention that I'm not a bad cook myself?"

She seems to be so much better today, but sadness overcomes me as I know it won't last. Her illness comes in cruel cycles. Every good day is followed by a day twice as bad.

While Alex heats the food and pours us each a glass of wine, Mom and I set the table. Lunch is an amiable and happy affair, a welcome change from last night's stiff hostility. It's obvious how much my mom likes Alex from the way she dishes up seconds on his plate and, after peppering him with questions, comes to the conclusion that he works too hard and needs a break.

Alex lets her serve the dessert and gladly accepts when she offers to make coffee. The kindness of the gesture isn't lost on me. Letting my mom prepare something puts her at ease in his house, making her feel even more welcome.

When we're seated at the indoor garden table with our coffee and a silence falls over the conversation, Alex clears his throat.

"Laura, I'd like to run something past you."

"Yes?" she says, giving him an encouraging smile.

"There's a new treatment center for rheumatoid arthritis near Deep Creek in North Carolina. The program is still very new, but it's already showing amazing results."

"Kate and I know about it," my mom says. "We looked into it, but it costs tens of thousands of dollars."

"And the results aren't guaranteed," I add.

"No, but it's worth giving it a shot," Alex says. "If you agree, I'd like to cover the costs."

"What?" Mom puts her cup down on the table. "Absolutely not. I'd never be able to pay you back."

Alex gives her a patient smile. "I don't mean a loan. Consider it a gift."

She blinks. "I appreciate the kindness of your offer, but I can't accept. It's too much."

Leaning forward, Alex takes her hand. "No price is too high for one's health. Besides, you and Kate are my family now—my only family. I'd appreciate it very much if you'd do this for me."

"Goodness, Alex." Mom shifts her gaze to me. "I don't know."

I'm as shocked as she is. What Alex is suggesting is beyond kindness. The costs my mom will incur will be huge. The treatment is only part of it. There's also the expense of board and meals in the private onsite clinic, as well as months of physiotherapy afterward. Tears of gratitude prickle behind my eyes. Even more than by his generous offer, I'm touched by his admission that he considers us family.

"It will make me very happy," Alex says, letting go of my mom's hand to pick up his cup of coffee. "In fact, I insist."

Mom's look turns pleading, quietly asking for my advice. I give a small nod, smiling through my tears. Alex doesn't say or do things he doesn't mean. He wouldn't have offered if he didn't really want to give her a shot at a better quality of life.

Blinking back her own tears, my mom says, "If you put it like that..."

Alex's smile is bright. "It's settled then. I'll get my assistant to make the arrangements first thing tomorrow morning."

The enormity of the gift only sinks in later when my mom says her goodbyes and Alex asks Yuri to bring the car around to drive her home.

"I still can't believe it," Mom says as we walk her to the car. "I don't know how to thank you, Alex."

"You already have," he says. "Anyway, no thanks are required. You'll be doing me a favor. Kate is important to me, and so are you."

My mom places a hand over her heart. "I'll be away for a few months, at least two or three."

"Don't worry about the apartment, Mom. I'll take care of it."

"*We* will," Alex says, giving me such a warm smile that my heart melts.

"Wait." My mom stops in her tracks. "That means I won't see you for a very long time. Will you come visit me? Both of you?"

Alex gets the door for her. "Of course. We will come down for Christmas. There's a quaint hotel not far away from the clinic. I've already looked into it."

My mom pats his cheek. "You're very kind. I'm so happy my daughter has met a man who deserves her."

"I'm not sure I deserve her," he says, "but I know how lucky I am."

I laugh. "Stop it, you two. You're making me self-conscious."

"It's the truth," he says, dragging a heated gaze over me.

My mom gets into the car. "You should come over for dinner more often."

"We'd love that," Alex says before closing her door.

She gives a little wave as Yuri pulls off. When the car turns the corner, Alex ushers me into the warmth of the house.

Standing face to face with him in the foyer, I say, "Thank you."

He wraps his arms around me and pulls me close. "You're welcome, my love."

I inhale his intoxicating scent and lean my cheek against his chest, feeling safe in the strength of his arms.

When he asks in a low, deep tone, "Shall we go upstairs?" there's only one answer to give.

24

The arrangements for my mom's admission to the clinic are made quickly thanks to Alex's contacts. One week later, we drive her to the facility and help her settle into her private room before meeting the staff and being present for her first meeting with the head doctor, during which he explains the treatment course to us.

We spend the night in a nearby hotel and go back the following morning to stock her cupboard with healthy snacks and drinks. It's hard for me to leave her, but it's for a good reason. If the treatment is successful, my mom will have a lot more mobility and increased flexibility. She'll be able to do things she hasn't been able to in years, such as low-impact sports and even adventures like paragliding and scuba diving. She'll be able to move without pain and sleep through a whole night without the help of painkillers and anti-inflammatories.

I'm simultaneously sad and filled with happy optimism when we say our goodbyes. Always in tune with my moods,

Alex takes my hand in the car and places it in his lap. When he catches Yuri's eyes in the rearview mirror, Yuri pushes on the button to pull up the partition, giving us privacy.

"She'll be fine," Alex says, kissing my hand.

"Yes." I swallow down my tears. "I know."

"I think she was making eyes at the male nurse."

"What?" I stare at him in shock. "No."

"Uh-huh." He grins. "So trust me. She *will* be fine. She may even have some fun."

"Alex!" I swat his arm.

He utters a soft laugh. "Didn't you say you wanted to go out with your friend and her boyfriend?"

"Joanne?" I search his face. "Yes, but I thought you'd be tired after the long drive."

He raises a brow. "Are you mocking my age, Miss Morrell?"

I grin. "I wouldn't dream of it. I have firsthand experience of your youthful stamina."

"Good, although I don't mind giving you a reminder."

"Yuri is only a seat away."

His voice turns husky. "It didn't bother you before."

"That's because you make me forget where I am or how to behave decently."

He does that finger-biting thing that sets my lower body on fire. "I prefer it when you behave indecently."

In a sudden rush of emotion, I cuddle closer to him. "I never thought it was possible to be this happy."

He puts an arm around my shoulders and kisses the top of my head. "Are you?"

"Ecstatically happy."

"Good," he says again, rubbing my arm. "I aim to please."

His tone is playful, but I have a sudden urge to be serious.

The words bubble up in my chest. Before I can stop them, they find a way to the surface and tumble from my tongue.

"I think I'm in love with you, Alex."

He stills. For a frightening moment, we're suspended in time. With my heart beating in my throat, I look up at his face. His expression is unreadable as he meets my eyes. For another terrifying moment, I consider that he may not be happy with this news. Yes, we've been moving fast, mostly by his instigation, going from non-dating to living together in a matter of weeks, but love is an entirely different ballgame, and I'm not sure he wants to play that way.

Have I just spoiled everything?

But then his lips tilt into the softest of smiles and the blue of his eyes heats to the shade of a warm summer's sky. My heart leaps with relief as he lowers his head and claims my lips. This kiss isn't wild and lustful or quick and urgent. It's reverent and meticulous. He's taking his time, making my knees weak and stealing my breath.

I'm panting when he finally pulls away.

"That, Katyusha, makes me very happy."

"Really?"

"Yes," he says, pulling me under the crook of his arm.

I sigh and relax against him. I wish he'd said the words back, but I don't want him to lie if he's not there yet, or if he's simply not ready to admit his feelings. Besides, actions speak louder than words, and everything he's done so far has all but shouted that I mean *something* to him.

We sit like that for most of the rest of the way, enjoying each other in silence until we're about a half hour away from home.

Nudging me gently, he says, "Call your friend. I'd like to meet them if they're free."

"You would?"

"I already told you so." He tugs a strand of hair behind my ear. "I think it will cheer you up."

"You're very kind," I say and mean it.

He smiles. "I know you've never been separated from your mother for so long. The two of you are close. It must be difficult, even if it's in her best interest."

Thankful that he understands me so well, I take my phone from my bag and dial Joanne.

She's happy to hear from me and says that they were planning on going to the movies but will gladly change their plans to meet us.

"I'll take care of the arrangements," Alex says before I hang up. "We'll send them a text message with the details."

I convey the message and sink deeper into my boyfriend's embrace while he takes out his phone and starts making calls to organize our evening.

I watch the snow sifting down through the windows as we enter the city. A few months ago, I never would've dreamed I could feel this complete and fulfilled. A few weeks ago, I was adrift, returning Alex's gifts and debating the wisdom of going out with him. And here I am, the luckiest, happiest girl alive. All because Igor got shot. Despite the terrifying fact that someone wanted to end Alex's life, I can never regret the way things have turned out.

AN HOUR LATER, JOANNE, RICKY, ALEX, AND I ARE SITTING AT A table in Romanoff's. Alex didn't book out the place, but he got a table at the back with a clear view of the stage. This way, we can enjoy the entertainment while still being able to make conversation.

Alex orders on behalf of all of us. Ricky is a vegetarian like me, while Joanne is an adventurous eater who gives Alex the green light to order her a traditional Russian dish.

"I'm so glad to finally meet you," she says to Alex. "It's good to see my friend so happy."

Smiling, Alex takes my hand under the table. "Consider her happiness my goal in life. What about you? Katherine tells me you work in finance."

"I'm an investment banking associate at Goldman Sachs. I just got the promotion a few weeks ago."

"Congratulations. That's a hectic job," Alex says with sympathy. "I admire your work ethic. It's not an easy profession you've chosen."

"Thank you," she says, grinning from ear to ear.

Alex turns his attention to Ricky. "I've been told you're an artist. When is your next exhibition?"

Ricky smiles. "I'm working with a gallery to have something ready in July."

"I hope you'll spare us an invitation?" Alex says.

"With pleasure," Ricky says. "Do you like contemporary art?"

"I like all kinds of art, but I lean toward contemporary in my personal style. I'm a minimalist at heart, and contemporary fits better with the decoration of my living space."

"Do you have some pieces?" Ricky asks.

"I own a couple of Jeff Koons's earlier paintings," Alex replies, "but my personal favorite is *Boxer* by Jean-Michel Basquiat."

Ricky's eyes bulge. "You own Jeff Koons's early work? Those are as scarce as hen's teeth."

"I was lucky. My interior decorator has a personal relationship with an art dealer. However, it's my dream to own a Cecily Brown one day."

"The gallery I'm exhibiting with in July works with Ms. Brown," Ricky says. "If you'd like, I can ask them to extend an invitation the next time she exhibits."

"That would be great, thank you." Alex glances at me. "I never make enough time for culture and entertainment, I'm afraid. Work-life balance is something I need to work on."

By the time the waiter arrives with our food, we've polished off a bottle of wine among the four of us. Alex has ordered a selection of starters to share, and the tasting menu for our main course.

During the meal, it becomes clear that my friends are as smitten with my boyfriend as I am. Alex possesses the kind of charisma one normally finds in the best politicians, and as I watch him interact with my friends, I can see how he was able to rise to the top so quickly—and why I've fallen for him so fast. His charm is downright magnetic, and it doesn't hurt that he seems genuinely interested in others' thoughts and opinions. I can't imagine anyone not liking him, never mind trying to kill him. Thinking about it always makes my stomach contract into a ball, so I shove the thought away. I'm having fun, and I don't want to spoil our good time with negativity.

We all dance and try to sing along to the Russian imitations of pop songs, much to Alex's entertainment. By the time the bill comes, it's long past midnight. A slight headache building at the back of my head tells me I've drunk too much.

Alex insists on paying, saying that it was his idea to invite everyone to the restaurant, and after much arguing, Joanne and

Ricky finally give in, but only because Alex promises to let them get the next dinner.

While Alex pays, Joanne and I slip away to the ladies' room.

"Wow, Katie girl," Joanne says once we're in the privacy of the bathroom. "You've hit the jackpot. Alex is loaded, hot, and he's crazy about you."

"Do you think so?"

"It's obvious. He couldn't keep his eyes or his hands off of you."

Leaning against the vanity, I bite my lip.

"What?" she asks. "You've got that look that says you've got something on your mind."

I regard her from under my lashes. "I'm falling for him. Hard."

"No one can blame you. On top of being ridiculously successful, he's also amazingly nice."

"He is, isn't he?" A warm, fuzzy feeling spreads through my body. "I told him I'm falling in love with him."

"Wow." She makes big eyes. "What did he say?"

"That it made him happy. In fact, I've moved in with him."

"What?" She squeals and grabs my hands, squeezing them tightly. "That's perfect then. I couldn't be happier for you."

"It's kind of scary," I admit as she releases me. "I've never had feelings this strong. It makes me realize that what I felt for Tony was closer to friendship than romantic love."

"That's because your decision to be with Tony was a logical one. It involved more of your brain than your heart. Alex is all about your heart, and we always feel stronger when it comes from the heart."

"Like Ricky?"

A dreamy look comes over her face. "Yes. Like my Ricky."

"*Your* Ricky? It sounds serious."

She utters a contented sigh. "We're perfect for each other. We both work long hours, so he understands that I'm not always available. It takes away the pressure of being in a relationship with someone who doesn't appreciate what my career involves. He respects my career choice, and he's very supportive."

"You do complement each other perfectly. He seems very caring and sincere."

"He is." She smiles brightly. "I'm so glad Alex and Ricky hit it off as well. It's not always easy for couples to get along."

"You're right, but I think it's because they're both making an effort."

"We're lucky," she says, "and we'd better get on with our business before the men come looking for us."

We slip into two open stalls. When I'm done washing my hands, I use the opportunity to swallow an aspirin for my headache.

"How's your mom?" Joanne asks when she steps out and squirts soap into her palm. "Did she settle in okay?"

"She looked a bit lost when we left, but she's strong. She'll be fine."

Joanne rinses her hands and dries them on a paper towel. "That was beyond kind of Alex. What a generous gesture."

"Indeed." I follow her to the door. "I feel a little indebted, though."

"Don't," she says from over her shoulder. "He wouldn't have done it if he didn't want to."

"That's what I've been telling myself."

The men are waiting just outside the door. I give a little start, not having expected Alex in the corridor.

"Did we make you wait long?" I ask. "I thought you'd be out front."

"Just making sure you're safe," Alex says.

He says it almost jokingly, but despite the casual tone, there's a strain to his voice. He really is obsessive about my safety.

Hooking my arm through his, I give him a smile. "Thank you for being my knight in shining armor."

He stiffens a bit, his expression darkening, but he says nothing as he leads the way to the coat room.

"Did I say something wrong?" I ask softly enough for only him to hear as he gets our coats.

He looks down at me. "No."

"Alex," I whisper while Ricky helps Joanne into the sleeves of her coat. "You're upset about something."

"Not upset." He cups my cheek. "Just hoping I'll never disappoint the image you're holding of me."

"You can't." I wrap my arms around his waist. "You're far too perfect."

"And only a man, I'm afraid," he says, kissing the top of my head.

"Shall we go?" Joanne asks as she and Ricky approach.

"We'll drop you off on the way," Alex offers.

"That's mighty kind," Joanne says. "Thank you."

As she and Ricky waltz out ahead of us, I steal a glance at Alex. His features are tight, the steely blue of his eyes hard. None of that takes away from the warm glow in my chest.

It doesn't matter that he's an oligarch and a kind of mafia in his own right. To me, he'll always be my white knight.

25

When we wake up the following morning, Alex pulls open the curtains to reveal a white landscape and snowflakes drifting down. The snowfall is heavy for November.

Alex doesn't involve me in his business, but living with him has taught me that he's a workaholic, jumping on calls with Russia and answering emails at all times of the day and night. The fact that he puts work aside to spend time with me whenever my schedule allows only makes me appreciate him more. When my shift starts at ten in the morning, like today, he insists on serving me breakfast in bed.

I nestle under the warm covers as he pulls on a robe and goes downstairs to return with a tray of coffee, French toast, and sliced fruit.

"Yum," I say, sitting up and resting my back against the headboard. "That looks delicious."

He hands me a mug of steaming coffee before balancing the tray between us. "You need your energy for that twelve-hour shift today."

I take the plate he hands me and leave it on my lap. "You never told me how you got hold of my schedule."

"I did," he says, holding my gaze as he bites into his toast. "I told you I have contacts."

I raise a brow. "At Coney Island Hospital?"

"Everywhere."

I consider that for a moment. "How did you make such powerful connections here in New York City?"

"Business."

"Mm." I give a mock-frown at his evasiveness. "Where else do you have connections?"

"Everywhere," he says with a glint in his eyes.

I pout. "You're making fun of me."

His smile is mischievous. "I wouldn't dare."

I take a sip of the strong, well-rounded coffee and leave the mug on the nightstand. "I suppose if I ask you where you own properties, you'll tell me everywhere too."

He laughs. "As far as my personal residences go, I have a hacienda in Mexico, a cabin in the French Alps, a penthouse in Miami, a loft in Moscow, a flat in London, a mansion in St. Petersburg, and an island in the Maldives. I also own a couple of hundred buildings around the world, but those are just investment properties." He puts his plate aside with a playful smile. "Does that answer your question?"

I gape at him. "How often do you visit them all?"

He stretches out next to me, bending his elbow to support his weight and resting his head in his hand. "Not nearly as often

250

as I'd like." Reaching out, he trails a finger over my naked shoulder. "I do happen to know you're due some time off in the spring."

His touch makes me shiver in a delicious way. "Obtaining confidential information is unethical."

He traces the length of my arm. "You would've told me if I'd asked."

Goosebumps break out over my skin. "Exactly."

"Then it's not confidential."

"Alex," I chide, picking up my toast. "You know what I mean."

His expression turns serious. "Come with me to St. Petersburg in April."

I stop with the bread midway to my mouth. "What?"

"Your mother will be home by then, her treatment finished. If you're worried about her, I can hire a private nurse to make sure she's well taken care of."

"I wasn't thinking about my mother," I say, dropping the bread back onto the plate. "Well, not only."

He tucks a strand of my hair behind my ear. "Then why the hesitation?"

"That trip would be huge. I mean, expensive."

He raises a brow. "Does it look like I can't afford it?"

"It's not that."

"Katerina," he says in a stern tone. "What is mine is yours. Stop thinking about the money." In a gentler voice, he adds, "I want to show you where I come from. It's beautiful in St. Petersburg in April. Do you know what white nights are?"

I shake my head.

"The sun doesn't set from April to August. Those months

are eternally day. That's why we call those evenings with a midnight sun white nights."

"Wow," I say, trying to picture something like that. "It sounds like magic."

"It is," he says softly, stroking my hair. "Let me show it to you. You'll like it, I promise."

My reservations about not being able to afford such a trip on my salary vanish as I take in the expectation on his face. In a way, he is my white nights, my everlasting day, my magic.

When we started out, I feared that he'd grow tired of sex with me and that we wouldn't last, but the longer I'm with him, the more that fear diminishes. I'm starting to believe that we are magic, that what we have is something truly rare and special.

"Okay," I whisper, giving him a soft smile.

"Good," he says, looking as excited as a little boy with a new toy. "I'll start making the arrangements. I have much to show you, and I want everything to be perfect."

Taking the toast from my plate, he holds it to my lips. "Open. You haven't eaten a thing yet, and it's almost time for you to get ready."

Obediently, I part my lips.

His blue eyes darken as I take a bite. Leaning in, he says as he aims for the corner of my mouth, "You've gotten some honey on your face."

THE UNCHARACTERISTIC SNOWFALL CAUSES A HUGE TRAFFIC JAM. Sitting in the back of the car, I check my watch for the fifth time. I'm going to be late.

Yuri catches my gaze in the rearview mirror. "Maybe you want to call in to let them know you'll be late."

"I can't be late," I say. "We're already understaffed as is. My supervisor is counting on me."

He shrugs. "You can't control the weather."

"Nope." Biting my lip, I stare at the white landscape outside. Cars honk as we come to a complete standstill. There are still three blocks to go to the hospital. At this rate, we'll get there in fifteen minutes.

"I'll walk from here," I say.

Yuri shoots me a dark look. "Mr. Volkov won't like it."

"Well, it's not Mr. Volkov who's going to be late, is it?"

"It's cold. The pavements are slippery." He taps a finger on the steering wheel, his frown deep, and then he comes up with another argument for why I should stay in the car. "You may catch a cold."

Gathering my handbag and the tote that holds my lunch, I say, "I won't melt. It's not as if I haven't walked to work from the subway in the snow before."

"Miss Morell," he says as I reach for the door handle. When I get out, he calls, "Kate!"

"See you later."

I close the door and cross the road. When I look back from the pavement, Yuri is regarding me with a mixture of helplessness and concern. I wave to reassure him, and then I'm on my way, blending with the other pedestrians on Ocean Parkway making their way to work.

It's not as cold as it is tricky to trudge through the rapidly thickening snow. My boots are waterproof, but in no time, my toes feel frozen. Like everyone else, I'm doing my best to navigate my way as I sink ankle deep into the white powder. The municipality services haven't yet cleared the roads and pavements.

I'm so focused on my path that I don't see the man slipping in front of me until he hits the pavement with a thud.

"Fuck," he utters, cradling his wrist.

Rushing over, I go down on my haunches next to him. "Are you hurt?"

He gives me a startled look, surprise etched on his face. It's quickly replaced by caution. "I'm good."

He's wearing a wool coat and dark, tailored pants. Expensive clothes. His face is square with hard angles, his blond hair cut military short. He reminds me of a Viking with his large, strong frame and the unforgiving look in his eyes that borders on something savage. He looks like a soldier or a warrior, or maybe a man familiar with hardships. He has a slight accent, but that's not what betrays him. Even at a glance, it's obvious he's a foreigner. Not surprising, seeing that this is the Eastern European area of Brooklyn.

His brown eyes are intelligent and assessing as he takes me in. "Why did you stop? No one in this city gives a damn."

His cynical comment only strengthens what I've already assumed about him.

"You took your full weight on your arm," I say. "You may have broken your wrist."

"I'll manage."

I hold out a hand. "Let me see."

He lets go of his wrist but groans when he moves his arm.

"That doesn't sound or look good." Gently, I take his arm. "Can you move your wrist?"

He scrunches up his face. "Motherfucker. That hurts like a bitch."

"Here." I take his good arm. "Let me help you up."

"You don't have to do this," he says but lets me.

With his weight, it's not easy, but he has strong legs. He pushes himself up without using his arms or leaning on me.

"I work at the ER. It's not far from here. If you come with me, I'll see what we can do about that wrist."

He grunts and says under his breath, "Not the kind of fucking injury I can afford right now."

"Are you right-handed?" I ask as I lead him down the pavement.

"Yes," he grits out.

"You're going to have to learn to use your left hand for a while."

"Not as steady," he mumbles, looking pissed as hell.

"Keep your elbow bent and your arm close to your stomach so someone doesn't accidentally bump into your wrist. We're almost there."

We make careful but quick progress, and five minutes later, we walk through the sliding doors of the ER. Some of the staff members still gawk at me because of my relationship with Alex, but at least they're not storming to the windows any longer to try to catch glimpses of him whenever he's dropping me off at work or fetching me himself. The novelty is starting to wear off.

I take my charge to the reception desk. Trying to lift his mood, I say, "I assume it's going to take you a while to learn to write with your left hand. The receptionist will fill out the form for you."

"Tillie," I say, recognizing the receptionist on duty. "This is Mr. …"

"Besov," he says. "Ivan Besov. But call me Bes."

That's a Russian name, though an unusual nickname. As I suspected, he's of Eastern European origin. "Please help Mr. Besov fill out the admission form and send him up when he's done. He may have a broken wrist."

"Sure thing, Kate," she says with a smile, already turning to the patient.

"I'll see you when you've filled out the paperwork," I say to Bes.

I'm five minutes late, so I don't linger any longer. I rush to the locker room and don my scrubs in record time. Three minutes later, I'm washing my hands. A male nurse pushes Bes in a wheelchair into the hall when I'm done. A doctor arrives shortly, ordering him to the radiography wing for x-rays.

My day gets busy, and I forget about Bes until he comes back to the ER with his scans showing a fractured wrist. I assist the doctor who gives him a shot for the pain and puts a cast on him from his wrist to his knuckles, leaving only his fingers free.

I'm already busy with another patient when Bes comes to find me, his arm in a sling.

"I came to say thank you," he says, his face oddly expressionless even as intelligence and curiosity burn in his eyes.

"You're welcome. How's the pain?"

"Bearable."

"They say a wrist hurts worse than an arm."

"I wouldn't know. It's the first time I've broken anything in my life."

I smile. "I hope it's the last."

"Thanks again, Miss...?"

"Morrell. Kate Morell."

"Thank you for your help, Kate. You be careful now. As you saw for yourself, it's easy to slip and fall."

With that, he turns and leaves.

It's not until later in the day that I discover my hospital access card is missing.

26

*A*fter declaring my card lost, I go through the red tape of filling out all the necessary forms, which takes a whole hour and makes me late for dinner. I send a text message to Alex to let him know what happened and ask Yuri to fetch me later, but I don't hear anything back from Alex. He must be busy with work himself. It's always hectic for everyone in the weeks leading up to the holiday season. Joanne says her workload doubles around this time.

I'm tired to the bone, cold, and hungry when I finally climb into the back of the car. As usual, Yuri doesn't say much as he drives me home. It gives me time to think. I need to decide what to do with my studio. Since I'm living with Alex, the cost of keeping the apartment isn't justified. Legally, I'm not allowed to sublease it. The only feasible solution is to give my notice to the landlord. To avoid paying the penalty for breaking the lease before the two-year period has come to an end, I'll have to find a tenant to take over my rent. I'll speak to Nancy tomorrow.

She's sharing an apartment with two other girls, but mentioned looking for a place of her own.

It's dark outside when we come to a stop, only the porch light illuminating the path. The angel is almost completely covered in snow, her form visible under a blanket of white. The broken tip of her wing and the curve of her hand where it's lying on the rim of the fountain look as if they've been sketched in white, a painting drawn in concrete and snow.

I climb the three steps to the door, shaking the snow from my coat and boots before venturing inside. Alex waits in the foyer. I grin when I see him, a sense of homecoming washing over me. I quickly shrug off my coat and leave it on the coat stand before walking over and folding my arms around his waist. Burying my face against his chest, I inhale his familiar scent of cardamom and spices and hug him tighter.

He holds me to him for a long moment, his embrace almost uncomfortably tight.

When I finally manage to untangle myself from his death grip, I pull away to search his face. Despite the soft set of his sensual lips, the line of his jaw is tight.

Marusya rushes downstairs with a pile of dresses thrown over her arm. Leonid follows in her wake, carrying two big suitcases.

The housekeeper barely spares me a glance as she shows Alex the dresses and says something in Russian while Leonid scurries past me and out the door. A few men I haven't seen before enter from the hallway. Judging by their dark suits, earpieces, and gun holsters, they're bodyguards. Their presence, and especially the weapons, make me nervous. I've never seen so many guards in Alex's house. What are they doing? Sweeping the rooms? Their postures are rigid, their expressions alert.

Turning my attention back to Marusya, I take in her flushed cheeks. Like the men, she's tense.

"*Da*," Alex says to Marusya in a brusque command.

She bobs her head up and down and flashes me a guilty look before running back up the stairs. I stare at the sequined fabric of the evening dress that trails behind her on the floor, a dress Alex bought for me.

Something is wrong.

My voice wavers with uncertainty as my heart starts thumping in my chest. "Alex? What's going on?"

Cupping my cheek, he brushes a thumb over my jaw. "Do you remember that trip we talked about?"

I frown. "To St. Petersburg in the spring?"

There's reassurance in the smile he offers, but I don't miss the vigilance that makes the blue of his eyes appear colder. "Yes."

That look in his eyes makes my throat go dry. "What about it?"

"I'm afraid it has to be accelerated."

The suitcases and the hasty preparations… It hits me like a fist in the stomach. "To when?"

His firm reply brooks no argument. "Tonight."

I must've heard wrong. "What? You want us to go now?"

"Yes, kiska," he says, reaching for my hand. "Right now."

I pull away, backing up. "We didn't discuss this."

He watches my retreat with the attention of a predator, but he doesn't move. His voice remains calm. "I'm aware of that."

"I can't," I exclaim. "It's a hectic period at the ER. They need me now more than ever. I can't leave them in the lurch. Anyway, I barely have any vacation days left for this year."

Watching me levelly, he says, "Actually, you're taking a leave of absence, as we may be gone for several months."

"What?" I utter a soft, hysterical laugh, backtracking to the door. "You're insane."

He allows the distance, studying me with a disturbingly unfaltering gaze. "No, kiska. Not insane. Just determined to keep you safe."

"Safe from what?" I look around the space as if I'll find the answer there. "From whom?"

The men are going through the room, sweeping an instrument that looks like a small metal detector over the furniture and fixings. Some of them are standing at attention by the door while others are hauling more luggage down the stairs.

"Katerina."

The stern yet gentle way he says my name brings my attention back to him.

"You know about the attempt on my life," he continues. "You know it's not safe here."

The beat of my heart accelerates until it pulses in my temples. "Has something happened?" I'm frozen in place with a mixture of dread and fear. "Did someone shoot at you again?"

"Not me," he says with an odd note of regret.

"If not you, then..." My mind connects the dots, but my lips go numb, refusing to form the word. *Me.* It takes me a moment to find my voice again. "How? What?"

Dipping his hand into his pocket, he takes out a plastic card with a clip and holds it out to me.

It's my hospital access card.

My mind is in shambles, my thoughts a jumbled mess. I read the name printed on the card three times before my brain formulates a sentence. "I lost it today. Where did you find it?"

He lowers his hand, tracing the letters of my name on the card with his thumb. "Someone tied it with a ribbon to the fence. The guard who patrols the garden found it at the back of the property twenty minutes ago, around the same time you left the hospital."

"Why?" I ask, my tongue tripping over the words. "It doesn't make sense. Why would someone take my card and leave it here? Unless... maybe I dropped it and someone found it. Everyone knows we're dating. Everyone knows I've moved in with you. You're a well-known figure in the city. It can't be difficult to find out where you live."

"If that were the case, that person would've rung the doorbell like normal people do. But why even bother to find out where I live? They could've left it at the hospital where it would've been returned to you immediately. No, Katerina. Someone stole your card."

My pulse jumps. "I don't get it." I pace in a circle. Someone simply returned a lost card. They must have. The alternative is too scary. I stop to face him and try again. "Why would someone steal my card only to leave it here?"

Raising a brow, he watches me quietly.

"They're sending a message?" I ask through dry lips.

A dark look crosses his face as he slips the card back into his pocket. "A warning."

I can only stand there like an idiot and repeat the phrase I can't make sense of. "A warning?"

He closes the distance between us in three steps and grabs my upper arms. "I want you to think back to the moment you realized you'd lost your card." He gives me a gentle shake. "Think, Katerina. This is very important."

"I—" Biting my lip, I run through the busy day in my mind.

"It was after lunch. I needed to access the dispensary when I noticed it was gone."

His gaze is imploring. "Before that, when was the last time you used it?"

"When I clocked in for duty."

"Do you remember anyone bumping into you or any out-of-the-ordinary distractions?"

I shake my head. "We were busy, but it was the same as any other day. I thought I'd hooked the card on something in my rush and the clip had come off."

"Obviously, that wasn't the case," he says.

"How can you be so sure it's a warning?"

Letting me go, he drops his hands. "This is how it works in my world. Believe me, I know."

A shiver runs through me. "You think it's related to the time Igor took the bullet for you?"

"I have no doubt. Someone is using you to get to me."

My knees buckle a little at the declaration. "Why? Why would someone target you?"

He rakes his fingers through his hair, messing up the short strands. "I have no idea, but I have every intention of finding out."

I take a few shallow breaths, trying to find calm. "We have to go to the police."

"Your police force won't be able to help. I have to deal with this myself."

"What are you saying?" I utter in a hoarse whisper. "You can't simply take justice into your own hands. There are ways of dealing with threats in America. We have to call this in and make a statement."

His laugh is sardonic. "And say what? That someone tied

your access card with a pretty ribbon to my fence? What exactly do you expect them to do about that? Take fingerprints and put a police officer in front of our door?"

"Okay," I say slowly. "I can see how that won't happen, but if you explain—"

"There's nothing to explain."

I flinch at his harsh tone. "Of course not. How could I forget? Your business is shady. You said so yourself."

He grabs my hands in his, the heat of his palms warming my icy skin. "I can keep you safe." He emphasizes the promise by massaging my palms with his thumbs. "You have to trust me."

I yank my hands from his. "Keep me safe how? By taking me to Russia? For several months? That's crazy. I can't just pack up and leave."

"Your clothes are already packed," he says as another man walks past us with my laptop bag in his hands. "We're leaving for the airport now."

I take a step back, my pulse speeding up further at the implacable look on his face. "I have a job. Friends. My mom."

"I've already stationed a dozen men at the clinic. Your mother will be safe there. Joanne and Ricky will have protection too. You don't need to worry. They won't even know the men are there."

Oh my God. "What about Marusya? We can't leave her here alone."

"I'm sending her and her family on vacation to a safe place."

Everything is moving so fast and sounding so bizarre I have a hard time processing what's happening. I shake my head to clear it. "I can't just run to Russia for a few months. What about an extended visa and the administrative logistics? I don't even have a passport."

He takes my coat, hangs it over my shoulders, and ushers me through the door with his fingers locked around my upper arms. "Everything is taken care of."

Just like that? "No." I twist out of his hold and spin around to face him. "I'm not going on the run with you. That's not a solution."

His eyes tighten, crinkling in the corners with resolve. "I'm afraid, Katyusha, you don't have a choice."

"What's that supposed to—"

Before I've finished my sentence, he grips my wrist and drags me to the car.

Yuri opens the back door.

"Alex," I cry out softly. "Wait."

Not paying my plea any heed, he pushes me into the back, gets in beside me, and closes the door. The partition is up, isolating us from Yuri and preventing me from begging him for help, not that the driver would listen to me.

The front door shuts, shaking the car gently, and a second later, the engine purrs to life.

"You'll be all right," Alex says, folding a broad hand over both of mine where I clasp them together in my lap.

I'm shaking with anger. I've yet to digest the shock. "Do I have a choice?"

"I've already told you the answer to that," he replies smoothly.

Yes, he has. The answer is no. I don't have a choice.

My future, whatever that entails, is now in Alex Volkov's hands.

MIDNIGHT DAYS

1

KATE

The full impact of the last twelve hours only hits me when Alex Volkov's private plane comes in for landing over St. Petersburg, Russia. I sit up in the double bed where I've been sleeping and look out the round window that's next to the bed. The sky is a magnificent thin, winter blue. Far below, a city is mapped out on the ground. Judging from the increased pressure in my ears, we're dropping in altitude.

I check my watch. It's seven in the morning in New York City. That makes it two o'clock in the afternoon in St. Petersburg.

The side next to me is undisturbed, the sheets unruffled and the pillow undented. There's no sign of Alex. When he ordered me to bed, he was in the middle of a hushed, intense discussion with the guards who boarded the plane with us. The usual guys, Igor, Leonid, Dimitri, and Yuri, were there, as well as a few new faces. Has he been working all night?

A knock falls on the door, startling me from my thoughts.

"Kate?" a gruff voice calls from the other side. "We're landing shortly."

Igor.

I have a good mind to tell him to go to hell, but it's not his fault I'm locked in here. Taking my anger out on the guard won't help.

He knocks again. "Did you hear me? You have to take a seat and buckle up."

I rub my eyes in an effort to clear the lingering grogginess. "Give me a few minutes to get dressed."

"You have ten."

I suspect Alex slipped something into the juice he insisted I drink with my dinner. My sleep was almost comatose. Under normal circumstances, I would've been too apprehensive to drift off after the events of last night.

Last night.

A shiver creeps over me at the memory.

After someone delivered my hospital access card to Alex's house, he had our bags packed in a hurry. Despite my protests, he bundled me into his plane and took me away from my home, my job, my mom, and my friends. For *several months* maybe. He delivered the blow with reserved regret but unstoppable determination, telling me in no uncertain terms that I no longer have a choice.

It's nothing short of a kidnapping.

Yet that's not the most troubling thought at the forefront of my mind. It's the knowledge that someone wants Alex dead. After the failed assassination attempt in New York, his life is still at risk. I thought—I hoped—that whoever shot Igor gave up when they didn't succeed, but the card delivery indicates otherwise. Whoever is after Alex is going to try again and is willing to do whatever it takes, including using me to get to Alex.

Not only am I a liability to him now, but my life might also be in danger—and Alex refuses to go to the police. He thinks they can't help, and maybe he's right. Other than my card going missing for a few hours, we don't have any evidence of foul play. Also, there's the possibility of corruption. I didn't consider that before, but it's not uncommon, especially where the Russian mafia is concerned. Alex's business dealings aren't exactly clean.

What a freaking mess.

Throwing the covers aside, I swing my legs over the edge of the bed. Without the warmth of the soft blanket, goosebumps run over my arms. I'm naked. I vaguely remember Alex undressing me and asking if I wanted a sip of water. After that, everything is a blank.

I look around for clothes and spot an overnight bag at the bottom of a closet alcove. I've never seen a plane like this. The cabin even has a vanity and en-suite bathroom.

After finishing my shift at the ER last night, I didn't have time to shower. Everything happened in a whirlwind of action. So now I have a quick shower and dress in the clothes Marusya, Alex's housekeeper, packed for me. They're not my own clothes —which would've meant my standard casual wear of comfortable jeans, a sweater, and Uggs—but the new ones Alex bought for me. The off-white slacks and matching cashmere sweater are more formal than my usual style, as are the similarly colored high-heeled boots.

I'm brushing out my hair when the door opens. Alex stands in the frame, still dressed in the black pants and shirt from yesterday. Stubble darkens his jaw, and his hair is messy, the short strands standing in every direction as if he's dragged his fingers through them several times. Despite those signs hinting at a sleepless night, his gaze is alert, as is his stance. His tall, powerful frame crowds the space, trapping me like a rabbit in a cage.

Bravely, I maintain our eye contact. I'm not angry at him for trying to keep us safe. What upsets me is how he's going about it. He took away all of my choices and dragged me onto this plane. His single-minded resolve is nothing if not scary. Only I'm not going to give him the satisfaction of knowing he intimidates me. I normally pride myself on being a self-assured woman, but Alex is in a different league from anyone I've known. Just how different, I'm still discovering.

The cold blue of his eyes matches the color outside the cabin window, yet appreciation warms those frosty blues as he takes me in from top to bottom. "Sleep well?"

My wounded pride makes me immune to the unspoken compliment. I can't help getting in a jab. "Why bother to ask when you already know the answer? What did you give me?"

A smile drifts onto his face, as if he finds my sarcasm amusing, but the strain doesn't leave his features. "Just something to help you relax. You worked a long shift and needed your rest."

I put the brush away. "How considerate. I suppose I need my strength for whatever lies ahead."

He doesn't acknowledge the not-so-subtle hint. Offering me his hand, he says, "Come. We're about to land."

Ignoring his proffered hand, I squeeze past him into the main cabin. The plane dips, making me lose my balance. When Alex grips my elbow to steady me, I yank my arm away and use the backs of the seats as support.

"Katerina," he says behind me, his voice carrying a hint of a warning. "I don't want you to fall and injure yourself."

"I can walk, thank you very much," I say without looking at him.

The guards sit up front, leaving empty a set of plush leather couches with a foldable table between them. I plop down next to the window, trying not to look at Alex as he folds away the tray table.

Reaching over me, he grabs the seatbelt and secures the clip.

"I could've done that," I say, finally meeting his gaze.

"Yes." He settles next to me, fastening his own seatbelt. "But I like to take care of you."

I grip the armrests of my seat, digging my nails into the leather to prevent myself from doing something disgustingly violent, like slapping him. "Does said care involve kidnapping and drugging? Because that's what this is."

His smile stretches, the gesture patient even as displeasure sparks in his eyes. "In time, you'll come to understand that I'm acting in your best interest."

"My best interest?" I whisper-cry, keeping my voice down so the guards won't hear. They know Alex is kidnapping me and they won't lift a finger to help. They don't need to witness my humiliating, helpless anger. "You're doing this against my will. Explain to me how forcing me to leave my job and home is in my best interest. Forcing me to abandon my *mom*." My voice cracks. "She's *sick*. You know she has no one but me."

"Your mother is in good hands." He cups my hand where I'm clenching the armrest, his big palm warm and dry on my chilled skin. "I don't expect you to fully understand my world. Nor do I want you to. It's much too ugly for someone as pure and beautiful as you." His eyes tighten, that spark of displeasure bleeding into something darker. "Just know that disobedience isn't an option, not where your safety is concerned. You can throw your little rebellion if it makes you feel better, but it's not going to change anything. Is that clear?"

I glare at him as painful emotions churn in my chest. He's just told me in not so many words that I no longer have a say in my life, that he's taking away my freedom and right to make decisions. How does he expect me to react? With gratitude? I'm angry and hurt. Most of all, I feel betrayed.

Tears prick at the backs of my eyes. Before he can see that weakness, I turn my face away.

Only he doesn't allow me the reprieve of the limited privacy. Even though he doesn't force me to look at him, the words he whispers over the shell of my ear won't let me off the hook. "I asked you a question, Katerina."

Taking a breath, I find a semblance of calm and force my voice not to quiver with the tears I'm desperately trying to hold back. "Yes."

"Yes, what?" he asks, brushing his lips over my temple.

I lean away from the touch. "You've made yourself crystal clear."

This time, he lets me escape. Not that I have anywhere to run or hide. There's no place to lick my wounds where the many eyes on the plane won't see. All I can do is pull into myself.

Unseeingly, I look out the window. This is not the future I envisioned when I told him I was falling in love with him. I've read articles about women who were seduced and lured to foreign lands with love, pretty promises, and luxuries, only to find themselves prisoners of the very men who were supposed to save them. The ones lucky enough to escape got to tell their stories.

You're such an idiot, Kate. You should've known.

Yes, I should've. I should've learned from those women's press interviews and recognized the signs. I knew from the start that Alex might be dangerous, but I never thought this would be my fate, not for one minute.

I have no one but myself to blame for the mess I'm in. Will I be one of the fortunate few who gets to tell her story? Or will I disappear like thousands of others, slipping through the cracks of a Russian city?

Alex's voice penetrates the fog of my tumultuous thoughts. "Hungry?"

"No, thanks."

It's not as if I'll be able to eat. Not that it matters. He'll probably threaten to hand-feed me if I don't eat everything on my plate, just like he did last night.

"It's past lunchtime in Russia, and you haven't had breakfast," he says. "I'll make sure a meal is waiting when we arrive."

I don't reply. What's the point? He's made it clear my opinion doesn't matter.

After a while, he releases my hand to check something on his phone, and I breathe easier. The anger and worry don't diminish, but I don't have a vent for those emotions. I have no choice but to bottle them up inside.

The buildings grow in size until gray, drab blocks dominate the view through my window. A control tower and runway become visible. Alex braces me with an arm around my shoulders even though the landing is smooth. The minute the plane touches down, he's on his feet, barking out orders in Russian.

The men don their jackets and weapons. Alex leans an arm

on the overhead baggage compartment above the window, scanning our surroundings with singular attention as the plane taxies to a hangar on the outskirts of the airport.

Leonid, who's examining a computer screen, says, "No interference detected."

Alex doesn't take his eyes off the window. "Keep the satellite surveillance active."

A convoy of black cars with tinted windows is parked on the tarmac. Men in dark suits with automatic rifles are stationed around the area in a circle. The blatant display of firepower makes my mouth go dry.

It looks like a war zone or a drug deal about to go down.

When the plane comes to a standstill, Igor appears with an off-white coat that he hands to Alex. Alex says something to him in Russian as he accepts the coat, at which Igor hurries to open the door.

"What did you say to him?" I ask, anxious to know what's going on.

Alex holds the coat open in silent instruction for me. "I told him to make sure it's safe before we go outside."

Stomach knotting with worry, I look at the armed men through the window as he helps me into the coat. "Why wouldn't it be safe? Who are those men?"

"Don't worry," he says, turning me to face him. "They work for me." He adjusts the lapels of the coat before buttoning it up. "Checking things out is just a precaution. I prefer to take nothing for granted."

"What does that mean?" I try to read his expression, but he's good at keeping a poker face. "That they'll betray you?"

He takes a scarf from the overhead compartment and winds it around my neck. "Unlikely, but a man like me shouldn't take chances. Now stop concerning yourself with these matters. I have everything under control."

Igor sticks his head around the door. "All clear. We're good to move."

"Come," Alex says, making his way to the front.

"Alex," I call after him.

He stops to look at me.

"You need to lay all the cards on the table. This is my life too."

There's no amusement or patience in his smile any longer. "I already told you that I'll protect you. You'll have to learn to trust me."

Yeah, sure. Treating me like a prisoner has destroyed our trust, and keeping me in the dark won't help repair what he's damaged. I want to say as much, but he's already taking a hat with a wool lining from a coat closet next to the door. He waits until I've caught up with him and hands me the hat. When I've pulled it over my ears, he gives me a pair of leather gloves the same color as my boots.

I watch him from under my eyelashes as I pull on the gloves. His stance is rigid. I've never seen him so tense, not even when Igor was being treated for the gunshot wound.

His stress rubs off on me. Whatever he's expecting isn't good, and his refusal to explain only makes my anxiety worse.

A gush of frosty air hits me in the face when he ushers me outside. The winter feels different here than in New York City. This cold penetrates the wool layers of my expensive clothes all the way to my bones.

Alex throws an arm around my shoulders, sheltering me against his side as he leads me to one of the cars. It's as if nothing is wrong between us. I try to break free, but he tightens his hold.

A man standing at attention next to the car opens the passenger-side door in the back. Alex helps me inside and takes the seat next to me. I scoot all the way to the window, leaving space between us. With how I feel about his actions, I'd rather be exposed to the subzero temperature than huddle against him.

We wait inside the chilly interior of the car while the men carry the luggage from the plane and load it into the trunks. It looks like Marusya indeed packed for several months. When the last suitcase has been loaded, Igor shifts into the front passenger seat of our car while Yuri takes the wheel.

The engine starts up. As the car rolls forward smoothly, the finality of the situation sinks in, followed by a wave of nauseating fear.

We're here.

There's no turning back.

The car picks up speed, transporting me to an unknown future.

2

KATE

*T*he drive passes in silence. I stare at the scenery through the tinted window, taking in the apartment blocks that eventually make way for statelier buildings. We follow a broad river for several miles before crossing a bridge. The signposts are in Russian. I have no idea where we're heading, and the uncertainty adds to my fear.

As if reading my mind, Alex says, "We're going to Krestovsky Island."

I have no desire to look at him, but the sound of his voice pulls my gaze to him in a reflexive reaction.

"I realize this is all new and strange to you," he continues. "If you want to know anything, you only have to ask."

One question runs on repeat through my mind. "How long before you'll let me go home?"

The tall buildings throw shadows over the road that intersperse with the bright winter afternoon sun. They play over his face as we speed along, making the laugh lines etched from his nose to his mouth appear deeper.

"Katyusha," he says after a tense beat. "I'm trying to be patient, but don't push me. Not on this."

"Fine." I shrug. "Why don't you just tell me what you want me to say? It'll make the road forward considerably smoother for both of us."

He clenches his jaw. "This doesn't have to be hard on you."

"Are you for real?" I twist in my seat, facing him squarely. "What did you expect? That I'd be excited about this trip?"

"You could be." He lays his arm on the backrest behind me and rubs a finger over the curve of my shoulder. "Think of this unforeseen getaway as a vacation."

I shift to the edge of my seat, escaping his touch. "This is *not* a vacation, and I'm not in the habit of lying to myself."

He lowers his arm to his side. "Your attitude is only making it worse."

My attitude? What about his? My nails dig into my palms. "What I think and feel doesn't matter, right? So why do you even care if it's new, strange, or scary for me?"

His eyes crinkle in the corners. "That's not true, kiska, and you know that. If you want a reminder that I care about you, you don't have to search very hard. The fact that we're here spells it out in bold letters, don't you think? Now stop being difficult. You're looking for a fight to appease your anger, and it's not going to happen."

I grit my teeth in powerless fury and angry frustration. This isn't about picking a fight, but there's no winning this argument with him. There's no way of making him see the situation from my point of view.

When he reaches for my hand, I wrap my arms around my

body. Rejecting him hurts me, especially when I fear more for his life than for my own, but I don't know if I can forgive him for what he's done, not when he doesn't show a stitch of remorse.

He drops his hand, letting it rest on the seat between us, close enough for his knuckles to brush against my thigh. "We're going to a house I own on the island. It's one of the best neighborhoods in St. Petersburg."

I want to ask if that's supposed to make me happy, but I bite my tongue. Things are bad enough, and further conflict won't help. We're talking in circles. A sudden spell of exhaustion washes over me. These bizarre circumstances are emotionally draining. I'm too tired even to think.

Leaning back, I sink deeper into my seat, escaping my thoughts by focusing on the sights through the window. We cross over another bridge and continue to drive along the river. My jaw drops as I take in the mansions set on generous, snow-covered gardens facing the river. The deeper we drive into the island, the more luxurious the properties become.

These aren't houses. They're palaces, and their gardens are parks.

One property is so big it takes up the whole block. A green metal roof, maybe oxidized copper, is visible through treetops from behind a high wall. The driver pulls up to eight-foot-high iron gates that swing open as we approach. The garden we pass through is a winter landscape dotted with naked trees. Right in the middle of it stands an imposing four-story sandstone palace with a turret on each corner and decorative balcony rails in front of the windows.

The tires crunch over the gravel driveway that has been cleared of snow. The car slows to a stop in front of the dwelling. Two cars from our convoy are already parked outside, the men carrying our luggage into the house.

I turn to look through the back window. Another two cars are entering behind us. Movement in the garden catches my eye. Men dressed in white combat pants, matching snow jackets, beanies, and yellow-tinted anti-glare sunglasses walk along the perimeter of the wall that surrounds the grounds. They're armed with automatic rifles and knives strapped to their thighs. They're so well camouflaged, blending into the white scenery and the stark, charcoal lines of the winter trees, that I didn't notice them until they moved. There must be at least two dozen of them. I stop counting at twenty.

When I turn back in my seat, Alex is studying me. Yuri and Igor get out. Igor heads toward the back of the mansion while Yuri gets Alex's door. Freezing cold air barrels into the car, but Alex doesn't make a move to get out.

"Ask me," he says.

I blink. "Ask you what?"

He lifts his gaze to the landscape beyond my window. "About the men."

I requested that he lay his cards on the table, and I'm not going to waste an opportunity to gain a better understanding of my situation. "What are they? Soldiers? Guards?"

"They're here for our protection."

Another vague answer. So much for hoping he was finally going to give me something. "Right." I look through my window. "I suppose a job title doesn't apply then."

"I don't tag them with a label like soldier or guard."

"Or mafia," I say under my breath.

"Look at me." When I obey reluctantly, he continues. "They're well trained and they're loyal. That's what matters."

If he says so. "How many of them are here?"

"Thirty, give or take a few. The rest are training at a base camp on the outskirts of the city. I want my men to keep in shape and up to date with their weapons."

"Thirty?" I exclaim. "How many are there in total?"

"I have two hundred men in this particular line of work in my employ at any given moment. They rotate between here and my offices, taking turns with patrolling, training, and resting."

Shivering from the cold that has invaded the car, I glance up at the façade of the house. The building is huge, big enough to house twenty people. "Do they all stay here?"

He takes my gloved hands and rubs them between his, warming them through the butter-soft leather. "They live in the barracks at the back of the property."

I gape at him. "You have a barracks?"

"It used to be a barn—storage space for foliage and a stable for horses. I had it converted into a dormitory for the men." He takes my arm. "Come. You're cold. We'll talk more in the house. I just wanted to put your mind at ease about the presence of the men before we went inside."

Not having a choice, I follow him to the front door, but I refuse his arm when he offers it for assistance. My heart is still aching too much.

A tall, blond woman, whom I judge to be in her fifties, greets us at the door. Once she's closed it behind us, she offers Alex a bright smile and launches into rapid-fire Russian.

He holds up a hand. "English, please. We don't want Katerina to feel excluded."

The woman's smile is much more reserved as she acknowledges me. "Your girlfriend doesn't speak Russian?"

"Not yet," Alex says, removing his coat. "Katyusha, this is

Lena, my housekeeper." He opens an entryway closet and hangs his coat on a hanger. "She'll take care of all your needs."

Politeness compels me to say, "Pleased to meet you."

In turn, she gives me a cool once-over when Alex's back is turned.

Since I'm rooted to the spot, overcome with the grandeur surrounding me, Alex takes charge of unwinding my scarf and unbuttoning my coat. Coming somewhat to my senses, I push off my coat, remove the hat, and comb my fingers through my hair.

While Lena busies herself with putting my clothes in the closet, I look around the foyer. The opulence is overwhelming. Downton Abbey has nothing on this place. The high, domed ceiling looks like the pictures I've seen of Michelangelo's painting on the Sistine Chapel ceiling, except this one depicts a czar and his court. A double staircase with a golden balustrade runs from both ends of the foyer to meet on the landing. Expensive-looking rugs cover the marble floors, and a red carpet runner decorates the stairs. Chandeliers throw soft yellow light over moss-green walls adorned with Russian baroque art. I'm not a connoisseur, but I've picked up bits and pieces in conversations with Ricky, an artist who's dating my best friend, Joanne—enough to know that if these paintings are originals, which I suspect they are, they must be priceless.

The housekeeper disappears down a hallway, her sneakers not making a sound on the floor.

"You look like you're miles away," Alex says. "What are you thinking?"

I wave a hand around the space. "This is very impressive."

"This palace belonged to a czar. Later, during the Communist era, it was used to house military officers. When capitalism was reinstated, one of the first oligarchs bought the property and restored it to its former glory. It came back onto the market after the death of its owner, which is when I acquired it." His voice holds a note of pride.

I wander to the foot of the staircase, staring up at the patterns on the pressed ceiling. "This is very different from the style of your house in New York City."

"To be honest," he says, his footsteps falling behind me, "I prefer the minimalism and simplicity of the house in New York, but this one has the best location in the city."

I turn to face him. "And location is important?"

He shrugs. "I prefer Krestovsky to the city. Would you like a tour of the house? If you'd rather rest, I can show you around later."

In spite of my turmoil, I can't help but be curious. Besides, if this is where I'm staying for the foreseeable future, I'd better get acquainted with my surroundings.

"I'd like to see it," I say.

Leading the way up the stairs, Alex shoots me a smile from over his shoulder. "Then I shall oblige."

As I follow him through corridors and up and down stairs, my astonishment grows. Every room is luxuriously decorated with its own theme, the furnishings fit for a king. Apart from ten bedrooms, each with an en-suite lounge and bathroom, we visit formal and informal lounges, reading rooms, a library, a study, and an indoor heated pool with a skylight. Next to the pool, a gym overlooks the garden. A sauna is nestled into the corner. Working out seems to be on Alex's list of priorities. Like in his New York home, there's every imaginable piece of equipment one would expect to find in a gym.

We finish our tour in a modernly renovated kitchen with

stainless steel shelves, where a man is chopping vegetables on an island counter.

"This is my cook, Timofey," Alex says. "Tima, this is Miss Morrell. She hasn't had lunch yet. Since it's only breakfast time in New York, prepare a light meal and have Lena take it up to the room."

Timofey salutes. "Yes, sir. One light meal coming up."

"His skill compares to that of a Michelin star chef," Alex says. "You're in for a treat."

Timofey clicks his tongue. "Michelin? Those stars mean nothing. Me?" He pulls away the collar of his shirt and points his knife at a tattoo of a star on the curve of his shoulder. "I earned this."

Alex chuckles. "Don't mind Tima. He can be overdramatic."

I take an immediate liking to the cook. "It's a pleasure to meet you, Timofey. I look forward to trying your food."

"The pleasure is all mine, Miss Morell."

"Please," I say, "call me Kate."

"Only if you'll call me Tima." He swings the knife, splitting a carrot down the middle. "You want something special? You ask Tima. I'll cook you anything you want."

His enthusiasm makes me smile. "I appreciate that."

Putting a hand on my lower back, Alex moves me along.

"Do all of your staff members speak English?" I ask, side-stepping his touch.

He steers me into a pantry the size of my studio apartment back in New York. "I insist that they take lessons. It's good to have language skills. But I can't take credit for teaching Tima to speak English. He was a chef in a high-end restaurant before he came to work for me. Speaking English was compulsory, not only for training, but also for conversing with the clientele."

Fragrances of dill and tarragon infiltrate my nose. Bunches of garlic and dried herbs hang on strings from a beam running along the ceiling. "Aren't chefs normally bound to the kitchen?"

"In those kinds of restaurants, chefs are often called to the table to be paid a compliment. It's the highest honor a diner can bestow on a chef. It will reflect negatively on the restaurant owner if a chef isn't able to thank an important English-speaking customer in his own language."

"That's a bit harsh." I duck to pass underneath a bouquet of parsley hanging upside-down from the beam. "Does that mean top-end Russian chefs are required to be polyglots like you?"

He acknowledges the unintended compliment with a crooked smile. "Most people can manage in English."

I look around the well-stocked space. The shelves are filled with jars of preserved fruit, pickled vegetables, and honey. A cured ham, partially covered with a linen cloth, stands on a chopping block. Baskets filled with fresh fruit and vegetables hang on hooks from the walls. A bigger one on the floor over-flows with bread rolls.

"You don't risk a food shortage here," I say.

"Tima cooks for the men who live in the barracks." He crosses his hands behind his back. "In their line of work, they have high caloric demands."

I nod like feeding an army of men is a normal household occurrence. "I see."

He stands aside, letting me exit ahead of him. "Let's finish our tour. I have to take care of business, and you need to rest."

We go down the hallway and through a dining room with a table that can seat twenty people. Until now, I hadn't truly comprehended how wealthy Alex is. His house in New York is on the upper end of the scale, but it's a lot humbler than this palace in St. Petersburg. It seems he has a full-time housekeeper in every house he owns, and there are two hundred men on his security payroll. I don't even want to know how many people his various businesses employ. Not to mention he smuggled me into Russia on his *private plane* with no passport or visa. Who can do that?

Who is the man I fell for in New York City? He's so much more powerful than I could've imagined, and it frightens me. I'm completely at his mercy. We're on his home territory, and he has all the control. It would be difficult, if not impossible, for a woman with no resources, no passport, no phone or money, and very limited knowledge of Russian to escape from such a powerful man.

At the top of the first-floor landing, he pauses. "You're very quiet."

"It's a lot to take in." And I don't just mean this house or palace or whatever you call it.

His expression softens. "You need a little time to adapt, I understand."

It'll take a lot more than time, but I swallow my retort as he opens a carved wooden door and guides me into a spacious bedroom with a big window that overlooks the front garden. A four-poster bed stands in the middle of the floor. The burgundy velvet bed curtains tied back with golden cords look like something from a medieval scene.

His voice drops an octave, the deep timbre sending a shiver down my spine. "This is where we sleep."

At *we*, my heart trips over a beat. Does he think our relationship will continue unchanged when he's made me his prisoner? I don't even know how I'm going to explain my disappearance to my mom or to my supervisor, June.

Below in the garden, the men in their white camouflage combat gear scout the property. The gigantic iron gates are closed. From this level, I can make out the spikes on top of the wall that make scaling over it impossible. A surveillance camera is fixed every few yards. Like creepy robots, they turn their heads constantly, scanning the surroundings with electronic eyes. There must be a control room somewhere.

It's like being locked up in a prison. I have no way of communicating with the outside world. Yet if I don't inform my mom and my employer about my impromptu trip, they'll be worried sick. They may even report me missing. With how meticulous Alex is in everything he does, he must've already thought up a plan to explain my absence, but I don't want to disappear without giving my mom some kind of explanation.

Whatever I tell her, I can't admit the truth. I won't put that burden on her shoulders. Besides, if she learns what Alex has done, she'll want to leave the clinic where she's being treated for rheumatoid arthritis. It's a ridiculously expensive program that Alex is paying for, and she'll refuse to benefit from the charity of a man who's kidnapped her daughter. This is her only chance at a better quality of life, and I don't want to ruin it for her. She's been in pain for so long, and she deserves this more than anyone I know.

I hate asking Alex for anything, but I don't have a choice.

Schooling my features, I turn away from the disconcerting sight of the unbreachable fortress wall. "Alex?"

He frowns. "You look tired. Did I wear you out with the tour after our long flight?"

"Where's my handbag?"

A shutter drops in front of his eyes. "You don't need it for now."

Renewed anger heats my blood, indignation burning like a flame in the pit of my stomach. For the sake of my mom, I swallow it down and say evenly, "I need my phone." The man facing me is dangerous. Ruthless. I remind myself of that fact as I carefully choose my words. "I can't just vanish without an explanation. I have to call the hospital and my mom. She'll worry if I disappear. You have to let me speak to them."

His easy agreement as he says, "Sure," and takes his phone from his pocket surprises me. Unlocking the screen with his thumb print, he hands me the device. "I was planning on letting you call later."

I take it gingerly, glancing at him from under my lashes as I type in my mom's number. Instead of giving me privacy, he eavesdrops unabashedly.

"Put it on speaker," he instructs, ignoring the cutting look I give him.

Not wanting him to snatch the phone away, I do as he says.

The call connects, and the ringtone sounds.

My mom answers with an uncertain, "Hello?"

"Hi, Mom." It's a battle to keep my voice normal. "It's Kate."

"Katie!" She sounds upbeat. "This is a surprise. I didn't recognize this number."

"I'm calling from Alex's phone."

I briefly meet his eyes. His intense gaze is unnerving.

"Aren't you at work?" Worry filters into her tone. "Is something wrong?"

"No." I force a smile onto my face, hoping she'll hear it in my voice. "Don't worry, nothing is wrong." Flinching, I brace myself for the lie. "Quite the contrary, in fact. We've taken an impromptu vacation." I've never lied to my mom, and I hate both myself and Alex for starting now. "A trip to Russia."

"Russia?" she exclaims. "Where in Russia?"

"St. Petersburg," I say brightly, trying to sound like an excited tourist. "Alex has a house here."

He holds up a finger and shakes his head, indicating I shouldn't say more.

"What about your job?" Mom asks.

I imagine the confusion on her face. "I really needed this vacation."

Her voice softens. "Yes, honey. You're right. You've been working too hard."

"If you need me..." I swallow, biting back an uninvited bout of tears. "I didn't activate roaming on my phone." I give Alex an inquiring look.

He nods.

"You can reach me on this number," I continue.

"All right," she says slowly. "But why doesn't Alex activate the roaming for you?"

The lies are piling up, drawing tighter around me in a web. Flustered, I look at Alex, who faces me stoically. My brain shuts down, unable to come up with a plausible explanation.

"You don't want calls from work," Alex whispers.

"I-I don't want the hospital to bother me on our break," I say.

"Oh." My mom pauses. "That makes sense, but it doesn't sound like you, honey. You're normally so dedicated to your job, you even go in on your off weekends when they ask."

I tuck a strand of hair behind my ear. "That's exactly why I don't want them to be able to call me. I'm taking a long, much-needed vacation with Alex to recharge, and I don't want work problems in the back of my mind."

"That certainly is a wise attitude." Mom sounds considerably more at ease. "I'm glad Alex has such a positive influence on you. I've been nagging you for years to take a proper vacation."

"Enough about me." Turning my back on Alex, I face the window. "How are you?"

"Wonderful. I'm already so much better, and with the new diet, I'm losing weight."

"That's great," I say, my chest warming with gratitude. All the more reason for keeping up the charade. If the treatment is working, I can't take this opportunity away from her. "I'm so happy to hear that."

Alex lays a hand on my shoulder, tightening his fingers lightly. In the reflection of the glass, I see him extending his other hand, asking for the phone.

"Listen," I say, holding back a fresh surge of tears, "I have to go. Promise you'll call me if you need anything, or if you don't feel well."

"Don't worry about me. I'm having the time of my life. Just enjoy your vacation with that generous and amazing man of yours. You deserve it."

Taking a deep breath, I let it out slowly. "I love you."

"Love you too, honey. Say hi to Alex for me."

I cling to the phone, unable to end the call.

Turning me toward him, Alex takes the phone gently and pushes on the red button. His gaze isn't entirely without sympathy when he asks, "Who's next? Your supervisor?"

Unable to speak with the tears clogging up my throat, I nod.

He swipes a thumb over the screen and selects a number. It doesn't surprise me that he has June's contact info programmed into his phone. When it rings, he gives me the phone.

"June Wallers," my supervisor answers. It's clear from her brusque but not unfriendly tone that she's busy and tired.

My guilt doubles. "Hi, June. It's Kate."

"Kate? Please tell me you're making your shift at ten. Rose is sick and Lettie is stuck in some mountain resort where the roads are snowed over. It's chaos here today."

Biting my lip, I drag in another long breath. "I'm so sorry. I have a family emergency. I'm afraid I have to take a leave of absence. I don't have a choice."

"Wow." A beat of silence follows. "I hope it's nothing too serious?"

"I can't—" Checking myself, I say, "I'd prefer not to discuss it. All I can say is that it's a private matter."

"If it were anyone else, I would have doubts, but you're one of our best and most serious nurses. For all the times you sacrificed your days off to stand in when we were short-staffed, I can only say take as much time as you need."

"Thank you." Her understanding makes me feel even worse. Glancing at Alex, I say, "I'll email HR and deal with the necessary paperwork."

He nods, giving his silent agreement.

"Good luck, Kate. I hope you sort out your emergency soon. I'll tell the girls you say hi."

"Thanks," I mumble.

Alex takes the phone and ends the call. "I'm sorry, but you can't be on the phone for too long. This number is secure, but I'm—"

"Not taking any chances," I say hollowly.

"Exactly. Eat something and rest. I'll check on you again later."

"Wait," I say when he turns for the door. "I need to call Joanne. I agreed to meet her for lunch today."

His tone is uncompromising. "Two calls are enough for today."

I take a step forward. "I can't just not show up. She'll worry."

He unlocks the screen and types something. A moment later, the phone pings.

"What did you do?" I ask. "What did you say to her?"

Turning the phone toward me, he shows me the screen. I read his text message and Joanne's reply. He told her the same thing I said to my mom, that we took a spur-of-the-moment vacation and that she can reach me on his phone. He said I'm tired from the flight and sleeping, but that I'll call her soon. She replied with several gasping emojis, telling him to have fun and to take good care of me.

"Happy?" he asks.

I can only look at him.

"I'll see you later, Katyusha."

When he bends down to kiss me, I turn my face to the side. My feelings are too raw to accept his advances. When he created this imbalance of power, he pushed an obstacle between us. I can't just give in. My self-respect won't let me.

He straightens with a tight smile. "If you need anything, let Lena know. I'll be home tonight, my love."

Not sparing me another glance, he walks through the door.

It takes me a good moment to come to my senses. Belatedly, I grab a decorative cushion from the loveseat and throw it at the door he closed behind him. It hits the wood with an ungratifyingly soft thump. It's an immature and pointless display, a sadly ineffective outlet for my cooped-up, frustrated anger. When the door reopens, I'm ready to hurl another cushion at him, but it's Lena who enters with a tray.

She walks over to the lounge area by the fireplace and leaves the tray on the coffee table. "Tima prepared French toast and a fruit salad. There's tea and honey." Straightening, she asks in a formal tone, "Would you like anything else?"

"No, thank you," I say, still battling to get my temper under control.

Nodding, she briskly leaves the room.

Movement outside draws my attention to the window. Yuri walks to the car we arrived in and opens the door. Alex exits the house, followed by Leonid and Igor. The four of them get into the car. Dimitri gets into a second car with some of the men who escorted us from the airport. Three cars pull out ahead of their convoy. The five cars roll down the driveway and through the open gates.

When the entourage is gone, I seize the opportunity. I approach the door and feel the handle. The heavy door swings open without a squeak. I stick my head around the frame. The corridor is empty. Somewhere, a grandfather clock strikes four times.

Tiptoeing into the corridor, I move quietly but swiftly. The study is one floor down. Thankfully, I don't see anyone as I climb down the stairs. My heart beats in my throat, but I make it to the study without running into the housekeeper or a guard. I close the door behind me and let out a shaky breath. My pulse jumps with relief at the sight of the landline phone on the desk.

I hurry across the floor and grab the receiver from the hook even though I have no idea whom I'm going to call. The American embassy? And say what? I don't know, but I want to test the limits of my imprisonment. I want to know the telephone number of the embassy just in case.

My hesitation only lasts a second. My best bet is to call

Joanne and ask her to look up the number for me. I'll say I lost my bank card. The lie bothers me even before it's left my mouth, but I don't think about it as I punch in her number.

Before I'm done, a voice sounds in my ear, saying something unintelligible in Russian. Giving a start, I almost drop the phone.

"Hello?" I say in a hushed tone.

The man on the other end of the line switches from Russian to English. "Good evening, Miss Morrell. What can I do for you?"

Swallowing, I ask, "Who are you?"

His Russian accent is heavy. "I'm Mr. Volkov's telephone operator. All calls from the house go through a central system."

Alex has a landline operator? Hiding my shock, I try to say in a normal voice, "I need to make a call home. Can you please connect me?"

"Sorry, ma'am," he says without missing a beat. "I'm only allowed to connect you to Mr. Volkov. Would you like me to dial him for you?"

"No," I say quickly, dejection setting in.

"All right, then. Good evening, Miss Morrell."

Stunned, I hang up without returning the greeting. I guess that answers the question about my limitations. How far is Alex willing to go? Why not just lock me in while he's at it?

Wait. He wouldn't. Would he?

When I leave the study, I'm no longer discreet about wandering through the house. I stride decisively to the front door. Once there, I take a deep breath. I don't really want to go outside into a garden from which I can't escape. I just *need* to know.

Gripping the doorknob, I turn it. It slips in my sweaty palm. I wipe my hands on my thighs and try again.

It's locked.

I can't believe it. Why I expected otherwise, I don't know, but being locked in only adds to the claustrophobia closing in on me. Running from door to door, I try each one, but the verdict is the same. They're all locked.

A baffled Tima stares at me as I storm into the kitchen and sprint for the back door. I yank on the handle, pushing with all my might, but the heavy door doesn't budge.

"Kate," he says, his tone apologetic. "Don't wear yourself out like this. It's no use, my poor little rabbit. You know it."

Leaning with my back against the door, I slide to the floor, finally admitting defeat. There's no sugarcoating this truth.

I'm Alex's prisoner.

"Come on," Tima says, discarding the spoon he was stirring something in a pot with and pulling me up by my arm. "Let's get you back to your room." He lowers his voice. "You don't want Lena to see you like this. You can't show weakness if you want to survive, am I right?"

I take a closer look at his face. His skin is marred with pockmarks and his nose is knobby. The light is his gray eyes is friendly.

"Tima, you have to help me."

"I am helping you," he says, guiding me to the door.

"You have to let me out."

He clicks his tongue. "Now, that won't be helping you, little rabbit. That'll be sending both of us straight to a shallow grave."

3

ALEX

*T*he security team jumps to attention when I enter the basement of my office building in the tech district of St. Petersburg.

"Anything?" I ask, loosening my tie as I walk down the aisle that separates the state-of-the-art workstations.

Igor and Leonid tail me, their weapons within easy reach, while Dimitri guards the door. With the measures I put in place, we're safer here than anywhere, but there's a weakness in the system I can never overlook—humanity. Human beings are fickle, and human nature is always an unreliable and inconstant variable in the equation.

Like I explained to my pretty, angry kitten on more than one occasion, I'm not taking anything for granted. That's the only reason I'm not six feet under.

The head of my security team, Pyotr Nelsky, waits at the wall-mounted monitors in the front of the room, standing in a military pose with his arms plastered to his sides.

"Nothing, sir," he says when I reach him, an undercurrent of fear in his tone.

I slide my gaze toward the flatscreens on the wall, which reflect the status of every workstation. The results of the data each employee is compiling are summarized in code. "Did you get the hospital security tapes?"

"Yes, sir. We're going through them as we speak."

Going over to one of the monitors, I press the button to wake up the screen. A mosaic of black-and-white photos is puzzled together. These makeshift mugshots are freeze-frames taken from the video feed, singling out the patients who frequented Coney Island Hospital's ER yesterday.

At best, the images are blurry. In some of them, only the backs of the patients' heads are visible.

Frustration eats at my gut. "What's the operation status?"

"We're in the process of trying to identify all the patients and visitors who were present in the building yesterday," Nelsky says to my back.

I turn to face him. "How long?"

"It may take us a couple of days." His Adam's apple bobs as he swallows. "We pulled the records of the patients who signed in. The staff aren't a problem since they clock in and out for work. It will be harder to trace the visitors and service providers, especially considering that there are camera blind spots."

"What are you saying?" I ask, drumming my fingers on his desk.

He fixes his gaze on a spot over my shoulder, not looking me directly in the eyes. "It will be impossible to draw up a list of everyone who moved through the building in the span of twelve hours."

The news infuriates me, not that I expected otherwise. Still, it's worth a shot. "What about Ms. Morrell?"

He stumbles over his feet in his eagerness to boot up the second of the five monitors on his desk. "I already put together a visual file for you."

He presses a button, pulling up a kaleidoscope of faces, some with Katerina in the picture and others without. Many of the faces are hardly discernible. Others are partially or fully hidden from the cameras.

"Patient list?" I ask, my irritation growing.

"Here, sir." Grabbing a printout from his desk, he offers it to me. "As you'll see, there are a lot of Russian names, but seeing that the hospital is situated in an Eastern European neighborhood, nothing out of the ordinary jumps out."

I scan over the names printed on the paper. The list is long. "Pull whatever records you can find on every one of them. Use my government contacts to speed things up."

"We're already working on it, sir."

"Good." I shove the paper back into his hands. "Report to me on the hour, and let me know the minute anything comes up."

The paper trembles in his hand. "Yes, sir."

I make my way to the door with long strides. My employees busy themselves as I pass, not daring to meet my eyes. I suppose I have somewhat of a reputation. People fear me, including the ones who feed their families on the generous salaries I pay. Good. In my world, you don't get very far with kindness. No one is complaining, though. They'll search long and wide to find better fringe benefits or working conditions.

The kind of work they do requires the room in which they spend eight hours a day to be underground. The walls, ceiling, and floor are fortified. No radio waves or infrared beams can penetrate the structure. That means the industrial intelligence I keep in this room is safe from unwanted eyes and ears, but it also makes the room blast-proof. A sophisticated system carefully monitors and purifies the air. The lights are bright without being harsh on the eyes, and the temperature never varies from a comfortable twenty-three degrees Celsius. Wallpaper depicting a mountain landscape covers the gray concrete bricks, and trees planted in pots provide greenery. A fountain in the corner creates the tranquil sound of a waterfall. It empties into a pond populated with koi fish. Apparently, the fish have a calming effect on the human psyche. As per the advice of the interior designer who specializes in Zen environments, the air purifier releases minute organic notes of bergamot and citrus into the air. The fragrances are supposedly uplifting and revitalizing. Yeah, there are worse bunkers to work in.

The metal door shuts behind me with a soft click. Dimitri straightens from where he leans on the wall. Leonid watches me from under hooded eyes.

"What?" I snap. "If you have something to say, say it."

Leonid's chest expands with a breath. "It's unlikely we'll uncover anything via this route. You've seen the quality of those tapes. A lot of people walk in and out of that hospital on a daily basis. Anyone could've snatched Kate's access card."

Spearing my hands through my hair, I practice the control I've mastered through the years to get a handle on my anger. I've come to the same conclusion, but I don't have anything else to go on. "What do you fucking suggest we do?"

Igor gives me a worried look.

Silence.

That's what I thought. No one has any better ideas. If only I knew who dared to threaten her. If only I knew why.

"I need answers," I say through clenched teeth, shoving my hands into my pockets as I circle the space. "Who? Why?"

"Maybe a competitor," Igor offers. "Someone who wanted to send a message."

It's not a new suggestion. We'd already considered this possibility after Igor got shot. Where my business is concerned, there's no shortage of competitors. Power is both a valuable and dangerous commodity in Russia. As the saying goes, the highest trees catch the most wind. Getting to the top takes hard work and dirty fighting, but the real war only starts when you reach that level. Once you're in the number one spot, you're a target for every man beneath you on the ladder. You have to fight twice as hard to stay at the top than to get there.

Threatening a woman who has nothing to do with my business just to send me a message is a low blow, but it's not uncommon. Women make men weak. Enemies have exploited that weakness since the beginning of time.

"For now, we wait," Dimitri says, always the pragmatic one. "It looks like we don't have much of a choice. Whoever took Kate's card wanted your attention. Now that he has it, he'll make known what he wants sooner or later."

Twisting the cord of the hospital badge in my pocket around my fist, I caress the name printed on the laminated card with my thumb. I've traced the letters so many times with my gaze that when I close my eyes, I see them behind my eyelids. "I'll be damned if I sit on my ass and sip tea while some *ublyudok* threatens Katerina."

"We'll get the motherfucker." Igor's upper lip curls. "Only a coward hides behind a woman's skirt."

I nod grimly. I won't rest until I put that cockroach in his grave.

"What do you want us to do?" Leonid asks.

"For now? Keep your ears on the ground. Ask around. See if we unknowingly stepped on any toes or if there are any changes in the power hierarchy we're not aware of."

"Yes, boss," Leonid says. "I'll talk to some guys in the city I know."

"Go with him," I tell Dimitri. "Igor, you stay with me."

Dimitri nods, already following Leonid to the exit.

When they're gone, I consider my options. I still hope we'll get lucky with the hospital tapes, but since we haven't found anything after ten of my best men and women have gone through every second of the security feed frame by frame, the chances that we'll pick up something are slim.

"Fuck." I kick the chair next to the door, nearly sending it flying. Frustration eats at me like acid.

"What do you want to do?" Igor asks. "It's dark. Shall we go back to the house?"

I'm eager to be with Katerina, but she could do with a little space to get over her anger. In time, she'll see this is the only way. For now, at least she's safe.

Somewhat calmed by the thought, I say, "I'm going to spend a few hours in the office." I may as well catch up on some work while I'm here. There are new contracts to sign off on and some investment opportunities I'd like to suss out.

Making my way to the elevator, I take my phone from my pocket to check if there's a message from Lena. There's still nothing, just like ten minutes ago when I checked. Before the door opens and I lose my signal in the elevator, I type a quick message and send it to Lena.

A reply comes a second later. Katerina is napping and all is well at home. Reassured, I pocket the phone, enter the elevator with Igor, and press the button for the top floor.

My executive assistant, Grigori, is a young man who reminds me of myself at his age. His desk stands in the foyer of the top floor where Igor and I emerge. Grigori always dresses formally and fashionably. Today, he's wearing a navy suit cut to the latest Italian fashion, paired with a red cravat. Very European.

Rising to his feet, he bows his head. "Mr. Volkov. Igor. I didn't expect you."

"I didn't plan on coming in," I say as I cross the floor. "Messages?"

"In your agenda, sir. I filtered the unimportant ones. The urgent ones, I emailed to you."

"Good. Anything new?"

Grigori is my eyes and ears when I'm not around. Whenever something happens, like when someone isn't happy with the way I do things, he lets me know.

"Nothing new, sir. Would you like me to order tea or dinner?"

"No, thank you. We're not staying that long. On second thought, bring a bottle of vodka and a chilled glass."

He acknowledges the instruction with another bow.

Igor takes out his phone and makes himself comfortable in the visitor's lounge area in the back while I push open the door of my corner office.

The furnishings consist of a glass desktop suspended on metal cables from the ceiling, a chair in which I've spent more hours than in my bed, and several monitors locked away behind a fireproof metal shutter that covers the entire wall facing the desk. A simple lounge area with a sofa and coffee table is set up against the window for meetings. A door on the side leads to an en-suite bathroom. One of my favorite paintings, a piece by David Hockney, hangs on the wall to the left of my desk. Other than that, there are no knickknacks or photos. Nothing to hint at an attachment. As the situation with Katerina has so effectively demonstrated, flaunting your weaknesses only gives your enemies ammunition to use against you.

While I make myself comfortable behind my desk, Grigori enters with a tray on which a bottle of premium vodka and a glass are sitting. He keeps the alcohol and the glass cold at exactly the right temperature. Once a month, a technician verifies that the bar fridge is set at two degrees Celsius—the optimal temperature for drinking vodka, not a degree more or less.

Grigori places the tray on the corner of the desk, uncaps the bottle, and pours a double shot while I unlock the fireproof shutter with my thumbprint on the electronic device attached to my desk. When the shutter lifts, Grigori gets the laptop I keep there for when I'm in the office and carries it to my desk.

"Shall I leave the bottle, sir?"

"No, thank you," I say, opening the laptop and booting it up.

He picks up the tray. "I'll be here until eight if you need me."

I acknowledge him with a nod before he leaves.

For the next hour, I try to lose myself in work. I've always enjoyed the challenges of running a business empire. The hard work and long hours ground me. Having a knack for figures, I enjoy playing the stock market and investing in high-risk projects. The financial part of the business is the most rewarding, especially when the money rolls in.

At six, a light dusting of snow starts to fall. I was going to give it another hour, but my mind isn't on work. Shutting the laptop with a sigh, I scrub a hand over my face. I haven't slept in twenty-four hours. It would be wise to get some rest, but the agitation and gnawing worry won't let me. The vodka hasn't taken off the edge as I hoped it would.

Pushing to my feet, I shove my hands in my pockets and stare at the lights of St. Petersburg shining through a veil of snow. Dinner isn't until seven. The thought of a warm house, a long shower, and Tima's food is inviting, but not as much as the idea of seeing my kiska, of touching her—when she lets me again—and reassuring myself that she's here and safe. It's that last notion that makes me decide against heading straight home. I should give her another hour like I promised myself. She'll come around.

Igor stands when I exit the office.

Grigori lifts his head. "Good night, sir." For a moment, his formal mask slips as he says to my guard by way of greeting, "Igor."

Well, hell. I would've never guessed. Who knew Grigori had a soft spot for my bodyguard?

If Igor picks up on anything, he doesn't show it.

At the reception area downstairs, Igor gets our coats where the clerk had checked them into the coat room. The clerk is gathering his satchel and umbrella, heading out for the day. The night guard is already there to take his place.

Yuri sits on a sofa near the exit, reading a book. After we go through the security scanners, he shuts the book and gets up to open the door.

Once we're seated in the car and the engine is idling for the heater to run warm, Yuri asks, "Home, Mr. Volkov?"

Rubbing a thumb over my lip, I consider my answer as I

look through the window. It takes me a second to make up my mind. "To the graveyard. The Orthodox one on the hill."

Igor shoots me a look from the front passenger seat, but he doesn't ask questions.

I've only been there once in recent years, not long ago. In fact, it was right before I left for New York City.

The traffic is heavy. We make it around the city and to the hilly part in just under an hour.

"Wait here," I tell Yuri, getting out of the car and unfolding my umbrella.

Igor exits, pulling a beanie over his shaved head. He follows a few steps behind as I make my way to the graveyard entrance. The pedestrian gate is locked. A sign on the driveway gates says the graveyard closes at six. An iron chain dangles from one gate, the attached metal lock hanging open.

Igor pulls out his gun as I slip through the opening between the gates. I know what he's thinking, because I'm thinking the same thing. Maybe some kids broke in to vandalize the graves and paint the walls with graffiti. Street gangs steal the fresh flowers and sell them on the sidewalks. The graveyard is also a popular place for drug dealing. The police are clamping down on the unlawful nocturnal activities, but cleaning the city of criminal elements is like trying to get rid of a cockroach infestation.

The graveyard is well lit. Spray lights cast a yellow glow over the family tombs in the back and the humbler tombstones near the gate.

Our shoes crunch on the gravel road as Igor and I make our way along the simple crosses and marble slabs. Keeping vigilant, I check in the dark corners of the shadows and prick up my ears. Below, the river flows strongly. The gush of the water reaches all the way up here. Except for the river and the noise from the traffic on the nearby highway, nothing else makes a sound.

When we get to a sheltered corner under a big tree in the back, we stop. Sadly, the yard seems to be empty of thieves and drug dealers tonight. I need a fight to vent my frustration and anger, and I was looking forward to one.

Igor hangs back on the road while I take the path to the double gravestone. The angel guarding it is a work of art. She kneels on the steps, one arm resting gently over the tops of the graves. The hem of her long dress drags on the grass. It's so well-crafted that the marble is almost see-through where the fabric gathers in soft folds around her hips. To have given her no grief in such a setting would've been a lie, and a lie would've distorted the beauty of the artist's work. She wears the signs of suffering and pain that I can't show the world. What I've locked in my heart, she displays in the quiet of the graveyard, her only audience the ghosts. She's perfect, down to the broken wing and the teardrop that runs down her cheek. The sculpture in the garden of my New York home is a copy of her. I had it made so I could look at it because the pain wouldn't let me come here.

While the artist was at work with the original, I visited his workshop every day. I oversaw the project in its finest detail. I knew once she was brought here, I wouldn't see her again. And I didn't for many years. Yet before I left for New York, something compelled me to visit. I'm not superstitious. I don't believe in premonitions. However, that day, as I stood on the same spot I'm standing on now, I knew in my gut something was going to happen in New York City. And it did. Someone tried to kill me, but Igor took the bullet.

Maybe that gut feeling was my parents trying to warn me.

I stare at the names engraved in marble.

Viktor Volkov.

Anastasia Volkova.

A shrill chirp cuts through the air. The leaves above me rustle as a bird lifts into the sky with a loud flapping of wings.

I turn. Igor is searching the area, his gun pointed in front of him. When a black cat saunters from behind the tree and crosses the road, he lowers his arms and blows out a long breath.

Shaking the snow from my umbrella, I say, "Let's go."

Since it wasn't my plan to come here, I didn't bring flowers. Just like it wasn't my plan to drag Katerina across the ocean and lock her up in my house. But it is what it is now.

I'll come back with roses.

My kiska will adapt.

She has to, because I won't let her refuse my advances for long. She's mine. We both know it. The world knows it. I'm carrying the proof in my pocket in the form of her access card.

Movement near the gates makes me stop in my tracks. A bent figure trudges over the snow-covered lawn. Igor draws his gun again, but I stop him with a hand on his arm. I recognize the drab black garb and thin gray hair that's plaited down the woman's back, sticking out from underneath a wooly hat.

I saw her here on my last visit. She's the grave keeper who lives in a small house inside the cemetery, not far from the gate. She asked my name and whose grave I was looking for, claiming to know every grave in the yard by name and date. The woman is as old as some of the graves themselves, practically part of the so-called furniture here. I didn't need her directions. Even though I hadn't been to the graveyard since my parents' funeral twenty-one years ago, I remembered exactly where to find them. But to appease her, I played her game. I gave her the names, and she pointed out the high spot with the weeping angel.

"Why have you never visited?" she asked in her croaky voice.

Not wanting to spew some bullshit, I didn't answer.

Now, she looks up at the sound of our footsteps, not seeming the least bit alarmed at our presence.

"Ah," she says, looking me up and down. "It's you."

I take in her worn shoes, shabby coat, and the holes in her mittens. "What are you doing out in the snow?"

"Came to lock up," she says, motioning at the gate. "We close at six. You should come back during the day."

"I'll do that." Taking my wallet from my pocket, I empty it of the stash of cash I always have on me and place the bills on her palm. "Go inside before you catch your death in this cold."

Looking from her hand to my face, she gives me a toothless grin. "May the dead protect you and God bless you, sir."

"Go in," I say. "We'll lock the gate."

Her grin stretches. "That's my job. I've been doing it for fifty years. Never missed a day of locking up in my life."

Igor holds the gate for me.

"God bless you," she says again, waving the money in the air as I walk through the gates.

Yuri gets out from behind the wheel to open my door.

"You know she's going to blow that money on booze," Igor says on our way to the car. "She reeks of cheap spirits."

"You'd rather I buy her a cup of soup at the soup kitchen?" I hand my umbrella to Yuri and shift into the back of the car. "She's eighty years old. Cut her some slack."

"Soup would've been better," Igor says, a rare reprimand.

I let it slide, not only because I owe him my life, but also because he's right. "Tomorrow, place a standing order for a meal delivery at the caterer we use for our office functions."

His mouth tightens, but he doesn't argue, seeing that he stupidly brought the task upon himself. I would laugh at the expression on his face if it weren't for a foreboding—that pesky premonition I don't believe in—that slithers down my spine.

The hair on my nape stands on end. My scalp prickles. Like the last time I visited my parents' graves, I have a feeling that something is about to go down. Something ugly. Maybe it's my imagination that my parents are trying to warn me, but I can't ignore my gut feeling. That feeling saved my life. It left me with an uneasiness, a strange awareness of doom, and when that sniper took a shot at me, I was alert enough to sense it, able to escape in the split second when my sixth sense told me to move.

The notion worming its way into my gut now is the same, yet different. This time, the hunch is far worse. This time, I don't fear for my life, but for the life of the only woman I've ever cared about.

4

NEAR DETSKIY SEVERNY BEACH, ST. PETERSBURG

*T*he club is pulsing with music and sweaty bodies. Naked waitresses strut around on spiky heels, offering drinks and blowjobs or other services in the back rooms. Officially, prostitution is illegal, but the club belongs to Vladimir Stefanov, one of the wealthiest men in Russia, and for the right price, the authorities turn a blind eye.

Tonight, Vladimir barely spares the women's perfectly proportioned bodies a glance. Pushing through the throng of people on the dance floor, he makes his way to the private room reserved for VIPs.

Under the jacket and waistcoat that stretch over his stomach, he's sweating. He's been on edge ever since word reached him two hours ago that Alex Volkov arrived in the city. Oleg Pavlov, like the coward he is, has already fled St. Petersburg with his family, jumping on a private plane to go hide in the States. If he thinks Vladimir believes his excuse of taking his wife and kids to warmer weather, he insults Vladimir's intelligence. Oleg is weak. Running with his tail between his legs is proof of that.

Vladimir has always known that Oleg could become a problem. It would take little pressure to make Oleg talk. He's certain Oleg is holding on to some of the evidence, just like Vladimir is. Vladimir has kept photos as insurance in case he has to blackmail Oleg with them one day, and Oleg likely has something similar. There's no telling what will happen if that evidence comes to light.

The situation Vladimir now finds himself in is a clusterfuck of epic proportions. He never should've trusted Oleg to deal with Alex Volkov. Things would've gone smoother if Vladimir had gotten his hands dirty from the start. But he wanted to keep a back door open by pinning the assassination of Volkov on Oleg if the shit hit the fan. Problem is, you can't trust any-fucking-body but yourself with your dirty work.

His bodyguards, having circled the room, shove the clubbers aside to create a path. A young woman who gets a rough push on the shoulder stumbles. She trips over her feet and goes down face first. A man dressed in a well-tailored suit crashes into his date, causing her to spill her cocktail down the front of her glittery dress.

No one says a word. No one dares. The clubbers stand aside, leaving the way to the lounge clear for Vladimir.

A bouncer wearing a microphone and a holstered handgun opens the door to the VIP room. Ivan Besov—Bes— is already there, reclining in a chaise lounge with one arm in a sling and a coffee cup in his free hand. A fucking coffee cup. After fucking up, he dares to sit there and drink coffee like he owns the place? The sight of that alone makes Vladimir want to break the assassin's fingers and let them mend crookedly so he can never hold a cup or pull a trigger again.

Two of Vladimir's guards enter the room ahead of him. Bes puts the cup on the table and gets to his feet, knowing what needs to follow. Once he's been patted down for weapons and none have been found, Vladimir steps inside. The bouncer stationed outside closes the door. His men stand at attention in each corner of the room. If Bes takes offense to the open display of distrust, he hides it well.

"Sit," Vladimir says, motioning at the seat Bes has already warmed.

Bes acknowledges the order with a humorless smile. "Why am I here?"

Vladimir walks to a liquor tray and selects his favorite brand of vodka. A waitress could've served the drinks, but he needs the distraction. If Bes notices how nervous he is, he'll lose face. It's important—paramount—that he's feared.

After pouring two glasses, Vladimir carries one to Bes and offers it to him like a generous host.

"No, thanks," the assassin says without accepting the drink. "Alcohol isn't advisable for a man who needs steady hands."

To be served a drink by none other than Vladimir Stefanov is an honor. Refusing it is an insult. Vladimir will take great pleasure in making Bes suffer for that slap in the face. Soon.

Tipping his chin toward the sling, Vladimir asks, "How's the wrist?"

"Almost healed." The assassin stares up at him with unblinking, emotionless eyes. "The cast comes off in two days."

Vladimir downs the liquor as he considers his reply. A guard rushes over to take his empty glass.

"Will you be able to handle a gun?" Vladimir asks.

Bes's gaze narrows minutely. "I'll hit the target, if that's what you're asking."

Vladimir downs the liquor in the second glass, stretches out his arm, and drops the glass. "That's what you said when Oleg paid you to take out Volkov."

The guard who hurries to Vladimir's side catches the glass just before it hits the floor.

The line of Bes's jaw turns hard, but his regard remains expressionless. "As I told Oleg, Volkov moved. One second more, and I would've had him."

Vladimir rolls onto the balls of his feet. "Unfortunately, one second is all it takes to blow a plan to pieces."

A muscle ticks in Bes's temple. "Mistakes happen in my business, but I've never failed to finish a job. I don't intend to start now."

"Mistakes." Vladimir utters a soft laugh as he crosses the floor, coming to stand in front of the glass wall that forms one side of a Perspex pool.

The turquoise water is lit. The filter pump causes a gentle current, the movement throwing soft waves of light over the walls.

"Once, maybe, it's a mistake," Vladimir says, studying the way the water distorts the figure of the woman who walks over the stage to the edge of the pool. "But twice?"

"Slipping and fracturing my wrist was an unfortunate mishap," Bes says. "If not, you would've had Katherine Morrell by now."

The woman looks straight at Vladimir. From behind the wall of water, he can't make out her face, but she knows for whom she's performing. She stretches out her arms in front of her and dives gracefully. Her naked body comes into focus as

315

she glides through the water and swirls like a ribbon, making a stunning live portrait in the Perspex frame.

"The truth is, Bes," Vladimir says, focusing on the way her nipples contract into hard points from the cold water, "I'm growing tired of excuses."

The dancer bends a knee and jumps elegantly with pointed toes. Her poise is regal. With eyes the color of the water and lips naturally red, like ripe cherries, her delicate face is classically beautiful.

"There won't be another mistake," Bes says in a flat tone.

"Yet you made one."

For that, the assassin deserves a bullet in the head. The thought alone makes Vladimir's hands tremble with violence. The urge to grab a gun is so strong he has to curl his fingers into fists to prevent himself from acting on it. He'd like nothing more than to crack Bes's skull and paint the walls with his blood, but he can't get rid of him yet. He has bigger plans for the assassin.

"What are you talking about?" Bes asks.

Vladimir allows the woman's graceful movements to calm him. Natasha is an accomplished but retired ballerina. She's one of Russia's treasures. She's too old for the stage now, but her ass is still firm, her tits pert. People flock to the club to see her show. Vladimir's personal favorite is the one where she performs with the water snakes.

"You made a grave mistake by delivering Katherine Morrell's key card to Volkov," Vladimir says.

"That was intentional. I've got him worried," Bes says, meeting Vladimir's gaze in the reflection of the glass. "Worried men make mistakes."

The naked male dancer dives into the water. His strong

body is lithe and well defined, his cock thick and long. He scoops up the woman, lifting her in a choreographed dance.

Vladimir follows the dancers' underwater ballet, moving his head to the side and up as they surface for air. "He also ran home to protect his lover, and we both know he's as good as untouchable here."

"An opportunity will come. It always does," Bes continues in a bored tone.

The arrogance makes Vladimir shiver with fury. Controlling it is difficult. He focuses on the couple diving to the bottom. The man presses the woman against the wall, flush against Vladimir's body. Only the glass separates them as the man spreads her legs and shoves into her from behind.

Not even the highlight of the performance is enough to abate Vladimir's anger. Natasha's breasts push flat against the glass. She snakes her arms around the man's neck and locks her legs around his ass, pulling her supple body into an artistic C-shape as the man pummels her splayed pussy for Vladimir's visual entertainment. A tongue of heat licks through Vladimir's stomach and stirs his cock, but with the nagging worry in the back of his mind, the spark of arousal doesn't catch.

"This is what you're going to do," Vladimir says, not taking his eyes off the show. "From now on, you're following *my* orders."

The woman throws back her head. A bubble escapes from her lips, floating to the surface.

"What about Oleg?" Bes asks.

"Oleg had his chance."

The male dancer meets Vladimir's gaze through the water, a wordless request for permission to end the show. Vladimir shakes his head.

"What do you want me to do?" Bes asks in his infuriatingly disinterested voice.

Vladimir clenches his teeth. The woman opens her eyes. She draws a line with her palm across her throat, indicating she's out of air and needs to surface.

"I have reason to believe Oleg is in possession of certain evidence," Vladimir says. "You're going to get it for me."

The woman starts to struggle. The man's face pulls into a mask of concentration as he pumps his hips faster to finish the performance.

"How am I supposed to do that?" Bes asks.

Turning to him, Vladimir says, "The instructions are encrypted on a flash drive."

A guard jumps forward, handing Bes the plastic casing with the drive.

"I'll let you figure out a way," Vladimir says with a cold smile. "Your file states you have a high IQ. I'm sure you'll get creative. You do this, and I'll turn a blind eye to your mistakes."

Thumping sounds rattle the glass behind Vladimir.

Bes weighs the casing in his palm. Wisely, he doesn't turn down the deal. "By when do you need this evidence?"

Vladimir turns back to the show. He's just in time to see the life wash out of the woman's eyes. At long last, the male comes, pulling out so Vladimir can see the jets of ejaculate he shoots into the water. "The sooner, the better."

Kicking with his feet, the man swims up to the surface, his heavy cock drifting flaccidly between his legs. Finally, Vladimir grows hard. Maybe he'll order the male dancer to his upstairs room tonight.

"Fine," Bes says. "But that doubles my price."

Natasha's body drifts like a four-pointed star in the water, her long blond hair billowing around her face. She makes a peaceful picture.

For the first time in weeks, Vladimir breathes easily again. All he needed was to take back the control. Facing Bes, he says, "Get the evidence and finish Volkov, and you'll get your money."

The assassin stands.

"If Oleg finds out what's going on, if he so much as catches a whiff of it, you're dead," Vladimir says. "Is that clear?"

Bes's gaze drifts over Vladimir's shoulder toward the pool. "Crystal."

"Good," Vladimir says, feeling much better.

5

KATE

*O*pening my eyes, I blink in momentary confusion. My emotionally drained mind wants to sink back into the relief of oblivious sleep, but something harping at the back of it urges me to wake up. Slowly, I surface to full consciousness.

I'm lying on a bed under a soft blanket. It's so dark I can't see my hand in front of my face, but I don't need my eyesight to know this isn't Alex's bed in New York City. This isn't the house I moved into with him. Then the cobwebs lift, and I remember. That little something in the back of my mind crystalizes into clarity as the memories flood back.

I sit up and stretch out an arm to feel my way. Velvet brushes against my fingertips. The bed curtains. Scrunching the fabric in my hand, I pull it aside. Light penetrates the inky darkness. A nightstand lamp throws a soft glow over the room. Someone must've closed the bed curtains after I'd fallen into an exhausted sleep. Lena, maybe. I find the idea of her being in the room while I was napping disconcerting.

Despite the comfortable temperature in the room, I shiver a little as I get up. The time on my watch says it's seven o'clock. I napped for two hours. My wrung-out body and mind needed the rest. I'd been working long shifts at the hospital for two weeks straight. Physically, I'm still playing catch-up, and the mini breakdown I had at discovering I'm locked in didn't help.

Pricking up my ears, I listen for sounds. The house is quiet. Eerily so. Rubbing my hands over my arms, I head to the dressing room and find a warm cardigan that I pull on over my sweater. I catch sight of myself in the full-length mirror. My slacks are wrinkled from sleeping in them. My hair is disheveled, the waves untamed. I smooth down my hair with my palms and don't bother to find shoes. I pad on my sock-clad feet to the window and pull the drapes open a crack. Whoever closed the bed curtains must've also closed these.

The powerful spray lights don't leave a single corner of the garden in the shadows. As earlier, men patrol the perimeter of the wall and stand guard at the gates.

Taking a moment to go over everything that's happened since last night, I consider my options. Now that I'm calmer, I can think clearer.

I'm locked in the house. Tima and Lena won't help me. I don't have access to a phone. Whatever liberties I'm allowed from now on will happen at the sole discretion of Alex, which means it's in my best interest to appease him. Somehow, I'll have to win back his trust. Seeing that he's broken *my* trust, that will be very hard for me to do. But how am I supposed to sit here and do nothing while Alex is out there risking his life? How am I supposed to bear the thought that something might happen to him while my hands are tied?

Lost in my troubled deliberations, I go downstairs to see if Alex has come home. A guard stands next to the front door.

"Good evening," I say.

He acknowledges me with a nod.

"Do you know if Alex—"

The door opens before I can finish my sentence, and Igor walks through it, dusting snowflakes from the shoulders of his coat.

He stops when he notices me.

"Igor," I say, part in greeting and part in relief.

I look over his shoulder, trying to see if Alex is with him, but he cuts off my view by closing the door, presumably to keep the cold from coming in.

"Where's Alex?" I ask.

"He'll be in shortly," he says, moving around me.

I take a step to the side, blocking his way. "Where is he?"

A beat lapses. "Getting an update from the men at the barracks."

Testing my boundaries, I ask, "May I please use your phone?"

His large frame sags with the sigh he blows out. "You know I can't do that."

"That's what I thought."

At least he has the decency to look guilty. "You can't call home. It's for your safety." Averting his eyes, he walks away.

"Miss Morrell?" a female voice says.

I spin on my heel.

Lena stands at the foot of the stairs. "Dinner is served in the dining room. Mr. Volkov will join you as soon as he can. He said you shouldn't wait." She drags her gaze over me, pausing on my socked feet. "Normally, Mr. Volkov dresses for dinner."

"Do you know where he's been?"

She waves a hand toward the corridor. "The dining room is this way."

"Alex showed me already."

She gives a cool smile. "In that case, you won't get lost." Without another word, she disappears down the hallway.

Clenching my hands into fists, I turn back to the guard at the door. If I was hoping for an explanation from him, I'm in for another disappointment. He's facing straight ahead, ignoring my presence as if I don't exist.

Not having anywhere else to go, I walk to the dining room. The table is set with a dozen dishes. None of the intricate pastries or colorful salads are familiar, but they're all beautifully presented with garnishes of radishes and tomatoes artfully carved to resemble roses.

My stomach grumbles, reminding me I didn't touch the French toast and fruit Tima had prepared earlier.

Tima enters with a steaming platter. Giving me a bright smile, he says, "I hope you rested well. Please, have a seat. You must be hungry." He places the platter in the center of the other dishes and pulls out a chair next to the head of the table where a place is set. "Here. Come. Make yourself comfortable."

A whiff of garlic and parsley reaches my nose. I want to decline out of spitefulness, but I'm starving. Grudgingly taking the seat and letting him adjust the chair, I say, "There's enough food here for an army."

He chuckles. "There *is* an army, in case you haven't noticed."

I scoff. "How could I have missed that?"

"I made you some comfort food." He motions at the dish from which the aromas are wafting. "Pasta with artichoke. It's an Italian recipe." Taking a serving spoon and fork, he scoops up a generous helping and places it on my plate. "There. Eat up before it gets cold. Then you can try the cold dishes and salads. Those are all local recipes. Delicious."

"Thank you," I say with reluctant gratitude.

Tima pours water into my glass before leaving the room.

The grandfather clock strikes once. The beat echoes in the quiet room. Half past seven. For a moment, I sit motionless, taking in the silence and how unreal this feels. A soft tick-tock follows as the clock continues to count off the seconds. It's a strangely depressing sound and a very awkward situation, sitting alone at a table made for twenty people. I do need to eat, though.

Twisting the hair-thin pasta around my fork, I bring a bite to my mouth. Flavors of garlic, parsley, and olive oil blend with the taste of the artichoke hearts. The combination is delicious, instantly igniting my appetite. Tima was right. This is comfort food and exactly what I need.

I devour the portion on my plate and contemplate going for seconds, but I'm curious about the other dishes on the table. Just as I'm digging the serving spoon into a salad of potato and what looks like dill pickles, Alex walks into the room.

I still as I meet his gaze. He wears a white button-up shirt and dark pants. His jaw is free of stubble, his lightly tanned skin perfectly smooth. The dark brown color of his hair forms a striking contrast to the icy blue of his eyes. His regard is vigilant and observant as his gaze slides from my face to my empty plate.

His smile is reserved. "My apologies for being late."

"This is your house. You can do as you please."

Taking the seat at the head of the table, he says, "I thought it best to give you a little time to cool down."

I'm far from having cooled down, especially after discovering just how much of my freedom he's taken away. It seems stealing my choices wasn't enough. When he takes my hand and lifts it to his lips, I try to free myself, but he tightens his grip and presses a kiss on my knuckles. The moment he lets go, I pull my hand away.

The set of his mouth turns strained. "It looks like time didn't do the trick."

Ignoring him, I finish serving myself a helping of the salad.

"What do you need, Katerina?" he asks, a bite to his tone. "How much time is it going to take?"

I pick up my fork. "How about giving me the truth?" For example, where has he been all afternoon?

He watches me with unwavering attention. "I gave you the truth. Someone stole your card, and I *will* find out who. Until then, I'm keeping you where it's safe." His tone hardens with resolve. "Here."

I clench my fingers around the fork. "As your prisoner."

His voice remains level, but the minute tightening of his eyes betrays his impatience. "As someone I'm doing my damnedest to protect. That's not going to change until I catch the perpetrator, so get used to the way things are. Asking my staff for a phone and trying to call home isn't going to work."

Stabbing a piece of potato with my fork, I glare at him. It's good to know his telephone operator and guards report back to him. At least I know who's on my side. No one, it seems.

A sensual aroma of cardamom and spices drifts to me as he reaches over the table and loads some of the pasta onto his plate. He showered. The smell stirs memories of happier times. I push them away, not wanting to remember him as a kind and skillful lover. The Alex who's serving me small portions of every dish on the table isn't the man who shared starters and kisses with me in Romanoff's. He's the man who brought me to Russia and locked me up in his house.

"Try the *oliv'ye*," he says, serving us wine. "It's my personal favorite."

My appetite for the food is gone. I take a big gulp of the red wine while he watches me with hooded eyes as he brings a forkful of pasta to his mouth.

After chewing, he says, "Don't be obstinate, Katyusha. It's not going to help. The sooner you accept the situation, the easier this will be for you."

I've already come to the same conclusion, but having my choices taken away isn't something I'll easily accept. Carefully, I ask, "Have you considered that you may be overreacting a bit?"

"Not where you're concerned."

"You're locking me in and denying me the use of a phone. What am I going to do? Run away in a strange city where I can't speak the language or call the police? I'm not stupid or naïve."

"I'm not taking any chances."

The jab hurts. He doesn't trust me either. "You could've protected me just as well in New York."

"You're wrong." He pulls the salt closer and adds a generous amount to his food. "I can't protect you if you're on the street or in a hospital with thousands of people passing you on a daily basis."

I lean back in my chair, digesting that information. What about him and the thousands of people who pass him on the streets? What if someone shoots at him again? What if, this time, the sniper doesn't miss?

"Katyusha?" He takes my hand and rubs a thumb over my

knuckles. "Are you unwell? You're very pale. Didn't you rest enough?"

The fear is crippling. "How long is this going to take? To track down the person who wants you dead?"

"I'm doing everything in my power to find the son of a bitch."

I swallow. "Do you at least have an idea of who it could be?"

"A business rival, maybe." His brow furrows as he lets go of my hand to draw his fingers through his hair. "I don't have any concrete leads for now."

"In other words, we could be here for months."

His jaw bunches. "As long as it takes."

The words rush from my lips. "Don't go out there. If you have a telephone operator, you must have a security chief or someone who can find out who's trying to kill you."

"Hey." He leans over and grips my shoulder. "Slow down. I know how to take care of myself. Don't worry about this. That's my job."

Easier said than done. I care about him. My feelings aren't going to vanish just because he brought me against my will to Russia. I've fallen for him, and now it's too late to protect my heart. If anything should happen to him—

I give a start when he pushes to his feet. The man staring down at me is wearing an expression that says he owns me. The heat in the cool blue of his eyes is the kind that can cut through iron. I imagine the blue flame of a welder melting steel as he rounds the corner of the table without moving his gaze from mine. His expression sharpens with intent. It should be a warning, but the magnitude of the power he exudes hypnotizes me, keeping me frozen in my seat.

He pulls my chair back as if the weight is nothing. Locking

his fingers around my waist, he drags me to my feet. I'm a puppet in his hands, overwhelmed with fear, worry, and the notion of being trapped in a dark, endless tunnel. I don't see a way out, not for the foreseeable future and not when he lifts me swiftly onto the table.

My heart is beating a mile a minute as I stare up at his face. The harsh lines are drawn in lust. It's been too long. Too long for us, at least. We're used to making love at least a couple of times a day. His hands on my waist feel right, but my mind can't make peace with the new imbalance of power between us.

He lowers me gently, cushioning my head with one broad hand and going for the button of my slacks with the other. His gaze holds me prisoner, radiating pretty promises of safety and warmth as he pops the button through the buttonhole. My body heats instantly, his effect on me devastatingly powerful. The zipper of my slacks makes a scratchy sound as he pulls it down. His actions are slow and meticulous, his attention focused on my face.

I gasp when he slips a hand inside my underwear and over my folds. The mere brush of the pad of his finger over my clit makes my body bow. If he slips that finger inside me now, I'll be lost, and the victorious look on his face says he knows it.

If this were any other day, I wouldn't hesitate to take the pleasure he offers. I would give him everything he wants and all I'm capable of. When he took me in the bed and again in the shower the day before yesterday, we were on equal footing, or so I thought. Did I ever have a say in our relationship, or was it just a sweet illusion?

The thought hurts, adding to the growing mountain of torment in my chest. If I've been blind and naïve, I only have myself to blame.

Gently, he parts my folds, finding the wetness that's proof of my arousal.

"Katyusha," he says in a rough voice, his features tight with desire as he plants one hand next to my face.

When he lowers his head to move in for the kill, it takes every ounce of my willpower to say, "No."

He freezes above me. Inside my panties, his fingers curl into a fist. I don't have to look at him to know his control is hanging by a thread.

Gripping his wrist, I pull his hand from my underwear. Tears burn in my chest as I whisper, "I'm sorry. I can't."

6

ALEX

Torn between disbelief and confusion, I stare at Katerina's face. Her beautiful features are drawn into a mask of regret and something else, something that looks a lot like disappointment. She holds my gaze with her large hazel eyes as I pull my arm from her grip and bring my hand to her mouth.

"You want me." I trace the closed seam of her lips with the finger I had in her pants mere seconds ago. "Here's the proof. Do you want me to part those pretty lips and make you taste it?"

She turns her face to the side.

Splaying my fingers over her delicate jaw, I bring her gaze back to mine. My voice is thick with the desire and frustration I try to suppress. *"You want me."*

And if I don't get inside her soon, I'm going to blow up in more than a physical way. The distance she's placing between us is driving me insane.

"Not like this," she says, slamming her palms on my shoulders and shoving me off her.

I straighten with reluctance, unwillingly creating even more distance. The gap between us feels like a vacuum, as if all the air is being sucked out of the room.

Not meeting my eyes, she sits up and fastens her slacks.

I'm like a pressure cooker, the mounting steam threatening to shoot the lid through the roof. "Katerina."

She looks at me again.

"Is this how you punish me? By withholding sex?" I home in on the heaving of her breasts under her sweater. "It's a very effective method, I have to admit, but I wouldn't advise you to go down that road. We both know this isn't a game you're going to win."

"A game?" Her tone sharpens. "You think this is a game?"

On the contrary, this is serious. Just how serious, I'm not sure she fully comprehends. Nor do I wish to enlighten her. What's the point of tormenting her with the knowledge that if she's captured, my enemies will most likely torture her in the most despicable ways to draw me out of my stronghold?

"I don't want it to be like this," she says. "But you made your choice when you took away mine."

I don't like the way this conversation is going, not one bit. If she's hinting at wanting to leave me, she can get that ridiculous idea out of her pretty little head.

It's not going to fucking happen.

Ever.

Ignoring the way her beautiful eyes grow large, I step between her legs, my hands balled into fists. It's all I can do not to reach for her. Biting off every word, I make myself clear. "There is no longer a choice."

"You knew." She leans away, supporting her weight on her arms. "You knew this could happen."

Feigning ignorance isn't going to work. Not with me. I pin her with a stare. "So did you."

She blinks. Emotions play over her stunning features. She's expressive, my kiska. It has always been easy for me to tell what she thinks. That's one of the things I love so much about her. With Katerina, I don't have to worry about manipulations and games. She's honest and straightforward. Maybe that's what the problem is. She's too honest, too good, to accept the ugly parts of my world.

An internal battle wages in her eyes. Yes, she knew what she was getting herself into when she agreed to move in with me. I've told her in not so many words that I'm a bad guy. True, I left out the gritty details of what goes on behind the closed doors of my empire. No one gets to where I am without blood on his hands, but there's no point in burdening her with that fact.

"I…" She wets her lips with the tip of her tongue. "This isn't what I expected."

Placing my palms on either side of her body on the table, I close some of that unwanted distance. "We won't be hiding forever."

"It's not the running or the hiding."

My voice is gruff with the need clawing inside me. "Then what is it, kiska?"

Her features contort, the brave mask she's wearing collapsing. "It's being treated like a possession."

The hurt etched in her expression hits me straight in the heart.

I get it. I'm not a foolish or insensitive man. Katerina is

independent. Up until now, she's made all her own decisions. She's used to running her life and taking charge. In her relationship with her mother, she seems more of the adult, taking responsibility for her ailing parent, and as a nurse, she's used to making decisions that mean the difference between life and death. Locking her up and taking away everything that gives her life meaning isn't ideal, but it's not for forever. It's temporary and for her own good. She'll understand eventually. She loves me. She told me so once, and I'm determined to hear those sweet words again. I'll do whatever it takes to get them.

Except letting her go.

I've never begged for anything in my life, not even for bread when I was starving. She's the first one to bring me to my knees. Pressing my forehead against hers, I say raggedly, "Let me touch you, kiska. Please."

A sob catches in her throat. She shakes her head, brushing our hair together. "This isn't me, Alex. This isn't who I am."

I clench my fingers so hard my nails dig into the table. "Tell me what to fucking do."

"If you can't give me freedom, give me time," she says, gripping my wrist and moving it away to break the cage of my arms. "I need time and space."

When she ducks under my arm and slides from the table, I don't stop her. When she runs from the room, all but fleeing from me, I don't go after her. I don't acknowledge how much it hurts that she treats me like an enemy. Instead, I go in search of a bottle of vodka and give her the time and space she wants.

7

CALIFORNIA, THE UNITED STATES

*O*leg Pavlov presses the phone to his ear and walks to the edge of the terrace where he's out of earshot. He drums his fingers on the rail as he waits for the call to connect, inconspicuously checking to see if his bodyguards are in place. Assured that they're in position, he takes a handkerchief from his pocket and wipes the sweat from his brow.

What is taking the assassin so long? Acid burns in his stomach. This fucking ulcer is going to kill him.

Finally, Bes picks up.

Oleg cuts straight to the chase. "What did you do?"

"I do a lot of things on a daily basis," the assassin says smoothly. "You'll have to be more specific."

Oleg glances over his shoulder to where his family is having breakfast. Lowering his voice, he grits out, "Alex Volkov should be dead by now. Instead, he's running around St. Petersburg, very much alive." Despite the control he's forcing, his voice rises in volume. "And working very hard on finding out who's behind the assassination attempt."

When his wife, Annika, looks up, he gives her a smile, indicating all is well when nothing could be further from the truth.

"Oleg," she calls, "your breakfast is getting cold."

He raises a finger to indicate he needs another minute and turns his back on her. "Explain to me what the fuck you were thinking, stealing Katherine Morrell's key card instead of snatching the woman herself. All it accomplished was chasing Volkov straight to his army in Russia."

"Patience, old man," Bes says. "All in good time."

Facing the vista of the vineyard, Oleg says, "My patience is running out. So is your time."

"It will happen when I'm ready. We moved too fast the first time. That's why you failed."

"You mean *you* failed," Oleg says.

Bes laughs. "You gave the order. That failure is on your head, my friend."

Oleg clenches his jaw. "Do you have any idea what Vladimir is capable of?"

He's ignored two of Vladimir's calls already, saying that he was in public places and couldn't speak, but Vladimir expects him to call back and soon. He'll want a report on what the fuck went wrong this time.

"I do, as a matter of fact," Bes says, his tone dry. "If you don't want the throats of your lovely family slit, I suggest you go back to your breakfast like your wife ordered, and let me get on with my job."

Oleg glances around, acid pushing up into his throat as he searches the faces of the tourists. The motherfucking assassin is watching him? *Oleg* is the one paying Bes. *He's* in charge. How dare that lowlife Russian sniper spy on him like he's the goddamn target?

"Have I made myself clear enough for you?" Bes asks.

"I'm the one paying you," Oleg says, fighting to keep the fear from his tone.

"Yes," Bes drawls. "But there's always someone willing to up the price."

Oleg grips the rail hard. "Listen to me, you lousy—"

"I'd be careful with the insults if I were you. I'm sure Volkov will pay handsomely to know who ordered the hit on him."

Oleg goes cold in the heat of the day. How the fuck did this happen? How did the power switch from him to the man he hired? Bes is a rat, a lowlife, a dirty son-of-a-bitch traitor. If Vladimir finds out Bes is threatening to sell them out, he—Oleg —is dead. Hiring an unreliable cleaner isn't something Vladimir will let go unpunished.

"What do you want?" Oleg bites out.

"Evidence."

Oleg drags the handkerchief over his face. "Evidence of what?"

"Evidence of the crime you and Vladimir Stefanov committed."

Oleg freezes with his hand in midair. "What did you say?"

"You heard me."

Impossible. "I don't know what you're talking about."

Bes laughs again. "You know exactly what I'm talking about."

"Listen here, you—" Oleg swallows the insult, remembering Bes's threat. "You know how the business works. Vladimir and I collaborated on many things."

"I'm talking about the reason you want Volkov dead."

Oleg tightens his fingers around the phone to prevent them from trembling. "How did you find out?"

"A man like me has his ways."

"Tell me," Oleg says, spittle flying from his mouth.

"It doesn't matter. All you need to worry about is delivering the evidence of Stefanov's culpability."

Oleg is all but shaking in his shoes. He can't believe his ears. "You've got to be kidding me."

"I never joke, Oleg. You should know that about me by now."

"Do you have any fucking idea what Vladimir will do to you if he finds out? To *me*?"

"What do you care about what happens to me?" Bes asks. "With regards to you, Stefanov will never find out. He'll be out of the picture before he has a chance to try."

"You want to bring Vladimir down?" Oleg casts a glance at his family and waves at his frowning wife again. "Why?"

"Stop asking questions that don't matter."

It fucking matters, because if Vladimir goes down, so does he. Oleg swallows. "Who's paying you for the information?"

"Don't worry," Bes says. "I'll keep your name out of it. Give me what I want, and you can continue your wine tour with your perfect family."

Oleg feels like he may be sick. "What about Alex Volkov?"

"You uphold your end of the bargain, and I'll uphold mine. Deliver the information, and I'll deliver Volkov's head on a platter."

The line goes dead.

Lowering the phone, Oleg stares at the screen. He's shaking with fury. How dare that assassin threaten his family? He'll skin him alive. The only reason he's not retaliating right now is because he can't let Vladimir find out that Bes knows the truth.

If Oleg kills Bes, he'll have a hard time explaining it to Vladimir. Vladimir is a highly intelligent and intuitive man. He'll see straight through a lie. Besides, hunting down Bes might take months. No, Oleg's best bet is to play along. He'll deliver the evidence and let Bes bring Vladimir down. Once Vladimir is out of the way, he'll kill Bes.

Taking a roll of Tums from his pocket, he pops the pill from its casing and slips it onto his tongue. The more he thinks about it, the more Oleg believes it will not only be the best solution, but also a blessing in disguise. Let Bes do him the favor of getting rid of the ever-present threat of Vladimir. And once Bes himself is dealt with, no one will ever know the truth.

When Oleg walks back to his wife and children, his heartburn is already fading.

8

KATE

*W*hen I wake up the next morning, the bed beside me is empty. A sliver of light falls through the crack in the bed curtains.

Pushing up on one elbow, I pull one curtain aside. Daylight spills through the windows. The bedsheets are wrinkled. I lay a palm on Alex's pillow. The fabric is cool, but his scent clings to the linen.

I drag a breath of cardamom and spices into my lungs. Even in his absence, his presence lingers in the room. The events of last night weigh heavily on my chest. Folding my arms around my knees, I take a moment to reflect on our fight.

He'd come to bed long after midnight with vodka on his breath. I pretended to be sleeping, but the soft "goodnight" he whispered told me he knew I was awake. He respected my wish and kept his distance, not touching me during the night. I was both grateful and disappointed, and there was a moment when

I almost gave in. In the scary, lonely hours of the early morning, I wanted to snuggle against him and throw an arm over his waist. A part of me wanted to anchor him to the bed, to prevent him from going out there, where it's dangerous. But another part of me couldn't—can't—forgive him. I don't know how to make peace with our new circumstances. I don't know who I'm supposed to be any longer. Our roles have changed, and I've yet to figure out where and how I fit into his life.

Am I his girlfriend or his prisoner?

Does he see me as a woman he cares about or merely his possession?

Ugh. I need to think, but my mind is clouded with confusion and emotions. Climbing from the bed, I go to the bathroom. The cupboards are stocked with all my usual brands of toiletries, and a box of contraceptive pills waits on the vanity. I pull out the sheet of pills. The pills have been popped out on the days of the month that have passed. It's not a new box. Alex thought about everything when he instructed Marusya to pack. I take today's pill and have a quick shower, which doesn't clear my head as I hoped it would.

The closet is stocked with many of the clothes Alex bought for me in New York, including formal wear and evening dresses. Thank goodness Marusya packed some of my own outfits at the bottom of the bag. With the way I feel, I need clothes that are familiar and comfortable.

After dressing in a pair of jeans, a warm sweatshirt, and my sneakers, I venture downstairs. The only sounds that greet me are the dong of the grandfather clock, announcing that it's ten in the morning, and the clanging of pots coming from the back of the house.

Finding the dining room empty, I walk to the kitchen.

Tima stands behind the stove. Pots simmer on the burners, steam rising from their contents. The space smells starchy, like porridge and potatoes.

"There you are," he says, wiping his hands on an apron. "Take a seat." He motions at the kitchen table where fruit, rye bread, jam, and cottage cheese are set out. "I thought it would be cozier to have your breakfast here than in the stuffy old dining room."

Grateful for his consideration, I plop down in a chair. "Thank you."

He goes to a counter set with several urns and flashes me a smile from over his shoulder. "Tea, coffee, or hot chocolate?"

"Coffee, please." I need the caffeine to clear the cobwebs in my mind.

"One coffee with sugar coming up."

It's not surprising that he knows how I drink my coffee. He prepared only vegetarian dishes last night. Alex must've briefed him on my preferences.

When he places a mug in front of me, I ask, "What are you cooking?"

"*Borscht* with *pelmeni* for lunch and roasted lamb with potatoes for dinner. That's for the men. I'm making vegetarian versions for you." He goes back to the stove, picks up a bouquet of fresh herbs, and chucks it into one of the pots. "You can never start the preparations too early. I also made oatmeal porridge. Alex told me you like to have oatmeal for breakfast."

I cup the mug, letting the warmth seep into my palms. "That's very considerate."

He serves a helping of the porridge into a bowl and carries it to the table. "It's the least I can do." Pushing a small basket of berries and a pot of honey toward me, he studies my face. "How are you doing today?"

I shrug. "I slept well, and I'm eating like a queen."

"That's not what I meant. How are you feeling in here, where it matters?" He pats his chest.

Unable to lie to his face, I look away. "Good."

"Mm." He goes back to stirring the contents of a big pot. "Alex left you English books in the library. The cable isn't connected, but there are DVDs." He looks over his shoulder again and winks. "All the seasons of *Downton Abbey* in case you're in the mood."

I utter a wry laugh. "Alex disconnected the cable? What does he think I'm going to do? Send Morse code via the cable connection?"

Tima's smile is so wide his whole face looks like a piece of creased paper. "You're certainly clever enough."

"Ha. Technology and I aren't friends."

"If there's anything you want, you only have to say the word. Alex will send for it."

"That's good to know," I say with a bite to my tone, even though my anger is already wearing off, leaving me with a confusing mess of emotions and the worry that Alex is an open target outside.

"I've known Mr. Volkov for some years now." Tima puts the spoon on a saucer, turns to face me, and crosses his arms. "I've never seen him as invested in anyone as he is in you."

I raise a brow. "Is that supposed to make me feel better?"

Leaning against the stove, he says with a sincere expression, "He obviously cares about what happens to you."

I consider that. Tima is kind, but I don't know him. I don't trust him yet. I'm not going to discuss my dilemma or my feelings with Alex's staff.

Another smile scrunches up Tima's face. "Eat up. Your oatmeal is getting cold. I'm sure you have better things to do than keeping me company in the kitchen."

Actually, no. What else am I going to do with myself? "Do you need a hand in here?"

His eyes grow round. "Absolutely not. Mr. Volkov will roast me like that lamb if I make you work in the kitchen."

I frown at the expression. I hope he means that figuratively, but after the last couple of days, it doesn't sound as farfetched as it should.

"On with dinner," he says, speaking more to himself than to me as he goes to the pantry.

By the time he returns with his arms full of ingredients, I've finished my oatmeal and coffee. I rinse my bowl and load the dishwasher while he whistles an unfamiliar tune.

"Thanks for the breakfast," I say on my way to the door.

He lifts his head and gives an absentminded wave before continuing to chop the stalks off a bunch of beetroot.

The sound of a vacuum cleaner comes from the front of the house. Making my way over, I spot Lena in the foyer, vacuuming with earbuds in her ears. She looks up as I mount the stairs, but she doesn't say good morning. In return, I swallow the greeting that was on the tip of my tongue.

For the rest of the day, I explore the house. I find the DVDs and books Tima mentioned in the library and manage to distract myself for a while, but the stories don't hold my attention. I'm too strung out to let myself get lost in fiction.

When I grow tired of reading, I pull on a T-shirt and yoga pants and go in search of the gym. A guard mans the door, but he steps aside for me to enter. A fancy sound system boasts a variety of music mixes. It's not complicated to figure out how it works. I select a lively pop compilation, surprised at Alex's taste in music. I expected him to be a jazz or classical guy, not a pop music fan. Maybe this is just the kind of music he listens to when he works out.

Choosing the treadmill, I set it on a comfortable speed and run until my legs feel like jelly. It's a good feeling. I ran cross-country in high school and did a few 10Ks on my own in college, but I've been working so much in the past couple of years that I've let my fitness routine fall by the wayside. Now I realize how much I've missed it. The exercise doesn't expel my turbulent thoughts, but it does lessen some of my cooped-up tension.

Thoroughly exhausted yet satisfied, I pull on a swimsuit, rinse off in the pool shower, and drift in the warm water of the Olympic-sized pool. Condensation runs down the sides of the skylight that lets in the sun. The smell of chlorine reminds me of vacations when I was little. The pleasant association relaxes me further, and by the time I stretch out on a lounge chaise with a view of the indoor garden, some of my level-headedness returns.

Lena surprises me, entering with an infusion that she deposits on the side table before leaving quietly again. I pick up the delicate porcelain cup and sniff the herbal tea. It smells like lemon verbena. A taste confirms I'm right.

As I sip the tea, I try to put things in perspective. What Alex did hurt me. The blatant way he executed my disempowerment without considering my opinion angered me. Yet I can't say it shocked me. Not really. Looking back, I now see the signs clearly—the way he insisted I go out with him, how he wouldn't take no for an answer until he'd worn down my resolve, how he moved my clothes into his house without consulting me, and how quickly he convinced me to move in with him. Then there was the unsettling fact that he always knew my shift schedule at the hospital.

The truth is he's always been this way, and despite the blinders lifting from my eyes, I don't want him any less. One touch from Alex is enough to make my knees weak. It's always been the case, right from the start, and I doubt the visceral pull he exerts on me will ever change. Last night was proof of that. My body always tells the truth.

I care about him more than I've cared for any man. If I want space, it's not because he's made me a woman on the run or put my life in danger. The reason I need to slam on the brakes is that he believes there's nothing wrong with keeping me locked up as long as he's convinced that it's in my best interest.

Can I tie myself to a man who won't give me freedom? Maybe Dania, the daughter of his business partner, was right. Maybe I don't fit in Alex's world. How much am I prepared to accept? Can I make peace with letting him dictate my life? No. Like I told him last night, that's not me. Then how do I take back my power?

A shadow invades my sunny spot. I glance up at the skylight. The sun is setting. I check my watch. It's close to five, and there's still no sign of Alex. A shiver of unease runs down my spine. I hate being kept in the dark while anything can be happening out there.

Seesawing between worry and anxiety is exhausting. I've been lying here, thinking this thing through until my brain hurts, and I still haven't decided on a course of action.

Putting the empty cup aside, I get to my feet. I find a

bathrobe in the adjoining bathroom and pull it on over my swimsuit. My hair smells of pool chemicals and my skin feels dry. I need a shower to rinse the chlorine from my body.

After I've had a warm shower, I moisturize my skin and brush out my hair. Remembering Lena's comment that Alex prefers to dress for dinner, I choose a blue cashmere dress. I don't care what Lena and Alex think about my attire, but being underdressed puts me at an unfair disadvantage, even if it's just in my own mind. After applying mascara and lip gloss, I'm ready.

At seven, I go downstairs. The big house is quiet. Alex and his most trusted bodyguards are still not home. Like the evening before, the table is set with a variety of dishes. I finish dinner in solitude, my only company the ticking of the clock.

Tima distracts me with his lively chatter, telling me the names of the dishes in Russian and explaining their ingredients as he serves dessert and finally clears the table.

Not ready to retire, I go to the library and curl up on a chair. Someone made a fire in the fireplace. I watch the shadows the flames draw on the wall and listen to the crackle of the wood. Soon, a warm glow spreads over my cheeks, and my eyes start to droop.

I give a start when the door suddenly opens. Alex stands in the frame, wearing a dark suit and a black button-up shirt without a tie.

"I didn't mean to frighten you," he says, studying me with cunning intensity.

Sitting up straighter, I rub my eyes. "I was dozing off."

He steps inside and closes the door. "I'm sorry I'm late. I had to take care of business."

I follow him with my gaze as he crosses the floor and comes

to a stop in front of the fireplace. "Business as in work, or business as in finding out who wants you dead?"

"Both." He props his forearm on the mantelpiece and stares into the flames. "I hope the dinner was to your liking."

"It was delicious, thank you." The concern I can't shake compels me to ask, "What about your dinner?"

He takes a log from the basket and throws it into the fire. "I ate at the office."

"Oh. Do you have a private cafeteria for your employees?"

His lips quirk. "We do. But for the executives, we have a standing order from a catering company."

"Convenient," I say, studying my hands.

He turns to face me. "How was your day?"

I blink up at him. "Do you really want to know?"

He unbuttons his jacket and pulls it off. "Yes."

Not in the mood for small talk, I shrug. "Good."

He drapes the jacket over the back of the sofa and walks to my chair. Towering over me, he asks, "What did you do?"

"Don't tell me you're interested in the meaningless actions that occupied my hours."

"Just because you didn't save lives today doesn't mean what we're doing here is meaningless."

"What *you're* doing here, you mean."

He gives me a patient smile. "Is it wrong that I'm interested in how the woman I care about spent her day?"

There are so many things wrong with the way I spent my day that I don't know where to begin.

Dragging a chair closer, he sits down next to me. "Joanne called."

I sit up straighter. "What did she say?"

"Just that she wanted to talk to you."

"What did you tell her?" I ask, holding my breath.

"That you were at the spa and unable to take the call."

I clench my hands on my lap. "Lying comes easily for you, doesn't it?"

"You can speak to her if you behave," he says without missing a beat. "In fact, I think it will do you good."

My mouth drops open. I don't know if I should be grateful for the concession or upset that he's bribing me with selective contact with my friends.

Taking my hand, he rubs a thumb over my pulse. "I need you to think back to the night outside Romanoff's."

"The night when I got mugged?" I ask with surprise.

The line of his jaw hardens. "Yes, but I don't think it was a mugging."

I pull free from his touch as shock washes away the warmth of the fire. "You think it was related to the stealing of my card?"

"Maybe," he says with regret.

I gasp. "Why didn't you say so?"

"I didn't put two and two together at the time. The more I've been thinking about it for the last couple of days, the more it seems like a possibility."

Unfolding my legs from under me, I shift to the edge of the chair. "But why steal my handbag? Was that also some kind of warning, a message to you?"

When he only stares at me with violence brewing in his steely eyes, another truth hits me between the eyes.

"You don't think he was after my bag," I say, jumping to my feet.

"Katerina." Alex follows my pacing with his gaze. "I need you to think. Tell me anything you can remember about that night."

The memory isn't pleasant, especially given what I've just

348

learned. "You were there. You saw what happened." More truths pierce me like arrows. "Did you even give a statement to the police?"

"My men do their job better than your police do theirs."

"Your men." Right. "What did they find?"

He scrubs a hand over his face. "Nothing. That means the police would've found even less. At the time, I thought like you, that maybe it was just an unfortunate mugging, but now I suspect differently." Getting up, he walks over and grips my shoulders. "I didn't want to put you through this, not then and not now, but you have to think back to that night. What did he look like?"

I dig into my memory, trying hard to give Alex something. "He was stocky and big with a bald head."

"What else?"

"He…" I swallow when I remember the cruel smile he'd given me. "He had bad teeth—crooked and yellow."

"Did he say anything to you? Could you make out an accent of any kind?"

A shiver of repulsion runs over me. "He just laughed in a creepy kind of way, like he enjoyed scaring me."

Alex's nostrils flare. "Did he have any discernable marks, like a scar or a birthmark?"

It suddenly hits me. I motion to the top of my scalp. "He had a tattoo here."

"What was it?" he asks, urgency lacing his voice. "Can you recall if it was a word or a picture?"

"A picture." Now that I think about it, I can see it clearly in my mind's eye. "An eight-pointed star."

He lets me go so suddenly I stumble.

"Are you sure?" he asks, his gaze drilling into mine. "Are you sure it was a star with eight points?"

"Yes," I say through dry lips. "Why? What does it mean?"

"Nothing." Grabbing his jacket, he presses a chaste kiss to my forehead. "Go to bed. Don't wait up."

And he's gone, the door slamming behind him.

9

ALEX

*R*ushing out the front door, I run into Igor.

"I parked the car," he says. "Yuri locked up the garage. Do you need anything else before I head out?"

I pull on my gloves. "Where are the others?"

"Having dinner at the barracks."

"Get them." I make my way to the garage with long strides. "Take three armored cars and bring a dozen men. Yuri too."

He doesn't ask questions. He jogs around the mansion as I unlock the garage door by pressing my thumb on the wall-mounted fingerprint scanner. The roller door lifts. The garage houses the cars I use for the city as well as a motorbike and an off-road four-by-four.

A hidden button at the back opens a false wall panel. Behind it is one of the several weapon vaults on the property. A digital lock requires a retina scan and thumbprint. I open the door and step inside the walk-in safe just as Igor returns with Leonid, Dimitri, Yuri, and twelve of the men not scheduled for the night guard shift. Three cars with bullet-proof windows and reinforced bodywork pull up outside, their headlights illuminating the snow-covered garden.

I take an AK-47 from the gun stand and hand it to Igor. "Take automatic rifles and grenades. Smoke bombs too."

Leonid hands the weapons to the men who gear up while Dimitri picks three drivers. I instruct them where to go, and in under a minute, we're leaving the property in four cars.

Leonid and I sit in the back. Yuri drives and Dimitri rides shotgun. No one handles a car like Yuri. He can maneuver a Land Rover down a cliff at a forty-five-degree angle. I don't trust any other driver. Plus, he's good with a gun.

Our convoy slips smoothly into the sleeping streets of the upmarket neighborhood. I don't expect a war, but I take nothing for granted where these motherfuckers are concerned.

The gang that uses the eight-pointed star emblem operates from a shady part of St. Petersburg. They're a bunch of lowlife scums who make their money by smuggling weapons and drugs, but they'll do any job for a price. They're not picky about the so-called freelance work they take on.

After leaving the historical center behind, we head toward Kupchino and park at the back of a warehouse with an eight-pointed star painted on the wall. That's where the gang stores their merchandise. I came here a couple of times in my youth when I was running deliveries. The attached building serves as their clubhouse, with the kitchen as a sorry excuse for a restaurant.

I scan the surroundings before we get out. Nothing stirs. They're not expecting a visit. They won't even see us coming. At my signal, the men exit their vehicles. Half of them follow me while the other half surround the building. Leonid goes ahead to scout the area, his gun pointed in front of him.

For now, we benefit from the cover of the dark night, but as soon as we hit the area illuminated by the streetlights, we move along the side where there are no windows. The place is exactly as I remember. The stench of rotting food and the pungent smell of piss hang in the alley. The bulb above the door burns. Good. A grin of anticipation splits my face. That means the motherfuckers are home.

Footsteps fall on the cobblestones. Leonid's beefy face appears around the corner. He creeps up to me before saying in a hushed tone, "The warehouse and the back are empty. No one on guard. There must be at least ten of them inside."

I take my gun from my waistband and tilt my head toward the entrance. My men move ahead of me to the door. We pass a small broken window that's boarded up from the inside—the toilet window.

At the door, I stop to listen. The noises coming from inside are faint. The walls are thick. There's a distinct clanging of metal, pierced by the occasional boisterous laughter. The cockroaches are dealing as usual.

I hold up a hand, counting down on my fingers. Leonid screws a silencer onto the barrel of his gun. On three, he shoots the lock open. Four men cover him as he kicks in the door. The sturdy metal slab swings inward, hitting the doorman squarely in the face. He stands frozen, a look of surprise trapped on his features, but he's as good as unconscious on his feet. After another beat, he falls backward like a dead weight. Not taking any chances, Leonid plants a bullet between the man's eyes as he steps over his body.

The silencer ensures there's minimal noise to attract attention, but the open door alarms someone who comes out of the back room, zipping his fly as he walks. His eyes grow large when he spots us. He utters a cry, reaching for the gun in his holster, but he's dead before he has his hand on the shaft.

All hell breaks loose.

Men fire at us from the back, forcing us to take shelter in the kitchen. It would've been easier to drop a grenade in the back room, but I want the man who attacked Katerina alive.

Men in dirty aprons are skinning rabbits at a big table. They look at us as if we're ghosts. The shortest one drops his knife and raises his hands. The other two follow suit when Leonid rounds on them with his gun. An old woman with a nose and eyes buried in folded layers of skin shouts insults from the stove, waving a wooden spoon.

Gunfire sounds from the hallway. The acrid smell of gunpowder hangs in the air.

The cooks are workers. The men are part of the gang, but the old woman gets paid to prepare their meals.

"Go," I say to her, motioning at the back door next to a storage area.

Instead of running, she grabs a pot from the stove and flings it at Leonid. The boiling liquid barely misses his shoes. With the distraction, the bravest of the cooks grabs his paring knife and throws it at one of my men, who ducks. The knife falls with a clatter on the floor.

Pop, pop, pop.

The three men drop like flies, each with a hole between the eyes. The barrel of Dimitri's gun is smoking. The woman goes berserk, grabbing a steak knife and charging at me.

Really? A steak knife? For fuck's sake. Give me a break.

Pop.

She falls on the floor, next to her minions.

I lower my gun. I don't feel bad about shooting a woman. I gave her a choice. She made it.

More shots come from the back room. It sounds like fireworks on New Year's Eve. They're giving it their all. We're not here to take prisoners, and they know it.

"Cover me," I say to Leonid.

I stealthily approach the door and steal a glance around the frame. The hallway is empty. Our targets are in the back, trapped inside the room. There's no way out but through the door we used or through the one in the kitchen.

Leonid takes an automatic rifle from one of our men. He sends a spray of bullets at the doorway of the back room while I move down the hallway. A man who dares to stick his arm around the frame gets his hand shot off. A howl of pain lifts above the noise of the gunfight. Another man dashes forward, firing blindly, but he goes down before his bullets can do any damage.

My men follow on my heels. By the time we're at the door, the shooting from inside has stopped.

"We surrender," someone calls from inside.

"Come out," I say harshly. "One at a time. And don't fuck with me, or I'll brick up every door and window and let you rot inside."

We line up on either side of the hallway, our weapons aimed.

The first man steps out, his arms hanging loosely at his sides.

"Put your hands behind your head," I say.

He sneers and reaches for something behind his back.

A sequence of rapid gunfire goes off.

His chest explodes, the gun he pulled from his waistband falling with a clang on the floor.

"Hold your fire," someone shouts from the room. "We're out of bullets. Unarmed."

"Come out now and I'll finish you off quickly," I call back. "You know you're dying here today."

A man walks out with his hands in the air. He's as tall as he is square, his puffed-up muscles steroid-induced. He wears a black shirt and pants with Italian shoes, apparently trying hard to imitate a crime boss. His shaved head shines under the bulb that dangles on a cable from the ceiling. A black tattoo of an eight-pointed star sits in the center of his skull.

Every muscle in my body goes taut with a need for violence. It takes all my self-control and then some not to off him right away.

Stopping in front of me, he spits at my feet. "Fuck you."

Three of my men filter into the back room while the others grab the man. He struggles at first, until they've tied his wrists and ankles with cable ties. Then he lies grunting on the dirty concrete.

"What's your name?" I ask, suppressing an urge to kick in his teeth.

"Vadim," he says with defiant pride.

He's brave but stupid. If he had one clever brain cell in that thick skull of his, he would've never laid a hand on Katerina.

One after the other, my guards shove the men from the back room through the door. There are four of them—three older men and a lanky young one with a dark stain on the front of his pants. The old men leer as they're brought to stand in front of me. They're hardened, old-school gangsters. They're not going to bow to me or anyone else. Too bad I don't give a fuck about their resilience.

Vadim went after Katerina, and these men are culpable by association.

I give the order with a nod of my head.

My men know what to do. They take them to the kitchen to finish them off. Only because of their age do they get to die quickly.

"Leave this one," I tell the guards, motioning at the one who's pissed himself.

He stares at me with owl-sized eyes, shivering in his shoes.

I point my gun at the bald-headed piece of filth on the ground. "Tie his ankles."

In a few seconds flat, Vadim has a thick rope strung around his legs. He hurls insults as Leonid and one of the guards drag his heavy weight to the bathroom. I grab the arm of the thin guy, tugging him along.

The bathroom reeks of a blocked drain and overflowing excrement. Brown water covers the floor. Vadim curses me to hell as they drop him face down in the water.

Turning his face to the side, he spits. "Go fuck yourself, you motherfucking fuck."

I go down on my haunches, studying his face with the passive curiosity of someone who's about to dissect an insect. He's red with fury, about to blow a gasket.

My voice is cold, collected. "You know why you're here, tied up like a dog and lying in shit and piss, don't you?"

His upper lip curls. "Because you're frightened."

I chuckle. "Do I look frightened to you?"

"You're scared of what's going to happen to you, Volkov.

Admit it. I'm here, lying in piss and shit because you're a coward."

"Wrong answer." My manner is calm, not betraying the cold fury inside. "You're here, about to die, because you laid your filthy hands on my woman."

"The American chick?" He gives a taunting laugh. "If I were in charge, I would've used her up nicely before delivering her."

My vision goes hazy. The urge to rip out his windpipe is so strong I have to curl my fingers in a fist to prevent myself from acting on a whim. That will be too merciful for the piece of scum.

"Deliver her to whom?" I ask coldly.

He laughs. "If you think I'll tell you that, think again."

Straightening, I say to Leonid, "Let's get on with it."

"What are you doing?" Vadim shouts as my men drag him to the toilet stall.

He squirms like a worm, wriggling and spewing gibberish as they lay a metal pole over the stall and throw the rope tied to Vadim's feet over the pole. It takes two men pulling on the long end of the rope to hoist him up.

Hanging with his head down, he twists from side to side. "You think you'll break me with torture?"

He's not worth the time or energy of torture.

When they carefully lower him, he starts to beg. He makes useless promises and offers futile bribes. His voice is an insult to my ears until his head dunks below the brown sludge drifting on the dirty water in the bowl. All that are left of his pleas are gurgles and another spout of indiscernible prattle.

I give it a few seconds before giving the signal. The men hoist him up until only his forehead touches the filth.

"Cut me down," he says, coughing up brown water.

I walk to his side. "What were you supposed to do with Katherine?"

"Take her to an address and leave her there." He gags and coughs again. "An apartment in Brooklyn."

The answer makes me as volatile as a volcano on the verge of erupting. "What's the address?"

"I don't know. I was supposed to call a number—a burner, I think—once I had the woman. Instructions with the address were supposed to follow."

"On whose order?"

He blows a string of snot from his nose. "Cut me loose."

I raise a hand. The men lower the rope.

"Wait," Vadim cries out. "It was Stefanov. Vladimir Stefanov."

My rage is so enormous it takes me a moment to digest the name. Vladimir Stefanov? One of the biggest bratva bosses in St. Petersburg? What the fuck is Stefanov's problem with me? We've never done business. We haven't even crossed paths.

"Why?" I grit out.

Vadim shakes his head, sending drops of filthy water flying. "I don't know. It's not my job to ask questions."

I believe him. Vladimir Stefanov is too high up in the hierarchy to share his plans or motivations with a lowly cockroach like Vadim.

I flick my fingers.

The men lower the rope. Vadim's head disappears under the slimy foam again. He makes ugly gargling sounds as he twists his upper body.

Gripping the neck of the piss-stained young man—the last enemy standing—in a fist, I push him closer and to his knees so he can witness what it looks like when a man drowns in shit.

He shakes and whimpers in my hold, slobber running from his mouth.

"You see this?" I say, pressing his face to the rim. "This is what happens to a man who touches my family."

He gags, trying to turn his face away, but I hold fast.

For such a big man, Vadim has a small lung capacity. Sadly, his fight lasts no more than a few minutes before his bulk goes still. The bubbling stops and the sloshing of the water over the sides of the toilet stills.

I let the fool on the floor go with a shove. The moment he's free, he scurries away on his knees and uses the wall for support to claw himself to his feet.

"You're the lucky messenger who gets to live another day," I say. "Go tell Vladimir Stefanov what happens to people who touch what belongs to me."

He backs up to the door, watching me like he expects me to say it was a joke, that I'm going to kill him after all.

"Go," I say icily, "before I change my mind."

He runs, tripping in his haste. My men don't laugh. The situation is far too serious. What could've happened to Katerina is no laughing matter.

Leonid covers his nose with a hand. "Do you want me to dump the body?"

"No." I spare the dead *ublyudok* one last look. "Leave him here." It will send a stronger message.

Dimitri lifts a foot and wrinkles his nose as he takes in the wet hem of his pants.

"Let's get out of this stinking hole," I say.

Our cleanup team is already getting rid of the other bodies and wiping away our tracks when we leave the building and walk into the night.

"What the fuck was that about?" Leonid asks in a lowered voice.

I clench my jaw. "I have no idea, but we're going to find out." And I know exactly who the best man for that job is.

Yuri gets my door.

"Put a man on Stefanov," I tell Leonid as I slide into the back. "I want eyes on him twenty-four-seven." Now that I've stirred up some shit—literally—Stefanov may get nervous. He may make a move that will shed some light on what the hell is going on.

"Do you want me to take him out?" Igor asks, getting in beside me.

"No." I rub a fist over my brow as I consider the implications. "Not yet. I first want to know what he's cooking up and who else is involved. Whatever he's planning, he might not be alone."

Yuri starts the engine and steers the car into the street.

"Home, Mr. Volkov?" he asks.

"The office." I need to change into clean clothes before I set foot in the house. I'm not facing my kiska smelling like filth. I keep a few changes of clothes at the office for when I don't have time to go home before business dinners.

Taking my phone from my pocket, I type up a message to Adrian Kuznetsov, the corporate spy, asking him to dig around and see if my name has blipped anywhere near Stefanov's dealings. As much as I despise Kuznetsov, if there's anyone who'll find something, it's him. After encrypting the message with a software application, I send it to Adrian's secure email address.

"What now?" Igor asks.

"For now, we wait," I say, repeating Dimitri's words from yesterday.

10

KATE

Something is wrong. I know it.

Kicking off the high-heeled shoes that pinch my toes, I pace the floor of the library. The fire has burned out. It's close to midnight.

Where is Alex? What's taking so long?

Whatever that tattoo means, it's important, or else he wouldn't have run out of here like his life depended on it. He clearly expected trouble because he left with enough men to fill four cars while I helplessly watched their exodus through the window.

I consider calling him for the tenth time, but I don't pick up the phone on the desk. If he's in the middle of something dangerous, the last thing I want is to distract him. Instead, I keep watching the windows. I've opened all the curtains so I can keep an eye on the driveway.

Being shut in the house and not knowing what's going on is driving me crazy. My stomach is tied in knots.

Movement at the gates draws my attention. Two guards run to the gateposts and stand at attention, one of them talking on a two-way radio. A car's headlights appear. They shine through the bars as the car comes to a stop in front of the gates. Rushing to the window, I grip the windowsill and crane my neck for a better view. The large gates swing open, and a convoy of cars enters.

Not bothering to pull on my shoes, I run to the entryway. As usual, a guard stands in front of the door. It's another reminder that Alex doesn't trust me. The knowledge chafes like a rough rope that's been ripped from soft palms. Whereas he betrayed my trust, I don't deserve his circumspection. I'm not stupid enough to run and put my own life and the lives of everyone I love at risk. I might not trust him with my freedom any longer, but I do trust him with my life. If there's anyone who's ruthless and powerful enough to protect me, it's Alex Volkov. But he is human, a man of flesh and bone, and very much vulnerable to bullets and blades.

My nerves are wreaking havoc on my emotions. I need to make sure Alex is okay.

"Please open the door," I say to the guard.

He stares straight ahead.

"Open the door," I demand in a firmer voice.

Just as I'm about to squeeze around him and do it myself, the door swings inward, letting in a dusting of snowflakes with a flurry of wind. The guard steps aside. When Alex enters, my chest deflates with the breath I was holding. My relief is so great I sag in a spell of weakness, feeling much like I do after an adrenaline crash.

Igor, Leonid, and Dimitri pass behind Alex, making their way around the house, but all my attention is focused on him.

For a moment, time stills as we stand frozen, our gazes locked with awareness and knowledge running between us like electric currents.

He could've been killed.

For every minute he's out there, there's a possibility he may never return. Do I want to waste our time together on nursing my anger and protecting my pride? The man I met in New York City was only a part of the complex puzzle that is Alex Volkov. He's so much more than the sophisticated oil tycoon with an unexpected caring side. There are layers to him I'm just beginning to uncover. The man standing in front of me now is one-hundred percent the Russian oligarch who's both admired and feared. This is his home. His history lies here in this palace, in this city, along with everything that shaped him into the man he is. Here, I have an opportunity to *really* get to know him, this dangerous man I gave my heart to. All I have to do is embrace the twisted chance fate has given me.

My throat closes up with fear. Ignorance is bliss. As much as I care about Alex, there's a good probability I won't like the full truth about him. If I push for it, I'm walking off a cliff, falling into an abyss of darkness. I have no idea what awaits me there, but once I open that door, there's no turning back. I'll either love him more or hate what I find.

This could be a new beginning or the end.

The insight is terrifying. If we make it through this, we'll make it through anything. If he's willing to trust me with my freedom and I can make peace with every hidden part of him, our relationship will be built on a rock. Together, we'll be unshakable. However, if our foundation crumbles, I won't have a choice but to walk away. I've done it once, and I'll be strong enough to do it again.

There's only one problem with that scenario. Now that I know Alex better, I suspect I never truly walked away in New York. He was always pulling the strings. Every move he made was perfectly orchestrated. Even when he gave me freedom, he was reeling me in. That freedom was nothing but an illusion.

No, he'll never let me go. If our relationship comes crashing down, there will only be one choice.

I'll have to run.

I tremble a little as insight after insight hits me like a tornado and the verity settles like broken branches in the destruction it leaves behind.

"You can go," Alex says to the guard, holding my gaze as he pulls off a pair of black leather gloves.

The guard salutes and closes the door behind him when he leaves. The click of an electronic lock sounds. The door must be fitted with an automatic locking mechanism.

Alex studies me with unsettling attention as he takes off his boots. "Why aren't you in bed?"

His manner is cool, my earlier rejection sounding like a bee sting in his tone. The distance he keeps is what I wanted a few hours ago, but everything is different now. My insight has brought me to another choice.

I rub my arms. "I was worried sick."

The cold fire in his blue gaze warms a few degrees. "As you can see, I'm fine." A smile plucks at his lips as he unbuttons his coat. "But your concern flatters me—not that I want you to worry."

Stepping closer, I study him for signs of injuries when he takes off his coat. Besides his slightly tousled hair, he looks just like he does when he leaves on a normal workday for the office. "Where did you go?"

"To deal with business," he says, turning his back on me to hang his coat in the closet.

"It has something to do with that tattoo. Did you find out something?"

Facing me slowly, he says, "Quite a lot, actually."

"What?" I ask through parched lips.

He only continues to look at me.

"What, Alex? Tell me. Please don't keep me in the dark. I can't stand it. You have no idea what it feels like to be locked inside, not knowing what the hell is happening and going out of your mind with worry."

He rests his hands on my shoulders in a soothing gesture. "You have an army of men to protect you. Nothing is going to happen. You don't have to worry about anything."

I twist out of his hold. "Stop patronizing me. How would you feel if you were in my shoes? Would you enjoy it if I locked you in here and went out to where someone wants to kill me without telling you what's going on? Would you be able to go to bed and have a sound night's sleep without knowing whether I'm okay?"

"Katyusha." He doesn't touch me again but beseeches me with his eyes instead. "I'm sorry for making you worry. I understand that this situation isn't easy on you."

I suck in a breath, trying not to cry. I'm not usually a tearful person, but I'm not myself. The current circumstances are getting the better of me.

"Wait for me in the library," he says. "I need a shower. Then we'll talk."

I don't argue. I go back to the library and pace the floor while I wait. Not ten minutes later, he joins me. His hair is still damp, and he changed into a pair of dark pants and a white shirt.

"Come," he says, draping an arm around my shoulders and leading me to the sitting area facing the fireplace. "You need a drink."

He gently pushes me down onto the sofa while he goes to the liquor tray. After pouring a stiff shot of vodka, he carries the glass to me. "Here."

Obediently, I take a sip. "What happened?"

In a blink, he clams up again, a closed-off look coming over his features.

"Please, Alex. Tell me."

"You don't know what you're asking."

"I'm asking you to show me the respect I deserve." Unwaveringly, I hold his gaze. "If you can't give me freedom, at least treat me like an equal in this."

He works his jaw from side to side. "I'm protecting you."

"You're not protecting me by cutting me out of parts of your life. You're keeping me ignorant."

A spark flashes in his eyes. "Are you sure you want to go down this road? There's no returning from this, Katerina."

I swallow. "I've already come to that conclusion."

Silence.

"Don't you believe I deserve your respect?" I ask softly.

"Fine." He takes a step forward, putting us so close that our knees touch. His eyes gleam as he stares down at me. "If you want enlightenment, that's what you'll get. Just remember, your judgment won't change a thing." Placing emphasis on the words, he says, "You're staying."

I've already come to that conclusion too.

A beat passes. When I don't take the opportunity he offers to back out, he gives a resigned nod. "The tattoo you recognized belongs to a gang that operates from a shady district in St. Petersburg," he says.

My mouth goes dry. "You went there."

"Yes," he replies in a level tone.

Our fingers brush as he takes the glass from my hand. I wait quietly for him to continue, unable to look away from his face as he brings the glass to his lips and takes a generous swallow of the liquor.

After another sip, he still says nothing, so I ask, "What did you find?"

Hardness fills his eyes. "The man who attacked you."

My heart thumps with loud beats. "He's here, in Russia? What did he say?"

Alex clenches his jaw. "That Vladimir Stefanov hired him for the job."

"To snatch me?" I still find it hard to believe that someone was planning to abduct me just a few blocks from where I work. Well, where I used to work. "Who is Vladimir Stefanov?"

He hands the glass back to me. "One of the bratva bosses who runs the underworld here."

I drink on autopilot, needing the fortification of the alcohol. "Why?"

"I have no idea." Muscles bunch in his temples. "But I'm working on rectifying that."

A mafia boss wants Alex dead. This is bad, much worse than the rival he imagined. I don't have first-hand knowledge of mafia workings, but I've read enough articles to know you don't want to get on the Russian mob's bad side.

I swallow hard. "Where is he now, this man you interrogated?"

"Dead," he says without batting an eye.

Dead.

The word refuses to register. I'm unable to process it. I stare up at his strong, masculine features as the truth I begged him for wars with denial in my chest.

He regards me with a mocking smile, wordlessly daring me to give sound to the thought in my head. That smile says he expected my judgment, and even so, he has no regrets. He's not sorry for what he's done.

"Say it, Katyusha," he says with narrowed eyes, his tone dangerous despite the endearment.

"You…" My voice is hoarse. I'm breathless with the realization.

"Killed him," he says, finishing what I'm unable to say.

My shock is palpable. It's charcoal black, a smoky odor that hangs in the air over the embers of the dead fire. My boyfriend —if that's what he still is—has killed a man. It's not the first time either. He's much too collected for someone who's committed his debut murder.

"He was a bad guy, Katerina," he says, a warning sharpening his gaze further.

The words slip from my tongue before I can stop them. "Like you?"

His eyes scrunch in the corners as his smile widens.

I didn't mean for that to sound like the judgement he so obviously expected from me, but the world I grew up in is a far cry from his. The people from my world have an inborn objection to killing. Not to mention, the oath I took to save lives won't let me justify taking one.

"Say it," he says again. "Tell me I'm a cold-blooded murderer and a monster. That's what you're thinking."

It's not. I clench my fingers around the glass. I don't know *what* I'm thinking. I thought *shady business dealings* involved handing money under the table to secure a few deals, not this. Yet despite what he's admitted, I can't label the man who conquered my heart a monster. The man who worshipped my body is not cold-blooded. The man who's paying for my mother's treatment isn't an uncaring psychopath.

"What's the matter, Katyusha?" Despite his arrogant smile, a flash of vulnerability passes over his face. "If you can't handle the truth, you shouldn't have asked for it."

"Shouldn't you have delivered him to the police?"

"Sometimes, my beautiful kiska, you can be so naïve." He leans down, resting one hand on the armrest of the sofa and brushing a curl behind my ear with the other. "But that's what I love about you."

"The police—"

"Are corrupt in my country." He straightens. "The bratva owns them."

"All of them?"

"Most of them. More often than not, they act as double agents, not only reporting back to the underworld bosses but also conveniently losing evidence or witnesses."

My throat tightens. "The police in the States—"

"The bratva has government officials from all over the world in its pockets. So does every man with enough money," he says in a harsh voice. "Same goes for successful Russian companies. Connections are essential both for success and survival. I don't trust anyone but myself. It would be stupid to do so." He leans closer again, resting his palms on either side of me on the sofa and trapping me between his arms. "I killed that man not because he was a threat to me, but because he touched you. And I'll kill any other man who lays a hand on you. I'll kill any motherfucker who as much as tries. Understand?"

I flinch at the outburst, my heart crumbling even as conflicting emotions battle inside me.

Alex killed to protect me. I can never condone his behavior, but yes, I understand what he's telling me. He's saying that this is his world and I'm a part of it now, whether I want that or not. He's reminding me that I no longer have a choice. That I never had one.

It's a lot to take in, but I did ask for it, and I don't shy away from the facts.

In the space of two days, I've come to realize that the assault on Alex's life isn't over. I've learned that my life is in danger, and therefore the lives of anyone connected to me. I've had my freedom and my choices stripped away. Most importantly, I've come to understand that Alex won't let me go. Not now, and not ever. And the part that hits me the hardest?

This isn't love for him. It can't be. At best, it's obsession.

Alex straightens. "If you have nothing to say, I suggest we go to bed. It's been a long day."

It has been. My head feels on the verge of exploding. But caring for someone can't be switched on and off with the press of a button. The nurse in me has to ask, "What about you? Are you all right? Did you get hurt?"

He smooths a palm over my hair and rubs a curl between his fingers. "Do you know why I was so attracted to you that first day when I saw you fighting to save Igor's life? Apart from the fact that it was impossible not to notice such a beautiful face and the alluring body under your clothes."

At a loss for words, I can only stare at him.

"You were so focused, so dedicated," he continues, "that you didn't even notice the other people in the room. You only had one goal, and that was to save the life of a critically wounded man. Gunshot wounds are related to criminal activities more often than not. You didn't ask what Igor had done. You didn't care if he was a bad man deserving of death. You saved him without casting judgment. As I watched, I wondered if you were some kind of angel." His gaze is intent on my face. "You fascinated me, Katherine Morrell. That kind of goodness was new to me." Slowly, he traces the line of my jaw. "Do you want to know something else? I was jealous of Igor. I was jealous of the dedication and care you gave him. I wanted you to care for *me*. I wanted the angel all to myself. I needed to know if you were for real." He gives me a soft smile. "And then I took you to dinner and to bed and discovered that's just who you are—pure and beautiful."

My breath catches at the admission. He's placing me on a pedestal, raising me to a level I don't deserve. "I'm not an angel, Alex."

"Maybe, but you're real." He runs a thumb over my lips before pulling away his hand. "Even now, hating me, you're real. You don't pretend to be someone you're not."

I want to say that I don't hate him, but he swivels on his heels and walks out of the room, leaving me with blood on my conscience and the sweetest declaration of obsession.

11

ALEX

*A*part of me hoped I'd never have to expose Katerina to every facet of my life. I wanted her to have the good and pretty portions I worked so hard at building. She doesn't deserve the ugliness, but it's part and parcel of who I am. If I'm keeping her, which I am, it's unavoidable that I peel away every rotten layer and give her the truth. She may hate me, but I'll work hard on winning back her affection.

She *will* give me her love again. I'm a determined man. Once I set my sights on a goal, I never fail to achieve it. I've worked for everything I have. My company, my properties, this palace… nothing was handed to me on a silver platter. I broke my back to build an empire from scratch. I earned every penny with my own two hands. Yes, these hands are dirty, but that's the price for living my lifestyle and not bending a knee to either of the forces ruling my country: the government and the bratva. Yet I've never worked harder for anything than I have for Katerina. I've pursued her with everything I've got. I've gone after her with every resource at my disposal, using every tactic in the book. I'll be damned if I lose her now.

I roll my neck to alleviate the stiffness of my muscles. After changing into pajama bottoms, I walk barefoot into the bedroom. The bed curtains are pulled closed. I slip a finger into the opening and lift the left one. The bed is empty. My kitten is probably hiding somewhere in the house, appalled at the prospect of sleeping next to a murderer.

I drop the curtain and leave the room. I meant it when I said I understood that the situation is hard on her. I said I'd give her space, and that's what I'll do, even though every cell in my body demands I take her to bed and make her say things she can't possibly mean, things I desperately need to hear.

All in good time.

At the study, I punch in a code on the electronic pad mounted on the wall to unlock the door. Until I'm certain Katerina won't run or call the police or the embassy, I'm keeping my laptop and cell phone locked away when I'm home.

Making myself comfortable in the swivel chair behind my desk, I pour another shot of vodka from the bottle Lena left for me and wake up my laptop.

A message from Adrian awaits me.

That was quick.

I upload it to the decryption app and read the text. Adrian did some digging into Stefanov's dealings as I requested. There's no mention of Vadim or the gang. Nothing out of the ordinary jumps out. I check the list of Stefanov's recent movements that Adrian attached. Stefanov had met with Oleg Pavlov, a bratva boss who's big in Moscow, in St. Petersburg a month before the assassin took a shot at me and a day after the event. On both occasions, they met at a club that Stefanov owns near

Detskiy Severny Beach. There's no information about the business they discussed, but in between those dates, Stefanov also showed up at Oleg's house in Moscow. I look more closely at that date. It was a couple of days after Katerina was attacked near Romanoff's.

Dread slithers down my spine at the memory. If Katerina hadn't walked into the restaurant that night… If I hadn't been there, having dinner with Mikhail… I can't even think it. I can't put into thoughts what could've happened, never mind into words.

Leaning back in my chair, I take a swig of the vodka as I consider the information.

Vladimir Stefanov and Oleg Pavlov.

The names are familiar, even though I've never had the unpleasant experience of crossing either's path. Like every businessman with a certain net worth in Russia, I know who they are. That's not the familiarity I'm referring to, though. There's something else, a faint memory at the back of my mind. It's a niggling awareness, like a word you can't remember that's hovering on the tip of your tongue.

And then it comes to me.

My mind flashes back to the apartment on Vasilevsky Island where I grew up. I remember myself at fourteen, lying on my bed and reading a comic book I'd smuggled into the house. My father didn't want me to read those books. He'd said the pictures would make me too lazy to read.

The hushed voices of my mother and father came to me through the thin walls of my room. They were having an argument. It was rare for them to fight, so rare that I pricked up my ears. That's when I heard them—those names.

Stefanov and Pavlov.

My mother whispered them frightfully. My father replied in a soothing tone, and when he repeated the names, his voice was harsh. A moment later, the sound of pots came from the kitchen where my mother was making *solyanka* for dinner, and the smell of my father's cigarette reached me from the balcony.

Eager to know Batman's fate, I went back to my reading.

The ping of my phone brings me back to the present. I pick it up and check the screen. It's the head of the cleaning team, letting me know the job is done. Vadim's body should be discovered not long after daybreak when his cronies come to collect the goods for their daily deliveries. Stefanov will get my message soon.

Good. I can't wait.

Drumming my fingers on the desktop, I knock back the rest of the vodka. The alcohol slips smoothly down my throat, warming my stomach and loosening my tense muscles. Why did my parents fight about two bratva bosses? My father was a high-ranking police officer. He never discussed work at home, at least not when I was around. Was he a bought man? Did Stefanov or Pavlov own him? Is that why my mother was upset? Because he'd sold information to them? I can see how that would've upset my mother. She was a good woman, a humble person who believed in right and wrong. Corrupt cop is not the image I have of my father, but I was just a kid. I was more interested in forbidden pop culture and in saving enough money for a skateboard than I was in my father's job.

Unable to think about my parents without experiencing the pain that tears my heart out of my chest, I push the nostalgia aside.

How do the dots connect? Is there a link between my parents' conversation and the events of the last couple of months? What's the likelihood of the same names popping up then and now? Stefanov paid Vadim to kidnap Katerina. Did he also pay the man who stole her key card? It's a logical deduction. That means Stefanov most likely paid the assassin who tried to kill me. But why? What does it have to do with my parents, if anything? How does Oleg Pavlov fit into the picture? His meetings with Stefanov around the time of the attacks on Katerina and me could be a coincidence—it's very likely that the two bratva bosses do business together—but the fact that my father mentioned them both raises a big red flag.

I don't have the answers, but I will find them. And when I do, I'll make Stefanov and every man involved in his scheme pay.

Firing up the encryption app, I send another message to Adrian, instructing him to keep sniffing for information on Stefanov and to do the same with Pavlov. I put a handsome sum of money for bribing informants at his disposal and log into my bank account to pay him for the job he's done. Nothing motivates like prompt payment. He'll drop whatever else he's working on to get me the information I need.

The earlier adrenaline has yet to work itself out of my system. I'm too hyped up to be able to sleep. To use the time productively, I take care of the red tape surrounding Katerina's leave of absence. Once all the paperwork is out of the way, I schedule an email to be sent to Joanne at a reasonable time in the morning, asking her what time is convenient for Katerina to videocall her. I might be ruthless, but I'm a man of my word. I said my kiska could have a reward if she behaves, and now that she knows there's no way out, she'll behave if it means that she can speak to her friend. Call it manipulation, but I'm not forcing Katerina's compliance to make *my* life easier. I'm doing it for her. The sooner she adapts to her new situation, the sooner she'll be happy again.

I'm not optimistic about uncovering anything via the hospital security camera tapes. Nevertheless, I log into the real-time workflow to check on the team's progress. As I expected, they haven't found anything. Hopefully, I'll learn more soon, either from Adrian or the man I've put on Stefanov's tail.

I type a command, telling my security chief, Nelsky, to shut down the search and instead focus on obtaining information on Stefanov and Pavlov's personal and professional operations. I want the blueprints of their homes and their offices. I want to know how many men they have on site and with what weapons they're armed. I want to know how many kids they have, where they go to school, where they keep apartments for their mistresses, what cars they drive, and what their wives eat for breakfast. I want to know everything right down to the brand of their underwear. I want to know their strengths but mostly their weaknesses. I want to know where their protection is breachable. They may seem untouchable, but if you look hard enough, you'll always find a vulnerability.

Standing up, I stretch. Killing Vadim hasn't appeased my fury, not by a long shot. I need a strenuous workout in the gym. Until I can lay my hands on Stefanov, the punching bag will have to do.

My phone rings just as I reach the door.

It's Igor.

I take the call with, "Yes?"

"I thought you'd like to know that Stefanov is having the house watched. There's a man outside. He's discreet, but we picked him up via infrared."

"Are you sure he's Stefanov's?"

"Yeah. We used a night vision camera and ran the face recognition program."

I smile grimly. We're already like old-time enemies, Stefanov and I, having eyes on each other. I can't wait to crush that motherfucker like a bug under my shoe. "Keep tabs on him."

"Already doing it. He entered a building across the river. He's making himself comfortable on the top floor as we speak."

"Good. Let me know if more men join the party," I say before ending the call.

It's never difficult to smoke termites from the woodworks. You just have to light a fire underneath them.

12

KATE

*D*rowning in guilt over being an accomplice to murder, I spend another two hours in the library. My mind goes round in circles until my brain feels like mush and I can't think anymore.

In the end, Alex gave me an easy out by taking away my choices. There's nothing I can do while being locked up and cut off from the rest of the world—for now, at least—and in a way, I'm grateful. Even if I had access to a phone, I could never tell on Alex. I'd sooner die than send him to prison—but this is not even an option right now. There's no one to call, no one to turn to. I can't trust anyone, not even the police. What's unfolding is bigger than I could've imagined. Two deadly forces are at war, and I'm caught in the middle. All I want is for Alex to get out of this alive. Selfishly, I just want this to be over so we can go back to our lives. I want to work and do what I do best—care for the sick and injured. Most of all, I want to be there for my mom when she comes home from the clinic.

Rubbing the heels of my palms over my eyes, I get up from the sofa. I'm tired, but I doubt I'll be able to sleep. Despite my mental exhaustion, I can't shut down my brain. Tonight's events keep running through my mind.

Maybe some warm milk will do the trick.

Lost in my thoughts, I make my way to the kitchen. As I turn the corner, I bump into a hard chest.

Gasping, I stumble back a step. Strong hands clasp my upper arms to steady me. Off balance, I stare at the naked chest at my eyelevel. A manly dusting of dark hair covers powerful pecs. Broad shoulders and well-cut muscles look as if they were carved from stone. Pajama bottoms ride low on slim masculine hips, exposing the deep lines of abs angling down to the groin. A thicker triangle of hair showing just above the elastic hints at what lies below the thin cotton of the pants. The fabric molds around a heavy cock, drawing a perfect outline of its impressive length, thick girth, and the groove that runs around the head.

Tearing my gaze from the sculpted body in front of me, I finally meet Alex's eyes. He stares down at me with heat sizzling in his blue irises, but his features are schooled.

"Alex," I say, cringing inwardly at how breathless my voice sounds.

He raises a brow. "Looking for something?"

I wet my dry lips. "I was going to warm up some milk."

A hint of sympathy warms his tone. "Are you having trouble sleeping?"

"Like you, it seems."

Crossing his arms, he takes a wide stance. "I need a workout. I was just on my way to the gym."

He's occupying all the space in the hallway, blocking my path. My pulse spikes, partly in anticipation and partly with a need to flee. My body is interpreting our positions as those of a hunter and his prey, and it likes the idea a little too much. It warms to the scenario, sending all of the heat straight to the juncture of my legs.

"I'll just…" Swallowing, I point toward the kitchen.

"Do you want me to get that?"

I blink, struggling to focus through the fog of desire that's invaded my senses. "W-what?"

Lustful intent narrows his eyes. In a low voice, he asks, "Would you like me to warm up some milk for you? I can bring it to the room."

"Oh, no." My reply is rushed. "I'll just, um, you know." Taking a breath, I pull my lecherous self together. "Do you want some?" When the icy blue of his eyes darkens a shade, I add hastily, "Milk. Do you want some milk?"

"Sure," he says slowly. "Why not?"

"Okay."

I move to the left, all but running in my haste to escape his presence. At the same moment, he takes a step to let me pass. The breath leaves my lungs with an *oomph* as our bodies collide for a second time. Like earlier, he catches me, testing my balance with his hands on my waist. I should pull away, but I don't. He should let me go, but he holds on.

Carefully, as if not wanting to scare me with a sudden movement, he wraps his arms around my body and pulls me close. His size and power envelop me, sheltering me from the harshness of our reality. How I've missed the warmth and safety of his embrace. Some of the tension leaves my body as I press my cheek against his chest and absorb the welcome relief of the security he offers. I didn't realize how much I needed the comfort of his touch until now.

Gripping my chin, he tilts my face. When he lowers his head, I don't turn away. I close my eyes and do the scariest thing I've ever done in my life. I step off into the abyss and tumble into the darkness—for better or for worse.

"Katyusha," he says in a rough voice, dragging his lips over my jaw to the corner of my mouth.

The kiss he plants there is dry and light. I've missed how warm and hard his chest feels against mine. I've missed dragging my hands through the soft strands of his short hair. Wrapping my arms around his neck, I act on the fantasy. A groan escapes from deep in his throat as I close my fingers and pull his hair gently in the process. The pressure of his hand on my lower back increases, arching my body as he draws me to him and rubs against me.

The hardness that grows against my hip makes me utter an involuntary moan.

"Yes," he growls, cupping my ass and pressing me tighter while he spears the fingers of his other hand through my hair.

In contrast to the roughness with which he palms my ass cheek, his hold on my nape is tender. Burrowing my face in his neck, I inhale deeply. His skin smells like a seductive mix of cardamom and musky man. His stubble pricks my lips when I bring them to his jaw. Trailing my hands over his shoulders and down to his chest, I trace the grooves that define his muscles. Under the solid slab of strength beneath my palms, his heart pounds with a wild beat. His callused palm catches on the wool of my dress as he smooths a hand down the outside of my thigh.

Skimming his fingertips over my nape, he brings his hand around and folds his fingers around my neck. The touch is possessive and tender. My breathing quickens as he aligns our lips, letting a second of anticipation pass before he presses our mouths together.

Fireworks explode in my belly. The house, the city, Russia, why we're here—everything vanishes as he parts my lips and slips his tongue inside my mouth. He drags in a breath, stealing my air. In response, I gasp into our kiss.

He sweeps his tongue over mine, teasing and testing. When I sag in his hold, all but melting against him, he pulls me closer by the gentle hold on my neck and kisses me with skillful precision. The strokes of his tongue are meticulous, designed to arouse, and he succeeds.

Every inch of my skin is on fire. The heat between my legs turns liquid. My breasts become sensitive and heavy. The way my nipples brush over his chest through the layers of my bra and dress makes me clench my thighs in need.

"Kiska," he groans between kisses, bending his knees and pulling me between his legs.

His erection rubs against me, stimulating just the right spot. Pinpricks of pleasure pierce my clit through my underwear. If he carries on like this, he's going to make me come right here in the hallway.

"Alex," I breathe, pushing on his chest.

He tightens his hold on my ass and neck, preventing me from pulling away, but he does slow the sensual assault of his mouth.

Brushing his lips over my ear, he murmurs, "I need this, Katyusha. How much, you have no idea."

I need him too. I was a fool to think I could fight him. He warned me it was a game I couldn't win, and as always, he was right. I'm a second away from surrendering.

"Let me take care of you," he says in a husky voice. Seductively, his soft lips press the words against my ear. "Let me remind you how good we are together."

I don't need a reminder. I remember only too well.

At my silence, he straightens to look down at me. The intention that sparks in his eyes is no longer out of control. It's more calculated but no less heated. The steely blue pools harden with determination as he holds my gaze, measuring my reaction while he slowly drags his fingers over my collarbone and down my chest. When he reaches the upper curve of my breast, my breath catches. Satisfaction bleeds into his expression. He studies my face with hooded eyes as he continues south, brushing his knuckles ever-so-lightly over my nipple. The tip pebbles into a hard point. Goosebumps run over my body, contracting my skin from the crown of my head to my toes.

The look of satisfaction on his face transforms into victory.

The test is over. The results are indisputable.

He's won.

Offering me a hand, he says, "Come with me."

This is moving faster than I anticipated—we still have a lot to talk about—but I've already made the decision. What's the point of delaying the inevitable?

Reaching out slowly, I place my palm in his. He folds his warm, dry fingers around mine and leads me to the staircase in the foyer. He climbs the steps confidently, like a man who knows he'll be obeyed.

My surrender doesn't come without a price. Shame and wounded pride squeeze my chest as I follow him into the bedroom. My only consolation when he turns me around and pulls down the zipper of my dress is that he'll make me forget.

"I want you," he says roughly, kissing the arch of my shoulder.

I close my eyes, focusing on the sensation of his lips on my skin while blocking out everything else.

He unclasps my bra with efficient, economical movements. A soft click later, the cups give. The temperature in the room is comfortable, but my nipples tighten as the fabric falls away. I stand dead still as he pushes the sleeves of my dress and the straps of my bra down my arms. I don't even dare to breathe. When the dress pools around my waist, he cups my breasts.

The feel of his warm, hardened hands on my naked skin is almost too much. I utter another gasp when he rolls my nipples between his fingers until they extend. Tipping back my head, I steal a glance at his face. He's watching the work of his hands, teasing me with light caresses by drawing infinity patterns around my nipples. He writes invisible words on the tops, sides, and undercurves of my breasts until my clit is swollen and throbbing with need. Too soon, he flattens his palms over my ribcage and drags them over my belly. I bite off a moan when he slips them under the dress.

Dipping both hands inside the elastic of my underwear, he pushes it down along with the dress. The fabric makes a rustling sound as it hits the floor. I'm left standing naked in front of him, his thin pajama bottoms the only barrier between us. He emphasizes that fact by pulling my back against his chest and letting me feel the hot, hard cock between his legs.

"Katyusha," he whispers, placing his hands on my hips and turning me to face him. "Tell me you want this."

It's not my desire as much as his need to hear the words that makes me give him the truth. "I want you."

I've scarcely uttered the words before he dives for my lips.

The earlier tenderness is gone. He claims my mouth with a kiss that devours. Gripping my jaw between the splayed fingers of his broad hand, he walks me backward to the bed while he eats my mouth as if he's starving for my lips.

My knees fold when the backs of my legs hit the mattress. I plop down onto the edge. He comes after me without breaking the kiss, pushing me down at the same time as he crawls over my body. Pinning me down with his fingers locked around my jaw, he tangles our tongues with the fervor of a deprived man. Breathing hard, I trail a hand over his chest, dragging my fingers through the coarse hair. A moan escapes my lips when he diverts to my neck and trails kisses over all the sensitive spots along the arch.

Catching my wrist, he guides my hand to his cock, showing me what he wants. I oblige, stroking his length through the cotton of his pants before squeezing my fingers around his girth. His flesh is hard and hot. Unable to resist, I slip my hand underneath the elastic and close my fingers around the thickly veined velvet skin. A groan reverberates in his chest.

He gives me another second to catch my breath before he goes back to kissing my lips while I work his pants over his hips. Supporting his weight on one elbow, he lifts his hips to help me finish the task. Finally naked, he stretches out on top of me, pressing the lengths of our bodies together. He's hard in all the right places, the personification of virile strength. I need the promise he presses between my legs, but I also need so much more. I need him on more than a physical level.

My jaw aches from our almost violent kissing when he tears his lips from mine to drag them over my body. He doesn't pause at my breasts or at the dip of my navel. Instead, he slides down my body, kneels on the floor, spreads my thighs, and goes straight for my pussy.

Holding my gaze, he licks my folds from top to bottom. The pleasure arches my back. Like earlier, when he caressed my breasts, he teases me by tracing the outline of my entrance with the tip of his tongue, avoiding the spot where I need his touch the most. After every full circle, he licks a little harder and goes a bit deeper, slowly driving me crazy. By the time he's tongue-fucking me, I'm shaking with need. When he finally draws my clit into his mouth and sucks softly, it only takes a few seconds before I come.

The orgasm spreads like languid heat from the center of my legs through the rest of my body. It creeps over me unhurriedly. The pleasure ripples like shockwaves after an explosion, rolling out in slow-motion and leaving goosebumps in its wake.

With one last, long lick, Alex raises his head to look at me. Pressing the pad of his thumb to my clit, he massages in a circle. Immediately, the ebbing need starts to build again. I always believed multiple orgasms were a myth, but Alex has proven me wrong. It's almost too much. I'm oversensitive. Instead of fighting it, I throw back my head and let go. Relaxing my hips, I lie still for him, letting him manipulate my body into another climax.

It takes longer than the first time, but when my release hits, it's quick and intense. The brutal pleasure makes my thighs quake. I'm still riding the high when he says in a hoarse voice, "Move up for me, kiska."

I do as he says, scooting to the middle of the bed. My back has barely hit the mattress before he's crawling over me again, his cock brushing over my inner thigh. Reverently, he kisses my belly and trails soft kisses on the undersides and upper curves of my breasts, working his way to my nipples. The reward for my patience is a sweet kiss on my left nipple. He circles the tip with his tongue before sucking on it with the same gentle treatment he gave my clit, while bringing a hand to my other breast to roll the nipple between his fingers.

I moan when he sucks a little harder. As if I haven't just had two orgasms, my folds swell with arousal. My sex clenches around nothing, begging to be filled, but Alex isn't to be hurried. He moves to the other breast, kissing and grazing my nipple with his teeth while laying a hand over the abandoned one. With his tongue and fingers, he works me into a frenzy, preparing me to take him.

He lifts his head to look at my face as he fists the base of his cock and aligns it with my entrance. Needing to hold onto him, I grip his shoulders.

"Tell me," he says hoarsely, parting my folds with the broad head of his cock. "Tell me if it's too much."

My answer is to wrap my legs around his ass. We've waited two days, and now that I've decided to take this step, I want all of him. He advances cautiously, driving an inch into me. My inner muscles clench involuntarily around the intrusion, but I make a conscious effort to relax and let him inside.

He moves with excruciating gentleness, giving me a few seconds to adapt after every inch he claims. Holding back takes its toll on him. It's evident in the sheen of sweat on his forehead and in the utter concentration etched on his features. When he's finally so deep inside me that our groins are flush together, he cups my face and kisses my lips. The kiss is sweet. It's both a tender compensation for and a subtle warning of what's to follow.

Even two days apart was too long. Alex is too virile, his

appetite for sex too insatiable. Framing my face between his palms, he holds my gaze as he pulls out until only the head of his cock is wedged between my folds. He holds still for a second before sliding back in. In spite of his size, my body accommodates him without difficulty. My arousal is slick, aiding his movement. Plus, he took the time to prime me. The stretch is intense enough to be just a little scary. If he's not careful, he can tear me. The tinge of apprehension fuels me with adrenaline, increasing my tolerance threshold, and when his control finally slips, I'm ready.

As if sensing my final surrender, he pulls out and thrusts back. My skin tingles as his cock slides over ultra-sensitive nerve endings. Oral sex with Alex is great, but nothing beats the feeling of him filling me inside. Perspiration beads on his skin as he gives a few softer strokes. His hips fall into a rhythmic pattern, rocking our bodies together. The coarseness of his pubic hair brushes over my clit. The pressure of his groin on the bundle of nerves quickly makes my need climb again. I've never wanted to come so badly.

Wrapping my arms around his neck, I roll my hips to urge him on. He clenches his teeth, trying to hold still when I pull him deeper with my inner muscles.

"Katerina," he warns.

I lift my hips, taking him faster and breaking his pace.

He lets loose with a growl. Pinning my waist to the mattress with his large hands, he keeps me still and pounds into me with a harsher rhythm. With every thrust, the breath leaves my lungs. The roughness is delicious, taking me to the crescendo I crave.

He punches his hips until his face contorts into a mask of

tormented pleasure. Raggedly, he orders, "Come for me one more time, kiska."

The sensual sound of his accent washes over my ears. The musky smell of man and sex intoxicates my senses. The connection between us is more than a joining of our bodies. It goes deeper than the heat that coils through my insides, but the pleasure momentarily overpowers all else as my body erupts into flames. The fire incinerates everything, burning away the barriers and protection around my heart, leaving me open, vulnerable, and susceptible to Alex Volkov's loving.

Because it *is* love, but only on a physical level. Even in the midst of mind-blowing sex, I'm lucid enough to understand how this works. I told him I was falling in love with him. He never reciprocated the words. His declaration is to empty his seed in my body, pumping until he's dry and I'm dripping with his release. It's a stamp of possession in the most primitive of ways, an instinctive act of a male leaving his mark.

Panting, I internalize the thoughts that take over as the sensations subside. I'm falling for him a little more every day. The web draws tighter, and like a trapped fly, I'm stuck here with nowhere to go. I have no way to protect myself from being consumed. Alex, on the other hand, doesn't have to suffer that sensation of slow suffocation. He already owns me wholly. He has me right where he wants me.

In his bed.

In Russia.

Pushing up onto one arm, he brushes the hair from my face. His voice is soft. "You're quiet."

"Exhausted," I reply honestly.

He searches my eyes. "What are you thinking?"

"That we didn't use protection."

"You're on the pill."

"Yes, but still."

"We're both clean."

I blow out a breath. "I know." It just seems more intimate and risky. It's a commitment without the safety net of love.

He gives me a surprised look. "You want to go off the pill?"

"No," I exclaim. "Of course not."

"Because if that's what you want—"

"It's hardly a subject up for discussion."

His eyes narrow minutely. "You're right. This isn't the moment. We should wait until after I've dealt with Stefanov."

What? Does he seriously think my refusal is only about the threat on our lives? Pushing away from him, I sit up. "I need a shower."

"Later." He catches me around the waist and drags my back to his chest. "I'll wash you myself, I promise. Stay like this for a while."

"I'll soil the sheets."

"Fuck the sheets. I like the idea of my cum inside you." Pressing a kiss to my ear, he whispers, "Way too much."

The implications of his words make me tense. I'm already a prisoner, not only of Alex but also of my own heart. I won't become a prisoner in blood too.

He curves his body around mine, trapping me in a comfortable but dangerous cocoon. We breathe in tandem while our hearts beat with different tunes. The darkness envelops us as he reaches over and closes the bed curtains.

We lie like that for a long time, awake and slumbering, at peace and at war. We're on the same side but at opposite ends of the spectrum. Even the arms he folds around me are a contradiction in terms. Depending on the perspective I choose, he's either imprisoning me or keeping me safe.

In truth, it's both.

He tightens his hold, pulling me closer, and I lay my hand over his where he cups my breast. Neither of us says the words the other wants to hear.

13

ALEX

*T*he gnawing worry is always present in the back of my mind, even in my sleep, but I wake feeling a little more at ease. The reason is the woman I'm spooning from behind, the woman I'll give my life to protect. Her close proximity calms me. As long as her slender body is pliant and warm against mine, no one can touch her. In the circle of my arms, no one can harm her.

Already hard, my cock rests snugly against the crease of her ass. For a moment, I fantasize about an ass wank, as dirty as the idea may seem, but I wore her out last night. The stress of our fucked-up situation is a lot for a delicate, kind-hearted woman to handle. The filth of the world hasn't desensitized her conscience, the way it has mine. She's like the angel on my parents' grave, a compassionate innocent who saves lives without asking questions. The hell I dragged her into is no doubt exhausting on both a physical and emotional level. She needs her rest.

Reaching for the bed curtain on my side, I pull it open. The room is dark. I check my watch. It's after ten. Even at this time of the year, the sun is up by now, but the heavy curtains in front of the windows keep out the light. I disentangle myself carefully from Katyusha and get up quietly, taking care not to wake her. The darkness is so thick I have to feel around to find my pajama bottoms on the floor. After pulling them on, I use the light of my phone so I don't bump into the furniture on my way to the bathroom, where I grab a robe.

I tie the belt around my waist as I make my way to the kitchen. Tima glances up when I enter. A knowing smile flashes over his face as he shifts his gaze from my unclothed state to the clock on the wall. I never sleep in. It doesn't take a genius to put two and two together, but he's wise enough not to make a comment. I have a high regard for his culinary skills, but my private life is none of his fucking business.

"I left breakfast in the warming drawer," he says. "Omelets with cheese and grilled tomato for the little rabbit."

I narrow my eyes at the term of endearment.

"I look out for her when you're not home," he says, pouring coffee into two mugs. "She could do with a little friendly company."

Only the fatherly way he says that prevents me from planting my fist into his face. Yeah, I'm a jealous asshole, possessive enough not to trust a sixty-year-old cook.

After Tima has set the omelets, quartered oranges, and coffee on a tray, I carry our breakfast back to the bedroom. The path to the sitting area is clear. I make it there without falling over anything and deposit the tray on the table before opening the curtains. Sunlight pours inside. The bright rays catch dust particles in the wedges they cut through the room. The sky is such a brilliant blue that it momentarily hurts my eyes. The thick blanket of snow that covers the ground sparkles like glitter. It's a glorious winter day, a good day for being outside.

The thought knocks my heart off kilter, punching me with an unpleasant dose of guilt. My world turns askew. I've always condemned keeping birds and animals in cages. Knowing I'll be walking through the door into the beauty of the winter's day while keeping my biggest treasure behind the lock of a gilded cage only adds to the weird notion that the pieces of my life are misplaced.

Misplaced, but for a good reason. Neither of us likes this situation, but it's necessary.

Tima is right, however. Katerina needs company, stimulation, and friends. The current arrangement is hardly healthy. Not to mention, I'm not being a good boyfriend. It's her first visit to Russia, and she hasn't seen anything apart from the inside of this house. It bothers me to restrain her freedom, but I'm afraid to let her out. Although… maybe if I plan it to the last detail and take the utmost precaution, I could show her some of the sights. She gave me a huge concession last night, letting me touch her while her heart is still unhappy with me. It's only fair that I show her I'm making an effort too.

To say I'm relieved at finally having access to her body again is an understatement. It's not just the physical relief of blowing off sexual steam. Reclaiming what belongs to me on every intangible level is much more important. I want everything—her body, her thoughts, and her love. She still feels betrayed. I get that. Which is why taking her outside of these walls will be good for both of us. One, it's important for her mental health. Cabin fever has never been conducive to anyone's wellbeing. Two, it will help me get back into her good graces.

The more I think about it, the more the idea grows on me.

The object of my thoughts stirs. A soft sigh escapes her lips as she turns on her back. Her dark hair splays over the white pillow, the waves looking soft and silky. However, the usual glow of her golden skin is absent. She looks so fragile, so utterly vulnerable as she lies there, a tiny shape under the mountain of blankets covering the king-sized bed, that I almost go back on the promise I've just made to myself to take her out.

Her long lashes lift. Blinking, she takes in the room. Her rich hazel gaze settles on me.

I feel the smile that stretches my lips somewhere behind my breastbone. It drifts to the cavity between my ribs and settles there with bittersweetness. "Good morning, my love. I brought you breakfast."

Clutching the sheet to her chest, she sits up. "What time is it?"

"Don't worry about the time. You needed your rest." I pick up the tray and carry it to the bed. "Tima made omelets."

"That smells good," she says with a weak smile.

"You must be starving." Heat shades my voice as I add, "After last night."

A flush works its way over her cheeks. She's not shy about sex or her body. What bothers her is her surrender. I know my kiska well enough to understand that she feels like she's lost a battle. Well, too bad. Our relationship isn't a war she should be fighting.

Balancing the tray on one hand, I put a plate and mug on the nightstand on her side. She watches me with her lip caught between her teeth, her waves deliciously untamed. I've always found a woman who's just woken up sexy. There's something alluring about that natural beauty before it's been touched by brushes and makeup, and there's no woman sexier or more alluring than my Katyusha, even when she's scrunching the sheet in her small fist as if her honor depends on it. We finally took ten steps forward last night. I'm not going to let her hide from me now and take us five steps back.

Hooking a finger into the sheet between the curves of her breasts, I tug gently. She holds on, clenching her fingers tighter. I don't let her off the hook. This isn't a war. There's nothing to lose. I'm not stripping her of her dignity or pride. I simply want things between us the way they used to be. I want her to be comfortable with her nakedness around me, like she'd been the morning after the very first time I'd claimed her.

After another beat of me tugging and her pulling, she lets go. The fabric slides over her breasts and pools around her waist, unveiling her like a stunning life portrait. Unabashedly, I stare at her curves and the pert pink nipples that top them like cherries. My cock comes to life, tenting my pajama bottoms and showing her in no uncertain terms what she does to me.

Her gaze moves south. She only graces my erection with her attention for a second before she focuses on my face.

My smile is like a door hanging on one hinge—crooked and unstable. I have a good mind to forget about food and have her for breakfast, but in the light of day, she's skittish. The moon was kind. It let us hide in the shadows and commit sins we can't face under the judgment of the sun. That's all right. I have patience, a lifetime of it where she's concerned.

"The food is getting cold," I say, breaking the tension by walking to my side and getting in under the covers next to her. I move carefully, making sure I don't topple the tray, and when I'm settled with my back against the headboard, I balance the tray on my lap.

She gingerly reaches for the plate on her nightstand. Once she's installed herself comfortably, I hand her a fork.

"Thank you," she says, watching me from under her lashes.

I choose a safe topic to keep the conversation light. "I told Tima you like omelets."

She takes a bite and hums her approval as she chews. The simple fact that she's enjoying the food warms my chest.

"Tima said he's cooking vegetarian portions for me," she says. "You don't have to cater to me. I'm used to adapting."

"You're my guest, Katyusha."

Her hand stills midway in the air, the fork hovering in front of her mouth. Too late, I realize my mistake. That was a bad choice of words.

Instead of commenting, she takes another bite, brushing the ugliness aside as if pretending it's not there will make it vanish.

Eager to maintain a pleasant mood, I say, "I'd like to take you sightseeing today."

She looks at me quickly. "Really?"

Her enthusiasm makes me grin. "I promised to show you St. Petersburg, didn't I?"

Her slender throat bobs as she swallows. "What about safety?"

Brushing a curl behind her ear, I say, "Don't worry. I'll take care of the security."

As I dig into my omelet, I make a mental note to tell Dimitri to plan a route and scout the roads in advance. I'll have to station men on every corner and have snipers on the roofs. It'll be a mission to organize, but nothing is too much effort for her.

"Thank you," she says with a small frown, as if she's doubting my motive.

I can't resist kissing her cheek. "You're welcome."

The fact that she doesn't flinch or pull away further warms my heart.

Glancing at me, she asks after another forkful of omelet, "Will you show me where you grew up?"

The request catches me off guard. I expected her to ask about the Peterhof Palace or the Fabergé Museum, the usual tourist sights. "Why do you want to see that?" The prospect of going there tightens my stomach, not that there's anything left to visit.

Fiddling with her napkin, she averts her eyes. "I thought it would be good to, you know…"

"Good to do what?" I ask gently.

"To get to know you better." She shrugs. "There are many things about you I don't know."

She sounds almost guilty and definitely apprehensive. She tries to hide her reaction, but she's not a natural liar. There's something more to delving into my history than she's letting on. Even so, *getting to know me* hints at making an investment in our relationship, which I like.

Scratching my jaw, I consider what to tell her. I don't normally talk about my parents, but she deserves the truth.

I finish the last bite on my plate, knowing I'll lose my appetite once I delve into the past, and set the plate aside. "I grew up on Vasilevsky Island, but there's no point in going there. There's nothing left of where I used to live."

She frowns. "Why? Was your building demolished?"

"No." Strain locks my jaw.

Her brown eyes soften. "You don't have to talk about it. I didn't mean to pry. I just wanted—"

"No," I say again. "You're right. You'll never have the opportunity to meet my parents like I did with your mother. It's good that you're asking."

She waits quietly.

"There was a gas leak in our building," I continue. "The whole top floor blew to pieces."

"Alex." Gasping, she lays her hand on my arm. "Were they…?"

"Yes."

Empathy fills her tone. "I'm so sorry."

"Eleven people were killed. I was at school when it happened."

A man from my father's unit relayed the news to me in the headmaster's office. With a stony face and factual words, he told me I was going to live in an orphanage. In just a few seconds, he condemned me to one of the cruelest systems in my country, one that was notorious for preying on the children it was supposed to protect.

I may have been more interested in comic books than in asking my father about his day, but at fifteen years of age, I knew enough to understand my fate. The bodies of children who'd been in the system turned up only too often. Every time my father opened a new case, my mother would light a candle. I could tell how many kids had died by the number of evenings a candle burned in the windowsill.

"I can't even imagine how hard that must've been for you," Katerina says, squeezing my arm.

"There was nothing left of my home. I couldn't go back to pack a bag. They took me straight to a halfway house, a dump on the smelly side of the Neva River's banks. The first night, I ran away."

She makes a small sound of distress. "You ran away?"

"What else could I do?" I don't give her the colorful details of the future that would've awaited me as a so-called system child.

Staring at me in shock, she asks, "All alone?"

"I was fifteen, man enough to brave the streets and earn a living."

She trails her fingertips over my forearm. "How?"

Her intention is to provide comfort, but my body heats at the innocent touch. Even the subject isn't enough to turn me off when she puts her hands on me. "I was lucky enough to secure a job as a delivery boy in a pharmaceutical company. The job can be danger-ous. Delivery boys are often attacked, and the pharmaceuticals they transport stolen for the black market. Not many people have the stomach for it. I was good at defending myself, and the head of the division took notice. He favored me with extra work. It allowed me to save enough money to enter a business school at the age of nineteen. When I graduated, I landed a job in an oil company."

"What happened then?"

Many years of bitter determination and back-breaking work. Taking my mug, I watch her from over the rim as I drink my coffee. "What do you want to know?"

"How did you end up as a powerful business magnate who speaks several languages?"

I smile. "Do you think because of my background I can't be an educated man?"

A flush darkens her cheeks. "That's not what I meant."

"It's all right." I finish my coffee. "You're not the only one who's asked me that question. I worked my way up and made a few good investments. I parlayed those funds into searching for oil in an area of Siberia that my employer had dismissed but that I thought held a lot of promise. I was right. I struck gold, discovering a large oil reserve. That allowed me to start my own oil company and then branch out from there."

She regards me with fascinated interest. "What about learning to speak all those foreign languages? Did you also go to language schools?"

"I've always enjoyed reading, and I pick up languages quickly. A crash course usually does the trick."

She pulls her hand away from my arm and drops it in her lap. "Your parents would be proud of what you've achieved."

I doubt that very much. My mother would be horrified at the crimes I've committed to get to where I am, but as long as I'm at the top of the food chain, I'm willing to make the sacrifice.

Handing Katerina a wedge of orange from the tray, I say, "I have some arrangements to make before we can go out. How about we have lunch in the old city and visit a few sights around there? I want to be back before sunset."

"Okay." Either excitement or relief brightens the honey flecks in her eyes.

"Given the time difference, you probably won't speak to Joanne until tonight," I say.

She bites into the flesh of the orange. "You'll really let me chat with her?"

"I can do better than that." Catching a drop of juice that runs down her chin with my thumb, I bring the pad to my mouth and lick it clean. "How about a video call?"

Her eyes grow large. "Really? That's not too risky?"

"I just need some time to put a few measures in place." With a warning, I add, "It won't happen every day."

"Thank you," she says, looking almost like the Katerina of old.

The fact that she's thanking me for a call that should be her right to make says a lot about how twisted this situation truly is. Not wanting to linger on that fact, I lean over and kiss her lips. They're sticky with sugar and taste of winter fruit. We never did have that shower I promised her. Like a selfish bastard, I didn't want to wash the stamp of my possession off her body. If anything, I want to come all over her and rub my cum into her skin.

The smell of citrus explodes in the air as she bends the peel to eat the orange. I put my mug aside and then do the same thing with hers before leaving the tray on the floor. The widening of her gaze when I take the peel from her hand and carelessly discard it says she knows what's to follow even before I pin her down.

14

KATE

*A*fter we shower together, Alex leaves me to get ready while he takes care of the arrangements for our lunch and tour of the city.

As I brush out my hair in front of a mirror, my cheeks heat at the recollection of how we spent an hour after breakfast in bed. The sex had been downright wicked. A lot of dirty Russian words and loud moaning had been involved. I hope the walls are thick.

I haven't forgiven Alex, but I can't deny that I need him, now more than ever. I can't help but enjoy his company both in and out of bed. What's the point of running from the truth? I can't pretend he doesn't affect my feelings.

What he told me about his past has shocked me. I can't imagine how tough it must've been to survive on his own at such a young age. To achieve what he has, and with no support, took an enormous amount of self-drive. My respect for him has multiplied tenfold. I can only admire his determination, intelligence, and skills. Not many people, if dealt the same cards, would end up where he has. His sad but victorious history only confirms what I already know.

Alex never gives up. He always gets what he wants.

My hand shakes a little as I set the brush aside. I'm both excited and nervous about getting out of the house. Living in constant fear is new to me, and I've yet to learn how to deal with it.

A knock on the door startles me from my thoughts.

"Katyusha?" Alex calls. "We're good to leave a little earlier. We can go as soon as you're ready."

"I'll be down in ten minutes."

"Take your time."

Not wanting to make him wait, I quickly grab some clothes. In five minutes, I'm dressed in a pair of jeans, a wool sweater, and boots. When I come down the stairs, Alex is talking on the phone in Russian in the foyer. A few guards buzz around, carrying laptops and other equipment outside. Lena stands quietly next to the coat closet.

Alex has his back turned to me, giving me time to study how well his body fills out his clothes. A black button-up shirt stretches over his broad shoulders, and dark pants hug his sculpted ass. His bicep flexes under his shirt sleeve as he presses the phone to his ear with his left hand. A fancy watch and a chunky silver bracelet are visible on his wrist where the cuff has been pulled up. He looks like a walking billboard for a high-end men's designer clothing brand. A whiff of cardamom and cedar reaches me at the bottom of the staircase. He's such a perfect combination of everything that's deliciously male that it almost hurts to look at him.

Judging by his professional tone, he's discussing business.

Spoken in his deep voice and with his commanding attitude, the foreign words sound sexy, even when they're work-related. Alex Volkov not only exudes power; he drips with sex appeal. It's not often that I have the chance to observe him unnoticed. I'm the one who's usually pinned under his dissecting stare. Making the most of the opportunity, I burn the incredible way he looks, sounds, and smells into my memory, so I can enjoy the stolen moment again later.

My steps are quiet on the carpet. I stop at a distance to give him privacy to finish his call. As if sensing my presence, he turns. A steely gaze collides with mine. The blue of his eyes warms several degrees as he takes me in from top to bottom. His visual evaluation contracts my skin as if he were running his fingertips over my body. The heated appreciation he shows for everyone present to see sends sparks to my belly. He finishes his conversation with a few short commands, sounding as in charge as ever while simultaneously devouring me with his stare.

Only Alex can direct his attention to two places at once and control both with precision and power.

Ending the call, he pockets his phone. "Ready?"

Sexual tension runs thick in the air. Our awareness of each other is visceral. It always has been, right from the start. Alex is an incurable disease. No matter what happens, I'll never get him out of my system. He's gotten too deeply under my skin.

Not trusting my voice, I nod.

Lena takes my coat from the closet and hands it to Alex. He helps me put it on before taking his own.

When we've finished pulling on our scarves and gloves, he offers me his arm. "Let's go."

The guard at the door opens it to let us out. Five cars are on the driveway. Men in dark coats wait next to the cars. They're dressed casually, presumably to blend in on the streets, but when the man in the front bends to get into the car, his coat falls open, revealing a gun in a body holster.

Alex and I get into the car in the middle. Yuri is in the driver's seat. He gives me a nod in the rearview mirror as he starts the engine. Alex says something to him in Russian, at which he pulls off.

Two cars lead the convoy, and two tail us. Alex takes my gloved hand in his and keeps it on his lap, caressing my knuckles with his thumb, but his attention is aimed outside. Tension fills the car as he keeps a vigilant eye on the surroundings. My muscles tighten. He wasn't this preoccupied on the drive from the airport to the house.

"Is something the matter?" I ask.

Turning his face to look at me, he makes a visible effort to relax his features. "Everything is fine."

I search his eyes. "Really?"

"I'm just being careful. How does your saying go? Better safe than sorry."

Why do I get the feeling there's something he's not telling me? "If the risk is too big, we can stay at home. I don't mind."

His expression softens. "We're fine. It's a beautiful day to be out. You deserve it."

Do I? Then why do I suddenly feel so guilty? I don't want to be the reason Alex risks our lives. I don't want him to get killed just because I couldn't handle a little claustrophobia.

"Alex?" I close my fingers around his hand. "Let's turn back. There's so much to do at home. There's a gym and a pool and a sauna. I haven't even explored the home theater yet. And Tima's cooking is better than any restaurant's, right?"

"Hey." He brushes his knuckles over my cheek. "Don't worry, kiska. I'd never take an uncalculated risk, not with your life."

"I don't need to go out and see the sights. I'm happy to—"

"Shh." Leaning over, he kisses my lips. "I want to do this. Now just relax and enjoy the day. That will make me very happy."

Not wanting to throw the enormous sacrifice back into his face, I shut my mouth and try to show him the gratitude he deserves.

"Excuse me," he says, taking his phone from his pocket. "I have to make a couple of calls."

For the rest of the drive, Alex is occupied on his phone. From the firm tone of his voice, it sounds as if he's giving instructions. He could be talking to someone at his office, but my guess is the calls have something to do with securing our safety.

When we park in the old city, the men accompanying us get out first. Half of them clear a path while the other half surround us as Alex helps me out of the car.

Despite the army of men and the disconcerting meaning of their presence, I pause on the sidewalk to take in the scene.

The clear blue sky forms a perfect backdrop for the historic buildings. I read up on St. Petersburg after Alex first suggested bringing me here. The domed towers are a distinguishing characteristic of Russian Revival architecture. The colors are so vibrant they look like icing sugar on cupcakes. St. Petersburg on a clear winter day is magical.

Wrapping my arms around myself, I brave the icy breeze as Alex shelters me against his body and leads me down the street.

While I stare at the gorgeous buildings, he sweeps the surroundings, his gaze alert.

After a short walk, we reach the Church of the Savior on Spilled Blood. With the snow covering its domes, it looks as if powdered sugar has been sifted over a rainbow cake. It's breathtakingly beautiful. Alex takes a selfie of us in front of the church that he sends to Joanne and my mom before we continue on our exploration. By lunchtime, we've visited the Palace Square, the State Hermitage Museum, and St. Isaac's Cathedral. Since my face and feet feel frozen, I'm grateful when we enter a warm restaurant and take a table next to the window. It doesn't surprise me that the restaurant is empty.

"Did you book out the whole place?" I ask Alex when he seats me.

He offers me a smile as he takes the chair opposite me. "I like my privacy."

"So you've said," I say, studying him as he picks up the menu.

Our dining alone has more to do with keeping us safe than wanting privacy, I'm sure, and the fact that he's downplaying it to put me at ease only makes me appreciate his effort more.

"Would you like me to order for you?" he asks. "We could share a selection of starters if you'd like."

Holding out my hand, I say, "I'll have a shot at it."

A broad smile warms his face as he hands me the menu. "I admire your eagerness to learn."

The double meaning of his words sends heat to my cheeks. He taught me dirty Russian words in bed this morning, and I'm still marveling at how much power an ill-pronounced *"ya hochu tvoy chlen"*—"I want your cock"—had on him. When I repeated the phrase he'd whispered in my ear, he turned animalistic. The memory alone is enough to turn my underwear damp despite the fact that we're in a restaurant.

Pushing the erotic flashback aside with effort, I skim over the dishes listed on the menu. I've studied enough Russian words in New York to order mushroom *pelmeni*, which are dumplings served with sour cream.

Alex gives me an approving look. "Great choice. I didn't know you were improving your Russian on the sly."

I brush it aside with, "I've picked up a few words." I don't tell him I was planning on ordering a self-study course before we left New York. I'm not ready to admit how serious I'd been about us before he shoved me onto a plane. He has enough power over me as is. He doesn't need an ego boost.

"I'm impressed anyway," he says, ordering the meat *pelmeni* when the waiter comes to our table.

The boiled dumplings are soft on the outside and fluffy inside. The tangy sour cream complements the savory flavor of the mushrooms perfectly. After a steaming cup of Russian Earl Grey tea, I'm fortified and ready to brave the cold again.

We spend the rest of the afternoon shopping. Alex takes me to a few boutiques, all of them suspiciously empty of customers. He twists my arm into letting him buy clothes for me and gifts for my mom and friends at home. At his insistence, I select a miniature Fabergé egg replica encrusted with rubies for my mom and one with emeralds for Joanne—never mind that I have no idea when I'll be able to give it to them. He loads armfuls of hand-painted matryoshka dolls into one of our guards' arms for my colleagues at the hospital and pays for everything with his credit card. When we finally make our way outside with a pile of parcels, the sun is almost setting.

The drivers have been following us, the cars always parked

nearby on the curb. Alex steers me to the car Yuri is driving and helps me into the back while the men load our parcels into the trunk.

Once we're settled inside, I turn to him. "Thank you, Alex. That was an amazing experience."

"You're welcome." He puts an arm around my shoulders and pulls me against him. "I'm glad you enjoyed it."

His smile is warm, but the tension doesn't leave his features. Even as he presses a kiss to my forehead, his attention is trained outside, as if he expects trouble at any moment.

FORTUNATELY, THE TRIP HOME PROVES UNEVENTFUL. LENA greets us as we enter the house, telling us that Tima has left refreshments in the library to hold us over until dinnertime.

"You go along," Alex says. "I'll be right there."

I stare after him as I remove my coat, unable to suppress my worry. Igor and Leonid enter with our parcels, carrying them upstairs. I haven't seen much of the guards since we arrived in Russia. They stay in the barracks and don't talk to me when I'm with Alex. I linger, taking my time to remove my scarf and gloves. When they come back downstairs, I busy myself with putting everything in the closet.

Leonid exits first. Just before Igor steps through the door, I put a hand on his arm, holding him back.

He frees himself carefully. "Is there something I can do for you, Kate?"

"Alex has been very tense this afternoon," I say, keeping my voice down. "Has something happened?"

He glances at the top of the stairs. "Nothing's happened. He's just taking the necessary measures to make sure it stays that way."

"It went all right today, didn't it?"

"Surprisingly."

I swallow. "Did you expect trouble?"

"It would've been foolish not to."

"Then why did Alex risk going out?"

"It was a calculated risk," he says in a level voice. "If something were to have gone down, you would've been well protected."

"But you didn't like the idea," I say, trying to read him.

"It's my job to protect both of you. I don't like taking any risks, no matter how small or well managed."

"What are you really saying, Igor?"

"This house is the best-protected place you can be. If I were you, I wouldn't ask Alex to go on another adventure."

"I didn't ask," I exclaim in a whisper. "It was Alex's idea."

"Yeah, well, maybe you should dissuade him of those ideas. I'm sure you can find effective ways of occupying him here."

I pull my back straight. "That was an inappropriate remark."

"If you don't want my opinion, don't ask."

He nods at the guard, who opens the door.

"Igor," I say when he steps through the frame. "What's gotten into you?"

He pauses on the threshold. "Look, we're all tense about what's going on. It's rubbing off on everyone, that's all. As I said, Alex wouldn't have taken the risk if he hadn't been damn sure he could protect you. It just took a hell of a lot of resources and energy that could've been better spent."

"Right."

"Ah, hell." He throws his hands in the air. "That's not what I meant."

"It's okay," I say, backtracking toward the hallway. "I get it."

"Kate." He tips his face toward the sky. When he looks back at me, his expression is composed. "I didn't mean you're not worth the effort. I only meant our priority needs to be catching the fucker who wants Alex dead."

"I couldn't agree with you more," I say, my stomach knotting at the reminder of the problem we're facing.

"Just forget I said it. You're caught in the middle of a war, and we don't even know what it's about. It's not your problem or your fight. We'll handle it."

"You're wrong," I say, a little too forcefully. "I'm a part of Alex's life, and that makes this my fight too, whether I like it or not."

"Leave the dirty work to us. We'll catch the bastard." Turning on his heel, he walks away.

The guard shuts the door behind him and takes up his position in front of it, making a silent but strong statement.

Contemplating Igor's words, I go to the library. Admittedly, I enjoyed the day and I'm more than grateful for Alex's consideration. Yet I can't help but agree with Igor. We should keep a low profile until we're safe again.

A tray with tea and delicate cakes is on the table in front of the fireplace. Someone made a fire. The flames leap up the chimney, radiating welcome heat. I pour a cup of tea and am about to take a seat when Alex enters, carrying his laptop.

"Joanne is available now," he says. "Would you like to chat with her?"

I nearly drop the cup in my eagerness. "I'd love to."

He puts the laptop on the table and activates the connection. A second later, my friend's face appears on the screen. From the logo on the wall in the background, she's in one of the meeting rooms at her office. It's almost six o'clock here, which means she must be on her eleven o'clock coffee break. Her red curls form a copper frame around her pretty face. There's a glow on her cheeks and a sparkle in her eyes when she leans closer to the screen.

"Hey," she says. "There you are, elopers."

"Jo." I take a seat on the sofa. With everything that's happened, it feels as if I haven't seen her in weeks instead of days. "How are you?"

Alex sits down next to me.

"Same old on my side. The question is how are *you?*" She looks from me to Alex. "How's Russia? Thanks for the selfie, by the way. The scenery is spectacular." Winking, she adds, "You could've told me about your plans."

"It was a surprise for Katerina," Alex says, resting a hand on my knee. "She didn't know."

"Wow." Joanne makes big eyes. "That's a biggie. Careful, Alex. You'll win the boyfriend of the year award."

He clears his throat. "How's Ricky?"

"Busy. He has an exhibition coming up in the new year. We hope you'll be there."

"We'll try our best to make it," Alex says.

She turns her attention to me. "When are you planning on coming home?"

I glance at Alex.

"We're playing it by ear," he says. "Katerina has been working too hard. She's taking a much-needed leave of absence."

"Really?" Joanne says, not hiding her surprise. "And the hospital let you?"

"I was heading for burnout," I say, cringing inwardly at the lie. "It was either granting me extended leave or accepting my resignation."

She blinks. It's the first she's hearing of my supposed burnout. I can almost see the wheels turning in her head, the suspicions forming. But then she must decide I've simply been swept off my feet because she says with a sly smile, "I'm sure they don't want to lose you. And you're right. You deserve the break. What about Thanksgiving and Christmas? Will you be spending the holidays there?"

"We haven't discussed that yet," Alex says.

If she notices that he keeps his answers vague, she doesn't comment. I'm guessing she's decided we're madly in love and doesn't want to get in the way of that. Instead, she splays her hands and asks cheerfully, "So, are you having fun?"

Infusing my tone with as much excitement as I'm capable of, I tell her about the sights I've visited and the food I've tried.

Joanne grins. "You make it sound so beautiful. Russia is definitely going on my bucket list."

"You and Ricky will have to come visit." Alex draws patterns around my knee with his forefinger. "There's plenty of room here for you to stay."

Goosebumps run over my skin, making me shiver.

Her grin widens. "That's very kind. We'll definitely consider it." Then she glances at something to the side and her face falls. "Oh, shoot, I have to go to a meeting. I'll call you again soon."

"Sure," I say, already regretting having to say goodbye. "Don't work too hard."

"Send me more pictures." She blows me a kiss before the screen goes black.

There's a moment of silence, during which I process a strange sense of loss. A part of me already feels disconnected from my old life.

Alex closes the laptop.

"Thank you," I say, keeping my tone upbeat. He has enough on his plate. He doesn't need an emotional girlfriend too. It's probably just PMS.

"You're welcome, my love."

We sit like that for a moment, neither of us saying anything.

"Would you like a cup of tea?" I ask to break the silence.

"No, thanks. I have to get back to work." He stands. "I have to attend a function in a couple of weeks. It will be a formal affair. I'd like you to come."

Igor's words still ring clearly in my mind. "I don't know, Alex. Do you think it's a good idea?"

"I wouldn't have suggested it if I thought it was a bad idea," he says with a quirk of his lips.

I leave my untouched tea on the tray. "Maybe it's best if I stay at home."

He narrows his eyes, giving me one of those piercing looks that sees right into my soul. "It'll send the wrong message if I go alone."

"What message?"

"That I don't respect you."

I blink. "Why would people think that?"

"When a man keeps a woman in his house but doesn't show her off in public, he's telling the world what her place in his life is in no uncertain terms."

"That she's his mistress?"

"Exactly. You're not a dirty secret I have to hide."

"My reputation is hardly worth your life." Or our lives, for that matter. "In general, do you have to go?"

He nods. "Not going will make me look like a coward. We can't let our enemy think we're scared. That's what he wants. I'm having the gala venue secured. I'll have men there before, during, and after the event. Besides, a lot of powerful government officials and private sector leaders will be attending. The security will be top notch." When I don't reply, he says, "Aside from the fact that I refuse to hide with my tail between my legs, my presence is imperative."

My hands turn clammy as I think about everything that can happen at a public event. "Why? What do you mean?"

"I'm in the process of entering into a joint venture with a company that manufactures small, portable nuclear reactors. If the Russian government gives the green light to this technology, we'll be able to provide clean, affordable energy to many of the outlying communities here and in the neighboring countries. This gala will bring together the key players in the energy sector and their decision-making government counterparts. If all goes well, it will speed up the approval of this technology."

Of course. Now that I know he grew up on the streets, I understand why this is important to him. There's more to this event than advancing his business agenda. It's evident from the passionate way he talks about it.

"All right," I say, not that I really have a choice. Pretending to give me one is just a way of soothing my bruised feelings. It's like inflicting a cut and making it better by sticking on a Band-Aid.

"Good." He offers me a disarming smile. "I'll make sure you have an appropriate dress."

15

ALEX

$\mathcal{T}$he morning is gray. I open the bedroom curtains wider. Thick clouds hang in the sky. Snow is forecasted from late morning onward. The river looks dark in the grainy black-and-white picture of the cold day. Just as well I took Katerina out yesterday when the weather was clear.

In the garden, the men are doing their rounds. I probably shouldn't stand naked in front of the window.

Turning my back on the monochromatic winter image, I face a much prettier view. My kiska is sleeping on her stomach with her small hand on my pillow. The covers have shifted down, revealing the golden skin of her naked back. My cock hardens even though I had her less than an hour ago. I'd woken her at nine with my face buried between her legs. I'd been gentle, knowing she was half asleep. The sex was sweet. Vanilla. But I'm far from sated. My body demands more. With her, I always need more.

My plan was to go downstairs in search of breakfast. I have

meetings scheduled at the office. After taking the day off yesterday, there's a lot of work to catch up on. I really should go get our breakfast, but instead, I walk over to the bed. With every step, lust heats my veins. By the time I reach the edge of the mattress, my body is primed with wicked intentions. I want to bury myself so deep inside her that there will be no question as to whom she belongs. I want to pummel her pussy until I've eradicated this need that consumes me. The satiation will only last half a day before I'll need her again, but at least it will afford me a few hours to focus on work.

I pull the covers slowly from her body until she lies exposed in front of me. Her legs are slightly parted, giving me a glimpse of the delicate pussy between them. Partly obscured, it's like a hidden treasure. The illusion of being unobtainable—out of sight and out of reach—makes it all the more alluring.

Climbing onto the bed, I crawl over her body. My cock pulses with need. The simple brush of the sensitive head over the silky skin of her inner thigh contracts my balls. The base of my spine tingles as my whole body tightens with pleasure. I straddle her hips and fist the base of my cock. A drop of pre-cum spills from the slit. Using it as lubrication, I rub the crest over the pink, plump folds between her legs.

Katerina stirs. She makes a sleepy sound, followed by a throaty moan as I get her wet. Her body responds beautifully. In an instant, she's slick. I wrap an arm around her waist and lift her lower body. Before she's fully awake, I'm already sinking inside her. Her body is supple and soft from sleep, her inner muscles easily letting me in.

Gasping, she gives me a startled look from over her shoulder. "Alex?"

I plant a reverent kiss on her spine. "Morning, kiska."

"What are you doing?"

I pull almost all the way out. "Isn't it obvious?"

She stretches around me, pretty like peaches and cream. Her back arches as I slam back in, her breath leaving her lungs on another gasp, but the moan she utters tells me she likes this.

Sliding out slowly, I admire the view. I like that she shaves. I like to see everything. From this angle, she's more open to me. I can watch as well as touch. Both her clit and rosebud asshole are accessible.

I cup her breasts and pull her into a kneeling position. Her nipples are already hard little pebbles, a telltale sign that she's turned on. I rub my palms over the tips, enjoying the slight weight of her curves for a moment before I smooth my hands over her sides to her waist to test her balance. When I'm certain she's stable, I start pumping my hips with an easy pace. Her body sways rhythmically to my beat. She's a beautiful instrument to play, and all her songs are mine.

Even at the slight escalation of my pace, pleasure already draws my cock harder. I thicken inside her as her inner muscles grip me like a velvet fist. I'm not going to last long. Slipping a hand around her body and between her legs, I pull back the hood of her clit with the pad of my thumb. I use my other thumb to press on her back opening, massaging with just enough pressure to add stimulation without risking accidentally hurting her by penetrating the tight ring of muscle.

"Alex," she cries out softly, sounding half panicked and half euphoric.

"Shh." I rub her clit and asshole with lazy circles. "I'm not going to take your ass. Not yet."

Her breath catches as she glances back at me, her eyes large with uncertainty.

If she's an anal virgin, she'll need a lot of preparation before she'll be able to take me. My pulse quickens at the idea of claiming that tight little hole, my lust burning out of control, but for now, I just let her get used to being stimulated on that forbidden spot.

When her moans get louder and she's scrunching the sheet in her fists, I pick up my pace and rub her trigger buttons harder. Our bodies rock in tandem as I thrust so deep that my groin spanks her ass. I move harder and faster, until the sound of our flesh slapping together drowns out her moans.

The way all her muscles pull tight is my cue that she's about to come. My release threatens to explode when she clenches around my cock, milking me, pulling me deeper. I grit my teeth, ignoring the raging need to spill already, and ride out her orgasm without breaking my speed. Only when she goes slack and collapses with her upper body flat on the mattress do I let go. The climax hits me like a cyclone. White-hot heat erupts as I empty my body inside hers. I pump until I'm dry before stretching out over her with my weight supported on my elbows.

Her panting is erratic, her ribs expanding and contracting with fast breaths. Brushing her hair over her shoulder, I kiss her nape and the arch of her neck. She smells of peaches. I can't resist sucking on the spot where her neck meets her shoulder, leaving a mark. My mark. If I could, I'd stay inside her and fall asleep like this, but I'm already late for work.

Regretfully, I pull out. She moans.

I kiss the shell of her ear. "Don't move."

Leaving her in a disarray of tangled, sex-drenched sheets, I wet a washcloth with warm water in the bathroom and carry it back with a towel. Once I've cleaned her up, I take out something I got for her from my dresser drawer.

I sit down next to her and show her the small box and the lube.

"What's that?" she asks with a frown, pushing up onto her elbows.

A wicked smile curves my lips. "I want your ass, Katyusha. I want every part of you." Lifting the lid of the box, I show her the silicone bullet with the sparkly head. "But I need to prep you before you'll be able to take me."

Her eyes flare. "Is that what I think it is?"

My smile widens. "A butt plug. You'll have to wear it all day. It will stretch you."

"I…" She wets her lips with the tip of her tongue. "I've never done that."

I brush the hair from her forehead. "Do you want to?"

She considers it for a moment.

"We don't have to do anything you're not up for," I say. "We can try, and if you don't like it, we'll stop."

"All right," she says slowly. "I guess."

Even spent, my cock twitches. "Kneel for me, kiska."

Obediently, she goes onto her hands and knees.

"That's good." I brush a hand over the firm curve of her ass. "Lean your upper body on the bed."

Watching me from over her shoulder, she bends her elbows and rests her cheek on her arm.

"Perfect," I say, caressing the other cheek.

The position pushes her ass into the air. Her globes are spread, giving me easier access to her virgin hole. Uncapping the tube, I lube the plug well.

"This is going to feel a little cold." I smooth a hand over her lower back. "Take a deep breath and hold it until I tell you to blow out."

She inhales deeply, looking a little frightened.

"This won't hurt," I say huskily, pressing the tip of the plug against her opening and letting her get used to the pressure. "Blow out now, slow and steady."

When she exhales the air from her lungs, I splay my fingers over her ass and spread her wider while applying a little more pressure.

"How are you doing?" I murmur, pressing harder slowly but surely.

Biting her lip, she gives me a nod.

"Words, Katerina."

"I'm good," she says in a breathy voice.

"Do you want me to continue?"

"Yes."

Gently, I twist the plug from side to side, stretching her sphincter until the ring of muscles gives and the toy pops inside. The white gemstone fits prettily in her crease, a jewel adorning a jewel.

"How does that feel?" I ask, stroking my palms over her ass cheeks.

"Strange." Her voice holds a curious tone. "Full."

Heat building at the base of my cock roughens my tone. "Wait until I take you while you're wearing that plug."

Her cheeks flush a little.

"It's so fucking sexy." I trace the outline of the brilliant stone. "Do you want to see?"

She nods.

I go back to the bathroom and return with a mirror. She cranes her neck for a look, her flush deepening as she studies the sparkly stone that adorns her asshole. I'm not into BDSM or anything like that, but I am an anal man, and without this preparation, I risk hurting, if not tearing, her.

After I set the mirror aside, I get back onto the bed and pull her legs straight so she's lying flat on her stomach. Ignoring my renewed need, I spend the next ten minutes massaging her shoulders, back, and buttocks to help her relax. When she's soft and pliant, I press a kiss to the top of her crease.

"Stay," I order. "I'll be back in a few minutes with breakfast."

As usual, breakfast waits in the warming drawer. Tima made *syrniki*. Served with sour cream, honey, and berries, the cottage cheese pancakes are my favorite. After feeding Katerina in bed, I rush through a shower and get dressed quickly. She's dozing off again when I kiss her goodbye. It takes much willpower to tear myself away from her and walk out of the room.

Igor and Leonid are waiting in the foyer when I get downstairs. Dimitri and Yuri are already in the car, the engine idling.

"Guard her with your life," I tell Igor. His orders are to protect Katerina when I'm not here.

He nods with a steely expression.

"Ready?" I ask Leonid.

He moves his jacket aside, showing me the pistol in his waistband.

We drive to my office in a convoy of five cars. I expect an ambush every minute we're on the move. I almost wish for it, just wanting to get the fight over with and kill the motherfuckers already, but nothing happens, and half an hour later, we arrive safely at my office building.

Grigori greets me with coffee and a stack of reports. A pile of contracts waits on my desk to be signed. Once he's briefed me on what I've missed in my absence, I spend the first hour catching up with the tasks on my priority list.

At noon sharp, Adrian calls on the secure line.

"What do you have for me?" I ask, swiveling my chair toward the window.

"Something big."

My body tenses with anticipation. "Go on."

"I've been keeping tabs on Oleg Pavlov, as you requested. A huge amount of money was recently moved from his bank account and distributed between various accounts. Some of those are offshore and others local. From there, the funds went dark. My finance expert managed to trace a portion of it. Some of the money ended up in Bitcoin and some in shell corporations. It's a real fucking maze. Whoever designed the system made sure we'd be taken on a wild goose chase." He pauses. "It turns out all the diversions lead back to one place, or should I say, one person."

"Who?" I demand.

"A hacker in Moscow. Goes by the name of Mukha. He's gone to great pains to keep his identity concealed. I'm afraid I don't have his real name for you yet."

A snowflake drifts down and sticks to the window. "What did Pavlov want with a hacker?"

"That's what I asked myself. So I did a little probing. I offered the money you provided. The fish took the bait. Apparently, Pavlov paid him to encrypt and deliver a file."

"What file?"

"He won't say."

"Then what information did my money buy?" I ask with impatience.

"He gave me the name of the person he delivered the encryption to. A certain Ivan Besov."

Turning back to my desk, I type a message to Nelsky, ordering him to run a background check on Ivan Besov.

"Guess what *my* hacker discovered when he followed Mukha's cyber trail?" Adrian continues. "Besov sent the file to Vladimir Stefanov."

I go still. "He did, did he?"

"Most certainly."

"In other words, Pavlov paid a hacker to deliver an encrypted file to Besov, and Besov delivered it to Stefanov."

"Correct."

I mull over the meaning of this. "What about Besov?"

"He's ex-military. He got kicked out on charges of torturing a political hostage. It looks like he took the fall for his team. The charges were dropped, but after that, he went on his own."

"What division?"

"Spetsnaz. Sniper."

The snow starts falling harder. "That would make a good assassin."

"My thoughts as well. He goes by the nickname of Bes."

Bes. Demon or evil spirit in Russian. How subtle. I hook a finger between my collar and my tie and pull on the knot to loosen it. "Any teammates we can question?"

"No." Paper rustles in the background. "He works alone."

A ping sounds in my ear.

"I've just sent you an attachment with the information I could gather on Besov," Adrian says. "He has an address in

Moscow. If he's been traveling lately, he's been doing it with a false passport. According to his records, he's retired, living on disability payments, and he hasn't left Russia since his military missions."

A message from Nelsky pops up on my computer screen. I click on the attachment. It's a photo of Besov. He has green eyes and blond hair. The listed information says he's forty-two years old.

I fire off another message to Igor, instructing him to put a man on Besov and check out his address.

"You did well," I say, saving the file in a secret folder. "I want to know what's in that file Pavlov had Mukha send to Besov."

"Mukha won't give up the file. He's afraid of Pavlov and Stefanov. Understandably."

"Where are you now?" I ask.

"Still in Moscow."

"Can you trace the hacker?"

"It'll be tricky, but I can try."

"Do it. In the meantime, offer him double the money for the file. Promise him however much he wants, but get me that file. I need it decrypted."

"Are you sure this is the route you want to go? Pavlov and Stefanov are dangerous men."

A slow smile curves my lips. "So am I."

16

KATE

*E*very time I move, I'm aware of the toy inside my body. At first, the sensation is odd, but by late morning, I'm used to it. I almost forget about it until I sit down for lunch. The foreign pressure isn't uncomfortable. In fact, it's strangely arousing, serving as a reminder of Alex's intention.

The idea of anal sex both turns me on and scares me a little, yet I'm curious. I'd never been adventurous with my ex-boyfriends, and the fact that Alex is pushing my boundaries and is so at ease with kink thrills me. In my past relationships, I've often been the one to instigate sex. I love that Alex is taking the initiative and suggesting we try something new.

Since I've whiled away the morning by sleeping late and reading, I decide to spend the afternoon more productively in the gym. I don't mind walking or lounging with a butt plug, but I doubt running will be comfortable. After reading the instructions that came with the box, which are thankfully in English, I remove the plug and clean it with soapy water before putting it away. Then I pull on my exercise gear and grab a swimsuit on my way down.

Igor sits in a chair in the foyer, reading something on his phone.

"Hi," I say, not certain where we stand with each other after yesterday.

For a change, he smiles. "Good afternoon."

I stop in front of him. "Are you babysitting?"

He shrugs. "Duty calls."

"Lucky you."

"Alex said he'll be home for dinner."

I raise a brow. "I suppose the fact that I don't have a phone makes you the messenger too."

Lowering the phone to his lap, he says, "I'm not complaining."

"I do feel better knowing I'm so well protected," I say from over my shoulder as I continue on my way.

His chuckle follows me down the hallway.

Like the previous time, I select a lively playlist on the central sound system before hitting the treadmill. The running releases some of my tension and clears my mind. It's good to focus on the rhythm of my feet and forget about everything else. When my life returns to normal—when I go back to work—I'll make exercising a part of my daily routine again. I forgot how purging a strenuous workout can be.

After a half hour of running, I rinse off in the shower and do a few laps in the pool. When my skin starts to wrinkle, I stretch out on a lounge chaise under the skylight. It's snowing hard outside. It feels odd to lie in my swimsuit in an indoor garden while a snowstorm is raging on the other side of the windows.

Lena comes to ask if I'd like to use the *banya*, a Russian

sauna. If so, she'll tell Tima to make a fire in the stove and heat the rocks. Not being a big fan of excessive heat, I decline the offer. Instead, I take a shower in Alex's bathroom. Stepping out of the shower, I wrap a towel around my body and take the sex toy from the drawer. I contemplate the box for a couple of seconds before making up my mind. As soon as I've made my decision, a pleasant wave of heat creeps over my skin. What I'm about to do feels forbidden and naughty. I use the lube from Alex's nightstand drawer to insert the plug like Alex had done this morning. Once it's fitting comfortably, I dress in a warm sweater and skirt and install myself in the library to watch a couple of episodes of *Downton Abbey*.

By teatime, I'm starting to feel restless again. I pass the time exploring the house in more detail, admiring the artwork and trinkets as I walk from room to room. The history of the palace fascinates me. I make a mental note to ask Lena about it. Maybe Alex can get me a book if an English translation is available.

I end my tour in the upstairs rooms. Standing in one of the luxurious lounges, I turn in a slow circle to take in the mural that runs around all four walls. The scene depicts a family out on a picnic. The clothes suggest an eighteenth-century period. From the quality of their attire, I'm guessing they're a wealthy, maybe even royal, family. The lady of the house is reclining on a chair while a woman in a housemaid uniform is serving her a cup of tea. The gentleman sits on the back of a stately black horse, his pose regal. Five kids of different ages are running after a puppy while three servants are chasing after them. A blanket is spread out on the grass, covered with grapes, bread, and wine. A richly embroidered tablecloth spills from an open wicker basket.

The detail is extraordinary. The fruit catches the rays of the sun, the fat grapes a translucent purple and green in the light. The craftsmanship of the painting is spectacular. I bet Ricky would love to see this. It's like being transported to the past. Did that scene play out here? The green lawn in the painting could easily be the palace garden in the summer. Alex did mention there used to be stables at the back.

An eerie quietness descends as I continue to study the mural. For a moment, it's just me and the family caught in the happy snapshot of a bygone era. A clock on the mantlepiece keeps time with a soft tick-tock. It's almost five o'clock and already dark outside. An inexplicable wave of loneliness washes over me. I feel suddenly isolated, alone with only the company of ghosts.

Needing a warm drink, I close the door behind me and go to the kitchen.

Lena is ironing table linen when I enter. Tima is presumably on his break. The kitchen is warm and humid from the vapor of the iron. The air smells like a mixture of starch and laundry detergent, transporting me to the weekends at my mom's place. Mom always did her ironing on a Saturday. Nowadays, that only happens if her health allows.

A pang of longing pierces me. I miss my mom.

"Can I get you anything?" Lena asks, glancing up from the hissing iron.

"I'm good, thank you." I walk to the fridge. "I just want to warm up some milk for a cup of hot chocolate."

She folds a napkin meticulously. "The cacao is in the top cupboard on your left, and the pots are underneath the sink."

After finding a small pot, I fill it with milk. "Would you like some?"

"No, thanks." She runs the iron along the seam of the

napkin. "If you'd prefer to wait, Tima will be back from his break in ten minutes."

"I can make a cup of hot chocolate," I say good-naturedly. "It's not as if I'm doing much else."

She gives me a fleeting look before leaving the napkin on a neatly folded stack.

I turn on the gas and find a mug while the milk heats. "Have you been working here for long?"

"Since before Mr. Volkov bought the house."

Leaning against the counter, I shove my hands into the pockets of my skirt. "Do you know its history?"

"Some of it." She takes a napkin from a laundry basket and shakes it out. "The previous owner's wife made a study of the architecture and interior decorating. She collected every book on the subject she could lay her hands on."

"Are there any in English?"

She wrinkles her nose. "Only Russian, I'm afraid."

"Oh."

The iron blows out a billow of steam as she drags it over the napkin. "All the more reason to learn to speak Russian." With a haughty air, she adds, "That's if you're staying."

Not forever. At least I hope not. I have a job and friends in New York, not to mention my mom. I have a life there. The nagging uncertainty tightens my stomach anew.

Busying myself with spooning cacao and sugar into the mug, I hide my expression from Lena. My tremulous feelings must be showing on my face. A part of me isn't sure if Alex will ever let me go home. What if he's decided to keep me here indefinitely? As kind as he's being, I wouldn't put that past him. He's made it clear he won't let me go, and if he decides to stay here, which is a very real probability, my life as I knew it will be in the past. This is home for him, after all.

The burner makes a hissing sound when the milk boils over. I grab the pot from the stove and blow on the foaming liquid.

"Will you start entertaining soon?" Lena asks.

I turn my head to look at her. "What?"

"The previous owners used to throw the most wonderful parties. They had a charity ball every year. The preparations took months. Mr. Volkov also entertains regularly, but mostly for business and on a much smaller scale. Of course, the previous mistress of the house was a direct descendant of Russian royalty, so they moved in circles that demanded lavish entertainment. Although, Mr. Volkov does mix with some families who have royal blood in their veins."

I pour the milk into the mug and carry the pot to the sink. "He does?"

"The Turgenevs, for example. Mikhail Sergeyevich Turgenev and his family are regular callers. Mr. Volkov is a close friend of the family. Maybe you met them in New York? Like Mr. Volkov, Mr. Turgenev has a house in America for business purposes. The family spends one month there every year. They returned shortly after you, I believe."

I still in the middle of rinsing the pot. "Dania Turgeneva? Those Turgenevs?"

"Ah." She gives an approving nod. "Then you did meet them."

"Briefly," I say, putting the pot on the drip tray.

"At least you already have a friend in St. Petersburg." She folds the napkin and sets it on top of the pile. "You should ask Mr. Volkov if you can invite Miss Turgeneva for tea. She's such a charming young lady and from a good family too." She gives me a sugary smile. "I'm sure he'll be happy to oblige, as close as they are."

No, thanks. Not after Dania told me she was destined to marry Alex.

Lena waves a hand in the air and says with a dreamy light in her eyes, "Those dinners are simply marvelous. That's when we take out the silver and crystal and polish everything to a shine."

So, Dania is a regular visitor. Why does that bother me? I've never been the jealous type, but then again, I've never dated a man like Alex, a self-made zillionaire who wants me to wear a butt plug.

Warmth travels to my cheeks, and not from the hot drink I'm sipping.

Lena's conversation has dried up. From the look on her face, she's still at one of those fancy dinners with the Russian royals.

I'm about to take my hot chocolate to the library when the door in the back opens and Tima enters from the mudroom.

Shutting the door, he rubs his hands together. "It's a blizzard out there." When his gaze lands on me, he smiles. "How's the rabbit today?"

His smile is contagious. My lips curve involuntarily in response. "I'm good, thanks."

Lena switches off the iron and picks up the laundry basket. As she walks from the room, she says with her nose in the air, "Dinner is served at seven sharp."

"Like every night," Tima replies, making a face behind her back.

I can't help the laugh that bubbles up in my throat. I catch it just before it slips out.

"Don't mind her," he says, taking an apron from a hook and tying it around his waist. "She thinks her shit doesn't stink."

"Tima!" I say with a chuckle. "That's mean."

He winks. "It's true."

"She says she's been working here for a long time."

He takes a pan from the shelf and puts it on the stove. "She grew up in this house. Her mother was the housekeeper before her."

"Wow. She didn't tell me that. What about you?"

"Nah." He takes a knife from the block and pulls it through the blade sharpener. "She was here way before me. That's why she thinks she's the boss."

"How long have you known Alex?"

"A few years," he says evasively.

"How did you meet?"

"Let's just say our paths crossed when mine wasn't very straight or narrow."

Not wanting to pry when he's obviously not comfortable discussing it, I drop the subject. Being used to working with people all day, I miss human contact. I'm enjoying the company and I'm reluctant to leave, but I don't want to be under Tima's feet when he has work to do.

"I'll be—"

I'm about to say I'll be in the library when the door crashes open with a bang, and Igor and one of the guards rush through it.

Tima's hand tightens around the shaft of the knife. His stance is tense, as if he's ready to pounce.

My heartbeat spikes. Are we under attack?

"What's going on?" I ask Igor tensely.

The guard stumbles into the kitchen, clutching a towel that's wrapped around his hand.

Igor shuts the door. "He's hurt."

My professional side kicks in, and I drag a chair out by the table. The man looks as if he might keel over.

"What's his injury?" I ask as Igor helps him into the chair.

"He got cut," Igor says. "Knife."

"Let me see," I say to the man, unwrapping the towel.

"He doesn't speak English," Igor says.

I direct my question at Igor. "Do you have a first-aid kit?"

"I'll get it," Tima says, leaving the knife in the block and dashing down the hallway.

The blood has soaked through the towel. The man flinches when I pull the towel from his skin. Blood seeps from a diagonal cut in his palm.

"What's your name?" I ask as I take his hand to inspect the damage.

"Stepan," Igor says.

"It doesn't look as if any arteries are severed, but it needs stitches." Meeting the man's eyes, I say, "You're going to be all right."

"The sight of blood makes him…" Igor pauses. "How do you say? Woozy."

Tima returns with a first-aid kit that he leaves on the table.

"Can you walk to the sink, Stepan?" I ask. "I need to rinse off the blood."

"I'll help," Igor says.

Igor puts his arm around Stepan's shoulders and leads him to the sink as I go through the kit and extract a bottle of saline solution.

At the sink, I open the tap and hold Stepan's hand under the water. "I need some clean dishcloths."

While Tima opens a drawer and takes out a stack of cloths, I pour saline solution over the cut. When it's clean, I grab a dishcloth and wrap it around Stepan's hand to help stop the bleeding.

"That's good," I say in a soothing tone. "Now let's get you back to the table."

Igor helps him back into the chair as I drag another one closer for myself.

"Do you have a local anesthetic?" I ask.

Igor motions with his head toward the kit. "In there."

I position Stepan's hand with his palm facing up and his forearm resting on the table. "Keep pressure on the wound."

Igor does as I ordered, freeing my hands to find the anesthetic. I fill a hypodermic needle from the vial and tip my head toward the cloth. When Igor removes the cloth, I inject the anesthetic in the fleshy part of the man's palm.

"Take a clean cloth and press it on the cut," I say, looking for surgical thread and a needle.

Stepan is pale, appearing close to fainting.

"A soldier who's scared of blood?" Tima asks with a condescending smile.

"Only his own blood," Igor says, giving Tima a cold look. "Your blood, for example, wouldn't bother him."

"Hey." I give the men a stern look. "We're all on the same side. Igor, tell him he can close his eyes or look away."

Igor repeats the words in Russian as I prick Stepan's skin with the needle to test if the anesthetic has taken effect. He flinches.

"Does it hurt?" I ask.

Igor repeats the question before translating for me. "He can feel the sensation of being touched, but there's no pain."

"How did this happen?" I ask, pushing the needle through Stepan's skin at the top of the cut.

"Training," Igor says.

I lift my gaze to his fleetingly. "You train with real knives?"

"It would defy the objective to train with toy ones, wouldn't it?"

I bite back a retort. "What about Alex?"

"What about him?" Igor asks.

"Does he approve of this training method?"

"He's the one who insists on it," Igor says.

I gape at him. "That's dangerous. I can't believe he'd be so irresponsible."

Igor straightens his back. "He's not asking anything of us that he isn't doing himself."

The implication makes me go cold. "What? Does he train like this too?"

Igor's tone is indignant. "Of course he does. That's why we respect him."

Tima blows out a sigh. "If you've finished bleeding all over the room, I'd like to disinfect my kitchen. I have cooking to do."

"Sorry." I offer Tima a watery smile. "I should've taken him to the bathroom."

"Don't worry, my little rabbit," Tima says. "It's not your fault. These guys should know better."

Fear pools hot in my stomach as I go back to work. I knew Alex was working out, but doing combat training with his guards? With real knives? And who knows what other weapons?

"What's going on here?" a deep voice asks from the door.

I look up. The object of my thoughts stands in the frame, dressed in a dark suit and wearing a thunderous expression.

"Stepan is hurt," Igor says. "Knife wound."

"I can see that," Alex says, stepping over the threshold. "But what's he doing letting Katerina stitch him up?"

I blink up at him. "You'd rather Igor do it? At least I'm qualified."

"This isn't a fucking hospital." Alex stops next to the table. "The men know how to take care of their wounds."

Igor rubs a hand over his head. "I just thought—"

"That because she's a nurse you'll run a fucking sick bay?" Alex's voice is harsh.

"Alex," I say gently. "I'm happy to help."

"You're not here to work," he says, sliding a frosty gaze toward Igor. "And my men aren't here to put their paws on you."

"Enough." I tie a knot in the thread. "Instead of being angry about my assistance, why don't you hand me the scissors?"

Alex grudgingly obliges.

I cut the thread and give him the scissors with an overly sweet, "Thank you."

"We're talking about this in the library," he says with a tight jaw.

"After I've disinfected and bandaged the wound."

He crosses his arms, watching me with a broody expression, but he doesn't argue as I finish my work and tell Stepan to take a couple of painkillers and an antibiotic for good measure before going to bed.

Tima starts wiping the table with disinfectant as soon as Stepan stands. Igor has scarcely left with the patient before Alex wraps his hand around my upper arm and pulls me to my feet.

"Now we talk," he says in a dark voice, all but dragging me to the door.

"Wait." I dig my heels in. "I have to wash my hands."

He lets me, but the minute I'm done, he steers me to the nearest room and pushes me inside. It's one of the lounges close to the dining room. I walk to the center of the floor, creating some distance. He's unreasonably angry, and I'm upset. We both need space to cool down.

Watching me with gleaming blue eyes, he closes the door and turns the key.

The act makes my pulse jump. "What are you doing?"

"I don't like it when you touch my men," he says, advancing on me.

I crane my neck to meet his gaze when he stops so close our bodies almost touch. "It's my job."

His jaw bunches. "Not here it's not."

"I touch many men on a daily basis in New York," I say with barely suppressed frustration.

A muscle ticks in his temple. "That doesn't mean I have to like it."

I prop my hands on my hips. "You never said it bothered you."

"As I said, that doesn't mean I liked it."

"This is ridiculous. There's a difference between a caregiver's touch and an intimate touch. You get that, don't you?"

He gives me a hard smile. "It makes no difference to me what kind of touch it is. I don't want your hands on them." His voice lowers with dangerous intent. "And if I catch their hands on you, I'll chop them off."

Anger bursts through my veins, heating my skin. "I love my job. I'm good at it. You said so yourself. If you have a problem with my job, it's going to be a problem for us, and I mean a *real* problem." I add with emphasis, "A make-or-break problem."

"I do admire your skill and dedication." His words are softly spoken, but there's an edge to them. "I admire the profession you've chosen, and I respect your decisions. I'm not telling you that you can't do what you love. What I'm telling you, Katyusha, is that I don't like to share. I'll never like your hands on another man's naked torso or dick, no matter how professional the intention."

"You're jealous," I say, startled to realize just how much.

"Exactly." He splays a palm over my lower back, tugging me against him while he slips his free hand under the hem of my skirt to cup my sex. *"This"*—he squeezes—"belongs to me." Flicking my clit softly, he continues in a tone that leaves no room for argument. "Only to me."

A spark travels from my groin to my belly, but I can't let him sidetrack me with lust.

"No." I push on his chest.

He regards me with a mixture of surprise, anger, and disbelief, but he doesn't pull his hand away.

"We're not done talking." I grip his wrist and pull his hand out from under my skirt. "I'm not going to cheat on you. That's not my style. But I'm not taking orders from you." I point at the locked door. "If you can't accept that, you may as well walk through that door now. My job isn't up for discussion."

A quiet storm builds in his eyes. "Your job isn't the issue."

"Then what is?"

"My men," he bites out. "You're beautiful. They're horny. Put two and two together, and what do you get?"

"If you don't trust them, trust me."

Clenching his jaw, he says, "You're asking too much of me, Katerina."

I back up a step. "Is trust too much to ask?"

He stabs his fingers through his hair. "That's not what I'm

talking about. I'm talking about not wanting them to enjoy your touch a little too much." The blue of his eyes turns cold. "If one of those motherfuckers gets an erection from looking at you, I'll chop off more than his hands."

"Alex, please. Stepan was in pain. I can promise you, turned on was the last thing he would've been while I was stitching him up."

"Just as well," he says, biting off every word.

I drop my hands to my sides. "I can't believe you. While we're talking about trust, why didn't you tell me you were training with your men?"

He frowns. "What does that have to do with anything?"

"You're training with knives, for crying out loud."

"Yes," he says, as if it should've been obvious.

"Someone got hurt today. *You* could get hurt."

"The point of training with actual weapons is making sure we *don't* get hurt."

"In a real fight, you mean," I say, hovering between anger and concern.

He closes the distance between us. "Precisely." Hooking a curl behind my ear, he asks with a quirk of his lips, "Are you worried about me?"

"Of course I am," I say incredulously.

"Don't be. I know how to take care of myself."

"Then don't be jealous," I deadpan.

Folding his hand around my nape, he pulls me closer. "Are you saying you won't worry if I won't be jealous?"

"I'll try." I swallow. "Will you?"

He considers me for a moment. "What are you asking of me, Katerina?"

"I'm here anyway. I might as well put my skills to good use."

Studying me with a piercing gaze, he rubs a thumb over the back of my neck. "Are you bored?"

I shrug. "A little."

He nods. "Fine. I fight. You heal. Happy?"

"Was that so difficult?" I ask with a strained smile.

He smooths his palm up my thigh under the hem of my skirt. "You have no idea." Walking me backward to the couch, he adds in a soft, low voice, "But you know I'd do anything for you."

Our bodies are pressed flush together, his erection hard against my stomach. I slide my hands over his chest under his jacket as he tightens his grip on my hip. Holding my gaze, he follows the elastic of my thong with a finger, drawing a path from my side to my lower back. When he realizes my ass cheeks are bare, his gaze darkens. He caresses my left globe with a callused palm, his skin rough on mine. His movements are lazy and gentle, but intensity burns in his eyes.

My body tightens with anticipation, uncertain what to expect when he brushes a finger down my crease. Approval and heat wash over his features when he finds the jewel. I gasp as he presses on the plug, applying soft pressure.

"You've been a good girl," he says in a hoarse voice, lowering his head to mine.

I tilt my face up to give him easier access. He catches my lips in a searing kiss, eradicating our fight, truce, worries, and insecurities. None of those things matter when he reverses positions, sits down, and draws me onto his lap to straddle him. I forget about the imminent danger and the distant future, focusing only on the sound of his zipper as he pulls it down, and on the hot, smooth head of his cock brushing over my inner thigh.

Pulling my thong aside, he tests my folds with a finger. Satisfied that I'm ready, he lifts me to my knees and positions his cock at my entrance. He lets me take him at my pace, reading my face as I lower myself slowly.

The fullness is almost too much, the stretch of his cock with the added pressure of the toy unbearably stimulating. He presses a thumb on my clit, massaging until my inner muscles are supple enough to take him to the hilt.

"Wait," I say breathlessly, catching his wrist. "I'll come."

"Not yet," he agrees, cupping the side of my head and dragging me closer.

Pressing our lips together, he kisses me with a skill that makes my knees weak. He sweeps his tongue over mine and explores the depths of my mouth before gently nipping my bottom lip. The kiss is unrushed. He keeps still, giving me time to adjust to the new fullness and to enjoy the sensation of him filling me.

After a long period of kissing, he starts moving slowly. I grip his shoulders for balance as he rolls his hips. The sensation is so intense, the penetration so deep, that I throw back my head and moan. He picks up his pace, adding friction to the already overpowering pressure. This pleasure is different. It's darker. More devastating.

The faster he moves, the higher my need climbs. It rises to a crescendo, but I don't go over. I can't, not without some kind of touch on my clit. I slip a hand between our bodies, needing to get there like never before, but he locks his fingers around my wrist, preventing me from touching myself.

I'll go out of my mind if this intolerable yearning doesn't stop soon.

He rocks me faster but not harder, keeping the thrusting gentle.

"Alex. I need—"

The rest of my words are cut off as he slams up and steals my breath.

His voice is heated. "I know what you need."

Moving a hand around my body, he grips the jeweled head of the plug and twists from left to right while pummeling my sex with shallow thrusts. That's all it takes. I break with a shudder, barely biting off a scream. Release tears through me like a violent storm. He follows a second later, his body going taut as he comes inside me. Instead of pulling out when he's empty, he makes me ride the aftershocks of my orgasm, prolonging them by keeping pressure on the toy with his palm.

I've never come like this, not with this much force and not from this kind of stimulation alone. Collapsing against his body, I rest my forehead on his shoulder and inhale the masculine aroma of his cologne. The familiar smell grounds me as much as his strong hands on my back.

"How are you doing?" he murmurs, nipping my earlobe.

"Mm." I'm not sure I'll be able to peel myself off his body, never mind rise to my feet.

"It's time for an upgrade," he says in a husky voice. "You're ready for a bigger size."

I don't have to ask what he means.

"Silicone or glass?" he asks, sending goosebumps over my arm when he sucks on the sensitive spot behind my ear.

"Silicone sounds softer." Just to tease him, I add, "I like red."

He chuckles. "A ruby it will be."

I pull away in surprise. "A ruby?"

He brushes the hair from my face. "What did you expect, my love?"

"Crystal?" I ask with a frown.

"Tsk." He shakes his head.

My lips part in disbelief. "You mean…?"

"A diamond, yes," he says. "You didn't think I'd put a common crystal in your ass, did you?"

The crass words shouldn't sound hot, but they heat my stomach.

"And just so we're clear," he says, gripping my hair in a tight fist. "I won't be walking through that door any time soon, kiska."

17

ALEX

A week passes with no action on the security front. Stefanov got my message for sure, the one I sent via that dead *ublyudok*, Vadim, but he's not making a move. He's biding his time, maybe waiting for a weakness to exploit. We're caught in a frustrating stand-off, each watching the other.

There's no new information from Adrian either. He's still trying to trace the hacker who calls himself Mukha. The guy—Mukha—is good. I have to give him that. Nelsky and my team are on his trail too, but they've come up with zilch. Adrian tripled my original offer to the hacker for the file he encrypted for Pavlov, and the pesky little fly said he'd have to think about it. He said if he were to hand the file over, he'd have to take on a new identity and disappear. He'd never be able to set foot in Russia again. Whatever is on that file is damn important, enough for the fly to be wary of selling it, even for three million euros, and enough for Stefanov to want to kill me.

What I still don't know is how Pavlov is connected to any of this. Like Stefanov, he's beefing up his army. You'd think they're preparing for war. My informants told me they've both ordered more weapons on the black market and hired more men.

As far as Besov goes, I'm almost a hundred-percent certain he's the fucker who took a shot at me, although I can't prove he was in the States when the shooting happened. According to the flight records I got from my contacts, Besov has been safely and soundly on Russian soil for years. That doesn't mean he didn't travel with a false passport. The man I ordered to watch Besov's apartment informed me that Besov isn't home. The neighbors said he keeps to himself and never speaks to anyone, but they haven't seen him in a good two months.

While I'm waiting, I use my restless energy to ensure that the upcoming event will be secure. The gala dinner will be held downtown in the Lion Palace Hotel ballroom. The event coordinator has provided me with the guest list. Stefanov and Pavlov aren't invited. The bratva bosses aren't the kind of influencers the government wants to associate with when it comes to nuclear power.

Since many government officials and leading businessmen will be attending, the security is already top notch, but I insist on putting extra measures in place. For one, I want every person searched before they're allowed to enter the gala venue. The hall has a separate entrance from the hotel, which plays in my favor. It makes controlling who enters and exits considerably easier. I'm an important enough guest to get my specifications met to the last T. My money lines the pockets of many of the attendees, after all. The fact that Mikhail Turgenev and his family will be present further aids my efforts. Turgenev, who's a stickler for security, seconded my suggestions. He even asked to have walk-through metal detectors installed at the entrance.

We'll also have checkpoints set up and all vehicles searched for explosives before they'll be allowed to approach the hall through a cordoned-off one-lane street. Our carefully screened valets will park the vehicles in the underground parking lot that will be watched by a team of guards before, during, and after the event.

In addition, Mikhail and I will have the building surrounded. Our men will be stationed around the whole block, armed with automatic rifles, smoke bombs, and grenades. Of course, they'll be discreet. The general public won't even know they're there. My security chief, Nelsky, will monitor the movements around the hotel via satellite. We'll also have drones positioned at strategic coordinates, both to have extra eyes on the venue and for additional firepower if needed. Those drones are loaded with missiles that can flatten a ten-story building. Lastly, I'll have men on the floor who'll be connected to Nelsky and me via a central communication system. Any enemies stupid enough to target anyone at the gala will be squashed like insects before they come within a five-kilometer radius of the building.

This doesn't mean we're going to leave the house defenseless. Even though Katerina and I will be attending the gala with an army of men, enough of them will remain at my residence to hold down the fort there. I've also put extra men on the watch at Stefanov's, Pavlov's, and Besov's dwellings. If they move so much as a meter, I'll know about it.

Katerina is surprisingly accommodating about all the precautions. I expected her to complain and sulk about her loss of freedom, but she bravely carries the undeserved burden I've dumped on her shoulders. In turn, I bend over backward to fulfill her whims and wishes, even if it goes against every instinct I possess. Letting her play nurse to my men isn't easy for me. I explained to her in detail why it upsets me, but she makes an effort not to worry every time I put a foot outside the house—or she's simply not showing how much the concern affects her—and therefore I try to keep my jealousy in check.

The men flock to the house as if Katyusha lives there for their fucking benefit. Igor and Leonid transformed one of the lounges into a sick bay complete with an examination bed and medical equipment. The men come to her with everything from sprained ankles to headaches. Since my kiska seems to be genuinely happy to help and less stressed when she's keeping busy, I grind my teeth and bear the wimps' presence in the house. They never complained about a cut on a finger before. I suppose the novelty of Katerina's presence has yet to wear off.

I've never compromised for anyone before, but Katerina is a first for me in many aspects. Besides, the reward for my suffering is most effective. She's been more open with me during the last few days, her advances both sweet and hot.

I'll do anything if it means she'll give me access to her body and her heart.

WHEN I COME HOME FROM THE OFFICE ON FRIDAY EVENING, I GO straight to the homemade clinic. The room smells of disinfectant as I open the door. It's empty. For once, there's no patient with a splinter in his skin to be pampered.

Urgency drives my steps as I walk through the house. I'm eager to see her. I left while she was still sleeping this morning and didn't get a chance to kiss her goodbye. Her laughter comes from the end of the hallway, the sound beautiful and clear.

Tima says something in his baritone that makes her laugh more.

I follow the sound of their banter to the kitchen. Tima is scrubbing pots in the sink, and Katerina is leaning with her backside against the table. She's wearing a tight-fitting sweater and a skirt that hugs her thighs. Paired with high-heeled boots, the outfit looks sexy as hell. She's been mostly wearing dresses or skirts for the past week, and the reason heats my veins and sends blood to my groin.

"Alex," she says, offering me a smile. "Tima was telling me about some of your less appetizing local dishes."

Tima acknowledges me with a nod from over his shoulder. Despite the fact that I'm jealous of the attention Katerina gives him, I'm grateful to him for keeping her company when I'm working late. He doesn't have to hang around in the kitchen. It's long after his usual sign-off time.

Advancing toward her, I take in her shapely form. "Is that so?"

"*Keeshka*," she says with an adorable accent, wrinkling her nose. "Intestines stuffed with meat and meal? Or pig blood?" She shivers. "He told me it's one of your favorites."

"I'm an adventurous eater," I say, stopping short of her.

The huskiness of my voice must betray my lust because her throat bobs with a soundless swallow as she stares up at me.

Tima dries his hands on a dishcloth. "I'm done for the evening unless you need me for anything else?"

I don't break eye contact with Katerina. "We're good."

"Good night then," he calls on his way to the door.

It slams behind him with a bang, enclosing us in silence.

"How was your day?" she asks after a beat, her voice a little hoarse.

"Good." I lean my palms on either side of her body on the tabletop. "Yours?"

She wets her lips. "The usual."

I narrow my eyes at the act. Innocent or not, it makes me want to kiss her. "I hope you didn't overexert yourself."

"It will take more than that," she says, ducking underneath my arm and escaping to the other side of the room.

Her walk is unhurried, but she's running all the same. On top of sensing my desire, she must also know intuitively that I have special plans for her tonight.

Going on tiptoes, she opens the overhead cupboard. "I was going to make tea. Would you like some?"

Smiling inwardly at her futile diversion attempt, I stalk to my innocent little prey. She stretches to grab hold of the tin of tea. I reach over her and take the tin, making a mental note to tell Tima to put the refreshments on a lower shelf. The action puts our bodies together. Her back presses against my chest and her buttocks against my thighs. I put the tea aside and lean closer, capturing her between the counter and my body.

Like a cornered rabbit playing dead, she keeps perfectly still. Only her ribcage expands with fast breaths. She knows what I want, and it scares her.

I lower my head and inhale the fragrance of her skin before kissing her neck. She smells like my favorite dessert—peaches and cream. Despite her fear, she tilts her head, giving me better access. Splaying one hand over her stomach and the other over the curve of her breast, I hold her close as I kiss her neck slowly and meticulously. I pay extra attention to the part where her neck meets her shoulder, knowing this is an erogenous zone for her. When her skin turns red from my stubble, I kiss my way up the arch of her neck to the sensitive spot behind her ear. She moans when I graze her earlobe with my teeth. As I draw my hand from her stomach down between her legs, her nipple hardens under my palm where I'm fondling her breast.

She sags against me with her eyes closed and her lips slightly parted when I reach my destination. Cupping her pussy, I hold her in place while I slip my other hand between our bodies to explore the crease of her ass. The jeweled head of the butt plug is hard beneath my palm.

"Good girl," I whisper in her ear, pressing a rewarding kiss on her jaw.

She mewls when I press two fingers on the plug and apply gentle pressure. I've been patient. We've been playing with butt plugs for a week now, using a bigger size every day. I've stretched her carefully and fucked her roughly, and she's loved everything I've done. She's ready to take my cock.

I rub her clit with the heel of my hand to get her wet. She arches her back, pushing her ass harder against my palm. Using both hands, I play with her front and back, massaging her clit and asshole in circles. Her breathing quickens as I increase my pace. Just before she breaks, I stop.

Wrapping my fingers around her wrist, I say, "Come."

She follows me wordlessly to the bedroom. No one is going to disturb us, but I turn the key in the lock for good measure. I like my privacy.

"Strip," I say in a voice rough with desire, peeling off my jacket.

She holds my gaze as she undresses, dropping the clothes in a heap at her feet. I do the same, tearing out of my shirt and pants as fast as I can.

When we're both naked, she turns toward the bathroom, presumably to remove the plug. "I'll just be a minute."

I watch her cross the floor, admiring the sway of her ass and the red gemstone that peeks out from between her globes.

The wait almost kills me. My cock is hard and ready, a heavy weight jutting out between my legs. I fist the shaft and pump twice, catching the drop of pre-cum and lubricating the head. When Katerina steps back into the room, apprehension widens her eyes as she trails her gaze over the work of my hand.

"I'm not going to hurt you," I say, reminding her of my earlier promise. "If you tell me to stop, I will."

She swallows when I open the bedside drawer and take out the lube.

"Kneel on the bed like I taught you, Katyusha."

Her obedience warms me in all the right places when she climbs onto the bed and kneels with her ass in the air and her elbows on the mattress.

I climb onto the bed behind her and spread her thighs to my liking. In this position, I have access to all of her body. Her asshole is nicely stretched, an inviting temptation. Arousal glistens on her bare folds. To be sure, I dip a finger between those plump lips. She's slick, as ready as I am.

Gripping my cock in a fist, I position the head at her pussy and part her carefully. She stretches around me, taking me easily as I slide in to the hilt. I hold still for a moment, giving her time to adjust while I uncap the lube and squirt a generous amount into her crease.

Using a finger, I spread the lube around her dark hole before working it inside. She clenches around the intrusion, her inner muscles gripping my finger tightly. I nearly come then and there, imagining what that tightness will do to my cock. As I start to pump with my cock, I do the same with my finger, synchronizing the pace to take her ass and pussy with shallow strokes.

She moans, letting me know she likes the double stimulation. I've taken her enough times while she was wearing a butt plug to get her comfortable with the feeling of being overfilled, and I've used my fingers to teach her how to enjoy having her ass played with. Meeting my undemanding pace, she pushes back with every thrust until I give her two fingers. I carry on like this for a while, slightly quickening the rhythm but keeping the thrusting in both holes gentle until she's so needy that she's grinding her ass against my groin.

I only pick up the pace when I'm fucking her back entrance with three fingers. Mimicking the pumping of my cock, I sink deeper and go harder to get her ready. When she arches her back and makes a sound that tells me she's close to coming, I give it to her, holding nothing back. She orgasms with a cry, her inner muscles clenching hard on my cock and fingers.

While she's supple inside and high on the euphoria of release, I pull out and align my cock with the pretty hole between her ass cheeks. I go painstakingly slow, applying steady pressure on the tight ring of muscle until it starts to give. She stretches perfectly, letting me in with little difficulty. Before she's come down from her climax, the head of my cock is buried inside her ass.

"How are you doing, kiska?" I ask roughly, rubbing my palms over her globes. It takes everything I have to exercise restraint, but I'd sooner die than hurt her.

She watches me from over her shoulder, her big brown eyes hazy with endorphins and her pupils already dilating with fresh need. "Good."

Dragging in a deep breath, I sink an inch deeper. Her ass

grips me like a fist. She's velvet soft inside, the slick heat of her body milking me so hard I have to clench my teeth so as not to ejaculate before I'm fully sheathed. The alluring sight of her forbidden entrance swallowing my cock doesn't help. It's one of the most erotic images I've ever seen.

The preparations have paid off. She's taking me exceptionally well. Resting her cheek on her arm, she lies quietly and, like a good girl, lets me do the work. My skin is slick with perspiration from the strain of holding back when she closes her eyes and blows out a contented little sigh. Good. I couldn't have asked for a better reaction. I want her first time to be perfect. I want her to enjoy this as much as I do.

With every inch I drive deeper, my balls draw tighter. The pleasure is excruciating. The need to pump is all-consuming. I brush a hand over the delicate line of her spine and caress her back as I take my time to own this part of her. When I'm three-quarters in, it gets impossibly tight. I slip a hand between her legs and work her clit the way she likes. She softens with a whimper, and I slide all the way in.

Fuck. My groin is flush against her ass. So hot. So pretty. I wish I could film this to show my kitten how beautiful she looks. If privacy weren't as important to me, I would. As for me, the picture is burned into my memory. I'll have wet dreams about this for the rest of my life.

Wrapping my hands around her waist, I keep her still as I pull out an inch and sink back slowly.

The action makes her gasp. This is where it gets intense.

I bend down to plant a kiss on her back. "Do you want more?"

"Yes," she says in a shaky voice.

"Open your eyes for me, kiska. I want to look at you."

She obliges, lifting her eyelashes and giving me a glimpse of those soft brown pools with the honey-gold flecks.

I pull out two inches before pushing back in. Her breathing picks up and her moans turn louder. I could drown in the noises she makes. The sexy sounds spike my arousal, and it takes every ounce of self-control not to move faster. I advance with herculean patience, taking care not to tear or hurt her. I'm well aware of my size and her small body.

A few more gentle pumps of my hips, and I'm taking her ass with long, slow strokes. She's panting now, her need evident in the crescendo of her moans. I could make her come quicker by playing with her pussy, send her tumbling over the edge by finger-spanking her clit, but for her first time, I want her to come from anal stimulation alone.

When I'm certain she's ready to take everything, I pivot my hips faster, taking her harder. She bites her lip and swallows her moans as she watches me obediently. Her eyes are like mirrors. A flinch tells me to slow down. A bat of her eyelashes tells me to move faster. The widening of those hazel pools tells me she's close.

So am I.

I go for the last sprint, keeping her in place with my hands on her hips as I increase the pace. My rhythm is grueling but controlled. I read her face as I slam my groin against her ass. Her expression is one of pleasure, not of pain. Intense pleasure. There are a million-and-one nerve endings in that part of her body, and I know just how to move to trigger them all.

One last thrust, and she comes with a soundless gasp. Her pretty lips part as her whole face pulls into a mask of ecstasy. It's my cue to let go. Hot ribbons of cum erupt from the sensitive crest of my cock, filling up her ass. The release is so powerful that, for a moment, I go weak.

Katerina's upper body collapses on the mattress. I follow her down, careful not to pull out too suddenly and hurt her. Supporting my weight on my arms, I cover her body with mine and kiss her shoulder. It takes a few moments before our breathing starts to calm, and I stay inside her, reveling at the possession. I've marked her in yet another way. Call me primitive, but it's hugely satisfying.

I brush a kiss over her temple. "How are you doing, my love?"

"Mm."

Her lethargic response makes me smile. "Take a breath and hold it. Blow it out when I tell you." I push up onto my arms. "Breathe out slowly, kiska."

I pull out gently as she exhales. Cool air washes over my cock. Already, I miss the heat of her body.

"Don't move," I say, caressing her firm globes as I get to my feet.

We need a shower, but it can wait a few minutes. I've thoroughly worn her out.

In the bathroom, I wet a facecloth and grab a towel. Gently, I clean her up. I even have enough brain cells left to call Lena and tell her to prepare a tray with the dinner and leave it in front of the bedroom door.

As I settle next to Katerina on the bed and pull her close, I can't help but bask in the knowledge that I own her on every physical level. It's only fair, seeing that she owns me, heart and soul. The words I never thought I'd say to any woman are on the tip of my tongue, threatening to spill over my lips, but she's already dozing off and this is hardly the moment.

I don't say things I don't mean. I don't make promises lightly. The day I tell Katerina I love her is the day I'll put a ring on her finger. The words are sacred. They deserve to be saved for a special occasion. And since she may not be on board with where I plan to take our relationship, she may need the consolation of those words when she realizes that in this matter also, I'm not giving her a choice.

18

KATE

One day rolls into the next, and before I know it, it's Thanksgiving. Nobody celebrates it in Russia, of course—it's a purely North American holiday—but I can't help thinking about the big home-cooked meal I'd be having with my mom if it weren't for the fact that she's at the treatment center while I'm halfway across the world. Worse yet, I might not see her for Christmas.

Alex must notice my mood because he encourages me to call my mom that evening, something I'm always more than happy to do. He has Lena make a cup of hot chocolate for me and then considerately gives me privacy.

By now, he trusts me enough to believe I won't ask my mom to contact the embassy or something along those lines.

Once I'm settled on the sofa with the cup of hot chocolate in my hands, I dial my mom.

"Hey, honey," she says, sounding out of breath. "How are you?"

"We're good. More importantly, how are you?"

"Great. We've just finished an aerobics session in the heated pool. The water is marvelous. Oh, and guess what? I'm losing more weight. My pants are so loose I'll have to go on a shopping spree soon."

I smile at her enthusiasm. "How's the treatment going? Are you feeling an improvement?"

"Absolutely. The diet makes a huge difference. I love the holistic approach here. It makes so much more sense than simply swallowing a few pills. I'm doing an electronic detox at the same time, and a break from social media is doing me wonders." She lowers her voice. "I dare say, I love the doctor the most. Dr. Hendricks is a charming man, not to mention brilliant. He's done so much for people suffering from my condition."

"Yeah, well, it's okay to admire him. Just don't take it beyond the professional."

She utters a forced little cough.

"Mom!" I press a hand to my forehead. "Please tell me you didn't."

"We haven't taken things to a physical level if that's what you're worried about. We felt we should wait until after the treatment. It wouldn't be professional, you know, to take it further now."

I leave my drink on the coffee table and shift to the edge of my seat. "You make it sound serious."

"Don't worry, honey. We're just enjoying each other's company and having fun. I'm not planning on marrying him."

"Still, I don't think it's a good idea to flirt with the staff."

"We're only getting to know each other." She clears her

throat. "In fact, he'd very much like to meet you and Alex when you come for Christmas."

I take a deep breath. "About that… We may not be back before Christmas after all."

There's a moment of silence on the line. "That's a long break from work you're taking, honey," Mom says finally. "Is something wrong?"

Crossing my fingers, I say, "Not at all. Alex is just very busy with some projects here, and I don't want to return to New York on my own."

"Ah. Well, don't worry about it, honey. I completely understand, although I was looking forward to seeing my future son-in-law."

I cringe. "Mom."

"He's serious about you, Katie. Anyone can see that."

"Do you need anything?" I ask, eager to change the subject. "Snacks? Toiletries? I can arrange for an internet delivery."

"That's sweet of you, but I have everything I need."

"Okay. Let me know if—" I catch myself. "Send a text message to Alex if you're running short on something."

"Will do. I miss you, honey."

I swallow down an untimely sob. "Miss you too, Mom."

Before she can hear the emotions tearing up my chest, I hang up.

AS THE DAYS MARCH ON AND CHRISTMAS APPROACHES, I FEEL increasingly homesick. No matter what I'm doing, my mind often drifts off to nostalgic memories of the holiday. On Christmas Eve, my mom and I would take a taxi to Manhattan.

We'd brave the cold to admire the Christmas lights and the giant tree at Rockefeller Center before having a special dinner at home and exchanging gifts.

Fortunately, the winter holiday spirit isn't lacking in Alex's house, even though I've learned that Russians celebrate Christmas on January 7th, as per the Eastern Orthodox tradition. Since that's considered a purely religious holiday, a lot of the Christmas traditions I'm familiar with—the tree, the gifts, the decorations—are instead part of the New Year's celebration in Russia. Thus, the cookies Tima has been baking, the ones that fill the kitchen with the aromas of cinnamon, raisins, and vanilla, are for the New Year's celebration, not Christmas. So is the tree with delicate glass ornaments that Lena has put up in the foyer, as well as the pine branches and red ribbons she's tied around the balustrades. The pantry is stocked with cured meats and pickled fish for the men's New Year's Eve party rather than for Christmas lunch. Decorations have also gone up in the street, but they're not visible from Alex's bedroom windows. I have to climb up to the top floor to get a peek at the fairy lights that span across the road along the river. The lights aren't colorful, like the ones back home, but white, depicting snowflakes, Christmas trees, and reindeer.

Not wanting to add to Alex's problems by burdening him with my depressive mood, I keep my feelings to myself. I can't say he's not accommodating. He lets me speak to Joanne, June, and my mom on the phone every week. It helps, but I still miss them. I can't shake this weird sense of sadness.

It's not that I'm bored. There's plenty to occupy me in the house, and Alex's guards keep me busy. More often than not, their ailments are minor, but I welcome the visits. It provides me with human contact, even if our different languages don't always permit communication. Sadly, my Russian isn't improving much. I asked Tima to teach me a few words, but with all the conjugations and male or female nouns, the language is much more difficult to master than I imagined. I try to stay positive, but even the walls of a palace can get to be too much after several weeks.

Alex is late for dinner almost every night. He's a workaholic, but he's also putting a big effort into finding the man who's threatening his life. He refuses to tell me much, always answering my questions with vague answers. Since he's also focusing a lot of his attention on preparing for the gala dinner, I don't bother him with selfish requests to go outside. We'll attend the ball soon enough.

In the meantime, I content myself with walks in the garden. At first, the heavily armed men unsettled me. Their weapons made me nervous. With time, I got used to the guns. The automatic rifles slung over their shoulders don't shock me as much as they did initially.

Three days before the party, a team of people arrive first thing in the morning for a dress fitting as well as a makeup and hairdressing trial. To my dismay, Lena is present to act as translator, her condescending smile never slipping.

The dressmaker, a middle-aged woman with exotic features, shows me three evening gowns to choose from. The first is white and figure-hugging with diamante detail, and the second is a red dress with a low back and wide skirt. Both are gorgeous, but the third is my favorite. The cut is simple. The skirt is long with a slit on the side that ends just above the knee, and the sleeves are off-shoulder. The pale pink fabric has a beautiful pearly shine. Crystal beads have been sewn onto the bodice, artfully creating delicate flowers.

The dressmaker suggests that I try on all three dresses, but I already know which one I want. She helps me put on the pink dress and positions me in front of the full-length mirror. The dress looks as if it were made for me. The only adjustment necessary is taking up the hem a few inches. She pairs the gown with high-heeled silver sandals and a matching clutch bag. The outfit is perfect.

After pinning the hem, she helps me remove the shoes and the dress. I put on a robe over my underwear and install myself in front of the mirror in Alex's dressing room for the makeup trial that follows next.

The makeup is heavier than what I usually wear, but the black eyeliner, smoky eyeshadow, and nude lipstick are suitable for a formal evening. The hairdresser takes my hair up in soft curls, leaving a few tendrils to hang down my neck. When the makeup artist and hairdresser are done and ask if I'm satisfied with the end result, Lena translates my answer, telling them I'm very happy. They both wear broad smiles as they pack up their equipment.

Lena stands at attention like a drum majorette in the dressing room while they clip their cases closed. She watches my reflection in the mirror as I wipe off the makeup with cotton swabs. I don't want to be rude, but the way she's studying me makes me uncomfortable.

"I won't keep you any longer," I say, trying to dismiss her politely. "Thanks for translating."

She lifts her chin. "I suppose grace is inherited and can't be learned."

I pause with my hand in midair. "Excuse me?"

The ladies wave and take their leave. A guard waits outside the door to escort them downstairs. If they're insulted about having their cases and persons searched before entering and exiting the house, they don't show it.

When it's just Lena and me, she says, "The white gown and subtler makeup would've been more appropriate."

I pull my spine straight. "I liked the way I looked."

"Well." She sniffs. "Just make sure you don't embarrass Mr. Volkov." She adds with meaning, "The whole of Russia will be watching the event."

"You can go now," I say in a firm tone, no longer making an effort to be polite.

"You're not done yet." She waves a hand toward the door. "What about the beautician?"

My smile is tight. "I'll manage."

"As you wish," she says, turning on her heel and leaving.

I'm definitely not Lena's choice of a partner for Alex. I suppose not being from royal ancestry doesn't help.

The beautician has already set up her makeshift salon in the indoor garden next to the pool. She gives me a wax and a full-body exfoliation before treating me to a massage. After a manicure and pedicure, I'm ready for the upcoming party.

It's not quite noon, but the sky is gray and it's snowing outside. Once again alone in the big house with no patients to treat, I put on my swimsuit and do a few laps in the pool. When I surface for air after swimming underwater, I come face to face with a pair of fancy black dress shoes.

I trail my gaze from the shoes to the dark suit pants and button-up shirt until I meet Alex's handsome face. With his hands shoved into his pockets, he's in a relaxed stance, but the underlying tension is ever-present in his body.

Propping my forearms on the edge of the pool, I smile up at him. "Hey. Playing hooky from work today?"

His smile is faint in return. "Having fun?"

"Just keeping fit. Or trying to, at least."

His smile doesn't widen at my attempted humor. Offering me a hand, he says, "I'm sure your fitness is great."

I close my fingers around his and let him pull me out. He takes the towel I left on the chaise lounge and wraps it around my shoulders.

Rubbing the towel over my arms, he says, "Katyusha, there was an incident with your mom."

I freeze. "What?"

"You don't have to worry. She's fine. She just had a little setback."

"Setback?" I take a step sideways, escaping his touch. "What kind of setback?"

"She had a dizzy spell and fell, but she didn't hurt herself and nothing is broken. The doctor examined her. Her blood pressure is fine."

A hollow feeling settles in the pit of my stomach. "Why wasn't I told?"

"I'm informing you now," he says in a reasonable tone.

Anguish and helplessness mix together, turning into anger. "When did you find out?"

"An hour ago. That's why I came home. I left the office as soon as I received the news."

I take another step to the side, creating more distance between us. "You could've called me. You *should've* called me. Immediately."

"Katyusha." He raises his hands. "I thought it was better to tell you in person."

"If I had a damn phone, this wouldn't have been an issue. I

would've known an hour ago." I march toward the door. "I want to speak to her."

Before I've made it halfway across the floor, he grabs my wrist and spins me around to face him.

"You have to calm down, Katerina. I know this is upsetting for you—"

I yank my arm from his hold. "You have no idea how this is for me."

He narrows his eyes. "As I was saying, I know this is upsetting for you, but she's in good hands. It was probably just a little low blood sugar from adapting to the new diet."

"You don't know that. It could be a more serious problem. I want to speak to her, Alex." I make my voice hard. "Now."

He clenches his jaw. "It's not even five in the morning there. She's sleeping. You'll speak to her later today."

"Now," I repeat. Unable to go to my mom or to offer my help is bad enough. His attempt to keep me from speaking with her makes me feel just a little hysterical.

"Katerina," he says harshly, grasping my shoulders. "Get ahold of yourself."

"No." I twist out of his grip. "I want to see her. She's my mother. Don't you get that? She's the only family I have."

"Katyusha," he says in a gentler tone, reaching for me again. "Don't upset yourself so much, my love."

I backtrack to the door. "She's sick. She fainted. She *fell*, for crying out loud. I'm not going to sit here like a pampered princess while my mom needs me."

The blue of his eyes hardens like glittering gemstones. "You'll stay here or wherever I decide to keep you safe, and you'll do as I say. That's the only choice you have in this equation, kiska."

The harsh words are like a blow to my head. We've been doing so great, getting along so well, pretending that everything is normal. Yet it's not. And I can't do anything about it.

Spinning around, I run for the door. To my relief, he doesn't follow. He grants me the reprieve of solitude as I lock myself in the library and come to terms with the truth. Over and over, I come to terms with it. *This is no honeymoon.* No matter how great or adventurous the sex, no matter how well he treats me, there are limits to this arrangement, and only one person makes the rules.

Alex. He holds all the power.

Now that I'm slightly calmer, however, I have to admit he's right about the hour. I'm not going to call my mom at five a.m. and wake her if she's sleeping. I don't have a choice but to wait until it's later in the morning in the States, at least nine or so.

A knock comes from the door.

"Katyusha?" Alex calls. "Come have lunch. You have to eat."

I have a good mind to throw a vase at the door, but he's right again. Starving myself isn't going to change anything.

Taking a few deep breaths, I get my emotions under control before unlocking the door. He stands on the threshold like a king, regal and imposing, his large frame dominating the space.

"I want to see her, Alex," I say quietly. "I want to examine her for myself."

"That's her doctors' job and what I'm paying them for," he says in an uncompromising tone. "This discussion is over." He holds out a hand. "Now come dress and have lunch with me."

He's not giving me a choice. Nothing has changed since we arrived in St. Petersburg. Maybe it will never change.

I don't accept his proffered hand. Gritting my teeth, I go upstairs, change, and join him for lunch in the dining room.

Our meal progresses in silence. He tries to draw me into a conversation a couple of times, asking about the dress rehearsal and if I like the ball gown, but when he remains unsuccessful at getting a response, he eventually falls quiet.

He does wait with me in his study until the clock strikes four p.m. He works while I pace the floor. The minute the grandfather clock announces the hour, he connects his laptop and activates a video call.

When my mom's face comes onto the screen, I collapse onto the sofa in relief at how well she looks. Her cheeks have a healthy glow, and her blond hair is prettily styled. She's wearing her favorite blue sweater and a lighter blue silk scarf that brings out the color of her eyes. Judging by the painting behind her on the wall, she's sitting in the lounge.

"Mom, hi." I swallow to contain my emotions. "How are you?"

"Katie," she says with a broad smile. "Alex. How good to see you."

I glance up to find Alex behind me, leaning with his arms on the backrest of the sofa.

"So," my mom says. "How are you two doing?"

I wave a hand. "Never mind us. Are you all right? I had such a fright. What happened?"

She utters an embarrassed laugh. "I didn't want to worry you. It's nothing. I told the doctor he shouldn't even have called you."

"Of course he had to," I exclaim.

"I got up to pee at night and tripped over the dresser, that's all."

Narrowing my eyes, I study her face. She looks thinner,

some of the roundness of her cheeks gone. "They said it was a dizzy spell. Are you eating enough?"

"The dietician is excellent." My mom adjusts her scarf. "I'm eating more than enough, and the food is delicious. The doctor already ran a few blood tests, and everything looks fine."

"Okay," I say slowly, unable to shake my concern.

"These things happen," my mom says. "I'd taken a hot bath earlier in the evening, and I might've undereaten a bit at dinner. It's possible my blood pressure might've been a bit low. In any event, they're monitoring me like a baby, so you can enjoy your vacation without any worries." She gives me a bright smile. "Speaking of your vacation, how is it going?"

"Great," Alex says. "Although, we haven't gotten around to as much sightseeing as we'd like."

My mom winks. "I understand. You're not getting out of the bedroom a lot, are you?"

"Mom!"

"I still have plenty to show Katerina," Alex says, not missing a beat at my mom's remark. "I want her to get to know my home country."

"Understandably." Mom checks her watch. "I'm afraid I have to go. I have a checkup with the doctor in five minutes."

"Let me know how it goes," I say. "And please take care of yourself."

"I will." She blows us a kiss. "Thank you for checking on me. Speak to you later, kids."

At *kids*, Alex chuckles. She's my parent, but she's only seven years older than Alex.

When the screen goes black, he leans over me to close the laptop.

"Thanks," I say, rubbing my palms over my thighs. "You

didn't have to be here for this." He could've gone back to the office to work in peace.

"It was the least I could do," he says, squeezing my shoulder. "Now I'm going to get some more work done, and then we'll grab dinner."

MY MOM TEXTS ALEX AFTER HER CHECKUP AND CHEERFULLY informs us that she's as healthy as a horse. Still, I worry about it all through dinner, and then I can't fall asleep at night. Alex does his best to wear me out with mind-blowing pleasure, but for once, even that doesn't help. So after I toss and turn for two hours straight, I get up. To my surprise and over my protests, he gets up too, and then he stays up with me, quietly working on his computer next to me while I watch some *Downton Abbey* in an effort to take my mind off things.

By three a.m., I'm completely exhausted, but my mind is still churning. To calm myself, I ask Alex to text my mom again, to check if she's had any other spells and he does. Mom replies right away, assuring me that she's perfectly fine and has had a great day.

Alex watches me with compassion. "Now that you've seen for yourself that there's nothing to worry about, let's get some sleep."

There won't be much sleep for him. He's up every morning at six to work out until seven before leaving for the office at seven-thirty. Sometimes, he exercises in the gym, and at other times, he spars with his men in the barracks. My stomach is always tied in knots when he's training with them, knowing how quickly an accident with a blade can happen.

Coming around the sofa, he sits down next to me. "Katyusha." He waits for me to look at him before he continues. "I know this isn't easy for you."

"My mom…" I swallow the lump in my throat. "She has no one but me."

"I know," he says, brushing a strand of hair behind my ear. "That's why I'm taking you to see her for Christmas."

"You are?" I ask with surprise.

"Yes, kiska."

"When did you decide this?"

He simply looks at me.

Ah. He's made a spur-of-the-moment decision to soothe my bruised feelings. He's made it all by himself without discussing it with me—not that I'm unhappy about the prospect. My battered ego doesn't want me to accept the olive branch he's offering, but if it means I'll get to see my mom, I'll gladly lay down my pride.

"Thanks," I say in a detached tone, pushing to my feet. "That's very generous of you."

The text reply from Mom has comforted me, yet something inside of me still feels broken. It feels as if I've been violated, which is exactly the case. My free will has been stripped away, and Alex won't let me forget it. His actions keep on reminding me of my inferior place in his life.

He follows my progress with a dark gaze as I walk out of the room, but like earlier, he doesn't come after me. He lets me go to bed alone. And when I wake up the next morning, he's already gone.

19

ALEX

I'm like a wounded bear at the office. Even Grigori stays out of my way. It's more than the lack of sleep. My kitten is docile—for now—but she's angry with me. She's unhappy about the choices I'm taking from her hands, and when she's upset, so am I, especially since I'm the reason she's upset to begin with. This whole damn situation is driving a wedge between us. I'm worried that by the time this nightmare is over, that wedge will have settled for good.

No matter. I'm nothing if not dedicated and resilient. I'll work hard to win back her adoration. Once she's taken my surname, I'll have all the time in the world to obtain that goal. In a few months from now, when we look back on all of this, she'll see that I was right. She'll understand that I acted in her best interest. Eventually, she'll forgive me.

My phone rings on the way from the boardroom to my office. It's Adrian. Igor follows closely behind me, keeping up with my long strides as Adrian tells me there's still no answer from Mukha and no sign of him either. The hacker is practically a ghost, untraceable and nonexistent as far as his trail goes.

I hang up with a curse and slam a palm on the door of my office. Igor catches the door before it bangs against the wall.

"Alex," he says as I plop down in the seat behind my desk.

The rare use of my first name makes me look at him. "What?"

"You're not your usual self."

"No shit." I push on the thumbprint scanner to open the wall shutter. "And your point is?"

He advances to my desk. "You need to remain level-headed. You have to keep your wits about you if you're going up against Stefanov."

I boot up the wall-mounted computer screen. "Three fucking weeks and we're not making any progress."

"It's more than the lack of progress," he says, giving me an even look. "You're upset because of Katherine."

I narrow my eyes. "Careful, Igor. I owe you for saving my life, but don't think for one second that gives you the right to put your nose in my private affairs."

He's undeterred. "Her stress is rubbing off on you."

Indeed. I'm not an unfeeling monster. I know how tough the news about Laura was on my kiska.

"There was an incident with her mother yesterday," I say, wiping a hand over my brow. "Everything is fine now. She'll come around."

"This has been going on since way before yesterday. She's in the dark. Put yourself in her shoes. Imagine how she must be feeling."

"Are you the expert on Katerina's feelings now?" I ask in a tight voice.

"She's not stupid. She's picking up on things. She asked me about you the day after you took her sightseeing."

"Is that right?" If Igor is discussing me with *my* woman behind my back, I swear I'll break his face. My tone is cool. Shrewd. "Asked you what exactly?"

"Why you were so tense."

I curl my fingers into a fist on the desktop. "If you told her someone is watching the house..."

I don't finish the threat. Igor knows me well enough to understand what would happen to him if he'd been so stupid. Katerina has enough to worry about. I'm not dumping information on her that can only give her nightmares and more sleepless nights.

He raises his hands. "I didn't tell her anything."

"But?"

"Maybe you need to share more with her."

He's really starting to get on my nerves. "Like what?"

"You haven't told her about Stefanov and Pavlov. You need to tell her what's going on. What if she gets it into her head to run?"

"There's a damn good reason for not telling her," I say, slamming my fist on the desk. "And it's none of your business."

He backtracks a step. "It's your call. I just thought—"

"Don't fucking think where Katerina is concerned. That's my job."

He drops his hands. "Whatever you say."

"Is that the reason why you insisted on accompanying me to the office today? To chew off my ear about how I treat my girlfriend?"

He shakes his head. "Alex."

"Mr. Volkov," I grit out. There are limits to what I'll tolerate. Katerina is definitely off limits.

"Mr. Volkov," he says, giving me a wounded look. "Leonid was long overdue for babysitting duty."

Looking at the door pointedly, I say, "I have work to do."

He nods. "If you need me, I'll be checking on the man who's watching Stefanov's house."

"You do that," I say in a frosty tone.

The minute he's closed the door behind him, I pop in my earbuds and dial Krupnov, the most prestigious jeweler in Eastern Europe. Katerina isn't going to run. She's too clever to attempt something so foolish—not to mention, my staff and the guards won't let her. Yet Igor's words have ignited a spark of unrest in my gut. All the more reason to follow through sooner than later on the decision I've made.

Just when I think Krupnov isn't going to pick up, he answers with a haughty, "Good morning."

"Alex Volkov on the line."

"Mr. V-volkov," he says, sounding flustered. "What an honor."

"I need a ring."

"Of c-course," he stammers. "What kind of ring?"

"An engagement ring. Send me a few designs."

"Y-yes. Absolutely. As you may very well know, all my rings are custom made, each one unique. There are no two of the same in the world."

"I don't need a sales pitch, Krupnov. If I'm calling you, it's because I've already made up my mind."

"W-well, yes, sir. It's just that I'll need to meet the lady to design a ring that will match her p-physique as well as her character. I don't have to tell you that w-women can be very particular in their tastes."

I pull up the forecast for the joint venture. "I want a diamond, the biggest one you have." Opening the spreadsheet, I glance over the figures. "And rubies. The best quality ones you can find. Set the stones in white gold. I'll send you the size."

It shouldn't be too difficult to obtain that. I can measure one of Katerina's rings. She has a ring shaped like a rose that she wears on her right hand. Her left ring finger should be no more than half a size smaller than her right. Or better yet, I can buy her a new ring and use the excuse to measure her finger.

Suddenly eager to set my plan in motion, I ask, "How long will it take you to design?"

"F-for you, sir, I'll put the job in the front of the queue."

I tap on the button to bring up the cost sheet for the construction of the new reactors. "How long, Krupnov?"

I'll have to move some funds around and liquidate a couple of other investments if I'm to put this much into the joint venture, but this is important to me. I know what it feels like to be poor and freezing. I send an email to my CFO with instructions to start the liquidation process.

"The d-design can be ready in a week's time, provided that you approve and don't w-want to make changes, but it will take me longer to make the r-ring. All my designs are hand crafted with—"

"Delivery date?"

"How about V-Valentine's Day?" he asks uncertainly. "It's always a g-good date for an engagement."

"New Year's and not a day later. I trust I can rely on your discretion?"

"Y-yes, Mr. Volkov. Of c-course, Mr. Volkov."

"And Krupnov?"

"Yes, Mr. V-volkov?"

"If it's not the prettiest ring that's ever been made, I'll kill you."

He gives a high-pitched laugh.

I hang up just as the door opens and Dania Turgeneva walks into my office.

Minimizing the screen, I watch with wary surprise as she crosses the floor. She's dressed in a red two-piece suit with matching heels. Her dark hair is drawn back in a high ponytail, and the makeup on her face is flawless.

It's not the first time she's been here, but she's never walked into my office unannounced. She's also always accompanied her father. The fact that she's here alone tells me this isn't a business visit.

"Alex Volkov," she says, stopping in front of my desk with her hands on her hips. "How un-neighborly of you to be back in St. Petersburg for three weeks already without so much as a call."

Manners dictate that I stand. "I've been busy."

"So I've heard." Her red lips stretch into a smile. "Lena told me you have a guest."

"Lena, huh?" I round my desk and indicate the sofa in the sitting corner. "I didn't realize the two of you were so friendly."

She sits with a graceful movement and crosses her legs. "I called your house to invite you to dinner." She shrugs. "Lena answered."

I take the chair facing the sofa. "I see."

"Friday night," she says, tapping her long, red fingernails on the armrest.

"I'm afraid that won't be possible."

She gives me a sly look. "Lena already told me you have nothing planned."

"Lena is my housekeeper." I add with an unfriendly smile, "She doesn't plan my agenda."

"Playing it safe?" She raises a brow. "Everyone knows about the attempt on your life. Is that why you keep your girlfriend locked up in your house?"

"Obviously, Lena talks too much." I make a mental note to reprimand Lena when I get home.

She waves a hand. "Don't blame poor Lena. It's pretty much common knowledge in town. You know how fast news travels, especially when you book out restaurants and boutiques for your girlfriend." She pauses with a dramatic air. "Or shall I say soon-to-be fiancée?"

If she weren't the daughter of a business associate whom I happen to respect and admire, I would throw her out of my office and have her escorted from the building.

Instead, I give her a hard look. "Have you been eavesdropping, Dania?"

"I was about to knock." She makes big eyes. "I couldn't help but overhear. Krupnov, mm? You're not playing around."

"Is there a point to this visit?" My calm voice doesn't betray my impatience. "I have a busy morning scheduled."

"I'm just a little surprised. I mean, you? Engaged?" She laughs. "Love has never been high on your priority list. Are you even capable of the feeling? I know you better than anyone, Alex Volkov. You've never said *I love you* to anyone." She gives me a polished smile. "But maybe I'm old-fashioned. Maybe in your book, marriage doesn't require love."

My jaw flexes. "I do love Katerina, very much, and I'll tell her so in no uncertain terms when I put that ring on her finger."

She gasps. "You haven't told her?" Her gaze narrows as her lips part wider. "You haven't said the big L-word yet. My, oh my. Are you sure you're doing the right thing? If it's that hard to say, maybe you don't feel as strongly about her as you should."

She couldn't be more wrong, but how I feel about Katerina is none of her damn business. "My feelings are none of your concern." I lean closer. "And if you mention a word to anyone and spoil the surprise, you will sorely regret it."

"Shame on you, Alex." She clicks her tongue. "How long have we been friends?"

I stand. "Not long enough to cross the line you're crossing now."

"Oh, calm down. I'm not going to tell anyone, if that's what you're worried about. I'll keep your little secret. I'm shocked at the bold step, that's all." She irons an invisible crease from her pants with a palm. "Are you sure it will be a good surprise for... What's her name again? Kate, right?"

"Katerina," I say through clenched teeth. "Katherine."

"Are you sure Katherine will say yes?"

My reply is filled with calculated determination. "Oh, she will."

Dania gets up. "A word of advice? Make sure she still feels the same as she did in New York before you pop the question." Winking, she adds, "This is Russia. Things are different here than in America. Not everyone can adapt to our way of living."

Our way of living doesn't refer to how we do things in our motherland. It refers to the kind of men Mikhail and I are, to the things we do to survive. Dania grew up in this world. Katerina didn't. That's what Dania is implying.

"Grigori will see you out," I say evenly. "Give my apologies to your father for not being able to make the dinner."

For a second, the well-practiced act Dania puts on for the world cracks, and a flicker of concern slips into her dark eyes. Going on tiptoes, she kisses my cheek. "Do take care, Alex. I hope you're making progress in tracking down whoever wants you dead."

"I am," I lie.

"You know my father would gladly help."

"I can take care of myself."

"Promise me you'll be careful."

"I promise."

She bites her lip, regarding me quietly for a moment. "You know, Alex, you and me—"

"There is no you and me, Dania."

Money is as important to her as it is to her father. She's always been more interested in my wallet than in my heart.

She puts on a fake smile. Just like that, her mask is back in place. "I suppose I won't see you before the party then. Papa is going to extreme measures with security. I guess the reason is you."

"I guess," I say, shoving my hands into my pockets.

Flashing me another practiced smile, she walks to the door. "Don't be a stranger, Alex," she says, pausing in the frame. "Papa considers you a friend."

I follow her with my gaze as she walks through the foyer and past Grigori's desk.

The minute she gets into the elevator, my assistant rushes over.

"I'm sorry, Mr. Volkov. I told her you were busy, but she wouldn't take no for an answer," he says before closing my door with an apologetic expression.

I blow out a breath to rid myself of the lingering annoyance and sit back at my desk. No one says no to Turgenev's daughter. Certainly not my assistant, who's considered way beneath her in the power hierarchy. She's her daddy's princess, and a spoiled one at that, one who's used to getting her way.

For once, though, Dania Turgeneva isn't getting what she wants. She's not getting my money or my status, and she's taking it surprisingly well. Then again, I've been very clear about my intentions. Perhaps she finally understands that there's only one woman destined to be Mrs. Volkova.

20

KATE

*T*he same team of women arrive on the afternoon of the gala to help me get dressed for the event. Thankfully, this time, Lena isn't present.

I'm ready half an hour before the time Alex said we needed to leave. A guard escorts the women downstairs while I add the finishing touches by dabbing on perfume and putting on the ruby earrings Alex gave me in New York.

By six, I go in search of Alex, who dressed in one of the other rooms to give the women space in his. The hallway I pass through is quiet, not a sound coming from behind any of the closed doors. Not knowing which suite he's using, I make my way to the foyer.

Since the incident with my mom, the atmosphere between us is still strained. Neither of us has brought up the argument again. We're maintaining peace by avoiding the subject. Alex came home late the following night, and we had dinner as if nothing happened. Later, in bed, we made love like he hasn't shattered my life and like the world around us isn't falling apart.

As I near the end of the hallway, voices drift from downstairs. I pause on top of the landing. Alex and a man I haven't met are conversing in the foyer. Alex is wearing dark suit pants and a fitted waistcoat over a white shirt. With his dark brown hair brushed back and his shoulders impossibly broad, he looks dangerously handsome. Intimidatingly so. The thin, short frame of the man facing him only aids in emphasizing Alex's formidable strength and size.

I haven't made a sound, but Alex pauses mid-sentence and glances toward where I stand. The blue of his eyes heats a shade as he trails his gaze over me.

"Katerina," he says in a deep voice, pronouncing my name with that Russian accent that always makes it sound exotic. "I'd like you to meet someone."

I pay closer attention to his guest. Like Alex, the man is dressed in a dark suit, but a less formal one. He's holding a metal case the size of a briefcase in one hand and a cane in the other.

Alex leaves the man standing there and climbs up the stairs to meet me at the top. Catching me off guard, he lowers his head and plants a kiss on the shell of my ear. It's a tender but possessive kiss, one that unmistakably stakes a claim.

"You look beautiful," he says softly enough only for me to hear.

It's not so much the words as the admiration in his eyes that gives weight to the compliment.

He offers me his arm. When I've placed my palm on his forearm, he carefully leads me down the stairs. I'm used to walking in heels, but I appreciate the gentlemanly gesture.

"This is Mr. Krupnov," he says when we reach the bottom of the staircase.

The man puts the case down and rushes over as fast as his cane allows. Extending a hand, he says in a heavily accented English, "A p-pleasure to meet you."

"Likewise," I say, accepting his handshake.

Placing a hand over mine where it rests on his arm, Alex smiles down at me. "Shall we go to the lounge? I have a surprise for you."

I look between Alex and the man, a tinge of nerves sparking in my stomach. Under normal circumstances, I like surprises, but with the situation we've found ourselves in, I've learned to be cautious. I don't like the disadvantage of being in the dark.

"Please follow me," Alex says to Mr. Krupnov, leading the way to the lounge.

Once inside, we stand stiffly in the center of the room while the man leans his cane against the sofa and places the case on the coffee table. When he clips it open, my breath catches. Rows of rings set with gemstones of all the colors of the rainbow fill the case. The designs range from elaborately bulky to plainly elegant.

"Choose one," Alex says, motioning at the box.

The craftsmanship of the rings is exquisite. I don't doubt each one costs a fortune. Of course, Alex can easily afford the whole case of rings. What bothers me isn't the price of the gift he's proposing but the reason for it. I've learned that Alex never does anything without a careful calculation.

"It's not my birthday," I say.

Alex gives me a crooked smile. "I'm well aware."

"Then why?"

He raises a brow. "Do I need a reason?"

I study his face, but his expression gives away nothing.

"I c-couldn't help but notice your earrings," Mr. Krupnov says with a wink. "May I suggest the ruby ring?" He picks up a golden ring with a big ruby in the center and smaller ones surrounding it. "This o-one is a classic design. Q-quite timeless."

"Try it on," Alex says.

When I don't move, Alex snatches the ring from Mr. Krupnov's palm and takes my hand. Holding my gaze, he slips it over my ring finger.

I look down. Wow. The somewhat old-fashioned design transforms on my hand, the tier of rubies taking on a three-dimensional effect as the gemstones catch the light and come to life as if each of them has a heartbeat.

Alex twists the ring to test the fit. "It's a little loose."

"T-that's not a problem." Mr. Krupnov takes a finger gauge set from his pocket. "I c-can easily adjust the band." He gives me a questioning look. "If t-this is the ring the lady likes? M-maybe you'd like to t-try some others?"

The ring is perfect, but I say, "I can't accept this. It's too much."

"We'll take it," Alex says.

Mr. Krupnov jumps on the sale. "I-I'll just take the young lady's finger sizes, and y-you'll have the ring by n-next week."

"Alex," I protest.

He gently wiggles the ring from my finger and hands it to Mr. Krupnov before kissing my hand. "I won't hear any arguments on the matter."

"Why?" I ask as Mr. Krupnov takes a notebook and pencil from his other pocket.

Alex presses a kiss to the corner of my lips. "Because I can."

Just like that, the discussion is over. Mr. Krupnov takes the measurements of my fingers and scribbles them in his notebook. He asks on which finger I'd like to wear the ring, writes that down too, and then he takes his leave.

When we're alone, I feel compelled to say, "Thank you," even though Alex didn't give me the option of refusing his gift.

He frowns. "You don't look happy. If you don't like that ring, I'll get you another one."

"The ring is gorgeous."

"Then what's the matter?" he asks, taking my hand.

"I'm not used to receiving gifts that must cost more than what I make in a year."

Resting a hand on my hip, he tips up my chin with a finger. "Get used to it."

I'm about to press him more for the motivation behind the sudden gift, but he stills me with another kiss on my lips.

"We'd better go." Tension flows into the set of his shoulders. "We can't be late. I want to get to the venue before everyone else."

Right. Because it's dangerous to go outside.

My stomach muscles knit into a ball when he leads me to the foyer where Lena waits with our coats and my clutch bag. Alex helps me into the tailored white evening coat before pulling on a stylish jacket and his own coat. Steering me outside, he helps me into the car idling in the driveway. As usual, Yuri drives.

We make our way to the old center of the city in a convoy of cars. Alex wears an earpiece and constantly communicates in Russian while checking his phone. After forty minutes, we arrive at a roadblock. Yuri lowers his window and says something to the man who approaches his window. Immediately, the boom gate lifts.

My stomach tightens further as I take in the men in combat gear armed with rifles who are lined up on either side of the road. It's as if we're entering a war zone. At the end of the block, we arrive at a stately building with columns in the front. It's snowing softly. The flakes are illuminated by the golden lights shining from the impressive façade of the former palace that has been turned into a hotel. Lena proudly told me that the venue had been the residence of Princess Lobanova-Rostovskaya in 1820.

We enter a heavily guarded underground parking garage. From there, an elevator with a thumbprint scanner takes us to the ballroom. Alex's bodyguards follow us to the hall, staying no more than a step behind. Alex hands in our coats at the coat room before wrapping an arm around my waist and keeping me close to him.

As we're the first to arrive, the hall is empty of other guests. Round tables are set with brocade tablecloths and gold-trimmed crockery. Some waiters are polishing crystal glasses and golden cutlery, while others are aligning the place settings. The centerpieces are flower arrangements of white lilies and peonies that perfume the hall with their sweet scents. The flowers must've been cultivated in hothouses or flown in from a summer region for the occasion.

When Alex has done a round of the room with me in tow, he leads me to our table and seats me.

"Champagne?" he asks as a waiter appears with a bottle.

"Thank you," I say, nodding at the waiter.

Not long after, the guests start arriving. Within minutes, the hall is brimming with women in gorgeous dresses and men in fancy suits. Alex is holding my hand under the table, but he's still busy on his phone, talking in rapid Russian. I don't mind. I'm entertaining myself by people watching.

The first guests to join our table are an elderly lady with a red sequined gown and a gentleman with a silver waistcoat and bowtie. Alex introduces them to me as the Dyatlovs.

Mrs. Dyatlova tells me to call her Elvira. Her British-accented English is impeccable, which she attributes to the years she studied in England. Mr. Dyatlov, on the other hand, has to rely on his wife's translations to follow our conversation and soon gives up, launching into a discussion with Alex in Russian instead.

The next invitees to arrive are a couple who look to be in their early forties. Mrs. Feba Zykova is a lively woman who explains that she owns a textile factory, while the subdued Mr. Zykov is in the import and export business. What kind of import and export, his wife doesn't say, and he doesn't seem to speak the best English either. Alex no doubt made sure the women at our table are fluent in English, a consideration I'm very grateful for.

Elvira gives me tips on sights to visit. I let her talk, not telling her I probably won't be able to visit any of the museums or ballets she recommends. Alex is still talking to the men, but he keeps a point of contact between us with his hand on my knee. The touch is both reassuring and possessive.

When Elvira stops talking to take a sip of water, Alex leans over and whispers in my ear, "Not too bored yet?"

I turn my face toward him. Like always, I'm hyper-aware of his presence. The smell of his spicy cologne and the electrifying touch of his fingers on my knee overpower my senses. It's impossible to stare into his eyes and not drown in those vivid blue pools. His lips quirk as his eyes crinkle in the corners. He knows the effect he has on me. With a single look, he renders me defenseless. The attraction between us is as strong as the first day we met. If I weren't so level-headed, I would say running into each other on that day was fate. But that would mean that Igor had been shot for the sole purpose of bringing Alex and me together. Ironically, it would mean that the very reason we're here in St. Petersburg and in this horrifying situation—the fact that someone is trying to kill Alex—is what's responsible for driving us into each other's arms. In some way, I'd have to be grateful to Alex's hunter. If not for him, we never would've met.

"Good evening," a polished female voice says.

I look over at the guests who have arrived at our table and freeze. Dania and her father, Mikhail, stand on the opposite side. My spine goes stiff as I recall my conversation with Dania at the cocktail party in New York, when she told me she was destined to marry Alex.

Dania and Mikhail do the rounds to say their hellos. Dressed in a white gown with a flowing skirt, Dania looks like a Disney princess. Her black hair forms a stunning contrast with her blue eyes and pale skin. Her makeup is light and youthful, giving her an innocent look. Virginal, almost. Classically beautiful. She looks like perfect marriage material, and from the way the men in the room are staring at her, she's undeniably desirable too. Is this what Lena was trying to tell me? That I haven't dressed the part? That I have no idea what I'm up against or how to fight the subtle war for a man's attention?

I steal a look at Alex while Mikhail shakes his hand. At least he's not gawking at Dania like the other gentlemen.

"I'm so glad we're at your table," Dania says when it's our

turn to exchange a greeting. "I was looking forward to seeing you when I heard you were in St. Petersburg."

To my dismay, she takes the empty seat next to me. Mikhail installs himself in the available spot on Alex's right.

"How are you, Dania, darling?" Feba asks with affection. She's speaking English, no doubt for my benefit. "It's been ages."

Dania waves a hand. "I've been traveling nonstop. You know how Papa's business takes us around the world."

"I hope you'll pay us a visit now that you're home," Feba says.

"We should organize a lunch," Dania says. "Women only." She winks. "I could do with a break from the company of businessmen."

"I didn't know you were so involved in your father's business," Elvira says with a tinge of disdain. "How's your mother?"

Dania meets Elvira's gaze head-on. "You know how Mama is. Unfortunately, always intoxicated." To me, she says, "In case you haven't heard the gossip yet, my mother is an alcoholic and not seen in public much."

That shuts Elvira up. The men are still engrossed in their conversation. Mikhail doesn't show any signs of overhearing what has been said.

"To answer your question about my involvement in the business, Elvira," Dania says sweetly, "as you know, I'm the only child. One day, I'll take over."

"More likely, your future husband will," Elvira says.

"How about meeting up at Chekhov's next week?" Dania asks, looking around the table. "They have a new chef and the reviews are outstanding." She turns in her seat to face me. "Kate, you have to come. I can introduce you to some friends who'll help you pass the time while Alex spends all those long hours at the office. Everyone knows what a workaholic he is. If you enjoy the opera and ballet, you must join me at my monthly culture club."

"That will be marvelous," Feba says. "I know you young people prefer the nightclubs, but if you'd care to spend a couple of evenings in an old lady's company, I'd love to introduce you to some of my artist friends. They make for the most entertaining company."

I'm about to make up an excuse of why I won't be able to accept the invitations when Alex says, "I'm afraid that won't be possible."

Dania gives him a wide-eyed look. "Really, Alex. This isn't the Middle Ages. I'm sure Kate is capable of making her own decisions." She fixes her gaze on me. "Aren't you, Kate?"

Alex tightens his fingers on my knee. "Katerina and I still have a lot to see."

"Yet you've done nothing but work since you've been back, as I've seen for myself when we met yesterday," Dania says with a reprimanding frown. "You're not planning on keeping your girlfriend all to yourself, are you?"

I tense even more. They saw each other yesterday, and Alex didn't mention it to me? Then again, why would he? He calls the shots. He only shares with me the facts he deems necessary.

"You know how it is," Alex says with a strained smile.

Dania bats her eyelashes. "Actually, I don't."

The smile on Alex's lips turns cold. "We're like newlyweds." His tone carries an unspoken warning. "Still on honeymoon."

Elvira gasps.

Feba picks up a menu and fans her face.

Apparently, sex before marriage is frowned upon by the older company at our table. Or at least discussing it is.

Dania's grin is smug. "You don't protect a lady's honor, do you, Alex Volkov?"

Mikhail clears his throat and reprimands, "Dania."

"Just watching out for my fellow sisters." Cupping my hand, Dania continues, "Don't let him boss you around even before he's put a ring on your finger. You're allowed to be your own person. We've moved with the times in Russia, you know."

I pull my hand away. "Thanks, but I'm too busy to accept any invitations at the moment."

"Busy doing what?" Dania asks. "Sitting home alone all day?"

"Nursing," I say in a tight voice.

"Nursing," Dania says slowly. "Yes, of course. You're a nurse in New York. Alex mentioned something like that. Who are you nursing?" She scoffs. "His bodyguards?"

Under the table, Alex squeezes my knee so hard it almost hurts, but his grip on the stem of his water glass remains light.

"Excuse me," I say, pushing to my feet. "I have to powder my nose."

Alex stands too. "I'll accompany you."

"To the ladies' room?" Feba exclaims, fanning her face faster.

"Please, Alex," Elvira says with a wink. "There are limits even for honeymooners."

Alex's polite humor is all fake. "No one has ever accused me of not being a gentleman."

"I'll accompany her," Dania says, getting up. "If it makes you feel better, Alex, my bodyguards can stand guard."

"Sit, Alex," Mikhail says, placing a hand on Alex's forearm. "Let the women be women and do whatever women do in the ladies' room."

"Gossip," Dania says conspiratorially.

I have no desire to let Dania accompany me to the bathroom. Going there is just an excuse to escape, but everyone is staring at Alex, Dania, and me now, waiting for Alex's call. He's already made me look like someone incapable of making her own decisions. He's announced to the whole table that we can't keep our hands off of each other when the older women have made it clear the subject is taboo in a public conversation. They already have a negative impression of me. If Alex insists on walking me to the bathroom, it will only make matters worse. After what was implied, they'll no doubt think we're going together to have a quickie.

A tense moment passes as indecision plays on Alex's face. I know how worried he is about our safety, but thanks to the measures he put in place, the hall is like Fort Knox.

"We won't be long," I say, taking back the only power I can as I push back my chair.

My heart keeps time with heavy beats. A second passes, then another, and then Alex slowly sits down, but not before catching the gaze of Igor, who stands not far away from our table.

Beyond relieved, I excuse myself and walk away. Dania hooks her arm around mine like we're friends, chatting amiably as I follow the bathroom sign to the end of the hallway.

I don't hear a word she says. My mind feels as if it's been stuffed full of cotton. All I can think about is how humiliated I feel, even though I logically know that wasn't Alex's intention. He was only trying to keep me safe, but in doing so, he told me and everyone else that I can't go anywhere without his consent.

"Hey." Dania nudges my shoulder when we enter the ladies' room. "Are you all right? You look pale."

I go to the vanity and face my reflection in the mirror. My cheeks are indeed pale despite the makeup and the natural olive tint of my skin. Taking a bronzer from my clutch, I brush a little over my cheekbones.

"Is Alex treating you well?" she asks, smoothing a hand over her perfectly styled hair. It's caught in a ballerina bun at the nape of her neck.

"I know what you were doing out there," I say, giving her a hard look. If she thinks I'm going to play her games when we're alone, she'd better think again.

She pats her hair. "What I was doing was looking out for you."

I chuckle humorlessly. "Is that right?"

"Look," she says with a sigh. "Alex told me what's going on when he reached out to me yesterday."

He went running to her with our problems? I don't believe that for one second. I study her face in the mirror as I take a tube of lipstick from my bag. "And what might that be?"

"He told me about the shooting in New York. He's worried."

"Damn right he's worried. Someone is trying to *kill* him."

She leans her backside against the vanity. "He can take care of himself. He's worried about *you*. You're a weakness."

I inhale sharply. "I didn't ask for this to happen."

"No." She gives a wry smile. "That much is clear. You're not here of your own free will. You're nothing but a prisoner. Sadly, now you're keeping Alex a prisoner."

I gape at her. "What?" Has Alex told her he's all but kidnapped me? Or is she just guessing? And what does she mean by that last bit?

She shrugs. "Alex feels responsible for you. He has to stick around now until he's certain you're safe. You're not doing him any favors by hanging around."

She is just guessing about my status, I'm almost sure. Either way, I have no reason to hide the truth. "Like you said," I say, capping the lipstick and dropping it in my bag, "I don't exactly have a choice."

"What if you did have a choice?"

I still. "What's that supposed to mean?"

"What if you could get away?"

I don't like the way this conversation is going. "I won't do that to Alex."

"Do what? Give him a chance to hunt his attacker without you being a ball and chain? You're not only hampering his efforts. You're also significantly reducing his chances of getting out of this alive."

Clenching my fingers around my bag, I turn to face her. "What are you trying to say, Dania?"

"If Alex were with me, like he's supposed to be, my father would've long since gone after my fiancé's attacker. By now, the threat to my future husband would be nonexistent."

My grip tightens. "Bullshit."

"You don't realize how powerful my father is." Her expression is rueful. "It's safe to say we're not going to be friends anytime in the future. The one thing we have in common is that we both care about Alex. It's the only fact we agree on, am I right?"

"Exactly." I narrow my eyes. "What point are you trying to make?"

"Hanging on to him is a selfish move, Kate. You're not from our world. I told you that once already, and if you didn't believe me then, look around you tonight. Look at the people at our table. Do you think you fit in? You can't even speak our language. If you cared about Alex at all, you'd set him free and let him live the life he's destined to live, a good and long life.

My father can make that happen. Once we announce our engagement, my dad won't leave a stone unturned to get the man who threatens his future son-in-law and therefore his only daughter's future."

"You're delusional," I say, making to walk away.

She locks her fingers around my wrist, holding me back. "Is this the kind of life you want? Forever under Alex's thumb? Doing as he says and only going where he lets you—*if* he lets you?"

I pull free. "You don't know anything about Alex and me."

"And you don't know how it works in our world, but I think you're beginning to realize that St. Petersburg isn't New York. You won't have a job here and go out to meet friends. Once Alex ties you to him for good, you'll be like a bratva wife. You won't have a say. Your opinion won't matter. You'll be lucky if you ever see your family again."

That strikes a nerve, a painful one, but I pull my lips into a mocking smile. "And it will be different for you?"

"It will be, because my father is Mikhail Turgenev, and I'm the sole heir to his business." Giving me a pitiful look, she asks, "Who is *your* father?"

The arrow hits me straight in the heart. Not knowing my heritage has never bothered me before, and I hate that this woman has the power to make it matter.

"One more thing you need to know about Alex," she continues, "is that he doesn't fall in love. Ever."

Of everything she's said, those words hit me the hardest. "You don't know that."

My mask must be slipping because her expression turns full of pity. "Why do you think he's never told you that he loves you?"

Her statement stabs like a knife into my stomach. It takes everything and more not to show her how much it hurts. Lifting my chin, I say in my most confident tone, "You don't know that either."

She crosses her arms and cocks a hip. "Oh, but I do darling." The pity in her regard intensifies. "He told me so himself yesterday."

If she'd impaled me on a sword, she couldn't have tortured me more. Not sparing her another glance, I walk out of the bathroom.

Igor and a few guards I don't know are waiting outside. Dania exits on my heels, smiling as if butter won't melt in her mouth.

The guards follow us quietly back to the hall. Alex and Mikhail stand when we arrive at our table. Two waiters jump to action, pulling out our chairs. The appetizers have been served. The others wait until Dania and I have been seated before picking up their eating utensils.

"Is everything all right?" Alex whispers in my ear, rubbing a thumb over my shoulder.

A shiver runs down my arm. "Yes." I force a smile. "Perfectly."

"I was starting to miss you," he says in a husky voice.

"Wine?" Mikhail asks.

"Vodka, please," Dania says.

Feba gives her an approving nod.

Mikhail flicks his fingers, at which a waiter approaches and pours vodka for Dania and wine for me. Mikhail goes on about the sweet wine that's paired with the starter, but I tune him out. All I can think about is Dania's cruel words.

There's a kernel of truth in Dania's argument. Two, actually.

One: will I forever be Alex's puppet? He likes being in control. Will he let me have my life back when all of this is over? And two: am I harming Alex by being in his life? Igor implied I was the reason Alex risked our lives by taking me sightseeing. True, Igor believed I'd selfishly asked Alex to take me out, but even though I actually suggested we stay home, Alex still took the risk for my benefit, and that makes me responsible. In an indirect way, my presence is having a negative impact on Alex's life. What if I *am* making him weak? What if his obsession with me is making him more of a target?

Throughout the five-course dinner, the questions keep churning in my head. I don't remember what I eat and drink, or what the women talk about. When it's time for the keynote speech about nuclear power, Alex considerately translates for me, whispering what is being said in my ear.

The content of the speech goes in one ear and out the other. What sticks is my growing conviction that this potential joint venture is important to Alex because he believes in affordable heat for everyone, including the less fortunate communities.

It feels like forever before we say our goodbyes, which takes a good hour as Alex has many people to greet. At last in the car, I relax marginally for the first time.

"What's wrong, kiska?" Alex asks, draping an arm around my shoulder.

I make another brave effort to smile. "Nothing."

He pulls me closer. "You barely said two words during dinner."

I escape his piercing gaze by looking through the window. "It was difficult to follow the conversation."

Gripping my chin, he turns my face back to him. "The

conversation was in English. That's why I made sure the women seated at our table were fluent in your mother tongue."

"Thanks for that," I say with genuine gratitude.

"It's only normal." He searches my face. "There's something else you're not telling me." Narrowing his eyes, he asks, "Did Dania say something to you in the bathroom?"

"Actually, yes." I study him right back. "She said she saw you yesterday."

"She did," he says slowly, a question in the admission.

Then she wasn't lying about that. "She said I'm your weakness."

In the soft, interior light of the car, his blue eyes darken. "You are." Tracing the line of my jaw with his thumb, he says in a low, deep voice, "The only one I've ever had."

I drag in a breath. "If I make you weak—"

His tone turns harsh. "Don't you even dare say it."

"I was just—"

He splays his fingers over my cheeks, pouting my lips, and growls, "I'm not letting you go. Not now. Not ever. Do you understand?"

The truth twists inside me, cutting a little deeper.

"This isn't love," I whisper. "This is obsession."

His blue eyes glimmer as he narrows them another fraction. My heartbeat picks up. The man looking at me is a predator with incredible intelligence and cunning human insight, one of the most business-savvy and intelligent people in the world. He's got power in spades, both the natural kind some men are born with and the kind that comes with money. He's the most powerful person I know, in fact, and he's observing me like a hunter who has no intention of letting his prey get away.

His voice is dangerously soft as he drags his hand down to my neck. "It doesn't matter what you call it. You're mine, and your life is here now." Locking his fingers around my neck, he holds me in a possessive grip. "It will be a happy life if you don't fight it so hard."

I swallow, my throat moving against the pressure of his palm.

Lowering his head, he brushes a question over my lips. "Is that clear, Katyusha?"

"Yes," I say, not daring to breathe.

I know where this is going when he pushes me down, yet I don't stop him. There's only a partition between us and Yuri, but it's not the only time he's taken me in a car. When my back hits the seat, I don't utter a protest. The taste of defeat is bitter in my mouth, but I try to take my loss without letting him see my tears. My stomach clenches with anticipation as I wait for the moment he slays me.

He doesn't make me wait long. Planting the gentlest of kisses on my lips, he dips a hand under my skirt and between my legs. My underwear is no match for his strength. The lacy fabric gives with a tearing sound that mixes with my gasp just before he forcefully sinks two fingers inside me. Barely giving me time to drag in air, he finger-fucks me with harsh strokes.

My body bows to his rhythm, responding with pleasure. He nips my bottom lip and feeds me tender Russian words as he spanks my clit with the heel of his palm while curling his fingers inside. It's a battlefield, and the war is over before it's even begun.

I come in seconds, surrendering like a beaten enemy. It doesn't matter that my release locks every muscle in my body with excruciating ecstasy, or that he presses sweet praise with kisses to my neck for my record-breaking performance. It's a loss all the same.

Because that's how it works in war.

There are only two outcomes, only two sides.

If you're not the winner, you're the loser.

21

ALEX

*I*t's quiet at work, the building deserted except for me, Igor, and a few bodyguards. The sky outside is still dark. A vista of city lights spreads out below my office window, twinkling on a blanket of snow. The streets aren't buzzing with the morning rush hour yet. I'm the first one in, which gives me time to catch up before everyone demands my attention.

Settling behind my desk, I study the report in front of me. The gala was a big success. Many influential business players pledged their support for nuclear power. The pressure is on for the government to give the green light to the new technology. As usual, there's a shitload of red tape, but it's only a matter of time.

I close the report and pull up my emails. After scanning through them, I file the less urgent ones in a folder for later and open the most important messages. The first is from Konstantin Molotov, checking on how the gala went and informing me about a few kinks his engineers have worked out in the latest version of the portable reactors. Konstantin is the brains behind the technology, and though we have yet to formally sign the papers for the joint venture, my engineers and I have been working with him for several months as part of our due diligence process.

The Molotovs are a powerful, well-connected family from Moscow. Their wealth and position in society go back generations, all the way to Czarist Russia. Konstantin Molotov is the oldest of four siblings and is widely considered to be a tech genius, while his younger brother, Nikolai, runs the business side of things—or did until recently. The youngest Molotov brother, Valery, seems to be managing most of their holdings now, though Nikolai is overseeing this particular project despite the fact that he recently married an American woman and is currently residing in a small mountain town in Idaho, in the States.

I reply to Konstantin, telling him that the event went well and that we're one step closer to getting government approval for his technology. Of course, all of this is predicated on the joint venture going through. If the Molotovs back out at the last moment or try to screw me over in any way, it'll take just a few words whispered in the right ears to choke the project with red tape. Naturally, I don't say that to Konstantin. I don't need to. He understands perfectly how things work in our world.

I'm about to launch into a review of the new safety regulations we're implementing at one of my oil wells when the screen of my phone lights up with a call. I usually send my calls to my voicemail until later in the morning, using the only time I have without interruptions from my employees constructively, but one glance at the caller ID and I take the call.

"Alex," Adrian says. "My apologies for the hour, but I know you're an early riser, and I figured you'd want to hear this without delay."

I tighten my grip on the phone. "Tell me you found Mukha."

"I did. It wasn't easy, but my hacker finally discovered a loophole in Mukha's cyber tracks. We planted a bug in the electronic currency I sent him as payment for the information he gave me. The bug piggybacked on the currency all the way to the Cayman Islands and back to Russia. It turns out he pays for his mother's care at a nursing home in Moscow. I paid her a visit."

"Spare me the details," I say with impatience. "Where is the son of a bitch?"

"He's renting a house on the outskirts of Moscow. I'm on my way there now."

I sit up straighter, anticipation tightening my gut. "Pay him any price he wants for that file, and if he's still not willing to sell, get the information any way you have to." I put emphasis on the next words. "At any cost."

"Understood. I'll get back to you tonight."

The line goes dead.

Finally. It's about time. If all goes well, by nightfall, I'll know the reason Stefanov wants me dead.

22

RESIDENCE OF VLADIMIR STEFANOV, ST. PETERSBURG

*V*ladimir bounces his leg under his desk. He feels especially on edge tonight. Alex Volkov knows he's behind the assassination attempt. That's the message Volkov was sending by letting Vadim's head soak in a toilet bowl full of shit. That's why Volkov is having his house surveilled. The only reason Volkov hasn't struck yet is because he doesn't know why Vladimir tried to put a bullet in his brain. The only people in the world who do know that are Oleg and Vladimir himself.

Oleg is the weak link. Why else did he run like a dog with his tail between his legs to hide with his family in California? The only thought soothing Vladimir is that this mess will soon be over. Before the clock strikes twelve, one more nagging worry will be something of the past. At last, he'll be able to seal that closet full of skeletons and let it sink to the bottom of the Neva River with the bodies he plans on dumping there.

As it turns out, Oleg Pavlov arrived a short hour ago at the airport and should be ringing his doorbell just about—

Ding dong.

Now.

Inwardly, Vladimir smiles.

For security reasons, his study is soundproof, but he's left the door open so that he can follow the sound of the footsteps as they advance.

Oleg's voice bounces off the arched ceiling of Vladimir's stately home. "How's the family?"

"Good, thank you," Vladimir's wife, Galina, says. "How about Annika and the children?"

"All good," Oleg replies in a strained tone.

Galina enters the study, followed by Oleg. "I'll leave you to your business."

"Galina," Vladimir says. "Go buy us some of that Napoleon cake that Oleg likes so much. The one from the bakery in Nevsky Prospekt."

Her smile is uncertain. "That's so far away. It'll take me an hour or more in the traffic. I'll just go to Lastochka."

"No." Vladimir's double chin quivers as he shakes his head. "That one is no good. Go to the one I told you. Tell the owner I sent you."

"All right," she says with a nod, giving Oleg a tight smile as she leaves the room.

Oleg's shoulders sag in obvious relief. Vladimir knows how Oleg's mind works. Oleg thinks that if Vladimir is sending his wife to buy him some cake, he has nothing to be worried about. He's less nervous about why Vladimir ordered him to fly all the way here from California. He feels exactly the way Vladimir wants him to—safe.

"Sit," Vladimir says jovially, motioning at the chair facing his desk.

Oleg pulls on the knot of his tie as he takes a seat. "What's so urgent that it couldn't wait until after my vacation?"

Vacation, his *zhopa*. After selling Vladimir out to Bes, Oleg was hiding in a hole like the rat he is.

Vladimir studies him with a sly gaze. "We have a problem."

Oleg sits up like a stick man. "What problem?"

"Volkov is on to us."

Oleg pulls on his tie again. "He is? How do you know that?"

Vladimir flicks the picture of Vadim's body across the table. For the purpose of setting today's plan in motion, Vladimir kept the news of Vadim's murder to himself. Better to catch Oleg off guard.

Oleg blanches as he studies the photo. It's not a pretty sight. "How do you know it was Volkov?" he asks, turning the photo upside down.

Vladimir points at the photo. "Because that's the man I sent to grab Katherine Morrell."

"I knew it." Oleg shifts to the edge of his seat, his voice growing in volume. "It was a mistake to interfere."

Vladimir adopts the appropriate hard look. "Are you criticizing me?"

"No, but..."

"But what?" Vladimir asks harshly.

Oleg clears his throat. "When did this happen?"

"Not that long ago," Vladimir says. "I asked you to come the minute I found out. But that's not all. Volkov is having your house watched as we speak. He probably had a man on your tail in California too."

"What?" Oleg's voice turns shrill. "How did he find out?"

"Who knows?" Vladimir shrugs. "What matters is why he came back to St. Petersburg."

Oleg's Adam's apple bobs as he swallows. "Why's that?"

"To start a war. We have to prepare. We need to get our men ready."

"*Mudak.*" Oleg drags a hand over his balding, liver-spotted head. "When do you think he'll attack?"

Vladimir doesn't miss the slight shaking of Oleg's hand. "Today. My informants tell me his men are arming up. You have to call your most trusted men here for a meeting. There's no time to waste."

"What about Bes? I need to tell him about Volkov's plans."

"Bes is wasting time going after the woman. He didn't get the job right the first time. And not the second time either, for that matter. It's up to us now."

Vladimir can almost see the gears turning in Oleg's head. He thinks Vladimir doesn't know that he's a traitor. He thinks Bes wants to fuck them both over, but he can't tell Vladimir that without admitting his betrayal. He thinks like Vladimir expects him to, and when he opens his mouth, he utters the words Vladimir predicted.

"We have to deal with Bes. He insults us. It's not good for our reputation."

Inwardly, Vladimir grins. "In good time. Our priority is Volkov. If we don't act fast, we'll both be dead tonight."

Sweat beads on Oleg's forehead. He takes a handkerchief from his pocket and dabs at his brow. "How much do you think Volkov knows?"

Vladimir puts on a grave expression. "It's hard to say."

"How did he find out?" Oleg asks again, blinking a couple of times. "Only you and I know the truth. That means the traitor is Bes." He mans up, saying with bravado, "That's double the reason to kill that no-good assassin now." As he says this, Oleg almost looks relieved. In his mind, killing the assassin will take care of all his problems. Little does he know.

"We need to destroy all the evidence that can point a finger at us," Vladimir says. "I got rid of everything on my side the same day Volkov escaped from foster care." Of course, he did nothing of the kind. Just like Oleg, he kept the evidence locked in his safe as insurance for the day he needed something to blackmail Oleg with. The only one who knows Vladimir never burned the evidence is himself. "Do you have anything that'll incriminate us?"

"No," Oleg says, averting his eyes briefly before meeting Vladimir's gaze again.

Vladimir smiles. Oleg has just given him a valid reason to off him. No one in the bratva will blame him for executing a traitor.

"Call your men." Vladimir checks his watch for dramatic effect. "We need to ambush Volkov before he makes it out of his house. If he catches us here, we're fucked."

Oleg clutches the armrests of his chair. "Between your men and mine, he'll be outnumbered."

"He's got Turgenev on his side, remember?"

"*Mudak*," Oleg says, now sweating so profusely that dark patches stain his shirt around his armpits.

Pushing to his feet, Oleg takes his phone from his pocket and dials his second-in-command with a swift instruction to bring the highest-ranking men in his organization to Vladimir's stronghold of a house. Fast.

"Let's drink to our victory," Vladimir says when Oleg ends the call, producing a bottle of vodka.

Oleg looks aghast. "You know it's bad luck to drink before the deal is done."

"Come on," Vladimir says with a mocking smile. "We have to behave like victors, not losers. Besides, we'll catch Volkov by surprise. He won't expect us to storm his house. He'll expect us to hide in our fortresses where we're best protected."

Oleg wets his lips. Hesitantly, he takes the glass Vladimir offers.

They drink a toast, and then another. Oleg's men arrive just as they finish the third. The five men who rank highest in his organization are his cousins, an uncle, and a nephew.

Vladimir gets to his feet with effort, his joints groaning under his weight. His words are loaded. He chooses the right expression to go with them, enjoying the little drama he's putting on. "Let's go talk where it's safe."

The men nod in unison. Vladimir sweeps his study daily for bugs, but the opposition and the clean players in the police force always find new ways. Their latest favorites are drones.

Vladimir leads the way. His men wait outside the door to his study. They let Oleg and his men pass, discreetly covering Vladimir's back before following the entourage to the basement.

Like the study, the basement is soundproof, but for a different reason.

Vladimir walks down the well-lit stairs to where a guard stands at the bottom. Taking his gun from his waistband, he hands it to the guard, who places it on a table where a bottle of vodka and shot glasses are set out to look like a preview to a celebration.

"Gentlemen," Vladimir says, motioning at the table for them to disarm as well.

One by one, they lay their weapons on the table.

When the guard pats them down for concealed guns and

knives, Vladimir says, "My apologies for the necessary precautions, but you know how heated we men can get when the testosterone levels run high."

Everyone laughs at that, except Oleg's uncle. He glances at Oleg. "I don't like this."

Lowering his head to Oleg's ear, Vladimir says in a conspiratorial tone, "I don't need to remind you that Volkov could already be on his way here as we speak. We have one shot at taking him out. If we fuck it up..." He leaves the sentence hanging, letting Oleg imagine the worst.

Oleg commands his uncle with a flick of his head. Like the rest of the men, his uncle disarms and hands over the gun strapped to his ankle.

"Through here." Vladimir motions at the door down the hallway that his guard opens. "I have a surprise waiting for you."

Oleg tenses at *surprise*. "What's inside there?"

Vladimir gives him a pat on the back. "Go see for yourself."

Oleg's uncle is the lamb who sacrifices himself for the slaughter and goes in first. Sticking his head back around the frame, he says with a frown, "It's a woman."

"A woman?" Oleg asks, sounding confused.

Equally baffled, the uncle replies, "Handcuffed."

"Go on," Vladimir says, hardly able to contain the spark of excitement igniting inside him.

Oleg catches that spark. His eyes gleam with wicked intent as he forgets to be frightened and goes inside to see which whore Vladimir is gifting him and his men. He's done it before. It's only natural that Oleg believes the lie.

When Oleg and his entire crew are inside, Vladimir's men pick up their guns and follow. The guard locks the door.

Oleg blinks at the fearful woman in the cheap, revealing clothes who's handcuffed to the metal frame of the bed. Her thin arms and legs are dirty, and her bleached hair is oily. Usually, they go for high-class hookers, and they like to play dress-up. Oleg's favorite is a dominatrix uniform and a whip.

"Why is she dressed like that?" Oleg asks, wrinkling his nose. "She looks like a whore you snatched from a street corner." He turns on his heel. "What's going on, Vlad?"

Vladimir's men pull their guns.

Oleg raises his hands, palms out. "Vladimir." His voice trembles. "What are you doing?"

"On your knees," Vladimir grits out. "All of you."

When they don't react, Vladimir takes a gun from one of his men and slams the weapon against the side of Oleg's head.

Oleg drops to his knees.

"Down," Vladimir says, pointing the barrel between Oleg's eyes.

One by one, Oleg's men kneel.

Good. They should be crawling in the dirt at his feet.

"Fucking traitor," Vladimir says. "Did you think I wouldn't find out?"

"Please." Oleg cowers with his hands in front of his face. "Bes blackmailed me. He said he'd kill my family if I didn't give him the information." When Vladimir only grins, Oleg cries out, "He tricked me."

Vladimir sneers. "I know that, you motherfucking stupid idiot."

"He told you," Oleg says, tripping over the words. "It's Bes who told you. He's playing us, Vladimir. He's playing both of us."

"Do you really think I'm dumb?" Vladimir caresses the

trigger with his finger. "It was a test. *My* test. One you failed miserably."

"Vladimir," Oleg begs.

And that, very fittingly, is the last word he says.

Vladimir pulls the trigger.

The whore screams as Oleg falls backward like the dead weight he is.

All hell breaks loose. Oleg's men try to disarm Vladimir's guards, but it's nothing but a futile show of bravery. They die like they should, with bullets in the backs of their heads.

Executed.

Wiping blood splatters from his hand, Vladimir says to his man in charge, "Clean up this mess and shut that woman up."

"Gladly," the man says, aiming his gun between her eyes and pulling the trigger.

The high-pitched screaming stops.

Finally. Sweet silence.

Vladimir climbs over the bodies, making his way to the door. "Next," he says to himself, looking back at the massacre from the doorframe, "is Volkov."

23

KATE

*W*hereas the gala dinner pleased Alex, it had the opposite effect on me. Dania's words repeat in my mind as I go downstairs for breakfast. Alex may never let me have a life again, and he may never love me. The more I think about it, the more I'm convinced that love isn't part of the equation. Would he have ripped me from everything and everyone I care about if he truly loved me? I doubt that. Love is selfless. Obsession, on the other hand, is selfish.

Whatever the case, I'm powerless to change my circumstances. My hands are tied.

"Why the long face?" Tima asks when I walk into the kitchen. "Didn't you enjoy the fancy party last night?"

I give him an honest smile. "Not exactly."

He's the only person in St. Petersburg around whom I can relax. For everyone else, I have to wear a mask. I don't trust them with my feelings. Sadly, that includes Alex.

"Were the women bitches?" he asks, putting a bowl of oatmeal in front of me as I take a seat at the table.

"Only one woman in particular."

Crossing his arms, he regards me with a sympathetic smile. "Let me guess. Dania Turgeneva."

I give him a surprised look. "How did you know?"

"I've observed her when she's come here with her father. She's been giving Mr. Volkov strong signals."

I pull the honey closer. "What kind of signals?"

"The signals a woman gives a man to let him know she's available and willing."

"Ah." I consider that as I dribble honey over the porridge. "She told me that she and Alex were promised to each other, like in an arranged marriage."

"Ha." He snorts. "I'm sure she and her father would like that."

I dip the spoon into the porridge, scooping up a helping of nuts and berries with the oatmeal. "Then it's not true?"

"If it were, you wouldn't be here." He winks. "Don't listen to anything Miss Turgeneva says. Jealousy makes you nasty. Isn't that how the expression goes? Besides, Mr. Volkov has never called her kiska. He's never used that term of endearment for anyone else."

I looked up the word. It means kitten. At first, I thought it was derogatory, like reducing a person to a pet, but then I read that the term is used affectionately for someone you care about, especially by a man for his female partner.

"Thanks," I say with a grateful smile, and I don't only mean for the reassurance and the breakfast. Because of him, the kitchen has become my refuge in the house.

"Eat up," he says with a mock-stern expression, just like my mom used to do when I was little.

I still can't believe Alex is taking me to see her for Christmas. It feels unreal, and I'm worried that he'll change his mind if something happens on the security front.

Tima goes back to preparing the lunch, letting me finish my breakfast in silence. When I'm done, I rinse my bowl and carry a mug of coffee to the library, where a fire is burning as usual. For a moment, I'm undecided about how to occupy myself. There aren't any men with ailments knocking on the door this morning. I've almost caught up with all the seasons of *Downton Abbey*. My job always kept me busy. I relished the time I had off, using it to either see my mom and my friends or to recharge by vegetating on the couch. Since we've been here, I've been mostly vegetating, and it's getting monotonous. The only positive about having so much free time is that my exercise regime is back on track, but right now, I don't feel like working out or swimming.

I settle on the sofa with a book, but by the time I've finished my coffee, my mind is drifting again. I can't stop thinking about what Dania said, that I'm hampering Alex's efforts to find the man who's trying to kill him. What if she's right? What if he's using most of his resources to protect me instead of tracking his enemy? Is he doing either of us a favor by keeping me here?

The answer is a tough one to face because I care. And because I care, the truth hurts.

I MUST'VE DOZED OFF BECAUSE I WAKE UP ON THE SOFA TO FIND myself covered with a blanket. The book I've been reading has been placed on the side table. Someone considerately left a bookmark to keep my place.

Blinking, I sit up. I'm not wearing my watch, but I can guess the hour by the fact that the curtains are closed. It must be dark outside already. Lena always closes the curtains when the sun sets. I've slept from this morning straight through the afternoon. We came home late last night, and I didn't sleep much when we went to bed. I tossed and turned, mulling over the scene with Dania in the bathroom and the way Alex had proven his possession of me in the back of the car.

I throw the blanket aside and stand. My stomach grumbles, reminding me I skipped lunch. I'm about to make my way to the door when it opens and Alex enters.

"You're awake," he says. "I was just coming to check on you."

I look at him with surprise. What is he doing home so early? He's still dressed for the office in navy blue suit pants and a white fitted shirt. He never arrives before dinner.

"What time is it?" I ask.

He checks his watch. "Just after five."

"Why are you home so early?" Concern tightens my stomach as I recall the incident with my mom. "What happened?"

"Nothing," he says with a smile, closing the door before crossing the floor. "You don't have to worry." Staring down at me, he cups my face. "It seems I've been neglecting you if you think something must be wrong for me to be home early."

I study him with uncertainty. "It's just not like you."

His smile turns sweet. "It won't always be like this. I know I've been at the office a lot lately, but the preparations for the gala and the due diligence for the joint venture have been consuming a lot of my time."

"And finding the man who wants you dead," I say, my body automatically tensing at the thought.

Regarding me with a soft light in his eyes, he caresses my

cheek with his thumb. "That's why I'm early. We made a break-through today."

My breathing quickens. "You did?"

"You remember the informant you met at the cocktail party in New York?"

"Adrian? The man you said I shouldn't trust?"

"Yeah, that one. He got me some information that will shed light on what's going on."

I swallow. "Should *you* trust him?"

"No. He's a man with no loyalty who's on no one's side. His only alliance is with money, but the information he delivers is always good. That's why he's built himself a solid reputation as an informant."

"I see," I say, even though I don't. I wouldn't trust someone like that, but I suppose Alex is experienced in unorthodox matters and has better judgment than I do. "When will you know?"

"Tonight, hopefully," he says with a gleam in his eyes.

The knowledge seems to excite him, but it only stresses me more.

"Hey, relax," he says, dropping his hand to my shoulder and massaging the tense muscle. "I'll take care of everything." Lowering his head, he adds in a soft voice, "I'll take care of you."

He sweeps his mouth over mine, barely brushing our lips together. He's testing the waters, gauging my reaction. We didn't make love last night, and it wasn't because he thought I was tired and he was being considerate. It was because of the way he took me in the car—with dominance and possession. It was meant to prove that he owns me. It wasn't an exchange of mutual desire or an expression of affection. It was a punishment. A lesson. He wanted the message to sink in. He wanted me to remember that leaving isn't an option. Not today, not ever.

I bend backward, putting distance between us before he can deepen the kiss. I still feel bruised inside about last night, not only because of how he treated me in the car but also because of what transpired at the party. I'm feeling all kinds of confused. I'm a mess, and burying my head in a fog of lust won't help me find clarity.

Alex locks his fingers around the back of my head, keeping me in place as he homes in on his target and claims my lips, not taking no for an answer. When I push on his shoulders, he grips my wrist and walks me back to the sofa.

Turning my face sideways, I whisper in protest, "Alex."

"Tell me you want me," he says, releasing my wrist to splay a large hand over my lower back. He presses our bodies together, letting me feel the hardness between his legs. "Because I sure as hell want you."

The words shouldn't ignite a spark in my belly. They shouldn't heat my body and make me wet, but I can't help my reaction to him. In a carnal way, the physical affection is a balm for my bruised feelings. I do need some kind of care. Despite my mind telling me this isn't wise, my heart wants him to hold me. Especially now. Especially after last night.

"Katyusha," he murmurs, nuzzling my temple. "I'm not going to force this if you don't want it, but you're torturing me."

I let last night happen because some battles aren't worth fighting. This time, it's not about choosing my battles wisely but about needing a substitute for love. When he touches me, he not only makes me forget. He makes me believe that what's between us goes deeper than purely physical need. That's why I don't object when he pulls down the zipper of my skirt and pushes it over my hips. When he reaches for the hem of my sweater, I lift my arms obediently. Item by item, he strips me until I stand naked in front of him.

Even though the room isn't cold, I shiver a little. He must've stoked the fire when he covered me with a blanket. The flames are burning high. The warmth leaves a pleasant glow on my skin. He trails a gaze over me, taking me in from top to bottom. The heat in his eyes warms me more than the fire, the desire he shows openly making electric sparks run through me. With a single step, he closes the distance between us, grabbing me so suddenly that a gasp escapes my lips.

Framing my face, he kisses me savagely. Abstaining last night has made him even hungrier than usual. He peels out of his jacket without breaking the kiss, devouring my mouth as he unbuttons his shirt and yanks the hem from his pants. His buckle makes a clinking sound, and then his belt is undone. He's already toeing off his shoes while he's unzipping.

A moment later, he's naked too, towering over me with his perfect body and masculine strength. There aren't any barriers left between us, at least not of the physical kind. On an emotional level, there are plenty, but he doesn't give me time to ponder them. He goes straight for the kill, dipping one hand between my legs while cupping a breast with the other as he resumes kissing me.

I expect him to be impatient, but the man consuming me with practiced skill is someone who's always in control. Parting my folds with a finger, he tests my arousal and groans when he finds me wet. My nipple hardens against his palm as he gently kneads the curve and starts moving his finger with leisurely strokes.

Lifting his hand from my breast, he closes his fingers

around my neck and uses the leverage to pull me flush against him. The stance presses my breasts flat against his chest. Letting my lips go with a nip, he searches my eyes to study the havoc he's wreaking when he sinks two fingers deep inside.

My inner muscles clench around the intrusion. A spark of nervous excitement ignites in my belly when he tightens his fingers marginally around my neck.

"*Skazhi mne trakhnut' tebya*," he says against my lips, a phrase he's taught me in bed. *Tell me to fuck you.*

"*Ya khochu chtoby ty trakhnul menya*," I say in my broken Russian. *I want you to fuck me.*

A predatory look mixes with male satisfaction in his eyes. When he pulls his hand from between my legs and applies gentle pressure on my shoulder, I go down on my knees willingly.

His cock is jutting out proudly, heavy and hard. Gripping the base, he says in a lust-roughened voice, "Lubricate it well, kiska."

I understand the warning. I know what he wants.

He stands stoically when I wet my lips and stretch them wide to accommodate his thick girth. Relaxing my jaw, I take him into my mouth. He watches with unwavering attention as I trace the crest of his cock with my tongue before sucking him deeper. Supporting the back of my head with one large hand, he holds the root of his cock in the other and pushes toward the back of my throat.

I breathe through my nose as he slides in and out. He's not going deep enough to make me gag. He pivots his hips with an easy pace, taking my mouth with slow, shallow thrusts. When I'm moving to his rhythm, he lets go of his cock to caress my cheek. The touch is soft and appraising, encouraging me to swallow.

He never forces me to take more than I can handle. He's not suffocating me or stretching my throat painfully, but my eyes nevertheless water from the effort. Sucking him off is a turn-on, making me even wetter. He's showing the utmost constraint, not losing an ounce of control, yet the earthy taste of his precum on my tongue tells me he's not unaffected by my performance.

Gripping his thigh for balance, I caress the heavy sac between his legs. A slick drop of salty liquid squirts onto my tongue. His expression remains stoic, but the line of his jaw hardens as he grits his teeth.

I double my speed, taking him faster. I want him to give me his power. I want him to lose this round and come in my mouth, but he has other ideas. He twists my long hair around his fist and carefully pulls back my head until his cock slips from my lips with a pop.

He looks down at the result of my work. His cock is slick and wet. Taking a cushion from the sofa, he dumps it on the rug in front of the fireplace.

When he catches my gaze again, his eyes are ablaze and his voice thick with lust. "Get on your hands and knees for me."

He grips my elbows and pulls me to my feet to facilitate my compliance. Not that I need any coaxing to do as he says. Facing the roaring fire, I kneel on the cushion and brace my palms on the rug.

"Keep your knees pressed together," he says behind me.

I follow that order too.

He smooths a hand over my spine, starting at my lower back

and ending between my shoulder blades. "Now place your elbows on the floor."

I bend my arms and support my weight on my forearms. The position puts my ass in the air, presenting both my openings for his use. I know what's coming. We've done this enough times before. All I have to do is place my cheek on my arm, close my eyes, and let him manipulate my body. Alex likes to be in control, but he's not a control freak in bed. When I need to take charge, he encourages me to do so. He loves it when I'm on top. But tonight, I need this. I need to escape, and I can only do it when he pushes my boundaries until the world around us no longer exists.

Something hot and velvety brushes over my clit, making me jerk. I open my eyes and lift my head to look back at him from over my shoulder. He's rubbing the head of his cock over my clit, massaging in circles with just the right amount of pressure. I bite my lip, fighting the pleasure that already curls in my belly like the lick of a flame. I don't want to come too soon, but it's no use. I agreed to be played like an instrument when I kneeled in a submissive position, and Alex will wrench the reactions he wants from my body at his will and pace.

Tonight, he wants me to come fast. Parting my folds with his thumbs, he slides his cock slowly inside. My toes curl from the stretch. The pleasure is different than earlier, but it's no less intense. He moves with lazy strokes, giving me time to adjust, and when my inner muscles soften around the intrusion, he thrusts deep and fast.

Perspiration beads on his forehead. His powerful chest is magnificently defined in the light of the fire. Deep shadows run over his face and the grooves of his biceps as he grabs my hip in one hand and slips the other between my legs. I want to watch the spectacular show, but when he rolls my clit between his fingers, my body arches with pleasure. My neck can't support the weight of my head any longer. I drop my face back onto my arm, experiencing the tightening of my muscles with every nerve ending in my body.

I don't have to tell him when I come. I'm clenching hard around him, every part of me locked in ecstasy. Before the climax has released me from its grip, he's pulling out, leaving me empty, but not for long. A familiar pressure builds around my back entrance. The orgasm ebbs, leaving my body boneless and supple in the aftermath. That's the moment he chooses to enter me, using my arousal as lubrication. I take him without difficulty, my ass stretching to accommodate him the way it's been trained.

This pleasure is different too. It's darker. It doesn't come without pain, but the discomfort only fires up my nerve endings anew, turning every inch of me hyper-sensitive to his movements and touch. I dig my nails into the scratchy wool of the rug as he sinks so deep that his groin is cushioned between my cheeks. My breathing is hard and fast, the way I suck air into my lungs uncontrollable. I inhale the smell of wool from the rug and smoke from the fire, every sensory detail imprinting in my mind. My need spikes, my sated body demanding release again.

When he finally starts pumping, my lips part on another soundless gasp. I swallow my moans as he slams into me, rocking my body to a much harsher rhythm. I'm experienced enough in our anal play to take it. I crave it, even. The pain intensifies until it becomes muddled with the pleasure, and I can't tell if I'm flying or falling. The only awareness left in my consciousness is the extreme need to come.

Orgasming like this is much more powerful. It feels deeper. It lasts longer. When I finally break, a wave of intense pleasure tears through me. Like a violent ocean, it rips me apart, slams me to pieces on the rocks and washes the devastation ashore. My mind is half present and half floating, only partially conscious of Alex still thrusting between my ass cheeks. He says something in Russian, but my mind is too mushy to translate the words. He shoves one last time before he freezes, his taut body locked deep inside mine. Warm liquid fills my insides, bathing my stretched skin and leaving a slight sting.

All my energy depleted, I can only kneel there and let the strange hybrid of pain and pleasure rack me. He leans over me, covering my back with his chest, and kisses my neck. He keeps me warm with his body and asks something—how I'm doing, I think. Unable to scrounge up enough strength to answer him, I let him stroke my side while I pretend I'm safe in the cocoon of his arms. He tells me how well I did, adding more words of praise, but I can only internalize the sensations and another kind of sting that reverberates in my heart.

"Stay," he says, pressing a kiss to my temple.

I flinch when he pulls out. I must be really tired because despite the fact that I slept all day, my mind is already going hazy again. I barely focus on Alex as he crosses the floor, grabs a box of tissues from the coffee table, and kneels behind me. After cleaning me up, he takes the blanket from the sofa, drapes it around me, and lifts me into his arms.

"Where are we going?" I ask as he carries me out of the room.

Undeterred by our lack of clothes, he makes his way to the closest bathroom, which is the one by the pool. Fortunately, we don't run into anyone on our way.

His aftercare is gentle. He washes my hair and body in the shower before patting me dry with a soft towel. When we're both wrapped in fluffy robes, he carries me to his bedroom and puts me to bed with an instruction to rest while he fetches dinner.

I can't stand it. I can't stand the uncertainty. Against my better judgment, I open my mouth, but I *need* to know. I have to know if Dania was lying.

"Alex?"

He stops in the frame and turns to look at me.

I brace myself for humiliation. "Do you—"

The phone rings shrilly on the nightstand.

Frowning, he walks over and lifts the receiver. "Yes?" His voice carries a hint of irritability.

His frown deepens as he listens. After a moment, he says with a clenched jaw, "I see."

He lifts his gaze fleetingly to mine and catches me watching. Turning his back to me, he continues in a tight voice, "That won't be necessary. I'm no longer at the office. I'll call you back in five minutes." The phone makes a click as he returns the cordless receiver to the base.

I clutch the blanket to my chest. "Is everything all right?"

When he faces me again, his expression is schooled, but the worry lines are still visible around his eyes. "There's been a complication. I'm afraid I won't have the information tonight on the man who's hunting me."

A stone drops in my stomach. "I'm sorry."

He gives me a strained smile. "It's not your fault. I'll get dinner, but I won't be joining you. I have to deal with this."

I swing my legs over the side of the bed. "I'll get the dinner."

"No," he says in a commanding tone. Softer, he adds, "Stay in bed, my love. You need to rest."

"Is there anything I can do?" I ask, the lethargic effect of my orgasms vanishing as fear brings a fresh wave of tension.

"No, but thanks." He checks his watch. "You wanted to ask me something before the phone rang."

I pull up my knees and hug my legs. "It's nothing important."

"We'll talk about it later."

I nod, though I have no such intention. My courage has already failed me, and in light of that telephone call, we have much more serious matters to worry about than whether Alex loves me.

24

ALEX

*T*ima is still in the kitchen when I go downstairs. I instruct him to prepare a tray for Katerina and a sandwich for me. While he's getting our dinner ready, I grab a T-shirt and a pair of sweatpants from the closet in the gym and get dressed. The food is ready when I return to the kitchen.

After delivering the tray to Katerina, who's already half asleep in my bed, I leave her with a kiss and go to my study. A gourmet sandwich and a glass of water is set on the desk. I dial Adrian and finish the sandwich in three large bites while I wait for him to answer.

He picks up after several rings.

"What the fuck happened?" I ask, chugging back the water.

"Someone other than us wanted to find Mukha. He was already dead when I got there."

"Fuck." I scrunch the napkin in my fist. "How?"

"A bullet in the back of his head."

That has a ring of Vladimir Stefanov to it. It's his favorite style of execution. He likes to shoot between the eyes, but when his men follow orders, they do it the dishonorable way, by not looking the person they're killing in the face.

"I managed to sweep the place before the police got there," Adrian continues. "There was no sign of a computer or laptop. All his equipment had been cleared out. If Mukha had made a hard copy of the file, whoever got to him took it."

I grit my teeth. "In other words, it's a dead end." Literally.

"Pretty much," Adrian says with resignation. "Is there anything else I can do for you?"

"Not for now." I push away from the desk and stand. "Keep your ear to the ground. If you happen to stumble upon anything useful, I want to know about it."

"I'll do that," he says before ending the call.

Fuck.

I slam a hand on the desk. Mukha was my only lead to what's brewing with Stefanov. There's still no sign of Besov. According to the man who's watching his apartment, he hasn't returned home. That leaves me with one alternative—a last resort. I'll have to get the information from Stefanov himself. I'm not opposed to the idea of torturing the motherfucker, but I won't be able to trust the filth that comes out of his mouth. I was hoping to have the information before taking him on. If he's going to such lengths to hide it, there's a good chance he may not spill the beans even when I pull off his fingernails one by one.

Walking to the window, I draw back the curtain. It's dark, and snow is falling in the yellow glow of the powerful spotlights that illuminate the garden. On the opposite side of the river, someone is sitting in a room on the top floor of an apartment building with a pair of binoculars, reporting the activity in my house to Stefanov right this very moment. The idea makes me want to go out there and slit the cockroach's throat before dumping his body on Stefanov's doorstep and getting the fucking information I want. However, if I've learned anything in life, it's that you win a war with patience and not with impulsive actions. There's still time. Stefanov hasn't made a move yet. I'll give it until after Christmas, until we've visited Laura in the States. After that, the gloves will come off.

I drop the curtain and dial Nelsky. It's after working hours, but my security chief takes my calls twenty-four-seven.

He answers in a shaky voice. "Mr. Volkov?"

"What's the status on finding that file?"

He swallows audibly. "Nothing yet, sir."

My temper ignites. "What the fuck am I paying you for, Nelsky?"

"We've tried, sir. Our hacker can't find anything."

"Is the hacker even worth the fucking space he's taking up in my office?"

"He's good, sir." If anything, he sounds uncertain. "The best."

"Then he'd better prove it. Get me something, or don't come into the office when I'm back next week."

"Yes, sir. Thank you, sir. We'll work around the clock."

"You do that," I grit out before stabbing the red button to end the call.

Too on edge for sleep, I open my emails on my phone. There's a message from Konstantin Molotov. His brother Nikolai is finally ready to sign the papers formalizing the joint venture. The only catch is that he wants to meet me in person to do so, which means coming to his remote compound in Idaho. Nikolai is cc'd on the email, so I reply, thanking Konstantin for the introduction and suggesting that Nikolai and I meet the day after Christmas. Katerina and I will be in America anyway, and I might as well kill two birds with one stone.

Nikolai replies promptly, confirming the meeting and saying that he'll send directions and safety instructions.

Good. Like me, he must be a stickler for security. Then again, in our position, we don't have a choice. We haven't gotten this far by not watching our backs.

I go to the liquor tray, pour a double shot of vodka, and down it in one go. Another double later, I barely feel a buzz. What I need is a good sparring with the men.

I may not be any closer to having the information I want, but file or no file, before the New Year, Stefanov will be dead. That's a guarantee.

25

KATE

On the morning of Christmas Eve, Alex wakes me early. He rushes me through a shower and breakfast, and forty minutes later, we're boarding his private plane with the gifts he'd insisted I buy for my mom and friends when he took me sightseeing and visiting boutiques. We'll be spending the night in Deep Creek, where Alex made reservations at a B&B. He must've booked out the whole place, seeing that Igor, Dimitri, Leonid, Yuri, and four other men are traveling with us.

I sleep for most of the flight, getting in some quality rest thanks to the comfortable bed in Alex's bedroom cabin. Being the workaholic that he is, Alex uses the time to catch up on business.

He wakes me up for the landing just before four in the afternoon. Like when we were arriving in Russia, he's constantly talking on a satellite phone, presumably making sure we're safe. Four cars are parked outside the private hangar our plane taxies into. The armed men exit the plane first. When they've checked the cars and the hangar, Alex and I get into a car with Yuri. Sandwiched between two cars in the front and one at the back, we make our way to Deep Creek.

From town, it's a short drive to the clinic. The modern building sits on a few acres of land near a lake. Snow covers the ground, and the blue lake is frozen, forming a beautiful picture.

My mom is waiting in the lobby when we arrive. Dashing across the floor, she pulls me into a hug.

"Katie." After kissing my cheek, she holds me at arm's length. "Look at you. You've lost weight." Her brow furrows. "Are you eating enough?"

It's hard to contain my emotions and not burst into tears. "More than enough. I'm so happy to see you."

"Me too." My mom turns to Alex. "This is the best gift ever."

Alex bends down to kiss her cheek. "You look great, Laura. It's good to see you."

My heart warms as I take her in. She indeed appears trim and fit. Her skin has a healthy glow, and her eyes are sparkling.

"Wow," I say. "Look at *you.*"

Raising her arms, she twirls in a circle. "What do you think?"

"Mom, you look amazing."

"Thank you," she says, beaming. "I'm so much better already. I still have a few painful spells, but it's nothing compared to how it used to be. I'm agile again. It's amazing to do normal chores without discomfort."

"I'm so happy for you." She deserves this and so much more.

She smooths a hand over her dress. "All because of you, Alex. I can never thank you enough."

"No thanks needed," Alex says with a warm smile.

Mom glances over his shoulder at Igor and Leonid, who stand just inside the door. "Are they with you?"

"Yes," Alex says. "Don't worry about them. Traveling with bodyguards is protocol for me."

Wait until she sees the men outside. At least their guns are concealed under their jackets. I don't even want to know how Alex got the clinic to allow weapons inside.

"Really?" Mom tilts her head. "Does that mean you're a kidnapping candidate, as in getting captured for ransom?"

"Not likely," Alex replies with a chuckle.

"We brought some Russian food made by Alex's chef," I say quickly to change the subject. "I hope you like it. We thought it would be cozier to have lunch here than somewhere in town."

"Not much in town is open tomorrow," Alex adds.

My mom throws an arm around my shoulders. "There goes my diet."

"Don't worry." Alex picks up the cooler bag at his feet. "I instructed my chef to only use ingredients that are allowed in your eating plan."

"How considerate of you." Mom flashes him a smile. "Just as well. Otherwise, I'll be in trouble with William."

"William?" I ask as she steers us toward the elevator.

The glow on her cheeks deepens to a flush. "Dr. Hendricks."

I make big eyes. "You're on a first-name basis?"

Lowering her voice, she says with a glint in her eyes, "We're on first base too."

"Mom!" I whisper-exclaim.

She winks. "I have a surprise for you." She ushers us into the elevator when the doors open. "You don't have to go to the B&B in town," she continues. "Someone pulled out of the program—family emergency—so there's a vacant room. William suggested you stay here to spare you the traveling to town and back. No charge."

The elevator stops on the second floor.

"That's very kind of him," I say, glancing at Alex, "but we don't want to impose."

Alex holds the door for us. "Katerina is right. We should probably stick to the plan and sleep in town."

"Nonsense." Taking my arm, Mom leads me down the hallway and says over her shoulder to Alex, "He wouldn't have offered if he didn't want to."

She unlocks the door at the end and goes inside ahead of us. "These rooms are a bit smaller than the ones on my floor, but they're still comfortable. What do you think?"

I look at Alex for an answer. He's put a ton of security measures in place. Changing everything will take major reorganization.

He surprises me by saying, "It looks great. If you're sure it's not an inconvenience to the management, we'll gladly stay."

"Great," Mom says. "That settles it then."

"I'll let Yuri know to bring our bags up," Alex says.

I look around as I unbutton my coat. The room is cozy. Despite the sleek, modern look of the building, the focus is on comfort inside. A double bed and nightstand take up one half of the room, and a desk, bar fridge, sofa, and coffee table the other half. The colors are neutral, soft shades of beige with accents of green. A large window frames the lake against the backdrop of the mountains, allowing for plenty of light.

"You can unpack your things here," Mom says, indicating a small dressing room that connects to a bathroom.

I hang my coat on the hook behind the door and unwind my scarf. "Some of the food needs to go in the fridge. I'll start with that."

Alex carries the cooler bag Tima had packed to the desk.

"Let me give you a hand." Mom takes the frozen dishes from the bag. "What's all this?" she asks, bringing them to the fridge. "Your chef shouldn't have gone to so much trouble, Alex."

"It was no trouble," he says, removing his coat.

"A lot of people didn't want to interrupt their treatment and decided to stay here over Christmas," Mom says as she stacks everything neatly in the fridge. "We're having a special dinner tonight."

"That's very thoughtful of the staff," I say, handing her the last plastic container.

She shuts the fridge and walks to the sofa. "They're all amazing. Everyone here is so kind." Sitting down, she looks between Alex and me. "What about you? How is St. Petersburg? Tell me everything."

Smiling, I take a seat next to her. "I've already told you everything on the phone. What about your apartment? Is your neighbor taking good care of it?"

She pats my hand. "Everything is fine at home. Are you sure you can't stay longer?"

"I'm afraid not," Alex says, taking his phone from his pocket. "I have some business obligations in Russia."

Mom grimaces. "I'm not complaining. I just can't believe you flew all this way for a couple of days."

"I took the liberty of booking one of the private lounges for our lunch tomorrow," Alex says. "I hope that will do."

Mom clears her throat. "Speaking of lunch, William suggested we have lunch at his place instead of in the visitors' lounge. He reckons it will be more comfortable for us."

I steal another glance at Alex. "What about his family? I don't want to put him out."

"He's a widower." She crosses her legs. "His kids are grown

up and are visiting their in-laws upstate this year, which means he'll be alone for Christmas too."

"Oh, I'm sorry he lost his wife," I say. "Did it happen a long time ago?"

"Five years. It was a drawn-out illness." Blowing out a sigh, she gives me a sidelong glance. "I think it was very difficult for him and the kids."

"I can only imagine."

Alex types something on his phone. "Give me his address. I'll get my driver to program his GPS."

More likely, he'll make sure the surroundings are safe.

"I'll send you a text message with the directions when I get back to my room." A smile softens my mom's pretty features. "You must be tired after the long trip. Do you want to catch a nap before dinner?"

"I actually slept a lot on the plane," I say, "but a shower will be welcome."

She gets to her feet. "I'll leave you to get settled. Shall we meet around seven?"

"That sounds good," Alex says, pocketing his phone.

"Just knock on my door when you're ready," Mom says on her way out. After giving us a wave, she disappears with a bounce in her step.

"She really does look good," Alex says after closing the door behind her.

Walking to him, I wrap my arms around his waist. "Thank you, not only for the visit but also for doing this for my mom."

He kisses the top of my head. "I already told you, Katyusha, your family is mine."

I melt against him, unable to help myself. When he's kind

like this, it's difficult to remember that he holds my free will hostage.

~

THE DINNER IS A JOVIAL AFFAIR. THE DISHES ARE PLANT-BASED, low in saturated fat and sodium, with plenty of vegetables and whole grains. The menu theme is Mediterranean, which includes a spread of baked artichoke, ratatouille, sundried-tomato-and-chickpea stew, and a delicious gazpacho of melon, garlic, basil, and mint. The dessert is strawberry soup served with paper-thin, dairy- and gluten-free ginger tuiles.

Dr. Hendricks—or William—isn't there. My mom says he wants to give us time alone to catch up. From how much she talks about him, it seems they spend quite a bit of her free time together.

We meet the other patients staying here for Christmas. The group is diverse, with men and women of all ages. Living together for a few weeks has created a camaraderie that's obvious in their banter.

Megan is ten years older than my mom and is originally from Hawaii. George is a veteran who owns a cattle farm in Texas. Daphne is forty and is opening a florist shop in the new year. I enjoy the lively conversation and meeting new people. It's a welcome change from my isolation in Russia. For a few hours, I forget about the awful reality of Alex's life and how it has impacted mine.

After dinner, we have homemade, alcohol-free ginger beer in the lounge by the Christmas tree, while Daphne plays the piano and George has us all in stitches with his impersonation of Billy Mack's "Christmas Is All Around" from the movie *Love Actually*.

By bedtime, my stomach hurts from laughing.

I give my mom a hug when we arrive at our room, still wiping tears of laughter from my eyes. "I had so much fun tonight."

Alex regards me with a warm curve of his lips. Even he had a few laughs.

"So did I," Mom says.

"Alex and I have a gift for you."

"Oh, honey. You shouldn't have." Waving a hand around the space, she says, "This is already too much, and your visit is the best gift I could've asked for, not to mention how costly and tiring the trip must be for you."

Taking her hand, I open the door and drag her inside. "Come on."

"You didn't think we'd come empty-handed?" Alex asks with a chuckle, following us inside.

"Shall I close my eyes?" she asks with a squeal.

I laugh. "It's wrapped. You can look." Taking the first gift from my bag, I hand it to her.

She shakes it and turns it on all sides. "What is it? I have no idea what to guess."

"Open it," I urge.

She tears away the wrapping paper and lifts the lid of the box. "Oh, Katie," she exclaims, pulling out the cashmere sweater. "This is gorgeous. And blue, my favorite color."

"I'm glad you like it. It's from a boutique in St. Petersburg."

She hugs first me and then Alex. "I love it."

I hand her the second gift. "This one is from Alex."

She leaves the sweater on the desk to tear the gift paper off the box. When she lifts the lid and unties the strings of the velvet bag, she gasps. "My goodness. This is gorgeous. Look at the detail."

"It's a Fabergé replica," Alex says. "Unfortunately, it's not the real thing."

"I love it." She lifts the delicate egg from the box and studies it in the light. "Are those...?"

"The gemstones are real," Alex says. "It's a collector's piece, part of a limited edition. The valuation certificate is in the box."

"Oh, my." She gapes at him. "I can't accept this."

"Now you sound like Katherine," he says with humor. "Of course you can. I insist."

"This is beautiful." She puts it back in the velvet bag before carefully returning it to the box. "Thank you, Alex."

"It's given with much pleasure," he says warmly.

"I can't thank you enough." My mom's eyes glitter with tears. "Not only for the gifts, but also for taking such good care of my daughter."

Alex doesn't move a muscle. His reply is smooth, practiced. "She takes good care of me too."

Some of my excitement evaporates. The lies we're feeding my mom are a damper on my short-lived giddiness. I feel despicable, like a traitor, but how can I destroy her illusion if she's doing so well and looking so much better? How can I tell her the truth if it will crush her? No, it's better that she believes the lies, no matter how awful telling them makes me feel.

Patting my cheek, she says, "I should let you catch some rest. Good night, kids. Thanks again for spoiling me."

"You're welcome, Mom," I say, my throat clogging up with darker emotions.

She turns at the door. "The best gift is still having you here."

Not trusting my voice to speak, I blow her a kiss before she shuts the door.

Shit. I'm a horrible person, deceiving my own mother like that. This isn't how she raised me. Living with Alex is forcing me to become someone else, and I'm not sure I like that someone.

Turning toward the window, I hide my expression from Alex, who thankfully busies himself with taking off his jacket. I don't want him to see what will be written openly on my face—that right now, I despise both of us.

I take in the moonlit scene. It's stopped snowing. The landscape is a clean white of fresh powder glittering under the lampposts of the garden. Pristine. Not murky and full of dirty lies. There are no other buildings nearby, but I nevertheless close the curtains. With everything that's going on, I'm becoming paranoid.

I jump when Alex touches my shoulder.

"Hey," he says, twirling me to face him. "Why so on edge suddenly?"

"Is it safe to sleep here?" I can't hide the strain in my voice. "I don't want to bring the danger straight to my mom."

"Everything is taken care of," he says in a placating tone, rubbing my arms. "The men are on watch, and we have satellite surveillance."

"What about the lunch at Dr. Hendrick's house?" I ask, not reassured.

"I've already sent Dimitri to check things out. I won't take any risks, Katyusha."

"Okay." I bite my lip. "I'm happy to be here, more than you can ever know. I just—"

"Leave the worrying to me." He squeezes my biceps. "The only thing I want you to do is enjoy the time with your mom."

"You're right." My smile is halfhearted. "I should make the most of it." Although it's easier said than done.

He studies my face. "You looked happy tonight. Carefree."

"I was." I consider how much to tell him. I don't want him to think I'm ungrateful. "It was fun. It made me forget."

Regret flashes in his eyes, but it's gone in a blink. Pulling me closer, he says, "I know how to make you forget."

His mouth is on mine before I can reply. He spears his fingers through my hair, strokes his tongue over mine, and, as promised, takes me to a place where danger doesn't exist.

26

ALEX

*T*he vibration of my phone on the nightstand wakes me. I'm a light sleeper. It's part of my conditioning to always be alert. Reaching out for the phone, I check the screen. Nelsky. It's barely five o'clock here but noon in Russia.

I untangle myself carefully from Katerina. Her features are illuminated by the faint blue light from the electronic thermometer on the fridge. She looks peaceful in her sleep. Vulnerable. Sparing her beautiful face one last glance, I get up quietly and go to the bathroom, where I close the door before flicking on the light. It's safe to talk in here. Dimitri swept the rooms for cameras and listening devices while we had dinner last night.

My gut draws tight with anticipation as I take the call. Nelsky wouldn't call me at five in the morning for frivolous reasons.

"I hope I didn't wake you, sir," he says with a soprano pitch to his voice.

"What's going on?" I ask, facing my reflection in the mirror.

"We found it, sir."

I go still. Time stops ticking.

"Sir? The file. We found the file."

My heart goes into overdrive, thumping with triumphant beats in my chest. "Where?"

"In iCloud, sir. Mukha hid a copy there, maybe to use as insurance if his life happened to be at risk."

Much good it did him.

"It wasn't easy," Nelsky continues, "but our hacker eventually unraveled enough cyber threads to lead us there."

"I assume you already downloaded it and wiped the original."

"Yes, sir. We couldn't risk someone else finding it."

"Good work," I say, keeping my voice down so I don't wake Katerina. "Send it to me."

He coughs. "There's still one little hiccup we have to deal with before I can send it, sir."

I clench my jaw. "What hiccup?"

"The file is encrypted and we can't break the code." He adds hastily, "Not yet."

"Fuck," I say under my breath.

"I'll let you know as soon as there's an update."

"Do that." I scrub a hand over my face. "No matter what time of the day or night."

"Yes, sir."

"And Nelsky?"

"Sir?"

"You're not fired."

He utters a nervous laugh.

I end the call.

Taking a few long breaths, I process the news. The file is in my hands. At last. If that hacker I'm paying a fortune per month is worth his salt, I'll have the information soon. Though I have a feeling I'm not going to like what I'll find.

I switch off the light and go back to bed. The mattress dips when I get in next to Katerina.

Frowning, she blinks her eyes open. "Alex?"

My name on her lips warms my chest and hardens my dick. I wrap my arms around her and kiss her forehead. "Go back to sleep, kiska."

"Is everything all right?"

"Yes."

The lie comes easily. If the price for her tranquility is an untruth, I'll gladly carry the burden of that sin.

Her voice is croaky with sleep. "Where did you go?"

"I just went to the bathroom for a sip of water."

"There are bottles in the fridge." She snuggles closer to me, nestling under my arm. "Do you want me to get you one?"

The offer warms me in a different way, a way I seldom, if ever, experience. No one else tries to take care of me without expecting something in return.

"No, kiska," I say in a soft voice, tightening my arms around her. "I'm good."

She settles with a sigh, resting her cheek on my chest. She's cute when she's like this—half asleep and not yet remembering to be angry with me. Now that I finally have that fucking file, her negative feelings will soon be a thing of the past. I'll tie her to me in every way imaginable. She'll never be able to get away, but I'll make her so happy she'll be too delirious to realize how effectively I'm spinning my web around her. And even if she does, she'll be too ecstatic to mind. I'll give her everything her heart desires, everything a man with money and power can.

Not that material things are that important to her. Sure, she likes pretty dresses and shoes and even the jewelry she says is too expensive. But what she really wants are the simple things —a job she enjoys, a happy home, friends, a family.

I'll give her a family.

Soon.

As soon as I've eliminated the threat on our lives.

The thought alone makes me hard. My semi-erection turns into a full-blown hard-on that tents my pajama bottoms. Sliding a hand along the curve of her spine, I push up the silk camisole top of her sleep set. She presses closer, throwing her thigh over mine.

The non-verbal permission is all I need. There's a sudden fire in my veins, an urge to plant my seed deep inside her. It's different than the desire I always feel for her or the compulsive necessity to show her constant affection. It's more primal and, at the same time, more of a conscious decision. This isn't an impulse. At the back of my mind, I've always known that this is where we're heading. And now that my mind and body have taken notice of my resolve, I'm impatient to chase that goal.

I slip a hand under the elastic of her shorts and trace the crease of her ass before cupping a cheek. She arches her hips, rubbing the sweet spot between her legs against my thigh. She's so wet I can feel her arousal through the fabric of my pajama bottoms. The fact that I arouse her, that her body is making all that cream and honey for me, satisfies a primitive side of me I didn't even know I possessed.

Locking my hands around her small waist, I lift her on top of me so that her body is stretched out on mine, her thighs straddling my hips and her breasts flattened against my chest. I drag her up a little, sliding her silk-covered pussy over my rock-hard cock. When she lifts onto her arms, the extended tips of her breasts brush over my chest through the silk of the camisole. I grab her face between my palms and kiss her hard, too hard maybe, but she kisses me right back, tangling her tongue with mine. The depth of her mouth is sweet, her moans an aphrodisiac.

When I grip the elastic of her pajama bottoms, she closes her legs so I can shove the shorts over her hips. I leave them just under her ass, too eager to reach my destination to undress her completely. Straining up, I don't break the kiss as I slide a palm over her globes and between her legs. I curl a finger to part her folds. She's not just slick. She's dripping wet. For me.

I'm eager to sink inside her, but I want to see what I do to her first. Slowing the kiss, I press our lips together one last time before I roll her off me and sit up against the headboard. She gives me a confused looked as I move the covers aside.

"Come here," I say, pointing at my lap.

She grabs the elastic of her shorts, making to remove them, but I shake my head and switch on the bedside lamp for a better view.

"Put your pussy in my lap, kiska." My voice is dark with lust. "I want to see it."

She looks uncertain.

"Ass up," I say, making sure my instructions are clear.

She bites her lip, considering the order for a moment before asking, "You're not going to spank me, are you?"

Amused, I raise a brow. "Not unless you want me to. Do you?"

"No," she says quickly.

"Then lie down."

She looks at my groin, where the head of my cock is pushing

through the elastic of my pajama bottoms and pressing against my stomach. "Don't you want to take those off?"

Her eagerness makes my lips quirk with satisfaction. "In a moment."

Slowly, she executes the order, watching me warily as she drapes herself over my lap so that her pussy is cushioned on my legs and her ass is in the air. There's something perverse about her being presented like this, with her shorts around her thighs and her ass naked. I like that she doesn't wear panties under those silky pajama bottoms. I like that I can see everything from this angle.

Flattening a palm on her lower back, I stroke her soft skin. Her body breaks out in goosebumps when I caress her firm globes. Her bare pussy glistens with wetness, the plump lips swollen and pink. I trace the seam slowly, making her shiver. She bends her elbows and rests her cheek on her arm, watching me, but she can't see how erotic the sight is when I part those pretty lips in the V of two fingers to reveal the little pearl hidden underneath. I draw the thumb of my free hand over the button. Even the light touch makes her jerk. She clenches her ass cheeks when I apply firmer pressure.

I tear my gaze away from the work of my hands to gauge her expression. Her eyes are closed and her lips slightly parted, her breaths coming rapidly. Focusing my attention between her legs again, I rub faster while applying more pressure. She lifts her ass a little, the involuntary movement giving me better access, enough to gather some of her slickness. Keeping her open between my fingers, I turn my other hand palm-up and sink two fingers inside her. She looks so hot with her ass in my lap and my fingers in her pussy that a hot jet of precum erupts from the tip of my cock.

I never thought I'd get off on pulling down a woman's shorts and making her come in my lap with my fingers, but here I am, ready to ejaculate in my pants, because this isn't any woman. This is *my* woman. I don't break the pace of my fingers as I lift my other hand and suck my thumb into my mouth. I lubricate it well before pressing on her back entrance. The tight ring stretches easily, letting my thumb in to the knuckle. It only takes a few pumps before she gets to where I want to bring her. I nearly explode when she comes with a cry, squeezing her inner muscles around my fingers. If it's not the hottest thing I've ever seen, I don't know what is.

Aftershocks are still racking her body when I peel the shorts from her legs. I take just enough time to push my own pants over my hips before lifting her into a sitting position so that she straddles my thighs. Fastening my hands around her waist, I help her onto her knees. I hold her in place with one hand and grip the root of my cock with the other to position it at her entrance. She does the rest of the work, lowering herself over me. With every inch I sink into her, my balls draw tighter. I'm not going to last long, but that's not the point. That's why I took care of her pleasure first.

She leans back, rocking gently while resting her hands on my legs. Her nipples are hard points visible through the silk of her camisole. Her curves bounce with her movement, the fact that they're hidden somehow making the sight hotter. I home in on the triangle between her legs, on how her pussy stretches to accommodate my cock.

That's all it takes. I grip her waist to hold her in place and pivot my hips, taking her with harsh thrusts. Sweat beads over my body as I pound into her, taking everything that belongs to me. The foreplay has been too much of a turn-on. Long before

I'm ready, the release builds at the base of my spine. Two more thrusts, and sweet, agonizing pleasure pumps through my body and blows my mind. I'm breathing hard, lost in the moment, forgetting crucial details such as being alert.

Wrapping my arms around her, I press her to my chest. I'm reluctant to pull out. My body is sated. It should be satisfied at stamping my possession on her, but now that the idea of earlier has taken root, it wants more. I want everything with her, including the family I never thought I'd have. I won't rest until it's done, until I've bound her to me with no option of escape. Before that can happen, I need to put a ring on her finger. The one I brought with me isn't the one that will tie her to me yet, but for now, it'll do.

Reluctantly, I move her aside. Sex with Katerina is always hot, but our morning sex is especially intense. After cleaning her up, I coax her into having a shower with me, and then I take her back to bed. It's still early, yet neither of us is tired enough to drift back to sleep.

After pulling on a pair of sweatpants and a T-shirt, I get two cups of hot carob almond milk from the vending machine in the hallway and carry them back to the room.

She gives me a smile when I offer her the drink. "You always spoil me with breakfast in bed." Teasingly, she adds, "You do realize I've gotten used to it and will now expect it for life?"

For life. Fuck, yeah. "I can live with that."

I leave my drink on the nightstand and get the gift-wrapped box from my bag. Getting back into bed next to her, I say, "Merry Christmas."

Biting her lip, she looks at the box I leave on her lap.

"Hey." I brush a strand of hair from her face. "What's wrong?"

Her smile turns sad. "I didn't get you anything. I would have, but…"

She doesn't say it's because I took away her access to her money and her freedom to go where she likes.

"We don't celebrate Christmas in Russia on this date." It's a poor excuse, a feeble attempt at brushing away the hurt that underlies the unsaid, but I tell myself this situation is only temporary. "Besides, I don't need anything."

She looks at me quickly. "That's not the point. Giving a gift isn't about offering something the recipient *needs*."

My words are gentle, soothing. "I know, my love." My smile is a consolation. "But I appreciate the intention. That's all that matters."

Judging by the pleat between her eyebrows, she disagrees. Not wanting to spoil the aftermath of our amazing sex with an argument, I opt for changing the subject. "Aren't you going to open that? I know you already know what it is, but it seemed like an appropriate time to give it to you."

"Thank you," she says, making a good effort to not let me see the sadness that remains in her eyes.

I keep my tone light. "Open it first before you thank me."

She tears away the wrapping paper and opens the lid of the box. "It really is exquisite."

I lift the ring from the box and take her hand to slide it onto her finger. "Rubies suit you."

"So that is what the ring is for? For Christmas?"

"Yes," I say, another lie sliding smoothly from my tongue.

"You shouldn't have."

"I wanted to." And that's not a lie.

"Thank you again." She holds her hand to the light, studying the ring.

"You're very welcome again."

"What about the gifts we brought for Joanne, June, and the girls at the ER?" Hope sounds in her tone. "Are we making a detour via New York?"

"No." I try to deal the blow with gentleness. "Leonid already mailed the gifts yesterday from town."

"I see." She nods a couple of times. "That was a good idea." Leaving the paper cup on the nightstand, she gets out of bed.

"Katyusha."

"I'm going to get dressed," she says, not looking at me. "My mom always gets up early. I'd like to have breakfast with her."

It takes every ounce of willpower I possess and more not to go after her, but my gut tells me to give her a moment. As close as we were during sex, she's pulling away from me again. Her behavior only confirms what I already know. Katerina isn't a woman I can buy with gifts and keep happy by showering with jewelry.

What she needs are things money can't buy, such as the freedom I can't give her yet... and that I'll never be able to give her if she doesn't say yes.

27

KATE

*A*lex just gave me an enormous gift, but instead of making me happy, it reminded me of what he'd taken away from me. I'm not ungrateful. I just can't forget that in reality I'm nothing but a prisoner, as Dania so kindly reminded me.

Determined not to let my sadness ruin what little time I have with my mom, I get ready and go downstairs at seven to knock on her door. She opens it wearing a pretty red dress and matching jacket. Red looks good on her. The color compliments her complexion and brings out her blond hair and blue eyes.

"Morning, honey," she says, drawing me into a hug. "Merry Christmas. Where's Alex?"

"Merry Christmas, Mom." I kiss her cheek. "Alex is taking care of something work-related. He's having breakfast in the room and will catch up with us later."

She runs her gaze over my jeans, sweater, and Uggs. Planting a fist on her hip, she says, "We need to go shopping."

I lift a finger. "Oh, no. I'm not walking into that trap again."

The last time my mom took me shopping, we spent hours trying on clothes. I had blisters on my feet by the time I finally managed to drag her home. To add insult to injury, she convinced me to buy a short black dress that'd cost an arm and a leg and that I've never had the courage to wear.

Gasping, she grabs my right hand. "Look at that. This ring is gorgeous." She meets my gaze with a twinkle in her eyes. "Let me guess. Alex?"

I nod. "My Christmas gift."

"That man is something else. I'm happy for you. You deserve it." She hooks her arm through mine. "Come on. Let's have breakfast, and then I'll take you on a tour."

Some of the heaviness pushing me down vanishes. Her enthusiasm is contagious.

"Let's," I say. "It might be the mountain weather, but I'm starving."

In the dining room, we take a small table on the closed terrace. With the view of the lake and the sun filtering through the window, it's gorgeous. While we sip a delicious brew of carob and cinnamon, my mom fills me in on her treatment process. I feel a little guilty about enjoying the breakfast of frozen berries and vegan yogurt, knowing Alex's money is paying for it, but I brush the thought aside. He's told me repeatedly he wants to do this. At first, I thought it was because he loves me, but now I know better. Alex is a very generous person, and he likes to give gifts. That's what this is—an enormous gift. Although for a man as wealthy as Alex, the price of this treatment must be small change. I was a fool to see more into it.

"Did you hear what I said?" Mom asks.

I pull myself back to the present with an internal reprimand. Now isn't the time to let my mind drift. "I'm sorry. I was daydreaming."

"Mm." She gives me an approving look. "Someone is in love. I asked if you'd like to see the rest of the place after breakfast."

"Sure." I finish my drink and pick up my fork. "I'd love to."

After we're done eating, my mom takes me on a quick tour, showing me the parts I didn't see during my first visit, including the gym, the heated pool, the yoga and meditation rooms, the dietician's office, the lecture hall where they have educational sessions, and the physiotherapy wing.

The physiotherapy treatment includes massages and mobility exercises, Mom explains. Next to the wing where they do the treatments is a small beauty salon where patients can have a haircut or a manicure. Most patients stay for a couple of months, which makes such a service necessary.

At the end of the tour, Mom checks her watch. "Oh my goodness. Look at the time. We'd better go grab the food you brought."

Alex is working on his laptop at the desk when we get to our room. After he and my mom exchange Christmas wishes, we get the dishes from the fridge while he packs up his laptop and locks it in the safe. Just before twelve, we make our way downstairs.

Dr. Hendricks waits in the deserted reception area. Tall and dark-haired, with gray creeping into his sideburns, he's a handsome man who looks both smart and relaxed in a button-up shirt and a pair of chinos. At our approach, he straightens from where he was leaning on the counter. When his gaze falls on my mom, his green eyes go wide.

"Laura." He crosses the floor and meets us halfway, taking the shopping bag from my mom. "You look amazing."

"Thank you." A flush darkens her cheeks. "This is my daughter, Kate, and her boyfriend, Alex."

"Kate." He extends a hand, shaking first mine and then Alex's. His smile is warm, his eyes friendly. "It's good to meet you both."

"Thank you for inviting us to your home, Dr. Hendricks," I say.

"Please, call me William. Thank you for accepting." He reaches for the shopping bag I'm carrying. "May I?"

We load everything in his car while he asks how our flight was. Alex replies with a vague answer, not mentioning that we came by private plane. As William helps my mom into the passenger seat of his car, he tells us about the local attractions in the nearby Smoky Mountains in case we decide to return in the summer.

He looks up when Alex's guards get into their cars, but he refrains from asking questions as Alex and I head to our car. Mom must've already briefed him about Alex's so-called protocol.

William's vehicle takes the lead, and we follow. I look around as we exit the clinic grounds. Where are the men watching out for my mom? Alex said she wouldn't even know they were there. Are they hiding out somewhere in a nearby cabin, or are they keeping tabs on her via satellite? Maybe both.

We take a road that snakes up the mountain. From there, the drive only takes fifteen minutes. William's house is a modern structure situated on an outcrop with a view of the lake and the mountains. While my mom unpacks the grocery bags, he takes Alex and me on a tour. The house is small, but the rooms are spacious and the minimalistic furnishings create an unobstructed flow between the living area, dining room, and kitchen. Two upstairs bedrooms share a bathroom and balcony. My favorite part is the outside terrace that overhangs the slope.

We stop at the rail to admire the view. Alex leans one elbow on the rail and drapes his other arm around my waist. As always, his closeness seduces my senses, making everything else seem insignificant. Not even the view can compete with him, although the vista is magnificent.

"This is spectacular," I say.

"I'm glad you like it," William replies. "I had the house built five years ago when I moved here from Oakland."

Alex casts a practiced glance toward the horizon, his blue eyes alert as he takes in the surroundings. Seemingly satisfied with his visual evaluation, he checks his phone before saying, "I'll go check if Laura needs help in the kitchen."

"Kate?" William says when Alex is gone.

I abandon the vista to look at him.

"I want you to know that you have nothing to be worried about where your mom is concerned. We like each other." A smile appears on his lips. "A lot. I love her optimism and her zest for life. She's an amazing woman. I also realize she's a bit of a free spirit, so I have no intention of rushing her into anything."

He seems so sincere I can't help but believe him. "That's good to know."

"When I take my vacation this summer, I'd like to visit her in New York City. I was hoping we"—he waves between us—"me and you, could also get to know each other better. I know you're busy. Your mom has told me about your job."

I return his smile. "I'd like that."

"Great." He utters a soft laugh. "I don't want to give you the wrong impression, like I'm rushing things when I said I wouldn't, but my kids will be in Florida. Maybe we can all go down there and spend a weekend together? I'd love for both you and your mom to meet them. And Alex, of course."

Brushing the windblown wisps of hair off my face, I say, "I'll keep that in mind when I plan my summer shifts." That is, if I'm back at work by then. "I'm sure I can finagle a long weekend."

"Wonderful." He raps the rail. "Shall we go inside where it's warm?"

When we get back to the kitchen, my mom and Alex have finished unpacking the bags.

"What do you think?" she asks under her breath as William pours us organic grape juice while Alex keeps him company.

"He seems really nice," I say sincerely.

She's all but glowing. "I knew you'd like him."

"Here you go," William says, handing us each a glass of juice. "Homemade from Californian grapes."

We spend an agreeable half hour together, sipping our drinks in the kitchen while we warm up Tima's dishes and William adds the finishing touches to the ones he prepared. I listen attentively as he tells me about the program and its development. On a personal level, everything regarding Mom's welfare concerns me, and on a professional level, I find the medical information fascinating.

Our lunch stretches well into the afternoon. It's dusk when we finally thank William, say our goodbyes, and drive back.

Despite the amiable afternoon, I can't shake my tenseness

when we arrive at the clinic. Knowing me as well as she does, my mom picks up on it.

"Is everything all right?" she asks as we enter the foyer.

"Yes," I say, smiling for her benefit. I hate myself for lying to my mom. "Everything is perfect."

SURPRISINGLY, I SLEEP WELL AND WAKE UP RESTED THE following morning. I thought the anxiety would keep me tossing and turning all night.

Other than opening my eyes, I don't move. Alex is lying on his back, still asleep. I use the opportunity to study him. His face doesn't carry the tenseness that strains his features during the day. For once, he looks relaxed. Stubble darkens his jaw. His eyelashes are long for a man, softening the straight, harsh lines of his strong bone structure. He looks vulnerable in his sleep. The way my heart squeezes reminds me just how susceptible I am to him.

Trying to be quiet, I slip out of the bed, but the minute I stand up, Alex opens his eyes. The unguarded smile he gives me is my undoing. His blue eyes are soft with sleep yet piercing as he evaluates me. A feeling like a flapping of wings stirs in my chest.

"Sleep well?" he asks in a bed-sexy voice.

"Yes, actually." I glance at him from under my lashes as I dig through my bag for clothes. "You?"

He shifts up and rests his head on the headboard to watch me. "Like a baby." His lips quirk. "Like always when I sleep next to you."

My gaze is drawn to the sexy curve of those lips. My reply is meant as a clever comeback, but my voice sounds embarrassingly breathy. "With the emphasis on sleep. I'm surprised you didn't jump on me when we went to bed."

That quirk stretches into a lazy smile. "You sound disappointed."

Rolling my eyes, I head for the bathroom.

"Katyusha."

I stop in my tracks.

His voice is apologetic. "I wish we could stay longer, but we have to leave today."

I didn't expect otherwise, but the news is nevertheless disappointing. "When?"

"After breakfast."

I nod. "I'll be ready."

When I've finished getting dressed in the bathroom, I step back into the room. Alex is on the phone, speaking to someone in Russian. He's still in his pajama bottoms, pacing the floor. I can't help but stare at the broad, well-defined expanse of his chest and the flat ridges of his stomach.

He places a hand over the microphone of his phone. "You go ahead, my love. I'll follow later."

Igor is waiting outside our door to escort me downstairs. I find my mom on the terrace having breakfast.

"There you are," she says when she notices me. "Where's that sweet man of yours?"

"On the phone. He'll be down shortly."

"He sounds like a workaholic." She scoots to the side. "I hope you don't mind that I started breakfast without you, but I thought you might sleep in."

Taking the chair next to her, I say, "Alex doesn't want to get home too late. I'm afraid we have to leave after breakfast."

"He's very conscientious."

If only she knew.

I'm half done with my breakfast when Alex arrives. The minute he walks through the doors, everyone looks. He has that effect on people. It's not just his imposing height or potently masculine features. It's the self-assured way he carries himself.

He offers us a smile and makes his way over. Despite the friendly gesture, the tension is back on his face. The square line of his jaw is more pronounced from the way he always clenches it a little, and his eyes are tight with awareness. He seems permanently vigilant, forever on his guard.

"Good morning, Laura." He takes in my mother. "You look beautiful. I really like that new hairstyle on you."

She pats her hair. "Why, thank you. What a charming man you are. Have a seat."

When he puts a hand on my shoulder, my body takes notice. Awareness tingles in my nerve endings and travels down my arm as goosebumps run over my skin under my sweater.

"If you don't mind, I'll grab a quick breakfast in the lounge," he says. "I have business to take care of. Besides, I robbed you of Katerina yesterday. You deserve to have her all to yourself this morning."

He gives my shoulder a squeeze before walking off.

"Oh, my," Mom gushes. "That man is perfection. Could he be any more wonderful?"

Great. Now she's in love with the idea of Alex and me. I bite my lip. What if things don't work out? She'll be so disappointed, and I can never tell her the truth.

"What's with the long face?" she asks, taking my hand.

I shake myself out of it. "I'll miss you."

"I'll be home before you know it."

I blow out a shaky breath, not telling her there's a good chance I may still be in Russia at that time. "Just enjoy the time you have left here. You deserve it."

"I have to admit, this feels more like a vacation than a treatment. I'm having so much fun with the other patients, and then, of course, there's William."

I nod. "He wants us to meet his children in Florida this summer."

Concern plays over her face. "Are you okay with that?"

"Of course." Again, provided I'll be back in the States. I push the disturbing thought aside. "He seems serious, but he told me he won't rush you into anything." My experience with Alex makes me say, "Promise me you won't make any rash decisions."

"You know me." She lets my hand go with a squeeze and pulls the juice closer. "I may be impulsive, but I take my time before committing to anything."

I don't want her to think I'm against her having a long-term relationship with William. "I only want you to be happy."

"I am," she says with an easy smile. "That's all I've ever wanted for you too, Katie. I'm truly happy you've finally found your match."

Avoiding answering, I take the juice she poured and hide my face behind the glass.

When it's time to go, she sees us off. We say our goodbyes, my mom hugging both me and Alex and making him promise not to work too hard. She waves until we turn the corner.

It's then that the emptiness hits me.

It's then that I think that maybe I should've run when I had the chance.

28

ALEX

$\mathcal{W}$e fly to a small private airfield in northern Idaho, where I leave a disgruntled Katerina on the plane with enough men to guard her. I don't tell her where I'm headed or about the contract I'm about to sign with Nikolai Molotov. If I did, I'd have to tell her why I'm not taking her, and I don't want her to worry about the fact that I don't trust Nikolai. Though I've been working with Konstantin for months and have no reason to think his brother wishes me harm, I don't put my faith in anyone I don't know personally.

I don't leave until we've set up perimeter alarms and Igor has satellite surveillance running on his laptop. A secure connection feeds the information to my phone. No one besides me, Igor, and the pilot knows our flight schedule. It's unlikely that anyone will come looking for us here, but I repeat my instructions, commanding the men to guard Katerina with their lives. Igor assures me he'll follow protocol the minute he picks up any movement close by, meaning he'll send a reconnaissance team to find out who's on the way. The pilot is ready for takeoff in case of an emergency. His order is to leave immediately if there's any threat. I can always find my own way back. I know how to take care of myself.

The drive to the compound is tense. Yuri is behind the wheel and Leonid rides shotgun. It's a cold, gray day with fog hanging thick in the air. I can barely see ten meters ahead.

As we get higher into the mountains, I call Igor. "How is she?"

"Still angry," he says in his gruff voice.

"She'll get over it." Even though I can see for myself on my phone, I ask, "How about the surveillance?"

"Everything is running smoothly."

The words don't reassure me. I don't like being away from my kiska.

Leonid glances at me from the front passenger seat when I end the call, his beefy face pulled into a frown. He doesn't like the fact that I'm practically keeping Katerina prisoner. My men respect her. They've taken a liking to her. Well, tough luck. I'm not taking risks with her safety. Leonid and everyone else can go fuck themselves.

I address Yuri in a terse tone. "How much farther?"

He shoots a quick look at the GPS. "Ten minutes."

The road zigzags up the mountain. Exactly ten minutes later, we arrive at a stately metal gate. At our approach, the heavy gate slides apart, revealing more dense woods and a narrow, unpaved road.

Why would Nikolai Molotov hide out here in the middle of nowhere? I suppose the isolation allows for heightened security measures, even more than my St. Petersburg residence. Maybe I should build myself a compound in the middle of nowhere too and keep Katyusha there. For her safety.

Yuri pulls up to a modern house. The lights shine golden through the vast windows. All those windows give me an uneasy itch that crawls between my shoulder blades. With no blinds or curtains, the occupants are sitting ducks, an easy target for any stalker or assassin. If Nikolai Molotov's reputation for being a mistrustful son of a bitch is true, the glass is bulletproof. Still, I've never liked feeling exposed.

The front door opens, and Molotov himself steps outside.

Leonid gets my door. He follows with Yuri as I make my way over and shake Molotov's hand.

Molotov ushers us inside and invites my men to have refreshments in the kitchen while he and I go to his study.

"In here," he says, standing aside for me to enter.

The vista behind the window is hidden by the fog. A few floodlights color the footpaths of the garden with an emerald light. The view must be spectacular on a clear day.

"Sit," he says, leading me to a round conference table near his desk.

When I'm seated, he takes a bottle of vodka from an ice bucket and pours two shots. "I believe you have an assassin on your tail."

I regard him from under my eyelids. "News travels fast."

"In our circles." He places a glass in front of me and takes the chair behind the desk. "Are you making headway in finding the man who wants you dead?"

Inhaling deeply, I exhale through my nose as I consider him. Like I said, I don't trust anyone, not easily. "As a matter of fact, yes."

When I don't elaborate, he asks, "And who is this person who wants you dead, if I may ask?"

My smile feels flat. "You may not."

"May I ask why then?" He traces the rim of his glass. "Power?"

"Power is always a good motive for killing."

A grin slides onto his face. He knows I'm not going to tell him anything. "What's with the evasiveness?"

Impatience slips into my tone. "What's with the curiosity?"

"I like to know with whom I'm doing business." Leaning back, he studies me with an inquisitive look. "Not so long ago, you were parading a woman around New York City, a woman you took to Russia with you. Katherine Morrell, am I right? It was all over the gossip magazines."

I tighten my grip on the glass. "If you value your life, you won't speak her name again."

"It's like that," he says, giving not only his agreement but also his understanding with a nod. "What happened? Did your hunter go after her to get to you?"

If I clench the glass any harder, it's going to break.

"Ah," he says when I don't answer. "I see that I'm right."

Narrowing my eyes, I say in a calculated tone, "You seem very interested in matters that don't concern you."

He regards me for a moment, both thoughtful and attentive. "You have a lot of enemies."

I raise a brow. "So do you."

"This joint venture will guarantee you an alliance with my family. To a certain extent. Is that the real reason for your interest in Konstantin's project?"

"It will also secure you an alliance with me. Is that why you're signing the papers?"

He smiles at my comeback. Silence stretches for a beat before the tension gives and a more amiable atmosphere settles.

"What's with the questions, Nikolai? I thought you were happy with my terms. Do you have doubts?"

Pulling his glass closer, he says, "Just making sure you'll stay alive for the project to actually get off the ground."

I give him a cold look. "I have no intention of dying."

"Good." He raises his glass. "To our mutual objectives."

I clink my glass against his. "To the joint venture."

We throw back the liquor in unison. When I put my empty glass aside, he takes a folder from the drawer and slides it over the desk.

I flip back the cover. As I read the contract, he pours more vodka. Satisfied that everything is stated as we agreed, I take a felt tip pen from my pocket and sign my name.

"This warrants another toast," he says.

After he signs, we drink twice more. When he lifts the bottle for a fourth round, I get to my feet.

"I'd better get going." I button up my jacket. "We have a long trip ahead."

He follows suit. "There's plenty of room here if you'd like to stay over."

"Thanks, but I'd prefer to get back."

Coming around the desk, he says, "I'll walk you out."

We go via the living room where Yuri and Leonid are watching television while stuffing their faces with a spread of snacks.

At the front door, I pause. "Tell me something, Nikolai."

He waits.

"What is a man who supposedly loves the opera more than anyone doing out here in the wilderness?"

His eyes tighten. "I like fishing."

Right. Does it have anything to do with the young American wife he took not so long ago? Either way, every man is entitled to his secrets, so I leave it at that. I'm halfway to the car when he speaks.

"It's my turn to ask you something, Alex."

Pausing, I face him.

"Why did you choose Konstantin's project?" he asks. "There are a hundred other investments with a much lower risk profile."

"Because everyone deserves affordable power."

He utters a low laugh. Yuri and Leonid join in. So do I. Let them think what they will. They don't need to know I mean it. As far as my reputation goes, I'm heartless.

Just as we get into the car, my phone rings.

It's Igor.

Every muscle in my body goes rigid. I take the call even before Leonid has closed my door.

"What's wrong?" I ask, my voice tight.

"Everything is fine here," Igor says. "Kate is safe. Something went down in St. Petersburg." He pauses, the silence grave. "I got word from our man who's watching Stefanov's house. I thought you'd want to know."

"Hold on." I put my phone on speaker for Leonid's benefit. If shit is going down, it will save time if I don't have to repeat the message. "What happened?" I bite out as we clear the gates of Molotov's property.

"Stefanov executed Pavlov and wiped out his whole senior commanding team."

What the fuck? "He did what?"

"That's not all." Another pause. "He decapitated the body

and delivered a headless corpse to Pavlov's doorstep, apparently to send a message."

"What message?"

"He claims Pavlov betrayed him," Igor says. "Sold him out."

Leonid catches my gaze in the rearview mirror. "Stefanov is cleaning up after himself."

Exactly my thought.

"What did our man see?" I ask.

"He says Pavlov arrived first and later his underbosses. He didn't see them leave, but their cars were driven away. That's when he suspected something was happening. Soon after, the bodies were carried out of the house in broad daylight for all to see. He reported it to your man in charge, who sent a drone. He's got footage of the body being dumped on Pavlov's doorstep."

That's a strong message to send. Everyone in Russia will think twice before double-crossing Stefanov. He may have set up the massacre to look like a justified bratva execution, but the fact that he silenced Pavlov means he's getting nervous.

Good.

I have a feeling more action is about to go down.

I can hardly wait.

29

KATE

$\mathcal{W}$e arrive back in St. Petersburg with the same strict security as before and make it to Alex's house with no incidents. Lena and Tima welcome us in the foyer. I convey my mom's and William's thanks to Tima for the food and excuse myself to have a shower.

When I come downstairs for dinner, Alex calls me into the library. I enter cautiously. He's sitting on the sofa with his laptop on the coffee table in front of him.

"Is anything the matter?" I ask.

Steepling his fingers, he gives me an examining look. "Not at all. Why would you think something is wrong?"

"Because you're being hunted by a killer? Because my mom is sick, and lots of bad things can happen while I'm not there? Because you look serious, and that always means bad news?"

His mouth tightens. "You're exaggerating."

I walk to the sofa. "Then what is it?"

"Joanne sent you a message to say Merry Christmas."

I tense. The fact that Alex is filtering my messages is wrong on so many levels. My voice comes out harsher than I intend. "How kind of you to convey the message. I hope you told her Merry Christmas from me too?"

His blue eyes narrow marginally, but he smooths it over with a smile. "How about telling her yourself?"

I glance at his laptop. "Now?"

"If that's fine with you. She's available. They visited Joanne's parents in Hudson for Christmas Day but returned home this morning. She's saving her vacation time for warmer days."

"Wow." I utter a laugh. "You know more about my friend's life than I do these days."

"Katerina," he says with a frown.

I shrug. "It's true. So? What did you tell her?"

"I told her we flew out to see your mom, but that we had to return straight away due to my business obligations."

"I see." My smile is wry. "Is there any point in me talking to her then? Since you've already told her everything you want her to know."

He gets to his feet. "Why are you so agitated about this? I thought you'd be happy to speak to her."

"You know what will make me happy? Reading the messages she sends me without having them censored and relayed by you."

He rounds the sofa. "What's wrong with you?"

"What's wrong with me?" I backtrack a step. "What's wrong is *you*."

I turn for the door, but he grabs my wrist and hauls me back. "Katyusha. This isn't like you. I thought we had a good time in Deep Creek. I thought you were happy to see your mother."

"I was happy to see her. Very. I already told you that."

"Then what's gotten into you?"

"Everything," I say, pulling free of his hold. "This." I wave around the room. "The fact that you lock me up here and filter my messages. And how about the fact that I don't have a life any longer? You land your plane in the middle of Idaho and leave me there while you do whatever the hell it was you did there. I don't know how you justify that behavior to yourself, but it's not okay, Alex."

His frown deepens. "I had a business meeting. That's all."

"It doesn't matter why you went there. What matters is that you're selective with the information you share with me. How do you expect me to trust you if you read all my emails but keep me in the dark about your affairs?"

He watches me quietly, his eyes gleaming with anger, but I'm too upset to care.

After a terse moment, he says, "I apologize for leaving you in the plane. It was for your safety. It won't happen again."

It's not even about having been stuck in a plane in the middle of the woods. To be honest, I haven't been myself since we left Deep Creek. My emotions are all over the place. This whole crazy situation is getting to be too much. The uncertainty is killing me.

Taking a few deep breaths to calm myself, I say, "I didn't mean to lash out at you like that."

"I understand." He wraps his arms around me and drags me against his chest. "It will soon be over, kiska."

I crane my neck to look at him. "Will it? Why? What's going on?" What isn't he telling me?

He kisses my forehead. "Do you want me to postpone the call with Joanne until you feel more like yourself?"

"No," I say quickly, freeing myself from his embrace and brushing my hands over my hair. "I'd like to chat with her."

Giving me another piercing look, he goes back to the sofa, takes a seat, and wakes his laptop screen to connect a video call. I sit down on the edge of the seat next to him.

Three seconds later, my friend's face fills the screen. "Katie! How good to see you." She's walking through a spacious room with raw brick walls. "You too, Alex. Merry Christmas again." She plops down on a brown leather sofa, folding one leg under her, and puts the laptop on a coffee table.

"Thank you," I say with a genuine smile, some of my tension lifting. "Merry Christmas to you too."

Ricky waves from behind an island counter stove where he's stirring something in a pot. "Merry Christmas, guys."

"We're at Ricky's place," Joanne says. "He's renting a loft apartment in the Meatpacking District." She smiles at him from over her shoulder. "He's cooking."

She's wearing makeup, and her hair has been blow-dried straight. I can count on one hand the number of times I've seen her without her spiral curls.

"You look amazing," I say.

"Thank you." A blush colors her cheeks. "It's a special occasion."

Ricky comes around the counter carrying a bottle of wine in one hand and two glasses in the other. "Once you two are done with your honeymoon," he says, taking a seat next to Joanne, "I'll invite you for dinner too."

"We'd like that," Alex says.

Ricky winks as he pours the wine. "I'll hold you to it."

"How's your mom?" Joanne asks. "I can't believe you flew all the way to North Carolina and didn't stop over to see us."

Alex throws an arm around me. "As I said in my text message, duty called."

"You work too hard, Alex." Joanne takes the glass Ricky offers her. "Coming from me, that says a lot."

Alex chuckles. "It's a busy period. It will calm down after the new year."

Joanne takes a sip of her wine. "Back to your mom, Katie. What's new?"

"She's feeling so much better," I say.

"That's awesome." Joanne snuggles closer to Ricky. "I'm glad to hear that."

"How about your parents?" I ask.

She shoots Ricky a puppy-eyed look. "They're doing fine. It really went well."

I look between them. "What went well?"

Ricky cups Joanne's knee. His smile is all teeth. "I decided to do it the old-fashioned way and asked Joanne's dad for permission to marry her."

"What? You got engaged?" I gape at Joanne. "That's fantastic! Congratulations. Is this what tonight is? A celebration dinner?"

Joanne glows. "We wanted you to be the first to know before we tell everyone else."

"Congratulations," Alex says. "That's very good news."

Placing a hand over my heart, I say, "I'm so happy for you. When's the big day?"

"Soon," Ricky says, his gaze heating as it lands on Joanne.

"I know it's rushed," she says, "but we know we're good together. Why wait?"

"Why indeed?" I utter a shriek. "My best friend is getting married! I can't believe it."

She shifts deeper onto her seat and rests an arm on the

backrest. "Ricky wants to elope. I think we should have a small, intimate ceremony."

Joy warms my chest as I study their happy faces. "I'm sure you'll work it out."

"I hope I can count on you," Joanne says. "I'd love for you to be my bridesmaid."

"Of course," I say on impulse. "It will be an honor." Belatedly, I glance at Alex and bite my lip, realizing I've just made a promise I may not be able to keep. The thought is a damper on the happy mood. Not wanting to spoil the moment, I quickly change the subject. "When are you going to choose the ring?"

"We're not getting rings," Ricky says. "We're getting tattoos. It's a cliché, but it seems like the right choice for us."

"Good for you," I say with a smile. "This is a wonderful Christmas surprise."

Joanne makes a face. "My mother is disappointed that I've decided against a ring and a big wedding."

"She respects your choice," Ricky says. "She just needs a little time for the idea to grow on her."

"Tell us about your visit to Deep Creek," Joanne says.

Ricky holds up a finger. "I'm going to give the sauce a stir, but I'm listening."

While he goes back to cooking, I tell them about the clinic and my mom's progress, but I refrain from mentioning William for now. There's no point in bringing him into the conversation unless their relationship, which is still in an early stage, lasts beyond the treatment center. I've learned my lesson with getting my hopes up too soon. My mom is a butterfly. Not many men hold her attention for long, and then there's her illness. Like her ex-boyfriend Martin, most men bail when times get tough.

Too soon, Alex checks his watch. "I'm afraid we have to leave you. We're about to have dinner, and we don't want your lunch to get cold."

More accurately, he wants to make sure we don't stay on the call for too long. It's one of his security rules.

"It was good to see you," Joanne says, unfolding her leg from under her. "We'll call you again soon."

"I'd like that," I say. "I want to know everything about your plans for the wedding."

After saying our goodbyes, Alex ends the call.

He regards me solemnly for a heartbeat before saying, "I'm sorry you can't be there for Joanne. I know you would've liked to help with the wedding arrangements."

I sit with a stiff back, waiting for the real blow.

His tone is regretful. "It pains me to say this, Katyusha, but we may not be back in time for the wedding, not if they tie the knot soon."

I turn my face to look at him. "You took me to see my mom for Christmas. I'm not asking to be there to help my best friend with her wedding preparations, but why can't we attend her wedding?"

"*If* they decide to have a ceremony."

"Hypothetically speaking then."

He blows out a sigh. "I'm sure they'll postpone the big day if you ask them to."

I stare at him with parted lips. "Are you for real? I'm not going to ask Joanne and Ricky to postpone one of the most important days of their lives to accommodate *me*. How selfish do you think I am?"

A moment of silence passes as he studies me quietly before

saying, "Suit yourself, but there will be no more traveling until the end of January."

I jump to my feet. "The end of January? That's more than a month away."

He regards me with an expressionless face. "I'm aware of the timeline."

"And when we get to the end of January, will it become the end of February?"

A muscle ticks in his temple. "It will be as long as it takes."

I utter a laugh. "You're unbelievable."

He gets up. "This is a difficult time for both of us. Don't make it harder than it already is."

Tears burn at the backs of my eyes, but I blink them away.

"If at all possible, you will be there." He takes my hand. "There are things that need to happen first, things that will compromise our safety if I don't deal with them first, and when I've taken care of them, we may have to lay low for a while."

"That's what you keep saying."

Wrapping an arm around my waist, he pulls my body flush against his. I lean back, but not far enough to escape his lips. He slants them over mine in a searing kiss, sending an instant fire to my lower body.

I push on his shoulders, fighting for distance until he loosens his hold.

"Katerina," he says, fixing me with a predatory stare.

"No, Alex." I grip his wrist and remove his arm from around me. "This time, you don't get to kiss yourself out of a fight."

Not sparing him another glance, I walk out of the room, my heart aching—and not just because I might not be able to attend my best friend's wedding.

30

ALEX

J'm up early the following morning. I had trouble sleeping because my kiska is angry. She told me goodnight and let me kiss her, but the message came through clearly when she turned her back on me and went to sleep.

After blowing off some steam in the gym, I have a shower and inform Tima that I'm staying home and will be around for lunch. I instruct him to prepare something special for Katyusha, one of her favorite dishes, and then I go to my study to get some work done.

I've barely settled behind my desk when Igor raps on the open door.

"Enter," I say, waving him inside.

"There's been a development you should know about," he says as he approaches my desk.

I give him my full attention.

He stops behind the visitor's chair. "Stefanov has put a price on Besov's head. Word has just been put out. The news is circulating in the bratva circles."

"Interesting." I rub a thumb over my lips. "What's his reason?"

"Stefanov claims Pavlov sold him out to Besov. According to him, Pavlov is a traitor and Besov a blackmailer."

"This drama is getting more intriguing by the minute."

It doesn't take much to connect the dots. Stefanov and Pavlov were in cahoots. One or both of them ordered the hit on my life, hiring Besov for the job. Stefanov has already killed Pavlov. Now he's putting a target on the assassin's back. If the price is high enough, someone will eventually find Besov and deliver his head on a platter. Stefanov is silencing everyone who was involved in his scheme to get rid of me. The only loose end left is me, which can only mean one thing. He's getting ready to come after me.

"Tell the men to be extra vigilant. I have a feeling it won't be long before Stefanov strikes."

Igor nods and leaves briskly.

I unlock my laptop screen with my thumbprint and pull up my emails. A call comes in from Nelsky. Since I'm back from the States, he reports to me on a daily basis.

I take the call from my laptop, which is connected to my phone. "You'd better have something for me."

"As a matter of fact, I do, sir."

I freeze with my fingers over the keyboard. "Did you crack the code?"

"Ten seconds ago, sir."

My body tenses with anticipation. "Did you have a look at the contents?"

"No, sir. I'm sending an encrypted file to you now."

A message from Nelsky pops up in my inbox. "Got it. I'll call you back if I have further instructions."

I end the call and download the message in the encryption application that descrambles the code. It's a security tape recording of a man tied up in a chair, his face beaten to a bloody pulp. I barely recognize the symmetrical features and square chin, but I do recognize the round table with the checkered tablecloth and the wooden bowl with fruit.

Our kitchen.

My father.

An untimely flashback hits me in the gut, a memory of coming home from school to the smell of my mother frying *blini*. I can see her smile as she told me to wash my hands.

"An orange first," she said, ruffling my hair as I stuffed a *blin* with honey into my mouth after washing my hands at the sink. "What are oranges for, *malysh?*"

"For not catching a cold," I replied dutifully with a full mouth, taking a seat at the table.

The lines around her blue eyes softened. "And why is that?"

I rolled my eyes. Could these questions have been any more basic? "Because they have vitamin C."

She put an arm around me, hugging me to her waist. "Good."

The scratchy fabric of her apron felt abrasive against the first man-scruff on my cheek. She smelled of frying oil and soap. I hugged her back, but then embarrassment made me pull away.

"I'm too old for hugs," I said in a gruff voice.

She patted my cheek. "You're right. You're almost a man now, my Sasha."

My chest swelled with pride. "I'm Alex. I'm too old for Sasha too."

"Alex," she agreed gently.

The memory fades, and my chest squeezes with pain. Had I known what would happen the next day, I would've hugged her longer and told her I loved her.

Snapping out of the past, I force my attention back to my laptop, pain and anger mixing to create a violent cocktail in my blood.

On the screen, two men face my father. Both are fat around their waists and flabby in their arms. My father, a police officer who regularly encountered the worst of humanity, had security cameras in the apartment, just in case. The men must be unaware of the hidden cameras because they turn their backs on my father, revealing their faces.

My pulse jumps.

Vladimir Stefanov and Oleg Pavlov.

Putting his head close to Stefanov's, Pavlov says, "He's not going to talk."

Stefanov grins. "Oh, he will." He faces my father again. "Tell us what evidence you have against us and where it is, and we'll let your wife and son live."

My father spits blood on the floor. "I have nothing. You're wasting your time."

Stefanov flicks his fingers at Pavlov. Pavlov walks somewhere, disappearing from view. A moment later, he's back, dragging a chair with him.

My heart stops.

My mother sits in the chair, her hands tied behind her back. He leaves the chair next to my father's so that their shoulders are touching. My mother cries softly, but she doesn't scream.

"You'll talk," Stefanov says. "Or you'll watch her die."

"She has nothing to do with this. Please, let her go," my father begs, a desperate entreaty in one eye and the other one swollen shut.

Stefanov bends down, putting him and my father at eye level. "Talk."

Pavlov grabs my mother's hair, fisting her dark curls in his fingers. She whimpers when he raises his other arm, poised to strike, but she doesn't cower.

"Stop," my father cries out. "Stop, please! I'll tell you."

"Where?" Stefanov demands.

"In the bathroom. There's a loose tile on the bath. It's behind the piping."

"Go," Stefanov says to Pavlov even as the latter hurries from the room. Then to my father, "You thought you could blackmail me?"

"No," my father says with disgust. "I was going to hand it over once I knew whom I could trust."

"Not very clever." Stefanov shakes his head. "I own the police force."

"Not everyone," my father says bravely.

Pavlov returns with a plastic bag dangling from his fingers. "Got it. He's got photos of us meeting with his superior and documents proving we pay him."

Stefanov nods. "You did the right thing, Viktor. Now you and your family will live. I'll even reward you handsomely for the trouble. Is there anything else you'd like to give me? For every other piece of information you hand over, I'll double the price."

My father's head drops. "No."

"I think he's telling the truth," Pavlov says.

Stefanov's voice is clear, his command cold. "Turn on the gas."

My mother blinks. Her head turns as she follows Pavlov with her gaze to the stove. "No." The whispered word is filled with dread.

Pavlov turns on the gas.

Stefanov takes a lighter from his pocket and lights the fat white candle that stands on the table, the one my mom used to save electricity.

"No," my mother cries.

"You said you'd let us go," my father yells, drops of blood splattering from his mouth onto his vest.

"The boy is almost fifteen," Pavlov says. "He'll be a problem for us later."

"No!" my mother says.

"Don't worry about the kid." Vladimir walks to the door. "He'll end up in the system. He'll be lucky if he survives."

"Goodbye, my friends," Pavlov says in a mocking tone, following in Stefanov's footsteps.

My parents sit side to side, facing each other. My mother gives my father a tremulous smile, and then the screen goes dead.

I clutch the edge of the desk so hard my nails leave imprints in the wood.

I see my surroundings through a haze of red.

Pavlov and Stefanov owned my father's superior at the police force. It's a pity that son of a bitch is long since dead, or I would personally torture him into his grave. I'd bet my left arm he was the one who pulled the security tape from the remote feed and handed it over to Oleg Pavlov. Pavlov then gave the tape to Besov via Mukha, who encrypted the file.

Why did Pavlov hand the tape to Besov? There can only be one reason. Besov threatened Pavlov's life. Besides me, who else would've wanted that tape? Stefanov. It's evidence connecting him to the murder of my parents. He would've wanted to make sure it never fell into my hands. I'd bet my right arm that Stefanov ordered Besov to threaten Pavlov for the evidence. The minute Stefanov had the file, he killed Pavlov. Now he's getting rid of Besov, and then me. Nice and clean.

One question remains. How did Stefanov find out who I am? Volkov is a common surname in Russia, and Alexander is a popular first name. After I dodged the system, there's no way he could've kept track of me. If he had, he would've killed me a long time ago. No, he must've found out recently that I'm the son of the couple he killed in cold blood, not long before Besov took that shot at me. I imagine his surprise when he discovered I didn't die in the system after all. It must've been his worst nightmare come true, learning that I've become one of the most powerful men in this country. He knew that if I ever found out about the murder, I'd come after him with everything I've got.

The cold rage doesn't show in my voice as I get to my feet, grab my phone, and dial Igor. "It's time," I say when he picks up. "We're going in."

"Don't you want to wait for Stefanov to make the first move?" he asks.

"It's no longer necessary." I walk from the office with long strides. "I got the information I wanted."

"I'll brief the men," he says with resignation.

I hurry to the back of the house, taking the shortest route to the barracks to weapon up, and nearly knock Katerina off her feet as she comes out of the kitchen with a mug in her hand. I grip her elbows to steady her, making sure I haven't accidentally burned her with the hot liquid.

"Alex," she exclaims as she stares up at my face. "What's wrong?"

"Nothing," I say, moving her aside. "Stay in the house. No walks in the garden today. I'll be back in a few hours."

"Alex," she says again, leaving the mug on a hallway table to run after me.

I don't slow my stride. "Katerina, not now, please."

Tima looks up from the stove, his face serious for once.

Taking Katerina's arm, I lead her back to the kitchen. "I have things to prepare, and I don't need you in the middle of it." Cupping her jaw, I plant a chaste kiss on her lips. "Now be a good girl for me."

She blinks, watching me with slightly parted lips and a frown as I turn on my heel, but I can't worry about her now.

Stefanov's time on Earth has come to an end. He will cry for his mother before I'm done with him.

31

KATE

"Wait," I call, going after Alex again.

"For crying out loud, Katerina," he all but growls. "Go to our room and stay there."

Catching up with him, I grab his arm. "Tell me what's wrong."

He spins around and says with narrowed eyes, "Don't make me tell you twice. If you can't follow the order, I'll lock you in there myself."

He'll what? This is taking the game to a new low.

I pull my back straight. "*Your* room, you mean, because it's never been *ours*."

He casts a glance at Leonid, who passes us in the hallway with brisk steps. When Leonid is out of earshot, Alex says in a low voice, "I don't have time for word games." Pulling free from my grasp, he continues on his way.

I jog ahead and stop in the doorframe of the kitchen,

blocking his way. "If you're planning on leaving this house, you'll have to go through me first."

"Katerina." He clenches his jaw. "I'm not going to lay a hand on you with force, so please step aside."

When I don't move, he reverses direction, heading for the front of the house.

I stand frozen to the spot, gaping. What's gotten into him? I understand that he's under enormous stress, but that's not a reason to behave like a jerk. I want answers, but now is obviously not the time to press him.

Dragging in a few deep breaths, I bite my tongue and march to the stairs as Alex crosses the foyer. Just as I reach the bottom of the staircase, the door flings open and Igor enters. Alex pauses in his stride.

"You have visitors," Igor says, closing the door behind him. "Mikhail and Dania are at the gate."

Alex pinches the bridge of his nose and tilts his face to the ceiling. "Fuck. What shitty timing."

Igor shifts his weight. "Shall I tell them to come back later?"

Alex blows out a sigh before facing Igor again. "No." His jaw bunches as he looks at the door as if he can see through it. "Mikhail will consider turning them away an insult. Let them in." Looking at me from over his shoulder, he tells me with a tight expression, "You'd better hang around for a while longer before you go to *our* room."

I ball my hands into fists. I'm getting tired of being treated like Alex's subordinate. He may be one of the most powerful men in the world, a self-made oligarch, but I'm still my own person. I've worked hard for my independence and confidence. I won't let him undermine those qualities just because he has more power than I do.

Before I can open my mouth to argue, Igor opens the door, revealing four cars pulling up in the driveway. Like us, Mikhail and Dania travel with bodyguards. A man exits the first car to open the back door of the second vehicle. A slender, pale leg is exposed as Dania gets out, her skirt riding a little too high. She unfolds her body gracefully and brushes a hand over her hip to straighten her skirt. Dressed in a red figure-hugging two-piece with matching heels and a fur coat draped over her shoulders, she's the epitome of elegance. Her stance is regal as she waits for her father to come around the car. Surrounded by men in black combat gear with caps depicting a labyrinth logo, which I presume to be Mikhail's emblem, they make their way to the door.

It's too late to escape, not that I'd leave her alone with Alex. I trust her as far as I can throw her. Her bathroom speech still rings clear in my mind.

Alex extends a hand when Mikhail reaches him. Except for the stiffness of his shoulders, he doesn't betray his stress. His face is composed and his manner controlled—a practiced mask. "Mikhail. This is an unexpected surprise."

Three guards stay outside. Four step inside the house before Igor closes the door. They stand at attention near the entryway, blending in with the furniture.

Mikhail shakes Alex's hand. "You couldn't make it to dinner, and we haven't heard from you since." His lips tilt as he casts a sideway glance at his daughter. "Dania insisted we check on you. She was worried." Dipping his chin, he studies Alex. "We both were."

"We were in the States," Alex says. "I told you."

"Yes, yes." Mikhail pulls off his leather gloves. "However, you didn't tell me that you're back."

Lena appears on cue, rushing across the foyer to take Mikhail's gloves and coat.

"Dania," Alex says, acknowledging her with a nod, but he doesn't kiss her cheek when she tilts up her face.

I don't miss the minute tightening of her eyes.

"I hope you don't mind the uninvited visit," she says, smiling sweetly up at Alex.

"Not at all," Alex says, returning her smile. It doesn't reach his eyes. "You remember Katerina."

Dania and Mikhail turn their attention to me.

Mikhail gives me a critical once-over, taking in my over-sized off-the-shoulder sweater and leggings. "Of course. How are you, Kate?"

Lifting my chin, I walk over with a straight back. "I'm good, thank you for asking. How about you?"

Raising his arms, he says with a condescending tilt of his lips, "As you can see."

"It's lovely to run into you again," Dania says to me. "You look…" She trails a gaze over me. "Nice?"

"Thank you," I say, matching her sugar-sweet tone. "You look… formal? Are you on your way to an event?"

Lena, who's taking Dania's coat, smothers a snort. When Alex gives her a hard look, she quickly busies herself with hanging the coat in the closet.

Dania chuckles. "This is my day wear, darling."

Alex holds out an arm, indicating the formal lounge. "Shall we?"

He leads the way.

Looking around, Dania falls in behind him. "Not much has changed around here. It's about time a woman redecorated this stuffy old place."

"Dania," Mikhail says with reprimand. "Alex will think you're insulting his taste."

"I know Alex's taste," she says, swaying her hips as she follows him into the lounge. "It's modern, like his house in New York."

The jab hits me hard, just as she intended. It's meant as a reminder that she's seen the inside of his house, and more specifically, the inside of his bedroom. It was before he knew me, but still. If I could claw her eyes out right now, I would.

"Would you like a drink?" Alex asks, motioning for them to take a seat on the sofa. "Vodka?"

"Tea for me, if you don't mind," Dania says, sitting down next to her father. "I'm parched."

Alex takes a seat on the couch and pulls me down with him. To Lena, who stands in the doorframe with her hands folded in front of her, he says, "Tea and vodka, please." Looking at me, he asks, "What would you like, Katyusha?"

"Tea is fine, thank you," I say.

"You know which tea I like, Lena," Dania says. "That lovely licorice and verbena homemade brew of yours."

"Yes, ma'am," Lena says before leaving the room.

Dania addresses me. "Tell us about your trip to the States."

Not in the mood to discuss my family or personal life with them, I answer vaguely, "It was great."

Alex stretches his arm across the backrest and brushes a finger over the naked skin of my exposed shoulder. "Too short, I'm afraid."

We make small talk for another few minutes, and then the discussion turns to business, which excludes me from the conversation.

Lena arrives with a tray that she puts on the coffee table.

She pours herbal tea from a small porcelain teapot for Dania and offers me a cup of Earl Grey. After serving everyone a slice of Tima's almond cake, she leaves.

Alex pours the vodka and hands Mikhail a glass. It seems early for drinking hard liquor, but I know it's a Russian custom. Mikhail drones on about the business while we finish our tea. He's in the middle of a sentence when Dania interrupts him by standing abruptly.

Placing a hand over her stomach, she says, "I don't feel well. Kate, can you please accompany me to the bathroom?"

"Of course," I say, already on my feet.

The men stand, their brows pleated.

"Shall I call a doctor?" Mikhail asks.

"It's just a little nausea, Papa."

I rush after Dania as she hurries to the door.

"Katerina is a nurse," Alex says. "She'll let us know if we need to call."

Dania knows her way around the house. She runs for the guest bathroom, banging the door against the wall as she opens it.

I follow and close the door for privacy. Her face is pale and sweat beads on her forehead. She looks like she's on the verge of vomiting. Just in case, I open the toilet lid.

"How do you feel?" I ask. "Only nauseated or do you also have stomach cramps?"

"Listen to me," she says, startling me by grabbing my shoulders. She continues in an urgent tone. "We don't have much time. In a moment, I'm going to be sick. *Really* sick."

I lean away, taking in her feverish face. "What are you talking about?"

"The tea. Lena slipped something into it."

"What?" I exclaim.

She gives me a shake. "Listen to me. This is your only chance to escape." She tips her chin toward the toilet stall. "There's a bag behind the door. Get changed. Soon, there will be mayhem. It'll look as if I'm dying. They'll think it's poisoning. My father is going to rush me to the hospital. I'll get into the car with him. While everyone is distracted, get into the second car. My bodyguard is the driver. Lie down in the back. He'll take you to the airport. Lena packed you a bag. It's already inside the trunk with money and a false passport."

Too shocked to find words, I can only stare at her.

"It's your only chance of getting away," she says, letting go of my shoulders. "I'm not going to poison myself twice for you."

"What about you?" I ask, battling to process what's happening. "What did Lena give you?"

"Don't worry about me," she says, wiping her brow with the back of her hand. "It was a small dose. I'll survive."

"I can't believe you did this," I say, shaking from head to toe. "It's so dangerous and irresponsible."

"Don't let it be for nothing." She pushes me toward the toilet. "Go. Hurry. We're running out of time." When I don't move, she says, "It's now or never, Kate. Do you understand what I'm saying?"

My brain goes into shutdown mode, even as my training dictates that I assist her. When her shoulders curl inward and her chest heaves, I take her arm.

"Come," I say, leading her to the toilet. "I'm calling Alex."

She shoves me away. "Take the fucking bag, Kate. Don't be an idiot."

I look at the bag in the corner behind the door. "How did it get here?"

"My bodyguard smuggled it to Lena," she says, kneeling in front of the toilet. "Does it fucking matter how it got there?"

Brushing her hair over her shoulder, I say, "I can't just leave you like this."

She utters a laugh. "I'll have enough people worrying about me. All you—" Violent retching cuts the rest of her sentence short.

I hold her hair as she empties her stomach. When the worst of it is over, I run for the door.

A knock falls on it as I'm about to reach for the handle.

"Katerina?" Alex calls. "Is everything all right?"

"No," I say, opening the door.

Alex and Mikhail stand on the threshold, their faces tense with worry.

"It looks like poison," I say in a shaky voice. "She needs to get to a hospital."

"Breakfast, Papa," Dania says meekly from the toilet. "*Blini.*"

Mikhail utters a string of expletives.

Alex says tersely, "I'll call an ambulance."

"No." Another heave racks Dania's body. Sucking in a breath, she says, "I want you to take me, Papa. I don't trust the ambulance."

"Tell your driver to start the engine," Alex says to Mikhail. "I'll tell my men to make sure the roads are clear. You'd better call home on your way and take samples of the breakfast. Maybe sweep the kitchen."

Mikhail gives a nod before running down the hallway.

"Can you hold down the fort here while I check on security?" Alex asks me, his words quiet but rushed. "I'll send Igor to carry Dania to the car."

My stomach twists as I nod. "Of course."

Offering me a fleeting smile of gratitude, he follows on Mikhail's heels.

Another bout of vomiting leaves Dania slumped over the toilet. There's not much I can do for her other than holding her hair out of her face. If the dose of poison she took isn't lethal, it'll work itself out of her system in a few hours. However, they'll still have to monitor her at the hospital to check for organ or nervous system damage. They'll probably pump her stomach to be on the safe side and hook her up to a glucose IV while running tests. After overnight observation, they'll discharge her and send her home. Her life will return to normal, and her suffering will have been wasted.

I look between her and the bag.

"Fuck you, Kate," she says, her chest rising and falling with rapid breaths. "I'll kill you if I went through this for nothing."

Shit. I don't know what to do. She's right about one thing. This is my only chance. There won't be another opportunity. The house is in chaos and I'm caught in the maelstrom, forced to make a rash decision.

Instinct kicks in, survival mode taking over. I drag the bag from behind the door to the vanity area of the bathroom. My hands shake as I pull down the zipper and take out a black T-shirt, a puffy jacket, a pair of combat pants, and a cap with a labyrinth logo.

Am I really doing this? I'm not thinking logically any longer. Pure adrenaline dictates my behavior. I yank off my sweater and drag the T-shirt over my head. I don't bother to remove my leggings. I only kick off my sneakers before pulling on the too-big combat pants. I'm in the middle of bundling my hair under the cap when the door swings inward.

Fright freezes me in place. If Alex catches me, I don't know what he'll do to me. I only know that it's too late. I'm guilty. I've been from the moment I unzipped the bag.

Lena steps into the bathroom.

I blow out a breath, nearly collapsing with relief.

"Come on," Lena says, taking a pair of combat boots from the bag. "Igor is on his way. You have to hurry." She hands me the boots and shoves my sweater and sneakers into the bag. "Put them on in the next room. I'll hide your clothes and take care of Dania."

I hesitate.

"Now, Kate," Lena says in a stern voice, prompting me to action.

I act on autopilot, taking the boots and peering around the open door. There's a commotion in the foyer, men running in every direction. The front door stands open. Mikhail is in the entrance, pulling on his coat while barking something in Russian to one of his men. Alex has his phone pressed to his ear, presumably alerting the security at Mikhail's house, or maybe he's warning the hospital of Dania's arrival.

Quietly, I slip around the frame and enter the deserted summer lounge next to the bathroom. It's one of the many rooms we don't use. I press my back against the wall behind the door, taking a deep breath as footsteps fall hard in the hallway. Scraping together all the courage I possess, I put on the boots. My hands tremble so much when I tie the laces that the effort is messy at best.

Igor's voice booms from the bathroom next door. He's saying something in Russian. Lena replies. Ducking my head, I hide my face behind the visor of the cap and scoot around the frame. My heart beats with deafening thumps in my chest as I walk briskly down the hallway.

Caught up in the havoc, no one looks up as I fall in line with two men carrying rifles. Igor comes out of the bathroom, carrying Dania in his arms. Alex ends his phone call and hurries toward them. Mikhail follows.

I use the opportunity to slip through the front door. Alex's men are carrying metal detectors and guns inside. After what's happened, Alex will make sure our security hasn't been breached. I walk toward the cars in the driveway, my heart threatening to burst from my chest with every step I take. It's too late to turn back. By taking action, I'm collaborating with Dania. Alex may even think I concocted this plan, but there's no time to ponder the possible consequences. There's only one way forward, and it's getting out of here. I'll figure out the rest when I'm on American soil.

The back door of the second car is open. The man next to the car gives an almost undetectable nod as he meets my gaze. I glance over my shoulder. No one is watching. I slide into the back, facing straight ahead. The man shuts the door. When nobody shouts and nothing happens, I slide down the seat and lie down flat. There's a blanket on the floor sticking out from under the passenger seat. I cover myself, not daring to breathe.

Mikhail's voice reaches me in my hiding place. Footsteps crunch on the gravel. When my lungs start burning, I realize I've been holding my breath. I inhale the scent of the leather seat and a feminine perfume that sticks to the cashmere blanket. The wool tents slightly with my exhale, the scratchy fibers tickling my nose.

Don't sneeze, Kate. Please, don't sneeze.

The engine starts. The car rolls forward slowly. I count the seconds. After fifteen beats, we pick up speed. The faster we go, the more my pulse quickens.

The man says something in Russian.

Syad', it sounds like. *Get up* or *sit up*.

Pushing the blanket aside, I stare at the sky through the window. The day is overcast. It looks as if it's going to snow. I straighten. We're still in the city, in a neighborhood I don't recognize, but there's a signpost with an airplane symbol up ahead.

I glance through the back window. We're not the only car on the road, but I don't see any of Alex's familiar black cars. We're not being chased.

The interior of the car is warm and the jacket I'm wearing is thick, but I still shiver. Instead of relief, an inexplicable sense of loss assaults me. I feel adrift. Lost. Torn and confused. I've yet to process what I've done. It was a spur-of-the-moment decision, not something I planned. And the stress is far from over. Nothing's resolved until I set foot in that plane. At that point, I'll be free. That's what I have to focus on.

Holy shit.

Dania did it.

I made it.

I rub my palms over my face. I still can't believe I'm out of Alex's stronghold.

Turning my face toward the window, I stare out with an unseeing gaze. My thoughts are focused on the future, on what I'll do when I get home. I'll let Alex know I'm safe. He deserves that much. But I'll make it clear that I'm not prepared to be a prisoner any longer. While he deals with his assassin, I'll disappear, take some time to think everything through. In the meantime, I'm not going to dwell on why Dania helped me. She didn't do it for selfless reasons, that's for sure.

The driver steps on the gas as we approach a traffic light.

It's green for us. A pair of headlights advances from the crossing, heading toward the red light, but the car doesn't slow down.

Blinking, I frown. Too late, I realize he's not going to stop.

"Look out," I yell, trying to warn the driver.

He yanks the wheel to the right.

The car smashes into us from the side, hitting the passenger door in the front. The airbags pop. Metal crunches and glass cracks as the momentum pushes us over the tarmac. My body is thrown violently against the door as our car folds around a lamppost.

Every bone in my body aches as I blink in shock, struggling to process what's happened. The driver of the car who hit us gets out. He walks around our car toward the driver's side. The window has exploded from the impact. The lamppost obstructs the door, and the other side of the car is banged in so badly that I'm not sure he'll be able to open the door. He'll have to call the fire brigade to cut us out.

He stops in front of the broken window.

"Help us," I croak, wiping away something wet that runs over my cheek. I'm trembling all over, the cold from the outside somehow already inside my body, the chill encasing my insides, scrambling my thoughts.

He offers me a smile. Taking a gun with a silencer screwed onto the barrel from under his coat, he pushes the gun against the airbag and fires a shot. A scream catches in my throat. A car pulls up next to us, presumably to offer assistance, but the driver's eyes go wide when he sees the gun. He pulls off without a word.

I scoot to the other side, yanking on the door with shaking hands, but it's stuck.

The man puts two fingers on the driver's neck, checking for a pulse.

Oh God. Maybe he just shot the airbag to deflate it.

I raise my hands, my stomach roiling with a mixture of terror and hope. "Please." Does the man even understand English? "Please, don't hurt us."

Aiming the barrel at the driver's temple, the man pulls the trigger.

32

ALEX

*I*gor takes the front steps two at a time and stops next to me where I stand on the porch. Flanked by Dimitri and Leonid, we watch Mikhail and his entourage leave.

"Poisoning?" Leonid says. "Who would want to poison Dania Turgeneva?"

The cars clear the gates. I follow their speedy departure with a thoughtful gaze. "Whoever he is, he's a dead man."

"You bet." Dimitri shakes his head. "No one messes with Mikhail's princess. I can't believe someone was so stupid."

"What about the operation?" Igor asks. "Do we still move out?"

"No." I shove my hands into my pockets. "Let's wait until there's news about Dania. It would be disrespectful to launch a full-blown war if Mikhail's daughter is dying. We should wait until Mikhail knows more about the poisoning and how it happened."

"What about Kate?" Igor's brows pull together. "Does she have any idea what kind of poison it may be?"

"We haven't had time to speak yet," I say. "Keep alert and double the guards around the house. Let me know if you pick up anything on satellite. I'm going to talk to Katerina."

The men nod in unison. I leave them in charge of the security and go back inside the house. The door clicks shut behind me, the electronic pad beeping as the lock activates. Two men guard the door. Another stands near the hallway.

"Anything?" I ask as I approach him.

"No, sir," he says, looking straight ahead. "The downstairs rooms are clear. We're checking upstairs as we speak."

I have the house swept on a weekly basis and immediately after I've had visitors. I trust Mikhail, but it can't hurt to be cautious. Especially in light of what has transpired.

Making my way past him, I go to the guest bathroom. A smell of bleach hangs in the air. Lena is mopping the floor. She looks up when I stop in the doorframe.

"Have you seen Katerina?" I ask.

"No, sir. Maybe she went upstairs."

On my way to the lounge, I check the library and my study. Both rooms are deserted. The lounge is empty. I try the room Igor converted into a makeshift clinic, but when I don't find her there either, I make my way upstairs.

The house is big. Three men are sweeping the second floor. I pass them in the hallway and open *our* bedroom door.

Empty.

Crossing the floor with big strides, I enter the dressing room.

No sign of her.

I knock on the bathroom door. "Katerina?"

No reply.

A bad feeling grows in the pit of my stomach. I open the door, already knowing what I'll find.

Nothing. No one.

Fuck.

I yank my phone from my pocket and dial Igor, already running for the stairs. When he picks up, I bark out, "Katerina is gone. Search the house, the garden, and the barracks."

"Yes, sir."

"You," I say, pointing at one of the men guarding the front door.

He jumps to attention.

"Did Miss Morrell leave the house after Mr. Turgenev and me?"

"No, sir."

"Fuck," I mutter under my breath, racing for the kitchen.

"What's going on?" Tima asks when I skid to a stop in the middle of the floor.

"Is Katerina here?"

"No," he says, frowning.

Still clutching my phone, I spear my fingers through my hair. "She's gone."

His face collapses, his eyes and mouth drawing down. "How long?"

"Not more than ten minutes."

He moves a carving knife aside and leans his palms on the counter. "She could be hiding in the house."

"I'm having the property searched."

"If she's not…" He looks at me from under his eyebrows.

"Then she slipped out while the emergency with Dania was unfolding." I feel sick merely saying those words.

"She couldn't have walked through the gates. The guards would've noticed."

I grit my teeth. "They also would've noticed if she'd gotten into one of the cars. She must be in the house."

He sucks air through his teeth.

"What?" I ask.

"If she's not in the house and nobody saw her leaving, you have to assume she left with Mikhail."

I slam a fist on the table. "Mikhail would never do that. He knows I'd kill him."

"What about Dania?" Tima asks, his eyes narrowing into slits.

"Dania was puking out her lungs."

"There's something wrong with this poisoning scenario." Straightening, he crosses his arms. "I've administered a few poisons in my day, and I can tell you that if Dania had been poisoned at breakfast, the symptoms she was having wouldn't have kicked in three hours later. They would've manifested almost straight away."

I still. "Are you saying she was poisoned here?"

"It couldn't have been the cake. Lena brought four empty plates back to the kitchen, so you all ate the cake, right? What did Dania drink or eat that no one else did?"

I slide my gaze toward the drip rack where the teacups and teapot are stacked. "Herbal tea."

The knowledge sinks into my gut like a stone. I know it instinctively as I walk to the drip rack and lift the teapot to peer inside.

"Lena washed it already," Tima says. "She cleans the porcelain with bleach to remove the tea stains."

"Thereby removing all traces of the contents inside," I say slowly, uncontrollable rage unfurling in my chest.

He gives me a level look. "Exactly."

My voice is calm, not betraying the violence flowing through my veins. "Bring her here."

Tima rounds the counter and walks down the hallway.

I dial Igor.

He answers with, "There's no sign of her yet."

"Check all the passenger manifests for domestic and international flights. I want men at every station and airport in St. Petersburg. Katerina may have left with Mikhail's entourage."

"Fuck. I'm on it."

Next, I dial Nelsky. "I want the satellite surveillance footage of my house from the last thirty minutes. Send it to my phone."

I cut the call when Tima leads Lena in by her arm.

She yanks her bicep from his hold and lifts her chin. "Is there something I can do for you, Mr. Volkov?"

I walk to the counter. "How long have you worked for me, Lena?"

"Since you bought the house, sir."

Taking the knife Tima was using, I study the blade in the light. "That makes it quite a few years."

"Yes, sir," she says, looking down her nose at Tima, who stands wide-legged in front of her, effectively blocking her path should she get it into her head to run.

"Are you loyal, Lena?"

She meets my gaze head-on. "Yes, sir."

"To whom?" I ask, wiping the knife on my sleeve.

She swallows visibly.

I approach her. "Were you loyal to the previous owners?"

"I was, sir," she says with a tremor in her voice.

"Why?" I ask, circling her.

"Sir?"

"Why?" I repeat, placing emphasis on the word. "What made you loyal to them?"

She blinks. "They were of royal descent. They were suitable inhabitants for this house."

I raise a brow. "And I'm not?"

She utters an uncomfortable laugh. "You're the new owner, sir."

Stopping in front of her, I look her dead in the eye. "Did you poison Dania?"

She blinks.

My patience is running low. "Did you or did you not put poison in her tea?"

No reply.

She utters a shriek when I fist my hand in her hair and push her to her knees. Stepping behind her, I pull back her head and press the sharp edge of the blade against her neck.

"Answer me, Lena, or I swear I'll gut you like a pig."

She grips my forearm and tries to pull it away. "Please, Mr. Volkov."

"Answer me. You know I never bluff."

"It was D-Dania's idea," she stutters out, spittle flying. "She told me to put the wormwood in her tea."

"Why?" I ask, pressing the blade until I draw a thin line of blood.

"Please..." Her throat works with a swallow, tears spilling down her cheeks. "She wanted to help Miss Morrell escape."

Rage blurs her features in my vision. "Did Katerina ask Dania for help?"

"I d-don't know," she blubbers.

I give her hair a yank. "Why did you do it?"

Tima regards her with disdain, his face pulled into an expression of disgust. "Because she's a royalist."

"Because Miss Turgeneva is a suitable mistress for this house," she cries out. "Please, I only wanted what's best!"

I let her go with a shove. "Lock her in the summer lounge. Take her phone and make sure she doesn't leave the room."

"With pleasure," Tima says as he grips her arm and pulls her to her feet.

I leave the task in Tima's capable hands and summon Yuri, Igor, and Leonid. On my way to the car, I inform Dimitri of the situation and put him in charge of the security at the house.

Leonid checks the GPS to find us the least congested route to the hospital while I dial Mikhail and tell him what I've learned.

We make it to the ER in record time. Mikhail waits outside Dania's private room, his cheeks colorless.

"How is she?" I ask, tilting my head toward the door.

"She'll be fine," he says with a troubled expression. "Let's not talk in the corridor. Best if we go inside."

Dania lies pale against the white sheets, her dark hair splayed over the pillow. She pushes up on her elbows when my men and I enter and her father closes the door.

"Alex," she says with surprise. "How nice of you to check on me."

I clench my jaw. "Cut the bullshit, Dania. Lena told me everything."

Her gaze turns shuttered. "I don't know what you're talking about."

I level a dark look at Mikhail.

"Dania," he says, "if you got yourself poisoned on purpose to help Katerina escape, you'd better tell us now."

"Papa!" She gapes at him. "Do you think I'd do this to myself?"

"I love you, princess, but this time you've gone too far. There's not a trace of poison in our house." He adds in an angry voice, "Which means you lied to me."

"Papa, I don't—"

He holds up a hand. "You've dishonored me and put a stain on our family name. If you don't tell the truth, you leave me no choice but to disown you. You'll be a nobody, out on the street alone, with no one to protect you and not a penny to your name."

A look of hurt flashes across her face. "Papa, please. You're the only one I have. Mama doesn't—"

"The truth, Dania, and think carefully before you open your mouth and tell another lie," Mikhail says.

Folding her hands on top of the covers, she looks desperately between me and her father.

"Tell us what happened," Mikhail says, "and I'll take responsibility for your actions."

She looks at the window.

"Dania," I say, my tone harsh. "You have no idea what you've done. Katerina's life could be in danger this very minute."

When she still doesn't say anything, I walk to the door. "So be it. You've made your choice."

"Wait," she calls, glancing at me from under her lashes.

I pause.

"Fine. I told Lena to put a few drops of steam-distilled oil of wormwood in my tea. I was only trying to help Katerina." She gives her father an imploring look. "You have to believe me, Papa."

Mikhail utters a cussword. Dania jumps when he kicks the visitor's chair.

"How did you do it?" he asks with flaring nostrils.

"My bodyguard smuggled a uniform to Lena when we arrived at Alex's house. Kate changed in the bathroom. While everyone was distracted, she got into the car my bodyguard was driving."

I clench my hands so hard my knuckles make a cracking sound. "Where did he take her?"

She drops her gaze to her hands. "To the airport."

I grab my phone from my pocket, dialing Nelsky as I grit out, "Without a passport?"

Dania doesn't look at me. "I arranged for a false passport. Lena packed her a bag."

"Where is she flying to?" I demand.

"America, I assume," Dania says, finally meeting my gaze. "I left enough money in the bag to buy a ticket to anywhere."

"Fuck," I say, dragging a hand over my face.

"Our men are at the airport," Igor says, his phone already in his hand. "I'll let them know."

"This was a premeditated affair," Mikhail says through thin lips, looking at his daughter with disappointment.

Nelsky answers in a high-pitched tone. "Sir?"

"She's at the airport. Destination unknown." I don't elaborate. He knows what to do.

"I know my apology can't make up for what Dania has done," Mikhail says, turning toward me. "I'll give you access to all of my resources. I'll do everything in my power to help you find her. Rest assured, Dania will be appropriately punished." His gaze hardens. "As for Lena, I trust you'll deal with her."

My phone pings with a notification. I check the message. It's an update from Nelsky. The team is checking the satellite footage of the roads leading from my residence to the airport, but they haven't found anything yet.

I'm shaking with both anger and fear. I feel like strangling Dania and watching the life bleed from her eyes.

"If anything happens to Katerina," I say to Dania in a cold, dangerously quiet tone, "I will hold you responsible."

"Alex." Mikhail splays his hands. "Tell me what I can do to help."

"Nothing for now," I bite out, leaving the room and slamming the door behind me.

I'm halfway down the corridor before Leonid and Igor catch up.

"We'll find her," Leonid says. "If she's on her way to the airport, she won't get far. You have enough connections to prevent the plane from taking off."

Yes, I do. But even if she's already in the air, I'll find her, and when I do, there will be hell to pay.

33

KATE

$\mathcal{M}$y mouth is dry when I wake up. It takes a moment to focus my eyes. The room is unfamiliar. An overhead bulb throws light on the concrete walls and floor. The only furniture is the bed I'm lying on.

My stomach twists. What happened? Where am I?

I try to sit up, but my arms are stuck above my head. I can't move them. Craning my neck, I take in the handcuffs around my wrists.

In a flash, it all comes back—the accident, the man who shot Dania's driver and then injected me with something.

My pulse speeds up. What does he want from me? Either he's kidnapped me for ransom, or he's the man who wants Alex dead. If the latter is the case, I don't have to wonder hard why he took me. A shiver runs over my body.

Who is he? Being in the dark only makes my situation worse. Knowledge is power. Right now, I have no power. All I have left is control. Losing my calm isn't an option. I have to breathe and keep a level head to figure out a way to escape.

Deep breaths, Kate. In and out. Focus.

The sound of a key scraping in a lock comes from the other side of the door. I strain my neck for a visual to assess the danger. The door swings open, and a man I don't recognize enters. A waistcoat stretches over his corpulent torso. Thinning gray hair frames his round face. He watches me with narrowed eyes as he advances to the bed.

Whoever he is, this man is evil. It's evident in the excitement that flashes across his ugly features as he takes in my restrained position. I swallow hard, trying to hide my fear.

Towering over me, he says in a thick Russian accent, "You must wonder what you're doing here."

No longer able to support the weight of my head with my neck muscles, I let my head fall back on the mattress. "The question has crossed my mind."

He seems amused. "I have to congratulate you. You're very calm for someone in your situation."

I'm not, but I'm glad he thinks so. "Who are you? Where am I?"

"Vladimir Stefanov." He sits down on the edge of the bed. "You're a guest in my house."

I scoot to the other side of the mattress, as far away from him as possible, as more dread fills my veins. I've heard the name before. Alex told me it was Vladimir Stefanov who'd hired the man to abduct me in New York. "What do want from me?"

"You're going to bring me Alex Volkov."

Even though it was the answer I expected, I go cold. "How?"

"A trade." He looks pleased with himself. "You for him."

My mouth goes dry. "How do you know Alex will do it? Who says he even cares that much about me?"

Stefanov chuckles. "Oh, he does. Why else did he come running to Russia to protect you when my hitman threatened your life?"

I suck in a breath. "My hospital key card. That was your doing."

"Yes," he drawls.

"Who took it?"

He raises a brow. "Remember Ivan Besov?"

It takes a moment before I place the name. When it comes back to me, I exclaim, "The man who fractured his wrist?"

"You were lucky that he slipped in the snow." Stefanov folds his hands over his stomach. "That part wasn't planned."

I go even colder as my suspicion is confirmed. When the attempt to kidnap me from the alley failed, this man, Stefanov, sent Besov to snatch me on my way to work.

How did Stefanov know I was on my way to the airport? My stomach turns over. Did Dania sell me out?

"How did you find me?" I ask in an unsteady voice. "Who told you where I was headed?"

"One of my men was watching Volkov's house from a building across the river. He spotted a small person getting into the back of a car and managed to take a photo. Imagine my surprise when it turned out to be you."

"You had us followed." Anger mixes with my fear. "You ordered the man who took me to crash into our car. We could've died in that accident." My voice escalates in volume. "He shot the driver."

Stefanov shrugs. "You didn't die."

"I'm an American citizen," I say, my heart thumping with a

wild beat in my chest. "You can't just kidnap me in broad daylight."

"Maybe not in America." He grins. "But this is Russia."

My pulse goes into overdrive. "Alex won't let you get away with this."

"He will. This time, I'm not planning on failing."

Breathless with fright, I ask, "How is this supposed to work? What happens now?"

"Now we wait for Alex to arrive. And then…" He pushes a finger against his temple and makes as if to pull a trigger with his thumb. "Bam."

It takes everything I have to maintain my pseudo-calm. "Why? Why do you want Alex dead? What do you want? Money?"

He gets to his feet. "If it were about money, I could've simply traded you."

"Wait," I say as he walks to the door, but he leaves without sparing me another glance.

Horror washes over me as the situation becomes terribly clear.

Alex and I aren't leaving here alive.

34

ALEX

*I*t's been an hour since I left the hospital, and there's still no news about Katerina's whereabouts. I'm pacing my study, checking my email and phone every few seconds. The lunch Tima brought stands untouched on my desk. Mikhail won't let Dania's interference go unpunished, but I feel like killing her all the same. I'm still undecided about what to do with Lena.

A knock falls on the door. Leonid enters, his face somber.

"Any news?" I ask.

He shakes his head. "What about Nelsky?"

My phone vibrates in my pocket. I take it out and look at the screen. I've been sending business-related calls to my voicemail, preferring to keep the line open in case there's an update from one of my men.

My heartbeat picks up as I register the name on the screen.

"Have they found—" Leonid continues.

I hold up a hand to silence him. "It's Igor."

Leonid's expression goes tense, reflecting what I feel inside.

I swipe the answer button and put the phone on speaker. "Tell me you have news."

"She's not at the airport," Igor says in a rushed tone. "No one matching her description has checked in."

I assume she would've changed into normal clothes before entering the airport building. We don't know what she's wearing, but my men have her passport photo on their phones. They're questioning both passengers and airport staff, asking if anyone has seen the woman in the photograph.

"What about the parking lots?" I ask harshly.

"There was no sign of Mikhail's car." He pauses. "We did, however, find the driver."

I tighten my grip on the phone. "Dania's bodyguard?"

"Yes."

Exchanging a look with Leonid, I ask, "Where?"

"At the morgue."

My heart slams to a stop.

Leonid moves closer, his troubled look intensifying.

"I'm here now with one of Mikhail's men," Igor continues. "He identified the body."

My order is brusque. "Tell me what happened."

"Car accident, but that's not the cause of death. Someone popped him in the head."

"Fuck." Ice fills my stomach. This is my worst nightmare come true. If anything has happened to Katerina... I can't even think it. Rage burns like acid in my chest. "Any sign of Katerina?"

"No," he says with regret. "But we did find the bag with the clothes, money, and passport Dania had mentioned in the trunk."

Dania wasn't lying. My kiska was in that car.

"What about satellite footage?" I ask, clenching the phone hard. "Are there any witnesses to the accident?"

"No one reported the accident when it happened," Igor says. "A good half hour passed before someone called it in."

"Inform Nelsky." Covering the microphone with a hand, I direct the order to Leonid. "I want that satellite feed. Now."

He hurries to the door. "I'll let him know."

"Comb the area where the accident took place," I tell Igor. "Tell our men to start searching in a twenty-kilometer radius. Knock on every door and ask every person living in that vicinity if anyone has seen something. Don't offer money. They may spew bullshit just to get the reward. Use fear instead." It's faster.

"Got it," he says and hangs up.

I shut my eyes briefly, praying I find Katerina before I have to make a call to Laura that will destroy her as surely as it will destroy me.

My phone pings a second later. I look at the screen, but it's not the satellite recording that I'm expecting from Nelsky. It's an image of Katerina lying on a cot in a cell, handcuffed to the bedframe. The text message is signed by Vladimir Stefanov.

Motherfucker.

Fury like I've never experienced rushes through my veins, even as fear rips through me, cold and terrifying.

Leonid walks back into the room. "Nelsky says you'll have the footage in five minutes." One look at my face makes him stop in his tracks. "What's wrong?"

I turn the screen of my phone toward him, shaking with rage as I show him the image.

He blanches. "Fuck."

"Weapon up." I clench my teeth so hard it feels as if my jaw is about to unhinge. "We're going after Stefanov. I'm bringing her back."

He pushes a hand on my chest as I take a step to the door. "It's a trap."

I grip his wrist and move his hand away. "Of course it's a fucking trap."

"Mr. Volkov," he says carefully, holding my gaze. "You have to consider the fact that she may already be dead."

Before he can blink, I grab him by the lapels of his jacket and smash his body against the wall. "She's alive and well." I need to believe that.

"For now, maybe," he says, unfazed by the violence. "Once Stefanov has you, he won't need her any longer. If we launch an attack on his house, what guarantee do you have that Stefanov won't slit her throat? He's not going to wave a white flag and simply hand her over. If he thinks he's going to lose, he'd rather take her with him to the grave than give her back to you."

That's not what I have in mind. I'm not going in guns blazing while hoping for the best.

Leonid must see the intention in my eyes because his jaw goes slack.

"You're going to suggest a trade," he says, sounding flabbergasted. "Your life for Kate's."

"What else?" I growl, letting him go with a shove.

"Think about it," he says, coming after me as I make my way down the hallway. "That's what Stefanov expects you to do. That's what he wants."

"Then that's what he'll get."

I send a text message to Dimitri, telling him to round up the men, all fucking two hundred of them. Then I fire off a message to Igor to bring him up to scratch and to inform him that our rendezvous point is Stefanov's house.

Outside, Yuri leans against the hood of my car. He straightens when I approach. I check that my gun is loaded and get into the car.

"Mr. Volkov," Leonid says.

I slam the door, cutting off further conversation.

Pounding a hand against his forehead, Leonid paces next to the car.

I wind down the window. "Are you coming or what?"

He drops his hand on his hip, regarding me with a defeated look. "I work for you because I respect you. We all do—Igor, Dimitri, and every guard in your employ."

"Are you getting sentimental on me?" I ask with a cold smile.

"None of us is the leader you are. That's why you're the boss. That's why we follow your orders. If you die, everything you've built will be wasted."

It'll go to Katerina. I've already set it up with my lawyer. Not that I have any intention of making it easy for Stefanov. "I'm leaving. If you're coming, get in. If not, it was good to know you, my friend."

With a curse, he gets into the front passenger seat.

Yuri starts the engine. We don't speak during the ride. I stare through the window at the familiar landscape, but inside, my blood is boiling.

On the way, I get the satellite feed from Nelsky on my phone. I watch the accident happen with balled hands, from the point when the fucker hits their car to where he carries an unconscious Katerina to a truck parked half a block down the road. From there, he drives straight to Stefanov's house.

"*Svoloch*," I mutter under my breath, squeezing the phone so hard the plastic casing cracks down the middle.

"We're here," Leonid says, pulling my attention from the scene I'm replaying on my phone.

I glance up at the imposing gates of Stefanov's house. "Are the men on their way?"

"They'll be here in five minutes. They left shortly after us." His gaze is pleading. "Don't go in there alone, Mr. Volkov."

If I don't, Katerina is dead.

Not bothering to answer, I dial Stefanov.

"Volkov," Stefanov replies in a jovial voice. "I was expecting your call."

My voice is tight with repressed fury. "I want to speak to her."

"Of course you do. Hold on."

Shuffling and footsteps sound, and then her sweet voice comes on the line. "Alex?"

I sag in my seat, physically weak with relief. "Are you all right?"

A choked sob.

"I'm coming for you, Katyusha," I say, my voice harsh as I imagine what Stefanov has done or could still do to her. "Hold on for me, my love."

"Don't," she whispers. "It's a—"

"As you can see," Stefanov's voice interrupts, "she's very much alive."

I'm going to crush that motherfucker. "How do you want the trade to work?"

"Come alone, unarmed, and I'll let her go."

Leonid, who's listening in on the call, shakes his head.

"Do I have your word?" I ask.

"I swear on my mother's grave," the fat bastard says.

In that case, "I'm here."

I end the call and hand my phone and gun to Leonid.

"Mr. Volkov," Leonid says with a plea in his voice as he takes the items. "Alex."

Opening the door, I step out into the gray light of the day. The snow has lifted momentarily. An eerie quiet has dawned on the landscape.

Leonid follows suit.

Four guards armed with automatic rifles walk through the gates toward us.

The one in the front says, "You're to come unarmed. No phone."

Raising my arms, I stand waiting, giving my consent to be searched. The man who voiced the command hands his gun to the one on his left before patting me down. When he's sure I'm not wired or carrying hidden weapons, he motions for me to walk ahead.

Leonid looks on with helpless anger painted across his face.

"Don't look at me like I'm already dead," I say, lightening the mood with a smile.

He doesn't reciprocate. He follows me with his gaze the way one would stare at a funeral march.

I don't hesitate. Leonid disappears from my peripheral vision as I walk through Vladimir Stefanov's gates.

35

KATE

The door rattles as it opens. A guard steps inside. I cringe on the bed when he approaches, flattening my body on the mattress. Without looking at me, he unlocks the cuffs around my wrists and stands aside. Another guard enters with a tray that he puts on the floor. Both men leave, and a second later, the sound of the key turning in the lock echoes in the space.

Rubbing my arms to get my blood circulation going, I push to my feet. The light in the room isn't overly bright, but it reaches far enough to illuminate the contents of the tray. They brought me food—a sandwich and a glass of water.

I'm not touching it. It may be drugged. Regardless, I'm unable to eat in the state I'm in. At least Stefanov doesn't want me dead yet. Otherwise, he wouldn't have sent food. He needs to keep me alive until he's lured Alex into his trap. In the long run, I'm dead, but Alex is still free. I just hope he's clever enough not to walk into Stefanov's trap.

I look around the room for a way to escape, but the only way out is through the door. I expect it to be locked and guarded. Nevertheless, as soon as the circulation has returned to my legs, I run to the door and feel the handle. The door doesn't budge.

My gaze falls on the tray. It's metal. I could whack someone over the head with it. If I hit hard enough, I could give my victim a concussion that would cause a blackout. Knocking out a guard will win me time, but I'll need more than a metal tray if I'm to make it over the threshold where another guard will be waiting.

I look around again. If there are cameras, they're well hidden. Still, I can't take any chances. I have to assume my kidnapper is watching me. In my circumstances, an aggressive outburst will be expected behavior.

Taking aim, I kick the tray with all my might. It goes flying and hits the wall with a thwack. The plate and glass shatter against the concrete. Water drips down the gray surface and the sandwich falls open, a slice of cheese on one side and the buttered side on the floor. Glass crunches under my boots as I walk over the mess and crouch down in the middle of it. Selecting the sharpest pieces of porcelain from the broken plate, I take them discreetly and hide them behind my back. Then I retreat to the far side of the room, sit down on the floor, and wait.

When the door opens again, I'm ready. I stand up, holding the broken pieces of the plate behind my back, but instead of one guard entering to remove the spoiled food like I expected, four of them enter.

My heart hammers as I make myself small in the corner and keep quiet, trying not to attract attention to myself.

The man in the front looks at the mess on the floor before lifting his gaze to me. He speaks English with a strong accent. "That was a foolish move." His smile doesn't reach his eyes. "Who knows? It could've been your last meal."

I feel like stabbing him in the eye, but I bite my tongue and look away. I have to be patient and bide my time.

The one who addressed me stands guard as the others carry buckets and brooms inside. They throw water over the floor and scrub the mess away with the brooms. A smell of chlorine reaches my nostrils. Stefanov must be making sure no diseases break out in his prison.

Since they're not attacking me, I dare a glance at the guard who spoke English. "Where am I?" I look around. "What is this place?"

"You're in Vladimir Stefanov's house." He says it with glee, as if he wants the information to scare me.

It does. It also explains why they're cleaning up. Smells and infections spread fast.

They sweep up the broken crockery and the wasted food. When the floor is clean, they mop up the water, rinse the concrete with clean water, and leave with their buckets and brooms.

Once again, I'm alone. It's only then that I become aware of how much I'm shaking. It's a natural reaction to the shock, but I don't like it. In an effort to both calm and warm myself, I walk around and stretch my sore muscles.

My isolation doesn't last long. A sound at the door alerts me. Backing up to the wall, I grab my makeshift weapons as adrenaline floods my veins. A plan takes shape in my head. I'll ask them for a glass of water and stab whoever delivers it in the neck. I have no idea what waits behind that door, but I'll just have to take my chances.

A sliver of light falls over the floor through the crack as the door opens. I remain immobile, measuring the danger, but the man who enters isn't one of Stefanov's guards.

It's Alex.

Relief and fear war in my chest.

He stumbles as someone pushes him, and then the light from outside disappears as the door is shut.

At a loss for words, I stare at him. Despite the situation, the moment is sweet. I thought I might never see him again. In his long, tailored coat and fancy dress shoes, he looks as formidable as ever. His thick dark hair is brushed back. His long lashes dip as he takes me in from head to toe. Signs of strain are visible on his hard-featured face. His blue eyes are marred with worry lines, and the couple of days' worth of stubble that darkens his jaw sets off the paleness of his skin.

His voice is rough. "Did they hurt you?"

The rasp of that timbre is like water to my ears. "No."

He looks at me as if he may consume me. "Come here."

I don't hesitate. When he opens his arms, I lay my makeshift weapons on the floor and run into his embrace. His body is strong and warm, the heat emanating from him enveloping me. I inhale the familiar scent of cardamom as I burrow my face in the scratchy wool fabric of his coat. He lets me soak up his presence before holding me at arm's length.

He conducts another visual evaluation, scanning the length of me. "Did they touch you?"

"I'm okay." My voice is meek in the aftermath of my relief, even though that relief will be short-lived.

A muscle ticks in his jaw. "I'll kill them for taking you. I swear it on my parents' graves."

I swallow away the dryness of my throat. "Why did you come? It's a trap."

His smile is crooked. "Did you think I'd leave you here?"

Wrapping my arms around him, I press my cheek against his chest. I only give myself another second to be comforted by his presence before I pull away. "I'm sorry for running. I shouldn't have done that. Everything just happened so fast. There wasn't time to think."

A smile softens his features. "I understand why you did it. I put you in an impossible situation." Regret fills his eyes. "If not for me, you wouldn't be in this place."

"You're not angry with me?"

"I'm furious, kiska," he says in a low, rough voice. "You put your life in danger."

"Dania—"

"I know what she did. She admitted everything."

"Is she all right?" I ask.

The line of his jaw turns hard. "She'll be fine."

His face swims in my vision. "We're going to die, aren't we?"

Stroking his hands up my arms, he tightens his fingers on my shoulders. "I won't let you die, Katyusha." He pulls me close and crushes me against his chest. "I was going out of my mind with worry. You have no idea."

I free myself from his embrace and go to the corner. "Look," I say, lifting my weapons from the floor. "I managed to get these."

His gaze widens, then narrows as he walks over to me. "I can't decide if I should feel proud or spank you for even considering something so dangerous." Taking the shards from my hands, he studies them in the light.

"We can take them out when they open the door," I say hopefully.

"*We* will do nothing." He fixes me with a hard look. "You will stay in the corner, as far away from danger as possible. I'll take care of it."

Before I can argue, footsteps sound on the other side of the door.

My heart beats wildly. There's only one reason why Stefanov's men could be coming for us now, and it's not to bring us food.

36

ALEX

*V*ladimir Stefanov himself steps through the doorframe.

Hatred pushes up my throat. I want to pounce on him and slash him to pieces, but three guards armed with automatic rifles follow on his heels. If I were alone in this hole, I wouldn't hesitate to rip out his heart. But I have Katerina to consider. I have to protect her, which I can only do if she doesn't distract me by putting herself in danger.

Tilting my head toward the corner, I give her a wordless command. To my relief, she backs away slowly until the shadows swallow her shape. I take a breath and clear my mind, letting instinct take over. I need to focus on survival and not on the woman I love, because love is a potent reminder of everything I stand to lose.

I square my shoulders as Stefanov approaches, discreetly sliding my hands behind my thighs to hide the porcelain shards.

His bloated face is smug when he stops in front of me. "I was wondering if we'd ever meet in person. If I were you, I would've hoped the day would never come."

I have a good mind to snap his thick neck, but that would be too easy. "You have me. Let Katerina go."

The layers of his chin quiver as he laughs. "You didn't think I'd let a witness walk away, did you?"

Gnashing my teeth, I hold back the violence that threatens to erupt. "A man who doesn't keep his word is a dishonorable man." Even in our unethical circles.

He curls a lip and says in a mocking tone, "I've been accused of worse."

My smile is cold. "No one wants to follow a dishonorable man."

"Who would they rather follow? You?" He laughs again, glancing at his men. At his cue, they all pipe up with chuckles. "In that case, they'd be following a ghost."

"Honor our deal and let her go. There's still time. In another minute, you won't have a choice any longer."

He scoffs. "Do you think you're in any position to negotiate?"

I close a step between us. "With the file that's fallen into my hands, I have *all* the power."

His gleeful expression slips. "What file?"

"Come on, Stefanov. You're a terrible actor."

His eyeballs bounce in their sockets. I imagine the gears turning in his head as he tries to figure out who betrayed him. He got rid of Oleg Pavlov, the only other man besides Besov who knew about their crime. He must come to the conclusion that Besov is the guilty party.

"You're wondering who gave it to me," I taunt.

"Gave you what?" he asks, keeping up the show.

My voice is cold, the hatred I feel for this man coloring every word I utter. "The video of how you killed my parents."

A gasp comes from the corner, but I tune it out. I need to focus on Stefanov. He's a snake at best, one who'll happily strike when my guard is down.

Fear creeps into his eyes, but he blinks it away quickly.

I laugh. "Did you think I wouldn't find out?"

He sneers. "It doesn't matter. You're a dead man anyway."

Stefanov isn't naïve. He knows I'd never trust him to keep his side of the bargain. He's prepared for a war, but it doesn't matter. My army is much bigger than the thirty men guarding my house. Stefanov won't know what's hit him. I'll burn this house to the ground before the day is over. He can stand there with his self-satisfied look, thinking the fifty men on his property will cut it, but soon, he'll beg for his life. Only before it comes to that, I need to know who betrayed *me*.

I watch him carefully as I ask, "How did you find out who I was?"

His grin says he's already savoring his premature victory. "The grave keeper told me a man came to visit the graves. She took a photo and sent it to me."

"The old woman? You paid her to inform you if anyone visited the graves?" No wonder I felt like my parents were trying to warn me after I visited them that first time, shortly before I left for New York. I chuckle grimly. "I have to give it to you, Stefanov. You don't leave anything to chance."

He looks pleased with himself. "In case you'd grown up and were plotting revenge. I have to say, I didn't think you'd survive on the streets."

"I survived rather well," I say with a mocking smile.

He gives me a sly look. "Who told you? Who gave you the tape? Tell me now and I'll finish you quickly."

I don't fucking think so.

Pop, pop, pop.

Gunfire comes from upstairs.

It's the distraction I've been waiting for.

Stefanov gives a start. "What the—?"

Before he's finished his sentence, I have an arm wrapped around his throat, holding him like a shield in front of me while I push the sharp point of the porcelain against his neck.

"Drop your weapons," I say to the guards. "It'll only take a little pressure to make him bleed out like a pig."

"Shoot him," Stefanov yells.

The guards aim their guns, undecided. If they shoot at my hand, they'll put a bullet in his neck. They can't shoot at my head without going through his skull. They've been trained to protect Stefanov, and that training won't allow them to take an uncalculated risk.

"Shoot the woman," Stefanov says, gurgling as I tighten my grip.

"You shoot her," I say, "and your wife is dead."

On cue, a woman's shrill voice sounds from the top of the stairs. "Don't shoot, Vlad! It's Galina. Please. They have me."

Stefanov curses as footsteps fall on the stairs. A group of men filter through the door. They're armed to the teeth, carrying grenades, combat knives, and AK-47s. Dimitri follows with Galina, pointing a gun at the back of her head. Igor comes in behind them, wiping his brow with his sleeve when he spots me.

"*Yob tvoyu mat'*," Stefanov mumbles.

I address Igor. "Take Katerina. Get her out of here."

"I'm not leaving you," she says as Igor rushes over.

She's too brave for her own good.

"You heard Alex," Igor says. "Let's go, Kate."

"Let's fight it out," Stefanov says defiantly. "Man to man."

"Don't do it," Katerina cries out when Igor takes her arm and drags her to the door. "He'll fight dirty. Come with me, Alex. Don't let revenge muddle your decisions."

Her voice washes over me, the sweet sound grounding instead of distracting me. I've never been more present in the moment. My mind has never been clearer.

"I love you," I say.

She stills at that. Momentarily, so does Igor. It's not the place or time, but I owed her those words. I needed to say them before things got even uglier.

Giving up her struggling, she nods. With that single gesture, she offers me acceptance. Her trust warms my chest with pride. I came here expecting many reactions. At the top of my list was blame. It's my fault she's in this mess. But when she follows Igor past me, her soft hazel eyes are like mirrors, reflecting what I feel in my heart. Her lashes lower and lift. In one blink, she tells me everything I want to know. She tells me that she's mine, and that she'll love me regardless.

The hatred dissipates, turning into icy calmness. I'm cool and collected. The power I've given Stefanov by hating him vanishes. Just like that, he doesn't count any longer. His actions don't touch me. He's just a bag of filth that needs to be dealt with. A loose end that needs tying.

Even though I've acquired all this power and wealth, I've never felt truly happy or free. My past has always hovered like an invisible sword over my head. I've blamed myself for my parents' deaths. I've lain awake at night, thinking that I should've smelled the gas leak, that I should've told my father not to smoke in the apartment. I've beaten myself up for reading my comic books and not paying attention to a faulty stove that was right under my nose. Now, for the first time since my parents' death, I taste the sweetness of freedom as the shackles of my past fall away.

Dimitri pushes Galina to the center of the floor. "The house is surrounded. Stefanov's men surrendered." He gives Galina a nudge. "Tell him."

"It's true," she says through her tears. "They've taken away all the weapons and locked everyone in the lounge."

"Casualties?" I ask.

"Two of Stefanov's men," Dimitri says. "We caught them by surprise."

Squeezing Stefanov's neck, I say to his men, "No one else needs to die. Lower your weapons."

Stefanov chokes out, "They'll kill you."

"You're outnumbered," I continue, ignoring him. "Don't be foolish. Put your weapons down. Unlike your ex-boss, we don't shoot unarmed men. I'll offer any man who pledges his loyalty to me a job."

Spit flies from Stefanov's mouth. "He's lying."

I press the point of the shard hard enough to break his skin. "Pavlov's family wants revenge. Not to mention Ivan Besov, on whose back you've slapped a target."

He goes quiet.

My chuckle is condescending. "By now, Pavlov's family has already retrieved Oleg's head from your freezer. You know that as well as I do."

He drags in a labored breath. "Kill me, and you're nothing but a cold-blooded murderer too."

I laugh coldly. "Which of us isn't? We all have blood on our hands. Still, no one wants to support a traitor." I turn to my men. "Take his guards upstairs and lock them up with the others."

Stefanov's guards don't argue. They walk from the room like a flock of sheep following their new shepherd.

When only Dimitri, Stefanov, and his wife are left, I address her. "Do you want to die with him?"

She shakes her head, making her blond hair fly to the sides. "No. Please, no."

"Piece of shit," Stefanov says under his breath. "Some wife you are."

She spits at his feet. "Damn you to hell, Vladimir Stefanov. May you burn there."

I nod toward the stairs. "Take her."

As Dimitri turns with his charge, Stefanov moves with startling agility for a man his size. Pulling back an arm, he slams an elbow into my stomach. The blow knocks the air from my lungs. The moment my grip loosens, he twists in my hold and plants a fist into my jaw. The force makes me stumble. Off balance, I barely have time to ward off the next punch he aims at my face.

Yanking the shard from my hand, he jabs it into my side where my coat and jacket have fallen open. The pain burns cold. It's a sensation I'm intimately familiar with. I was assaulted with various sharpened objects while I lived on the streets. I know how to block it out and use the adrenaline to focus on my opponent's moves.

Dimitri doesn't fire. Our fights are always fair. Stefanov takes a wide stance, breathing hard. He's severely overweight and unfit. He hasn't done his own fighting in years. In the second he catches his breath, I strike. Slicing with the other shard, I cut his face from his eyebrow to his lip.

Blood spurts over his eye. It looks worse than it is—a head wound always pisses blood—but he squeals like a pig being slaughtered.

Galina screams.

Stefanov comes for me, but the blood pouring over his face blinds him. He's stabbing at air. Grabbing his wrist, I squeeze hard enough to crack his bones. He utters a cry and splays his fingers, dropping his weapon.

"That's better," I croon, bending his arm behind his back.

Dimitri throws me a pistol.

I push the barrel between Stefanov's shoulder blades. "Walk."

We go up the stairs, following in Dimitri and Galina's wake. I move my coat away and steal a glance at my side. Blood drips through the tear in my shirt. The cut needs stitches, but it'll have to wait.

"Get everyone out of the house," I tell Dimitri. "Leonid will know where to take them."

While Dimitri and Galina go to the lounge, I shove Stefanov ahead of me to the kitchen. "Don't move. If I shoot you in the back, you'll finish your life in a wheelchair. I don't imagine it's the kind of life a bratva boss wants."

He says nothing, complying with silence.

I keep the gun aimed at his back as I go through the drawers. It doesn't take me long to find what I need. It's a child's skipping rope, shoved into the drawer with crayons and pens. His daughters are in college. The skipping rope must be a keepsake. Good. That seems fitting.

I make quick work of tying him up in a chair. He regards me

with hatred until I walk to the stove and switch on the gas. Then he starts to beg.

"No, please," he says, blinking away the blood that colors the whites of his eyes red.

I stop in front of him. "My father said those same words. Except he didn't beg for his own life, only for my mother's." I cock my head, studying his features so I'll always remember the look of defeat on his face. "You didn't show mercy then, but now you ask for it?"

"I have money," he says through slobber and tears. "Lots of it."

I bend down, putting us on eye level. "Do you think I need your money?"

"I have power. I can make anything happen. What do you want?" His manner turns feverish. "A nice big house full of women? You want men to kneel when you walk into a room? Say it," he urges, leaning toward me. "Say the word and it's yours."

"Spare your breath for the devil," I say with disgust.

"No," he yells as I take an ornate candle from a shelf and put it on the table in front of him.

The odor of gas already taints the air.

"Please, Volkov," he says, stumbling over the words.

I take the box of matches next to the stove. Pulling one out, I bring the flame to the candle. The wick catches. An orange flame springs to life.

"I'm a father," he cries. "I have two daughters."

I don't listen to more. I throw the charcoaled matchstick over my shoulder as I exit the room.

Dimitri waits by the front door.

"Did you evacuate the house?" I ask.

He nods. "Leonid and the rest of your men drove the guards away, sir. Galina called her sister to fetch her."

I didn't give her time to take anything valuable from the house. Stefanov left me with nothing. His family will be left with nothing too.

"Where's Katerina?" I ask as I make my way down the driveway.

"She's waiting in the car," he says, lengthening his stride to keep up with me. "Igor is with her. Yuri is waiting by your car for your instructions."

My chest expands as I drag in a breath.

"Sir. Alex?"

The way he says my name makes me look at him. "What?"

He motions at my side. "You're bleeding."

"It can wait."

He knows when not to argue with me.

We stop outside the gates. Igor leans against the hood of the car, smoking a cigarette. I can count on one hand the number of times I've seen him smoke. I breathe even easier when I spot Katerina in the passenger seat of the car. She clutches the dashboard with both hands, her eyes brimming with tears. I need to get her out of here. She's encountered violence in her profession, but she hasn't experienced it firsthand. I just need a moment longer.

I turn around. Dimitri stands next to me, our backs straight and our faces solemn as we face the house. It's quiet, like when I arrived. The eeriness rides on the brilliant sunlight that's broken through the clouds. The rays make a fan of light, and then the gap closes and everything goes gray. The birds are quiet, as if they know.

Boom!

An explosion rocks the house, blowing the roof tiles into the air. Billows of orange burst through the windows, creating heatwaves over the white landscape. Flames leap into the air, their black-tipped tongues curling with smoke.

"Come on," I say to Dimitri. "There's nothing left here." Physically or emotionally.

"Do you want me to drive?"

"Go with Yuri and Igor. I'll follow." I need to be alone with Katerina.

"Straight home or via the hospital?" he asks, glancing at my side again.

"Home." Katerina can stitch me up there. "Meet us at the house."

"We'll start interrogating Stefanov's men," he says, already making his way to the car where Yuri waits. "We'll determine who'll come over and whom we need to get rid of."

Straightening, Igor puts out the cigarette and drops the butt in his pocket. He gives me a respectful nod before getting into the car with Dimitri and Yuri.

I stand in the road as they pull off, watching their car until they turn the corner. It feels a lot like the end, like closing a chapter that didn't end happily. After that last full stop lies hope. A new page. Time to let go of the past and move on.

Galina is on her own, but she has what my mother didn't have—her life and her children. How she builds her new future is up to her. In a warped sense, that has a ring of freedom to it.

I owe Mikhail a call to tell him what's gone down. But not now. I'll call him when we get home.

Impatient to be with Katerina, I close the distance with hurried steps. Even as I grip the door handle, sirens sound in the distance.

She gives me the minutest shake of her head, tears pouring down her face as I get in beside her.

I close the door and lay the gun in the console. "Hey." Cupping her face, I drag her closer. "It's over. You're all right. We're going to be fine."

A shadow that moves in the back catches my eye. In a flash, I understand Katerina's reaction, that slight shake of her head.

Someone is hiding in the back.

A man sits up. "Famous last words."

Fighting instinct takes over, but before I can dig my fingers into his eyes, he presses a gun against Katerina's temple.

My insides shake with fury. The sight of that gun against her head makes me want to break every finger of the hand clutching the gun before shooting out the man's brains.

Engulfed with helpless anger, I meet his gaze in the rearview mirror. He has square features and blond hair. I recognize him before he says, "The name is Ivan Besov. It's a pleasure to finally meet you, Alexander Volkov."

37

KATE

The barrel of the gun is cold against my temple. I stare at the one Alex left in the console. How quickly can I grab it?

"Tsk, tsk," Besov says, reaching between the seats for Alex's gun.

"You're a dead man," Alex grits out.

Besov laughs. "In case you haven't noticed, I'm the one with the weapons."

Alex turns in his seat. "What do you want?"

Besov shrugs. "Nothing."

"Then why are you here?" Alex asks with a glacier stare.

"I never leave a job unfinished." Besov smiles at me in the rearview mirror. "And I never fail. It's not good for my professional reputation. Besides, you've been such a challenging prey. It'll be an honor to finally kill you."

Blinking back my tears, I glare at him. He must've slipped

into the car while the action was going down in the house. Igor and I—everyone—had been too distracted to think about searching the cars. It wasn't until I was already inside the vehicle that I realized I wasn't alone.

"The police will be here soon," Alex says.

The lights of the sirens are already visible in the distance.

"Drive," Besov says, pushing the barrel harder against my temple.

Alex gives me a reassuring smile. His voice is soft. "Put on your seatbelt, Katerina."

It's easy to follow his order. It's always been easy to follow him. He's the kind of leader people trust.

He secures his own seatbelt before starting the engine. "Where do you want me to go?"

"Back to the main road," Besov says, lowering the gun to my side. "Left at the intersection."

Alex's knuckles turn white as he grips the wheel. His body is like a tightly coiled spring, but he drives smoothly, turning the car around and heading toward the main road. We go left just as the police cars round the bend and speed down the road.

I crane my neck to look at them as we drive in the opposite direction, my heart pounding. Maybe I can flag one of the men.

Besov nudges me in the ribs with the gun. "Eyes in the front."

Not having a choice, I face forward. Anyway, what would I have said if the police had stopped us? Alex just blew up Stefanov's house. With Stefanov inside it.

The bleakness of our situation suddenly crashes down on me. We're screwed. Ironically, in the cell, I had hope. But out here? Our chances aren't looking good. We have no weapons and Besov, a skilled assassin, has two. Plus, Alex is bleeding. I glance at his side where his coat has fallen open. Underneath the jacket, his shirt is torn and soaked with blood. It looks like a stab wound. He needs stitches. If the bleeding doesn't stop, he'll soon be too weak to drive, never mind defend himself.

"Turn right here," Besov says.

The fancy neighborhood with the big houses makes way for apartment buildings. We cross a bridge and drive alongside the river. It starts to snow, flakes drifting down onto the windshield. Alex switches on the wipers.

We drive for another few minutes, following Besov's directions, until the buildings run thin and we finally leave St. Petersburg behind. We're on a road leading toward the countryside. He must be taking us somewhere isolated to kill us.

The silence in the car is stifling. The road runs straight for as far as I can see. Besov isn't giving directions any longer. With no witnesses around, he raises both guns, pushing one against my head and the other against Alex's.

Alex flexes his jaw, but he keeps his eyes on the narrow road, navigating us through the snowfall that turns into a storm as the wind picks up. The wipers make swooshing sounds, batting left and right as Alex puts them on maximum speed. Our visibility diminishes. The snow falls down harder, the flakes illuminated in the headlights of the car.

Trees dot the sides of the road. They quickly grow denser. We're entering a forest. Clutching the edges of my seat, I look at Alex. He's pale, a tell-tale sign of blood loss. Turning his head no more than an inch, he fleetingly moves his gaze from the road to my face.

"I love you," he mouths.

The words are silent, but their meaning is powerful. Charged.

Scraping together all the courage I can muster, I give him a smile. Our gazes lock. He's no longer focused on the road. It only lasts for a second, but I know instinctively that this is the moment our lives are supposed to flash in front of our eyes.

With a sharp movement, he jerks the wheel to the left. Our bodies are thrown to the side as the car skids across the road. The seatbelt cuts into my chest. I scream. I can't help it. At the same time, the momentum propels Besov through the air. Arms flailing, he hits the door, but not before a shot goes off.

Pain lances into my shoulder.

The car crashes through a barrier and barrels down an embankment. I'm tossed forward as the tires lose grip. We torpedo ahead, hitting a ditch at full speed. The thick snow breaks our velocity. My neck jerks violently as we come to an abrupt halt. The nose of the car dives, and the weight of the back pulls it over. The world tumbles past my window as we roll onto the roof. The crash jolts my spine. The car condenses, metal groaning and windows exploding.

Then silence.

I'm still for a moment. Disoriented.

It's snowing too hard to make out anything other than that I'm upside down, squeezed into a narrow space.

"Katerina!"

Alex's voice penetrates the strange numbness encasing me.

A warm hand touches my arm. "Katyusha, talk to me."

I force my vocal cords to function. "I'm…" I swallow. "I'm all right."

He utters something in Russian, a curse or maybe an exclamation of relief. "I'm unclipping your seatbelt. Brace yourself."

The clip makes a clicking sound. The breath leaves my lungs with an oomph as my back hits the roof.

"I'm coming for you," he says, unfastening his seatbelt before pushing himself through the window.

Dazed, I lie in the wreck. We've crashed. I scan the space in front of me. Besov is slung sideways, his neck bent against the window. The guns are no longer in his hands. They're nowhere in sight.

Pain burns in my shoulder. My left arm feels numb. Crossing my right arm over, I brush a hand over the aching spot.

It's wet.

I lift my hand to my face.

Blood.

I've been shot.

"Katerina," Alex says next to me.

I turn my head. He's kneeling in the snow, his face pinched into a mask of concern.

"Push your upper body through the window," he urges. "I'll drag you out."

I try to do as he says, but my left arm won't cooperate.

"Just a little more, my love." His tone is calm, but he can't hide the anxiety that shows through the forced tranquility of his expression. "I've got you."

Hooking a hand under my right arm, he pulls me through the broken window. The glass has shattered into tiny pieces, but the puffy jacket protects me against the roughness of their broken edges.

"You're going to be fine," Alex says, cradling my face in his lap.

"Alex." My voice is scratchy. "I've been shot."

His lips flatten. Chaos swirls in his icy blue eyes, telling me the truth even as he offers me a smile. "You're going to make it."

I moan when he lifts me into his arms and rises to his feet.

"Your phone," I say, breathing through the sharp waves of pain. "Call for help."

"I have to get you to safety first."

We must have a guardian angel, because the wind stills to a breeze and the snowfall calms enough to allow visibility.

Sheltering me against his chest, he takes a step. The snow is so thick he sinks knee-deep. On the other side of the ditch, a field stretches out before the forest. He has to cross that distance before we can hide in the denser vegetation. We won't make it far like this, not with him wounded and carrying me while trudging through the snow.

"Put me down," I say raggedly. "Make the call."

He pauses, hesitates.

"You've lost too much blood. You can't carry me all the way there. The snow is too deep."

Indecision flashes in his eyes. He knows I'm right because after another second, he lowers me carefully. The snow is cold beneath me. Soon, my jacket will be damp. If I don't bleed out, hypothermia will set in. If the bullet has severed an artery, I'll need surgery and fast. The professional side of me calculates the risks on autopilot as he shrugs off his coat and lays it out like a blanket.

"No," I say through bloodless lips. "Keep it on. You'll freeze to death."

He flashes me a grin. "I'm used to this cold. I grew up in it, remember?"

I'm not from Florida either, but that doesn't make either one of us immune to simple science. Once his body temperature drops below ninety-five degrees, he's dead.

"Alex, please." I protest some more as he picks me up and lays me on his coat, but he's not to be deterred.

Crouching next to me, he brushes the hair from my face. "I can't leave you lying in the wet snow. You'll go into hypothermic shock."

A movement by the car draws my attention. Alex is partially blocking my view with his body, but when he straightens, I spot Besov climbing to his feet.

"Alex," I cry out, my insides turning to ice.

Following my gaze, he spins around.

Besov leans against the car, pointing a gun at Alex. Judging by the blood running down the side of his face and the way he sways on his feet, he's taken a hard knock. Alex positions himself in front of me, sheltering me with his body, but I see the horrific picture unfolding through the wide stance of his legs.

"You lose," Besov says, laughing as he aims the gun at Alex.

Alex charges.

My scream tears through the air.

Besov pulls the trigger, but his hand is unsteady and the bullet hits the snow left of Alex. Besov stumbles sideways. Before he's found his balance, Alex dives through the air. The gun flies from Besov's grip as both men go down. They roll through the snow, fists and elbows flying.

Ignoring my numb arm, I struggle to my feet. My boots sink into the snow. The messily tied shoelaces don't help. My feet fit loosely, slipping inside the oversized boots. The left one gets stuck in the muddy ground beneath the snow, and I go down face first. I push up onto my good arm, dragging myself off the ground. Male war cries and grunts come from where the men are fighting. I wipe the snow from my face and spit out the mouthful I've eaten before forcing my legs to move again.

Alex and Besov are trying to kill each other with their bare hands. They roll down a second embankment to the edge of a frozen river. Adrenaline pumps through my body, vanquishing the cold. I pick up my speed, my lungs burning from exertion, and in a few more steps, I reach the gun.

The metal is cold when I haul it up from the snow. The weight is heavy in my palm. I've never fired a gun, but my finger curls instinctively around the trigger. Bracing the arm on my injured side against my body, I run as fast as the snow allows while pointing the gun in the direction of the fistfight.

Both men are bleeding worse than before. A trickle of blood runs from Alex's nose, and Besov's eyebrow is split open.

"Alex," I scream when I reach the embankment. The snow is thinner here, almost iced. Before I can catch myself, I slide down the slope. My feet slip out from under me. Pain shoots up my spine as my tailbone hits the ground, but I don't let go of the gun. I grip it tightly, holding on for life and death.

"Alex!" I aim blindly in front of me.

The men don't stop. Grunts follow the dull thuds of their fists as they rain punches down on one another. Alex is on top. He gets in a blow that sends Besov's face flying sideways. A jet of blood flies from Besov's mouth and paints a red streak over the snow. Besov jams a fist into Alex's injured side. Alex howls, his head thrown back. It gives Besov a chance to fling Alex around, reversing their positions. Cartilage cracks as he slams a fist into Alex's nose.

I don't have a clear shot. If I pull the trigger, I may kill Alex. Aiming the gun in the air, I fire.

Pop!

The gunfire echoes in the space. A flock of birds lifts from the trees in the forest and rises noisily into the sky.

Both men freeze. I slide to the bottom of the embankment on my ass, lifting my feet to prevent my heels from digging into the snow and stopping me.

With Alex momentarily distracted, Besov breaks free. Instead of running up or down the embankment, he beelines straight for the frozen river. When he's halfway across, far enough to feel safe from my amateur aim, he stops.

One of his eyes is swollen shut and his lip is split, but that doesn't prevent a mocking smile from curving his lips. "You may get away now, but I'll be back for you." His voice rings out over the expanse. "You'll never sleep soundly again. That's my gift to both of you." He blows me a kiss before resuming his escape, this time walking at a mockingly normal pace.

My vision goes hazy. It's like a scene from a movie where the bad guy gets away. You look at the screen, waiting, because no one deserves to live in fear, but then the screen turns black, the music plays, and the credits roll. I watch it happening now, see our future like a spectator who looks on from the safety of her sofa. I see Igor's unconscious form in the ER and the bullet the doctor extracted, the bullet the bodyguard had taken for Alex. I see Alex on that bed, no longer breathing, his blue eyes no longer alert. I see myself, my mom, Joanne, my friends, and everyone else Besov will use to get to us. Because he won't stop. Not unless I stop him.

Without another thought, I aim at his feet and pull the trigger.

Stopping, he shoots a surprised look at me from over his shoulder. A moment of silence follows as the smell of gunpowder fills my nostrils. Alex moves in my peripheral vision. I don't know if he's telling me to back down or calm down, but I don't do either as Besov's laugh tears through the air.

I pull the trigger again. The ice around his feet cracks. His laugh dies. The sound drifts away with the snow.

Crack.

He stiffens, his eyes widening.

It's too late.

The frozen layer gives. It breaks. His weight pulls him down.

A beat passes. And another. My heart slams against my ribs, each thud painful. Another second ticks into nothingness, but Besov doesn't surface.

The ice that cracked is now in my veins.

I killed someone. I didn't shoot him, but I pulled the trigger. And I'm not sorry. I'm not sure what shocks me most. That I did it or that I don't feel remorse.

"Katerina!"

I look toward the sound of that voice. Alex is making his way through the snow, using his hands for purchase on the steep part.

Just as he reaches me, my legs buckle. The gun drops from my hand as I go down.

He falls onto his knees next to me, grabbing my face between his hands. "Katerina, look at me. Look at me, my love. Stay with me. Stay with me, damn you. I'll get you out of here."

I fight to comply, but the screen is fading, the credits already rolling.

"It's a happy ending," I whisper as he holds me to his chest.

He smiles down at me, looking at me as if it's the last time he'll see me. He seems like he wants to argue, but he doesn't.

Instead, he brushes a hand over my forehead and says in the saddest voice I've ever heard, "Yes." He seals it with a tender kiss. "It is."

Yes.

It was.

38

ALEX

The room of the private clinic in St. Petersburg is basked in the dusk of day. The ceiling light is set on dim so as not to disturb Katerina. Her face is pale on the pillow, the same color as the white linen.

Placing a hand over hers where it lies on top of the covers, I study her like I've done for the past four hours. Her eyes move behind her lids as in a deep sleep, and her breath tickles the fine, almost invisible hair on her skin as she exhales.

Those are signs of life, as are her vitals that beep on the monitor next to her bed. Still, I feel a compulsion to watch her, a need to reassure myself. I almost got her killed. It can never happen again. The mere thought sends my mind into a tailspin and makes my insides clench into a tight ball.

Igor enters with a paper cup that he hands to me. "How is she?"

"Stable." At least, that's what the surgeon said. I won't relax until she opens her eyes and tells me herself.

His rugged face softens as he looks at her. "I guess we have something in common now. Both of us took a bullet for you."

He says it jokingly, trying to lighten the heavy atmosphere, but my jaw clenches involuntarily. As I've just told myself, *it can never happen again.* I'll make damn sure of it. Ivan Besov is no longer a threat. Stefanov is no longer around to hold a sword over my head. And since no one will dare rat me out to the authorities, I'm a free man. After the message I delivered by blowing up Vladimir's house, nobody will fuck with me.

"Any news on Besov?" I say his name with disdain.

The way Igor's upper lip curls tells me he feels the same about that fucker. "The body will probably wash up in the summer when the ice melts."

I take a sip of the hospital coffee, needing the caffeine to keep alert. I haven't slept in two days.

"Why don't you go catch a few hours of sleep?" I tell Igor. He's been on his feet for as long as I have. "The staff prepared a room for us. Leonid can take over."

Rubbing his eyes, he gives me a grateful nod. "I'll be back in four hours."

"Take six." He's no good to me half asleep on his feet.

Downing what's left of the lukewarm coffee, I crumple the cup in a fist and dump it in the trash can.

"Do you need anything?" Igor asks on his way to the door. "Dinner?"

"The nurse already offered."

He leaves with a nod.

I turn my attention back to Katerina. She's lucky. The bullet hit her in the fleshy part of her shoulder, and no vital organs were damaged. The surgeon said she'll be up in a couple of days and back to normal in a few weeks. That may be so, but she'll always carry a scar—a reminder of how close I came to losing her. I haven't stopped beating myself up about the accident, even though we had little chance of surviving any other way. If I'd allowed Besov to drive us to his destination, overpowering him in my injured state with no weapon would've been suicide on my behalf and murder on Katerina's. Rage consumes me just thinking about it.

Her eyelashes flutter. A soft moan escapes her lips.

I lean closer. "Katyusha? I'm here, my love."

She opens her eyes. Those gorgeous honey-tinted pools are hazy until she blinks them into focus. Her voice is raspy. "Where am I?"

I pick up a glass of water from the nightstand and bring the straw to her lips. "In a private clinic in St. Petersburg." Supporting her neck, I help her take a sip. "More?"

She licks away a drop. "I'm good."

A wave of tenderness rushes through me. "How are you feeling?"

Her smile is faint. "High on morphine, I guess."

"Good." I don't want her to suffer from pain.

"Did you find the body?"

I grind my teeth at the memory of her bleeding out in the snow on the banks of the frozen river. "No. It'll wash up in the summer."

Her pupils dilate even as her eyes grow large. "What then?"

"Then nothing," I say, stressing the *nothing*.

Biting her lip, she gives me a pained look. "I killed him."

I squeeze her hand in mine. "You defended our lives." My unspoken message is clear. I don't consider her a murderer. I won't allow her to carry that burden. "Understand?"

The frown pleating her forehead doesn't smooth out. "What

I mean is I don't feel bad about what I did." She searches my face. "What does that make me, Alex?"

"Human," I say without hesitation.

Which also means she'll have post-traumatic stress from the events. Nightmares. Guilt trips. Anxiety attacks, maybe. No matter. I've already secured the best psychiatrist in New York City.

"Thank you," she whispers, relaxing slightly as she accepts the absolution I offer.

The heaviness of the situation sinks into my chest. I've made her a part of my world by falling in love with her. I've dragged her into the filth, and there's no going back. Not now. Not ever. She's been mine and I've been hers from the moment I laid my eyes on her.

Cupping my cheek, she says in a soft voice, "We'll get through this together. We'll get through everything together." Her gaze is imploring. "Okay?"

Gratitude brushes away the darkness, igniting a spark of excitement for the future we're about to embark on together. "Thank you."

"For what?" she asks, letting her hand drop back to the bed as if holding up her arm takes too much effort.

"For knowing who I am and loving me regardless."

"I do. I love you, Alex," she says with a gentle light in her eyes, giving me the confirmation I crave.

A smile starts in my chest and works its way to my lips. It feels good, this smile that comes from inside. Normally, it's the other way around. Normally, a smile is nothing but a nonverbal form of communication that my mind dictates in suitable circumstances. But this one comes from the heart. I haven't smiled like this since my parents' deaths.

It's been so long I've forgotten how a man is supposed to smile.

"What?" she asks, her lips curving in a similar fashion.

Brushing her hair away from her forehead, I take in her beautiful face. "Here we are, in St. Petersburg, only not under the circumstances we imagined."

"No," she agrees. "It didn't exactly turn out the way I expected. Did you call my mom?"

"Not yet. I wanted you to wake up first." I figure it's her call to make.

"Good." She relaxes visibly. "I don't want her to worry. I'm thinking..."

"Thinking what, kiska?"

"That she doesn't need to know everything."

I nod. "I respect your wish."

She searches my face. "When can we go home? I mean, to New York?"

"As soon as you're back to normal."

Her expression turns hopeful. "Do you mean that?"

Another bout of guilt tightens my chest. "Yes. Nothing prevents me from running my business from New York, the way I'd been doing when we met. We'll have to come back here every once in a while, but I promise you it will be under much more pleasant circumstances, and I'll make sure it doesn't inter-fere with your job."

Exhaling a breath, she says, "I can live with that."

I lift her hand to my lips and kiss every finger while I weigh my words. This is hard for me to say, because I'm going to ask something of her I don't deserve. "Katerina," I start, my tone serious. "About bringing you here..."

"I forgive you," she says before I can continue.

I stare at her, processing the gift she offers. There's only one way I can repay her. Solemnly, I promise, "I'll never make you sad again."

She grins. "I'll hold you to that."

"One more thing."

She raises an eyebrow, waiting.

The extreme lack of romanticism in our surroundings isn't lost on me, yet it feels right. Our relationship started in a hospital, so it seems fitting that I pop the big question in one. "Katyusha, my love, will you wear my ring?"

"You mean become Mrs. Volkova?"

Fuck, that has the perfect sound to it. My voice is hoarse. "Yes."

Her answer mirrors mine. "Yes."

I never expected my life to ever turn right again, but here in this room, in this city that held so much misery for me, it's as perfect as it can get.

Just as well.

Because regardless of her answer, I was never going to let her go.

They say little changes in the so-called sleeping neighborhoods of St. Petersburg. People are much the same. We have an inborn resistance against change. I'm no different. I will never be a good man. Cruelty and kindness will always live side by side in me. But whereas my enemies will always encounter my darkness, Katerina sparks the light I thought I'd long since lost. That's what I intend to hold on to, to the good memories and the new ones I'm making with the woman I love.

My Katyusha.

EPILOGUE

KATE

"*K*iska," Alex says, pulling my attention from the gravestones. Interlocking our fingers, he lifts our hands and points in the distance. "There it is."

The diamond ring on my finger sparkles in the sunlight, the stone seeming to catch and lock the bright rays inside. It's a princess cut surrounded by rubies—timeless and perfect.

I follow the direction of his gaze. It's impossible to miss the angel with the broken wing who mourns on the steps of a tomb. Her concrete dress drags on the grass, the hem damp from the sprinklers.

Silence falls between us as we make our way over. As I read the names engraved in the marble, I hold on to Alex's hand, offering my husband as much comfort as I can.

Viktor Volkov.

Anastasia Volkova.

The Russian Orthodox graveyard in St. Petersburg is beautiful. The grass is a bright green, and colorful iris and canna lilies grow around the trees. The perfume of honeysuckle is sweet in the air. The summer day is pleasantly warm. With the birdsongs and the buzzing of bees surrounding us, it's peaceful. It's a good resting place.

Not so long ago, when the graveyard was covered in a white layer of snow and I was recovering from a bullet wound in a private clinic, Alex found the old grave keeper near the gate, frozen to death. It's just as well. He wasn't going to stop until he'd made everyone pay for their part in putting our lives in danger.

Ivan Besov's body washed up on the shore of the river when the ice melted, just like Alex had predicted. The police opened an investigation when it became known that Stefanov had placed a price on the assassin's head, but it was closed due to a lack of evidence. The explosion at Stefanov's house was declared an accident due to a gas leak. I can only assume Alex's influence played a role in the speedy resolution of both cases.

Lena was fired. Alex made sure everyone knew she'd poisoned Dania, but he left out the finer details of the conspiracy. With that stain on her reputation, the only work she could find was doing laundry in a prison. For such an eternal snob, washing the sheets of the *lower class* she despises must've been her worst nightmare come true. A few weeks later, she fell down the stairs and broke her neck. The witnesses said she slipped because the floor was wet, but I suspect Mikhail had a hand in her untimely death. At least I hope it was Mikhail. I can't entirely rule out my husband's hand in this—a thought that should keep me up at night but strangely doesn't.

As for Dania, her father arranged a marriage to an old oligarch, a man who keeps her under his thumb. Eventually, she may still take over his business, but for now, she must deal with her father working closely with Alex, the man she's come to despise.

"Ready to go?" Alex asks.

When I turn my face, he's studying me with those piercing blue eyes, like I catch him doing so often. "Are *you?*"

"Yes," he says.

The word carries quietly on the breeze. It's soft, tranquil. The undertone of torment that was present when Alex told me about how his parents died is no longer audible in his voice. There's still sadness, but underneath the sorrow lies a tone of acceptance.

I study him back with the same intensity. The lines around his eyes are tight with awareness. He's eternally vigilant, but there are also times when he lets down his guard completely. Such as in bed.

"What?" he asks gently, a smile plucking at his lips as he brushes a wisp of hair from my cheek with his thumb.

"You're ridiculously handsome." And I'm giddily happy.

He chuckles. "You must be the only one who thinks that."

He's wrong. He's not handsome in a conventional way, true, but I'm not referring only to the strong features of his face and to the muscles bulging under his clothes. I'm talking about what's inside, about the man I've gotten to know. He's dangerous. Lethal. But he's also trustworthy and protective. He's a good husband, not only supporting my career as a registered nurse, but also encouraging me to complete my Doctor of Nursing Practice degree. He accepts my friends, and he loves my mom as if she were his own.

He searches my eyes. "Sometimes," he says softly, "I have to touch you to be sure you're real." He accompanies the words with action, gripping my hand tightly in both of his palms.

What happened to me has left a mark on him. I'm long since over the trauma of getting shot, both physically and emotionally, but he's still waking up in the middle of the night, sweating with nightmares.

Going on tiptoes, I kiss his lips. "I'm here."

The blue of his eyes darkens, the fierce intensity of his attention solely focused on me. "Yes, and you're not going anywhere."

"Nowhere," I agree. "Not without you."

He relaxes at the promise, the worry lines on his face smoothing out and the hard set of his jaw softening.

"Come," he says, tugging on my hand and turning toward the car where Yuri waits.

Not far behind Yuri, an entourage of guards is stationed. Their formal black jackets conceal guns and knives. More weapons are hidden under the floorboards of their cars. Alex never lets me go anywhere without at least six bodyguards, but I've grown used to them. Igor now reports to me. Well, sort of. He's the head of my personal detail, but he still answers to my husband.

"I'm glad you brought me here," I say as Alex grips my elbow to steady me when my heel gets stuck in the thick carpet of grass.

"I'm glad you came with me," he replies.

As if I would've missed this.

I understand now why he commissioned the statue in his garden in New York City. It's a replica of his parents' gravestone.

At the bottom of the slope, he stops to inspect my sandal. Going down on his haunches, he grasps my ankle in his large hand, his fingers overlapping around the circumference, and wipes away the mud and tuft of grass stuck to my heel. I grip his shoulder for balance, waiting patiently while he takes care of me. I've learned that he needs this. He needs to provide, protect, and comfort. In turn, he lets me do the same for him.

Staring down at his dark head, his thick hair shining in the sun, I ask, "Do you still miss them a lot?"

He glances up at me. "Yes." A second passes before he straightens. "But that's the past, and we're the present. You're my family now." His voice lowers, the timbre dark and heated as he brushes his knuckles over my stomach. "And soon, we'll have a bigger one."

A flush of heat creeps over my cheeks. I know the guards are watching. "It may take time," I warn. I've only been off the pill for a month.

Lowering his head, he holds my gaze with unmistakable intent as he breathes the words over my lips. "I have time. Lots of it if I get to practice every day."

That makes me laugh. "You just want to impress me like on the first night, making me believe you're virile for your ripe age."

His eyes crinkle in the corners. He purses his lips, trying hard to hold back his smile. My heart soars.

Gripping my wrist, he yanks me against him, making our bodies collide. "Are you teasing me, Mrs. Volkova?"

The sudden move makes me gasp. The moment my lips part, he steals inside, swallowing my sounds and sweeping the depth of my mouth with his tongue. My knees grow weak. I cling to his arms, feeling the muscles flex under my palms as he splays his broad hands over my back and presses me impossibly close, close enough to arch my back and let me feel the hardness that grows against my stomach.

A graveyard is hardly an appropriate place. The men discreetly facing forward and pretending not to see make it even less appropriate, but I couldn't extract myself from his embrace if I tried. He renders me helpless. Flames burst over my skin, burning through my body to my core.

He clasps my ass, jerking me tighter against him. The men in their black suits and the black cars fade away. Where we are doesn't matter any longer. The feeling of summer that rides on the air grows into a bubble that isolates us in happiness. In euphoria.

My phone rings.

Alex groans.

Flustered, I pull away and say breathlessly, "Not here."

"You're right," he says in a gruff voice. "You should get that." He spears his fingers through his hair and messes it up in that way I love so much. "You make me forget where I am." His lips tilt in one corner. "You have that effect on me. Always have, since the first night."

Tearing my gaze away from his, I dig in my bag for my phone and look at the screen. "It's my mom."

"Take your time." He fishes his own phone from his pocket and wakes up the screen, already scrolling to his messages. Turning sideways to give me an illusion of privacy, he says, "Say hi to Laura for me."

I take a steadying breath before I press the phone against my ear. "Hi, Mom."

"Katie! You sound out of breath. Did I catch you at a bad time?"

I glance at Alex's imposing back. "Um, no. I've just been walking."

"How's the honeymoon?"

"Great. Alex has taken me to see all the popular tourist attractions we missed on our first visit. He's taking me somewhere a little less crowded tonight. How about you? How's your vacation?"

"Fabulous. William and I decided to give the nudist beach a try."

"I thought you were in Croatia?"

"We are, honey. We found a place here where I can work on a full-body tan."

Despite her enthusiasm, I can't help the nagging worry at the back of my mind. "How's married life treating you?" Carefully, I add, "Not feeling too claustrophobic yet?"

"Oh, no. William is going hiking in the mountains with a guide tomorrow. That gives me a couple of days to myself on the beach. Afterward, we'll meet up at that fancy hotel I told you about."

"That sounds wonderful." I'm glad they found the formula that works for them.

"How's Alex?"

"He's good. He says hi."

"Give him a kiss from me." Her voice turns rushed. "Oh, gosh. Look at the time. I've got to go, honey. We're going out for dinner. I'll call you again in a couple of days."

When I put my phone away, Alex asks, "Is she happy?"

"Ecstatic."

"I'm glad to hear that." He grins. "I've been to more weddings with you in the last six months than in my whole life."

I smile up at him. "Are you complaining?"

He takes my hand and continues on the path we set out on before we got sidetracked. "Not about ours. How are Jo and Ricky doing?"

"They just got back from Brazil. They want to invite us for dinner when we're home."

"Only if Ricky cooks." He makes a face. "Jo could do with some lessons."

I swat his arm. "That's not nice."

He adopts a serious expression. "But true."

"Okay, fine. I'll admit her moussaka was a bit on the burned side."

We arrive at the car. Yuri gets the door with a stoic expression. Alex makes sure I'm comfortable in the back and gets in beside me. Taking my hand in his lap, he points out the sites on our drive back home. Whenever we're together, he always needs to touch me, but I'm not complaining about that. I love his obsession with me. I need it as much as he needs to take care of me.

"Hungry?" he asks when we're back in our bedroom.

"Starving. It must be all the fresh air."

He nods with approval. "Good. I already asked Tima to prepare a spread."

On cue, there's a knock on the door. Alex opens it to let Tima enter with a trolley set with dishes. One by one, Tima lifts the silver lids to reveal every imaginable Russian starter and bite-sized food.

"Enjoy," Tima says with a grin, offering me a wink on his way out.

"I thought we'd just nibble on a selection," Alex says when Tima has left. "The dishes are all served cold, so you have time for a shower if you like."

My stomach heats at the nuance of his tone. "Sure. I could do with one."

As I walk to the bathroom, I'm aware of him following. His

steps are quiet, like those of a lithe, feline predator, but I know he's there. His presence is too big to ignore, his male energy too overwhelming for me not to be conscious of how it lurks in the room, close on my heel. The hair on my arms raises with awareness.

Before I can reach for the zipper at the back of my dress, he catches the puller. He drags it down slowly, letting his fingertips brush over my spine as the sound of undressing reverberates with the rasp of the zipper. When the dress falls open from the top to the small of my back, he brushes the sleeves over my shoulders. The cotton tumbles to my feet, draping around my ankles.

Next, he works on the clasp of my bra, unhooking it with fluid efficiency. I stand quietly as he hooks a finger into the elastic of the matching thong. Instead of dragging it down my hips, he gives a sharp tug. A tearing sound cuts through the space, the lace digging into my skin for a second before cool air washes over my skin. The brusqueness of the act is in sharp contrast to the gentle way he got rid of the rest of my clothing, and that brief show of urgency makes liquid heat gather between my legs.

Clasping my waist, he turns me to face him and slowly goes down on his haunches, dragging his big, warm palms over my arms, my thighs, and finally, my calves. I swallow as I hold his gaze, taking in the dark, hungry intent in those magnificent blue pools.

Tenderly, he removes one sandal and then the next. When I stand completely naked in front of him, he straightens. Cupping one of my breasts, he rubs a thumb along the undercurve. My nipples harden instantly. I want him so much I'm aching. His hand is big enough that half of his palm covers my ribs. He holds me like this for a moment, simply caressing the underside of my breast as he stares into my eyes. He likes to read my reactions when he touches me. He likes to learn how to make me scream.

Seeming to have had his fill of my eyes, he drops his gaze to my lips. His eyes cut a slow path over me, pausing on my breasts. I grip his shoulders for purchase when he lowers his head, aiming for a nipple. The moment he closes his lips around the hard tip, a moan escapes my mouth. His tongue is hot, his teeth wicked. He knows how to make me come undone by doing nothing but caressing my breasts, but tonight, he doesn't make me beg. He goes lower, kissing his way down my body until he's crouching in front of me again.

I gasp when he hooks my leg over his shoulder. I already know where this is going. Still, I'm unprepared for the onslaught of pleasure that slams into me as he goes straight for his prize. He licks and nips, and in a matter of seconds, I come. My legs are like jelly in the aftermath of that quick and intense release, but he doesn't give me a reprieve. He strips with lightning speed, baring his hard male body and sizable arousal.

We don't make it to the shower. He catches my face between his hands and kisses me like he needs my air to breathe. I taste myself on his lips, the evidence of how badly I want him. When I fist a hand around the velvet flesh of his cock, he grips my hair in a ponytail and pushes me to my knees. I reciprocate, taking him into my mouth and licking the crest until his breathing speeds up and he pumps his hips as I suck him in deeper.

Like always, I swallow every drop when he comes, owning his release just like he owns mine. Coming like this takes the edge off, but it doesn't slow him down. If anything, it makes him greedier for me. Hauling me to my feet, he swings me into his arms and carries me into the shower. He holds on to me with one hand, splaying his fingers over my waist as he opens the tap with the other. While the water heats up, he kisses me, making sure to shelter me from the cold mist of the drops with his body.

When the spray is warm, he takes me underneath it, entering me with one thrust and then pausing to let me adapt. The heat that burns me up inside is different, greater than the pleasure of earlier. It's the kind of ecstasy that steals my mind. It robs me of my senses and makes me forget everything else.

After a few beats, he starts moving slowly, working himself deeper. My moans spur him on. My whimpers make him punch his hips harder, but it's when I scrape my nails over his shoulders that he plunges inside and owns me. The tiles are cool against my back. Every thrust moves my body up the smooth surface. The ridges of the tiles' corners grate my skin, but I'm barely cognizant of the discomfort. As long as he's driving me toward an unbearable peak, every other sensation is mere background noise.

He palms a breast and tweaks my nipple. The sensation ignites more sparks in my core. He stops kissing me to look into my eyes. Drops cling to his dark lashes, glistening like diamonds against the backdrop of his blue irises. The color is arresting, but it's the fierceness of the possession sparking in their depths that I focus on. It's the all-consuming love reflecting back to me that holds my attention as he slips a hand between our bodies and finds my clit. He rubs the pad of his thumb in the way that always brings me to my knees, and when my legs buckle, he pivots his hips and comes just as I break and my inner muscles lock around him.

To say I see stars is a cliché, but that's what he does to me.

The pleasure ripping through me is like an explosion of mete-orites blasting through the atmosphere. When I close my eyes, the white-hot pinpoints of the stars as they burn out in the sky are like the static noise on a television screen. But that's not what causes the height of my euphoria. What drives me to that point is the bond between us. It's always present, no matter what we do, but I feel it strongest like this, naked in his arms, vulnerable and exposed. This is when both our bodies and our souls are bared.

Pressing his forehead against mine, he says with a tremulous breath, "Katyusha."

The endearment washes over me, filling me with warmth.

He kisses my lips, catching the bottom one with his teeth. "You make me crazy. *Sumashedshim.*"

"*Sumashedshim,*" I agree.

His voice is gruff. "Say you want me."

"*Vsegda.*" Constantly, always, eternally, forever.

A glint of satisfaction lights up his eyes when he pulls away to look at me. "Your Russian lessons are paying off."

Lethargic, I lean against him, letting him carry my weight. "Mm."

"Come on," he says, his voice tender. "Let me take care of you."

After he's washed my body and my hair, he wraps me up in a fluffy towel and pats me dry before taking me to bed. He serves me dinner there, feeding me small bites and petting my hair as if I were the kiska—the kitten—he calls me.

When I'm sated, he pours us each a glass of wine. After a few sips, he lets me nap. It's close to midnight when he wakes me with a kiss on my shoulder.

"Katyusha." His deep voice penetrates my sleep. "Wake up, my love."

Blinking, I rub my eyes. "Is it morning already?"

"No," he says with a quirk of his lips. "It's almost midnight. Come."

He helps me from the bed and holds my robe open for me. When I'm protected against the cooler air of the night, he takes my hand and leads me to the rooftop terrace.

Folding his arms around me from behind, he rests his chin on the crown of my head.

"Look," he says.

I take in the vista. The colorful domes of the baroque-style buildings shine in the copper light of the sunset. Like a ball of gold, the sun hangs on the horizon. Above it, the sky is a fragile, delicate white, like the veil of a bride.

"A white night," I say in awe.

He kisses the top of my head. "A midnight day."

Turning in his embrace, I look up at the sharp angles of his face.

He chuckles. "The view is over there."

"No." I cup his cheek. "What I want to see is right here, in front of me."

"Yes," he says softly. "So it is. You. It's always been you."

When he lowers his head, I offer my lips, letting him kiss me under the midnight sun.

SNEAK PEEKS

Alex and Kate's journey ends here. Thank you for following their epic love story!

To be notified about our upcoming books, sign up for our newsletters at www.annazaires.com and www.char-mainepauls.com. All of our titles are available in print and audio as well.

Craving more edgy, suspenseful romance? Check out *Terrible Beauty* by Anna Zaires and *Imperfect Intentions* by Charmaine Pauls. And don't miss our action-packed enemies-to-lovers collaboration, *Darker Than Love!*

Turn the page to read excerpts from *Terrible Beauty* and *Imperfect Intentions,* and to learn more about our books.

EXCERPT FROM TERRIBLE BEAUTY BY ANNA ZAIRES

A family contract. A dark bargain. No escape.

Eleven years ago, I met him. A year later, I was betrothed to him. Now he's come to claim me, slaughtering anyone standing in his way.

My husband-to-be is a monster from a family as ruthless and powerful as mine, a man who deals in violence and destruction... a man terrifyingly like my father. For over a decade, he's stalked me, shadowing my life.

I fear him. I hate him. Worst of all, I want him.

My name is Alina Molotova, and Alexei Leonov is a fate I can't escape.

~

Cool lips brush my throbbing forehead, bringing with them a faint aroma of pine, ocean, and leather. "Shh... It's okay. You're okay. I just gave you something to ease your headache and make this easier."

The male voice is deep and dark, strangely familiar. The words are spoken in Russian. My fuzzy mind struggles to focus. Why Russian? I'm in America, aren't I? How do I know this voice? This scent?

I try to pry open my heavy lids, but they refuse to budge. Same goes for my hand when I attempt to lift it. Everything feels impossibly heavy, like my very bones are made of metal, my flesh of concrete. My head lolls to one side, my neck muscles unable to support its weight. It's as if I were a newborn. I try to speak, but an incoherent noise escapes my throat, blending with a distant roar that my ears can now discern.

Maybe I am a newborn. That would explain why I'm so ridiculously helpless and can't make sense of anything.

"Here, lie down." Strong hands guide me onto some soft, flat surface. Well, most of me. My head ends up on something elevated and hard, yet comfortable. Not a pillow, too hard for that, but not a stone either. There isn't much give in the object, but there is some. Also, it's oddly warm.

The object shifts slightly, and from the foggy recesses of my mind, the answer to the mystery emerges. *A lap.* My head is lying on someone's lap. A male someone, judging by the steely, thickly muscled thighs underneath my aching skull.

My pulse accelerates. Even with my thoughts sluggish and tangled, I know this isn't normal for me. I don't do laps or men. At least I haven't thus far in all of my twenty-five years.

Twenty-five. I latch on to that sliver of knowledge. I'm twenty-five, not a newborn. Encouraged, I sift through more of the tangled threads, seeking an answer as to what's happening, but it eludes me, the recollections coming slowly, if at all.

Darkness. Fire. A nightmare demon coming to claim me.

Is that a memory or something I saw in a movie?

A needle biting deep into my neck. Unwelcome lassitude spreading through my body.

That part feels real. My mind might not be functioning, but my body knows the truth. It senses the threat. My heart rate intensifies as adrenaline saturates my veins. Yes. Yes, that's it. I can do it. With strength born of growing terror, I force open my leaden lids and look up into a pair of eyes darker than the night surrounding us. Eyes set in a cruelly handsome face that haunts my dreams… and my nightmares.

"Don't fight it, Alinyonok," Alexei Leonov murmurs. His dark voice holds both a promise and a threat as he gently threads his fingers through my hair, massaging away the throbbing tension in my skull. "You'll only make it harder on yourself."

The edges of his calluses catch on the tangles in my long hair, and he pulls his fingers out, only to curve his palm around my jaw. He has big hands, dangerous hands. Hands that have killed dozens today alone. The recollection roils my stomach even as some knot of tension deep inside me unravels. For ten long years, I've dreaded this moment, and finally, it's here.

He's here.

He's come for me.

"Don't cry," my husband-to-be says softly, brushing away the wetness on my face with the rough edge of his thumb. "It won't help. You know that."

Yes, I do. Nothing and no one can help me now. I recognize

that distant roar. It's the sound of a plane engine. We're in the air.

I close my eyes and let the hazy darkness take me.

～

Order your copy of *Terrible Beauty* today at
www.annazaires.com!

EXCERPT FROM IMPERFECT INTENTIONS BY CHARMAINE PAULS

I never dreamed of getting married.
I dreamed about freedom.

When my stepfather promised Leon Hart a partnership in his clandestine software company, he offered me as part of the package deal. It's a win-win situation for both men. My stepfather gets rid of his damaged stepdaughter, and Leon becomes second-in-command of the biggest underground IT operation in the country. I'll do what I must to escape my fate.

Even if it means turning my powerful and dangerous betrothed into my worst enemy.

Note: Imperfect Intentions *is Book 1 of the Beauty in Imperfection duology. Violet and Leon's story concludes in* Imperfect Affections *(Book 2).*

~

Violet

Kneeling on the floor, I pack away the cleaning products. I'm putting away the bucket when the door clicks open and a sliver of darkness from the hallway creeps into the room. I look over my shoulder and freeze. Leon Hart stands in the door, wearing dark jeans that hug his powerful legs and a leather jacket that stretches over his broad chest. A pendant carved from wood hangs on a leather string around his neck. It matches the braided leather bracelet on his wrist. His ring finger on his right hand sports a gold signature ring. His left hand is bare.

He leans in the frame with one arm above his head, studying me quietly yet intensely. Those are the two words that describe him best. Quiet. Intense. I've tried hard to remain invisible, particularly here. In my circles, it's dangerous to be noticed, especially by men like Leon Hart. He's different than the other men who work for my stepfather. He's not a brain or a muscle. He's both. And more. There's a darkness to him that only dangerous men acquire. I should know. I grew up with dangerous men.

He pushes off the doorframe. His movements are unhurried and precise. Premeditated. I stare, hypnotized like a rabbit by a snake. When he steps inside and closes the door with a soft but firm click, my heart starts pounding in my chest. Being at a disadvantage in my kneeling position on the floor, I grab hold of the shelf to pull myself up.

Before I've straightened, he's behind me, gripping my arms to assist me. I spin around, looking up at his face as he takes one elbow and places a palm on my waist to test my balance. He holds on too long, not setting me free. The pounding of my heart turns into a wild gallop. I know enough by now to know men like him take what they want. I know enough to know women like me can't win. Our only chance is fighting smart.

He studies me as I study him. His face is handsome, too much so. Black wavy hair flops over his forehead. His jaw is square and strong, darkened by stubble. A straight nose adds to the hard lines of his symmetrical features. Sensual lips soften the harsh angles. The color of his eyes reminds me of Guinness. Instead of just brown, they glow with a deep ruby undertone. He's so perfect it hurts to look at him. It's the kind of male beauty no wise woman will fall for. It's like my mother's beauty. It's too desirable. Men like him can never be faithful.

I pull a little, testing his intention. He holds fast, not letting go of my waist or breaking eye contact. My throat closes up. When I swallow around the lump, his gaze follows the movement. He visually traces the arch of my neck before focusing on my heaving chest. I try to control my breathing, but my fear is a biological reaction. Instead, I let my mind take over, looking for a weakness and an opportunity to exploit.

Setting my elbow free, he plants his hand on the closet door next to my face and lowers his cheek to mine. His stubble grates lightly over my skin before he turns his face and inhales with his nose in my hair. He's sniffing me like a dog, but the animalistic behavior doesn't shock me. I already know he's not a gentleman. What frightens me is when he moves his hand from my waist up my side, inviting a shiver.

He must feel my reaction, because when he meets my gaze again, satisfaction burns in his eyes. He drags his fingers over the side of my breast, the pads barely brushing my T-shirt. Goosebumps run down my arm.

Slowly, he reaches for my throat. Wrapping his splayed fingers around my neck, he pushes my body gently against the shelves. The bottles and brushes rattle as I grip the edge behind me for leverage. Still holding my gaze, he brings his mouth to mine.

I go still. I know what's coming, but the warmth of his lips when he slants them over mine shocks me. What shocks me more is that it's not unpleasant. Something stirs in my belly. My pulse flutters. Anticipation mixes with fear, sending heat to my lower body. Like a trapped animal, I keep perfectly still as he explores the curve of my bottom lip with his tongue.

Blood gushes like static noise in my ears when he parts my lips and slips his tongue inside my mouth for a more thorough exploration. I don't kiss him back. I'm too busy processing my reaction, trying to get a handle on what's happening while waiting for the right moment. I'm waiting for him to get carried away before I knee him in the balls, but he doesn't grow weak. He's meticulous, tasting the depth of my mouth with too much control.

What is he doing? Men like him don't go for girls like me. They go for the pretty ones who aren't broken, the ones who aren't afraid to kiss them back.

At my lack of response, he lifts his head and tilts his hips forward, letting me feel the hardness between his legs. He's thick and long under his jeans, hot on the naked strip of my stomach where the hem of my T-shirt has pulled up.

Studying my face, he says with certainty, "You want me."

That's what this kiss was? A test?

He turns me on, but he's wrong. He's the furthest thing from what I want. "Do you always take what you want?"

His gaze dips to the pulse in my neck that beats under his fingers. "Yes."

I lift my chin as much as his hold allows. "Even if a woman doesn't want you?"

A lazy smile curves his lips. "As I said, you want me."

I don't falter under his scrutiny. I let him look into my eyes because they don't lie. "You mistake my aversion for arousal."

His eyes tighten minutely. To my surprise, he backs off, not easing his grip on my throat but putting space between us.

"Have dinner with me," he says. "We can talk this through."

"There's nothing to talk about."

He brushes his thumb along the curve of my neck. "You have to eat, don't you?"

I try to repress a shiver and fail. "It's midnight."

"Have you eaten dinner?"

"No."

He raises a brow.

"I don't have money on me," I say.

"My treat."

"No thanks. I don't want your money."

The line of his jaw hardens. "Because it's dirty?"

"Because I don't like to owe people."

He smiles again, seeming amused. "No strings."

There are never no strings. Not in our world.

His tone is quiet, but it's not a soothing kind of quiet. "I never ask twice."

Ah. He's the arrogant type. If a woman says no, it's her loss. He won't chase after anyone. With his handsome face, I should've known. Only more reason to stay away from him.

My laugh is wry. "Good for me, because my answer would still be no."

He leans closer, placing his nose millimeters from mine. Throwing my earlier words back at me, he says, "You mistake my meaning. I'm not giving you an option."

~

Order your copy of *Imperfect Intentions* today at www.charmainepauls.com!

MORE FROM ANNA ZAIRES AND CHARMAINE PAULS

If you enjoyed *White Nights: The Complete Duet,* check out the following titles from Anna and Charmaine!

Other Collaborations by Anna & Charmaine:

- *Darker Than Love* – Yan and Mina's action-packed enemies-to-lovers romance

Dark & Contemporary Romance by Anna Zaires:

- *The Molotov Obsession Duet* – Nikolai and Chloe's addictive, all-consuming love story
- *The Twist Me Trilogy* – Nora & Julian's dark, twisted love story
- *The Capture Me Trilogy* – Lucas & Yulia's breathtaking enemies-to-lovers romance

- *The Tormentor Mine Series* – Peter & Sara's intense captive romance
- *Wall Street Titan* – a sizzling contemporary romcom featuring a billionaire and a cat lady

Dark & Contemporary Romance by Charmaine Pauls:

- *Beauty in the Broken* – a dark forced-marriage romance about revenge and salvation
- *The Diamonds are Forever Trilogy* – a dark romance featuring a hot French mafia kingpin
- *The Beauty in the Stolen Trilogy* – romantic suspense set in South Africa's criminal underworld
- *The Loan Shark Duet* – a dark mafia romance with a *Beauty and The Beast* theme
- *The Age Between Us Duet* – an older-woman/younger-man romance that will melt your e-reader
- *Catch Me Twice* — a heartbreaking second-chance romance about betrayal and redemption

Sci-Fi Romance by Anna Zaires:

- *The Mia & Korum Trilogy* – an epic sci-fi romance with the ultimate alpha male
- *The Krinar Captive* – Emily & Zaron's captive romance, set just before the Krinar Invasion
- *The Krinar Exposé* – Anna's scorching hot collaboration with Hettie Ivers, featuring Amy & Vair —and their sex club games

- *The Krinar World stories* – sci-fi romance stories by other authors, set in the Krinar world

Sci-Fi & Paranormal Romance by Charmaine Pauls:

- *The Krinar Experiment* – alpha alien kidnapping at its hottest, set in Anna Zaires's Krinar world
- *The Krinar's Informant* – an alpha alien captive romance, set in Anna Zaires's Krinar world
- *7 Forbidden Arts Series* – a dark, forced-mates paranormal romance

Laugh-Out-Loud Romantic Comedy by Misha Bell, the geeky, raunchy pen name by Anna Zaires and her hubby, Dima Zales

- *Hard Code* – a workplace romcom about a quirky coder tasked with quality testing sex toys, and her mysterious Russian boss, who steps in to help out
- *Hard Ware* – a hilarious slow-burn romance featuring a sex toy company CEO, a hot, mysterious stranger, and star-crossed puppy love
- *Hard Byte* – a fake date romcom about a prime-number-obsessed Anglophile who makes a deal with the Devil, her boss, to save her dream project
- *Royally Tricked* – a raunchy royal romance featuring a daredevil prince and a germaphobic, movie-obsessed magician
- *Femme Fatale-ish* – a spy rom-com starring aspiring femme fatale Blue Hyman and a sexy (possible) Russian agent

- *Of Octopuses and Men* – an enemies-to-lovers rom-com featuring Olive, one of the Hymen sextuplets, and her sizzling hot (and infuriating) new boss

Sci-fi and Fantasy Collaborations by Anna Zaires and her hubby, Dima Zales:

- *The Girl Who Sees* – the thrilling tale of Sasha Urban, a stage illusionist who discovers unexpected secret powers
- *The Bailey Spade Series* – the mind-bending saga of a girl who can explore dreams and steal memories
- *Mind Dimensions* – the action-packed urban fantasy adventures of Darren, who can stop time and read minds
- *Upgrade* – the mind-blowing technothriller featuring venture capitalist Mike Cohen, whose Brainocyte technology will forever change the world
- *The Last Humans* – the futuristic sci-fi/dystopian story of Theo, who lives in a world where nothing is as it seems
- *The Sorcery Code* – the epic fantasy adventures of sorcerer Blaise and his creation, the beautiful and powerful Gala

ABOUT THE AUTHORS

Anna Zaires is a *New York Times, USA Today,* and #1 international bestselling author of sci-fi romance and contemporary dark erotic romance. She fell in love with books at the age of five, when her grandmother taught her to read. Since then, she has always lived partially in a fantasy world where the only limits were those of her imagination. Currently residing in Florida, Anna is happily married to Dima Zales (a science fiction and fantasy author) and closely collaborates with him on all their works. To learn more, please visit www.annazaires.com.

Charmaine Pauls was born in Bloemfontein, South Africa. She obtained a degree in Communication at the University of Potchestroom, and followed a diverse career path in journalism, public relations, advertising, communications, photography, graphic design, and brand marketing. Her writing has always been an integral part of her professions.

When she is not writing, she likes to travel, read, and rescue cats. Charmaine currently lives in Montpellier with her husband and children. Their household is a linguistic mélange of Afrikaans, English, French and Spanish. To learn more, please visit www.charmainepauls.com.

Printed in Poland
by Amazon Fulfillment
Poland Sp. z o.o., Wrocław

24826873R00389